W9-BIS-703

FLORIDA STATE
UNIVERSITY LIBRARIES

APR 2 6 2001

TALLAHASSEE, FLORIDA

WOMEN'S TALES FROM THE NEW MEXICO WPA

La Diabla a Pie

FLORIDA STATE
UNIVERSITY LIBRARIES

APR 0 9 2001

TALLAHASSEE, FLORIDA

Recovering the U.S. Hispanic Literary Heritage

Board of Editorial Advisors

Ramón Luis Acevedo
Universidad de Puerto Rico

José F. Aranda, Jr.
Rice University

Antonia Castañeda
St. Mary's University

Rodolfo J. Cortina
University of Houston

Kenya C. Dworkin y Méndez
Carnegie Mellon University

José B. Fernández
University of Central Florida

Juan Flores
Hunter College of CUNY

Erlinda Gonzales-Berry
Oregon State University

Laura Gutiérrez-Witt
University of Texas at Austin

Luis Leal
University of California at Santa Barbara

Clara Lomas
The Colorado College

Francisco A. Lomelí
University of California at Santa Barbara

Agnes Lugo-Ortiz
Dartmouth College

A. Gabriel Meléndez
University of New Mexico

Genaro Padilla
University of California at Berkeley

Raymund Paredes
University of California at Los Angeles

Nélida Pérez
Hunter College of CUNY

Gerald Poyo
St. Mary's University

Antonio Saborit
*Instituto Nacional
de Antropología e Historia*

Rosaura Sánchez
University of California at San Diego

Virginia Sánchez Korrol
Brooklyn College of CUNY

Charles Tatum
University of Arizona

Silvio Torres-Saillant
CUNY Dominican Studies Institute

Roberto Trujillo
Stanford University

FLORIDA STATE
UNIVERSITY LIBRARIES

APR 0 9 2001

TALLAHASSEE, FLORIDA

WOMEN'S TALES FROM THE NEW MEXICO WPA

La Diabla a Pie

Edited by Tey Diana Rebolledo and
María Teresa Márquez

With an Introduction by
Tey Diana Rebolledo

Recovering the U.S. Hispanic Literary Heritage

Arte Público Press
Houston, Texas

This volume is made possible through grants from the Rockefeller Foundation and the City of Houston through The Cultural Arts Council of Houston, Harris County.

Recovering the past, creating the future

Arte Público Press
University of Houston
Houston, Texas 77204-2174

3 1254 03527 1192

Cover design by Ken Bullock

Tey Diana Rebolledo and María Teresa Márquez.
    Women's tales from the New Mexico WPA: *La diabla a piel*
edited by Tey Diana Rebolledo and María Teresa Márquez.
With an introduction by Tey Diana Rebolledo.
        p.   cm. — (Recovering the U.S. Hispanic literary heritage)
ISBN 1-55885-312-X (pbk. : alk. paper)
    1. Mexican American women—New Mexico—Social life
and customs—Anecdotes. 2. Mexican American women—
New Mexico—Interviews. 3. Mexican Americans—New
Mexico—Folklore. 4. New Mexico—Social life and customs—
20th century—Anecdotes. 5. New Mexico—Biography—
Anecdotes. 6. Folklore—New Mexico. 7. Tales—New Mexico.
I. Rebolledo, Tey Diana, 1937. II. Márquez, María Teresa, 1938.
III. United States. Work Projects Administration (N.M.)
IV. Recovering the U.S. Hispanic Literary Heritage Project
publication.
F805.M5 D53 2000
305.868'72073—dc21   00-056589
                                                              CIP

F
805
M5
W 66
2000

⊗ The paper used in this publication meets the requirements of the American National Standard for Information Sciences—Permanence of Paper for Printed Library Materials, ANSI Z39.48-1984.

Introduction © 2000 by Tey Diana Rebolledo
Printed in the United States of America

0 1 2 3 4 5 6 7 8 9   10 9 8 7 6 5 4 3 2 1

Para todas/todos que compartieron sus estorias.
For all who shared their stories.

And:
For all the Teys in my family: My great-aunt, Esther Galindo (Mama Tey); my mother, Esther (Tey) Vernon Rebolledo; my daughter, Tey Marianna Nunn; my niece, Tey Mariana Stiteler, and my great-niece, Tey Diana Stiteler. May there be many more.

And, as always, for Mikko.
—*Tey Diana Rebolledo*

For Tony and Chris.
—*María Teresa Márquez*

CONTENTS

APPENDIX (BATCHEN)

PREFACE

THIS BOOK IS THE WORK OF MANY PEOPLE. Many years ago, Erlinda Gonzales-Berry and I spent several afternoons in the New Mexico History Library Archives in Santa Fe looking at the WPA files, then stored in manila folders in filing cabinets, and easily accessible to anyone who wanted to look at them. We read some of the stories and laughed with them. We wondered at how easily anyone who wanted to could simply steal those typewritten and yellowed pages. We thought about the translations and asked if the original Spanish versions were anywhere to be found. To this date, I have been unable to find any of the Spanish originals. Subsequently, I traveled to the National Archives in Washington, D.C., to see if I could piece together any more of the stories, some of which were missing from the New Mexico files. I published several of the stories in my anthology *Infinite Divisions: An Anthology of Chicana Literature* (with Eliana Rivero) and continued to think about them and to teach some of the stories in my classes.

In 1994, Teresa Márquez received a grant from the Recovering the U.S. Hispanic Literary Heritage Project to microfilm the collection that was at the New Mexico History Library Archives. At the same time, she made some photo copies of the women's stories, which she allowed me to use. In the summer of 1996, the Research Opportunity Program of the University of New Mexico provided me with an undergraduate research assistant, Barbara Gonzales, who spent the summer copying some of the stories into the computer and analyzing them. For her project, she wrote a research paper on the Women's Stories of the WPA. In 1997, I applied for a grant from the Recovery Project in order to finish inputting the stories into the computer. After we received that grant, Barbara, now a graduate student at the University of New Mexico, finished that task. A Spring 1998 fellowship at the Bogliasco Foundation Institute of the Arts and Humanities on the Ligurian Coast of Italy provided me with solace, the Mediterranean, delicious pasta, and uninterrupted time to finish my research and write the introduction. At that time, Teresa Márquez also finished a WPA bibliography. In the fall of 1998, Xochitl Shuru, my graduate research assistant, and Teresa carefully read the computer-ready stories against the original xeroxed ones. Rosita Pickle made the corrections and input additional stories. Lastly, Derek Roff suffered through the scanning of the typewritten stories, with all of their crossed-out letters, handwritten remarks, and other software hair-raising difficulties. Hazel Romero of the New Mexico History Archives found some of the original illustrations I had been searching for these many years. On that rainy day in Santa Fe, she and I jumped up and down with glee. Finally, Francisco M. Sánchez put the remaining stories told to Lou Sage Batchen (the ones that were not about women) into an appendix, as we had decided that the entire collection needed to be included. All these people have left their marks on this collection.

The outstanding pioneer work that Marta Weigle has done on the WPA and its history has informed and shaped this book. Marta's many articles and books on the New Mexico WPA and its impact on New Mexicans have been invaluable guides in this study. In addition, the work done by Suzanne Forrest on Placitas enriched the background of this collection.

It is evident that not all of the stories in this collection are told exclusively by women. The stories collected by Lou Sage Batchen in Las Placitas, New Mexico, especially reflect a community storytelling experience which also included men. We chose to include these stories because to include the women's stories only would have excluded much of that context. We did focus, however, on the stories in which women were the central characters or upon ones told by women. The rest of the stories form the cultural and historical context in which the women in the community lived their lives. The stories that do not focus on women but which complete the Placitas stories are collected chronologically in the appendix.

We learn a great deal here about family and community life, local customs, herbal remedies, and other realities of everyday life. Perhaps the most difficult part of these stories for some contemporary readers will be the cultural interactions between Hispanos and Indians. Particularly in the Las Placitas stories, the memories of the conflict between the people of Las Placitas and some Indian tribes are vividly described. While Hispanos traded, intermarried, and had generally positive neighborly relations with the Pueblo tribes close to Las Placitas (such as Sandía Pueblo), their attitudes towards the Navajos were fraught with terror and hate. Navajos are described as savages: They raided Hispano livestock and their towns, and, in the people's memory, kidnapped or killed several young shepherds. People were afraid of them, and this fear is captured in their stories. Yet a careful reading of the stories reveals that not only did many people follow some native customs, but some were at least part Native Americans themselves.

Moreover, the relationships with the Anglo-Americans who came later are also often ambivalent. The Anglos are portrayed here as being mostly concerned with money. While there is a necessary interaction with the newcomers, there are only a few stories where Anglos are described in a positive manner.

Often in the stories the values of the community are held up for examination. We are told that bad things happen to people who are miserly, and that good comes to those who are generous. Miserly parents beget miserly children. We see the importance of religion, the value of home and place, and how people helped each other in times of need.

From the outset, Teresa Márquez and I had agreed not to change drastically the language, spelling, accent marks, or grammatical structure of the original stories, in either English or Spanish. We felt that if we began to correct the spelling and the grammatical structure, much of the flavor of the stories would be lost. Many archaic spellings, pronunciations, and other language variations existed in the Spanish. These features also existed in the English. We felt that these language variations were important for the flavor of the stories (even if they were in stilted English) as the stories had been translated from the Spanish into English. They also contributed to the feel of English as it was written in the 1930s. Finally, we did not want to add another layer of editing or translation to what was already multiple-layered. However, the readers of this collection felt that some problematic grammar and spelling made the stories difficult to read. With this in mind, we have slightly corrected the spellings. For example, Annette Hesch Thorp insisted on putting the apostrophe in contractions before the contraction, as in *did'nt*. She also spelled *tortilla* as *tortiall* (something perhaps she heard). Batchen often made gender mistakes when reporting Spanish words. For example, she often spelled *arroyo* as *arroya*. This sort of error was corrected in later entries. We also have put accents on Spanish words that need them. Thus, minor errors have been corrected. The stories, except for some obvious typographical errors, are much as they were in the originals. Thorp's stories are organized, in the most part, chronologically by dates they were collected or turned in. Batchen, too, is organized in the main by date, but occasionally, a story is placed within its thematic context, such as in "An Old Native Custom."

The WPA stories are in the public domain. As such, no one has the copyright to them. But here, for the first time, they are accessible to a wider readership. We hope that you enjoy them.

INTRODUCTION

The Federal Writers' Project

In the late 1930s and early 1940s, the administration of Franklin D. Roosevelt sponsored the Federal Writers' Project, designed to help destitute writers during the Depression. As part of a larger federal back-to-work project, the Works Projects Administration (previously known as the Works Progress Administration), the writers collected materials for a series of State Guides. Central features of the project were interviews with older residents; these were meant to document culture and history as a "human interest" section of the guides. Much valuable material was collected, including slave narratives from the southern states and a series of folk songs from throughout the country.

New Mexico was one of the states that participated in the project. The first activities here began in 1933 under the Civil Works of Art Project. According to Suzanne Forrest, however, "the idea reached its greatest development in New Mexico under the famed Federal Project One of the WPA with its Federal Art Project, Federal Writers' Project, and Federal Music Project" (119). The first state director was Ina Sizer Cassidy, hired in 1935. She, in turn, hired workers from the relief rolls throughout the state, and faculty from the University of New Mexico provided some research and editorial help. Many of the workers, however, were not trained professionals.

In addition to the writers' project, there was also a series of photographs taken under the auspices of the Farm Security Administration that documented the people and places of the time.

The New Mexico Federal Writers' Project tapped a vein of folklore and culture as the writers interviewed *ancianos*. Among the many Project workers (around fifty-five in all) were two women, Lou Sage Batchen, working in Placitas, New Mexico, and Annette Hesch Thorp, working in Albuquerque and Santa Fe, who were notable for the emphasis they placed on Hispana women's stories. In addition, Bright Lynn collected stories and folktales from Guadalupe Gallegos in Las Vegas, New Mexico. Therefore we have some remarkable materials about life and culture from the perspective of women. Most of the WPA stories have never been published and remain in their type-written form in the New Mexico State History Archives, the State Archives in Santa Fe, and in the Library of Congress. Recent funding from the Recovering the U.S. Hispanic Literary Heritage Project helped microfilm these stories and make them available to a larger public.

Hispanic Folklore: The Early New Mexican Collectors

The collecting of folklore in New Mexico certainly did not start with the WPA. New Mexico has a long history of rich oral traditions beginning from colonial times. During the years from the first Hispano colonists until the early part of the twentieth century, New Mexicans were fairly isolated from their mother countries, Spain and (after 1810) Mexico. Because it was an isolated outpost, there were few schools; only children from the wealthier classes were taught to read and write, and these were mostly boys. The extensive cultural and imaginative history of the common people was instead passed down by word of mouth, from elders to youngers.

In general, as Stanley Robe says, "the New Mexicans were left to shift for themselves in their isolation. They had to provide their own food and satisfy any other needs through their own devices. Their way of life likewise continued under these same circumstances" (Robe, *Hispanic Folktales*, 3-4). In particular, in the small rural northern settlements, the people lived traditional lives. The practice of storytelling was especially deeply ingrained. Annette Hesch Thorp, for example, recorded people who said that,

> Storytelling was looked forward to on winter nights. All the family, big and little, gathered around the fireplace, and by the light of a kerosene lamp, or ocote wood, "pitch," would shell corn, or the women sewed while some grandmother or neighbor viejita, "old woman," told stories until time for bed . . . The stories that were told by these grandmothers were religious ones. About santos, and the miracles they used to perform. And about brujas "witches," and those who have been embrujada, "bewitched." (Thorp, "Stories.")

Interest in collecting this people's lore began early in this century with the work of such folklorists as Aurelio Espinosa, his son José Manuel Espinosa, Juan B. Rael, and Arthur L. Campa. They were later joined by Aurora Lucero-White (who did some of her collecting under the WPA) and

Helen Zunser. More recent folklorists working in New Mexico include R.D. Jameson, Stanley Robe, Enrique Lamadrid, Elba C. de Baca, and Nasario García, among others.

The outlook on the collection and analysis of folklore has greatly changed, however. Early folklorists such as Espinosa and Rael were interested in identifying New Mexico folklore with that of Spain. Therefore, they examined the tales to compare common aspects with Spanish and European ones, and to gauge the influence those tales had on local folklore. Other folklorists followed the structural folklore classification method, identifying the various tales as to "universal" folklore types and motifs. Recent folklorists focus on the cultural content of the folklore. I do not want to enter into these arguments, nor do I want to discuss the so-called magic tales and stories that are linked to European tales. Rather, I want to focus and analyze the local, historical, and cultural content of New Mexico found in these tales and, in particular, the literary and cultural contributions and influence of, and by, the women in the tales. Before I discuss the stories themselves, however, we must examine the scope and perspective of the WPA and why it sponsored the collection of folklore in New Mexico, the Southwest, and elsewhere in the United States.

The Federal Writers' Project: "A Significant Experience in National Self-Discovery"[1]

The administration of President Franklin D. Roosevelt sponsored the Works Progress Administration and a subsidiary unit, the Federal Writers' Project, programs designed to help the destitute during the Depression and support public works at the same time. The people employed by the WPA had to show need and were put to work doing such things as building public parks, roads, and trails through public lands; artists adorned public buildings such as community centers, libraries, public monuments, and post offices; and writers in the Federal Writers' Program were sent out to collect information and folklore in order to produce an organized system of State Guides. Part of the collecting of information for the State Guides involved interviewing older residents to document culture and history; identifying cultural events that might attract visitors; and cataloging the origins of name-giving to places, roads, and streets. Many of the individual state Federal Writers' Projects were especially rich in folklore and culture. The New Mexico Federal Writers' Project was seen as a great resource in folklife and culture as the writers were sent out to interview *ancianos*. These activities are commonly associated with rural, and especially Southern, grassroots life (Weigle, *New Mexicans*, xiii). However, they also had significant impact in the Southwest in terms of its arts and literature projects.

The Great Depression had a profound impact on northern New Mexican villages as Nancy Wood shows in her study *Heartland New Mexico*. A report in 1935 from a team of experts from Washington related that "the relief load is between sixty and seventy percent of the people of the area and most of the people not receiving relief are indirectly depending for a livelihood upon relief orders" (Wood, 26). Wood also shows that the New Deal programs in New Mexico had limited success in addressing the problems of the Hispanic villages:

> due to the fact that bureaucrats, reams of forms and regulations in hand, swept in from Washington, ignoring local agricultural agents who had managed to form a fragile link between villagers and the bureaucracy. The newcomers spoke no Spanish; few villagers spoke English. The result was that, except for direct emergency relief, little attempt was made to discover the roots of Hispanic misery, or to educate the Hispanic people in matters of food production, job training, or health. So great was the bitterness toward all things federal that in rural Hispanic New Mexico the WPA became known as "*el diablo a pie*"— the devil on foot. (26)

Doubtless, the problems were many and serious, but Wood here fails to recognize the jocularity and linguistic playfulness of the phonetic and mimetic recognition. Thus, the way the phrase "the WPA" was pronounced in Spanish, sounding like "*el diablo a pie*," mockingly incorporated Nuevomexicanos' attitudes towards it.

The mixed results of the Project were apparent in the New Mexico Guide as in other New Deal projects. The Federal Writers' Project series of Guide Books was originally meant to be a five-volume regional encyclopedia but later was expanded into individual State Guides, written and edited locally. This proved at times to be a problem, with neither editors or writers specifically trained for the task. As letters from a state director reveal, the editors of the New Mexico guide "did not know the New Mexican scene very well and did not at all grasp the kind of writing that must go into a Guide . . ." (Weigle, *New Mexicans*, xvii).

The final product, *New Mexico: A Guide to the Colorful State*, was not only late but it was ugly (it had a blue-on-orange cover), and, in addition, had been purged of any individual interest or perspective. Marta Weigle characterizes it as an "essentially anonymous record of hundreds of submissions and interviews" (*New Mexicans* xviii). The documents that remain, however, many unused in the Guide and unpublished, are important to scholars today as the primary material for an understanding of New Mexico's history, people, employment, arts, folklore, and literature.

During an early phase of the Federal Writers' Project, emphasis on the study of folklore was successfully urged by New Mexicans Nina Otero-Warren and J. F. Zimmerman (president of the University of New Mexico) in a proposal to the national office arguing the value of regional difference. "It is a person who is a product of the soil, who lives closely to it, that is able to give us the regional and varied aspect of America" (quoted in Weigle, *New Mexicans*, xix). Their proposal, according to Weigle, helped shape questionnaires sent out to collectors working for the Writers' Project in 1936. The questionnaire, in turn, shaped the form of the interviews:

1. Are there any Indian legends that tell stories of your community? What are they? Give the exact location of the scene of the story.
2. Are there any geographic features, canyons, mountains, peaks, headlands, etc., named for Indian legends? What are they?
3. Are there recognized things such as wishing seats, wishing wells, swamps, or quicksands with sinister properties, localities with beneficent qualities, proposal rocks or lanes, etc.?
4. Are there any stories concerned with animals or animal life, or the relation between human beings and animals, that are native to your community?
5. Are there any festivals celebrated at special times of the year designed to insure good luck, good crops, good weather, etc.? Describe them.
6. Can you discover any songs or ballads sung or commonly used by any group of people or passed down in any particular family? Copy them or get them by word of mouth.
7. Are there special fairs or market days, particularly if they are significant as related to local products or local life or industry? Describe them.
8. Is there a particular kind of costume common to a sect or group worn in your district? Describe it. How did it originate?
9. Are there special customs relating to particular days in the year, such as Fourth of July, Halloween, Christmas, etc.? Describe them.
10. Are there special customs observed at the birth of a child, upon the death of a person, at marriages?
11. Are there community gatherings such as quilting, singing, schools, etc.? Describe them.

12. Are there any peculiarities of table service or dining routine, such as serving the husband first, serving of bread by the father, etc.?

13. Are there religious customs, such as public denunciation of wrong-doing, Easter services, blessing of crops or rivers, camp meetings? Describe them.

14. Are there rodeos, joustings, log-rolling contests? Are there localized ghost stories, witch stories, etc.?

Addenda:

1. Are there any words, phrases, or expressions peculiar to your section, such as dialect, slang, unusual "graces" at table, drinking toasts, short rhymes, dance calls, "play party" songs, etc.?

2. Are there any of the so-called "tall tales," where the story teller gets the effect either through exaggeration or understatement, stories that are not in print but that are passed around by word of mouth?

3. Are there any jokes, anecdotes, about some local character or unusual person of the present or past that are passed around by the campfire or where two or three good fellows meet together?

4. Are there any unusual epitaphs in old graveyards, or signs about abandoned mines or starved-out towns, or painted on wayside stones?

5. Are there any persons in your community who are believed to possess power to see into the future? Tell some of the current stories about such persons (Weigle, *New Mexicans*, xix, xx).

The very nature of the questionnaires was designed to get at, in specific ways, the folklore and customs of a people, and to direct the interviewers to ask the necessary questions to find the material. It is not clear if these questionnaires were distributed to all interviewers in all regions or if they were taken seriously by the directors of the state programs, or if they were uniformly applied in the field. The Arizona WPA, for instance, did not solicit such material from the Hispano informants, but some apparently was solicited from Anglo informants. It appears that the questionnaire was distributed to the New Mexico collectors as it was handed out in a mineographed form.

In addition to the stories and interviews collected, there were many photographs taken by the Farm Security Administration. Generally taken by a team of photographers led by Roy Stryker, the photographs were to document rural life and even later functioned as a sort of propaganda or publicity campaign for a "democratic America." Many of these photographs contained or sought out what Roy Stryker called "the significant detail," meaning that "special billboard, kitchen cupboard, or pair of work boots," which would articulate the "particular character of rural life" (Wood, 2). Wood notes WPA officials believed that these sorts of special detail did the following:

> They connect Americans to one another. They make people laugh. They create a nostalgia for the kind of uncomplicated innocence that perhaps the country never really had. And yet, the photographs spell it out. Details of kitchens. Backyards. Store windows. One-room schoolhouses. Parlors. Soda jerks. Migrants. Storekeepers. Gamblers. Schoolchildren. Fortunetellers. Old ladies with sturdy shoes, black leather purses, long baggy dresses, low-crowned hats with veils and faces that reflect an indomitable will. The pictures show suffering and despair, but they show a singular courage, too. (4)

Like the photographs, the stories people told were full of such significant details, and perhaps the interviewers were told to keep their eyes on those details. Thus, Annette Hersh Thorp would describe the interiors of the houses in her narratives, and Lou Sage Batchen would inscribe every detail of a *remedio* (herbal remedy) and its use. In her book *The Preservation of the Village: New Mexico's Hispanics and the New Deal*, Suzanne Forrest claims that the New Deal was a cultural invasion far more pervasive than anything Hispanic New Mexicans had yet experienced. She believes that the interviewers romanticized the work and culture of the rural villages and "cleaned up" the Mexican heritage. In so doing, they invented a romantic Spanish heritage for the state. This was the beginning of a "Spanish" revival, the creation of a "utopic" arcadia of Hispanic village culture. According to Forrest, the Federal Writers' Project was part of the implementation of a widespread cultural agenda,

> proporting to value cultural pluralism they extolled the virtues of Hispanic arts, crafts, music, and folklore, but worked mightily to extradite such other aspects of Hispanic ethnicity as the "superstition" or "irresponsibility" that brought Hispanos to put devotion to church, family, and culture over secular and monetary values. Other aspects of Hispanic ethnicity were variously and pejoratively labeled as docility, lack of ambition, and just plain ignorance. (103)

Forrest believes that the planners behind the Federal Writers' Project saw this interpretation as valid because it was some sort of "behavior modification." On the other hand, "many villages were also invaded by urban intellectuals, both Anglo and Hispanic, eager to record and transcribe old Hispanic myths and legends, songs and musical rhythms, dances and ceremonies, folk customs and folk medicine" (Forrest, 104). As she sees it, while the Federal Arts Project was supposed to help destitute writers and artists, the people themselves seized upon this opportunity to advance a Hispanic cultural agenda as they believed that their customs and culture were being lost, and that this would be one way to preserve them (Forrest, 119).

Unlike in Arizona, particular emphasis was put on the collection of Hispanic folklore by the New Mexico state director Ina Sizer Cassidy, in spite of the problems that she was to have dealing with the various administrative people and details in the program.[2] Many of the interviewers who collected the stories were not fluent in Spanish, and what is left in the archives is not in the original language of the storytellers. Most stories are bastardized texts, at times creatively imagined by the interviewer, often romanticized. Yet the basic rituals and customs remain, and often, too, the voices of the narrators come through the discourse.

With the advent of World War II, the entire WPA education program was put at the service of the U.S. Army, and the collecting stopped altogether.

Edited Voices: Approaches to the Hispano WPA Cuentos

In terms of the Hispano cuentos of the WPA, we need to ponder an approach to the "originatory" stories. By the time the stories were deposited, in English, in the WPA repository, many layers of editing had already taken place. Unlike the information available with the California testimonials,[3] whose interviewers kept copious notes on the process of information gathering as well as on individual interviews, we have little information on the process of folklore collecting in the New Mexico WPA. While we have a list of some of the questions asked, we do not know if the list was adhered to in a meticulous or casual fashion. There are only hints of how the material may have been collected (in the days before recording devices were used). There are also some interesting language issues involved that will be discussed later.

Two of the main collectors of the folklore and folktales were men, Lorin Brown and Bright Lynn. Both were competent in Spanish, or so it appears. Brown was a "coyote"[3] whose mother was Nuevomexicana, and he grew up in his maternal grandparent's home in Taos (she was Juanita Montoya de

Martínez). Lynn was a Spanish-language student at New Mexico Normal University in Las Vegas (*normal* meaning a college for training teachers), and it could be supposed that he had good Spanish-language skills. Both men appear to have had access to the Spanish-speaking Nuevomexicano community and to women's stories. One can only imagine, however, that very personal matters would not have been related to these men by older women.

As for the two women collectors, Lou Sage Batchen and Annette Hesch Thorp, it is difficult to say what their language skills were. They have left little indication whether the stories were told in Spanish and then translated by them (or some other WPA worker), or if the stories were translated for them already and told in English and then transcribed by them. Perhaps because they were women, they were entrusted with a few intimate details by their female informants. Several other collectors, Simeon Tejada and Reyes Martínez, were primary Spanish speakers and did their own translations or translated stories for others. Thus, the issue of the "authenticity" of the stories becomes complicated.

To complicate matters further, many of the directors in Washington, at various times, found the writing of the collectors in New Mexico, specifically the few Spanish-speaking collectors, to be very simplistic. Moreover, there was a great deal of discussion as to how their material should be arranged. One can imagine that the same sort of chaotic direction was being given to the other writers in the project as well.

Of the collectors, only Lorin Brown has left an indication of his collecting methods. In their interesting biographical and historical sketch of Brown, Marta Weigle and Charles Briggs quote Brown as saying,

> I spent my days renewing old acquaintances, particularly the elders whose conversations I enjoyed because they smacked of old times, old customs, and traditions. Thus, I would spend my afternoons and evenings talking here and there first with one and then another, until it was time for them to retire. I would then take myself to my room, light the kerosene lamp, put the old #5 Remington into action, and start typing the salient features of that evening's conversation. I would type until about two or three in the morning, at which time I would hit the hay, sleep late, and saunter forth next day after a brunch to resume my pleasant conversations around the village. I mailed all my manuscripts in to the head office, rarely going in except on occasions . . . (20)

From this statement we can surmise that the "salient" features that were retained contained the main thrust and important narrative features of his "conversations," but that details might have been added from memory or imagination. There is no indication that the texts were in any way approved by the storyteller. On the other hand, there is also no indication that the collectors were untrue to the original stories. In addition, as Weigle and Briggs explain, the outcome of Brown's manuscripts reflected his own interests and those of his family, who were native to the region, in recording the folklore of village history. Consequently, according to Weigle and Briggs, "he chose the oldest inhabitants of the village as his primary informants. Much of the information he recorded was drawn from such individuals' childhood memories and from their parents' and grandparents' stories" (Brown, 21).

Brown apparently had conflicts (as did many of the other collectors) with Ina Sizer Cassidy, the director of the New Mexico Writers' Project, over many issues. One of them was the fact that Cassidy was apparently not as concerned with quality as she was with quantity. Brown said, "I never received any word of approval; Ina just demanded a constant flow of material" (Brown, 24). In addition, some questions about the Spanish translations, not only those from Brown but also from the other collectors, are evident: questions that point out the constant struggle between the purists of the Spanish language and those who tried to duplicate and authenticate the native language variants. As Brown states, he had translated a song in which the phrase "*vente chinita comigo*" appeared, translating it as "come away with me, my little curlyhaired one" (in Spanish *chinos* are curls). He tells us:

> Mrs. Cassidy objected to the translation, saying that couldn't be possible, that the words really meant "come away with me, my little Chinese lass." Despite my efforts to prove her wrong, being the person she was, I could not make my point and so the translation had to go through as she had decided it must be. (24)

With this sort of comment over something so simple, one wonders what kind of confusion would be caused over something complicated. Moreover, Brown goes on to state,

> I'd been asked to repeat the conversations of a group of men around the campfire or bonfire (which) I had described as being one of the highlights of a "*velorio*," wherein the men would build a bonfire outside in the patio and hunker down round the fire carry-

ing on conversations and narratives on different subjects like horse trading, planting of crops, hunting, and highlights in the life of some individual who was outstanding because of his feats, whether humorous or prodigious in strength or so on. I was asked to prepare a typical conversation around these bonfires and submit it for some special request made by a Washington official perhaps, anyway, the higher-ups of the Writers' Project. This I did, putting down the conversation "just about verbatim," just in the Spanish as it is spoken up in the villages. I used the archaic and historic nuances of the language as it was spoken up there. For instance, I used the word *ansina* for *así*, *croque* for *creo que*, *p'alla* for *para allá*, *alao* for *alado*, *parao* for *parado* and so on. These distortions, if you will, were common and part of the language up there. My manuscript was submitted and sent to higher authorities for evaluation and was returned with the notation that it was at best, very poor pedestrian Spanish and as such could not possibly be entertained as a worthwhile contribution. In my benighted understanding, I had thought that that was what the Writers' Project was striving for—authentic reproduction of particularly the languages of people, and it was a blow to see this interpreted in such a manner. It is possible that whoever reviewed this, perhaps a graduate of Spanish from some university where academic Spanish was taught, did not realize the fact that in New Mexico the Spanish of three hundred years before has been preserved.

. . . This rejection of my efforts made me strive for a permission to hie myself back to the villages and keep a low profile . . . (24-25)

Some of the folklore work was checked by Professors F. M. Kercheville and Dr. Arthur L. Campa, of the University of New Mexico, both experts in language. It does not seem likely that Dr. Campa, a noted folklorist himself, would have affected such purity of language. Weigle and Briggs comment, "This is a serious charge against the Project, and it should be borne in mind by all who consult the New Mexico Spanish-language materials" (Brown, 25).

Problems apparently existed also with the writings of Reyes Martínez, one of the few native Spanish-speaking interviewers. The directors and editors in Washington were very disparaging of the writing found in his tales and critical of his writing style. In one commentary of several stories turned in by Martínez, the editor found his work to be "badly over-written" and "somewhat flowery." The sum of the critique said "each article contains a splinter of folklore, folk belief, etc. written in the somewhat lively style of an enthusiastic adolescent with a gift for expression. All the stories need editorial revision, in particular reorganization and condensing." This harsh criticism came from a Mrs. Turner. Ina Sizer Cassidy had sent Turner's letter to Alice Corbin, who was then directing the New Mexico Project, and Alice Corbin, in turn, wrote to Cassidy defending Martínez. Corbin said,

> The charm of Reyes Martínez' copy is its extreme simplicity — and lucidity. His descriptions of Spanish customs are, of course, authentic; he needs no "sources" other than his own knowledge (though he gives others). In a write-up of such a village as Arroyo Hondo, his work needed practically no editing or revision (far less than that of some of his "Americano" confreres); his description of the Arroyo Hondo church I should say was perfect . . . and anyone would be hard-put to better his description. And all his accounts of historic-legendary happenings in Taos county are genuine and of the soil . . . I hope we may have the opportunity to help to develop such talent. We have other conspicuous examples of it in the work handed in by other Spanish-Americans from San Miguel country, and elsewhere. (Letter from Alice Corbin to Ina Sizer Cassidy, September 29, 1936)

Such strong defense from Corbin did not remedy the matter. In a patronizing tone, Mrs. Turner wrote to George Cronyn on October 19, 1939:

> . . . I have been rather drastic in my criticism of Mr. Martínez. If he is very young and without much cultural background, his work may be taken to have some promise. He shows a sense of color and might, after learning to express himself simply, do adequate feature stories for a Sunday newspaper. If, however, he is mature in years and has had average school advantages, I regard his work as rather hopeless. He certainly shows none of the "extreme simplicity and lucidity" claimed by Alice Corbin. The general impression, after reading the papers submitted, is one of an adolescent who has been encouraged beyond his native ability.

Clearly these sorts of appraisals plagued the project as the central power, Washington, tried to force some control of uniformity over all the material that was being submitted. They failed to understand the unique viewpoint of the Hispano contributors in their efforts to extol the "American" aspect while at the same time giving lip service to "regional" values. At this moment of collecting and compiling the "American" Guides, there emanated from Washington a sort of Master Narrative for what was considered to be American.

New Mexican regional diversity in terms of culture and language was not necessarily included within a broad spectrum of what was America; rather it was viewed as exotic.

Thorp and Batchen:
The Women Collectors and the Women's Narratives

The language problem also enters into the narratives collected by Annette Hesch Thorp and Lou Sage Batchen. To begin, we do not have much information about them. We know that Thorp was married to N. Howard (Jack) Thorp in 1903. Her father was a sheep rancher. Her husband Jack, composer and collector of cowboy songs and stories, was employed by the NMFWP and Writers' Program. After he died in 1940, Annette was also qualified for the Program. Throughout, she is noted as "elderly" (Weigle, "Some New Mexican Grandmothers," 94-95).

As for Lou Sage Batchen, according to the foreword of the *Las Placitas* book, her husband had a mining interest in the Las Placitas area in the late 19th century. Batchen "developed a deep and warm feeling for the village and its people. . . .Lou Sage Batchen lived out her long life in the village that she loved so well." In his thesis, "The People of the San Antonio de Las Huertas Grant," Andrew T. White stated, "Lou Sage Batchen was not native to the area. . . At the time the testimonies were collected the Batchens lived in Ojo de la Casa. Though the Batchens were not the first Anglos to live in the area, they were the first to reside for a considerable length of time. By 1942, Lou Sage Batchen owned the second highest number of water rights in the grant" (White 10). He also comments on her language ability and collecting methods. According to White, Batchen's Spanish-language skills were poor. She could speak and understand Spanish but did neither well. Thus, she used one of the Las Placitas women, Christina Gonzales, as an interpreter (White 10). In a recent account of the Las Placitas Presbyterian Church, *Century of Faith*, Suzanne Forrest examines the establishment of the church, often using Batchen's stories as a basis for her history. Forrest states,

Lou Batchen was physically handicapped and could not get around easily. For that reason, and because she did not speak enough Spanish to carry on the interviews herself, she employed Max DeLara and Christina Gonzales to help her. Max was an enterprising twelve-year-old when he started working with her in the early 1930s. He recalls that she paid him fifty cents an hour, a magnificent wage for the time, to visit with old timers and get them to tell him stories from their youth. They were delighted to pass on the local wisdom to the eager, bright-eyed young man. Max's favorite storyteller was his grandfather, José Gurulé. Since all the villagers told Max their stories in Spanish, he had to translate them mentally as he retold them to Mrs. Batchen. He made it a point to mimic the way the stories were told to him as closely as possible, so she could get the right "feel" for each tale. She listened intently and wrote the stories down on her old typewriter as fast as he told them to her. Max devoted about six hours each week to the project, and the $3.00 weekly wage helped his father buy a lot of groceries. In 1936 Max DeLara left Placitas to work in the Civilian Conservation Corps (CCC), and Batchen employed Christina Baros Gonzales to help her. (12-13)

That Batchen's Spanish was not very good is certainly verified by the fact that often her tense, agreements, and spelling in Spanish are wrong. For example, she calls *arroyos arroyas* and refers to *madrinas* as *padrinas*; she also makes extensive errors in verbs, gender, agreement, and spelling, errors that cannot be explained away as regional variations. At times she cannot decide whether a name should be spelled in English or Spanish, so we have both variants— Nicolás and Nicholas. She would anglicize a Spanish word, *peón*, to *peons* in the plural when it should have been *peones*. She regularly does this with such words as *colchón, colchons*.

White claims that some insight into her methods can be seen in her letters to her director. "I shall get the stories. . . These older people at Las Placitas are grand to me, and they do all they can to get me the information I need. It may take many sittings with each source of information, but usually after hours of assorted suggestions and various memory aids, they do recall the things that their forefathers did, or whatever it is I am after" (White 11). Forrest also goes on to state,

Batchen's stories cannot be taken literally. . . .Batchen sometimes related different versions of the same story, with varying names and dates. At other times she probably winnowed out contradictory or apparently irrelevant details to make a better story. Some of her informants may also have embroidered their tales with imaginative details to amuse themselves or to cover up failing memories. Even Lou, we suspect, was not above adding her own literary details and giving an occasional O'Henryesque twist to the ending. (13)

Such changes are, however, the expected composition of storytelling, and changing the details of the story, or making them more dramatic, does not necessarily detract from the authenticity of the story itself.

José Librado Arón Gurulé was one of Batchen's principal informants, and he was quite elderly; nevertheless, with a bit of prompting he was very knowledgeable. He died in 1943, shortly after Batchen had stopped working with the WPA. Batchen herself died in 1953.

I concur with White when he says that the best part of Batchen's procedure was that she listed her informants, their ages, and often their relation to other informants and to the original settlers of the grant.

Thus, it is probable that neither Thorp nor Batchen had good Spanish-language skills. Thorp's narratives include many concepts and terms in Spanish, particularly if they have to do with implements, tools, and concepts she considered different or archaic. She then immediately translates the terms for her readers. This happens less often in the original narratives that Batchen collected. She would, at times, would include the Spanish words or phrases, but places less emphasis on them than Thorp does. By the time we reach the book published on Batchen's original narratives, *Las Placitas*, the language has almost totally changed and has become Batchen's narrative and not that of the original tellers. In fact, it is interesting to note that in *Las Placitas*, a book she had reworked and rewritten, the English also takes on a very antiquated and archaic tone; when a Spanish-speaker is quoted, he speaks in a sort of pidgin English.[5] This perhaps harks back to the idea that rural New Mexicans were part of that nostalgic, Arcadian, romanticized past. Certainly there is little mention of modern-day problems or remedies.

A directive from the main office may have spurred part of the Arcadian notion. In a letter from Hanau on the Placitas material, he says:

> The scheme of grouping the material into sections on the villages is perhaps a good one, but by trying to arrange the stories in chronological order within these sections nothing is gained, and much is lost, it seems to us. A possible way of handling the material would be to give the present picture: What Las Placitas looks like today, who lives there, and how they live. Then tell the old stories in some way that suggests, at least, how the material was gathered. Perhaps a visitor could be the narrator, and the old people, gathered together or singly, could tell him about life in the old days and tales they heard as children. These talks would of course not be verbatim translations; the general atmosphere can be created, however. . . To sum up: Do not try to edit, revise, and

> correct the text as it now stands. Hold the original material intact
> until it can be reconsidered and rewritten according to some more
> imaginatively conceived scheme.

This, of course, was a disaster for those of us interested in the original material, but it also may have been what preserved it in its present state.[6] We must hold in mind, however, that even the original material was not verbatim.[7]

It is interesting to note that the state directors in New Mexico recognized the value of the material that both Batchen and Thorp had collected and tried in vain to get it published and to save it in some sort of format. On November 8, 1940, state supervisor Charles Ethrige Minton signed what appears to be a grant request from the Coronado Cuarto Centennial Commission asking for funds for "Some New Mexico Grandmothers," which he explains as the "life stories of some old crones in New Mexico villages." With that money they would have two people working, and the project completed in one year. (Thorp is not mentioned as the collector). They also apparently expected to have some photographs accompany the text. Later, in a letter to the director of the Federal Writers' Program, J. D. Newsom, November 13, 1941, Minton, writing about "Some New Mexico Grandmothers," complains bitterly and sarcastically about Thorp's dismissal from the Writers' Project:

> Almost half of this material was in when the writer who was work-
> ing on it received her 403 (notice of termination) because she had
> managed to save $200 toward a down payment on a little adobe
> house. The possession of this vast wealth made her ineligible for
> WPA employment, so nothing further has been done with this
> exceptionally interesting material. (Cited in Weigle, "Some New
> Mexican Grandmothers," 96)

Later, in a progress report for February 2, 1942, Minton again comments on Thorp's dismissal,

> This is the material, roughly one-third complete, on which work
> was stopped when the worker was 403'd several months ago. It
> was insufficient for separate publication and too good to lose, so it
> has been incorporated in *The Deep Village* (also never published).

There is a bit more information about the problems and ideas raised about Batchen's "Las Placitas" material. The material was sent, largely unedited, to Washington along with a request for the advice of the Central Office on how to organize it. In a letter from Minton to Newsom on November 6, 1941,

Minton lays out the problems, asking if the work is suitable for publication, or if a publisher could be found for it. He also thinks "it needs a fresh eye."

Because of these "problems" with the text, we are able to find out some of the history of its collection. Interestingly enough, part of the problem with the text, according to Minton, is that

> The original material has been difficult to edit. Full of inverted phrases and archaic expressions, and with a sentimental style that becomes cloying, this first revise is simply to smooth it out, so it will be easier to see how it might be shaped up. . . . The section of Las Placitas is much the longest, for the reason that the population is centered there now. Tejón is entirely in ruins, only three families live in Ojo de la Casa, one family in Las Huertas, and La Madera is some distance away. (2)

He also believes that although the definitions of Spanish words and phrases are "given parenthetically, we thought we should prepare a glossary of terms for the back of the book, having only long phrases translated in parenthesis." Later he goes on to comment that the Spanish used in the phrases is "not classic or academic Spanish, but that spoken by the people. We plan to leave this as it is, for the reason that its value as folk material is enhanced thereby."

In addition to the stories, there were plans to include pen-and-ink drawings with the text, a map illustrating the places mentioned in the stories, as well as illustrations of specific local phenomena such as Juan of Tecolote's mill. Apparently, there was also a children's book planned for this material, to be named *Before Your Time*. Minton states, "We hope some day to adapt this material, leaving out most of the gore and the witchcraft, for a child's book of about 35,000 words, or less . . . What do you think of this?" In fact, he gets so enthusiastic that he comments, "It might be that this kind of material has more value than some in the category of National Defense."

The answer came on January 27, 1942. Hanau concurs that the material is "unusual and provocative" but states, "As the text now stands, however, it lacks atmosphere, the visual pictures are not sufficiently well drawn to orient the uninitiated reader, and the characters do not "come alive." He is puzzled by the text and considers it verbose and undistinguished. He asks, "Has the original perhaps been too drastically changed, thus losing something in flavor without gaining anything in readability?" He is at wit's end as to how to improve it, but gives some general suggestions as a guide. One of the strongest suggestions is to condense the history of the stories. "The lengthy historical passages need to be subordinated and cut; . . . the historical material and quotations from old records might be used as interludes between some of the reminiscences to give the necessary factual background" (2). Perhaps the critic did not understand that none of this local material had ever been written down, and might be lost without its inclusion.

Although Ina Sizer Cassidy's staff did not find her supportive, Thorp and Batchen appreciated Minton. He wrote encouraging letters to them, telling them how good their work was and asking informed questions. He expressed enthusiasm for their work. On more than one occasion Thorp and Batchen wrote thanking him for his encouragement, as well as commenting on local happenings. Batchen wrote, "I cannot tell you how very much I appreciated your letter. Those letters, as I told you before, are like Green Lights that tell me to go on—I am as eager to read the flash of that signal now as I was at the beginning of this work. I work harder now, for the field of information is narrowing, but I love the work more. It is like calling something back to life that is fast slipping away" (Batchen to Minton, May 22, 1942).

The End of the WPA

By 1942, the United States was deep into the Second World War, and its resources were needed for national defense. The WPA and its writers (those who had not been 403'd, as were Thorp and Martínez) were put at the service of the nation. The material from the WPA went into steel filing cabinets in history and state archives in Santa Fe, and most has remained there until this day. Some selections from Thorp's "Some New Mexico Grandmothers" have been published in various articles and books by Marta Weigle. She also published some of Batchen's stories. In 1972 Batchen's revised but unpublished collected material, which she had rewritten and reconceptualized, was published by the Placitas Garden Club as *Las Placitas*. In the publishing of this book, some of the stories were incorporated into other stories, and the order was changed around. Charles Ethridge Minton used the material as the basis for a creative work, *Juan of Santo Niño*, published in 1973. In this book, with the place name of Las Placitas changed to Santo Niño, Minton used Batchen's stories, but did not refer to the informants because "names have been changed because the story is authentic and because the descendants of the people of Santo Niño still live there" (Minton, iv). He does not credit Batchen for all her hard work; the only oblique reference to her is a cryptic dedication, "Tía Lou, here is your book."

Many of the Las Placitas stories were later used by Andrew T. White to create a historical ethnography of the area in his 1973 unpublished master's thesis, "The People of San Antonio de Las Huertas Grant, New Mexico, 1767-1900." In addition to Batchen's stories, White corroborated dates and events with other historical documents, such as archival records, census records, and New Mexico land grant records.

In this book, we have gathered together all the Thorp and Batchen stories in their original form, those contained in the Santa Fe History Archives as well as those in the New Mexico State Archives. We have also gathered as much material about them and the informants as we could find. The material, published here for the first time, is a rich representation of Hispano life and culture in New Mexico.

The Hispano Informants
Annette Hesch Thorp: Informants

We do not know much about Thorp's informants. The title of the book based on her material was to be *Some New Mexico Grandmothers*. The stories that are included in the WPA files were collected from at least seven different informants, all of whom lived in different areas of the state. We can discern the following from the stories themselves.

Catalina Viareal was from Alcalde, New Mexico, and was about eighty years old when interviewed. Her father was Antonio Viareal, her mother María Vigil. Her narrations were written as if they were mostly answers to questions asked. We know that she was the youngest daughter of her family and that she chose to help her parents and not marry. She thus inherited her parents' house and land. She described the furnishings and contents of her house, in particular her *nicho* of the Santo Niño and his story. Her story is the first, collected on September 17, 1940, and is told as a conversation, with Catalina answering Thorp's questions.

Cesaria Gallegos told her story on September 23, 1940. She thought she was close to one hundred years old. Her parents were from Agua Fría, a small town near Taos; her father was Vicente Ortega, her mother Dolores López. Cesaria married Antonio Gallegos when she was fourteen. This story was also told as a conversation.

Manuelita Romero (Tita) was the daughter of Natalia Urioste. She did not know who her father was. At fifteen, when she married Lino Romero, her troubles began. Lino was an alcoholic and went crazy after he fell off a wagon. Tita thought her husband was bewitched. She was around eighty years of age when Thorp talked with her.

Cresencia Atencio, also known as Chana, was about ninety years old when interviewed by Thorp. She was unsure of her actual age. She lived in the village of El Santo Niño on the Santa Cruz River. The daughter of Policarpio Montoya and Antonia Valencia, she had married Manuel Atencio when she was quite young. Her stories were about local customs, and she was very knowledgeable about the way things were made or obtained in her youth. She gave vivid descriptions about making molasses, gathering salt, and about customs such as singing and praying in the church, and local celebrations. Moreover, she had definite ideas about the importance of sharing food, and other necessities, with both the poor and the departed souls. She was one of the first whom Thorp interviewed, since the date of her story is December 3, 1940. Also, Thorp had not yet begun counting the number of words she was writing.

We do not have information about Antonio Vigil.[8] On the story of "Nuestra Señora del Rosario," there is an annotation saying that it was told by Antonia Vigil. In a letter from Thorp to Minton (December 23, 1940), she confirms this information, stating that she took it out of her collection "because she could not find anyone who knew a complete story." Here the informant is identified as Antonio [sic] Vigil of San Ildefonso, who died ten years earlier. She says that she obtained this story from him about fifteen years ago. The "Casorios" story was told on the same date (or written on the same date), December 10, 1940, and it is possible that they were told by the same person. The note also stated that it was part of the Chana material. The same note is listed on "Witch Stories. The Story of a Headache."

Marcelina García was sixty-eight years of age when she was interviewed. She was the niece of Josefa Vigil, who brought up Marcelina after her parents died. We do not know Josefa's importance. Marcelina, also known as Lina, talked many times to Thorp, and the dates of her stories range from December 31, 1940, to March 25, 1941. At least seven narratives seem to come from Lina, and perhaps even more that are not specifically marked. She was from Pojoaque, New Mexico, and was married to Tiófilo García. Most of Lina's narrations are about the parteras, curanderas, and remedios. She knew so much that we might surmise that she herself was a curandera and that perhaps her Aunt Josefa was also. Lina discussed important community and personal rituals: the misa on the first anniversary of her husband's death, the importance of godparents, and the significance of various fiestas. The dates of "Velorio" and "Mortaja" suggest that Lina was also the informant for them.

Barbarita Nieto, from Cedar Grove in the San Pedro Mountains, tells stories about the death of her husband, Merejildo Nieto, and attendant customs surrounding it. Merejildo was a *penitente*. Barbarita was the daughter of Luis Chávez and Manuela Gallegos.

Juliana Martínez, also from Agua Fría, was around seventy or seventy-two when interviewed by Thorp. We have little personal information about her. She told "Fabiana, a Witch Story," and "Satan and the Girl." The dates on her narrations are April 1, and April 8, 1941.

The final informant was Vicenta Sánchez from Albuquerque, who was between seventy and seventy-eight when interviewed. She must have been quite talkative, for many of the stories come from Vicenta. The earliest date is April 15, 1941 and the last is June 17, 1941. The daughter of Juan José Sánchez and Juanita Chávez, Vicenta had a grandfather who was a miserly old man. She obviously disapproved of his miserliness as she commented on it, as well as on that of the father of Amalia Lucero, one of the people in her stories, and of Amalia herself. She told the wonderful story about Alvina and the buffalo hunters, and explained cheese and wine making, local customs (observances of Holy Week), and children's (especially girls') games. In her stories, we also see the encroaching of the modern age.

It is a pity that Thorp did not keep notes. (If she did, we have not found them.) The language issue is especially difficult. We do not know if Thorp was fluent in Spanish or if she had a translator to help her. She is good at leaving specific items or concepts in Spanish, which she then translates into English. The words she left in Spanish are often spelled differently from standard Spanish; at times they are words or concepts known only in New Mexico. Thorp's English was not that of a polished writer. In her texts we have corrected some of the minor spelling discrepancies to make them easier to read. In particular, she was fond of inserting an apostrophe into plurals and omitting it from the possessive. It is difficult to know if this was to simulate what she might have thought was a simple use of language or if, indeed, it was her own style. One of the original texts, "Parteras," shows signs of heavy editing. In some paragraphs almost every word is crossed out and the entire sentence restructured. Again, it is difficult to know if Thorp edited the text herself or if it was edited by someone in the central office. But the reader can see that the layer of editing was transformative.

Thorp was also not very careful about putting dates on her collected narrations. The numbering system is not consistent so it is impossible, except for the dates, to tell the order in which they were collected. Moreover, there are no field notes to help us determine what sort of methods were used in the collecting. It is highly suspicious that the narrations are dated, in most cases, exactly a week apart. It is as if the narrator would delay telling the story until the next week, instead of telling it all at once. More probable is that the dates come from the times that Thorp typed the stories, carefully counting the words, and turning them in so that she could collect her money, or show progress in her work.

Lou Sage Batchen: Informants

The information contained in the stories collected by Lou Sage Batchen came down in different ways. José Antonio Gurulé, one of Las Placitas' *mayordomos* (a person who looked after community water rights), provided a list of the twenty-one founding families of the San Antonio grant who had rights to the water. The heads of the families were kept on the mayordomo's list which was passed on to José Librado Arón Gurulé, one of Batchen's most frequent informants. His name appears on many of the stories and tales as a source. There is also other written information from the Trujillo family. These are records of Juan Tafoya given to his grandson, Dave Trujillo, Sr. Other sources are collective storytelling and historical records, such as Twitchel and others. At times, the informants told stories by themselves, but if we look at the records carefully, Batchen often lists the names of several who told a particular story, thus verifying it in group process.

Batchen tried to establish a genealogy or some sort of historical/family connection to the stories. We know, for example, that José Librado Arón Gurulé was the son of Nicolás and the grandson of Juanita. We are also told the connections of the storytellers to the story, such as the fact that the teller knew the subject, or was a friend. What we are not told, and what emerges as a fascinating accompaniment to the stories, is that most of the storytellers were related in one way or another, by blood or by marriage. If we pay careful attention, we also discover, as in "Antonia and her Saints," that there is great suspicion in the town that the priest from Bernalillo took the old saints away to sell them to art collectors. José Librado Arón Gurulé and others in Placitas became Presbyterians and thus were against the statues (regarded as idols).Often the religious perspective of a story changes, depending on which part of the family is telling it, and whether the informant was Catholic or Presbyterian.[9]

Informants were interviewed from 1938 to 1942; for that reason, their ages are different at various times. The following is information on them culled from various biographies, and stories.

Josefa and Miguel Trujillo, subjects of "Josefa and Her Sons." Josefa Tafoya was born in 1823.

Dave Trujillo, Sr., inherited family records from Juan Tafoya, his grand-father. He and his brother José were direct descendants of the twenty-one families of the San Antonio de Las Huertas Land Grant.

David Trujillo, (ages forty-five to forty-nine) of Placitas, New Mexico, a grandson of Josefa and Miguel Trujillo, son of Dave Trujillo, Sr. and great grandson of Teresa Chávez, born in Las Huertas.

José Trujillo, forty-seven, of Placitas, New Mexico, a grandson of Josefa and Miguel Trujillo, son of Francisco Trujillo, son of Josefa, and brother to Dave. His family had lived continuously in the old town of Las Huertas since the land grant was given to the twenty-one families in 1765.

Josefita Lucero, forty, of Placitas, New Mexico, a granddaughter of Josefa and Miguel Trujillo, a daughter of Dave Trujillo.

Avelina Gurulé, fifty-five, of Placitas, New Mexico, a granddaughter of Josefa and Miguel Trujillo. A daughter of Dave Trujillo and wife of Nicolas Gurulé, she was also the niece of Francisco Trujillo.

Carolina Mascarida, sixty, of Placitas, New Mexico, a daughter of José Librado Arón Gurulé. She was married to the youngest brother of Miquela, wife of Francisco Trujillo.

José Antonio Gurulé was a freighter and traveled to Los Estados (the United States).

Nicolás Gurulé, son of José Antonio Gurulé.

José Librado Arón Gurulé, born circa 1850, son of Nicolás Gurulé and nephew of Lucas Gurulé. He appeared at various ages (eighty-eight to ninety-four) during the course of the stories. From Las Placitas, New Mexico, he was a direct descendent of the twenty-one families of the San Antonio de Las Huertas Land Grant. At fifteen he was traveling with his grandfather on a trading trip to Los Estados when the musket he was carrying went off and blew off part of his arm. He cured himself and saved his own life. He became a schoolteacher and a Presbyterian and began teaching in Placitas when he was twenty-six. He was the grandson of Antonia, "Antonia and Her Saints," and nephew of Juana, whose Old Saints he buried. In "An Old Native Custom," his aunt is further identified as Juanita Gurulé de Zamora. His father was a contemporary of Mateo of "Mateo y Raquel." He was the son-in-law of Francisco Gonzales and Conception (Chonita) Tafoya de Gonzales, as he was first married to Rosita Gonzales, who was born March 6, 1853, and died April 15, 1906. He was one of the pupils of El Indio Viejo of that story. He was the head of the house Placida and Preciliano built by the side of the road. He saw early peddlers and Arab traders. Petra, of the Juan of Tecolote story, was his aunt. José L.A.

Gurulé, as he is also referred to, was born on August 15, 1851 by one account, and died shortly after Batchen stopped collecting stories on April 2, 1943.

Rumaldita Gurulé, aged sixty-six to sixty-eight, Placitas, New Mexico. A descendant of one of the twenty-one families to receive the San Antonio de Las Huertas Grant from the King of Spain in 1767, she was the second wife of José Librado Arón Gurulé. She knew the younger children of Piedad and Feliciano of "An Old Native Custom, Madrecita Piedad." Her grandmother was Quiteria, the young curandera or "witch nurse." She was the daughter-in-law of Gabrielita.

Cristiana Baros, aged twenty-eight to thirty-three, Placitas, New Mexico, was the daughter of Rumaldita Gurulé. Her knowledge of old folk-ways came from her great-grandmother, Gabrielita Gallardo.

Nicolás Gurulé, fifty-nine, Placitas, New Mexico, grandson of Francisco Gonzales and Conception Tafoya de Gonzales. Born November 7, 1882 and died March 26, 1964.

Avelina Gurulé (María Avelina Trujillo), fifty-eight, wife of Nicolás Gurulé and niece of Francisco Trujillo. Born September 27, 1883 and died September 5, 1955.

Pedro Gurulé, seventy-four, brother of José Antonio Arón Gurulé, son of Nicolás Gurulé, who was born in Las Huertas, and Catalina Bustos, born in San Felipe.

Auralia Gurulé, forty-seven, grandniece of the curandera, Jesusita. Wife of Pedro Gurulé. She explained how a few families of French descent arrived in Placitas, descendants of Victoria Alary, mother of Jesusita.

Catalina Gurulé, aged forty-five to forty-eight granddaughter of Nicolás Gurulé, daughter of Pedro by a former marriage, friend of Jesusita, La Curandera. She was the grandniece of Petra, wife of Juan of Tecolote.

Gracia (Grace) Trujillo, twenty-three, daughter of Pedro and Aurelia Gurulé.

Ferminia Durán, aged seventy-one to seventy-five, Las Placitas, New Mexico. Her grandmother was a friend of Petra. She married Salome Gonzales, son of Francisco Gonzales and Conception (Chonita) Tafoya de Gonzales. Salome died in 1890. Her parents, Juan Lucero and Chona Pacheco, came to Placitas from Alameda with Juan Armijo in the late fifties,or early sixties. She was a descendant of Pablo Pacheco of "La Cuna y La Muñeca." She saw some of the dolls he made when she was a child, and she had vivid memories of just how they looked.

Benino Archibeque, aged seventy-four to seventy-five, Las Placitas, remembered how his mother's *telar* and *malacate* were made. He was the son of Francisca and Salvadoro of "Clotilde and Francisca," and was born after the death of Marcelino. He helped take care of the old saints for so many years. He bitterly opposed exchanging the old saints of "Antonia and Her Saints" for new saints. His maternal grandparents were contemporaries of Mateo and Raquel. His father and Juan of Tecolote were good friends. He was the youngest brother of Juan Archibeche of "Juan y el Oso Ladrón," but was born after Juan was grown.

Concepción Archibeque, (aged sixty-nine to seventy-one), Las Placitas, wife of Benino Archibeque, remembered the telar and the malacate of the old days. She had a *malacate* she prized, made by her husband in the early days of their married life. A pious member of the church, she remembered the capilla of long ago and spent much of her time caring for Antonia's saints. She opposed giving up the old saints for the new ones. She was the daughter of Francisco Gonzales and Conception (Chonita) Tafoya of "Life in the Old Houses," and of Chona in "La Cuna y La Muneca." Chona died when Conception was about three, and she was reared by a friend who lived close to the home of Chona, Gabrielita. The child was familiar with the things in her mother's home, and played with dolls her mother had made.

Patricio Gallegos, aged sixty to sixty-four, Ojo de la Casa, New Mexico, was a direct descendant of the twenty-one families of the San Antonio de Las Huertas Land Grant. He helped build the new church in Las Placitas, and favored exchanging the old saints of Antonia for new saints. His father was Juan María Gallegos (d. 1930), and his mother was María de los Angeles Zamora de Gallegos. His father played with the older children of Francisca and Salvadoro of "Clotilde and Francisca." He was also a nephew of Piedad of "Madrecita Piedad," and of Juan Chaves and Calletano Chaves. His grandfather Cassimiro (also spelled Casimiro) Gallegos was a friend of Francisco Gonzales. He was the grandson of Valentino Zamora of the story "Life in the Old Houses: Hunts." Petra Gurulé, wife of Juan, was the sister of Juanita Gurulé Zamora, his grandmother. He was the great grandson of José Antonio Gurulé.

Magdalena Gallegos, aged fifty-eight to sixty, of Ojo de la Casa, wife of Patricio Gallegos, was born in Tomé, New Mexico. She was reared and educated by the Sisters of Loretto at Bernalillo. She was the daughter-in-law of Juan María Gallegos who played with the older children of Francisca and Salvadoro.

Teresita (at times spelled Terecita) Baca, aged thirty-four to thirty-five, was the daughter of Patricio Gallegos. Her grandmother was María de los Angeles Zamora de Gallegos, and her great-grandmother was Juanita Gurulé. Her grandfather was Juan María Gallegos.

Adelaida Chaves, fifty-five, Placitas, New Mexico, was the wife of Predicando Chaves and descendant of the Armijo family who came to Placitas before 1870 from Alameda, New Mexico. Her grandfather was Juan Armijo. Tomás Lucero was her uncle by marriage.

Auralia Chaves, fifty-seven, Las Placitas, New Mexico, was a niece of María of "El Cajón Bonito."

Predicando Chaves, sixty-four, Placitas, New Mexico, was the son of Juan P. Chaves and Paulita Zamora de Chaves, descendants of the settlers of Las Huertas who applied for the San Antonio de Las Huertas Grant from the King of Spain in 1765. Nephew of Juan María Gurulé.

Todosio Chaves, seventy-four, Santa Barbara, New Mexico, was the son of Calletano Chaves and María de Rayo Zamora de Chaves, descendants of the settlers of Las Huertas who applied for the San Antonio de Las Huertas Grant from the King of Spain in 1765.

María Chávez, aged thirty-five to thirty-eight, Ojo de la Casa, Las Placitas, New Mexico, was the granddaughter of Nicolás Mora, one of the founders of Ojo de la Casa. She married into the family of Felicia The Bruja. The husband of Julianita was her distant cousin. She was a descendant of the José de Luz of "Out of Bondage."

José García, ninety-two, Albuquerque, New Mexico was a member of the García family, who built Tejón among with the other holders of the Tonque and Tejón Grant given them by the Mexican Government in 1840.

José Gurulé y Trujillo, ninety-four, Albuquerque, New Mexico, was born in Socorro and came to Albuquerque as a youth.

Antonio García y Sánchez, sixty-eight, Albuquerque, New Mexico, who got the story of "An Old Native Custom" from his father. He was born in Belen, where his father was also born. Lola García de Salazar, Albuquerque, New Mexico, was the daughter of Antonio García y Sánchez.

Lucas Salazar, twenty-eight, Las Placitas, was a great-grandson of Juan of Tecolote.

Venturo Escarcido, sixty-four, Las Placitas, knew Juan Archibeque of "Juan y el Oso Ladrón," and grew up with his younger brothers.

Guadaloupe García. No information.

Onofre Gonzales, fifty-eight, Las Placitas, was a descendant of Rafael of "Dos Hombres Sabios De Las Placitas."

Ramón Nieto, seventy-six, Placitas, New Mexico, was a descendant of one of the twenty-one families to receive the San Antonio de Las Huertas Grant, in 1767.

Barbarita Lucero, fifty-three, Placitas, New Mexico, was the grand-daughter of Gabrielita.

Nina Montoya de Pearce, forty-four, Las Placitas, New Mexico, confirmed the story of Pablo Pacheco's dolls (her mother had one). Her family on her paternal side held a land grant covering a portion of the James Mountains and knew of Mateo.

Antonio de Lara, forty-five, of Las Placitas, New Mexico, was a direct descendant of one of the twenty-one families to receive the San Antonio de Las Huertas Grant.

Federico Otero, fifty-eight, Albuquerque, New Mexico, was the son of M.S. Otero, cattle and sheep man and banker, one-time owner of town of Tejón Grant.

J.P. Batchen, sixty-eight, born in Louisville, Kentucky, was a mining engineer who came to Algodones and Ojo de La Casa in 1897. He lived in Ojo de la Casa and was Batchen's husband.

In 1938, Batchen wrote a letter to Ina Sizer Cassidy, in response to a request for more information about the families. She comments on the family relationships of her informants:

Patricio Gallegos is a descendant of the Archibeque family. His father's mother was Gertrudes Archibeque . . . Gertrudes was born about 1825, Patricio thinks. Her father was Neberto Archibeque, born in Las Huertas. His father was Juan Archibeque. The father of Juan was Antonio of twenty-one families of 1765, who settled Las Huertas. Gertrudes was born in Algodones. Patricio Gallegos says they went there from Las Huertas, as all the families left Las Huertas in 1823, and most of them did settle in Algodones . . . From the record used in the enclosed manuscript, there was an Antonio Archibeque on a ranch near Bernalillo, which was sold to the Pueblo of Santa Ana about 1755. This might be the Antonio in the records of those receiving the San Antonio Las Huertas Grant in 1765, but this is not certain . . . The Gurulé family say their family sprung from two Frenchmen who married Chimayo women and came to the vicinity of Algodones with other men who married Chimayo women and were the ones to help found it and Las Huertas. From what the descendants of these old families say, nearly all of the twenty-one families receiving the grant of Las Huertas came from the vicinity of Santa Fe. (Letter from Lou Sage Batchen to Ina Sizer Cassidy, October 8, 1938)

La Diable a Pie: The Women's Cuentos

The stories told by women informants in the WPA follow some of the same narrative structures found in the cuentos told collectively or told by the men. There are fairy tales that follow the European model, and there are tales of local folklore and local events, as well as of local history. What distinguishes the stories told by the women is that there are often traces of resistance to the traditional roles assigned to them. Many cultural complexities and struggles by women are depicted in these stories. In particular, there is emphasis on regulating the normative by repressing women's sexuality and desire. The result of these tales may be an unhappy or tragic end for the particular woman in question. The stories may have been cautionary, yet they are also incipient stories of rebellion and the creation of new role models for women. Why is there the need for cautionary tales, one might ask, if the rules and mores of the time were being followed?

Another interesting aspect of these tales is the often humorous description of women's fashion, women's work, and women's housekeeping. There are also many funny stories of the follies of men. The details of these humorous stories were clearly intended to validate the listeners' own moral values. And, finally, we have rather intricate descriptions of the kind of work that women did, from plastering adobes and building their own houses, to gathering water at the stream and bringing it home in large jars placed on their heads. This description of the work done in the "old days" is told with a sense of the hard work that women had to do, but not with complaint. Rather it shows a sense of pride in the contribution of women in the building and sustenance of the community. We are also told of the behavioral expectations for women. There are also stories of the health of the community, a general medical knowledge sustained by the *curanderas* (in these stories, the healers were generally women), and their immense knowledge of remedies.

To begin, I will briefly discuss the stories collected by Annette Hesch Thorp. In the inventory of her manuscripts, Marta Weigle counts twenty-two separate narratives, many including several sections; we have counted thirty-seven narratives. All are accompanied by a word count, as it appears that the writers were supposed to submit a certain amount of words in their stories in order to be paid, or to show progress, and Thorp would often split the longer stories into several segments and submit them one at a time.[10]

What we learn from the stories Thorp recorded is that women had hard lives. Not only did they have to work from the time they were children, but they were often mistreated by their husbands, fathers, and sometimes brothers. There is quite a bit of violence against women in these stories. Brothers are treated better than sisters; often, the girls work while the brothers loaf. This was especially true if there were several girls in a family and only one boy. Sometimes, it appears that men cared more about their livestock than their families (in the story about Fabiana the witch, the husband forgave her for making his wife sick, but when his three cows became ill, he confronted the witch and killed her).

On the other hand, it is also clear that women had fun; they went to dances, flirted with boys in church, and formed lifelong friendships with other women. Sometimes, they even rebelled, as Alvina's story reveals. However, her story's end is tragic; she is killed in a violent manner, a warning against wives that are too uppity. Alvina's story is a tale about gender relationships within Hispano society.

To be the wife of a "cibolero," or buffalo hunter, during the early 1800s was to be special, for "on those hunts the best men went, leaving behind the old men and boys and men who were afraid." Thus, *ciboleros* were heroic, hard-working,well-fed, and good providers. Alvina, a woman in the village, had a husband Marcos, known as Marquitos because he was a small man and, perhaps, a reference to his personality—Marcos was a worthless man. One day, when the regular wagon driver had an accident, Marquitos was asked to go along on the hunt as the driver. He said he was too ill. Alvina knew he was faking so she asked the *ciboleros* if she could do the job. They accepted. After four months the *ciboleros* returned, having had a fruitful hunt. Alvina was proud that she had done a good job and had provided well for her family. A handwritten note, perhaps penned by Thorp, accompanies Vicenta's narrative: "This is an early instance, usually thought to be of very recent occurrence, when the wife went out to provide for her family while the husband stayed home." However, the author of the note failed to state the consequences of the wife's independence. The end of the story goes like this: "Marquitos behaved very badly towards his wife. He was not glad to see her, but quarreled with her day and night. About a week after her return, early one morning, one of Alvina's children (she had five) ran crying to a neighbor's house, saying that her mother was dead. The neighbors went and found Alvina lying on the floor stabbed to death." Having determined that Marquitos had done this deed and fled, the *ciboleros* found him, dragged him out, and hung him to a cottonwood tree until he was dead. They then cut off his right hand and nailed it to a pole in the center of the village, as a warning to other men who were "mean to their wives." This story is very understated, with the dire result of death called only "mean." Regardless of this punishment, as in many of the *Diabla a Pie* stories in which women disobey fathers or husbands, fate is often violent.

At least one of the women in Thorp's stories gets her heart's desire. Even though she was sixty, Manuela did marry her childhood sweetheart Donicio, and she did so with the help of her sister Torrivia, who was no longer afraid of their brother's threats. They had listened to their father that Manuela should not marry the man she loved, but the sisters were not about to listen to their brother, especially one who had not only been a sloth, but who lost all their money. The women in these tales share their food, their lives, their stories.

We learn a great deal about family and community life, local customs, herbal remedies, and ways of doing things. We also learn about cultural interactions between Hispanos and Indians, and about attitudes towards Anglo-Americanos. We are told that bad things happen to people who are miserly, and that good comes to those who are generous. Miserly parents beget miserly children.

One of the most interesting stories is about molasses-making. People had parties and danced while they took turns stirring the pots so the "miel mexicana" would not burn.

We also have many, many *remedios* . . . fairly specific notes on what herbs cure illnesses. It is curious that while folk religion played such an important part in the lives of *la gente,* we witness the stories about el Santo Niño, in which organized religion seems far away. It is only on occasion—funerals, weddings, baptisms, and other formal occasions—that a priest is even mentioned, but many lay religious persons, such as the resador and the cantador, are important people in the community.

The encroachment of the modern world is not far away in these stories. Manuela gets taken to the big city. For Amelia, all the americanos want to do is spend money; it was Charlie, an americano, who wanted to marry her for her money. According to Tita, only americanos get divorced. Perhaps it did not occur to her that her husband was playing crazy so she would leave him.

Batchen's stories tend to be more historically oriented. Perhaps because they relate to a history of a specific site, they are dealing more with a community memory. We learn about Las Placitas and its environments, the houses and the people who lived in them, the village characters and their quirks. We also discover young women whose sexual behavior disgraced themselves and their families, and women who were deserted or well loved. As in Thorp's tales, we learn about healing, remedies, and customs. In these stories told in great detail and with great relish, the informants were conscious of their ancestors' heroic and not-so-heroic deeds. What comes through, in particular, is how people cope in times of trouble and develop survival skills.

Class differences are discussed, as is injustice, in the stories about peonage. In the story of Mateo and Raquel, it is clear that the women were enterprising. They received credit for establishing herds of sheep and goats to meet the necessities of their families. Other women, such as La Curandera, La Pelona, Petra, and Eufemia, were courageous. Some, such as Camila, liked pretty clothes and bright colors and rebelled against limiting community social mores. Their lives, their suffering, and their laughter speak to us across the ages. How these women protected their children and how they connected with each other are a large parts of this community history.

In many of the stories collected by Lou Sage Batchen, the messages are even more problematic than in the tales collected by Thorp. Because Las Placitas and Las Huertas were small and close-knit communities, most of the villagers were related by blood or marriage. Three stories, "Guadaloupes'[11] Transgression," "El Pelón y La Pelona, or The Fall of Paquita," and "Camila" are related in theme and moral, but reflect different attitudes.

The theme of "Guadaloupe's Transgression" is arranged marriages, virginity, and honor in the small town. Guadaloupe García, born in 1842, became a hard worker early in life, at age six. She looked after the house, cooked, washed and worked in the garden. By age twelve she was considered an adult, "She could no longer appear in the plaza, nor outside the walls of the town . . . nor anywhere abroad without a chaperone . . . under no circumstances must she meet masculine glances, nor even speak to one of the opposite sex, unless they be members of her intimate family" (248). But at fourteen, Guadaloupe, gave her heart (a euphemism) to a youth in Tejón. Without consulting her, her father had arranged a marriage for her to another man, a custom in those days. Her godmothers were to prove that she was a virgin (the story does not discuss the details as to how this was ascertained.) Guadaloupe was found not to be a virgin. The entire village reacted to the news, "Because human nature dwelled within the walls of Tejón there were 'ahs' and 'ohs' whispered everywhere and shocked madres and padres on every side of the plaza" (249). This did not deter the wedding plans but it did alter the process of the wedding. "There was something amiss with the wedding party. The little bride-to-be was without veil and flowers . . . should a maid be found without her virginity, straightway she forfeited the right to veil and flowers or bouquet of any sort at the altar when her marriage service was said" (249-250). This did not, however, stop the usual wedding festivities of wine, cakes and a feast. The godmothers took the bride and put her in a new dress, "arranged her hair in a knot on top of her head" and "returned her to her husband, a matron in good repute" (250). Thus, aside from the public embarrassment and a bit of indignity, Guadaloupe's good repute was restored at the end of the story. The story, of course, was to warn girls about what would happen if they should transgress and lose their honor.

However, in "El Pelón y La Pelona or The Fall of Paquita," the consequences of such transgressions take on a more sinister and somber tone. These stories begin with a focus on hair, which symbolized virtue. Long descriptions of the meaning of hair enhance the descriptive and oral imagery of the story. Men at that time wore their hair long and in two braids. "These braids proclaimed him a good and honorable citizen. He would fight to preserve them . . . without them, he would be called "El Pelón," and that name applied only to the criminals, for in those days only the criminals who came from the prisons had shorn locks . . . Short hair identified a man as an outcast" (259). Women wore their hair long and knotted upon their heads. Maidens wore one long braid. If a woman should "fall from virtue," her hair was cut and she was called "La Pelona" (259). One day a new man appeared in Placitas; he was wearing his hair short, and he was not a criminal. He was an explorador from Los Estados (The United States). Thereafter, some of the men in Placitas began to wear their hair short. The men who had gone to war (the Civil War and the fight against the Texans) returned without braids.

These customs are related to the story of Paquita Gurulé who was beautiful and wore her hair in a braid down her back. She was raised strictly, but while her father searched for a suitable husband for her, her heart was "set aflame by a dashing trifler, who played the violin. His music raised the tempo of the maidens' pulses and even caused matronly hearts to skip a beat" (262). Paquita's father chose Juan de Aragón as her husband. Paquita had actually loved Juan, but "she realized now that it was too late, that the light-hearted violinist in his passion . . . had even caused her to forget Juan" (263). Paquita is found to be without virtue; moreover, she has not only dragged herself into perdition but the good name of her entire family with her. The family would become despised unless they publicly denounced and punished her. As the community gathered to denounce Paquita, "their harsh voices cried out, not for the blood of Paquita, but for her long black hair" (264). Paquita is shorn of her long locks, becomes a slave in her father's house, and is punished by every member of her family. Then she is ordered to name her seducer. Because she refuses, she is tortured. Juan, however, still loves her and breaks with his family. He, too, is branded a criminal, made a *pelón*. They could not be married by the church, and their hair is cut off "with ceremonial regularity."

However, in 1823, the community of Las Huertas was ordered to abandon the town because of Indian raids. Paquita and Juan took the opportunity to escape to the nearby mountains, taking their time to let their hair grow long again, and moved to Socorro, where they and their descendants lived and prospered.

In this story the loss of honor by Paquita is described as regrettable, as is Juan's break with his family. Nevertheless, the two are also saluted for their love and devotion to each other in spite of all their travails. Although life is hard, the end of their story is uplifting. It seems, indeed, that Juan and Paquita are not condemned; rather, the community is condemned for inflicting such harsh punishments on those who made mistakes.

A similar theme is found in the story of Camila. Born in Placitas in 1841, she was always different from her brothers and sisters. At an early age she went to work for the owners of a great house in Bernalillo, where she learned to sew and weave and put colors into the clothes she wore. In this story, clothing; rather than hair, symbolizes downfall and redemption. To color cloth, Camila learned to use two natural dyes—pietra lipis for green and *azafrán* for orange. She also made dresses with slim waistlines and sashes, clothing that was different from the loose clothing worn by other villagers.

Camila's father, Felipe, arranged a marriage for her to Ramón, the son of his best friend, but Camila was in love with Andrés, the son of the great house. Neither Camila nor Ramón wanted to marry each other, but they obeyed their parents. Although the union was unhappy, Camila managed to compensate by working. She returned to making clothes (as the story says, "an ageold remedy for women grieving over lost dreams"). She fashioned beautiful clothes, made up her face with natural powders and brushed brilliance into her hair.

All of this made the villagers condemn Camila. Her husband did nothing to counter the whispers about her. She and Ramón begged their parents to let them live apart. When they refused and nothing would do, Camila took her two children to her mother, went to Andrés, and they fled Bernalillo. Followed by the "enraged Ramón," he "laid her lovely head open with a stone machete . . . Church and society condoned it" (285).

In recounting these stories, we see some curious anomalies. We are led to identify with the sinners, learning about their lives, their hopes, their desires. These are women who confronted a repressive society and defied it. They often tried their best to meet their obligations but either made mistakes or openly resisted. Paquita manages to redeem her life, and Guadaloupe is disgraced but accepted into society. Alvina and Camila, the ones who transgressed their roles, are killed, yet their stories, rather than serving as examples of bad morals, turn them into heroines and victims of a repressive society.

It is hard to determine the desired results of these stories. Are they warnings to independent women? Stories of heroism and valor? Early hints of independence and rebellion? Or merely meant to entertain? Possibly they were intended to be all of those things: rich in detail, high in drama, heroism, and tragedy. Yet the images of Alvina, Paquita, Guadaloupe, and Camila, their dreams and hopes, populate our imaginations with the concrete details of their desires, struggles, punishment, and redemption.

And finally, to give a quick example of the humor of Batchen's stories, let me point out "The Snow Bride." The title may give, as is surely intended, an indication that this will be a fairy tale. But the story itself is quite different. It makes fun of contemporary fashions. In 1881, Beneranda Gutiérrez was to marry Terencio Lucero, and according to custom, Terencio bought his bride-to-be the customary wedding finery (the groom was the one who provided a trousseau). He had acquired the latest in fashion, a dress with hoops. "That fashion had finally made its way into this remote village, and Beneranda was the one to introduce it." The day of the wedding was cold and snowy, and after the formal marriage in the church in Bernalillo, the wedding party arrived at Las Placitas for the party. The story goes:

> When they saw them coming, they rushed out to meet them. Old Pedro, the simple one, had loaded an old gun, and as the burros approached, he fired to the right and the left, clearing their path of evil spirits. The burros took fright as the bullets cut the air about them, and became unmanageable. Beneranda lost her tapalo when her burro jumped and kicked up the snow and made a sudden rush forward. The hoop skirt bounced up and down. It was a funny sight. The gentle ripples of amused laughter fell upon the ears of old Pedro. He thought it was the crowd's approval of his good work. Up went his old gun and he blazed away again and again. The people shouted at him. Beneranda screamed hysterically as her burro kicked high in the rear and gave a summed nosedive. Off she went in the snow, her veil somehow caught in the animal's flying hoofs. Her hoop skirt was wrecked, her bodice torn.

This is just a small sample of these wonderful stories from the *Diabla a Pie.* We hope you enjoy them and that you take away a sense of the complex, marvelous life and lives reflected in the oral traditions of New Mexico.

Tey Diana Rebolledo
University of New Mexico

Notes

1. Alfred Kazin as quoted in Weigle, *New Mexicans,* xiii.
2. Please see Marta Weigle, "From Alice Corbin's Lines Mumbled in Sleep," pages 54-76, for a full analysis of this.
3. The California Testimonials were oral histories collected in the 1880s by H.H. Bancroft in order to write his histories of California and the West. Many older Hispanos were interviewed by Bancroft's assistants to document happenings in California. His assistants, Nino Cerruti and Thomas Savage, kept journals and copious notes as to how they collected their information.
4. Coyote is a term to denote a person of mixed heritage, originally Hispano with French, now Hispano with Anglo.
5. This book, published by the Las Placitas Garden Club in 1972, was edited by someone, possibly Batchen. The book does not contain all the stories collected by Batchen, and the stories vary from the original manuscripts. Republished by The Friends of Placitas, Inc., 2000.
6. While outside the scope of this introduction, the approach and use of all this material by the WPA, as well as by Minton, in terms of ignoring the original informants, is a complete appropriation of their stories at worst. This appropriation was seen by Cleofas Jaramillo, for example, when she worried about people "stealing" her stories.
7. Robe, commenting on folktales collected by Jameson, talks about the difficulties in the translation of oral narratives, stating, "The preparation of these New Mexican texts in English causes mixed feelings for the folklorist. Certainly in English they are available to a much more numerous community of scholars and students of the folktale than were they presented in Spanish. Many of them show evidence of having been narrated in Spanish or perhaps even in a mixture of Spanish and English, but when they are turned into English, any dependence by the narrator upon language effect has been completely lost. At the same time, the relationship between the tale and its cultural background is modified and obscured. Thus, it is often difficult to discern the role of an individual tale in the community where it is told" (Robe, 18). He goes on to lament the quality of details that may be lost and the fact that the narrator's style is not reflected faithfully.

8. Letter from Thorp to Minton, December 23, 1940. "These two stories were given to me by Antonio Vigil, who lived in San Ildefonso about fifteen years ago. He died ten years ago."

9. Forrest and White both say that Batchen identified herself with the Presbyterians and therefore had a bias against the Catholics.

10. Weigle states that it is erroneous to say that the collectors were paid by the word, as they received a salary. Brown claims that Cassidy wanted quantity. Whatever the reason, whether it was to show that they were making progress, or that they were paid according to the number of words, both Thorp and Batchen carefully counted words.

11. This is a case of English/Spanish spelling confusion. In Spanish, it should be Guadalupe.

PART I

ANNETTE HESCH THORP

SUBJECT: Stories
WPA: 5-5-53 #5
December 17, 1940
Words 760

STORIES

Storytelling was looked forward to on winter nights. All the family, big and little gathered around the fireplace, and by the light of a kerosene lamp, or ocote (wood pitch) would shell corn, or the women sewed, while some grandmother or neighbor viejita (old woman) told stories until time for bed. The beds were made down on the floor. The colchones (mattresses) were stuffed with wool, and folded on bancos against the wall in the daytime. At night they were laid on the floor.

The stories that were told by these grandmothers were religious ones. About santos, and the miracles they used to perform. And about brujas (witches) and those who had been embrujada (bewitched). Brujas were taken for granted by all. The men as well as the women believed in brujas and were careful not to offend anyone they were not sure of. To prevent brujas from casting a spell over you, these old women used to say, you should carry a piece of garlic in your pocket that had been given to you by a person named Juan or Juana. Brujas hated garlic and could not get near anyone who had garlic about him or her.

Also, if you were suspicious that some neighbor or friend was a bruja, all you had to do was the next time she, or he, came in your house, put two needles or straws in the doorway in the shape of a cross unseen by the person and if they were brujas, they could not go out the door until the cross had been removed.

You should never eat food given to you by anyone whom you did not know, for when brujas wanted to cast a spell over you, they usually offered you some tempting morsel, which if you ate, would harm you.

2

It is also good luck if a golondrina (swallow) builds its nest in your house on the vigas. If it builds it for seven years in succession, at the end of that time you will find a little white stone in the nest, which is called piedrita de virtud (magic stone). And brujas cannot harm you as long as you carry it in your pocket.

SUBJECT: Catalina Viareal
WPA: 5-5-52 #68
September 17, 1940
Words 1074

CATALINA VIAREAL

Catalina was all of eighty years old. Very small and thin, with white hair, and brown eyes that sparkled when she talked. Such a contrast to her little brown wrinkled face. She had on a black dress, blue apron, and a grey cloth tied over her head.

She lived alone in her two-room adobe house, which was part of the big house her father and mother had owned.

Her father's name was Antonio Viareal, and her mother's was María Vigil. They had four children, two boys and two girls. All were born in the same little village in Alcalde.

Catalina was the youngest of the children. Her brothers died when small. When her sister became a young lady, maybe fourteen years old, she married, and with her husband moved to Taos.

So that left Catalina alone with her parents. Yes, she could have married if she had wanted to. Ever so many men had asked for her. But no, she would not leave her mother and father alone.

And she stayed single, took care of them, and when they died, they left her the house and land. From then on she lived by herself, planting her garden in chili, onions, calabasas, and melons. The rest of the land she gave out on partido (shares). One part for her and three parts for the one that planted it. Of course, the planter furnished everything and did all the work, and when the crop was ripe, he gave her her share.

No, she was not afraid to live alone. She knew everyone in the placita and was related to most all of them. A little girl stayed with her at night. Her sister had tried for years—before she died—to get her to sell her house and land

and go live with her. But no, she did not want to give up all her father and mother had left her. Why, her land was the best in the placita!

Her father had bought it from an Indian, when he was married, paying the Indian two serapes (Navajo blankets) and a fanega of wheat. A fanega is twelve almudes. An almud is a wooden box twelve inches square, and six inches high. The almud was used for measuring grain. Then he built a room, and later on added four more rooms. There used to be dispensas (store rooms) and corrals, but they fell down years ago—also, three of the rooms. The remaining two were still good, and warm. No, she did not like stoves, but had a small one in the kitchen to cook on. In her room she used her fireplace. Heat from stoves gave her headaches.

Catalina's house was more or less like all the other houses in the village. With white-washed walls, and corner fireplace, and the vigas (beams or logs) on a roof almost black with age. Her room was small, but clean and cool. In a corner stood an old spool bedstead, piled high with freshly washed bedding. On the floor was a gerga (carpet) woven from natural colored wool, in black-and-white checks. Against the wall were two or three chairs with gay-colored cushions on them stuffed with wool, so high they had to be removed before sitting down.

In a tin nicho hanging on the wall was a figure of a child, sitting in a chair, with a cloak around its shoulders, and on its head a wide-brimmed hat with a long plume. In its right hand he held a shepherd's crook, and under it's left arm a lamb, very old and quaint.

When asked what the name of the santo in the nicho was, Catalina said it was El Santo Niño de Las Buenas Obras (The Holy Child of the Good Deeds). Her grandmother told her this story about the Holy Child, for it happened right here in this placita, when her mother's grandmother was a child.

There appeared one day in the village a little boy whom no one knew, and could not find out from where he came. He went around doing good deeds, and helping all those who needed help. If a cow or horse strayed off, and the owner could not find it, the little niño would come up to him and say, "I will go and help you hunt for them," and no sooner had they left, when the stock was found. His feet were sore and bleeding always, from walking miles to help someone. There lived a woman in the village, who had been married quite a few years, before she had any children, and was always sad because she had none.

At last a little child was born to her, and of course she loved it very dearly. The child became very sick when it was about a year old, and all the curanderas (women who doctor the sick) from far and near came, but the child got no better. After ten days it was thought that there was nothing that could be done for it. The mother was crying, for she knew her baby was dying. Just then the little boy appeared at the door and asked for a drink of water. She told him there was none in the house, but to stay with the baby, and she would go to the spring and get some. He went in, and stood by the child's bed, and the mother went for water. When she returned, to her surprise and happiness, she saw her child sitting up playing with a little lamb, perfectly well. And the strange thing about it was, that there were no sheep in the village or close in the surrounding country. The woman called her neighbors, and they came to see what was the matter. She told them about the niño taking care of the baby while she went for water, and when she came back, she found it well and the little niño gone.

The wise men of the placita talked it over, and said that he must be the Holy Child, and he was. The santero of the village made a fine big figure of him out of wood, and the women spun, and wove little clothes, and dressed him. Then he was put in a nicho in the church, and when the padre came was blessed. So there he sits today in his chair, and the devout ones go to him and pray for help. They take little shoes as an offering, for he wears out a great many pairs, by walking at night helping those in need.

SUBJECT: Cesaria Gallegos
WPA: #153
September 23, 1940
Words 829

CESARIA GALLEGOS

There was no respect for the old any more, and she was muy vieja (very old). She did not like the way young people behaved nowadays. When she was young, children always said, sí, señora, or no, señora. Now if you speak to them, they answer, sí, no, or what do you want, said Cesaria Gallegos, who lives with her son Antonio and his wife.

She has nine grandchildren—married—and twelve great-grandchildren. Cesaria does not know how old she is, but thinks she must be close to a hundred. She is bent, and walks with a cane. Her brown face is wrinkled, and she has very little hair. What there is of it, is grey, and still streaked with black. She had on a black dress green with age, a grey calico apron, and a faded blue handkerchief tied on her head.

She cannot see very well anymore; on cloudy days it is bad, and she stays home. But when the sun shines, she goes to church. Oh, yes, she walks muy despacio (very slow).

Her son is good to her, and his wife cooks her food. But it is not like the food they used to eat. When she was a young woman, she made her own tortillas de maíz azul (blue corn). She had a metate and ground them fresh every day. There is no food como la Mexicana (like the Mexican) frijoles, and chili con carne seca (dried meat). Jerked or dried meat is made as follows. Fresh beef or mutton is cut thin, sprinkled with salt, and hung in the sun to dry. When wanted, it is placed in the oven, and heated. While hot, it is pounded on a metate stone until soft, then mixed with chili.

Her mother's name was Dolores López, and her father's, Vicente Ortega. They lived in Agua Fría, where she was born.

When she was a little girl, they used to go to the hills and gather piniones. One year they got so many, her father took them to Albuquerque and sold them. He brought back muncha comida (lots of food) and a barrel of vino mexicano (native wine). When she was maybe fourteen, she married Antonio Gallegos and came to town to live. She had two children: A girl who died of smallpox when small, and a boy with whom she now lives. Oh, yes, she could have married again, but did not want to be bothered with any more children. So she remained single, and did washing and ironing for a living. Those were the days when there was a lot of money.

There are no remedios (remedies) like the Mexican remedies. Why, one time she was walking downtown, and a car was backing out of a side street—she didn't see it, nor the driver her—and knocked her down. She was not hurt, but the man was scared; he picked her up and wanted to know for sure if she was not hurt. When he found out she was all right, he gave her five dollars and took her home. In the evening when her son came, she showed him the money, and told him about the car hitting her. He got very angry and told her she should not have taken the money, but should have sent for him. He would have made the man pay a lot more, or go to jail. But what good would that have done? The man might have preferred to stay in jail rather than pay a big sum of money. No, her way was the best. She got five dollars, and maybe the other way, she would not have gotten anything, "Porque el que todo lo quiere todo lo pierde." (He who wants it all, loses all).

But the next day her leg pained her, where she struck the cement. No, she was not worried. She boiled some hojas de rosa de castilla (wild rose leaves) and bathed her knee, and the pain left her in three days.

Oh, yes, she had worked very hard when she was young, and if her eyes were not so bad, she could still work. But there was one day in the week she never washed, and that was Friday. Because on that day Nuestro Señor (our Lord) died. And it was sacred. And she didn't want to come back to this world again, after she died, to do penance, like the woman her mother told her about.

Her mother had told her that her grandmother had told her that there was once a woman who always washed on Fridays. No other day would she pick. But every Friday she went to the river and built a fire under her calentón (boiler) and washed. Her friends used to tell her not to pick Fridays, but to wash on some other day. But she would not listen to them. And when she died, the people could hear crying every Friday down by the river. And some had even seen her, gathering palitos (chips) for the fire. Her soul came back every Friday to do penance.

SUBJECT: Tita
WPA: 5-5-52 #75
October 1940
Words 1092

TITA

Manuelita, or Tita, as her grandchildren call her, has had una vida muy triste (a sad life). She does not know who her father was or anything about him.

Her mother's name was Natalia Urioste, and was born and raised on a ranch. She married José Lión Romero, who two years later lost his life in a forest fire trying to save three cows. After his death Tita's mother came to town with her baby girl to live.

She found work washing and ironing for the Americanos. Twelve years passed, then Tita was born and went by her mother's name. When she was small ("does not know just how old, probably eight or ten years old"), she was taken to live with Martín El Cojo (the lame one) and his wife, Gregoria.

They lived on a ranchito some ten miles from town, and had no children, all having died when small. Martín and Gregoria had promised her mother that if Tita would stay and take care of them, they would leave her their ranch when they died.

Tita had to do all the work in the house and help with the outside as well. Old Martín had goats, she can't remember how many, but there were munchos because she used to help milk them, and it took a long time. Gregoria and she made cheese, and Martín took them to town on his burro to sell. While he was gone, she herded the goats.

They also gathered remedios (herbs) especially on San Lorenzo's day, fifteenth of August, because on that day San Lorenzo blessed all the yerbas.

They gathered Añil de Muerto, a tall weed with yellow flowers, something like a sunflower only much smaller, which is very good for dysentery, when boiled and the tea drank. Yerba de la bíbora (snake weed), you boil it

9

then bathe in the water, cures rumos (rheumatism). Snake weed is called broom weed by the stockmen in the southwestern part of the state. It is one of the first green weeds to come up in spring, and is bad for cattle. They also got Chimaja, "a small plant that looks like a fern, and grows on sandy soil. The leaves taste like celery." Chimaja tea is very good for dolor de estómago (pains in the stomach).

Then one day she left the dispensa (storeroom) door open, where Martín had three large sacks of pinion, and the goats got in and ate them up. Gregoria whipped her and sent her back to her mother. She stayed with her mother until she was about fifteen, then married Lino Romero, and her troubles began.

Lino was good the first few months, but after that took to drink and had no time for work. She had a child every year, but they died when small, maybe eight in all. The last one was a boy, and she took good care of him. She wanted him to live so he could take care of her in her old age.

In the meantime, Lino kept on drinking, and one day he fell off a wagon and struck his head on a rock, which caused him to lose his mind. Well, she didn't know what to do with him. Finally, he was taken to an asylum, where he remained a year, then was sent home. When he came back, he told her he did not want to live with her anymore, but wanted a separation. She paid no attention to that, because when you married, it was for life. "Only Americanos got divorces in those days." Then he fell once more, and struck his head in the same place and lost his mind again.

He would go out at night, and walk around praying, and singing until the neighbors complained. But she could do nothing. When she tried talking to him, he would say she was to blame, that if he were not living with her, he knew he would get well. So she let him go. Six months later he drank himself to death.

She did not think it was his fault the way he behaved, but thought it was maleficio (witchcraft). Someone did it. Yes, she believed there were persons who could harm you, maybe not so much nowadays as they used to. Many years ago a friend had told her of a woman who had been maleficiada (bewitched). This friend told her a young man wanted to marry a girl whom his mother didn't like, and refused to give her consent. But the boy married her in spite of all, and took her home to live with his parents. After a short time the girl developed a cough, and said she knew there was a wad of hair in her throat. She went to several curanderas; they gave her teas, and rubbed remedios on her, but she kept on coughing. One day her husband heard of an old man, who was a very good curandero, and took his wife to him. The old man looked her over, then told her she was maleficiada (bewitched). But not to worry, he would cure her in a short time. He locked himself in a room, and after a while came out with an egg on a plate. He told the girl to break the egg. She did, and instead of a yolk, there was a big tight ball of hair inside the egg. The girl's throat cleared up at once, and her cough was gone. The old man told her it was her mother-in-law who had done it.

So Tita thinks something like that might have happened to her husband, and that was the reason he lost his mind so often.

Her boy grew up, and married a muy buena muchacha (good girl). He too took to drink, and wouldn't work, but Mela, his wife, did work and took care of them all. She has two grown grandchildren, a boy and a girl. Pero Dios sabe (God knows) what they will turn out to be.

Tita must be all of eighty years old. She is tall, very dark with grey hair. Dresses in black, and when she goes out, always wears her tapalo negro (black shawl).

Yes, she has always lived in the little three-room house her mother left her. She does not like the way things are nowadays, but thinks old times were better. Why, nowadays, the Mexicanos want to be Americanos, and the Americanos want to be Mexicanos.

SUBJECT: Chana
WPA: 5-5-52 #71
October 8, 1940
Words 783

CHANA

Women think they work nowadays. Pero no, they don't know what work is. The Americanos have made it so easy for them now. They would die if they had to work like she did when she was young, and strong, said Chana, a very old woman who lives in the country with her granddaughter.

Cresenciana, as she was named, does not know in what year she was born. She looks close to ninety, is small, thin, and has very little hair, and what there is of it is white. Her skin is light brown. Sí, she was muy blanca y bonita (white and pretty) when she was a girl. She cannot see well anymore, and has to walk with a cane. She wears dark calicos for every day, but on Sundays her black dress, which she likes the best. She can't do much anymore, but sits on the shady side of the house, and watches that los niños (the babies) don't fall in the acequia (ditch) or the chickens get into the garden. But when she was young, and had her own home, how she could work.

She had four sisters and one brother; they are all dead now. Her mother and father, whose names were Antonia Valencia and Policarpio Montoya, were born and lived in the same place as she does now. No, she does not know how to read or write—there was no need for an education in those days. They never got letters, and if they did, there was an escrivano, who read and wrote their letters for them. Oh, yes, he charged, twenty-five cents for writing a letter, but nothing for reading it to them.

She was muy joven (very young), when she married Manuel Atencio. He was a good man. His father gave them a piece of land, and they built two rooms. Manuel laid the adobes in the walls and put on the roof, then turned the house over to her. She mixed her own mud con muncha paja (with straw) and plastered the walls so smooth, and then white-washed them with yeso (gypsum). Oh no, the men did not do the plastering or whitewashing; that was women's work. Men could not do it as nice as the women did.

She cooked in a fireplace. The food tasted so good cooked that way, much better than on a stove. She had a tinamaiste (iron ring with three legs) to put her pots on. Not like the pots they have nowadays, but ollitas de barro (clay pots). She rubbed them inside and out with grease and put them on hot coals to burn. That kept them from leaking. There are no beans like the ones cooked in ollitas de barro. Her tortillas de maíz she cooked on a comal (flat stone, or iron like a griddle pan). She also built an orno (oven) outside to bake in. Oh, what good bread de harina de trigo (wheat flour) she used to bake. And in the fall, she roasted green chili in it, peeled and hung it up to dry for winter use. She planted much chili, melons, onions, and garlic to put in the chili. Yes and punche (native tobacco). No, you cannot get punche any more. She always raised a lot, and knew how to cure it, too. Chana picked the leaves off, and piled them in a corner, put a blanket over it, and when the leaves were yellow, put them in the sun to dry. Then it was ready to smoke, with ojas de maíz. (corn husks). And you never got tos (cough) like you do now smoking Americano tobacco and paper.

Chana had many children, but raised only four, a boy and three girls. While they were still small, Manuel died. After that she did all the work, besides raising her family. She taught her children to respect los mayores (the old). When she was young, children were taught to be very respectful and to obey their elders. If you asked for a jumate (dipper) of water, and if there was a child present, he or she jumped right up, ran to bring you a drink, and stood with arms folded until you had finished. Pero ahora, if you ask for a drink, they push it towards you and run. No, no, there is no crianza nowadays.

Now all her daughters are dead, and her boy married, and lives somewhere in the north. They tell her he has a big family, and is getting old. She has not seen him for many years. Chana has a great many grandchildren, and great-grandchildren. But likes Carmel, with whom she lives, the best.

October 15, 1940
Words 612

CHANA

Chana believes you should share whatever you have with the ánimas (souls of Purgatory). She always did. You had better crops, and good luck in everything, if you gave to the ánimas. The portion you give is called el don de las ánimas (the gift for the souls). And this was the means of many old people making a living.

When a friend or neighbor butchered, baked bread, or set a hen, they always gave some old woman the portion that belonged to the ánimas, and in return, the one who received the gift had to pray for the repose of the souls.

Like when setting a hen, if a neighbor asked for the soul's portion, before giving it to her, you marked an egg, and held the hen over the nest and said this little verse to San Salvador.

San Salvador,	San Salvador,
Todas Pollas,	All pullets,
Y un cantador	And one rooster

When the egg hatched out it would be given to her. But first she had to lock herself in a room, and pray for an hour or so, then she could take the chick home. And the egg that was marked always hatched, because it belonged to the ánimas. Oh, no, Chana never forgot the dead. When tying chili in the fall, there was always one string set aside. Or when the crops were gathered, there was a certain amount of grain given.

Crosses by the roadside are called descansos (resting places) for the ánimas, for it is said that every night at midnight, souls come back to this world to pray and do penance for their sins. And that is the reason these spots are marked for them.

Oh, sí, they had their good times also. Días de fiestas (feast days). Y bailes (dances). She liked Día de Santiago. It came in the summer, on the twenty-fifth of July. Chana always had a lot of company on that day. But she managed very well. The green chili was just about right to eat, and she saved carne seca for that day. And as it was warm, she could make beds outdoors for those that did not fit in the house.

The men would all take part—except the old ones—in the corrida del gallo, while the women watched. A rooster was buried with its head sticking out of the ground. The men galloped by on their horses, and as they passed, reached down and pulled it out of the ground, by its head. This game was in honor of the saint. And at night they had a baile (dance).

The next day, the twenty-sixth, was Santa Ana´s feast day, and that belonged to the women. Then the men stood around and watched, while they rode horseback. No, they didn't play games, just rode up and down. And at night also gave a dance. But instead of the men asking them out to dance, the women asked the men.

Then they used to have mielero dances in the fall. They were the best of all. Miel (molasses) was made at some house that had a large space, or patio outside. A hole was dug, and a fire built in it, then the big copper kettles with cane juice were placed over it to cook. This was done at night. The owners of the cane juice got the músicos, and asked all their friends and neighbors to come. They danced and took turns stirring the juice in the kettles, until the molasses was done; then the dance was over. Sometimes there was molasses cooking and dancing for a week or two.

October 22, 1940
Words 675

CHANA

Miel mexicana was known by no other name, and was made from sugar cane. The seed was first brought in from Mexico, on the old Chihuahua wagon trains. These went to Mexico every year, and it took six months or longer to make the round trip. The native people planted this for miel (molasses) only.

Some planted three or four acres, others smaller patches. It all depended on how much land they had, and could spare from other grains. Sugar cane did not grow or thrive as well here as it did in Mexico, or the southern parts of the state, then a territory.

It was planted in rows, and when about six inches high, was thinned out. In the fall, about the later part of September, the cane was cut. The heads or seed was spread on the ground to dry for planting the following year. The rest was cut up into lengths about two feet or smaller, and hauled in wagons to la prensa (press). These prensas were crude affairs, mostly made out of wood. They also were brought from Chihuahua. A horse or burro was hitched to the prensa to do the turning, by being driven around and around. The drivers usually were boys. Under the prensa was a trough hewed out of a cottonwood log, into which the juice ran.

In each village there was some family who owned a prensa, and it was used by all those who planted cane. The owner of the press furnished the horse or burro, and driver, and the owner of the cane paid him a quart of juice out of every four. Afterwards the juice was taken to the mielero in ollas or tinajas (large clay jars) to be made into miel.

The mieleros were at some house that had a large patio or space, and who owned copper kettles. These kettles were also brought from Mexico, and held from five to ten gallons, and were handed down from father to son. These kettles were also used for scalding hogs, frying lard, and as wash pots.

The patio or ground at the mielero was sprinkled with water and goats driven around on it, three or four days before, to pack it hard. Holes were dug, about two feet deep, with tinamaistes (large iron rings with three legs) over them to place the kettles on, under which a fire was built. In the afternoon, the owner of the juice that was to be cooked that night, would send his son or someone else's, on horseback or burro to get the músicos, and invite relatives and friends, while he took the juice to the mielero.

He paid for the music and the wood that was used for cooking, and also the use of the kettles by giving a portion of the miel when done. One quart out of every four. The músicos were given whatever the owner thought was right—sometimes a half gallon or more, it all depended on how much miel he had. They left it to him to be fair.

The invited friends went to the mielero dance as soon as it became dark, taking all the children with them and stayed until dawn. When the babies got sleepy, pallets or beds were made down for them in the kettle owner's house. And they slept through the night, while mother and father danced cunas and polkas to the music of violin and guitar.

The juice required constant stirring to keep it from scorching. So turns were taken by the dancers, in stirring the kettles with long, iron-handled spoons. While one group danced, the other stood around the fire tending to the molasses. Miel making was done at night, because the cooking required so much attention, and by giving a dance, it kept them awake, and they got free help.

October 29, 1940
Words 843

CHANA

It took from eight to nine hours to make miel. When it was done, the dancers left. Those who lived some distance hitched horses to their wagons, put the sleeping children in, and drove home. Others, who lived close by, walked. The owner of the miel stayed at the mielero until the molasses had cooled enough to be divided. Then ollas were brought out, and the miel measured. Three parts or quarts to the one who owned the miel, and one part or quart to the mielero owner.

Afterwards the miel was taken home, and buried in the dispensa (storeroom). Every house had a storeroom. And like the rest of the house, the walls were plastered with mud, but not white-washed. The floor was mud also. Holes were dug in the floor, or ground of this room, and the ollas placed in them, so that the top of the olla was on a level with the floor. A small board or piece of tin was put over the top of the ollas for a cover, then mud was mixed, and plastered over all until the floor looked smooth again.

A small rock was placed above, where each olla was. This was done to seal the miel until it was needed. Two or three days later when some other neighbor's or friend's juice was ready to cook, and the gente (people) rested, the cooking and dancing was repeated, until all those who had cane got their miel cooked.

Later in the fall when the harvest was all in, about the last of October, or the first of November, wagons would be loaded with strings of chili, sacks of onions, and five-gallon kegs of miel. These kegs were borrowed or rented from someone in the village who was a little more prosperous than the others, and were used by one after another. Empty kerosene cans were also used.

Then these wagons would be driven to villages in the northern parts of the state, then a territory, to sell or barter their goods.

The reason for driving three or four days to get to these places was that it was higher, and the summer seasons were short. The people who lived there could not raise cane or chili. So when the miel sellers came, they bought all they had.

It was sold for fifty cents a quart, or traded for the same amount in grain. One quart of miel was traded for an almud of beans, wheat, or garvanzo (cow or hog peas). An almud was used in those days for measuring grains. An almud is a wooden box twelve inches square, and five inches deep. The larger grains like beans and peas were piled high (colmado). But smaller grains like wheat were measured level with the box (razo).

Miel was traded also for other things. Old sheep or pigs and chickens. Sheep in those days were cheap, also pigs—and for two quarts of miel a fat old ewe could be bought, or a small pig. They drove from house to house, until everything was sold. Then they started back home with beans, wheat, garvanzo, a sheep or two, pigs and chickens, in their wagons.

At home there was always enough miel left to last through the winter months. For as soon as spring came, and the weather got warm, what miel was left over would ferment and spoil. It was only a winter luxury, and sweets were scarce. For the people who planted cane did not know how to make sugar from the cane. So only miel was made.

There were different ways the miel was used. Chana used to make buñuelos enmielados. A quart of miel was placed on the fire in an iron puela (skillet). The tortillas made from wheat flour, with a hole in the center, were fried in lard. When the miel was boiling, the fried tortillas were dropped in, and left for a few minutes, then taken out, and eaten when cool. And when Chana had fresh goat cheese, she served it with miel poured over it. And for the muchachos, who had such good teeth, esquite was made. At night sitting around the fireplace, puelas of white corn would be toasted, then miel poured over it. They would eat it while listening to stories grandmother told about brujas, and the miracles the santos performed.

But all this is gone, and the growing of cane, and miel cooking was given up many years ago. The younger generation grew up, and are now middle-aged men and women. They find it cheaper to buy Karo, and other brands of molasses at the stores than to make it.

The houses where the mieleros were held have been fixed over with red tin roofs. The prensas fell to pieces and were burned for firewood. And the old copper kettles, sold to curio dealers. One of Chana's cousins sold a muy grande copper kettle, "probably a ten-gallon one," to some Americanos who were buying copper during the last world war. And he thought he was very lucky to get the large sum of six dollars for it.

November 5, 1940
Words 983

CHANA

Cresenciana, or Chana, as she has always been called, does not know how old she is, for in the days when she was born it was not important to keep any record of your age. Of course, if you had to know how old you were, you could go to the church where you had been baptized, give the Padre the names of your father and mother, also your padrinos (godparents), and he would look it up. And give you your Fe de Bautismo (baptism certificate), only charging a dollar.

Chana is a very old woman, looks as though she might be close to ninety years old. Her mother and father had five children, the oldest was a boy, the rest girls. Chana is the youngest of them all. Now they are all dead, with the exception of Chana. Her mother's name was Antonia Montoya, and her father's name Policarpio Valencia.

She thinks they were born and raised in El Sombrio in La Cañada de la Santa Cruz. Her father was a small man. She says she took after him, for she is small and thin. But her mother was a very big woman, and very strong. They were good people, and believed in raising their children to be respectful, and good workers. Chana remembers how she used to help her father with his planting. As there was only the one boy, the girls helped with the outside work as well as the inside. She used to drop corn seed in the furrows, while her father or brother plowed.

He did all his planting and hauling with oxen. Horses were expensive then, and only the well-off gente had them. Her parents were poor. The oxen were stronger than horses, and did not require so much care or feed.

Her father always used a wooden plough. These were made from green cottonwood logs, and when dry were very tough. Chana thinks these logs were about three and a half to four feet long. One end was pointed, and on the other end was a short pole to guide it with. Close to the pointed end, an iron ring was bolted; this was to hitch the oxen to. Her father liked these Mexicano ploughs better than American ones, and used them as long as he lived.

They got up when the resador sang the Alba, long before the sun came up. She and her sisters would go to the river, which was close, for water, carrying it back on their heads in ollas. In the fall the chili was picked, and tied in bunches of three and four, then woven on a mecate (string). These strings at the time were made from palmilla (amole plant or yuca). When this was done, they were hung on the walls of the house outside to dry. Then corn was gathered, piled in the patio, and the whole family shucked it, saving the thin inside husks for smoking hojas. These were tied in bundles and hung from the vigas in the storeroom. The blue and white corn was separated. Blue corn was mostly used for tortillas, atole (cornmeal gruel), and mush. The old-time people claimed that the blue corn had more strength and a better flavor than the white, and that was the reason why it was used more. But the white was also good, and was used for posole, tamales. Also fed to the stock. Wheat was also planted, not as much as corn. The wheat flour was kept for baking bread, only when there was company, or bautismos, or weddings. This was baked in the outside horno. And what a treat it was when they had wheat flour bread. Sometimes when her mother baked in the winter, three or four calavasas (pumpkins) were scraped out, and a cup of miel poured inside, then placed in the horno to bake with the bread.

Late in the fall when all the crops were in, her father and five or six, sometimes more, men in the neighborhood, would go in their wagons to the salinas (salt lakes).

Chana does not know where these salinas were, but thinks somewhere in the south, probably the salt lakes east of the Estancia Valley. Until about 1904 or 1905, these lakes were on government land, and a great deal of salt used to be hauled from there. The salt was free to all. After the above date, a man by the name of Julius Meyers, then sheriff of Torrence County, filed on these lakes under the Homestead Act, then charged the salt haulers, or salineros, as they were called, twenty-five cents a hundred pounds, weighing it at the lakes. This discouraged the poor Mexican people, who could not afford to pay. So the salt hauling and selling was discontinued. There used to be five lakes.

It took about six weeks to go and come back with a load of salt. This salt was then taken to Tierra Amarilla, and sold or traded to the sheepmen there, for old ewes. Her father brought back as many as seven or eight sheep. The salt was sold for one dollar a fanega (twelve almuds razo) or traded for a fat sheep, then brought home and butchered for winter meat. The meat was salted, then hung up to dry. The wool was sheared off the pelts for colchones (bedding) and pillows, or the weaving of blankets. The zaleas (skins) for rugs on the floor.

As they were taught how to work, they also were taught their prayers. The resador of the village would gather the children at some neighbor's house, winter nights. He taught them prayers, and prepared them for their first communion. They learned everything by heart. And how hard they tried to memorize all he taught them. For no boy or girl was allowed to dance at the bailes until they had made their first communion.

November 12, 1940
Words 651

CHANA
The Resador

In Chana's youth, the resador was a highly respected person, and no one cared to offend him, for they never knew when he might be needed.

The resador usually was some man whose father had been a resador before him, and from whom he had learned los resos, and alabados (prayers and hymns).

Some of these old men in their youth had been placed with the padre of their village church by their parents, to learn the ways of good Christians. These boys worked for and waited on the priest, and went with him on his journeys to the different placitas, assisting at mass as altar boys. In return for this, the padre taught them their prayers, and catechism, and sometimes to read and write.

It was with the hope that their boys would become priests, that the parents so willingly gave them to the church. But very few ever took Holy Orders. Instead, when they became old enough to marry, they usually did. As they knew the resos, they became resadores. In small places where mass was said but once a month, the resador taught the village children their prayers, and saw to it that they made their first communion. When anyone was very sick, or dying, he went to pray over them. Often both he and the curandera were called at the same time to some sick person's bedside.

He also played an important part at the velorios, not only for the dead, but for the saints. When a certain saint had granted some favor, such as making the sick well again, or bringing back father or husband safe from some long journey, a velorio (wake) would be given, or held, in honor of the santo who had been appealed to.

An altar was erected, by placing a table or bench in a room against the wall, covered with a sheet, and the santo placed upon it surrounded with tinsel and gay-colored paper flowers. The women baked bread in the ornos, and cooked other foods, chili, beans, and meat if they had it.

In the morning of the day on which the velorio was to be held, some boy would be sent out to invite friends and relatives. The man of the family would make arrangements with the resador, who was to take the leading part in the velorio, do the praying and sing the alabados. He was paid in grain, or as it sometimes happened, a load or two of wood was hauled for him in pay. Just as soon as it became dark, those invited would arrive in wagons, on horseback, and on burros, bringing all the children and the viejitos (old ones.) These viejitos loved velorios, and unless sick, never failed to attend them.

As soon as all were there, singing and praying would go on until midnight. Then a supper was served. After supper the singing was continued until dawn when the Alba was sung. Then all would leave for home.

The Alba hymn was the song of dawn. In each little settlement the resador arose at dawn, and walked around the placita singing the Alba. That was a call for everyone to arise, day was coming. Anyone—unless sick—that was found in bed after the Alba had been sung, was considered lazy, and a disgrace to the village. The Alba was also sung at dawn at all velorios (wakes).

LA ALBA	IN THE ALBA
Cantemos la Alba	We sing the Alba
Ya viene el día	Day is coming,
Daremos gracias a Dios,	And give thanks to God,
Y Ave María.	And Ave María.
Viva Jesús	Long live Jesus
Viva María,	Long live Mary,
Cantemos todos	Is what we will all
En este día.	Sing on this day.
Bendito seas	Blessed be
Sol refugente	The shining sun,
Bendito seas,	Blessed be
Sol del oriente.	The sun from the east.
Bendito sea	Blessed be
Su claridad	Its clearness,
Bendito sea	And blessed be
Quien nos la da.	The one who gives it.

The resador often was the santero also. The poor people could not afford to pay the prices that were asked for sacred pictures brought from Mexico. So they had them made at home by the santero, or resador, who, after hewing and smoothing pine boards of different lengths, painted on them the pictures of Mary and the saints to the best of his knowledge. The people bought or bartered for them, then waited for the padre's next visit to their church, which was usually once a month, to have them blessed.

It was also the resador who was appointed by the priest to collect the church's fees. The head of each family paid a dollar and fifty cents a year to the church but very seldom in money. In the fall the resador went in his wagon from house to house, collecting whatever the people could give. This was mostly corn, beans, cornmeal, and goats. The grains were kept by the Padre, or sold. The goats were given to the resador on shares for his work. If there were ten goats, at the end of three years, the resador gave the priest back twenty, the same ages as the ones he had received.

The old resadores are all gone. The younger generation can read, and write, and do their own singing and praying.

SUBJECT: The Curandera
WPA: 5-5-52 #70
November 19, 1940
Words 705

THE CURANDERA

The curandera was also an important figure in the lives of those who lived in little placitas. It was she who doctored the sick and attended at the birth of the babies. They were not only called curanderas, but parteras (midwives) also.

They were middle-aged or old women whose mothers, grandmothers, or aunts had been curanderas before them, and from whom they had learned about remedios, and what each one was good for. There were good curanderas, and others who were not so good. They were busy most of the time, being sent from far and wide, especially so if they had the reputation of being good curanderas.

Some would go for them in wagons, others on horseback or burros. Those on horses would let the curandera sit on front on the silla or saddle, while the man mounted on behind, the two riding the same horse. Before she left home, she gathered all the remedios she thought might be needed, and took them with her. She stayed at the patient's bedside treating them with the remedios, until the sick one either got better, or died. She would use one remedio after another, and sometimes two or three at the same time. If the sick got well, she was praised for it. If she or he died, it was because God willed it so, and she was not to blame. The curandera never charged for her work. When asked how much was owed her—they knew she would not charge them—she would reply that it was nothing, "just what you want to give me."

And those who appreciated what had been done for them gave her in pay or correspondencia, things like flour, corn, beans, chili, and sometimes fifty cents or a dollar. Then take her home again. But there were others who had no gratitude, and just said gracias, and let the curandera walk, or get back home any way she could.

Some of the remedios that were used by the curanderas were gathered at home, along the rivers, fields, and on the mesas. Some were grown in gardens. Like anís (anise seed)—this was not only used for remedio, but for flavoring little cookies (biscochitos). Then there was jilantro (coriander seed), mostasa (mustard), alegría (cocks comb), polello (pennyroyal), and yerba buena (peppermint).

Some remedios that grew in the north were brought back by the chili sellers, and those that could only be found in the south were brought, and sold to the curanderas by the freighters. Then there were some remedios that were brought from Mexico; these were bought at the little tiendejons in town, such as coral molido (ground coral) and oro bolador (gold leaf).

The remedios that grew in the Sierra, such as altamisa and oshá roots, some man would make a special trip to get these for the curandera. Also when hauling wood pitch and cedar bark, other yerbas would be brought home.

Here are some of the remedios, and what they were used for by the old curanderas.

For calentura (fever), flor de sauco (elderberry) flowers were placed in a jar of water, and soaked for twenty-four hours, then strained through a cloth, and the water given to the sick one. This was used either fresh or dry.

Polvos de coyote is like a small tomato bush. In the spring it has a white flower, later a small green berry, which looks like a tiny tomato, about the size of a small marble. In the fall this berry dries up into a pod, and inside this is a grey powder. This powder was blown into the ears to cure sordera (deafness). The reason for its name, polvo de coyote, is that it grows on the mesa, where the coyotes roam.

Yerba de la golondrina (swallow's herb) was used as an ingüente (salve). This yerba was picked green and hung up to dry. When dry, it was ground into a powder and mixed with sheep tallow for a salve. It was used for wounds, cuts, and sores. Yerba de la golondrina, or swallow's herb, grows close to the ground and has small round leaves, and looks like a small fern. The reason for the name is that the swallows eat the leaves of this yerba.

Yerba de la golondrina grows only in the southern part of the state.

SUBJECT: Remedios
November 26, 1940
Words 908

REMEDIOS

These are some of the remedios that were used by the old curanderas.

Canutillo (some called it carrizo grass) grows on river bottoms and looks like tall jointed grass. This canutillo was boiled and the tea from it drank three times a day for kidney trouble.

Then there was a cure for hives or (gervor de sangre). Cedar bark from small cedar trees was also boiled, and the water used to bathe in; also the water was given as a drink.

Pagua was for inchasón (dropsy). This was mashed when green, into a pulp, then a poultice of this was bound on the joints—ankles, knees, elbows, and wrists. In about three days, the skin would break, and the water drain out. After the swelling went down, an ingüente (salve) was made from soft pitch, from pinion trees and the yolk of an egg mixed, and applied to the joints to heal the sore places.

Pagua grows in vegas (meadows) where it is damp. This yerba was also used for stomach trouble, by boiling it for tea to drink.

Copper rings and bracelets were worn by those suffering from neuralgia, headaches, and rheumatism. These were made by the old plateros. The copper they used was bought in towns, where it had been brought in by freighters from the different mining towns. Copper was also brought in from Chihuahua. And sometimes old copper kettles, that were battered up and not used, were bought by the old platero, and cut up for rings. These old plateros made silver rings also. But silver being more expensive than copper, there was less sale for them.

The prices were twenty-five cents for a ring, and fifty cents for a bracelet. But mostly they were traded for the same amount in products.

Sometimes when the platero had a number of these rings and bracelets made, he sold them in other placitas. For he also waited until fall, then in his wagon or on his burro would take his wares to sell or trade to those who had no platero close. These copper rings were kept to use only in case of pain, and were loaned to neighbors and friends who suffered and did not have any of their own.

These rings were called anillos de corimiento (neuralgia rings).

Alegría (cockscomb) was grown at home in gardens. It grows about from two, to three feet high, and has a large red leaf. These leaves were mashed or squeezed, and the juice rubbed around the eyes. This was supposed to cure weak or sore eyes. It was used by the young girls for rouge. In those days the cheeks were painted but not the lips. Alegría was also used in making dyes for blankets and clothing.

Cota is a tall grass-like weed that grows in corn and bean fields. This was used for a blood purifier. The weed was boiled and the tea drank three times a day. The tea from cota yerba is red and bitter. It was also used as a wash for wounds and sore eyes. Many of the old people drank this tea with their meals instead of coffee or atole. Cota was gathered in the summer months, and hung on the vigas in the storerooms to dry for use in winter.

When babies became ill, and none of the curanderas' remedios helped them, and they lost weight, and would not eat, it was called tristesa or melarchico (sadness or melancholy). So to cheer and make them well again, red wool strings were tied on their wrists and ankles so that baby could look at these gay strings, and forget its tristesa, and brighten up again.

Babies were harmed by mal ojo (evil eye). It was said that some persons could hurt babies with evil eye or mal ojo unconsciously. When baby was made sick by anyone who had mal ojo, the mother called the curandera, who would ask who had last played with the baby. When told, she would send for, and tell this person to give the baby water, rub salt on its head, and hold it in his or her arms while a prayer was said. Then the baby would get were at once.

To protect little children from mal ojo, strings of coral beads were tied around their necks. And when anyone played with a baby, they were supposed to give it a little slap on the head to break the spell, in case they might have mal ojo.

Orégano del campo (wild sage) was boiled and the tea drank for colds and coughs. It grows wild on the mesa and foothills. When it comes up in the spring and is still tender, many of the native people cook it for greens, especially on ranches where vegetables are scarce.

The curandera made little woolen cords, some white, others colored. And, on San Blas Day (Saint Basil), the twenty-seventh of February, had them blessed. These cords were to be tied around children's necks to prevent sore throat or any other throat ailment during the year. And the mothers would send her gifts in correspondencia, like cornmeal, flour, or whatever they had.

December 3, 1940
Words 919

CHANA

Chana was born and raised in the little village of El Santo Niño, on the Santa Cruz River.

When she was probably fourteen or fifteen, she married Manuel Atencio, who also lived in El Santo Niño. Two of her older sisters and her brother were already married. One sister Dolores remained single, and stayed at home, and took care of her parents until they died.

When Chana married, she and her husband built a two-room house at first on a piece of land Manuel's father had given them. Later they added two more rooms. She had many children, but only four grew up, a boy and three girls. Rafael, the boy. Madalena came next. Then Carmel and Paulita.

When her children were still young, her husband died. Then she did the work, and as the children grew older, they helped. When Madalena, her oldest daughter, was about fifteen, she married and died the following year after giving birth to a little girl who was named Carmel. Chana raised this grandchild, and now lives with her at Jacona. Her other two daughters married and had children. They also are dead. And now the only one of her children left is the boy, who lives somewhere in the north. She has many grandchildren and great-grandchildren in different towns and villages.

It was the Santa Cruz River from which all those living close to it carried their water. Chana's father's land ran down to the river, and the house was not far from it. In those days, anyone living close to the river or ditches did not bother digging wells. All had large families, and it was the girls and women who carried the water.

Most everything of any weight was carried on the head by the women. The ollas with water, and all the bundles. It was said to be much easier, and the weight was not felt so much.

These ollas were bought or bartered for from the neighboring Indian Pueblos. Ollas from one to two gallons were used for water carrying. It was carried early in the morning, while it was still clean, before the stock went down to drink. Washing was done by the river. This required a lot of water; it was easier to wash on the river bank than to carry water. In late fall the women plastered their houses with mud. Some mixed the mud, while others put it on the walls. Then the inside of the house was white-washed, and bedding washed for winter. After this the blue corn was shelled and toasted in the ornos, then sent to the molinos (mills) to be ground. The rest of the corn was left to be shelled later, in the winter when there was not much work to do, except wood hauling or a few things that could be done inside the house.

The bailes, or dances, were looked forward to by the young girls and boys in the winter time. For it was then that they were held, and casorios began. It was very seldom that any of the young people married in the summer. Summer was the time for work, and to raise enough food for winter. When that was over, then the casorios and bailes commenced.

When young girls heard there was to be a baile, they watched to see if the combidador (the one doing the inviting) came to their house to invite them. Dances of pleasure, or casorios were always by invitation. In the morning of the day on which the baile was to be held, a boy or young man was sent on horseback to every house to invite the people who lived there to the dance. When he came up to the house, mother or father went to the door, and was told that they and all their family were invited to the dance. And they understood what was meant by you and family, for they all went, down to the baby. Only the very old who could not get around well stayed at home.

When mother had told the girls they had been invited, and would be taken, they started to get ready. First amole roots were pounded, and soaked in warm water, and a lather made in which they washed their hair. Then their best dress—usually calico or gingham, only the rich could afford silk—was washed and ironed. As soon as it became dark, father would hitch up the wagon, if it was some distance, and all would get in and were driven to the sala. If the sala (hall) was not far, then they walked. But mother always went with them. If for some reason she could not go, then grandmother or an aunt went. They never went without some older woman along to watch them.

When they arrived at the sala, mother took them in, and sat beside them on bancos, which were placed around the hall for the women only. The men stood in the doorway or outside until the dance began. When the music start-ed, they came in and asked the girls out to dance. There was no laughing or talking. A girl was considered brazen or forward if she was seen talking to her dance partner, and mother would threaten never to take her again.

SUBJECT: Casorios
WPA: 5-5-52 #67
December 10, 1940
Words 907

CASORIOS
(Weddings)

When a young man wanted to marry a certain girl, he went to his father, and told him he wanted him to ask for her. His father would tell him to wait until fall when the crops were all in.

Sometimes the boy and the girl were secretly engaged, he having asked the girl through his sister. So in the late part of October or early November, when all the crops were in, the boy's father went to the young man's padrino (godfather) to tell him that his godson (ahijado) wanted to marry. After finding out who the girl was, the padrino would set the date for the asking, and write the letter. If he could not do it himself, he would get someone who could.

When the day arrived, father, godfather, and an uncle or two went to the girl's home, usually after supper, when they were sure her father would be home. When they arrived, and were asked in, and sat down, they would talk about the weather, crops, or any other subject except the one which their visit was made for.

After staying an hour or more, they would get up and leave. As the boy's father bid the girl's father good night, he handed the other the letter, which he had in his pocket all the time. When the company had left, the father read the letter. If he could not read, he got some friend or neighbor who could to read it for him, and talked it over with his wife. The next day the girl's madrina was sent for, and told that her godchild had been asked for in marriage, and by whom. The madrina then took the girl in a room by herself, and told her she had been asked for, and asked if she wanted to marry.

If the girl was bashful, she would not reply then, but when her madrina left, would tell her little sister or brother to tell her mother and father that the answer was yes, or no. If the answer was no, the family waited a week "Ocho días," then her father would write or have a letter written, saying his daughter had refused the offer, and give it to some male member of the family to take to the young man's father.

This was called giving the calabasa (squash), meaning his offer had been squashed. The boy would be disappointed, but soon would try his luck somewhere else. Sometimes he would ask for four or five girls before he was accepted.

But when the girl's answer was yes, the father and mother would wait, usually two weeks, sometimes longer, to answer.

In the meantime, the house was cleaned from top to bottom, the walls white-washed with yeso, and the patios all swept, and the bride-to-be fitted out in a new dress. Then, a letter was sent saying their daughter had accepted the marriage offer, and that the young man, and his family could come on a certain day—about three days after the answer was given—and receive her.

On the day of the prendorio (receiving the bride), the girl's family prepared a fiesta. About sunset the boy's family arrived, with all their close relatives, and the madrina and padrino. They brought with them the donas (gifts for the bride). This consisted of a colchón de lana (wool mattress), blankets, pillows filled with wool, and a trunk in which there was clothes for the bride, such as calicos, ginghams, shoes, and the wedding dress, veil, and wreath of wax flowers. And sometimes she was given money, ten or twenty dollars.

After supper when all had feasted, there would be a baile, and they danced until daylight. The next morning the house would be turned over to the groom's family, they doing all the work and bearing all expenses of everything, until the wedding was over. The bride's family had nothing to do, or bother about, but were treated like guests.

About three days after the prendorio, on the wedding day, which was any day of the week except Tuesday (that day was considered unlucky, and the saying was, Los martes no te cases ni te embarques, on Tuesdays never marry or go on a journey), the bride was dressed by her madrina de casorio (matron of honor) whom she had selected. Usually a married couple acted the part of matron and best man. Before leaving for church, both bride and groom knelt, and received their mother's and father's blessing, then left for the church where they were to be married. Just the four went, bride, groom, madrina, and padrino. The families stayed home, and never went to see their children get married.

After the ceremony they came back to the bride's home, where a wedding feast was served; this lasted all day. At night there would be a baile, where they danced until dawn. After the dance, relatives, neighbors, and friends, with the músicos, would accompany the bride, and groom back to her parents' house. There the bride would be given to the groom's family, and the groom to the bride's family.

This was called la entregada de los novios (the giving away of the bride and groom). After this, breakfast was served to all, and as each left for home, they wished the bride and groom munchos años de vida y felicidades (many years of life and happiness).

SUBJECT: Antonia Vigil
WPA: 5-5-52 #73
December 10, 1940
Words 550

A handwritten note at the top of the page says, "Part of the Chana material to be included in part about stories around the fireside. These were told Mrs. Thorp by Antonia Vigil of San Ildefonso, who died about 10 years ago" (later identified as Antonio Vigil).

NUESTRA SEÑORA DEL ROSARIO

Nuestra Señora del Rosario was the patron saint of those who traveled. In the days when freight trains were sent to Mexico, Nuestra Señora del Rosario (Our Lady of the Rosary) was asked to take care of the men who drove the wagons.

The story is that once many years ago a train of wagons was sent to Mexico for goods, by a very rich man. There were about thirty men in all. They went to Chihuahua, and loaded up the wagons with merchandise, then started back. When they were about halfway home, they were attacked by Indians. All their stock and goods were stolen.

While the fighting was going on, one of the drivers ran away to try and get help, or see if he could. And wandered for days and nights without any water or food. Finally he came to a cave in the side of a mountain and crawled in to die, for he knew he was lost.

When he got halfway in, he saw a pool of water, and standing by it a woman who spoke to him, telling him to come in, and drink. So he did, and when finished, the woman told him she was Nuestra Señora del Rosario, and that she watched over all travelers, and to go down to the foot of the mountain, and there he would find his companions.

When he went down, he saw all his mates sitting around a campfire eating. They had killed a deer, and were very happy to see their lost friend again whom they thought dead. After eating, they saw in the distance another wagon train, and went to meet it, and found out that it was on its way to their hometown.

The one who had been lost told about his experience in the cave and the woman there. Then all fell on their knees and gave thanks to Nuestra Señora del Rosario. So after that she became the patron saint of all those who traveled, and was always asked to take care of them.

SUBJECT: Witch Stories
WPA: #539
Words 550

Part of Chana's biography to be included in section that mentions storytelling. Told to Mrs. Thorp by Antonia Vigil of San Ildefonso, who died about ten years ago. (Later identified as Antonio Vigil).

WITCH STORIES
The Story of a Headache

In a little village, there lived a man and his wife and small son. The wife suffered a great deal from headaches. She had tried all the remedios that the curanderas gave her but nothing helped.

One day while at play, her little son and the next-door neighbor's little girl went into the girl's house, and into a back room, and there saw a lot of clay figures. The boy asked the little girl what they were. The girl told him, they were people her mother made sick, and that her mother was a bruja (witch).

Looking around, the boy saw a figure with thorns stuck in its head, and asked what that was for. The little girl said that the figure with the thorns represented his mother, and that when her mother wanted his mother to get a headache, she pushed the thorns in the figure's head, and when she wanted her to get better, she pulled them out.

Then the boy went up to the clay figure, and pulled out all the thorns, saying "Mother has a headache now, and I am going to pull these out so she will get well." When the girl saw what the boy was doing, she told him not to touch them, but to leave them alone. "My mother will get very angry if she knows you are even looking at them."

At that the boy jumped up, kicking the clay figure over, and breaking it to pieces, then ran home. When he went in the house he saw his mother cooking supper, and said, "Mother, I thought you were sick?" "Yes I was," replied his mother. "My headache left me all of a sudden, and now I feel well again."

SUBJECT: Lina
WPA: 5-5-52 #74
December 31, 1940
Words 263

LINA

Marcelina, or Lina as she is called, was born and raised in Pojoaque. Her parents died when she was a baby. She was raised by an aunt whose name was Josefa Vigil.

Lina's husband, Tiófilo García, died last year. She has five children, three boys and two girls, also many grandchildren. All her children are married. One daughter, who is a widow, lives at home with her.

Lina's husband left everything to her: A large piece of land, with a small orchard on it, a good four-room house, three cows, two horses, and a pig. She does not know how many acres there are, but has the deeds that say how much land there is.

Tiófilo did not leave their children anything, because they were still young, and could work as he and Lina had, and buy land for themselves. Had he left them a share, now they would sell it and buy automobiles, and Lina would be left without a home. Anyway when she died, they would get it all, and she wouldn't be here to see them quarrel over it. Lina is sixty-eight years old, of medium height, and quite fleshly. She and her daughter do most of the work. She gave out some land on shares, the rest she looked after. She raised wheat, beans, and corn, and dried a lot of fruit. She has enough food to last her a year.

Now Lina is all through with the misa de cabo de año for Tiófilo (mass on first anniversary of a death). This misa is a very important event to country people, and is looked forward to, like a wedding or feast day. Tiófilo died a year ago, on the ninth of November, and ever since Lina has been preparing for this misa.

First she went to see the padre, and he told her he would have to say the mass on the sixth, because that was the only day he could spare. Lina thought it was too bad, but then that was only three days earlier, and after all, it did not make much difference. She had one of her granddaughters write to the sons and daughters who lived away, to be there on the sixth instead of the ninth. She also invited all her relatives and friends.

Then she began to get ready. First the bedding had to be washed in amole. Amole grows on the mesas. There are two kinds, palmia ancha, palmia angosta (wide and narrow leaf). The wide leaf is considered the best for washing; it makes the best lather. The roots are the only part used. They are dug up and placed in the sun to dry. When needed, they are pounded on a stone until shredded, then placed in a tub with a little water to soak for about fifteen minutes. Then the roots are stirred around, and around, until the tub is filled with suds. The roots are then taken out, and hot water added. In this, blankets and clothing are washed. And the walls inside the house were white-washed with yeso, and the patios swept. Then she and two other women went, and cleaned the church and draped it all in black, and wound a black ribbon around two dozen wax candles she had bought. This was done because everything had to be in mourning.

Lina sold some of her wheat and two cows. These cows were in the hills, and might be stolen this winter, so she thought it best to sell them and get the money for the misa.

January 7, 1941
Words 527

LINA

Two days before the misa, bread, empanaditas (small turnover pies), and panocha were baked in the outdoor oven. These ovens resemble beehives, having a small door on one side, and a hole on top for a chimney. A fire is built inside, and when thought hot enough, the fire is raked out and tested by holding a small piece of wool on a wooden paddle inside of the oven. If the wool should scorch a dark brown, the oven is too hot. Then a piece of sacking or cloth is dipped in water and the inside swabbed and tested again. When the wool comes out a light brown, the oven is right. The bread is placed inside and the door and chimney sealed up with mud. Telling the time by looking at the sun, they left the bread in the oven for about an hour. This is baking on a large scale, and is only done for wedding and feast days.

Panocha is a pudding made of wheat sprouted in a dark place, after which it is ground into flour. This is mixed in boiling water like making mush, then put in an olla or pot and placed in the oven, and left to bake for a day and a night or twenty-four hours. It comes out an amber color, is very sweet, and considered a great luxury.

The day of the misa, quite a number of people came, arriving at the church in wagons, trucks, and cars. All her children and grandchildren were there, as well as neighbors and friends. After the mass, the padre spoke a few words about Tiófilo. He said he missed seeing him in church, and that this day, the sixth, was a very happy day for all. Lina was glad the padre had said such nice things about her husband.

After the misa, all the people went to Lina's home, where she served dinner to them. After everyone left, Lina told her family that now that the misa de cabo de año was over, they could lay off their mourning and go to the bailes, but that she would always wear black. She was sixty-eight years old, and it was not proper for old women to wear colored clothes.

43

She had spent a lot of money for this misa—something like forty-five dollars in all. First she had paid the priest twenty-five, then the choir fifteen for singing, besides buying material to drape the church with. Lina said she might marry again. A man who lived close by had wanted to marry her for sometime. He had been married before and had eight children. All were married except two. The only thing that kept her from saying yes was he wanted her to deed her land over to him, so it would all be in one name, "his land and hers." But she didn't know what her children would say or do. She wishes she knew what to do. She needed someone to look after her land. Owning property was such a care.

January 14, 1941
Words 600

LINA

When Lina was young, godfathers and godmothers were as important to children as their parents were, and were chosen with a great deal of care by the mother and father. The belief was that children took after their padrinos and not their parents. If a child had a good or bad disposition, it took that from its padrino or madrina, but never inherited anything from its parents except looks. And all good or bad habits of any kind were laid at the godparents' door.

The padrinos had as much right to the child as the parents had, and were consulted, and their opinion asked about raising the child. If the father and mother thought their way of handling the child was the best, and the padrinos wanted it another way, then it was done so. They had a great respect for their comadres and compadres (co-mothers and co-fathers, or second mother and father). The parents called each other comadre and compadre. Children were taught to always obey, and love their godfathers, as they did their mother and father.

When the first child was born to a couple, the wife's mother and father were asked to be the padrinos. Then when the second one came, the husband's parents were asked. Always the mother and father of both husband and wife were asked first. The reason for this was the belief that on the day of judgment, when all were judged, that in the great crowd only comadres and compadres would recognize each other. This gave the hope of seeing mother and father again.

After the parents had been padrinos, then came relatives and friends. When a child was born, the father or some other member of the family looked in the almanac to see what saint's day it was, so the baby could be named after it. If they did not have an almanac, they asked someone who did. All children in the old days were named for the saints. Then a little girl or boy was sent around the neighborhood to let them know of the new arrival. These words were repeated at every house: "Tiene otra criada o criado más a quien mandar" (You have another servant to command), and from within the house, the answer would be, "Dios se los empreste por muchos años" (May God lend him for many years). This was an old custom, and all friends expected to have the birth announced to them. Sometimes a next-door neighbor or friend had attended at the birth, but that made no difference; when they went home, they awaited to be told about it.

Then wife and husband would pick the ones whom they wanted to ask to be their child's padrinos. A letter was sent by some friend—never anyone belonging to the family—to the couple that had been decided upon.

In about three days, or sometimes a week, the godfathers-to-be went to see the baby and pay the parents a visit, and asked on what saint day it was born, also what other name the mother and father wanted added to Juan or José. The parents would tell them to choose the extra name, which they did. Then the day was set, which was most always Sunday when the padre came to say mass.

The madrina then bought material and had the christening robe made. And the padrino got the gift for the child, which was a horse, a cow, or a piece of land. And sometimes if he could afford it, gave it as much as five dollars.

N.D.
Words 631

LINA

Most every little village has its church, and patron saint for whom the church was named. These churches were built by the people all doing their share of the work. One gave land, others made adobes (mud bricks), and laid them in the walls. Others cut the vigas from pine trees, and when dry, hauled them in, and put the roof on. The village carpenter made the altar and other woodwork. When the men were through, it was turned over to the women. They plastered it inside and out with mud, and when dry, whitewashed the inside with yeso (gypsum).

Afterwards, once a year a fiesta is held on the saint's day. These saint days or fiesta days were the big days of the year. Two mayordomos—husband and wife—are appointed by the people, and are called mayordomos de la fiesta. Mayordomos have quite a lot to do during the year. They collect all church dues for the padre. They take care of the upkeep of the church, and their wives saw that it was kept clean. A month or six weeks before the fiesta day, the mayordoma, as the wife is called, hires several women to help her. The church is freshly plastered outside and whitewashed inside. Women always did this work. Then the dresses or robes are taken off the santos, washed and ironed, or new ones made. The altar is decorated with colored paper flowers. Beads and jewelry are borrowed from the village women to adorn the saints with, and after the fiesta, returned to the owners.

The mayordomo made arrangements with the padre to have mass said on the saint's fiesta, for fifteen to twenty dollars. The cantador (singer) was some old man who had learned the mass responses from the priest. He went from fiesta to fiesta to sing. He was paid from two to two dollars and fifty cents. Women in the old days were not supposed to sing in church. No mayordomo wanted to have it said that he didn't have as good a fiesta as the one the year before.

The mayordoma made new clothes for her children, for on fiesta day, her family had to look nice. Invitations were sent to all friends and acquaintances on ranches, and other placitas, to be sure to come to la fiesta. The mayordomo sold two or three cows—if he had them—grain, or a piece of land, to get money to buy the fiesta with.

In their wagon, he and his wife went to town where they bought candy, canned goods, and vino and other liquors. Fiestas without drink were not fiestas. At home, meat was butchered, if it was summertime, cut up and salted, and hung on lines to dry. Bread was baked in hornos (ovens) and patios swept. Everyone who expected company prepared food, but the mayordomos were the ones who gave dinner to most everyone. Special food was cooked for the padre. It was considered quite an honor if the priest ate dinner at the mayordomo's house.

The day before the fiesta, in the evening, lumunarias (small fires of pine or pinion wood) were lighted before the church, and the rosary said. The santo was taken out of church and placed on a platform, and carried by four men or girls, followed by all the village people. Singing and shooting off guns, this procession went around the church. After this, the men gathered at the sala (dance hall). This was to name the mayordomos for the next year. Two or three names were voted on, and the names that received the most votes were given to the priest the next day, to be announced to the people in church.

February 4, 1941
Words 551

LINA

On fiesta day from early morning until time for mass, people began to arrive in wagons, buggies, and on horseback. When it was time for church, all went in. The men stood on one side and the women on the other. Never together.

After the mass, and once the names of the next mayordomos were given out, a procession was formed again with the santo. And marched again around the church, and village, with singing and shooting. After this was over, the fiesta began. The mayordomos were escorted home by the people followed by músicos. At the house the músicos were seated in the best room, where fiesta was passed around.

After dinner was served to all, the men raced horses or visited with friends whom they had not seen for some time, but were now at the fiesta, and the young men and girls danced. But the old women, who never liked the bulla (noise) went to church to pay la vesita (a visit), to pray and ask for help in sickness or other misfortunes. It was said that sometimes these santos grant-ed favors on the day their fiesta was held, like the one that Lina's aunt had told her about.

This happened about sixty or sixty-five years ago, when the aunt was a young girl. There lived a man by the name of Francisco Mendosa and his wife on a ranch. They had had many children, but all died at birth. The woman, whose name was Lus, became very ill, and then tullida (paralyzed) from the waist down. Curandera after curandera had been called, but all their remedios failed to help her. A few days before the fiesta of San Pedro was to be held in the little village of San Pedro, she asked her husband, Francisco, to take her there. He put bedding in his wagon, and laid her upon it, and drove to San Pedro where they stayed at a friend's house. On the day of the fiesta, in the afternoon, she asked to be taken to church and left there for a while. After being placed on some sheepskins in front of the santo, she told Francisco to go and come back for her after a while. She wanted to be left alone. When her husband thought she been in church long enough, he went for her. As he entered the door, he saw his wife standing, and when he called to her, she turned and walked towards the door. From that day the tullido (paralysis) left her.

At night the fiesta baile was held. Those who did not go to the misa were sure to be at the dance. Young mothers coaxed grandmothers to go with them, to hold the babies while they danced. A bastonero (dance manager) was appointed to keep order. It was usually someone who did not drink. He carried a bastón (small stick with a knob on one end) and was given authority to use it whenever he thought it was needed.

The next morning breakfast was served to those who remained at the mayordomo's house. Then wagons and buggies were hitched up, and adiós said, telling the mayordomos what a grand fiesta it had been.

SUBJECT: Partera, Midwife
WPA: 5-5-53 #8
February 25, 1941
Marcelina, age 68

PARTERA
(Midwife)

Juana Romero had been a partera (midwife) in the days when Lina was married. She had attended when Lina's children were born. In those days the partera had a tenedor (holder) who always went with her to help at the births.

The tenedor was usually some old man who was still strong. He was taken to help the partera in case the birth should turn out to be a difficult one.

When a woman labored two or three days, which they sometimes did, the tenedor had plenty to do. A woman in labor was kept on her feet until the child was born. If she were not so very ill, she walked up and down by herself, but in bad cases, when the mother was too weak to stand alone, the tenedor had to hold her up and keep her walking, sometimes dragging her back and forth for hours. If she fainted or showed signs of fainting, the partera placed coals in a barro (dish) and sprinkled ground horse hair and trementina (resin or hard pitch from pinon trees), then held this smoke to the patient's nostrils until she revived. When she did, she was again made to walk, while the tenedor held her up. When a birth was easy, the tenedor had nothing to do, but was always taken along in case he should be needed.

Parteras learned their profession from their mothers or grandmothers, who had been midwives before them, and sometimes they started by helping at a delivery.

The partera often was the curandera also, but not always. The curandera treated all, men, women, and children, while the partera cared only for women.

51

Sometimes the partera's husband was the tenedor—that was if he were strong. In that case both were gone most of the time. Their children and relatives attended their work, such as planting and wood hauling, for a good partera and tenedor not only cared for the sick women in their own village, but received calls from others. They never charged for their services, but left it to the patient's family to give what they thought their services were worth. Some were generous, and gave corn, beans, chili, goats, and sometimes money if they had it; but usually the pay was in grain. And if someone did not have very much and could not pay with grain, the father of the child helped the partera's husband with his planting or gathered his crops for him; or sometimes the women would go in the fall and plaster the partera's house. All tried to pay, for they never knew how often they would need her.

The partera was called or sent for at all hours. Some came in wagons, others on horses or burros. If it were a burro or a horse, the partera and tenedor rode the same animal, she in front holding her bag of remedios and the tenedor behind. There were times when she had to walk, for some were so poor that they were unable to provide any method of transportation.

There were two things that the old midwives dreaded, a first birth and births in the last quarter of the moon. They believed the moon had much to do with childbirths. The first quarter meant that the moon was weak, and it could not do much harm. A full moon meant that the moon was happy. In the last quarter it was dying and would try to do all the harm it could before being succeeded by another moon.

March 11, 1941
Words 600

PARTERA
(Midwife)

When a partera felt that she was getting old, and needed help, she looked around among her family and friends for someone to take her place. The one she picked had to be married, and close to middle age, for then she was through having children. A young woman with small children never became a midwife, for she was either raising a baby or expecting one, and had no time to spare. If one of her married daughters were strong and fearless, she would take her; but if her own daughter were not considered sufficiently courageous or intelligent, a friend or relative who was suitable was chosen.

The partera first taught her helper about the remedios, what each one was good for, and how to use them. After the pupil knew about these remedios, she was taken along with the midwife to help at birth. If it were an easy one, the helper did all the work under the direction of the partera; but if a difficult one, she helped only. After going to four or five cases she was considered a midwife. She did not compete with her tutor, however, but only attended cases when the partera sent her as her substitute.

These old parteras were jealous of their position, never giving up their calling except for sickness or some disability. If this were the case, she would send the new one in her place. But as long as she lived, she expected to be consulted and told about everything when the helper got back.

Two parteras in the same village—and sometimes there were—never were friends. They were rivals and envious of each other. If one partera were called, the other felt aggrieved, and when called by some member of the family who had summoned the other partera, she would refuse to go. The only ones approved were those they themselves had trained.

It often happened that when a partera delivered a child, she was asked to be its madrina. The midwives did not like this, because then they received nothing for their work; moreover, the madrina had to get the ropón (christening robe) and go to some expense for the baptismal. This often occurred because the parents were so poor, they did not have much to give the partera, and were ashamed to give too little. They knew that the partera told her family and friends what and how much were given by each one. Those who gave the most were held up as examples to the others. The result was that each tried to outdo the other in presents of food, work, and grain.

Año bisiesto (leap year) was considered a very unlucky year. More women died in childbirth in these years than in any other. Why this was thought unlucky, no one seems to know; but the old midwives used to say it was a very bad year.

When a baby was born dead, the partera had it buried next to the house under a canal (water spout) so it could have water whenever it rained. This was done because the child had died before it could be baptized. These children were called niños de limbo, a place or region assigned to unbaptized children.

When someone came to call the partera, she was sure to ask if it were a primeriza (first child), if she did not know the woman. If it were and the moon were full, she would feel no anxiety; but if it were a first child, and the moon was in the last quarter, she would be very fearful, saying, "I will do all I can, and I will leave the rest to God."

Lina had been told by old Juana that the moon did not like women, and would try to hurt them when they were expecting children, that expectant mothers had to be very careful, especially if there were an eclipse of the moon, for that was a sign that the moon was angry, and would do as much harm as it could. Also, women who were expecting a child were told to hang the door or padlock keys at their waists. This was the only thing that could prevent the moon from hurting the unborn child. And on moonlight nights windows were covered over, doors closed, and keys taken to bed with them. The reason for this was that in case there should be an eclipse late at night, the moon would not see and harm them while asleep.

The moon was blamed for deformed or crippled children. These old parteras used to say that through the child it could hurt the mother. And this, according to old Juana, was what happened through one woman's ignorance.

This simple-minded inocente lived on the outskirts of the village. She was married and had one child about two years old and was expecting another. One night there was an eclipse of the moon. She had heard about the keys, but did not know quite how to use them. She had heard that they had to be placed on someone to save a child from harm. So she took her keys and fastened them on her young child's head.

In about three months she gave birth to her second child, a little boy. One of its arms was much shorter than the other and the hand had no fingers. When the partera asked her if she had tied the keys around her waist during the eclipse, she replied that she did not know that she was to wear the keys, but had placed them on her child. Because of this, Juana said, the baby was born deformed.

Difficult births and cases of long labor were believed to be punishments for being ill-tempered, or disrespectful to their elders. If the partera could find out, or if she knew what the suffering woman had done, she would have the patient make amends, and everything would turn out all right. This was illustrated by Juana's story of a woman she knew.

This woman had borne several children, but all had died at birth. She was expecting another one. She was a very selfish, stingy woman, who never loaned, gave, or shared anything with anyone. She lived in a placita where there were many small children. If these children asked her for bread, she refused and sent them home. She ate her meals in the open doorway. Hungry children came and stood by watching, but she never gave them so much as a crumb of bread or tortilla; she just let them watch her eat.

The time came for the birth of her baby, and her husband brought the partera. She was very ill for two days and nights, but the child did not come. The partera used all the remedios she knew of, and the tenedor was exhausted from holding and walking her. On the third day her strength was gone, and she was thought to be dying. The partera as a last resort went to a neighbor's house to borrow San Ramón, the patron saint of all expectant mothers. (The story is that San Ramón was not born, but taken from his mother when she was dying. He was called San Ramón Nonato, and women prayed a novena to him, asking to be delivered safely.) When the partera asked for the santo, the neighbor asked her how the mezquina (stingy one) was. The partera asked why she called the woman a mezquina. The neighbor then told about the sick woman, how selfish and mean she was to little children. When the partera heard this, she handed back San Ramón Nonato, for he was not needed; she knew exactly what to do.

She returned to the house and went into the kitchen, where she found some wheat flour. This was considered a great luxury and kept for company and feast days only. Then she made a large number of tortillas in the fireplace. When they were done, she took them to the sick woman and told her that she was going to call in all the little children she could find, and when they came in, the sick woman was to give each child a tortilla with her own hand.

The children came in and went up to the sick woman, who by now was so weak she could barely lift her hand. But she managed to give each child one. No sooner had the last child gone out with its tortilla than her child was born. The next day the partera told her that the reason she was so ill and had almost died was because she was so selfish, that her child did not want to be born to a selfish mother.

She changed completely from a selfish person to a generous one, and instead of being called mezquina, she was known as la dadivosa.

WPA: 5-5-53 #6
N.D.

THE PIE AND THE PLATE
A Witch Story

In a village there lived a woman, whose eldest daughter was sick with some kind of fever. One day the village people took the statue of the virgin out to pray for rain. When the procession went by this woman's house, the sick girl stood in the doorway to see the people pass by. A woman who lived next door came out to watch the procession also. When she saw the girl standing in the doorway, she went back into her house, and came out again with an empanadita (small pie) on a small clay plate and handed it to the girl. Her mother, who was standing close by her, whispered, "take it, but don't eat it." The other woman heard her and went home.

The girl took the plate with the pie on it and held it by her side, while she watched the people go by. When it was over, she went back into the house, then thought of the pie, but she did not have it—it had mysteriously disappeared.

That night the girl became very ill; she complained of having a pain in her side. The mother sent for the curandera, but nothing could be done for her. Days and weeks went by, and the girl was getting worse. She had a large lump on her side by now, and the pain never left her. Her mother knew she had been embrujada (bewitched) but by whom or how was hard to tell.

One day the girl's madrina (godmother) came to see her, and after talking it over with the mother, also said the girl was embrujada, but that she knew of an Indian who was an arborlario (witch doctor) whom she was sure could cure the girl.

The Indian was sent for, and when he came and looked at the girl, also said she was bewitched. He also said that he could cure her if they would pay him a fanega (180 pounds) of wheat. The mother agreed to it. Then the Indian took some roots out of a bag he had tied around his waist and boiled them down to thick paste. When this was done, and cooled off, he put it on the girl's side, and in a few minutes the lump broke, and he took the little clay plate with the pie on it out of her side. And it was just as fresh and nice-looking as the day it had been made. They then cut the pie open to see what was inside, and this is what was found: horse hair, pinion, pebbles, and little toads.

Now they knew that the woman next door was the witch who had done the harm, and went to her house to punish her. But all they found was a large owl that flew out of the door, and was never seen again, nor the woman either. The girl got well.

WPA: 5-5-53 #8
March 18, 1941
Words 960
Marcelina

PARTERA
(Midwife)

One old partera by the name of Candelaria, whom Lina's aunt had told her about, was called one night to go and attend an unmarried girl. This girl was about to give birth to a baby, and had been ill for two or three days. Her mother had not called the midwife in hopes that the child would be born without anyone knowing about it, but at last had to get Candelaria. When the partera arrived, the girl was dead, but the baby was alive.

The dead girl's mother wanted to give this baby away, and asked the partera if she knew of anyone who would take it. Candelaria knew of no one, but asked them to give the baby to her.

The partera's children had all died when small, with the exception of a son who was married and lived in another village. He had many children and would have given one of them to his mother. But his wife did not like Candelaria and refused to let any of her children stay with their grandmother.

Candelaria lived alone and wanted to raise a child so she could have someone to care for her when she became too old to take care of herself. She had wanted to adopt a baby, but no one would give up their child to her.

She took this girl baby home with her, and asked one neighbor after another, who had a small baby, to feed it for her. One woman who came to feed the child wanted Candelaria to give it to her, and teased every time she came. The partera refused to give the baby to this woman. After a few weeks she became worried that the baby might become attached to this woman, and then there would be nothing she could do but give it to her.

One morning she got up very early and went to a friend's house and borrowed a goat from him. This goat had a young kid. She took the goat home, and nursed the baby on it. Bottles were unknown in those days. She kept this goat tied outside by the door, where she fed it weeds, and grass she cut along the acequias.

Whenever the child needed food, she took it out to the goat, and at night took the goat inside the house with her and the baby.

She became very fond of this baby, and whenever she was called to attend some woman in childbirth, she took the baby and goat with her.

If she were taken in a wagon, the goat was tied and put in also. Or if it was a horse or burro, she rode holding the child and bag of remedios, while the one who had been sent for her walked behind, leading the goat. Sometimes she was asked to leave the baby and goat with some neighbor. But this she would not do, saying that if they wanted her, they had to take the child also, and that if the baby went, it had to take its food with it. So the baby and the goat always went with the partera.

This baby grew fat and very healthy. The conscience of the grandmother (the dead girl's mother) began to bother her, and she regretted giving the baby away. She went to see the baby every day and tried to wean it away from the partera, and finally asked her to give her the baby back again. Candelaria refused, saying the baby belonged to her.

The grandmother kept on asking for the baby, and when she saw that the partera would not give it up, she told that she was going to steal it. This frightened Candelaria.

One morning the neighbors missed the goat outside the door, but thought that the partera had been called in the night, and as she always took the baby and goat with her, they thought nothing of it.

After three or four days went by, the neighbors began to ask whom Candelaria had gone to. But no one knew where the partera was. The village people hunted, and asked, but could not find her. One or two children were born, and the partera from another placita had to be brought.

After two or three weeks, a wood hauler came into the village and told the people he had seen Candelaria in the mountains. Some eight or ten men from the village, with the wood hauler, went to the place in the mountains where she had been seen.

They found her and the baby under a tree, the goat grazing nearby. When the men asked her what she was doing there, and why had she left home, she told the men that she was going to a village on the other side of the mountain where the baby would be safe. She was afraid to stay home, because the grandmother had threatened to steal the child from her.

She was only making about a mile or two a day, because she had to let the goat graze as she went on. Her food consisted of tortillas, and these were almost gone. But she was not worried about herself as long as the baby had plenty of milk.

The men then told her to go back with them, and that they would see to it that the baby was never taken from her. So Candelaria went back to the village, and the women were all happy to see their old partera again. The men kept their word. The first thing they did was to tell the grandmother not to bother Candelaria about the baby again, for if she did, they would punish her.

WPA: 5-5-53 #3
March 25, 1941
Words 834
Marcelina, age 68.

REMEDIOS

Yerba del lobo (wolf herb). This herb or plant grows high up in the mountains and looks like a currant bush. It grows from two and a half to three feet high. It has a small white flower when in bloom. The leaves are small and round and dark green. The roots of this bush are the only part used. The roots are dug up and spread out to dry in the sun—and when dry, are ground very fine, and mixed with beef or mutton tallow, and used as a salve. It is said that this salve is good for burns, sprains, sores, and bruises.

Enmortal. This yerba also grows in the sierra or mountains. It is a small plant with long narrow leaves, and grows in shady places, under bushes or beside rocks. The roots are dug up, and a brown skin peeled off. Then it is mashed and boiled. The tea is put into a jar or ollita (small clay jar) and left to stand for five or seven days. It is supposed to cure colic, and any other pain in the abdomen. The same amount is given children and adults, about two ounces three times a day.

Copalquín. This remedio comes from Mexico. It is a thick, hard, brown bark. It is broken with a hammer or stone, then boiled for about three hours. The tea is a dark red, and small doses are drunk three times a day. This is supposed to cure coughs and heart and lung trouble. In the old days the curanderas treated those affected with tuberculosis, or "el tis," with baked onions and copalquín. The onions were eaten, and the copalquín tea drunk afterwards.

Guaco/Waco. This herb or weed grows in fields, and along the roadside. When full grown, it is about two to three feet tall. The leaves are long and narrow. It has a purple flower. The scent from these flowers is strong, something like burnt rubber. On account of this odor, cattle, sheep, and goats keep away from it. The leaves from this weed are boiled down until it turns into a thick black paste. This paste is used as a poultice for lumbago, and other pains in joints. This black paste was also used by Indians, for painting pottery.

Contra yerba. This has a long smooth leaf, and grows along the river banks. The roots of this plant are white. They are ground, and mixed with warm water, and used as an eye wash. It is also used as a gargle for sore throat.

Estafate pardo. Known as grey sage, this was used as a cure for rheumatism. The tops of the bush were boiled, and the water used as a bath. The water is also drank for colds and dolor de estómago (pains in the stomach).

Malvas. This is a small plant, it has round leaves, and small white flowers, said to look something like a strawberry plant. Malvas grows in gardens and along the ditches. It is used for calentura (fever). The leaves are boiled, and the tea drunk.

Raíz de entraña. Cactus roots—any kind—are boiled, and hair is washed in the water. This is said to make hair grow and prevent it from falling. In the old days when a man began to lose his hair, he washed his head in this water made from cactus roots, to keep from getting bald.

Hiel (gall). This remedio was used in the old days for chilblain. When anyone had chilblains, a calf, goat, or mutton was killed, and the gall taken out. The fluid from the gall was rubbed on the feet, and they say it cured chilblains within a day or two. It was also used on the hands and face of smallpox patients, to stop itching and irritation.

Chiquete de embarrañada. This embarrañada is a grey weed that grows on the mesa. It does not need much water. It grows about a foot to a foot and a half tall, and has no leaves, just jointed stems. In the spring it has a very small yellow flower. When this flower dries up, little drops of gum or rubber, green in color, form on the stem joints, and become hard. Children used to pick these rubber drops off these plants and chew them for gum. But the curanderas used this gum for sprains, backache, and inflammation of the joints, by melting these little drops, or gum balls, until they were soft; then this soft gum was put on pieces of cloth and placed on the back, or tied to ankles and knees. These poultices stuck to the skin like glue and were painful to take off, so were left to wear off. This gum was also eaten while warm and soft by those who had stomach trouble. It is said to be very bitter. It was used also for boils and sores. For these, it was mixed with marrow from beef bones.

SUBJECT: VELORIO
February 11, 1941
Words 710
Barbarita Nieto, Cedar Grove.

VELORIO

Merejildo Nieto owned a ranch in a little settlement in the San Pedro Mountains, now called Cedar Grove. He had filed on this homestead, and lived there for twenty years. This ranch consisted of a hundred and sixty acres of dry land. They hauled their water from a spring five miles away.

Merejildo and his second wife, Barbarita, and their two children, a boy and a girl, lived in a three-room pole house. This house was plastered with mud. The inside walls were whitewashed, with dirt floors, which were also plastered over with mud. On the walls of one room were hung old santos, and mirrors in tin frames. In the corner of this room was a wooden bedstead painted blue, and piled high with bedding. A small homemade table with photographs of uncles, aunts, and cousins upon it, stood in another corner. And on the dirt floor were sheep and goat skins.

The next room was smaller. A bed was folded on the ground floor, where there also were skins.

In the middle of one of the walls was a fireplace, with a rock chimney built on the outside. There were one or two santos on the walls, and a very large cross, "maybe six feet by three," with the figure of Christ on it, with blood running down his face and side. This hung on a wall by itself. This was called La Sangre de Cristo (The Blood of Christ).

The kitchen had boxes, one on top of the other, for shelves; on these the dishes were kept. There was a small cook stove, and two wooden chairs without backs. Outside was a pole corral, an horno for baking, and a small room which was used as a storeroom.

Barbarita was about thirty or thirty-one years old. When she was sixteen or seventeen, she had given birth to a child, de padre no conocido (by an unknown father). And no young man wanted to marry her because she no longer was a doncea (maid). So she remained single until her boy was four years old. Then she married Merejildo, who had lost his wife the year before. He had no children of his own.

She was short and fat, with coarse black hair, and her skin was dark brown. She was born and raised on a ranch in the same settlement where she lived with Merejildo. Her father's name was Luis Chávez, and her mother's Manuela Gallegos. Her mother died when she was about thirteen years old. Afterwards she kept house for her father and two brothers until she married Merejildo. She was now married about ten years. They raised corn and beans when the season was rainy, but nothing when it was dry. She helped her husband cut wood, which he hauled, and sold in town. This way they managed to make a living.

Merejildo was seventy years old. Tall and very thin, he had no hair except a little grey hair around his ears and on the back of his neck. He was in very bad health, and had been for years. He coughed constantly. But he continued to work until he became so weak he had to give up and go to bed. He had some skins placed on the dirt floor, and upon these he lay. Barbarita wanted him to lay on the bedstead, but he refused to do so, for Merejildo was a Penitente, and belonged to the order of Los Esclavos de Jesús (The Slaves of Jesus). And for this reason was not to lay upon wood or have it touch him. Their belief was that there was a curse on wood because Jesus had been nailed and died on a wooden cross. He also insisted that he should do penance until he died, and would not have any bedding placed under him, just the two goat skins on the dirt floor, with a thin blanket for covering.

While he was sick, Barbarita and her two children—the boy thirteen or fourteen, and a girl eight years old who had been born to her and Merejildo—did the work on the ranch, and cared for the sick man. She and the boy cut wood, and hauled it to town, and with the help of the children, planted and took care of the crops.

Merejildo lingered sick all summer and fall. In December he became very ill, and Barbarita knew he had but a few days longer to live, so she began to get the velorio ready.

February 18, 1941
Words 890

VELORIO

Barbarita asked a neighbor to kill her pig, which she had been feeding and keeping for the velorio. The neighbor's wife helped her with the meat. After the hog had been scalded and scraped, the meat was cut from the bones. The bones were roasted and hung up on a line in the storeroom. Then every bit of fat was cut from the meat, and cut into small pieces and fried in pots until brown. These were called chicharrones (cracklings). Ollas of chili were prepared with orégano (sage) and much garlic. The meat was put into these ollas of chili for carne adobada (preserved meat). When all this was done, it was also stored. The chicharrones were sprinkled with salt, put in tin pails, and put away. The hide or pig skin, was cut in lengths and hung on a line. These were to be cooked in the posole (hominy). The corn for this was boiled in lime water until the hulls came off, then it was washed in several waters. Then bread was baked in the outdoor orno.

Two days after this food had been prepared and put away, Merejildo died. Barbarita sent her boy to tell the neighbors. Two men came and laid him out. Instead of cloths, a mortaja (shroud) was put on him, with a piece of rope tied around his waist, then laid on the floor—without the skins—in the same room where he had been when ill.

This mortaja had been made a month before he died. He had his wife send to town for the black cloth, and showed her how to make it. She made it and put it away.

When evening came, the neighbors began to arrive for the velorio, coming in wagons and on horseback, the women bringing all their children with them. The men built fires outside, and stood around them talking. The children ran in and out playing and laughing, while the women stayed inside to condole with Barbarita, who cried and wailed whenever a new arrival came in.

When it became dark, the resador came. He was the hermano mayor (head of the brotherhood). He went into the room where Merejildo lay, surrounded by lighted candles, followed by the men and one or two women, and began to pray.

When the praying was over, he sang alabados, with the men joining in. This praying and singing continued until about ten o'clock. Then the resador asked everyone to go into the next room and close the door, because the hermanos were coming to pray for their departed brother.

When all had gone into the next room and closed the door, the resador put out the candles around the dead man. Soon afterwards the hermanos arrived, singing alabados, and playing on a pito (fife) as they went in. When they finished singing, all was quiet for five minutes. Then they began calling on the dead to come. Salgan vivos y difuntos, aquí estamos todos juntos (Come dead and living, we are here together), the meanwhile rattling chains, and pounding on a small cowhide drum. This noise lasted for ten or fifteen minutes, then all was quiet again.

The resador went into the room where the men and women were waiting, and whispered to Barbarita. She went to the blue bed in the corner, and took the bedding off and laid it on the floor. The resador removed the springs from the bedstead, and carried it into the next room.

Nothing could be seen when the door was opened, all was dark. When the door was closed again, the spring was taken outside, and Merejildo placed on it. The hermanos then took this up, and carried him off, over the lomas and arroyos, singing and playing the pito as they went. This was the despedida del mundo (taking the dead to bid the world goodbye).

The men then went out to their fires, the women talked, and the children went back to sleep on their pallets on the floor. After an hour had passed the singing and pito were heard. They were bringing Merejildo back.

As they came closer, the men went back again into the room, and closed the door. The hermanos came in singing and praying, laid Merejildo on the floor again, and went off.

The resador opened the door, and told all they could come out. Three or four women went to the kitchen and prepared the media noche cena (midnight supper). When this was ready, the men were called first. The food was placed on the floor, where they sat around the pots of chili, meat, and posole, eating. When the men had finished, the women and children were called. They also sat on the floor.

After supper when men and women had finished smoking their cigaros, the resador called them in, and praying and singing went on until dawn.

When the sun came up, the bed spring was again taken outdoors. Two men carried Merejildo out and put him upon it. Barbarita handed the resador a bag containing salt, about five pounds. Four men picked up the spring, one at each corner, and followed by the rest of the men—the women stayed home—only men went to funerals and the resador carrying the salt. Merejildo was taken down to a field north of the house, where a grave had been dug the day before. He had chosen this place before he died. When they arrived at the burial place, he was lowered into the grave with two ropes. A cloth was put over his face and the bag of salt at his feet—this salt was supposed to keep the body from decaying—and the earth was put back in. All stood around until the last shovelful was thrown in. After this was over, they returned to the house, where the women had breakfast ready. After breakfast, horses were saddled, teams hitched to wagons, and the children put in. They all bid Barbarita goodbye and drove home.

Now that Barbarita was a widow, she was not to wash her face or comb her hair for eight days. If she did, people would say she was glad that Merejildo was dead.

February 25, 1941
Words 238

MORTAJA
(Shroud)

The cloth that Merejildo's mortaja was made of is called lacre by the Mexican people. Lacre is a cheap, coarse cotton cloth, like calico, and is about thirty-six or thirty-eight inches wide. At that time the cost was about twenty cents a yard.

Mortajas are all made about the same. Two lengths of cloth, long enough to cover the feet, are sewed up the sides, with an opening left for sleeves. These sleeves are square pieces of the same cloth, sewed together, then sewed in the side openings. The sleeves are about eight inches wide when finished. A slit is cut at the top of this bag for the neck. A band of the same material, some five inches wide, is sewed on for a neck band, and comes up to the chin. An opening is made at the back, and fastened with strings made out of the black material.

A piece of rope was tied into a knot around his waist. The ends of the rope were also knotted, and reached a little below the knees, one knotted end being shorter than the other.

The salt that was used at this burial was Sal de las Salinas (coarse salt taken from the salt lakes). This salt is considered the only pure salt, and is still used in most religious ceremonies.

SUBJECT: Satan and the Girl
WPA: 5-5-53 #4
April 1, 1941
Words 277
Juliana Martínez, 70 or 72, Agua Fría.

SATAN AND THE GIRL

There once lived a woman in a small village, whose only daughter died, leaving a small baby girl. The grandmother took and raised this child. When the girl was fourteen or fifteen, she was very pretty. But she would not obey her grandmother, or behave the way young girls were supposed to. She had been seen several times talking to boys, and it was rumored about that she had a sweetheart.

One night she slipped out of the house when her grandmother was asleep, and went for a walk with a boy. They had not gone far when the young man asked the girl if she knew with whom she was walking. She replied that she did, and said she was out with her sweetheart. Then he told her she was mistaken, that he was not her sweetheart, but that she was walking with Satan.

He no sooner said this when chains began to rattle, and out of the darkness appeared a big ball of fire, and the smell of sulphur. The man disappeared.

The girl fainted, and when she revived, found herself on a great mesa, so far from home that it took her four days to walk back. When she arrived at home, she told her story, and after that was ill for more than a year. She was shunned by all the village people, and no young man would marry her. After her grandmother died, she lived alone the rest of her life.

This story was told to young girls by their grandmothers, as a warning of what might happen to them if they talked to, or went out with boys.

SUBJECT: Fabiana
WPA: 5-5-52 #69
April 1, 1941
Words 600
Juliana Martínez

FABIANA
Witch Story

There appeared one day a woman in a little village, and no one knew who she was or from where she had come. She was not very old, about middle age, but very dark and ugly. She went to one house after another asking for food, which was given her. When asked what her name was, she said it was Fabiana, but would not tell them from where she had come.

One day she went to a certain house where a man and his wife lived alone. They had no children, and took the stranger in. This woman sat around all day, and never offered to help with the work, or do anything to pay for this couple's kindness.

One morning the wife, thinking they were alone, told her husband she was getting tired of having Fabiana around, and thought she was a lazy, worthless woman, and wished she would go some where else. Fabiana, who was standing outside by the door, heard all that the woman had said to her husband. She stepped into the house and asked the wife to lend her an escobeta, saying she wanted to brush her hair. An escobeta was a small brush made of fine straw. The woman brought the escobeta and gave it to her, and then left the room. When she came in again, Fabiana told her she was going to go and stay with another family that lived on the other side of the village. She placed the escobeta on a banco, and left. When she had gone, the other woman picked it up and put it away.

Two or three days later her arm began to pain, but she thought nothing of it until it started to swell. She went to the curandera, but got no relief. After trying all the remedios she was told to try, her husband decided to take her to Los Ojos (Hot Springs), which were somewhere north. He got his burros ready, and leaving three cows that he owned in care of a friend, he and his wife left.

Now the old people used to say that if anyone who had been bewitched bathed in these springs, the water would throw them out, and start to boil and get so hot that they could not even put their hand in. But if it were anything else except maleficio, the springs would be calm and warm, and would cure their sickness.

When the man and his wife arrived at the springs, the water was warm and calm. But the moment she stepped into the pool, the water began to splash and boil, and finally washed her out. She tried to go in several times, but the water became so hot it burned her. When she stood a way's off from the pool, the water calmed down. Now she and her husband knew what her trouble was; she had been embrujada (bewitched) and there was nothing else to do but go home. The man and his wife got on their burros, and started for home. When they had gone some distance, and it was getting late, they stopped at a ranch house they saw at the foot of the mountain. The people who lived there made them welcome, and after hearing about the woman's sickness, and how the water in the spring had acted, said she was embrujada. But they knew of an old Indian woman who lived in a Pueblo a few miles from their ranch, that could cure maleficio.

April 8, 1941
Words 818
Juliana Martínez

FABIANA
Witch Story

The old Indian woman was sent for, and after looking at the sick woman, said she had been harmed by some bruja, and that she would cure her if the husband would pay her as many almuds of beans as she had fingers, "Ten." The man said he would give her what she asked for.

The Indian then asked his wife if she slept with her mouth open or closed. The woman told her she did not know. The old squaw took a piece of buckskin string from around her waist, and threaded a bead on it, and told the woman to tie this around her head at night when she went to bed, with the bead over her mouth, and the knot at the back of her neck, and that when she woke up in the morning, if the bead was not in her mouth, it was a sign that she slept with her mouth closed. But if it was, she slept with her mouth open, and to be sure to let her know.

The next day the sick woman told the Indian that when she awoke the bead was in her ear. The squaw said this was a good sign, that it meant she kept her mouth closed, but her ears open. And that she wanted her to drink a remedio which she had prepared in water. This water was green, and she told her to stand in the open doorway the next morning just as the sun came up, close her eyes, and drink the remedio.

The sick woman did as she was told, drank the green water as the sun came up with her eyes closed. After a while she felt better, and towards evening she said she thought she was almost well, that her arm did not hurt, but it was still swollen. The old Indian woman told her she was not cured yet, but would be by morning.

The next morning when she opened her eyes, her arm was all right again, the swelling had gone, and there by her side was a small package, or bundle wrapped in skin. The Indian took this and cut it open, and inside found the escobeta the woman had loaned Fabiana.

The next day the man and his wife left for home telling the Indian woman he would be back in eight days with the beans he had promised her.

On their way home husband and wife talked it over, and decided to say nothing about knowing that Fabiana was a witch, and the harm she had done. But that they would be very careful, and have nothing more to do with her.

Upon their arrival home, the husband told his wife he was going at once to the friends house to get his cows. These cows were the pride of his heart. He had traded a big milpa his father had left him for these cows. He herded them himself in the daytime and locked them in the corral at night. He had had many offers for them, but had refused them all. When he got to the place where his cows were, his friend came out to meet him, and told him he had bad news, that for the last three days the cows had not been able to eat or drink, because their heads were getting so big they could not hold them up. He went to the corral, and there stood his three cows, their heads swollen so big that their eyes could not be seen.

This made the owner very angry. He went to the house where Fabiana was staying, and found her standing under a cottonwood tree by the acequia. He went up to her and told her he knew she was a witch, and had harmed his wife, and that he was willing to forgive her for that, but now she had cast a spell over his cows, and that he was going to kill her if she didn't cure them at once.

He had no sooner spoken, when in the place where Fabiana had stood, there was a big owl, which flew up into the tree. The man picked up a large stone and threw it at the bird, striking it on the head. It came down and struck the ground, and there laid Fabiana dead with her head crushed in from the rock.

The village people all said they were glad he had killed the witch. She was taken to the hills and buried in an arroyo. When the owner of the cows, on his return from burying the witch, went to look at his cows, he found them eating. Their heads were their normal size again, and looked as though nothing had happened to them.

SUBJECT: Vicenta
WPA: 5-5-53 #1
April 15, 1941
Words 1167

VICENTA

Vicenta Sánchez lives with her daughter in Albuquerque. She is the only one left of her family. She thinks she is seventy-six or seventy-eight years old, but does not know for sure. Vicenta is tall, with brown skin and many wrinkles; she says that when she was young, she was quite stout and strong but now is very thin, and from her looks, weighs about a hundred pounds or less. She is not well and has not been for years. She thinks her ill health was caused by childbearing and work.

Vicenta has had fifteen children. Some died when small and others when grown. Now all she has left is a son and daughter. Her father's name was Juan José Sánchez, and her mother's Juanita Chávez. They were both born and lived all their lives in Peña Blanca. Vicenta and her brothers and sisters were born and raised there also. When her mother and father married, they went to live with her grandmother.

Her grandfather, whose name was Moisés Chávez, had been dead for three or four years. Her grandmother had two sons and two daughters. María, the oldest, had been married only three months when her husband died. She went back home to live with her mother, and never married again. Next came two boys, and then Juanita, Vicenta's mother. María was about seven or eight years older than Juanita.

Her grandmother's house where she was born was a big square adobe house, had many rooms with small windows high up in the walls, and a placita in the middle. At one end of this big house were the despencias: one for grain and the other where food was stored. Vicenta and her sisters used to follow their mother or grandmother when they saw her going to get food out of the big cajones (boxes or bins). Sometimes they were given a piece of piloncio (brown sugar cones). Brought from Mexico, these big cajones had large iron padlocks which were kept locked; mother or grandmother carried the keys in their bolsas (pocket).

These bolsas were made out of some strong material, and were about eighteen inches long, and from eight to ten inches wide, sewed up on both sides and one end, like a bag. One end was open with two strings sewed at the corners. This pocket was tied around the waist under the dress. The skirt had a slit in it to put the hand through. In these bolsas were carried all the keys, cigarrera (small boxes of metal or wood in which tobacco was carried), hojas (corn husks), and many other small objects.

Her grandmother's name was Francisca, but her grandchildren called her Nanita (Mamy or Nannie). Her grandfather while living, she had been told, was a very industrious man. He worked from daylight until dark, and expected his family to do likewise.

This old man was a miser, and was supposed to have money, but no one knew for sure. He sold cattle, goats, and grain. But his family never knew what he did with the money, for he never spent any if he could help it. He very seldom hired help, but made his family do the work. And when he did hire anyone, he paid them in grain, or goats.

Her mother had told her this story about her father, that when she was a small girl, there was once a scare about the Indians coming. These rumors used to be spread around every once in a while. And when they were, the people would bury or hide anything of value they had, drive their stock into the bosque (cottonwood thicket) for sometimes the Indians did come, and when they did, would ransack the houses and take whatever they wanted, and drive off the stock, and set fire to haystacks and corrals, while the people fled with their children to some hiding place.

This time when word went around that the Indians were coming, her father told Juanita—Vicenta's mother—and her sister María, one evening that he wanted them to do something for him, and that when it became dark to go out to the corral, he would tell them what it was, but not to tell anyone what he had said.

After supper the father sent his two sons on some errand. When it became dark, María who was about seventeen or eighteen years old, and Vicenta's mother who might have been eleven or twelve years old, went out to the corral, and there found their father waiting for them with two horses saddled. He told María and Juanita to mount them, and placed in front of them on each horse, a cowhide bag. He told them to take these bags to the old goat corral, bury them, and hurry back.

This goat corral was about two miles up the river from the house, and was not used anymore, in fact was falling to pieces. The two girls were afraid of the dark, and also that the Indians might catch them. They cried and begged their father not to send them, but he insisted so they went. When they arrived at the goat corral, they dismounted and dug a hole with an old talache (pick) their father had tied to one of the saddles, and put the bags in, and then covered them over. Then they rode back home. When they got there, their father told the girls that he would punish them if they told where they had been, and what they had done, and to tell their mother when they went to the house, that they had been out with him hunting for a calf. So they did as they were told. About three or four weeks later, when the Indian scare was over, and the Indians did not come, the father again called them to the corral one night after dark, and told the two girls to mount the two horses he had ready, and go and bring back the two bags they had buried in the old goat corral. Again they went to the corral, dug up the rawhide bags, put them on the horses, and went back. On their return the father was waiting for them at the corral. He took the bags off the horses, and told the girls to go to the house, but be very careful and not say where they had been. After quite a long time, their father came in and went to bed without speaking to anyone.

Vicenta's mother, Juanita, asked her sister what was in the bags, and why their father had sent them to bury them, instead of sending one of the boys or going himself. Her sister María told her that the bags contained money, and thought their father was afraid his sons might follow him, if he went, and see where the bags were buried, and afterwards dig them up.

April 22, 1941
Words 800

VICENTA

About six months afterwards, the father was killed by being thrown from a horse. When this happened, the two girls told their mother about the money bags their father had given them to bury in the old goat corral. The mother said she knew her husband had money, but did not know where he kept it, he had never told her.

The mother and two girls and their brothers hunted for it. They went to the old goat corral and dug there, and also in the corrals at home. They hunted every place they could think of, but could not find where the father had hidden the money.

Three or four years after the father's death, one of the sons married, and went to live with his wife's people. The second son got a job herding sheep. This left the mother alone with her two daughters. She tried to care for the land with the help of the two girls, but found it was too much for them. So after talking it over with her children, the mother decided to rent the land.

She and the two girls moved into a small house which had been left to the mother by her father, then rented the land on shares to a man by the name of Juan Mata. This man was from Mexico. He and his wife had come to the placita some years back, as helpers on a wagon train from Chihuahua.

They had six children, and lived in a one-room house at the end of the village. He was a very good worker; both he and his wife used to hire out to the people—he for fifty cents a day, and his wife for twenty five cents. They took their pay in food and stock, such as a goat or a sheep.

He took the land for three years. He was to plant it and give one-third of the crops in payment for rent. Juan Mata took the land over in the early spring, and planted it and seemed well satisfied. But in the fall, after taking in the crops, he told the grandmother he was going to leave, that he could not take care of the land anymore. Several months later they heard that Juan had bought a place further down the river.

This place was considered a very good ranch. It had quite a large house on it, an orchard and much land. He also bought goats, pigs, and was living very comfortably. Vicenta's grandmother and her children knew that the renter had found the grandfather's hidden money, but having no proof, they could do nothing about it.

A few months afterwards, Juanita, Vicenta's mother, married Juan José Sánchez, and with the mother and sister moved back to the old house again. There Vicenta and her sisters and brothers were born and raised.

In the days when Vicenta was a child, most everything they needed was raised on the land: corn, wheat, beans, and chili. Her father had a few cows and quite a number of goats. The children all helped with the work. Vicenta was a big strong girl and used to help her father as well as her mother, and when she was not working, she was taking care of the baby. There always was a baby brother or sister to be cared for.

Sundays and días de fiestas (feast days) were the days the children liked best. On those days they did not have to work.

They dressed in their best clothes of gingham and calico, and with papalinas on their heads were taken to church. These papalinas (sunbonnets) were not starched, but had narrow lengths of cardboard inserted in the lining to make them round. They looked like a covered wagon. Sometimes their father took them in the wagon. That was when their grandmother went. But if her rumos (rheumatism) were bad, and she stayed home, the family walked. When they did, Vicenta and her sisters carried their shoes until they got close to the church, then sat down and put on their shoes, and afterwards took them off again when they came out of church.

This was done to keep their shoes from getting dusty and wearing out. Very few children had shoes in those days; the ones who had, took good care of them. They were worn only on Sundays to church, or días de fiestas. Shoes were bought two or three sizes larger than needed, but this was done so children would not outgrow them. Boys and the smaller children went barefooted. After church they went home, took off their clothes, and put them away until the next Sunday.

April 29, 1941
Words 765

VICENTA

Sundays were the only days children were supposed to play, when Vicenta was young. Relatives and friends came on that day to visit bringing their children with them.

Little boys went off by themselves to play with each other, while the girls stayed close to the house and played. Boys and girls never played together. If they were seen playing, they were called hombradas and mujereros (tomboys and sissies).

One of the most exciting games little girls played was called El Coyotito (The Little Coyote). A stone was placed on the ground for a base and one of the little girls chosen for El Coyotito, usually the smallest one. She stood with her eyes closed, while the others hid. Then called out, "Aquí viene El Coyotito" (Here comes the little coyote). The ones who had been hiding came out and ran towards the stone before the Coyotito could catch them. But if one was caught, she then had to take her turn as El Coyotito.

They also played comadres, and called each other comadres like older people did. But before doing so, one little girl linked her right-hand little finger with another little girl's right-hand finger, and while swinging their linked hands back and forth said:

Comadrita, comadrón   Little comadre, Big comadre
La que se bale a la comadre   We promise to be comadres
Lo ase de corazón.   With all our hearts.

This was called, balerse a la comadre (promising to call each other comadre). After giving this pledge they were not to quarrel, or be selfish with each other. And many girls in the old days, after they married, asked their childhood comadres to be a madrina to one of their children, to make the tie closer.

80

Playing house was another game little girls played with their dishes and dolls. But their dishes were made out of clay or mud, taken from the acequia banks, and dried in the sun. Their dolls were ears of corn, with two or three corn husks left on for hair. All little girls liked muñecas blancas best (white dolls) and picked white, yellow, and sometimes red ears of corn, but never blue. Because blue corn ears were supposed to be Indian or black babies. Late in the afternoon the children were called in for café, or merienda. Company was always given merienda or café, with biscochitos (little cookies) or bollitos (rolls) made from wheat flour. Children as well as older people drank coffee when it was served. Café was kept for company, or Sundays. The rest of the week they drank atole con leche (cornmeal gruel with cow or goat milk).

On weekdays there was no time for play. Children were taught to work. In the summer time they made cheese. Everyone arose at daybreak, and while mother and aunt cooked breakfast, and made up the beds, Vicenta and her sisters milked the goats, which were afterwards herded on the hills by her little brothers. The girls poured the milk into ollas, and stirred cuajo into the milk, then placed the ollas in a warm place so the milk would curdle, either by the fireplace or in the sun.

Cuajo was made by steeping the stomach of a young animal, either goat or calf, in hot water. This water was called cuajo and was and still is used for making cheese. Afterwards the curd was put into clay or wooden molds, with rocks placed on top, until all the whey was pressed out. This cheese, "queso de cabra," was considered very good while fresh, but after two or three days it became sour, and then it was eaten with miel or sugar.

After the cheese was made, it was sold to the village people who did not have cows or goats of their own. Not for money, but traded. Every evening little boys or girls were sent by their mothers to Vicenta's house for cheese, bringing small ollas of flour, cornmeal, and sometimes a bar of homemade soap, to exchange for a quesito (small cheese). The small ones were worth about five cents, the larger ones ten cents. The cabritos (kids) were also sold the same way. Her father sometimes used to take a wagon load of live cabritos to town, and peddle them out. They sold for fifty, and seventy-five cents a piece. And with the money he got for the cabritos he brought back cloth for clothes, coffee, and sometimes sugar.

VICENTA

In the fall there was the wine making. The uva Mexicana (mission grapes) were picked by the children as well as the older people. When picked they were put into the artesa. These artesas were made out of cowhides. While still green or fresh, the hides were soaked in lime water, and the hair removed by rubbing the hide with sandstones. Then holes were made in the hide like a sieve; it then was laced or bound on a frame made out of four small poles, and left to dry. When dry, this was placed over a wooden trough, and grapes put into it, to be pressed.

The boys and girls went to the acequia, and scrubbed their feet with sand and water, then took turns treading on the grapes in the artesa until all the juice was pressed out. The juice was poured into barrels—these barrels were brought from Mexico—and left to ferment. Some of the wine was sold, and the rest was kept for bautismos and casorios. Children did not like this wine because it was not sweet, but the men did.

Winter nights Vicenta's mother and aunt sewed by the light of the fireplace. Small scrapes or pieces of cloth was given to the little girls, and their aunt or grandmother taught them to sew. They made colchitas (little bedspreads) for their dolls, using ebreros (or ravelings) for thread. Thread was very expensive in those days. A spool cost as much as twenty-five cents. They were told that when they learned to sew neatly, they would be given cloth to make big ones like the ones their aunt made.

This aunt sewed very well, and was paid to make colchas (bedspreads) for those who could afford to buy them. These colchas were made out of canton flannel and unbleached muslin, which was brought in by wagon trains from the east. Birds and flowers were drawn on these pieces of cloth, with a piece of charcoal, then embroidered with fine spun wool. The wool was dyed with native dyes, then spun very fine. The color that was most used was red, the dye made from the alegría plant. Chamizo was used for yellow, and blue from añil (indigo). This last dye came from Mexico.

In the spring when Semana Santa (Holy Week) came, all children had to fast as well as the older people, with the exception of the real small ones who could not be reasoned with. Monday and Tuesday they worked hard, and enough bread was baked in the ornos, and other foods cooked to last through Wednesday, Thursday, and Friday. No meat was eaten on these days, but many other good things were.

The grandmother took the children who fasted out walking to keep them away from food, and on these walks remedios were gathered. Many of the remedios came up early in the spring. When the grandmother thought it was noon—telling the time by the sun—they went back home and the exchange of food began.

Before anyone ate their dinner, dishes of food were sent to relatives and neighbors, and they in return sent other dishes of food back. The little girls had to carry the trays of food to many houses and bring others back before they could eat their dinner. This was an old custom—the sharing of food.

And the little girls, no matter how hungry they were, did not dare to taste or eat of the food they carried. They were afraid of the duendes (dwarfs)[sic]. The grandmother had told them the duendes were a little race of people who lived in the bosques—that if they were good, and obeyed, the duendes came at night and did their work for them, and killed snakes and other harmful animals that might hurt them. But, on the other hand, if children were lazy, selfish, or disobedient, the duendes came and hid behind trees, and threw stones at them, and put snakes in their paths, and would undo all their work. It was very seldom you had to tell a child twice to do what he was told. At night children would not go out of the house alone, fearing they might meet a duende.

After the food had been exchanged, then the fasting children were given their dinner. On these holy days they were not allowed to play or work. But had to be quiet. But sometimes they could not resist the temptation, and went to the acequia to play in the water. If one of them had the misfortune to fall in and get wet, they felt sure it was a duende, who had pushed him or her in for disobeying their parents.

May 13, 1941
Words 998

VICENTA

This is a story the grandmother told Vicenta and her brothers and sisters when they were small, and is supposed to be true.

In the days when the grandmother was young, it was the custom for men to go buffalo hunting. In the fall, wagons were put in order, while the women baked bread for days in the ornos, getting ready the vastimento (food) for the men to take with them on their hunting trips. On these hunts, the best men went, leaving behind the old men and boys, and men who were afraid and had made some excuse or other so they would not be asked to go. The excuses mostly given were that they were sick, but as soon as the wagons left, they recovered.

Sometimes these wagons would be gone from their homes for three or four months. The men were killing the buffalo, and drying the meat for summer use, bringing back many wagon loads of carne seca (dried meat or jerky) to the different villages.

While on these hunting trips, they watched for Indian camps, and when they found any where the squaws were alone, raided them, and stole the Indian children. These Indian children were brought back, and sold to "ricos" for servants.

Women were very proud to be called the wife of a cibolero, especially so if their husbands went on these hunts two or three years in succession without a mishap. And they felt sorry for the women whose husbands could not go or were afraid to go.

When the wagons left in the fall, the people all gathered around them to see them off, and wish the hunters good luck. The children would sing or call out:

Se fueron los ciboleros.	The buffalo hunters have gone,
Todos hombres de bien,	All brave men.
Se quedaron los sin vergüensas	The shameless ones stayed home
Comiendo esquite con miel.	Eating esquite con miel (toasted corn rolled in molasses).

And the women whose husbands remained home, bowed their heads in shame. They knew that this song was meant for their husbands.

There was one woman in the village by the name of Alvina, whose husband was a lazy, worthless man. Alvina was big and strong. She did most of the work on their land, while her husband spent his time sitting around the village talking. She used to ask the men to take her husband with them on these hunting trips, but was always told that workers were needed, not lazy men.

One fall when everything was ready, and the hunters were about to leave, one of the wagon drivers fell, and broke his leg. This made them short a driver. After talking it over with the rest of the men, the carrero (wagon boss) decided to take Alvina's husband in the place of the one who had been hurt.

The night before leaving, the carrero went to Alvina's house, and asked her husband—whose name was Marcos, but was called Marquitos, because he was small—to go with them, to help drive a wagon. But Marquitos made all kinds of excuses, at last saying he was sick, and had been for several days, with a pain in his stomach.

Alvina knew this was not true. The reason he would not go was because he was afraid. She pleaded with him after the men left, pointing out how they would have plenty of dried meat that summer, and that she could be called the wife of a cibolero. But Marquitos would not listen to his wife, he would not go.

When Alvina saw that she could not persuade him to go, she left the house and went to the men, and asked them to take her, in her husband's place. They refused at first, saying it took men with courage. But she begged so hard, that they finally consented. She went home and told Marquitos that she was going with the wagons. That since he would not go himself, he could remain home, and take care of the children—they had five.

He forbade her from going, but Alvina was a big, courageous woman, and was not scared by Marquito's threats.

The next day the hunters left, with Alvina as one of the drivers. They were gone about four months. And when ciboleros returned, women and children went out to meet them, and cheered as the wagons halted. Marquitos did not go to meet the wagons, but locked himself in the house.

The men praised Alvina, and said she had been a great help to them. She did not kill any buffalo, but did the camp cooking, and helped dry the meat.

When the meat was divided, Alvina got a large share. She was quite happy to think there would be enough meat for her family to last through the summer. But what made her still happier was that she could now hold up her head among the ciboleros' wives. Her husband had not gone, but she had.

Marquitos behaved very badly towards his wife. He was not glad to see her, but quarreled with her day and night. About a week after her return, early one morning, one of Alvina's children ran crying to a neighbor's house, saying that her mother was dead. The neighbors went and found Alvina lying on the floor stabbed to death.

The men said it was no one else but Marquitos who had done this, and looked for him, but he was gone. The Ciboleros went hunting for him, and found Marquitos hiding in the bosque. They dragged him out, and hung him to a cottonwood tree until he was dead. They then cut off his right hand, and nailed it to a pole in the center of the village, as a warning to other men who were mean to their wives.

SUBJECT: Manuela
WPA 5-5-52 # 72
May 20, 1941
Words 906
Vicenta

MANUELA

Many years ago there lived in the small village of Galisteo, Leandro Chávez and his wife, Juana Padilla. They had five children, four daughters and a son. The daughters' names were Torrivia, the oldest, next Manuela, then Clara and Ramona, and last Carlos, the son. This boy was a hunchback, and not very bright, but being the only boy was pampered by his father and mother, and the girls made to wait on him. He had his own way in everything.

Don Leandro had two or three flocks of sheep and a good many head of cattle. He was considered very well off. In the summer he took his family to live on the ranch, which was a long day's drive from the village. While there, the girls worked very hard. While his daughters were on the ranch, their father would not have any men around except some old man or a very young boy to help with the work. He used to say he did not want young men looking at his girls, that he would never allow them to marry.

When they became young ladies, boys who were of marrying age, would tell their fathers to ask for one of Don Leandro's daughters for them in marriage, a la buena fe (in good faith).

These boys' fathers, with other men members of their family, would go to visit Don Leandro and present their letters of pidimiento. When these men came to his house, Don Leandro received them very coldly, for he knew at once what they had come for. He never told his girls they had been asked for in marriage, and forbade his wife to tell them. But the son Carlos knew, because when anyone came to the house he sat and listened to everything that was said, and his father confided in him.

When Don Leandro received these letters, he would go to some friend who could read and write—Leandro or any one of his family could not read or write—and have him read the letter for him, and write another saying no, or giving the calavasas (the squash). He then would send the letter by Carlos. He never waited the customary week, or eight days, but sent it off the next or the day after. The girls found out they had been asked for, because Carlos would tell them that Juan or José had asked for one of them in marriage, and that he Carlos, had taken, or was going to take the letter with calavasas. They felt bad about this, for they wanted to marry like other girls did. They feared their father, and would not dare say anything to him about it.

He had told them time after time, that as long as he lived, he would not let them marry, that he did not want any man to speak harsh to his daughters or mistreat them. He thought there was no one good enough for his girls.

Don Leandro loved his daughters in his own way. When he sold his wool, lambs, or cattle, he went to town for supplies. And he brought back silk dresses, hats, and shoes for his girls. They admired them, and after trying them on, would put the clothes away, for they had no place to wear them. These girls were never taken to bailes, or fiestas, were not allowed to have visitors or go visiting, but were kept shut up in the house. Church was the only place they were taken to, and that was once a month when the padre came to say mass. Then the girls dressed up in their fine clothes, and their father and mother took them to misa.

The father watched them closely, to see that the boys standing in the churchyard did not make eyes at them. This was called "asiendo ojos." When the Sunday came on which mass was to be said, the village boys gathered in the churchyard early, and stood on either side of the church walk to watch the girls go by. The girls, if their parents were not watching them too closely, looked towards the boys. If a boy smiled at a girl, and tried to speak to her with his eyes, and she approved of him, she always managed to smile back at him. After this went on for two or three months, the young man would be sure that he would not be given calavasas. And would tell his father he wanted a certain girl to be asked for.

The young men who asked for Don Leandro's daughters in marriage did not want them for their looks. They were seldom seen, and with the exception of Manuela, the second daughter, were very dark and homely. Manuela did not look like her sisters. She was small, while they were big. Her skin was almost white, and she had big black eyes, and a very pleasing personality. But these boys knew old Leandro had a great deal of livestock, and it was said he also had money. A story that was told was that he had a friend who needed ten thousand dollars to pay off a very pressing debt, and that he went to Don Leandro who gave him the money in gold pieces. Some of these boys made their fathers ask for one of the girls, two or three times. But this did not do any good. Don Leandro always sent them calavasas.

May 27, 1941
Words 1157
Vicenta

MANUELA

There lived in this village a young man whose name was Donicio Aragón. He and his mother lived together. His father had died when he was quite small. An uncle had given Donicio some sheep on shares, and the boy was doing very well. He was a good son to his mother, and very industrious. Fathers of other boys used to say they wished their sons were like Donicio, smart and sensible, that if he continued the way he was going, that before many years went by, he would be rico (rich).

One Sunday when mass was to be said, Donicio was standing with the boys by the church walk. Don Leandro drove up in his wagon with his family. After tying his horses, he and his wife and the four girls walked up to the church door. The girls walking in front, the mother and father behind. As they were about to enter the church door, a gust of wind blew Manuela's hat off. This was a large straw hat loaded down with flowers and feathers. The boys all turned to catch the hat. But Donicio was quicker than the rest. He caught the hat and gave it to Don Leandro, who was standing in front of Manuela. She put the hat on and went into mass. When they came out of church, Manuela looked up at Donicio, who was standing as close as he could by the walk. He smiled at her and she smiled back at him. For three or four months, Manuela and Donicio managed to look and smile at each other in the church yard.

Manuela was very happy. She told her sister Torrivia that when Donicio asked for her in marriage, to tell their father for her that she wanted to marry him. Torrivia, who was kind and loved her sister, promised to do so, but knew it would not do any good. In the fall of the year, when Donicio sold his wool and lambs, he told his uncle he wanted to marry Manuela Chávez, and for him to ask Don Leandro for her.

His uncle told him he was foolish, that Don Leandro would not give him his daughter, that he would have the same luck the other boys had, who had asked for her before he had. But Donicio insisted. So his uncle had a letter "de pidimiento" written, and asked two or three relatives to go with him to ask for Don Leandro's daughter.

The night that Donicio's uncle asked for Manuela, Carlos went into the room where the girls were sewing, and told them that Donicio's uncle had been there, and had given their father a letter and that Don Leandro had gone to a neighbor to have it read. When Manuela heard this, she could not sew any more. She called Torrivia into the kitchen, and again told her to tell their father she wanted to marry Donicio.

Four or five days went by and nothing was said about the letter. Manuela asked Torrivia if she had told their father that the answer was yes. Torrivia said she had not, because their father had not asked, or mentioned it. But she asked Carlos if he knew what their father intended to do. Carlos told her that the letter with calavasas (squash) had been sent two days before. At this news Manuela felt bad and disappointed, but could do nothing. She had hoped her father would give his consent, because everyone spoke so well of Donicio.

One day Donicio sent Manuela word by a cousin's little boy that he wanted to speak to her, and would be outside of the south corral wall that night, that when she heard a pebble thrown against the kitchen window to go out, he would be waiting for her. Manuela told Torrivia about this and asked her to help them.

The house in the village was a large adobe. A long hall ran in the middle with three rooms on either side. On the front was a big portal. The back of the house was enclosed by high adobe walls, and was called the corral because chickens and goats were kept there.

As soon as it became dark that night, and supper was over, Torrivia told her mother, she and Manuela were going to remain in the kitchen for a while, grinding corn for the next day's tortillas. When the two girls were alone, they called in the two dogs into the kitchen, so they would not bark when Donicio came. After a while a clink was heard at the window. This window was two small panes of glass, high up on the wall. Torrivia told Manuela to hurry out, while she watched, that if she heard the father or Carlos coming, she would warn her, by throwing out some water.

Manuela went up to the wall and coughed. Donicio, who was outside, answered by climbing up on the wall. The first thing he asked, was why she had given him las calavasas, that he thought she cared for him because she had liked and smiled at him so often in the church yard. Manuela said she did care, and wanted to marry him, and had told her sister to tell their father she did. But that he had sent the calavasas without asking her, or letting anyone of his family know. Donicio then told her he would again ask for her in the spring.

When spring came, Donicio told his uncle he wanted him to ask for Manuela again. His uncle at first refused, saying he would not be laughed at by the people, they would think he was a fool. Donicio insisted, saying that he was sure this time that Manuela would say yes, and that her father would have to consent.

The uncle had another letter written, and this time asked only one friend to go with him. They did not stay long at Don Leandro's house. After asking after his and his family's health, they handed him the letter and left. Two days afterwards Don Leandro sent Carlos with the calavasas letter. Donicio realized when he heard this, that there was no hope of marrying Manuela as long as her father lived. So he went off with his sheep herd, and stayed for about a year.

Carlos told Manuela that Donicio's uncle had again asked for her in marriage for his nephew and that he, Carlos, had already taken the letter saying no.

For days Manuela wept. Torrivia tried to comfort her sister by telling her that if God had made her and Donicio for each other, they would marry in spite of all, that he would work out some way by which it would come to pass. This made Manuela feel better, and gave her new hopes.

MANUELA

After this their father took them to the ranch, where they spent the summer, helping to build fences, and herding small flocks of sheep. Carlos was never asked to do anything. He sat most of the time or stood around watching his sisters work.

In the fall when the family came back to the village, Manuela looked forward to the Sunday when mass was to be said. When they were taken to church, she looked to see if Donicio was among the boys outside in the churchyard. But she could not see him, either when she went in to church or when she came out.

That winter Donicio's mother died, and his uncle advised him to marry, saying now he had no one to take care of him. Donicio was not interested in any of the other village girls; he still wanted Manuela but knew there was no hope of marrying her. His uncle talked and talked to him about getting married until he finally gave in, telling his uncle to ask for any girl whom the uncle thought would make him a good wife. The uncle picked a girl by the name of Aniceta Sandoval. She was not pretty, but was a good girl, and a neat housekeeper. They were married and Donicio seemed satisfied with his uncle's choice.

That year when Don Leandro sold his wool, and was preparing to leave for the city to bring back supplies, Manuela told her father not to buy her any new clothes, that all she wanted was a tápalo negro (black shawl). Her father said he would bring back two, one for her and one for Torrivia, that they were getting too old to wear hats. Manuela was about twenty-five and Torrivia about five years older.

Years went by. Then Don Leandro died, and shortly after his wife also died. When Don Leandro died, he left the care of his family and management of his affairs to Carlos. The girls knew nothing about business. All they knew was how to work. Carlos, through his ignorance and poor management, in ten years lost all except a few head of cattle, perhaps fifty head. On this they lived. Carlos and his four sisters spent most of their time on the ranch, taking care of the few remaining cows. The four girls now were elderly women. Manuela maybe sixty-three and Torrivia sixty-eight.

While Don Leandro's family were losing their stock, Donicio prospered. His small flock of sheep grew into two or three large flocks. He bought cattle, and owned several ranches. He and his wife had only one child, a daughter who was married, but had no children. Then one winter Donicio's daughter died of pneumonia. About a year later his wife also died. People said it was grief for her only child that killed her. Donicio missed his wife, but he missed his daughter more, for he loved this girl very dearly. He was not well himself, and had not been for years.

He remained single for two years. Then one day he asked two of his old friends to ask for Manuela for him. His uncle had been dead for years. These friends had a letter written, and took it to the ranch where the girls lived. When they arrived, Torrivia received them and was given the letter of pidimiento (asking letter).

When they left, she showed the letter to Manuela, but as they could not read or write, could not find out its contents. They knew it was a letter of pidimiento, but did not know for which one of them. Torrivia thought it might be for one of the youngest girls, Clara or Ramona.

Torrivia hitched the team of horses to the wagon, and drove eight miles to a neighbor's ranch, and had the neighbor's husband read the letter for her. When he finished reading it, he told her it was from Donicio asking for Manuela in marriage.

When Torrivia got back home and told her sisters the letter was for Manuela, they were very happy. But Carlos was not. He told them he stood in his father's place, and forbid Manuela to marry. He said he would have the calavasas letter written at once and send it off.

But Torrivia, who was not afraid of Carlos, took things into her own hands. She asked Manuela if she still cared for Donicio and if she wanted to marry him. Manuela told her sister she had never forgotten Donicio, and would marry him if they would let her. Torrivia waited the customary two weeks, then had the same friend who had read the first letter, write one saying Donicio could come and receive Manuela on a certain day. She sent this letter by the neighbor's oldest boy.

These old ladies who were up in their sixties, cleaned house, and prepared the prendorio fiesta. The sisters were as happy as Manuela, who felt like a young girl again. On the day of the prendorio, Donicio, with a few relatives and many friends, went to receive Manuela. He took her a large trunk that contained many donas (gifts). Three days after the prendorio, they were married. Manuela was dressed like a young bride, in a white satin dress, with veil and wreath. This outfit had been given to Manuela by Donicio.

Manuela was very happy. Her husband was good and kind to her. He took her to the city, where Manuela for the first time saw big stores and a train. She had never been away from the village except when they were taken to the ranch.

After being married three years Donicio died. Before he passed away, when he knew he was getting quite ill, he sold his stock and ranches, and invested the money in real estate in the city, putting everything in Manuela's name.

Manuela now is somewhere in the seventies, and Torrivia in the eighties. The two sisters live together in town. Carlos and the two younger girls died several years ago. When Manuela talks about her marriage, she says that her sister Torrivia was right. She told her years ago. Lo que es de cada uno, nadien se lo quita (what is to be yours no one can take away).

SUBJECT: Amalia
WPA: 5-5-53 #7
June 17, 1941
Words 773.
Vicenta

AMALIA

Amalia Lucero lives alone in a two-room adobe house by the river. Many people who do not know who Amalia is, think she is just another poor old woman. She is about seventy, small and thin, dark and her hair is almost white. She dresses in cheap grey or black calico, and wears an old faded black shawl on her head. But the persons who know Amalia say she is quite wealthy. She owns valuable real estate, and has money in the bank.

Amalia is the daughter of Juan Lucero and Rufina Montoya. In the old days her father was said to have had a great deal of livestock such as cattle, sheep and horses. He was one of the old ricos. He and his wife lived on a large farm or ranch on the west side of the Rio Grande, close to the village of Corrales. They had four children, three boys and a girl. Amalia is the youngest. Don Juan was supposed to have been a good businessman, but was very close and miserly. His wife, who did as she was told, was also known as a miser, and as stingy as her husband was, or worse. They were brought up in the belief that they were very poor, and made them work and save.

When the two older boys were in their early teens, through the advice of a priest, Don Juan sent them to a Catholic school in Saint Louis, where they remained four years. He never brought them home during vacation, because it was expensive. He said it was cheaper to keep them there. After four years he received word that the oldest boy was very ill and to come at once. But it took many days to get there, and when he arrived, the boy was dead.

Don Juan brought the other boy back home with him. This son had become very wild, and liked the things that money could buy, and spent most of his time in town. When Don Juan saw he could do nothing with his son, he put him on one of his ranches to look after the stock. A short time afterwards, he was killed by a sheep herder over a game of cards.

This left the two younger children, Enriques, the boy, and Amalia, the girl. These children were given a very limited education in the town school, just enough to be able to read and write. Enriques was like his father and mother, saving and miserly. He never would spend any money if he could help it. When he was in his twenties, he married a girl by the name of Josefa Sena. He took her home to live with his parents. But after two years she left him, and with her year-old boy, went back to her mother and father. She said she could not live with Enriques and his family because they were so very miserly that even the food was measured out for every meal by her father-in-law. If there was enough for all, well and good, but if not they went hungry. And when she asked for clothes, she was told that they could not afford to buy her any, and told her that the ones she had brought from her home were still good. Enriques tried to get his wife to come back to him. But she refused to do so. It ended by him having to pay her a certain sum of money each month for her and the child's support.

Amalia was about nineteen or twenty, when her brother's wife left him. She would have liked to marry, but no young man ever asked her. She was not even good-looking, was homely and very dark. Men who might have married her for her father's money knew that it would be for nothing because Don Juan would not part with any of his wealth, but would expect them to work and support his daughter, and get nothing for it except Amalia. And they did not think she was worth it.

Amalia was a good girl, and worked very hard, and seemed contented with her home life. She did not have pretty clothes like the daughters of other rich men. Nor was she taken to bailes and fiestas. Sundays she and her mother went to church, and once in a while Amalia was taken to town. On these occasions she wore an old blue dress that had been her mother's before her.

June 24, 1941
Words 1012
Vicenta

AMALIA

When Amalia was about twenty-five, her father bought a windmill to put on a deep well he had dug on the farm. At first he tried using a rope and buckets, which was cheaper, but when he saw it took such a long time to water the stock this way, he decided to buy the mill. The firm that sold the mill to Don Juan sent a young man—Anglo—out to the farm to put up the windmill for Don Juan.

This young Americano whose first name was Charlie—last name unknown—went to the ranch, and while working on the mill, would hear the other men who were working for Don Juan, talking about how rich the patrón Don Juan was. Then he began to ask questions about how much stock Don Juan had, and how many ranches. He was told that the patrón was muy rico (very rich), that he had many herds of cattle and sheep, besides much money. This interested the young man. He decided to try and marry Amalia. She was flattered by the attention this Americano paid her—unknown to her father and mother—when he finished the work, he asked Amalia to marry him. And she accepted him. Not knowing the Spanish custom of asking by letter, the young man went to Don Juan and asked him for his daughter's hand in marriage. Don Juan said no. And told him to leave and never come back again. He then scolded Amalia, and told her she could not marry anyone, much less a gringo, that all Americanos were spenders and wasters.

But this young man had made up his mind that he was going to get Amalia and her money one way or another. He came back to the ranch one day and hid until evening. When Amalia went to the corral to milk the cows, he came out of his hiding place. He asked her if she would elope with him. Amalia told him she would. He made plans with her to be at a certain place on a certain night, and asked her if she could manage to get some money—saying he had none, and that they would need some. Amalia told him that she knew where her father kept his money, and that she would take it and be at the appointed place.

Don Juan did not bury or hide his money, like so many other ricos did. When he sold land, wool, or livestock, he put his money in the bank. He invested some of it in real estate when he could get a bargain. He also loaned money out at twelve percent interest, taking mortgages on homes as security. And if the money was not paid back promptly, he would foreclose on the people, leaving many homeless. In this way he acquired a great deal of property. To pay his working men on his many ranches, he kept some money at home. He never paid by check; he did not want anyone to know he had money in the bank. This money was kept in a small satchel, maybe fifteen hundred, or two thousand dollars. Don Juan locked this satchel up in one of the big cajones (bins or boxes) where the food was stored. He always carried the key to the big padlock.

On the day that Amalia was to elope with the Americano, she asked her father to lend her the key to the cajón, saying she needed flour. Don Juan who was busy at the time, and could not go with her, gave her the key, and told her to hurry back with it. She opened the cajón, put some flour in an olla, then from under the sacks of grain took her father's satchel with the money. This she hid in a corner of the storeroom behind a pile of sheep pelts. After locking the box, she took the key back to her father, at the same time showing him the flour she had taken out.

All that day Amalia was very nervous and excited. Enriques, who was very suspicious, noticed how Amalia behaved. He wondered why she washed her hair in the middle of the week, instead of Saturday as she always did. And once when he went into the storeroom, he saw Amalia tying clothes up in a bundle. When he asked her what she was doing with her clothes, she said they were just some rags she was putting away. But Enriques had seen part of Amalia's blue dress—the one she always wore when she was taken to church or town—in the bundle. He went to his father and told him that Amalia was wrapping up her clothes, and that he thought she was up to something. Don Juan told Enriques to say nothing about this to his mother, but that they both would watch.

Amalia slept in the same room with her mother, and father, and Enriques in the adjoining one. She went to bed at her usual time, and when she thought her parents were asleep, arose, dressed and went out. She had no sooner got outside when Enriques and her father were up, and following her. They saw her going towards some trees where a man and two horses were. When Don Juan saw this, he called to her, and Amalia started to run. But her brother caught her, and between him and her father was dragged back to the house. Amalia was so frightened, she told all—that she was going to go with the Americano, who was waiting for her.

When they went to look for the young man, he and his horses were gone. They never saw or heard of him after that night.

Amalia was whipped and locked up by her father. And afterwards she was watched very closely. She never again was given the key to the cajón. If anything was needed, Don Juan or Enriques got it for the women.

About two years after Amalia's attempted elopement, her mother died. Amalia then kept house for her father and brother. She was not a neat housekeeper, but did what she could. Her father would not pay anyone to help her. And as the years went by, she became like her father and brother. Mean and miserly.

July 1, 1941
Words 1280
Vicenta

AMALIA

Don Juan was getting old and could not look after his interests so well anymore. Enriques was no help to his father in a business way. Don Juan sold his stock and ranches and invested his money. He kept the home ranch. Enriques and Amalia were well up in years when their father died. He left everything to his two children. The brother and sister continued living in the old home.

This house was a big square adobe, with a patio or placita in the middle, into which the many rooms opened. This old house needed repairs badly. The mud plaster was washing off, the roof leaked. But nothing was done to it, because it meant spending money to fix it up. When certain rooms became so bad they could no longer live in them, they piled their household goods into other rooms that were still good. And so the years went by. Instead of using some of their money to live on, they sold their furniture piece by piece, as they needed money to buy food with, for by now they were living in three rooms, and their excuse was that they did not need so many things. They never went any place, except to town to buy food. Then Enriques hitched up an old, old horse to an old-fashioned top buggy, whose broken parts were tied with wire, and Amalia and her brother would go to get their groceries.

Amalia and her brother, who were getting old, began to receive unsigned letters, threatening them with death if a certain sum of money was not placed at a certain place. These letters scared Amalia, but not Enriques. Whenever one came, he would bar the big placita doors with an extra log or two. Amalia wanted to move into town. They owned several houses there, where she said they would be safe. But Enriques would not listen to her.

One night about midnight two masked men climbed on the house roof from the outside, and jumped into the placita, and broke into the rooms where the two were sleeping. They tied Amalia and Enriques up, then ransacked the house, taking thirty-five dollars, which was all they found. Before leaving, one of the men untied Amalia, and afterwards left. When they were gone, she untied Enriques. The next day the two went to town to report the robbery. After three or four weeks the case was dropped, and nothing more was done about it. Some people said the robbers knew the brother and sister, and had felt sorry for Amalia, so they untied her.

Amalia was now frightened. She begged Enriques to move. But he refused to leave the old place. Finally she told him he could stay, but that she was going to move into town. So she did, taking with her as much as her brother would let her have. She moved into a house on a very nice street, which had been left to her by her father. It needed repairs also, and when the tenants could not get Amalia to do anything, they moved out. It had been vacant for a long time. So Amalia lived in this house.

When Amalia left the ranch, Enriques got two watchdogs, and kept them shut up in the placita day and night, where they barked at the slightest noise. He felt safe. About two years later, while driving home from town late one evening, Enrique was in a buggy that was struck by a loaded truck. The horse was killed, and the buggy broken to pieces. Enriques was seriously hurt and was taken to a hospital, where he died the next day. Enriques' son, who was married and lived in some western state, came to the funeral. He put in a claim for his father's estate and got it. This made Amalia very angry. She expected to get at least half of her brother's property.

Amalia owned much real estate, including a large business building on one of the main streets in town. This building was badly in need of repairs, but Amalia would do nothing about it. Through complaints that the building was unsafe, the court took over Amalia's affairs, and appointed a firm of lawyers as her guardians. She was not found insane or weak-minded because she was smart enough to keep her taxes and insurances paid. The first thing this firm did, was to repair this building. When Amalia saw they were tearing down old walls, and building new ones, painting and plastering it, she went to the place and quarreled with the working men and tried to send them away. When they paid no attention to her fussing, she went to the lawyers and told them what she thought of them. She became such a nuisance that they told her, that if she did not stop it, they would have to send her away. This firm, by order of the court, was to give Amalia two hundred dollars a month to live on. They did. But she would not take it. When she received her check, she went to their office and gave it back to them, saying that since the gringos were spending all her money, they could have the two hundred dollars also to spend. And no explaining did any good. So when each month comes around, Amalia sends back the check. She wants her property back again the way she had it, to do as she pleases with. She will not accept what is given her.

But Amalia needed money to live on, so she rented the old ranch—which was half hers, and some way left to her management—on shares. She had nothing to spend on this arrangement, which was very pleasing to her. When she gets her share of the crops, she sells it, and saves most of it and lives on the rest. It was decided that the house in which Amalia lived needed new plumbing and other repairs. She was told that the house was to be fixed, and new plumbing installed.

This made Amalia furious. She said that at the rate the Americanos were spending her money, she would not have any left. And that they never so much asked her permission. She went to a friend, who owned a two-room adobe house down by the river, and asked him if she could live in it. She told him she could not pay rent, because all her money was being spent by the gringos, fixing houses that were still good, that the Americanos loved to spend money.

This man, knowing how miserly Amalia was, knew there was no use asking for rent. So he told her that as the house was vacant, she could move in.

And that is where Amalia lives. She was told by the firm that as soon as the house was fixed, she could move back again. She refused to do so. She says she is happy where she now lives, because this house does not belong to her, and cannot be repaired with her money. Also it is much cheaper. She does not have to buy very much fuel. She picks up driftwood along the river.

Amalia is not a public nuisance in any way. She never begs, or takes anything that does not belong to her, or disturbs the peace. She bothers no one, and nobody bothers her. While her income is piling up, she goes around in old, faded calico dresses, and old, worn-out shoes, and picks up wood to keep from buying it.

PART II

LOU SAGE BATCHEN

SUBJECT: Placitas
August 13, 1938
Words 1828
Sources of information: José Librado Arón Gurulé and records of José
Antonio Gurulé Grandfather of José Librado Arón Gurulé, Nicholas and
Belina Gurulé, Pedro Gurulé, David Trujillo, José Trujillo, Catalina Gurulé.

PLACITAS

Placitas is located at the center of the San Antonio de Las Huertas Grant on the Loop Drive, seven miles east of Bernalillo. The altitude is sixty-one hundred feet. It is a village of charm to the visitors and one of interest to those who know its history. Its adobe houses follow the simplest lines of native architecture; they are scattered about promiscuously with a narrow crooked lane zig zagging about to reach the doors of most of them. This winding road is dotted with many fruit trees. Small orchards and vineyards flourish close to each house. Placitas presnts an exquisite picture in cherry-blossom time. A pretty little Presbyterian mission, with its yard full of trees and lilac shrubs, stands on the lane, and farther along up the hill on the plaza is the Catholic mission and the public school.

Within a mile of the village on the north and east lie the crumbled ruins of the old walled town of Las Huertas (The Gardens) where the forefathers of these people lived and waged war against the marauding Indians almost two hundred years ago. one half mile east of Placitas is the old Montezuma Mine of fact and legend. And there, also, is the dead-and-living village of Ojo de La Casa. On the southeast stately and beautiful ridges of the Sandía Mountains hem in Placitas and pour out an abundance of pure crystal water upon it. Off to the west is a far-flung mesa terminating in an exciting view where the Cabezón and the Valle Mountains are silhouetted against the western sky.

Placitas is built upon the ruins of a long-forgotten Indian pueblo, so say José Trujillo, fifty-five, Placitas, New Mexico, son of Francisco Trujillo, Civil

War veteran, and grandson of Miguel Trujillo who died in Las Huertas in 1853 and Nicholas Gurulé, son of José Librado Arón Gurulé, fifty-nine, of Placitas, New Mexico and his wife, Belina Trujillo de Gurulé, fifty-seven, Placitas, New Mexico, and Cataline Trujillo, forty-five, of Placitas New Mexico, granddaughter of Nicholas Gurulé, and present reminders of such a vanished people significant. Just to the north of the village is a reddish mountain with its upper surface deeply indented with Indian symbols. At the base of an escarpment of the Sandías near where the highway enters the village from the west is a tumbled ruin which was once a small round house with peep-holes near the roof. According to all the older generation now living in Placitas they, when little children, went inside this house. They say it was too small to have a bed in it, but that it was good to hide in and shoot out at the enemy. They say when their fathers came to Placitas, the place was covered with ruins and everywhere they found potsherds and metates, manos, stone axes, obsidian arrow and spear heads, and beads. In 1934, when a new tank was being excavated in the mountains east of Placitas, they found what was believed to have been an old Indian burial ground. David Trujillo, son of David Trujillo of old Las Huertas, who now lives in Las Placitas was one of the workmen and he said that skeletons were unearthed there and pottery bowls were found with them.

The exact date of the reoccupation of Placitas is indefinite. According to records kept by José Antonio Gurulé, grandfather of José Librado Arón Gurulé and inherited by him from his father, Nicholás Gurulé, there were sixteen families living in Placitas in 1843. These names are from his records and were copied from them by Pedro Gurulé, brother of José Librado Arón Gurulé; Andrés de Aragón, Antonio Archuleta, Juan Baldez, José Chaves, Miguel Gallegos, Antonio Galban, Juan Garcia, Antonio Gurulé, Matías Gutiérrez, Pedro Jurado, Francisco Labero, Alberto Montano, Nicholas Montoya, Juan Mes, Bisente Sena, Antonio José Balencia. José Librado Arón Gurulé, eighty-eight, is a direct descendant of the Serafin Gurulé listed among the twenty-one families who received the San Antonio de Las Huertas Grant from the King of Spain in 1765 and who also brought land from the San Felipe Indians and settled Algodones some years prior to that date. These sixteen families are, according to traditions, as told by Nicholás and Belina Gurulé and José Trujillo, descendants, of the twenty-one families who lived in Las Huertas and Algodones some two hundred years ago. As to why they came to settle Placitas, there seems a difference of opinion. Some say because there is plenty of water in the mountains; others say because they wanted to get away from the Indians; yet others say because the tribute exacted from the people by the Spaniards was so heavy, there were forced to find more land for crops. In around about way José Gurulé says it was the "call of the blood," that from some cause they do not understand, the scattered people traveled from afar at the same time back to the home of their fathers and to the land of their inheritance.

Sometime in the late 1850's three families came from the vicinity of Alameda to settle among them. They were Francisco Gonzales, Tomás Lucero and Andrés Armijo; and from Las Huertas came Francisco and Joaquín Trujillo, descendants of the twenty-one families. Together these families built Placitas and their children have intermarried until the people are as one large family made up of clans.

Three men from Placitas answered Governor Connelly's call for volunteers to resist an invasion "by an armed force from the State of Texas," in 1861. Otherwise, this was a call to join the Union forces in the Civil War. Two of these men returned. They were Francisco Gonzales, who dies in 1919 at the age of 101, and Francisco Trujillo who died in 1914. The third volunteer seems a matter of conjecture. All the early settlers engaged more or less in Indian warfare to protect their women and their homes. According to Pedro Gurulé, one of the men who came back to Placitas in 1843 from Algodones where he had gone from Las Huertas, told of the capture of an Apache warrior, but all he could remember of the tale was that there was Apache blood in Placitas, not much, but a little. And the present men of Placitas have upheld the war record of their fathers. Six of them are World War veterans: David Baca Trujillo, Jr., Ysidoro Lucero, Juan Gurulé, Ameliano Baldonado, Ventura Escarcidea, and Pablo Baca.

In 1860, the present system of irrigation including the El Tanque de La Ciruela (the tank of the plum), a large reservoir, just east of the village was built. In accordance with the territorial law which made it compulsory for a settlement to hire and pay a teacher fifty-cents for each pupil per month, the people of Placitas hired José L.A. Gurulé to teach their first school. Nicholás Gurulé, son of José L.A. Gurulé, said that his father was born in 1850, taught school in San Felipe when he was twenty-two years of age, left San Felipe when he was twenty-four and came to Placitas to teach in 1876. Placitas established a school in their mission and it continued for several years. José L.A. Gurulé taught the first public school of Placitas; his pay came in the form of beans, chili, goats, and wheat. he had taught for three years in the San Felipe Pueblo. José's first teacher was Pedro Sarna, an old man of Ojo de La Casa, the only men in the whole vicinity who could read or write. Later José went to

Algodones as a priest's boy and there gathered sufficient learning to teach. According to his people he was a "gusano que roe los libros" (bookworm) and even the priests lent him their precious books.

But this José Librado Arón Gurulé had other talents. At the age of fifteen he aided his Grandfather, Antonio Gurulé, a freighter on the Santa Fe Trail to drive his oxen team to the "estados" or specifically to Kansas City. It was on his first trip that the musket he carried for protection against the Indians exploded prematurely and tore off his arm. This boy of fifteen himself hacked off his torn limb and cared for the stump and saved his own life. For over fifty years, this dominant character has been the advisor of his people and shaped events in Placitas.

There are seventy-five heads of families, owners of water rights in the community. Placitas is the home of about three hundred and seventy-five people. They keep San Juan Day with feasting and horse racing. They brought their patron saint here with them, San Antonio de Las Huertas. By virtue of special permission from the church in Bernalillo, they celebrate San Antonio's Day on November 13th, when the harvest is gathered and the wine is in the barrels, that there may be fitting feasting. The community life in Placitas is still a distinctive feature. They work together on the community irrigation system; they work together in the harvest time, in husking bees, in ristra (string of chili)—making time, and house-raising bees. The old custom of group singing in the night prevails here. In the present Placitas the work is done much in the mode of 1843. Wheat is still tramped out by horses on a hard mud threshing floor, when it is raised. Pinto beans are still beaten from the pods with sticks and winnowed by hand. Corn is till ground into meal with the metate and the mano. Spanish is still the language of the people and English is taught and spoken only in the school.

But for all the unchanged customs of Placitas, there is today, nevertheless, a new Placitas. In the spring of 1933 eight boys from the village were called to the CCC Camp in the forest reserve in the Sandía Mountains. Into the homes of these boys came a regular income. In October of 1933 thirteen heads of families were placed on the CCC rolls. Since then successive government projects have been carried out in Placitas. The money which has come into Placitas so regularly has worked a subtle change in the lives of the people. Their standard of living has been raised probably beyond their dreams, and almost without exception the people have improved their old homes or built new ones. This prosperity has brought to Placitas a trading post which meets the demands of a new demanding people. The old winding lane through the village is unchanged, but new life looks out upon it. There is a new public school in the plaza.

When Congress created the United States Court of Private Land Claims (1891), the people of Placitas were forced to test the legality of their title to their land grant. They had no funds for this purpose. José Librado Arón Gurulé appealed to his two friends, Mariano Otero, Albuquerque banker and sheepman, and Thomas Catron, an attorney of Santa Fe, for aid. These two men had the grant approved by the Land Court; the price for their services was the east one-third of the grant, with exceptions. Thus, the people of Placitas wrote the final chapter in the history of the old San Antonio de Las Huertas Land Grant.

PLACITAS FOLKLORE
August 27, 1938
Words 1608
Sources of information: Rumaldita Gurulé, José Trujillo, Catalina Gurulé.

DOÑA TOMASA–THE WITCH NURSE

Señora Rumaldita Gurulé, age sixty-seven, Placitas, New Mexico, wife of José Librado Arón Gurulé, told this story, and her grandmother, Quiteria, plays an important part in it.

Margarita was very sick and in pain enough to die. Her baby would not come. For two days Quiteria, the midwife, had been wringing her hands and weeping. She had done all she knew to do. Narciso, Margarita's husband, haggard and worried, stood by making up his mind to go for old Doña Tomasa. That was what was wrong. With their other four children they had called old Doña Tomasa. Now, for the new baby they called Quiteria because Quiteria lived much nearer and was a much younger woman. But he would go and bring Doña Tomasa. He rushed from the house and brought his pony, and soon he was riding on the narrow trail to Doña Tomasa's house up in the mountains four miles away. The horse would not trot. At last he came to her house. She was sulky and angry.

"You must come to see my wife; she will die if you do not hurry," Narciso said.

"I will not go! Keep your Quiteria!" said the angry Doña Tomasa.

Then Narciso knew that he had been right. Doña Tomasa was jealous. Oh, his poor sick Margarita! What would this wicked old woman do to her. Now he became angry.

"My wife, she will die. You will go or I will lasso you and drag you behind my horse to my house!"

Doña Tomasa knew the man meant what he threatened. She said, "You go. I will follow you."

Narciso left the place. Now his horse went trotting along since he was going home. But every little while he looked back, but no Tomasa followed. He grew uneasy, but he rode on; she said she would follow. When he reached home, there by the fire sat Doña Tomasa, warming herself, for the day was cold. Margarita was begging her to hurry and help her. Quiteria was begging her to hurry and help Margarita lest she die. Narciso watched old Doña Tomasa roll and smoke cigarettes and warm her hands, not at all surprised to find her there before his fireplace, for she was always suddenly appearing or disappearing. He, too, pleaded with the old witch nurse to do something quickly to save Margarita. But all Doña Tomasa did was roll and smoke cigarettes, warm her hands at the fire, and putter about the room looking at this or that while Margarita groaned in her sufferings and begged her to help her baby to come. Hour followed hour. Margarita screamed in pain. Doña Tomasa glared at Quiteria and walked to the bed.

"Give me your hand, you coward!" she demanded.

Margarita laid her hand in the hard palm of the witch nurse and at that moment they all heard a baby's cry, and there was Margarita's baby right before them. Doña Tomasa gave them all a look of triumph—Margarita's baby had come when she willed.

TESORO DE LA CIRUELA
(Treasure of the Plum)
As told by José Trujillo

According to José Trujillo, these people were treasure hunters as well as home seekers. Long they had heard of the "Tesoro de La Ciruela." When the Indians drove the Spaniards from the soil of New Mexico, they seized what treasure they could find and hid it. Some of it they buried in the mountains east of the Sandía Pueblo. The Sandía Indians guard the place to this day; some of it they buried in the little town at Ojo del Oso: a door and a bell from a mission church, two big bars of gold, and many bars of silver. In their treasure hunt these home seekers dug up the mountainside, but to this day the treasure is still there somewhere. Many years ago when these people made a tank at El Oso, they found a hole filled with bark, made tight together with resin; they pulled it out, and in the bottom of the hole, they found many bows and arrows. The old story of el tesoro de la ciruela goes that the treasure is buried near the gate of the cemetery of Ciruela. In 1934, when a tank was being excavated at El Oso, what might have been an old Indian cemetery was unearthed. Public interest in the old tale of the treasure was revived, and eager treasure hunters and the curious flocked to Placitas. Now and then they still come to the village inquiring the location of the old Indian cemetery of La Ciruela. José said their Great Fathers said that the cemetery of La Ciruela was in the mountains east of the Sandía Pueblo.

❧ ❧ ❧

113

EL ABUELO–THE WHIPPING MAN

Catalina Gurulé, age forty-five, the granddaughter of Nicholás Gurulé, tells this story of the old days of her grandfather.

Long time ago the people of the village chose an old man, called an abuelo, to whip their lazy and disobedient children. So in the darkness of the night the old man went about the village, his face stained with bright colors and his chin masked with a long beard made of wool. He carried a whip made of long, narrow thongs of leather which cut stinging stripes on the backs and legs of the lazy, disobedient children. He would come quietly up to the door and knock loudly on it.

"Who is there?" the father or the mother would ask.

"El Abuelo" would come the answer, and the door would fly open and there he was. "Any bad, lazy children in the house?" he would ask, flourishing his whip.

The father or mother would say, "Juan (or whatever the child's name might be) would not do his work today."

The culprit would quake with fear when the abuelo would turn upon him.

"Dance and sing if you promise to do your work and mind your parents, and kiss the feet of El Abuelo," commanded the old man.

If the guilty one was repentant and made his promise, he stepped out to the middle of the floor and lifted up his hands and danced while he sang:

Baile, Paloma, Señor Gorrundú	Dance, Dove, Sir Clown
Alta las alas y baile la tú.	Up with your wings and dance yourself

Then he would stop his dance and kneel down and kiss the feet of El Abuelo, who would then vanish quickly into the dark. If the culprit did not sing and dance, he received the cut of the lash.

❧ ❧ ❧

FRANCISCO AND HIS SAINT

This, too, was told by Catalina Gurulé.

Francisco went to the Ojo del Oso to get a piece of cottonwood to make an artesa (trough) for his burro. He brought home a good, straight piece, on which he set to work with his daga (hunting knife). He hollowed out the log, leaving thick, strong ends. He made it level on the bottom that it would not roll or tip over. When it was finished, he had a smooth end left, about thirty inches long. What should he do with that? It was too good a piece of wood for the fire, and Francisco never wasted anything. Ah, he would carve out a saint. He again set to work with his daga. But saints were much harder to make than artesas for burros. The head and the hair were hard to carve. The eyes must be made to look at you. The arms must not be too long, and the hands must look right and fit the arms. And the feet—they must be made to fit the body. Francisco knew just how the saint's feet should look for he had kissed so many of them. For days he worked on his saint, that is, a little while each day, until it was finished. He named his saint San Benito. And then he took it to the priest to be blessed. All the people of the village went to witness the ceremony and to kiss the feet of the newly blessed San Benito, but Francisco did not go.

"Where is Francisco that he does not come to kiss the feet of his saint?" they asked each other, and then they asked the priest. But no one seemed to know why Francisco stayed away. Then one day the priest met Francisco when he was feeding his burro at the new trough.

"Why did you not come to kiss the feet of your saint?" the priest asked.

"Because," promptly answered Francisco, "I made the saint from the piece of wood I have left from the artesa."

SUBJECT: Folklore
WPA: 5-5-49 #s 1 to 6
September 17, 1938
Words 2723
Sources of information: José Librado Arón Gurulé, Rumaldita Gurulé,
Catalina Gurulé, Benino Archibeque, Conception Archibeque, David Trujillo,
Patricio Gallegos.

PETRA'S FAITH
As told by José Librado Arón Gurulé

It was in El Oso a very long time ago. Juan José built a house for his bride, Petra. He built it one room on the top of the other to keep them safe from the Indians and the wild animals. He brought Petra's two small brothers to stay with her for he was away much with his patron's sheep and goats. But Petra was afraid. Every night when Juan José was away, she was sick with fear. She wanted to bring food and water to the top room and stay there with her brothers while her husband was gone, but that could not be. They must take the goats out where they could find grass and water, and wherever they went, Petra was frightened at every noise she heard. The Indians and the wild animals might be coming. Then Petra prayed to the Holy Mother for a benediction. If the Holy Mother would bless her, she would no longer be afraid. So every day she prayed for the Holy Mother's benediction. Then one bright morning she saw a halo. She could not see the head under it for the light, but she could see arms stretched forward and hands moving up and down in a benediction. "The Holy Mother! The Holy Mother! She gives me her benediction." Petra cried and ran toward it. Her small brothers called after her, "Ho, it is a hare. The sun on the fur, it makes the light." But Petra did not hear them. "I am not afraid anymore," she sang out, as the halo disappeared, she knew not where.

❧ ❧ ❧

THE BRAVE LITTLE SHEPERD
As told by Benino Archibeque

Benino Archibeque, age seventy-two, is the son of Salvador Archibeque, who lived in Las Placitas in 1843, the earliest date found in the records inherited by José Librado Arón Gurulé, regarding habitation of the present Las Placitas.

It happened in the days when "wild Indians" raided the herds of sheep and goats and drove them off. The boys must tend the flocks because the men were busy in the fields or away on hunts or on long trips with the wagon trains to Kansas City for their patrón. On this day, Marcelino and his three young companions herded their flock in the mountains near El Oso. In the afternoon they saw the Indians coming up on them. They cried out, "The Indians!" and they ran and ran to hide where they would be safe—all but Marcelino. He stayed behind to defend the flock with his bow and arrows. When it was late the boys crept from their hiding place and went to their houses. All the flock was gone, they told the people, and Marcelino did not come with them. Maybe the Indians took him away to make him a slave. It was too dark to search for the boy. They must wait for the morning. No grown person slept that night. When it was light enough to see, they went to hunt Marcelino and the flock. They found a few goats that had strayed from the herd but no Marcelino. They hunted all morning. Then they found a track where something had been dragged. They ran along the track and there by the willows they found him and his bow and arrows. His flesh was cut to pieces with willow switches. The next day some of the people carried his body on a ladder (made to bear their dead) to Bernalillo to bury it, while the rest of the people hunted the mountains for the Indians and the flock. But they could not find them. Then the people held a meeting and talked it over. After that the boys went alone no more to tend the flocks. A grown person must go with them. And this was done until the "wild Indians" were conquered.

❧ ❧ ❧

THE COYOTES SEND THE WARNING
As told by Catalina Gurulé

Catalina Gurulé de Gurulé, age forty-five, is the great-granddaughter of José Antonio Gurulé, direct descendant of one of the twenty-one families who received the Las Huertas Grant from the King of Spain in 1765. José Antonio was the Gurulé who kept the old records, which are now in possession of José Librado Arón Gurulé.

This is how Catalina started her story: "Maybe it was in the days before people have a saint, I don't know."

It was over a hundred years ago and the people in Las Huertas had a hard time keeping their goats from the Indians. Many times when they had big flocks the Indians came and fought with them and drove off the goats, but something told the people the coyotes would help them. So the men went to the mountains where the boys herded the goats, and made holes. Then they covered the holes with boughs from the pinon trees. The men told the boys to run and hide in them whenever they heard the coyotes talk loud to the dogs. Then one day while the boys herded the goats, they heard the coyotes away up in the mountains howl and howl and say, "Yip, yip, yip." They raised a big noise. The dogs heard them and they howled and howled and told the dogs down by their houses that the Indians were coming because the coyotes had told them so. The boys ran and hid in the holes. The men got their bows and arrows and climbed the mountains. They hid behind the trees and rocks. And then the Indians climbed the mountains. The men shot arrows at them. The Indians could not see where the arrows came from. They got afraid and ran down the mountain. The men ran after them shooting at them. They followed the Indians down Las Huertas Cañón and there they saw a flock of goats the Indians had left there. Now the men fought hard with the Indians and drove them away. Then the men took the Indians' flock of goats up to the mountains. The warning of the coyotes saved their own flock and gave them another flock.

❧ ❧ ❧

EUFEMIA'S SOPAPILLAS
As told by Catalina Gurulé de Gurulé,
José Trujillo, and Patricio Gallegos

This is a story of the days when the forefathers of the Placitas people lived in the walled town of Las Huertas, just to the north of the present Placitas.

One day the men went to the mountains to hunt. They said they would be back before dark and told their women to lock the gates and keep all the children inside the walls. So that day the women worked in their houses and kept the children with them. Then a band of "wild Indians" came. They found the gates locked. They thought the people must be hiding somewhere, so one of them climbed on top of the house that formed the corner of the wall and another climbed up to look into the very small window. It was old Eufemia's house but the Indian could not see her because she was busy at the fireplace frying the last of her sopapillas (buns fried in deep fat). She had fried a lot of them because her men would be hungry when they returned from the hunt. There was no smoke from her chimney now for the fire was low. The Indian thought somebody might be hiding down there, so down came his long stick with a spear head on the end of it. It went right into the tinaja (pottery cooking utensil) of sopapillas. The poor old woman was frightened, but her mind worked fast. Because the spear head hit the bottom of the tinaja, the Indian would think he had speared somebody and would look for blood on it. She must do something to keep the Indians out there until the men came back. She put a sopapilla on the spear head and watched the stick go up the chimney. Then the stick came down again and she put another sopapilla on it. Again and again the stick came down until at last Eufemia had only one sopapilla left. And still the men had not come. It would take too long to make more sopapillas. What could she do? She moved back from the corner. She happened to look up. There was the Indian at the window eating one of her sopapillas. She must do something quick. She took up the tinaja, and fast as she could move, she stepped upon the adobe bench against the wall and threw the hot fat in the Indian's face. He cried out in pain. The other Indians thought he had been shot with an arrow. They ran away as fast as they could go, leaving their companion screaming with the pain. Then the men came back. They put a rope around the Indian's feet and pulled him up over a tree and cut his throat—just as they would do an animal.

❧❧ ❧❧ ❧❧

QUITERIA OUTWITS THE WITCH NURSE
As told by Rumaldita Gurulé

"Quiteria is the best nurse and she is young," the people said, and it made Doña Tomasa, the witch nurse, very jealous. So Quiteria was afraid of her and she tried to keep out of her way. The witch nurse might play an evil trick on her. Then one day somebody whispered to Quiteria that if she stood on Tomasa's shadow, Tomasa could not move and then she would have power over Tomasa. At noon one day Doña Tomasa came to visit Quiteria. Ah, thought Quiteria to herself, I must keep her until her shadow grows a little. So she invited the witch nurse to eat dinner with her. The woman was hungry so she stayed and drank the good atole (a drink made of milk and the meal of the roasted and ground pueblo corn) and ate the tortillas. But she was in a hurry and soon she was leaving. Quiteria picked up her new reboso and followed Tomasa out the door. "See how fine my new reboso is. Touch it." And Quiteria came very close to the witch nurse and stood on her shadow. The witch nurse tried to move. She could not. So she acted very natural as if she did not wish to move. She talked of the people to Quiteria. She talked of the crops. She rolled many cigarettes and smoked them. Hour after hour passed. Then she knew Quiteria was keeping her there on purpose. She must get away. She cried out, "I am sick. Run quick. Get me some water!" Quiteria saw that she looked very pale, so she ran into the house for the water. When she returned Doña Tomasa was gone.

❧ ❧ ❧

THE FIRST SAN ANTONIO
DE LAS HUERTAS
(El Primero San Antonio de las Huertas)

As told by David Trujillo, who told it as it was told by his grandfather, Miguel Trujillo, who died in Las Huertas in 1854.

When our fathers first came here, they had no god (meaning saint) to take care of them and cure their sick, and watch over their land and take care of their wheat and corn and their goats. No god to save them and their goats and their fields of wheat and corn from the Indians. They must have someone to take care of them. So they held a meeting and talked it over. One of the men, Miguel Trujillo, could carve many things from the wood. The people chose him to carve them a god. So he brought the root of an old cottonwood and carved the image from it. The people had no church, so the man made a capilla (little church) just big enough to hold the god. But where should they keep the capilla? They, each family in turn, promised to keep the capilla in their houses where all the people could come to pray to the god. Now they had someone to take care of them and cure their sick and save them from the Indians and look after their land and all they planted on it. Now there was much rejoicing. The people carried the god to San Felipe Pueblo, where there was a priest to bless him. They called the new god, San Antonio de Padua de Las Huertas.

Many years after that the people of Las Placitas built a little church. A woman named Antonia started to build it herself, then the other people of Las Placitas helped her. On the altar in the little church was an old saint carved from the root of a cottonwood. The people called him San Antonio de Padua. Once the candles about his capilla set it on fire, and one side of the head and along the lower body of San Antonio was burned, "not much but bad to look at." But he stayed on the altar of the little church until 1920 when a new church was built. Then it was that San Antonio disappeared. There are many who say, "I think the priest took him away." The people ordered another San Antonio de Padua from Texas, a new and modern one. David Trujillo, Sr., an old man at the time, ridiculed the people and condemned them for the lack of loyalty to their fathers' ancient grudge against the Texans. "You have a Texas San Antonio, not a New Mexico San Antonio," he lamented, as if the Texas San Antonio would leave them to shift for themselves. David Trujillo, Sr. died in 1920.

The last part of the story of "The First San Antonio de las Huertas" was told by David Trujillo and Conception Archibeque, age sixty-seven, who is the daughter of Civil War veteran, Francisco Gonzales, who came to Las Placitas prior to 1850.

Conception said, "No one today knows where the old San Antonio came from."

SUBJECT: Las Huertas
WPA: October 8, 1938
Words 1813
Sources of information: José Librado Arón Gurulé, David Trujillo, Patricio
Gallegos. Archive No. 88, Translated Title Papers, U.S. Pub. Survey, Book 3
pp 993-999. Private Land Claims in the Library in the Palace of the Governors.
Records Inherited by David Trujillo from his father.

LAS HUERTAS

There is no town outside the territory adjacent to the Río Grande with a more colorful history than the old town of Las Huertas. The place is about a mile north of the Loop Drive where it cuts through Placitas in Sandoval County. There, a gate on the Drive admits to the road, which joins Las Huertas with Placitas.

Las Huertas is situated in the historic Las Huertas Cañón at the foot of the north end of the Sandías, its length bordered, on both sides by ridges of the mountains. The north side slopes to a mesa, which stretches to Algodones. On the south side of the mountains, the mountains rise wall-like and their crests command a sweeping view of the Río Grande and the villages and pueblos in the broad area from the Jémez Mountains to Bernalillo. Look out mountains they are, commanding a scope in every direction, advantageous points in the hazardous days of hostile Indian invasions. This tillable cañón watered abundantly by six springs, where surrounding mountains offered water and pasturage for livestock was but five miles up the Las Huertas Cañón from Río Grande del Norte (Rio Grande) and Camino Real (Royal Highway) along which life in the Kingdom of New Mexico, South of Santa Fe, centered in 1755. This place was the answer to the long ago home seekers' prayer, and it was at that time, according to José Librado Arón Gurulé, David Trujillo, and Patricio Gallegos that their forefathers built houses and cultivated the land in Las Huertas and their family tradition is confirmed by Archive No. 88 U.S.

Public Survey Office, which also gives the names of the first families who registered, they all has large families and he (Juan Gutierres) was compelled to sell the ranch which supported them all to the Pueblo of San Ana in order to enable him to pay off some debts. The families were: Andrés de Aragón, (one of his sons called José), Javier Gutierres, a half-breed, José Antonio Rael, Antonio Archibeque, Miguel Gallegos, Matías Gutierrres, José Gonzales. There is no account of these families receiving the San Antonio de Las Huertas Grant, but in Archive #88 U. S. Public Survey Office there is a record of the settlers of Las Huertas petitioning his Excellency, Tomás Valdez Cachupín, in 1765 to bestow upon them, in the name of the King, the land whereon they had settled and cultivated. This record seems to confirm the family traditions of the descendants of the people who founded Las Huertas that the people did live in Las Huertas many years before they applied for the Grant of San Antonio de Las Huertas. Twenty-one families are named in this record: Andrés de Aragón, Vicente Sena, Antonio Calban, Serafino Gurulé, Juan Maise, Francisco Lobera, Antonio Archibeque, Antonio Gurulé, Juan Valdez, Alberto Montoya, Juan García, Pedro García Jurado, and José García.

Governor Tomás Valdez Cachupín died before the grant was completed and the decree was declared by "Pedro Fermín de Mendinueta, of the Order of Santiago, Colonel in the Royal Armies, Governor and Captain General of this Kingdom of New Mexico do declare that I do make this grant XXX on condition that they make the settlement in accordance with the provisions of the Royal Laws." The foregoing is quoted from Archive 88 U.S. Public Survey Office. The same source discloses that it was not until the month of January in the year 1786 that Bartolomé Fernández, Chief Alcalde and War Captain, got around going to the spot and informing the settlers of Las Huertas of the decree and the provisions and conditions thereto. This mention of San José further corroborates the family traditions of the descendants of the Las Huertas founders that they lived in Las Huertas many years before 1765. On the old grant maps, location of ruins are marked just west of the ruins of the old Plaza of Las Huertas. The Alcalde found, so says Archive #88, that the people had already divided the land and had it cultivated and were satisfied with the division, so "I designate to them the unimproved lands. I took them by the hand and led them over said lands and they all plucked up weeds and cast stones and we all exclaimed three times, Huzza for the King and may God preserve him." Then the Chief Alcalde and War Captain set about laying out the settlement in accordance with the Royal Laws. He measured off a plaza and allotted each family sufficient ground for his house and a corral for his livestock. The houses and corrals must be made of adobes and built in such a way that the plaza would be enclosed on its four sides only opening at the corners. The plaza was large enough to permit street opening in case of increase in population; for no one was permitted to live outside the walls. They must stand together in case of hostile invasions. Also they must plant and cultivate corn, wheat, and garden edibles, and they must plant fruit trees. The remaining ruins of the old plaza clearly indicate that the plan of building was carried out.

And here, the first families of Las Huertas lived and supported themselves. The tales that have come down from them stress their hard times. Indians raided their fields at harvest times. If the Indians won the battle, the Las Huertas citizens lost their crops and faced a bare winter. The Indians raided the mountains. If they won they drove off the goats, which were the chief source of supply of food and clothing and household furnishings for Las Huertas. There were grasping officials who exacted toll in the way of wheat of corn. And there were droughts. According to José Librado Arón Gurulé and David Trujillo and Patricio Gallegos, the people went down the cañón to the vicinity of Algodones for aid in seasons of distress, for they say, the people who settled Las Huertas also at the same time settled Algodones on land they bought from the San Felipe Indians, and that they were all members of the twenty-one families who received the grant of San Antonio de Las Huertas. It is true that to this day, the descendants of the first families in Algodones and the descendants of the Las Huertas settlers now living in Placitas and Ojo de La Casa (House of the Spring) are related.

According to David Trujillo, the people living within the walls of old Las Huertas never had a church or a priest. They made themselves a saint and had him named and blessed by the priest at the San Felipe Pueblo. The people kept their saint in their houses. They carried their dead on ladders (made to bear the dead) to the San Felipe Pueblo and buried them in the cemetery there. The way between Las Huertas and the pueblo was dotted with crosses and stone monuments where they had rested the dead on the sad journeys. Many there, who found such markets are yet living. The old Montezuma mine is at the North end of the Sandías and there is the ruin of a smelter in Las Huertas. Many years ago, he said, a bar of bullion was plowed up in a field in Las Huertas Cañón. He believed as did David Trujillo and Patricio Gallegos that the old working in the mine has long ago been lost; either filled up or caved in by mountain floods, or the Indians. And from David Trujillo came the statement that the older Trujillos born before the year 1800 said that Las Huertas became a town of one thousand people.

And so the people of Las Huertas lived within their walls, worked, prayed, and fought with the Indians until the fateful Order of 1823. "The order in the archive of the government of this province relative to requiring the settlements scattered through the mountains and valleys to attach themselves to the body of settlements situated on the Río del Norte." The foregoing information is found in Private Land Claims, Volume 3 pp 993-999, in Library Palace of the Governors, as well as the following, "I direct that without loss of time you appoint a committee of the corporation in your jurisdiction, who by virtue of this order, will cause the inhabitants of Las Huertas to remove to your jurisdiction, and with the corporation you will provide lands for them to cultivate which said corporation will see it done, informing me of its receipt and execution. God & c April 23, 1823." Communication from Governor Don José Antonio Visearrar to San Carlos de Alameda regarding the circumstances of protecting citizens against hostile Indian invasions.

Thus the inhabitants of Las Huertas were forced to abandon their walled town, their fertile cañón, and plentiful pasturage for their goats. Calletano Chaves who died in Ojo de La Casa in 1913 lived in Las Huertas at the time of the evacuation. His nephew, Patricio Gallegos, related the following story told by Calletano many times for it had made a vivid impression on his memory: "I was fifteen years old. I well remember the people putting their things together to leave the place. I went with some other boys to take the goats to the mountains for feed. Our father told us when we brought the goats in that they would be gone and for us to drive goats down the cañón to Algodones. They would be there looking for us. When we brought in the goats, the houses were all empty and nobody was there, so we drove the goats down to Algodones.

SUBJECT: Tales of the Towns settled by the Las Huertasanas
November 12, 1938
Words 2320
Sources of information: Patricio Gallegos, Predicondo Chaves, Teodosio
Chaves, Archive No. 88, Translated Title Papers, U.S. Pub. Survey.

OJO DE LA CASA
(House of the Spring)

Ojo de La Casa is a quarter of a mile south and thence a short distance east
from the point where the Loop Drive crosses the Hagen Road at the east end
of Placitas in Sandoval County. It is an area of about one hundred fifty acres
in Cañón de Las Huertas (Cañon of the Gardens) and it is divided into approximately two equal parts by the Las Huertas Arroyo, or as the forest maps call
it, Las Huertas Creek. The south end of Ojo de La Casa extends into the Cibo-
lo Forest. On the east a high ridge of the Sandías delays the hour of sunrise
almost an hour, and the high mesa on the west completely hides it from the
Loop Drive and cuts off another near-hour of sunshine. In good seasons, fruit
is abundant in this fertile area, and once the inhabitants supported themselves
from their corn and wheat and goats, for then there was virgin pasturage for
livestock. The soil is noted for its production of chili, and in all the generations it has yielded chili no disease has ever attacked it. It is not definitely
known when the first people came to this place to build homes, for the area is
but two miles up Cañón de Las Huertas from the settlement of Las Huertas,
which had its beginning about 1765, from information given in Archive 88
relative to San Antonio de Las Huertas Grant, which states that there was a
town and cultivated land in the place called Las Huertas before 1765, when
the citizens of the town petitioned for the land grant on which they had settled. It would be possible that these settlers cultivated this land as it has a fine
spring and there are evidences of another one.

The following story of Ojo de La Casa was told by Patricio Gallegos, Predicondo Chaves, and Teodosio Chaves:

The first families known to settle in Ojo de La Casa came about 1858. They were: Valentino Zamora, Feliciano Archibeque, Marcelino Archibeque, Juan Archibeque, Pedro Sarna, Nicolás Mora, Rumulo Maestas, Julian Pais, and Cornelia Archibeque. They called their new town Cañón de Las Huertas (Canyon of the Gardens). Within a few years additional families augmented the population. They were: Cassimiro Gallegos and his wife Gertrudes Archibeque de Gallegos (and not of the same direct family as the families of Archibeques who came with Valentino Zamora). Upon their heels came Calletano and Juan Pedro Chaves from the vicinity of Santa Rosa. All of the other families now settled in the cañón were either from Algodones or Tejón (Badger). And then there was Santos Lavota, who kept all his secrets to himself— even the place from which he came and when and where he was going.

The tale of Ojo de La Casa is one of those "short and simple annals of the poor" until later on the tale was embellished a bit by the advent of a young prospector with his gold pans and spoons late of the Black Hills, South Dakota, and Leadville, Colorado. Valentino Zamora and his wife Juanita Gurulé de Zamora had a large family, so large they say, that two of the girls received the name of María—the oldest and youngest of the family. When the padrinos (godparents) were told what they had done, they laughed and said, "Nobody could remember the names of Juanita's children." So to meet future use of the name, they added a suitable name to the one given the child, making her María de Los Ángeles. The older María had been frightened once by a bolt of lightning which felled a tree near her. She was immediately called María de Rayo, and so were the girls called throughout their lives. María de Rayo married Calletano Chaves, and her sister wedded his brother Juan Pedro Chaves. This sister was Paulita. Rosalie Zamora married Nicholás Mora, and Marcelino Archibeque took Florentina Zamora to wifehood. These daughters were married at the time they settled Cañón de Las Huertas. María de Los Ángeles had not reached her teens. And then she fell in love with Juan María Gallegos, son of Cassimiro. He was sixteen years of age. It was the first love affair in the new settlement. But María of the Angeles was much too young, they all said. The husband-to-be was far too young. The affair became the issue of the day. Cassimiro Gallegos and the two Chaves brothers, the last comers, had something aside from the youthful lovers on their minds. In all communities the life-giving water is of first importance. Here the spring and its abundance of pure water was open to people and animals alike. The spring gushed into a hole made hard with adobe mud. The place was bemuddied by the hoofs and feet of every animal about, and it was utterly unfit for the women to walk upon, and the water was filthy and needed to be settled after it was in the tinajas (pottery vessels). Something must be done. So the meeting was called to discuss the matter. As a result the community built an adobe house, which enclosed the spring. The name of the place was changed from Cañón de Las Huertas to Ojo de La Casa and María of the Ángeles and Juan María became the first bride and groom of Ojo de La Casa, for they demanded the right to marriage and an adobe house and land of their own. By now the girl was thirteen. She wore the merino wedding dress other brides of the family had worn, and padre (father) Cassimiro Gallegos, who was the owner of a carreta and a pair of oxen, drove the wedding party to the priest at San Felipe Pueblo. They left Ojo de La Casa about three o'clock in the morning and it took until nearly eight o'clock for the oxen to plod down the Cañón de Las Huertas and up the Camino Real (Royal Highway) and across the Rio Grande to the church in San Felipe. While they were gone the village of Ojo de La Casa hummed with festive activities. The wedding feast was prepared and a room made ready for the baile (dance). Then the wife of thirteen years and the husband of sixteen set about the business of building a house for themselves, a task that was lightened by community aid for the whole settlement was so closely related as to be as one big family. The house that they built is still occupied, though the builders of it lie in the little city of the dead, at the foot of the Sandías a short distance from the house she helped build, for in those days it was the woman who practically built the house.

Cassimiro was a progressive spirit of his time. A trader by nature and somewhat of an adventurer. His stout carreta he made himself without tools except an axe. The clumsy thing was a load in itself for his oxen but it never broke down. It was lined inside with tough hides. He had dreams of gain. Eagerly his neighbors gathered about him to hear of these dreams. He would build another carreta; he would use his young oxen and they would gather piñón nuts to fill the whole inside of the two carts. It was a good piñón year. The task of filling the carettas would not be too hard. He set to work, and by the time the piñóns were ripe for gathering, he was ready for the trip. He said, "Fill my carreta with piñons and I'll take my boy and some men to help keep off the Indians and we'll go down to Chihuahua and trade our nuts. We'll bring cloth for the women and things for the houses." With that golden promise they set to work. They carried their tinajas all over the mountains, and soon the small caravan rolled out of Ojo de La Casa. They were gone a half a year.

There is a brass kettle left in the house of María de Los Ángeles which is supposed to be a relic and reminder of this long-ago trip. But there was an aftermath to this glamorous trip into a far and exciting land. Cassimiro Gallegos could no longer content himself in the Cañón de Las Huertas where mountains hemmed him in on every side. The hidden village lost its charm for him. The adobe house he had helped build over the spring, the many-roomed house he and Gertrudes had built and dwelled within so many years, all irked him, so he loaded his belongings into his carreta and moved to Tejón, where there was an immense vista and a winding road where men and wagons and oxen went on their way to Estados (the states, particularly Kansas City).

Time marched on. Valentino and Juanita Zamora were no more. The Archibeque families, craving more of life and people, moved to Albuquerque. Others drifted away. Santos Lavato went silently on his trip from Ojo de La Casa leaving or selling, no one knows which, his property to the gringo, the young prospector. The older ones in Ojo de La Casa shook their heads, cursed Lavato roundly to each other and predicted that the gringo would never be satisfied until he had others of his kind around him and that in time they'd have the fertile Cañón de La Huertas. The prophecy was not an idle one. An American owns about half of Ojo de La Casa today.

The descendants of the families who settled and named Cañón de Las Huertas and who afterward with newcomers built the adobe house enclosing the spring and renamed the settlement Ojo de La Casa, fell to wrangling over the waters that came down from the mountains in the acequia madres (mother ditches) that were built and used in peace before them. They disputed boundaries and use of the spring. A general hegira ensued until more than half of the adobe houses stood ghost-like on the deserted slopes overlooking the fertile fields. One, it is said, picked up his axe and ruthlessly destroyed a fine orchard he could not take with him, others removed the vigas from their houses (the heavy pine timbers which support the ceilings and mud roofs) and put them in other houses. Some of the old dwellings were rebuilt and one or two have remained intact: one the old school room where Juan P. Chávez, the first teacher in the settlement, taught the children of Ojo de La Casa to read and write. Before that, Pedro Sarna, one of the first settlers taught the boys of Placitas and Ojo de La Casa who were ambitious to write their names and tell their letters. He went with them to the mountains where they herded their flocks and there held open-air classes. His one surviving pupil today is José Arón Librado Gurulé, age eighty-eight, of Placitas. But to this day, the name of Pedro Sarna is spoken in tones of deep respect by the descendants of the men whom he taught. And out of old Ojo de La Casa has come a story of a mother's ingenious way of solving a problem which worldwide caters to the appetites of small children alive today. There was but one food for the children, atole. This atole is a drink of milk and meal made from roasted and ground blue, or pueblo corn. The little children had to drink it whether they liked it or not, and this mother overcame their reluctance by making a bit of paste of bright red chili powder and the milk, and floating tiny bits of it in the small tinajas (pottery bowls) of atole. She told the children that the red flecks were birds floating on the little lakes and that they must drink all the atole away from the birds so they would not drown. It became a game to drink off the atole and leave the little red birds in the tinajas.

Also this story came out of old Ojo de La Casa. Old Miguel and his wife, Juana, lived in a little house on the point of the hill. Their field down in the cañón grew high in weeds and the corn had a hard time to come up. Old Miguel said he was sick and what could a sick man do? Juana bent over her chili melga (bed) and weeded it and scratched up the hard adobe with sharp sticks and faithfully watered it, so they had chili. Juana somehow found strength to keep her house and climb the mesa and gather wood for the little corner fireplace, where she did her meager cooking. Old Miguel seemed never to be sick when the dinner was in the tinaja. All the friends and family of Juana wondered what to do. Then one night someone rapped sharply on the tiny high window of Miguel's house. He woke up. Juana woke up. He told Juana to ask who knocked like that on their window in the dark of the night. "I cannot call, so afraid am I," said Juana. Miguel cried out, "Who knocks at my window and what do you want?" A strange voice answered, "I am the angel come for you because you are so sick." Old Miguel shook with fear. "No, no, angel, I am not sick. It is Juana. She is so sick she cannot call to you." After that, old Miguel attended his field religiously and brought the wood for the fire.

SUBJECTS: Tales of the Towns Settled by the Las Huertasanas
November 26, 1938
Words 2593
Sources of Information: Teresita Gallegos de Baca, Patricio Gallegos,
J.P.Batchen, (William Eckert), (Juan María Gallegos).

THE PEACE PLOT
As told by Patricio Gallegos

The settlers of Ojo de La Casa had been in their new homes but a short time when something happened that might have had disastrous consequences had it not been for the quick wit of Valentino Zamora (El Jefe), their leader, who averted a panic and saved the settlement. His son-in-law, Nicolás, possessed a span of burros. In those days of the Civil War period, burros cost not less than fifty dollars a span, and fifty dollars in Ojo de La Casa in those days was no small fortune. Burros could scale mountains like goats, they could carry heavy loads of wood on their backs; in short, they could be driven to do any sort of work and they were the only burros in the settlement, therefore, they were a community charge. One stormy night Nicolás herded them into a sheltered cañoncito (little cañón) to graze. They would be safe enough there, and he would get up very early in the morning and bring them in.

When he left the settlement about dawn, no one but old Valentino saw him. He hurried along, for the high wind of the night before still swooped down on them from the mesa, and the air was frosty. He had not gone far when he sighted one of his burros. Where was the other one? He ran as hard as he could to the cañoncito, but he found no sign of the beast there. He ran along the trail they had made for their goats, on and on, searching the ground for tracks. He stopped short. What was that red stain there on the ground? Blood! And there were tracks of tewas (moccasins). The Indians! They had butchered his burro for meat and carried it away. In his grief and rage he shook his fists and swore vengeance. He would rouse the men, and they would track down the Indians and kill them.

He started back to the village, then stopped. There was old Valentino coming to meet him. Nicolás called out, "Come quick, see where the Indians have killed my burro." Together they looked at the blood-stained earth. "We will hunt them down and kill them. We will make them pay for my burro. Now I will go to get the men."

He gave a bound, but the strong hand of the older man stayed him. "Sh-ee, sh-ee, my son," and he laid a finger across his lip, "sh-ee, not one word of this or Juanita (the old man's wife) will stir up the women. You know if they hear that an Indian has been here in the night, not one of them will stay. They were afraid to come to this hidden place; one word of this and they're gone. We'll cover this spot, and I'll lead them to believe the burro wandered off, wandered down to that shaft we discovered and fell in and broke his neck. The earth is loose around there. It is dangerous to go there. They will not investigate." With hope of revenge dying in his heart, poor Nicolás walked silently and dejectedly back to his house.

🍃 🍃 🍃

EL INOCENTÓN
(The Innocent)
As told by Teresita Gallegos de Baca

One day Lucas and Tomás and Juan sat in the shade of a piñón tree eating the roasted corn they had brought from home for their lunch. Their goats were grazing nearby. All at once Juan caught sight of an Indian. He was so frightened for a moment he could not speak, then he said "Look, the Indians!" The boys scrambled off on all fours to the nearest arroyos. Not for just one arroyo. No, their parents had told them never, never to hide in the same arroyo, but for each boy to hide in a different arroyo and then it might be that the Indians could not find them all. So into different deep arroyos jumped the young shepherds, and sat very still.

Three Indians circled the herd of goats and hunted for the shepherds. Alas, they found Lucas and dragged him from his hiding place and started off with him. One boy would have to do, for there were no others in the arroyo. Poor Lucas fought and tried to get away, but they dragged him along with them. Tomás, in his joy at being missed by the wild Indians, jumped up and down and shouted, "Tú no mi hallarse! Tú no mi hallarse!" (You did not find me! You did not find me!) But his joy was short lived. The Indians returned and routed out the poor simple one from his refuge and carried him off with Lucas into slavery.

ॐ ॐ ॐ

EL OJO
(The Eye)
As told by Teresita Gallegos de Baca

It happened many years ago. Tules took her young baby and went on a long hard trip with her husband to visit her sister Rosalie, who was ill. While on the brief visit a strange old woman came to the house of Rosalie. "Ah," said she, "what a pretty baby." She looked at the infant with longing eyes; she half held out her arms to it, but the young mother ignored her. The old woman went her way, and soon Tules and her husband started for home. All the day as she jogged along on the burro Tules tried to quiet her fretting baby, but it only cried the more. It was dark when they came to their home in Ojo de La Casa. At once Tules called to her mother, "Come quick. See my baby. What shall I do?"

"Who saw your baby while you visited your sister?"

"A strange old woman," Tules told her. "She wanted to hold my baby and love it, but I did not let her."

"Alas, my child, you should have let her hold your baby—if only for a moment. Now a spell is upon your baby—only that woman could undo it, and you do not even know who she was. The journey back to try to find her is too hard for the baby." And she shook her head, "There is nothing we can do. When someone looks longingly with their eyes at your baby and for some reason they do not take it in their arms and caress it, the look in their eyes casts a spell on the baby and it will die—unless you can find the person and he will sprinkle the baby with water from his mouth. That will take away the spell. You do not heed what we older ones tell you."

And so to this day, some say, many babies die from the spell cast upon them by the unrequited look in the eye.

❧❧ ❧❧ ❧❧

LUZ DE LA LUNA
(Moonlight)
As told by Teresita Gallegos de Baca

Antonia's baby was born. "God have mercy," cried out the midwife, "his little feet have no legs but grow out from his knees." Everybody came in for a peep at the unfortunate baby before Antonia knew anything of what was going on in the house. "She should know better," wailed the old grandmother, "and be careful. How often have I told these young mothers to watch and never let the moonlight fall upon them in their beds when they are carrying their babies. Now Antonia has caused her baby to be born without legs. When the moonlight falls upon a mother in bed before her babe is born, she must not blame anyone but herself if it has some part missing. And listen, if she allows the shadow to fall upon her when the moon has an eclipse, her baby will be very sickly or die—unless she is wise enough to wear a string around her waist with keys upon it." And so they think it is to this very day.

❧❧ ❧❧ ❧❧

LEGEND OF MONTEZUMA MINE

(As related by the Mexican people and the Indians in the section around Ojo de La Casa where the mine is located.)

They say the old mine was known to the Indians long before the Spaniards set foot on American soil. When Coronado wintered at the pueblo near Bernalillo, he visited the mine which was worked by the Spaniards and the enslaved Indians, who were compelled to labor long hours with the crudest tools to dig out and smelt the ore for their cruel masters. The gold they dug from the mine was sent on the backs of burros to Mexico. When the Indians revolted and drove out the Spaniards in 1680, they filled up all the pits and shafts of the mine. They carried new soil and spread it deeply over all the places they had covered, that weeds and other vegetation might grow over them and destroy forever all traces of the workings. They carried all the rock and ore on the dumps to arroyos and rivers where it would be washed away. Thus there would be no signs left of the mines where they had been compelled to slave.

❧ ❧ ❧

GOLD FEVER IN Ojo de La Casa
As told by Patrico Gallegos

(Stories of William Eckert and Juan María Gallegos, retold by J. P. Batchen)

Whenever men gathered along the old Santa Fe Trail and told of tales they had heard of New Mexico, there was repeated by someone the legend of the old Montezuma Mine located somewhere at the north end of the Sandía Mountains. Dick Wooten heard of it at Trinidad and at Ratón Pass. He became interested to the point of trying to locate it. As the legend goes, every sign of the locations was obliterated. He could find nothing. But he did find an old Indian in the vicinity who lay sick on the floor of his little house. No one lived near him and he was too ill to rise to his feet. Wooten gave him some of the food he had brought with him. He nursed the old Indian back to health. Then he asked him where the Montezuma Mine was. The story goes that it took Wooten several days to persuade the old Indian to talk, then he was told that he could not tell anyone of the spot. Wooten waited and continued sharing his grubstake. Finally the old Indian confided to Wooten that he was most grateful for the care he had given him and he felt that Wooten had saved his life and while he could not tell him, he told Wooten to watch him as he walked along the mountainside and note the places he stopped. And so it was that later Wooten discovered arrows cut in the rocks pointing in one direction. He located a spot and set to work with his pick and shovel. He did unearth a working that had been filled in, or else had caved in. For years the mine, or rather, workings that resulted were called "The Wooten Mine."

But it was in the late 1870s and the early 80s, that things happened in Ojo de La Casa to break the monotony of goat herding, wood hauling, and food problems. The young prospector who had somehow possessed himself of the house of Santos Lavato started a hunt for gold, urged on by the tempting legend of the old Montezuma Mine. And the hunt was stimulated by the fact that there was an awakening in New Mexico to the possibilities of hidden mineral wealth in the area from Santa Fe to the south end of the Sandías. On the high tide of the excitement a prospector named Wilson came into Ojo de La Casa. He located claims at the north end of the Sandías where legend located the old Montezuma. Many prospectors followed him and soon the whole Sandía ridge, the length of the Las Huertas Cañón, was staked with claims and the locations registered at Albuquerque, the county seat.

All this meant assessment work if the claims were to be held, according to the law. Ojo de La Casa was alive to the earning power of the pick and shovel. Digging started, times prospered, and everyone became accustomed to the chink of silver in his pocket. Wilson opened a saloon, and the inevitable gaming table of the day went with it. The peace and quiet of the hidden village was lost in the din of blasts of gunpowder, and the noise of drunken brawls originating at Wilson's saloon and terminating anywhere and everywhere.

The sudden and mysterious slaying of Wilson and the looting of his place closed the saloon. He was buried with scant ceremony in his door yard, for he had a highly developed ability for piling up ill will against himself. The murder never came to the notice of the law and so it passed.

Through legal steps his mine came into the possession of the young prospector. However, by now the gold fever had burned itself out in Ojo de La Casa. Besides, the Bland gold fever was on.

Before Ojo de La Casa settled back into lethargy, old Francisco staged a last gold hunt. He thought backward and forward, dipped his hands into his empty pockets, then he sought the prospector, who was not so young anymore but who still believed in tales of hidden treasure. Francisco told him a tale of his youth, how one day while he was herding his goats in the mountains, one kid strayed from the flock and became lost. He hunted everywhere, up and down the mountainside until he himself became lost. Then he heard the cry of the kid in a thick underbrush. Oaks grew so thick that he could not see through them, so he crawled along peering, breaking his way with his hands. Suddenly he came to the edge of a deep cave with a ladder sticking out of it. He wanted to see what was in the cave, so he went down the ladder, and there at the bottom of the cave he saw a little room dug out of one side. In that room he saw piles of shining gold and silver bars. He was so frightened at seeing so much treasure right there before him that he did not hear anyone come down the ladder. The first thing he knew somebody threw a blanket over his head and he was carried up the ladder and a long way off from the cave. Then rough hands stood him on the ground and jerked the blanket from his head and he saw angry Indians looking at him. They told him if he ever came near that cave again they would kill him. So none of them ever tried to find it.

The prospector hired him at a dollar a day and his dinner to take him over the ground where the cave was located. Francisco's old eyes lighted, and for a week they scoured the vicinity where the cave was hidden in the thick brush, but no evidence of it could they find. When old Francisco sensed that the prospector was ready to give up, he said, "That be a long time ago. Big rains come every year. He fill up holes, he make big change, now no can find."

SUBJECT: Tales of the Towns Settled by the Las Huertasanas
WPA: 5-5-31 #1
Dec. 17, 1938
Words 2630
Sources of information: Rumaldita Gurulé, Teresita Gallegos de Baca,
Catalina Gurulé, Vol. 111, Private Land Claims in library at Palace of
Governors at Santa Fe.

LA MADERA
(The Timber)

La Madera (The Timber) or Madera, as the forest maps call it, is located on the old La Ceja del Camino de San Pedro (Road of the Mountain Summit, of San Pedro) about five miles south and east from the place where the Loop Drive crosses the Hagan Road at the east end of Placitas in Sandoval County. La Ceja del Camino de San Pedro in times gone by was the main highway through the Sandías from points around Bernalillo and Placitas to La Madera, Tijeras Cañón (Scissors Canyon), and San Pedro Viejo (Old San Pedro) the site of an ancient pueblo, now excavated by a government project. This old road was made by Dame Nature, and Father Time through Perdizo Cañón (Partridge Canyon), which opens into Las Huertas Cañón (Canyon of the Gardens) at Ojo de La Casa (House of the Spring).

In 1839, Ramón Gurulé and his daughter Josefa petitioned the Mexican government for the land grant of San Pedro Rancho, which was the land of the ancient pueblo. They stated that they were descendants of the people who settled Las Huertas and received the San Antonio de Las Huertas Grant from the King of Spain in 1767, and that they had no lands whereon to live or to cultivate and no pasturage for their livestock. They received the grant in 1840, and they, with other descendants of the settlers of Las Huertas, went to live at San Pedro Viejo. Five years later they sold the grant to José Ramírez. The information in the above paragraph is contained in Vol.111, Private Land Claims, in the library in the old Palace of the Governors in Santa Fe.

These people from San Pedro Viejo became the founders of La Madera, though the exact date is a guess. It is thought to be around 1850, though it was probably before that, according to Rumaldita Gurulé, whose mother was born there some time after her grandparents came there from San Pedro Viejo. Among those first families were: Benerando Gutiérrez, Manuel Baros, Francisco Gurulé, José Gonzales, Marco Maestas, and a Lucera. Ramón Gurulé may have been one of the new settlers, along with his son Francisco. These people built their new town in a clearing on a thickly wooded mountain slope not far from the source of Perdizo Cañón. Most of the houses were built of logs and chinked with mud, for the local soil was not adaptable to the making of adobes. But a few of the new settlers were ambitious and industrious enough to bring in adobes with which to build their homes. On this mountain slope, rainfall and not irrigation determined the harvests. In rainy seasons the bean crop was heavy and corn grew abundantly. Vineyards and kitchen gardens were almost nil. Pasturage for their goats was sufficient.

🐝 🐝 🐝

THE GOOD SAMARITAN OF LA MADERA
As told by Rumaldita Gurulé

Fate played a prank on Manuel Baros when she wove La Madera into the pattern of his life. By virtue of his fairness and wise counsels and his worldly goods, which he turned to charitable account, he became El Jefe (the leader) of the community. He was a lover and tiller of the soil. He owned several spans of oxen and good wooden plows. Every spring he generously parceled out his precious hoard of seed and offered the use of his oxen and plows to anyone desiring them; but his seeds were neglected in the ground, or not planted at all, and his oxen grew fat and lazy for want of work. The heavily timbered area made haulers of wood of his people and not tillers of the soil. El Jefe was always at hand to relieve cases of distress and sickness; but it seemed that most of their illness and suffering required the incantations or brewed herbs of the witches to cure them. Manuel Baros sought to teach thrift and honesty. He fought witchcraft with reason, not switches, or tried to do it. For all he sought to do of good to his fellow men his reward came to him through his son Perciano Baros, who became one of the early Presbyterian missionaries in the vicinity.

❧ ❧ ❧

LA CITA DE LAS BRUJAS
(Rendezvous of the Witches)
As told by Rumaldita Gurulé,
Teresita Gallegos de Baca and Catalina Gurulé

La Madera, built in the woods, was isolated and although only four miles from San Pedro Viejo, a spooky old place. There was a weirdness about the whole location which made one shiver and think of ghosts and witches. La Madera had always been the rendezvous of witches. They simply abounded there-abouts in little houses higher in the mountains. Witch doctors, witch nurses, and just witches who played their evil tricks upon those they envied or hated. In La Madera, outdoor gossip must be conducted in low voices, for none could tell who might be listening from behind the trees. But it happened that all the witches did not live in houses far up on the mountainside. There were some right in the village who practiced the arts of the evil ones. There was Pepe, for one, who had a slight cast in his left eye. They must lock the doors to houses where babies were being born. If he chanced to enter a room and look at a newly born baby, for certain that baby would die. If he entered a kitchen and looked at a cake about to be set in the fireplace to bake, nothing could prevent that cake from falling and being unfit to eat.

And at night, when the wind was blowing and the pale moon was just a crescent, balls of light would jump about through the woods and around the houses of the witches. The balls of light would hop and run forward then backward, just as in a dance. It was the witches. Then the people clustered about their doorways in the dark to watch but no one ventured abroad. None but those named Juan had any power over the witches. If a witch had cast evil spells upon any of them, they set a Juan to watch her. The Juan would go out into the night and watch. When he saw the witch coming, he would jerk off his shirt, turn it wrong side out, and fling it in the witch's path. She would never see it. She would fall over it and for the life of her she could not move. Early in the morning the people would come and take her to the houses of the ones she had put an evil spell upon. They would make her cure them. They threatened to kill her if ever she bewitched them again. Then they took switches and lashed her out of the village.

🙞 🙞 🙞

EL MISTERIO
(The Enigma)
As told by Catalina Gurulé

Refrigia lived at the edge of La Madera with her old mother. She was very pretty and had large eyes and long lashes that hid them, and she put her hair high upon her head and made herself look very beautiful. Who would ever have thought that she was a witch? But none of them ever saw her eyes when she thought of Quita. Then they were balls of fire like cats' eyes and her fingers reached out like cats' claws that wanted to tear the flesh of someone. Refrigia hated Quita because of Felipe. Refrigia loved Felipe. Quita loved him also. But Refrigia felt that she could not live without him. One night she sought him out and confessed her love for him. Felipe was very gentle with her, but he told her he loved Quita and they were soon to be married. Very soon after that their padrinos (godparents or attendants) went with them to the priest and they were wed. No sooner was the service ended than Felipe seemed queer. He ran around Quita and laughed and pulled at the wedding veil as a child would do. When they came home, he cried at the wedding feast and would not eat of it, but asked for a tinaja (bowl of pottery) of atole (a drink made from milk and roasted and ground blue or pueblo corn) just as a child might do. All the wedding guests thought the handsome bridegroom was making a clown of himself for their amusement. But he did not change as time went on. Always there was a pain in his head. More and more he became like a small child. To satisfy him, his people made him a crib. Quita must always be playing with him. She tried to hide her grief and do what he wished to please him. Her youth and charm faded. Refrigia never showed her face anymore. Some said they thought they saw her go up into the mountains. "Could it be possible that Refrigia had brought all this misery upon Felipe and Quita?" The moment Quita heard of the suspicion she ran to the house of Refrigia, but she found only harshness and a command to be gone as Refrigia shut her door in Quita's face. Then one day Felipe suddenly became himself again.

Quita, too, looked as she did on that fateful wedding day. What of Refrigia? They ran to her house. There on her floor she lay dying and beside her was her witch doll and in her fingers was the big thorn she had pulled from its head. She had relented when death struck her and freed Felipe from the spell she had cast upon him.

And to this day there are those who believe that witches cause them to suffer or become demented by thrusting a thorn or a pin into their witch doll wherever they wish to cause suffering to the ones they envy or hate or to whom they wish to do harm.

🎜 🎜 🎜

EL HOMBRE ALEGRE
(The Jolly Man)
As told by Rumaldita Gurulé

But life in La Madera was not all made up of the goodness of El Jefe (or Manuel Baros) and the wickedness of the witches. There was Marcos Maestas, the jolly man, who was born to gamble. Should two of his neighbors go for a load of wood at the same time, he hunted someone to lay a bet with him as to which of the men would return first with his wood. He made a race course for the young men. Exciting foot races were weekly events and betting was heavy. A burro race is impossible, but he accomplished them. And that was something to bet on! Anything constituted legal tender when it came to offering bets: corn, beans, wood, goats, and some money, but money in hand was scarce. What difference did it make what they bet? The fun was in betting. And Marcos liked to see his neighbors enjoy themselves.

He reserved one room in his house for the playing of betting games. The favorite and most often played game was Cañuto (Pipe or Flute). For this game a pile of sand was placed in two corners of the room diagonally opposite and upon the mud floor. Navajo blankets were hung as drapes to conceal these corners. The game was played with four hollow sticks or reeds and a slender stick that could be inserted in the hollows, all the sticks being about eight inches long. The hollow ones had distinguishing marks upon them and each had a different value. The highest was called Mulato (Tawney) and scored four points. The next was called Cinchado (meaning to grip or cinch).

Its score was three points. Dos (Two) was next with two points, and Uno (One) was the lowest, scoring one. The slender stick placed in any of these hollow sticks doubled the score of that reed. Two leaders chose sides; each side had four players and each side possessed one of the corners. When the game was on, everybody in the village who could leave his house was there to watch and bet on the side that would score the most points during the evening's game. The side that was to start the game repaired behind the blanket in their corner. The slender stick was inserted into one of the reeds and the four sticks buried in the sand pile. The drape was pulled aside and the other four rushed in to the draw. They had but one draw. If the reed pulled from the sand pile contained the slender stick, they were entitled to a second draw; if not, they retired with the score given them by the one reed they did draw, and with all the reeds that were now to be hidden in their own sand pile. And so it went, with betting and drinking on the outside. Each time the players rushed to the draw everybody sang:

Paloma Lúcida	Beautiful dove
Lúcido Palomar,	From beautiful dove house,
Vengan atinados	Come ready to win
Vengan a jerrar.	Come ready to lose.

SUBJECT: Tales from the Towns Settled by the Las Huertasanas
WPA: 5-5-31 #1
January 6, 1939
Words 2158
Sources of information: Rumaldita Gurulé, Cristiana Baros.

LA MADERA: PART II
LUXURIES COME TO LA MADERA
As told by Rumaldita Gurulé

It was in the late seventies that the last teams of oxen and a wagon left La Madera for Kansas City, that great market at the other end of the Santa Fe Trail, with the usual excitement that accompanied the preparations for the six-month trip. But it was not the trip or the preparations for it that was the big event this time; it was the happy homecoming of Rumaldo Candelaria, who had made several trips before this one for his patrón, taking wool to market and bringing back precious cargo of merchandise. He had always gone with empty pockets. This trip he had some money of his own to spend. For this, the pick of his flock of goats had been sold. He had brought back goods like those bought for his patrón. When he arrived with his treasure, his neighbors crowded about his door to see what he had brought. They looked on breathless as he unwrapped the bundle. There was a whole bolt of muselina (muslin) and two large copper kettles! And last and most glorious of all was a bolt of calico! At sight of that, the women opened their eyes in surprise and sighed aloud with pleasure. What a present for Rumaldo to bring home to his wife and daughters. Señora Candelaria could scarcely believe the evidence of her eyes. When she was a girl, calico brought over the trail from Kansas City sold for ten dollars a yard in Santa Fe. Even now it was so expensive that only the rich could afford to buy it. And the snowy white muselina! The first bride in the family should have a dress and a veil of it.

And that first bride did wear a dress and veil of it. The veil was fastened to her hair at one side of her head and had wildflowers pinned on it where it touched her skirt, as well as where it was fastened to her hair. This dress and veil were borrowed and worn by other brides who preferred it to the merino outfits woven at home from the wool of their goats.

❧❧ ❧❧ ❧❧

THE SNOW BRIDE
As told by Rumaldita Gurulé

All the old-timers of La Madera delight to tell the story of Beneranda Gutiérrez and Terencio Lucero. Beneranda was seventeen. Terencio was twenty. It started one day in late autumn in the year 1881. That autumn day was summery, a perfect day for the trip such as Terencio planned. He and two of his friends started early that morning from their home in Las Placitas to walk to La Madera. Terencio was dressed in his fiesta best, not because it was a fiesta day but because he was going a-hunting for a bride. The maidens of Las Placitas had failed to build a fire in his heart, and he wanted a wife and a home of his own. He owned a flock of goats and some land and he worked often for his patrón, Pedro Perea, of Bernalillo. He was a tall, broad-shouldered youth and he looked well in his suit, which was bought at a store, and his brand-new leather boots which had been ordered specially for him. He took care that he did not scuff them as he and his compadres walked along rocky Perdizo Cañón (Partridge Canyon), which was the road through the Sandías from Las Placitas to La Madera. If he wished to charm some maiden, then he must look the caballero (gentleman). They reached La Madera in mid-morning, for the distance was only a little over five miles. Terencio had never been there before, and he looked about him, wondering where he might find someone he knew. And then he rubbed his eyes and stared; never had he seen such a lovely maiden. Down the trail she came like a little frightened deer. Her feet were bare and the dust rose like little clouds about her slender ankles. She steadied a tinaja (pottery vessel) on her head with her two graceful arms. She was on her way to the spring a half mile from the village, to fetch water for her family to drink. Her heels kicked out her many petticoats as she hastened along and the flush deepened in her cheeks as she thought of the audacity of the young man staring at her and of her own ill looks on such a momentous occasion. Not often did a maiden see such a handsome youth. The young man sighed as she disappeared among the trees. "Who is she?" he demanded of his companions. "Beneranda Gutiérrez," said one of them. Without another word Terencio turned on his heel and started for his home. He had found his bride. The rest was up to his father.

The next morning his father, accompanied by a small delegation of good citizens of Las Placitas who would vouch for the reputation and financial standing of young Terencio, appeared in La Madera before the house of José Gutiérrez. José saw them and came out to offer greetings. For a long time the men spoke together in low, confidential tones, then they went into the large kitchen where Beneranda was making tortillas, for it was nearing dinner time. "This is my daughter, my friend," José said to the elder Lucero, who, before Beneranda knew what it was all about, asked, "Do you wish to marry? My son says he will have no other wife but you."

Visions of the handsome youth she had seen the day before filled her mind. "Yes," she said.

Her father accompanied the men back to Las Placitas. The next day the two fathers went to consult the priest in Bernalillo, the date was set for the wedding, and the plans made. The rest was up to the young man and his family. They had but two weeks, as the wedding had been set for an early date.

Meanwhile Terencio was busy. Señor Pedro Perea of Bernalillo had need of him there, so he could not call upon his promised wife. But, following the old Spanish custom, he bought her wedding finery and it came to her at La Madera by burro. It was a bewildered bride-to-be who looked at her wedding dress. The curious about her shook their heads. The dress had hoops in the skirt! That fashion had finally made its way into the remote village, and Beneranda was the one to introduce it. The dress was of cashmere and the veil of sheerest lawn gathered into a small wreath of wax flowers. For her feet there were zapatos de Castellano as the people in those days called shoes from the store. The other dress, and there must be one in every trousseau, was of blue sateen.

The day before the wedding was cold and snowy. Late in the afternoon, Terencio and two friends who were to attend him arrived from Las Placitas on burros. The wedding party left for Bernalillo very early the next morning to reach the church for the sacrament before the marriage ceremony at eight o'clock. Beneranda was well wrapped in a large black tápalo (shawl), and it was no easy task to get her and the hoop skirt on the back of the burro. The burros, six of them, for there were four padrinos (attendants or godparents), padded through the snow down Perdizo Cañón. They passed through Ojo de La Casa before the village was astir and on through Las Placitas like ghosts in the cold gray dawn. When they reached Bernalillo it was snowing. When they came out of the church the storm was raging. By noon the sky cleared and they started for home.

It was a long, cold, and difficult ride, but at last they emerged from Perdizo Cañón in sight of home. According to custom, the groom's family had prepared the wedding feast and brought it to the home of the bride to serve. All was ready, and the guests were waiting to welcome the bride and groom.

When they saw them coming, they rushed out to meet them. Old Pedro, the simple one, had loaded an old gun, and as the burros approached he fired to the right and the left, clearing their path of evil spirits. The burros took fright as the bullets cut the air about them and became unmanageable. Beneranda lost her tápalo when her burro jumped and kicked up the snow and made a sudden rush forward. The hoop skirt bounced up and down. It was a funny sight. The gentle ripples of amused laughter fell upon the ears of old Pedro. He thought it was the crowd's approval of his good work. Up went his old gun and he blazed away again and again. The people shouted at him. Beneranda screamed hysterically as her burro kicked high in the rear and gave a sudden nose dive. Off she went in the snow, her veil somehow caught in the animal's flying hoofs. Her hoop skirt was wrecked, her bodice torn. Terencio carried her into the house and the women repaired the damage to her wedding clothes the best they could.

But the bride had another chance to look fresh and lovely. At midnight, there was a pause in the dance, and her two padrinas (lady attendants) took her away, arrayed her in that other dress, and put her hair up on her head in a knot. Until now it had been down. This putting the hair up in a knot on the head indicated that she was no longer a maiden, and the change of dress had a similar significance. Then she was returned to the dance.

This old custom is not longer observed, and the other dress had completely lost its meaning. But the old Spanish custom of the man buying the trousseau for his bride-to-be persists, as well as the custom of the groom's family furnishing and preparing the wedding feast and serving it at the home of the bride.

❧ ❧ ❧

THE BURIAL OF OLD JOSÉ
As Told by Cristiana Baros

Old José Gutiérrez lay dead in his house. Outside the wind rose and the snow piled up all over the mountainside. La Madera was but lost under the white drifts, and no one knew what to do. José must be buried. The little cemetery was hip-deep in snow, and the icy wind had crusted the top. No grave could be dug there. Nicolás, old José's son, made up his mind. He and his father had brought in all the timbers, the windows, and the doors that went into the building of the little church. They had helped to build it. Their wives had helped to lay the cement-like adobe floor and helped build the altar. He would bury his father there. So the men dug a grave in the adobe floor. They broke a path to the church door and carried the homemade box that contained the body of the old patriarch into the church, and there the mourners held the last rites and buried him.

Within a short time the priest came to them on his monthly visit. He learned in consternation of what the people had done. He ordered the body removed at once, and left the village. Another month rolled around; and the priest returned, and found to his amazement that nothing had been done. His order had been ignored. He lectured them soundly and demanded that without delay the body be taken from the church.

Again he came on his monthly visit. The body of old José was still in its grave in the church floor. He commanded Nicolás to remove it. The man remained obdurate. The priest appealed to others, but they refused to do anything that would wound Nicolás.

The matter went to the Archbishop at Santa Fe. Then the church at La Madera was closed, and the monthly visits of the priest suspended, until such time as the orders were obeyed. Time passed, one year and then many, when no longer voices were lifted in prayer or in the singing of the mass in the La Madera church. And then the Archbishop was found dead! Another succeeded him. The case of La Madera came to his attention. The years of silence in that little church were considered punishment enough. The regular monthly visits of the priest were resumed and now again voices in prayer and the singing of the mass are heard in the little church.

WPA: 5-5-31 #1
January 29, 1939
Words 2521
Subject: Tejón
Sources of information: Federico Otero, José Librado Arón Gurulé, Ramón
Nieto, Patricio Gallegos, Predicando Chaves, Adelaida Chaves, Miscellaneous
Book 2 pp 399 to 401 and Land Office Records pp 250 to 257 at the Country
Court House in Bernalillo. Record Book G p 574 at the Court House in
Albuquerque.

TEJÓN
(Badger)

Tejón is located on the Hagan Road about four and a half miles from the point where the Hagan Road crosses the Loop Drive at the east end of Placitas in Sandoval County. While the name Hagan is a comparatively new one, the road now bearing the name is an ancient and an historic one. It is a natural roadway and the only opening through the mountains from Placitas to Tejón and Hagan. It is a part of the main road from Bernalillo to Golden.

The story of Tejón is not merely a story of the people of Tejón. It is a story typical of the dramas enacted or lived in most of the old Spanish and Mexican Grants given to the early native people and their descendants.

It was on November 17, 1840 that Salvador Barreras appeared before Citizen Antonio Montoya (who signed his name Antonio Montolla) at the place of Angostura, Jurisdiction of Sandía to request for himself and others that their certificate of possession of the tract of 12,801 acres given them by the Mexican Government and called the Tonque and Tejón Grant be judicially executed and placed upon record. And by virtue of the authority vested in him as Constitutional Justice of the Peace, Antonio Montoya granted the request and gave copies of the papers into the hands of Salvador Barreras.

By 1846 Tejón was a flourishing town. On June 21, 1860 the Tonque and Tejón Grant was examined and confirmed by the Congress of the United States, which meant that the government gave a quit-claim deed for the grant to the people of Tejón. On February 11, 1882, Congress approved the grant, calling it the Town of Tejón Grant. The foregoing information is gleaned from Miscellaneous, Book 2, pp. 399-401, and Land Office Records, pp. 250 to 257 at the Court House in Bernalillo, Sandoval County.

Among the first families who built Tejón were: Salvador Barreras, Jesús Barreras, Juan Antonio Chaves, José Chaves, Juan Antonio Zamora, Bonifacio Zamora, Simón Gallegos and Pedro Montoya and others. They built their town on a flat, fertile, and well-watered tract not far from where Tejón Cañón suddenly emerges from the mountains. A ridge of the Sandías rises a short distance to the south of the place and off to the north is San Pedro Mountain. A wide arroyo-scarred area stretches west to join the lands of the San Felipe Pueblo, which forms the boundary of the Tejón Grant. The town was built according to the old Spanish law, which decreed that the house and corral of each family be built in such a manner as to form a wall about the large plaza and with openings or gates left only at the corners. They built their town thus for protection from hostile invaders, just as their ancestors had been compelled to do when they built Las Huertas. That deserted, walled town was less than five miles away, and a well-defined road, through cañons and arroyos, joined them.

Tejón had an abundance of pasturage for their goats and less than two miles away was Uña de Gato (Cat's Claws), an old watering place. There was plenty of water for irrigation and for many household purposes, but this water was salty and unfit for drinking or cooking. In the early days of Tejón, before there were any beasts of burden, the women carried all the water used for drinking and cooking on their heads in tinajas (pottery vessels) from the spring at San Francisco, which was nearly two and a half miles up Tejón Cañón. This carrying of water was not accounted a hardship; it was merely one of the things necessary that life might go on. There was plenty of water for their fields—that was of more importance than having drinking water at hand. That could always be carried from somewhere.

Time passed, the village population increased. Their flocks of goats multiplied. Burros and oxen now lifted body-breaking work from both men and women. Homes were built outside the walls, for there was no more room inside the walls. Then, on a hill not far from the place where the road entered the town, they built a church. It stood like a sentinel outside the walls. Over at the foot of the Sandías they now buried their dead, instead of carrying them on a long, hard journey to the cemetery in San Felipe. Now they placed an old hand-carved San Juan on their altar and held their own fiesta days. Life teemed with interest in the little town. Oxen and heavily laden wagons on their long trips to Estados (The States) plodded their way through the village, for there was the highway and the gates of the town now were always open. Then gold fever struck the section, and prospectors and burros, their backs loaded with "grub" and picks and shovels, wended their way through the town, bound for San Pedro and the hills around Tejón. This gold excitement around Tejón spelled the beginning of the end of that quaint little walled town.

About this time, M.S. Otero, a wealthy sheep and cattle man became interested in the grant. The 12,801 acres of land would naturally interest a sheep man. Then gold was found in the San Pedro Mountains. There was the possibility that much of the grant might be rich in minerals. The Town of Tejón Grant had been confirmed by Congress, but it must also be approved by Congress. That act required money. More money than the people of Tejón could ever pay, for the grant must be surveyed and the boundaries fixed, and legal services must be engaged to make out all the papers and prepare the case and present it to Congress. Such services meant a large amount of money, a small fortune in fact, in the eyes of the people of Tejón. But the Grant of the Town of Tejón was approved by Congress in 1882.

Life went on in the village. In the year 1890, March 28, M.S. Otero filed suit in the District Court at Albuquerque against Luis Chaves, José Antonio Zamora, and others for possession of the Town of Tejón Grant. That meant that every owner of the grant was in court, and their lands and their homes were at stake. But it required money to go to court. More money than the people of Tejón could possibly raise. Besides, M.S. Otero was a banker. The thought of all his money, and of the strange and unaccountable and mysterious ways of the gringos and their courts, bewildered them and left them in a state of apathy. José Librado Arón Gurulé of Placitas made frequent trips to see his kinsmen at Tejón, to advise them and do all he could to stir them to action. "Fight, fight for your homes and your land!" he would shout at them. "There must be something you can do!" But he failed to arouse their long-sleeping spirit of aggression—that paradoxical trait in his people which caused them to endure unspeakable privation and hardships with true heroism, yet which occasioned them to shrug their shoulders and say, "No podemos remediarlo" (We can not help it) whenever calamity overtook them.

It was on May 23, 1893, that the final decree in the case of M.S. Otero vs. José Antonio Zamora and the other citizens of Tejón, was handed down by

the second district court, which gave M.S. Otero the Town of Tejón Grant
except "The claims of Individuals of the Town of Tejón as a corporation, its
successors and assigns. But this exception in this decree is not to be construed
in any manner as affecting the findings by this court. There is not now or ever
has been any such corporation as The Inhabitants of The Town of Tejón." This
information was gathered from Record Book G, p. 574 and from Record of
Case 2942, at the County Court House in Albuquerque.

And so the people of Tejón found themselves with nothing left but the
houses in which they lived and the plaza. They were duly notified of the
owner's intention to close the land of the grant to them. But for a time they did
plant their fields and garnered their harvests. Two or three families saw the writing on the wall and moved away to seek other homes and start life over again.
The rest of them remained obstinate. Then small sums were offered for their
homes. One man, Louicio Barreras, son of Salvador Barreras, accepted twenty
dollars for his holdings. This, said José Librado Arón Gurulé and Ramón Nieto,
as far as we know, is all the money ever paid for the whole of Tejón.

Then the first of a series of decisive blows fell upon the heads of the people of Tejón. An order came demanding them to remove their flocks of goats
from the land of the grant. The grant was closed to them for that purpose.
Some of them sold their flocks, some placed their flocks in the keeping of
people on other grants and divided the increase, and a few sought public land
whereon to pasture their flock. Then one day old Juan Antonio Barreras called
the men together to tell them that hereafter they must go a long way for their
wood. They had been ordered to take no more off the grant. They discussed
the order, and shrugged their shoulders. Their ancestors had lived through
years of dangers, hardships, and privations in this town, surely they could go
on supplying themselves with wood to burn, even if the grant was closed to
them. But the next order was a visitation of doom to them. No longer could
they plant the fields. Those fields were a part of the grant. The grant was
closed to them.

Now the wall around Tejón became indeed a wailing wall. The path outside
the wall to the little church became more beaten than ever from the constant
pounding of feet of the black-shawled women going there to implore aid of the
Patron Saint San Juan. Praying for the restoration of their lands. Praying as all
their people did, to something in which they had faith, in their hours of need.

On September 28, 1904, death called M.S. Otero. His two sons shared in
the Town of Tejón Grant, in the distribution of his estate. They had been reared
in luxury; the tragic side of life had been no part of their experience. They

were visionary. Tejón became a part of their vision. They carried on the work of emptying the town. What a perfectly splendid layout it was for a museum! They were right, but born thirty years too soon for the scheme. Here was a walled town in the manner of 1690. Just outside the wall, depicting the March of Time, was the little church and the houses near by built to accommodate the increase in population. The narrow road through the town, the gates; all so picturesque and so reminiscent of the days of the conquistadores. The houses of adobe and the adobe corrals adjoining them, all facing the plaza they enclosed stood there, striking reminders of the days when, for the sake of protection against hostile invaders, a family and their livestock lived side by side. For a never-to-be-forgotten image of the towns of the long ago, here was Tejón! The church and all the things in it; the old hand-carved San Juan and all the other old handmade wooden saints kept there for occasions other than Tejón's own feast day, the fine altar cloth with its handmade lace, the quaint old candle holders and candelabra made by the hands of the people in Tejón; all now belonged to the new owners of the grant. They bought the church, they said. This story of their vision of Tejón as a museum was told by Federico Otero, one of the owners of the Town of Tejón Grant.

Old Salvador Barreras and his wife Victoriana were the last to leave the town they had helped to build. No one remembers where they went. The new owners now hired old Antonio José Gallegos to watch the place. He was installed in the house on the left-hand side of the south gate, which was the gate nearest the church. But the gates of Tejón could not be closed. Too long the road through the town had been a part of the highway—since the early forties. The watchman found it impossible to protect a wide-open town and he could not be at the church all the time to guard it. His eyes were keen and his limbs nimble enough, but somehow somebody looted the church of all that made it desirable as a museum feature or as anything else, for that matter. The heavy timbers supporting the roofs of the houses mysteriously disappeared, as did doors and windows.

In time the walls crumbled, whole houses fell in ruins, but it did not concern the Otero heirs. The Town of Tejón Grant had slipped through their hands and into the hands of their lawyer, Neil B. Field, who also had a dream, a vision for Tejón. He saw it as a mineral grant and an elaborate prospectus, so exploiting the grant, was written. The above information was also given by Federico Otero.

Today Tejón is fast crumbling into the dust from which it was raised. Its people are scattered far and wide. Its fields lie brown and barren beneath the summer suns and the winter snows. The waters which were once turned into irrigation ditches to flood those fields, flow down through an arroyo and eventually reach the Rio Grande. The name of M.S. Otero is but a memory, and Neil B. Field sleeps beneath the dust. But the story of Tejón will live, just as the stories of old battle grounds have lived.

🙚 🙚 🙚

THE NAMING OF PLACITAS

José Trujillo, age forty-seven, Placitas, New Mexico, told this story. He is a direct descendant of one of the twenty-one families who received the San Antonio de Las Huertas grant from the King of Spain in 1765. His family has lived continuously in the old town of Las Huertas since that date.

"It be a long time ago, my great father tell my father how Las Placitas get the name."

And here is the story of Las Placitas that tradition places at about 1820.

A long time ago some of the descendants of the people who settled Las Huertas wandered back to the home of their fathers. They found the fields of old Las Huertas were no longer broad and fertile, for the water no longer came down to them in abundance from the mountains springs. The few who had remained there, the Trujillo family, had no more than they needed. So, the home seekers went about a mile to the south, where there were a number of little towns in ruins; one little town at Ojo del Oso (Spring of the Bear), just to the east of the present Placitas; a little town by the red mountain with the Indian writing on it, north; a little town by the big arroyo, west; a little town back of the house of José Trujillo, south. These people picked out a place for their new homes and laid out their small fields where water could come down to them from el Oso, and there they built a big town spreading out to the four corners. They called this new village Las Placitas (Little Towns).

Subject: Old Houses of Placitas
WPA: 5-5-49 #23
February 10, 1939
Words 1577
Sources of information: Rumaldita Gurulé, Cristiana Baros, Catalina Gurulé,
José Trujillo, Conception Archibeque.

OLD HOUSES OF PLACITAS

The old houses, like the old villages, were unique. The old villages still remain so where no modern highways have cut through them and robbed them of the charm of primitive simplicity and their narrow lanes which zigzagged about as if to touch every doorstep in them. Placitas is one of those villages to escape the modern touch; the highway went around it, and its winding main street is as always, the only road through it. But the old houses of Placitas are gone with its past. They have been remodeled, expanded about patios, or zaguanes, and another wing added, until the characteristics of the original houses have disappeared.

There was both art and utility in these old houses and their uses were manifold. At once they were home, sanctuary, fortress, storage, and factory. They were the dwellings. They were the places where the patron saint of the village was kept; for there were no churches in the villages in those early days. They were the walls within which the people fortified themselves in cases of hostile invasions. Everything the families possessed in the manner of supplies must be stored in their houses, and everything the families wore was made there and everything the families ate was prepared there.

In Placitas the old houses were built mostly of rocks, of any size and any shape. They were joined together and held intact in a wall with adobe mud, quantities of it, until the walls were as much adobe as rock. The houses were low and the walls from twenty to thirty inches thick. The ceilings were sup-

ported by vigas, the trunks of pines peeled and dried, as they are today, and the ceilings were slender saplings laid evenly and close together crosswise of them. On these saplings was spread a layer of tough, dry grass and over that was spread a layer of adobe mud. The thick mud roof was laid up on top of that. The width of the houses was determined by the length of the pine trunks they could get. In those early days few, very few, possessed beasts of burden. Men and women must bring in their own building material with their own hands or on their own backs. Usually the houses contained two rooms. The windows were small, not much more than peep holes arched high in the thick walls, and the doors were for dwarfs or children, for no others could go through them without doubling over. The floors were adobe mud, made hard by proper drying, and they were not cut into by heels of shoes, for then the people had only tewas (moccasins) to wear, or else they went barefoot. The door and window frames were made of pine logs split into boards by stone axes and stone wedges; for they were all the tools they possessed at that time. The doors were made of these boards put together with wooden pins. If there were any shutters for the tiny windows, they were made in the same way. The house inside and out was plastered with adobe mud. There was left no trace of the rock, and so long as this mud was kept in good condition on those walls the rocks and adobe underneath were unaffected by time or weather.

But it was the inside of these old houses that was quaint and different. The kitchen was the living room. In one corner was a commodious fogón compaña (family fireplace) and adjoining it on one side was the tapanco (porch). Strange to say, this word belongs to the Philippines and means awning. The tapanco was a replica of the porch outside carried out in lesser dimensions, being about two feet from the wall, which would constitute its width, and between four and five feet high. The length depended upon the available space from the fogon compaña to the corner of the room. The columns of the tapanco formed its front and the even, smooth mud roof made a place to store tinajas (pottery vessels), for these vessels were used for every conceivable household purpose, and they were the only cooking utensils and dishes and containers they possessed. Most of the tinajas in the old houses at Placitas were carried here from San Felipe Pueblo. On the tapanco roof were pottery receptacles of varying sizes. The large ones in which meat was cooked, meat in great chunks, the large ones in which the fat parts of animals

were rendered into lard, and pottery bowls for cooking beans and peas and the blue cornmeal; all sizable bowls, and there were small ones for individual use, and there were the tall ones for carrying water, and the low wide ones for carrying food materials.

On the floor of the tapanco the great tinajas were stored. These vessels held food supplies. One was filled with blue meal, another held the lard, another wheat flour, if such there happened to be. Another held the cheese made from the milk of the goat, and this was an important food and was an ingredient of many of their dishes. Here also was stored the large smooth slab of stone and the thick hand-sized ones (the metate and manos for grinding the corn into meal). In fact the floor of the tapanco was the storage place for those household possessions too valuable to be left outside the house. At certain times of the year dried meat was kept there in tinajas. And there was the precious salt. Each year the men made trips to the salt region, in the vicinity of Estansia of today, to bring home salt. It was a trip of around ten days, and large bands of men went together, most of them on foot.

On another side of the room in the kitchen of these old houses a low adobe wall was run about two feet from the wall of the room and parallel to it. Adobe partitions were put in at desired intervals, thus forming bins for the storage of corn, beans, peas, onions, and whatever else they may have harvested. These bins were tragically empty in drout years or in times when the Navajos raided the fields and reaped the harvests.

The center of the floor was the living room and the feasting place. There were no chairs nor tables, and the clean, smooth adobe floor must be used in their stead. The room adjoining the kitchen was the sleeping room. On one side of this apartment was a long, slender pole extending the length of the place and the ends imbedded in the walls; for the pole was placed there as the walls were built. On this pole was hung the blankets—Mexican blankets they were, woven by the women of the family from the wool from their goats, upon the looms which were a vital factor in the lives of the people in these old houses. A loom was in every kitchen. At night these blankets were taken from the pole and made into beds for the family. If the nights be cold, they were folded into snug sleeping bags, if the nights be mild they were simply made into pallets and laid on the floor. These floors of adobe, laid at least eight inches below the threshold, were warm, as no wind could possibly creep in to chill them. These blankets and the pole on which they hung in the daytime and a crude handmade wooden chest were the furnishings of the sleeping room.

The older inhabitants of Placitas say that these old houses were built before 1840, amid the ruins of an unknown pueblo at an unknown date. There were little if any changes made in these dwellings until the eighties, though some articles of furniture were introduced to make living in them more comfortable. There is still to be seen some evidence of the style or these old houses. In the house of José Trujillo the old forms one corner of a new house built around a patio and it is readily distinguished from the later addition by its construction. The old one was bought by Francisco Trujillo in 1854 from one whose name has long been forgotten. But José said the house was an old one when his father purchased it. A one-room house of the early type, belonging to José Baldanado, is still intact. Aside from these the old houses have been lost in the rebuilding and additions, and their quaint interiors are but a memory.

SUBJECT: Life in the Old Houses: Part 1
WPA: 5-5-49 #13
February 24, 1939
Words 2686
Sources of information: David Trujillo, José Trujillo, Josefita Lucero, Avelina Gurulé, Carolina Escarcida. Records of Trujillo Family given to Dave Trujillo Sr. by his grandfather, Juan Tafoya, David Trujillo, José Trujillo, Josefita Lucero, Avelina Gurulé all were grandchildren of Josefa and Miguel.

LIFE IN THE OLD HOUSES: PART I
The Story of Josefa and Her Sons

In the year 1806, in the settlement of Las Huertas, one mile east of Placitas, Theresa Chaves was born. She was the sister of Calletano and Juan Pedro Chaves, who later helped to found and name Ojo de La Casa. Before she was sixteen she was married to Juan Tafoya. In the year 1823, Josefa, their first-born, came into a troubled world, and for her the Fates managed somehow to keep it a troubled world; for Josefa's life was one of toil and sorrows. It was in 1823 that the Mexican Governor at Santa Fe ordered the inhabitants of Las Huertas to abandon their walled town and take up their residence in one of the settlements on the Rio Grande del Norte for protection against the hostile and unrestrained Indians. The infant was taken by her parents and grandparents to Algodones, where they lived for a time. Then Theresa and Juan went to Cienega, not far from Santa Fe. There they built their house, and there many other children were born to them.

As the oldest child, Josefa became her mother's helper. Many responsibilities, and the work of a woman, fell upon her childish shoulders. Her mother taught her all the household arts and duties that fell to the woman's part in the business of living as it was in that day. Josefa was taught to cook, to prepare and conserve foods, to plant and tend the kitchen garden, and to safely carry tinajas (pottery vessels) of water and goats' milk upon her head. She learned to weave cloth from the goat's wool and to fashion the material she wove into garments for the family—blankets for household use and serapes (shawls) for the family to wear about them in the cold weather. She was taught to make the red dye from an herb, that the color might be combined with the natural wool of gray and black to make the blankets more attractive. Josefa could grind the blue corn into very fine meal, she could make tortillas and sopapillas (fried buns) expertly and as well she could plaster adobe walls with mud and lay even smooth adobe mud floors and build fogón compañas (fire places for the family) and keep them in repair, and she could help build adobe houses and make the tapanco, which was a porch built into the kitchen to be used as a cupboard.

Josefa was both pious and lovely of face and form. They said she managed to find time to keep her black hair neat and shining and her dress clean. Her little brown feet were calloused on the bottom, for barefoot she ran over the fields and rocks like a deer. Her small hands were hard from toil but there was a light in her black eyes, and she was ever ready to turn work into play.

Then one day the Fates caused a gay young caballero from Mexico to stop at Cienega. He met Juan Tafoya, who offered the handsome stranger the hospitality of his house. It happened to be dinnertime. Theresa had just placed a large tinaja of meat in the middle of the floor, the tortillas were ready to be eaten, and the family was gathering for the meal. As they squatted on the floor in a circle about the tinaja of meat, the flashing brown eyes of the gay caballero met the twinkling black ones of Josefa. The auburn-haired youth had no father to conduct his love affair with the father of Josefa, so he undertook the matter himself. In a short time they were married by the priest in San Felipe.

It must have been that the young couple came down to the deserted town of Las Huertas to live, for all their children were born there. The young wife of the gay caballero, whose name was Miguel Trujillo, could have been no older than fifteen years when she bore a son in 1838. To this day ruins of the first house built by the couple are to be seen in old Las Huertas. When the house was finished, it was the usual two-roomed abode constructed after the manner of the day. Thick fortress-like walls, low ceilings made of slender saplings laid evenly and close-together crosswise of the vigas (trunks of trees peeled and dried and laid across the walls to support the ceiling and mud roof). Small windows high in the walls, one to a room, and doors not five feet high. The rooms of the very early houses were small and were built primarily for protection and storage: Protection from the weather, hostile attacks, and wild animals; storage for all their possessions. It was a place to sleep in safety, and to carry on the work so necessary to their existence, but the real living room was the great out-doors and the sun-bathed adobe walls were the real lounges.

It was very probable that Josefa and Miguel repaired and occupied a house within the walls of the abandoned town until they made another ready. It must have been that at least two or three other families came with them; for at that time life was not only hard but fraught with dangers, yet no traditions among the descendants of the Trujillo family tell any. They say Josefa and her husband were alone in Las Huertas, but she had cousins, uncles and aunts from Algodones who were building homes for themselves in Placitas at that time.

A few years passed and the light-hearted Miguel carried on the work which befell the head of a family. He tended his flock of goats and his fields, while Josefa daily practised the housewifely arts learned in the home of her father. And there were her babies: Francisco, Rufrigia, and Virginia. They must have food and clothing, all of which must be materialized by the moth-er. More and more the duties of parenthood were forgotten by the still care-free Miguel, who dreamed of the open roads and the adventures of the day. Eagerly he gave ear to the tales of the world outside, of the rumbles of war in Mexico. His feet itched to be on his way, to be going somewhere. He related to Josefa the tales he had heard as the family squatted about the big tinaja of meat and beans in the middle of the floor, each helping himself from the pot with his fingers. Josefa listened, not once thinking that her brown-eyed, auburn-haired Miguel longed to become a part of it all. More babies came: Melesia, Rosalia. With patience Josefa tended her kitchen garden, cooked and washed her tinajas, and kept them in neat array on the tapanco. She scoured and combed and wove the goat's wool into cloth. She no longer had the time to weave blankets. One man at Placitas, his name long ago forgotten, was an expert weaver. For portions of the wool or other considerations such as hides, milk, cheese, and corn, he did much of the weaving for the community.

It was the year 1846. General Kearny floated the Stars and Stripes over the Old Palace at Santa Fe and declared the land and the citizens to be Amer-ican from that date. That momentous event meant nothing to Josefa but to Miguel it spelled adventure. Leaving his eight-year-old son to tend the flock, he slipped away. Josefa, who had no understanding of wanderlust, mourned him as dead, and because she knew no creed but work, she bent her energies to the task of rearing her family. Little Francisco became the shepherd but also at evenings when his flock was corralled at the side of the house, he helped his mother feed the other children their supper of atole (a drink made of milk and the roasted ground blue corn) and helped her fold the blankets into pallets and put the children to bed. Time passed and Josefa carried on, though much of the time some kinsman watched over the family in their lonely home, even if they could not aid materially; for in those strenuous times most of them were poor.

As the family grew Josefa found that they needed more and more corn. That, she could not provide. But there was plenty of milk from her goats. So she carried tinajas of it, one at a time on her head, to the Pueblo of San Felipe, where she traded it for the precious meal, which she brought home with her in the tinajas on her head. The journey to San Felipe was five miles but always she was home again with her children in the early afternoon. Nearly always she must leave them alone. She felt worried about it. So early and late Josefa toiled to wring a living for her brood from the place she had chosen for a home. But there were a few days of pleasure in her years. The fiesta day in San Felipe and now and then a baile (dance) in nearby Placitas.

After two years of the free life of the open spaces, the gay caballero came home again. But Francisco continued to tend the flock, the flock that had increased considerably; and Josefa went on shouldering the responsibility of providing for her children. In due season a son, Joaquín, was born. Rufrigia was now past eight years and old enough to share her mother's burdens. She could care for the younger children while indulging her love of play, for they said she was a merry child just as her mother was. Work and hardships were endured as always. Then came David. Miguel waited only long enough to see that the baby had brown eyes and hair like his own, as most of the other children were black-eyed, black-haired. And then he vanished, never to be seen by them again.

Josefa with her added though loved burdens faced relentless toil alone once more. For a time she kept the fogón compaña going and the tinaja full of meat, but her old strength and driving power were dwindling. None of her people could desert their own homes to stay with her, and she would not listen to their plea to bring her family and make her home with some of them. Finally she lost her health; there was nothing to do but to scatter her children among her relatives. Her girls were taken to Cienega to live in the house where the gay young caballero wooed their mother. Fourteen-year-old Francisco, with the experience of a man, struck out for himself, bought an old house in Placitas, repaired it, and took his brother Joaquín to live with him. With her youngest son, Josefa lived with a sister in Algodones until she should recover. Francisco tended his flock and cared for his small brother. Thus went

the family fortunes until the year 1861. Francisco answered Governor Connelly's call for volunteers to engage in the Civil War, which strife had spread
to New Mexico. Joaquín was now ten years of age and able to look out for
himself. Just when Josefa returned to her home is not known.

Soon after the close of the war Francisco drove a double span of oxen in
a wagon train loaded with wool bound for Los Estados (The States). When he
returned about six months later, he brought from Kansas City the first real
wedding dress ever seen in Placitas. It was made of heavy brocaded silk,
creamy white, the first piece of silk ever owned by any person in the village.
This beautiful silk wedding gown was made with a long, very wide skirt gathered on to a very tight bodice with puffs at the shoulders and with long
sleeves. The arrival of this wonderful dress created a furor, and every maid and
matron hastened to the house of the Armijos to see and touch the silken material with her own hands. For it was there it was taken by Francisco himself to
his bride-to-be, Miquela Armijo, daughter of Juan Armijo who was blessed
with more worldly goods than the rest of them.

In a short time Francisco and Miquela were married at San Felipe, and
they started life together in the old house Francisco had bought. There their
children were born. As the years passed they added rooms to the original
house leaving it to form a corner of the new. An adobe wall was built to complete the patio at the rear of the house and thus it is to this day.

Soon after the marriage of her son Francisco, Josefa made her last trip over
the old trail down Las Huertas Cañón and up the Camino de Real, across the
Rio Grande to the San Felipe Pueblo. But this time she did not return. She was
carried there on the ladder made for bearing the dead. Her son Dave, now nearly nine, went to the house of Juan Armijo, there to pay his way with his labor.
He was given a flock of goats to tend. Time passed. When he had acquired a
flock of his own, he returned to the house of his mother, claimed the whole of
Las Huertas Cañón, where the original settlers of the place built their walled
town and cultivated their fields. There he too built a house and corrals, a home
for Juliana Baca of Bernalillo, his bride. There he lived and reared his own children, most of them with brown eyes, auburn hair, and light skin.

After making adventurous trips over the old Santa Fe Trail to Los Estados, Joaquín married and lived in Bernalillo. They said that somewhere he
found a sheepskin bag of money that was somehow lost when the great and
wealthy dons along the Rio Grande sent out servants to hide their treasure
when they had word of a raid from the South. But true it was that Joaquín used
to make trips from Bernalillo to some secret place in Las Huertas Cañon and

always after the mysterious visit, on which no one was ever allowed to attend him, he had gold in his pockets. Many have searched for this treasure in vain. But even had it existed, it would be spent by now for Joaquin lived to be an old, old man.

In the house of Francisco Trujillo was an old hand, carved wedding box. It was carefully and reverently guarded through the years for inside it, like a rare jewel, reposed the silken wedding dress of Miquela. In time it came to be the inheritance of Melecia, oldest daughter of Francisco and Miquela, who lived out her life in the house with her brother Jose and his family. Melecia was sickly all her days. Her dreams of marriage, of children, never came true. In spite of her broken health she lived a half a century. In later years she mourned in bitterness the barrenness of her life. The wedding dress in the box became a symbol of what she had missed. On her death bed she commanded that it be her shroud. So to the grave went the wedding dress brought from Kansas City by Francisco Trujillo just after the Civil War. And that is why the women of Placitas today know so much about the wedding dress of Miquela. Melecia died in 1921.

SUBJECT: Life in the Old Houses: Part II
WPA: 5-5-49 #14
March 17, 1939
Words 3323
Sources of information: Adelaida Chaves, Predicondo Chaves,
José L.A. Gurulé.

LIFE IN THE OLD HOUSES: PART II
Life in the House That Juan Built
As told by Adelaida Chaves

It was shortly before the year 1860, that Juan Armijo and Guadalupe Barelas de Armijo, his wife, of the vicinity of Alameda, decided to bring their family, attendants, and effects to Placitas and there build a house and live out their days. Why they abandoned their property on the Rio Grande is not definitely known, but it is believed to be because Juan thought he could better protect his livestock from the raids of the Indians if he had them in the mountains around Placitas than he could along the Camino Real (Royal Highway), where every adventurer and raider in the Southwest roamed at will. Juan was plentifully blessed with cattle, herds of sheep and goats. He was considered a man of means-consequently, a target for the thieving invaders.

Excitement was rampant in Placitas the day he arrived. It was as if a small army was passing along the winding lane through the village, on its way to encamp upon a rise overlooking the village near the foothills of the mountains just southeast of the place. There were heavy, creaking carretas drawn by slow-plodding oxen. To the height of their sides the carretas were piled with corn and wheat and hay and forage, all for the cows which were bringing up the rear of the long train. There was a carreta loaded with household pottery and blankets being piloted along the rough road as carefully as the driver of the oxen could steer them. Another and yet another cart and more were loaded with the family and the female servants. There was a goodly company of retainers, for Juan required much help in the management of his livestock and his household. Whether these families were slaves or peons in bondage for debt was not known, but they were brought to Placitas with the Armijo family and were members of the household. There was Juan Pacheco and his family who had charge of the many sheep. There was Nativido Escarcida and his family, and Soledad, who spent most of her days on her knees with her stones, grinding the blue corn into meal. Her family name has years since been forgotten. There were many more servants in the Armijo house but their names, too, have passed with them from the memory of the descendants of Juan and Lupe. If Juan and Lupe possessed any house furnishings besides their countless tinajas (pottery vessels) and their blankets and serapes (shawls), they left them behind with their deserted valley house along the Camino Real. The noisy, troublesome part of the train which passed through Placitas on that long-ago day were the herds of sheep and goats. But by nightfall the entire assemblage was in temporary quarters on the sloping hill Juan had previously chosen for his building site.

The tumbled ruins of an ancient pueblo on the spot where Placitas was built furnished an abundance of rock for everybody, with no effort other than to pick them up. In a short time Juan and his sons and his band of servants had the new house well started. Plenty of rock and plenty of adobe mud, to lay into walls while some of the servants with oxen brought timbers from the mountains, and others made adobes; for the house was not all to be built of rock. While the building was in progress, the usual work of the day; cooking, preparing food, caring for the livestock, milking the cows, and other necessary labor went on and required the time of many persons to do it. Juan found that he must hire labor to help build his house. Of those he engaged of his new neighbors, Francisco Trujillo remained with him and became a trusted leader of his servants. It was Francisco who helped him engineer his marketing trips, with wagons and carretas loaded with wool for the buyers in Los Estados (The States). It was Francisco who married his eldest daughter, Miquela.

When the house of Juan was finally completed, it resembled in miniature the walled towns of his early fathers in the days of Spanish rule. A placeta entirely enclosed by rooms with doors opening out on to it and with but one direct entrance into the placeta and that was through a zaguán. A second zaguán opened from the placeta into the corral bordering the house on the west. All the rooms had tiny windows built high in the thick walls of the house, and the doors were small and made by joining boards at the top and bottom to poles with wooden pins, the poles extending beyond the boards at one side. These two poles fitted into holes made for them in one side of the doorway, through the jamb and into the wall, thus the door was held in place. These doors were called puertas de sambugo. The word sambugo could not be explained but it is probably a form of samblaje that means joinery. In the daytime these doors were removed and set against the walls, handy for replacement at night or in cases of danger. The shutters for the little windows were made in the same manner. In Juan's house there were four huge rooms on the south side of the placeta; they were protected by a long porch in the placeta. The first was the family sleeping room, next was the cocina (kitchen) the most important room of the house. A big fogón compaña (family fireplace) filled one corner and extended well out into the room. An iron bar projected from the fireplace in a position convenient for holding meat. On that bar meat was roasted or broiled daily while a large tinaja of meat cooked in a deep bed of flowing embers below. Adjoining the kitchen was the largest room in the row. It was the storeroom and beyond that was the tapanco (porch). In the small old houses the storage bins of adobe and the tapanco for storing pottery and tinajas of food and other things connected with food, were built into the kitchen, but in this big house of Juan there were rooms, large ones, devoted to the purpose. All around the storage room except at the doorways a low adobe wall was run about three feet from the walls of the room and parallel to them, with adobe partitions set in to form bins. All these bins were filled with supplies of grain, corn, beans, peas, onions, dried fruits, and with whatever else was harvested for food, as well as feed for the cows. The tapanco, which held the tinajas that served for every household purpose practically filled a room; the rest of the space held the loom. Weaving blankets and serapes in the Armijo household was an art and a profession and a hobby. It was Juan himself who did all the weaving, not because he must, but because he was an artist and he worked his dreams out in wool. He produced his blankets only in gray, white, and black. He refused to bother with the herbs and flowers which gave a gay color to the wool, a gorgeous red, but which never survived a washing nor wear in the sun. Juan's loom was a heavy affair with a malacate (hoisting apparatus). Among the effects of María Armijo de Lucero, one of the older of the ten children of Juan and Lupe, who died in 1933 at the age of eighty-five, there was an old loom which is thought to be the one made by Juan Armijo and used by him for so many years before his death.

    In the house that Juan built there was a sala grande (great room). This and one sleeping room enclosed the placeta on the north. This sleeping room was the guest room. Many notables of the day passed the night there. Juan's house was known for its fine hospitality. Priests and politicians were frequent guests. On his monthly visit to Placitas the priest was at home in this guest room in the northwest corner of the placeta, for in those days of slow travel the good padre must remain over night in the villages he visited. In stirring political campaigns the Armijo placeta was the scene of many a scheming political huddle and the guest room was never empty of republican leaders, for Juan was heart and soul Republican, and he could and did deliver votes to his chosen candidates on election days. Under his sway the popular vote of Placitas never varied.

To return to the house of Juan, all the rooms on the east and the west sides of the placeta were sleeping rooms—some for the family, others for the servants.

🐾 🐾 🐾

A BUSY DAY IN THE HOUSE OF JUAN

No one greeted the rising sun from his bed in Juan's household. In fact it was always the sun that was the laggard. Its first rays fell athwart the placeta humming with activity. When the sun shone straight down on them, it would be noon and dinner must be ready, and dinner was a matter of converting the raw materials at hand into eatables. That process consumed both time and labor. Everywhere about the placeta women were on their knees performing various tasks: some grinding the blue, or pueblo corn into meal between the stones, one grinding dried peas in the same manner, into a fine meal to be used to brew a drink, the substitute for coffee, one on her knees before a large smooth slab of stone making the bread that would be baked in the hot ashes in the fogón compaña. Another washing the breakfast pottery in a large pottery bowl, another kneading and smoothing a large quantity of tallow and then placing strings in the proper places on the flattened tallow and molding it into candles with the hands, which was more simple than melting the tallow and pouring it into molds made for the purpose. Juan's household required many candles and the supply must be replenished frequently. Another worker made the cheese, huge quantities of it. In this large household a big tinaja of it was consumed at a dinner. Then much of it was used in the making of bread puddings, the finishing dish for occasions. While this work was in progress in the placeta Lupe was in the kitchen cooking the meat. Always meat was cooking in the tinaja in the fireplace or was broiling or roasting on the iron bar above the embers; venison, buffalo meat, mutton, goat meat, with now and then wild fowls or beef adding zest to the appetites of the meat-eaters.

But there was other work, not much but some, to be done daily besides preparing food and cooking it. Each sleeping room must have the blankets from which the pallets were arranged, taken up from the floor, dusted well, and hung on the long pole which was made into the room as a line to hold this bedding in the daytime. The hard mud floors must be carefully swept. For this purpose there were homemade brooms of long stiff grass bound together and tied at the upper portion. The placeta must be swept and the tapanco and storeroom must be set in perfect order each day. Often the walls of the kitchen must be cleaned of smoke and dust, and laying new adobe floors was an oft-repeated task. Aside from all these labors there was the weaving of wool into cloth and the making of it into garments for the women and children and into shirts for the men. Many skins of animals tanned to perfection by a member of the great household were made into breeches for the men and boys and leggings and tewas (moccasins) for the whole clan. This work with the skins was full-time employment for one member of the household. It was said that there was much merriment on rainy days caused by the shrinking of these breeches; when they got wet they came only to a point midway between the knee and thigh of the wearer and were skin tight. Often the wearer had to be pulled out of them.

The men of the clan were as busy as the women. Sheep and goats to herd and then guard in the night. Their wool to be sheared and packed for market. Cattle to herd out to graze and drive back in the corral west of the house at evening, and the milking and the feeding of them. The continual hauling of wood for fuel. The seasonal cultivation of the land, the going on hunts; the killing and dressing of animals for food, food necessary to their existence. Making the annual trips for salt to the region of the present Estancia; and through it all on the constant alert for Indian raids.

And now on this busy day came the dinner hour. Down on the spacious kitchen floor they squatted about the big tinajas of meat and cheese. Small tinajas and calabazas (gourds) served to hold the "coffee," for such they called the beverage made of ground dried peas. Meat was lifted from the tinajas on the points of hunting knives and eaten with fingers, as were the other varieties of food eaten.

It was not strange that Juan should cling to this simple mode of life in spite of his money. He was born with the breath of freedom in his nostrils and a disregard for the frills of civilization. His father was a Navajo prisoner of war captured by an Armijo family somewhere near Alameda. In consequence the name Armijo was given him. He became a trusted member of the family. Almost nothing is known of him except that, and the fact that he had a son, Juan, with Spanish blood in his veins. It was this blood in Juan that gave him a genius for putting others to work for him and creating money and power for himself. It was the blood of his fathers in him that bound him to the primitive ways of living. And as for Lupe, she was too engrossed in childbearing and rearing and the heavy responsibilities of her large household to trouble her mind about the method of carrying on.

Then Nicolás Gurulé, father of José Librado Arón Gurulé, made a table and some benches for his kitchen, making and smoothing the boards himself he split from trunks of large pines, fixing them together neatly with wooden pins; even some hand carving was attempted. That revolutionary idea in dressing up a kitchen ushered in the furniture period in Placitas. Juan Armijo at once conceived the notion of making a trip to Kansas City with carretas of wool and bringing back things for his house. Francisco Trujillo helped engineer the venture, which turned out most successfully. Most of the cargo was copper kettles and brilliant-hued clothing and real coffee and sugar. The next year another journey was made over the Santa Fe Trail to "Los Estados" (The States). Juan's dreams expanded. He would make yearly trips to the markets in Kansas City with his wool: he would enlarge his sala grande and establish a trading post. Placitas was growing. La Madera was only four miles away and on La Ceja del Camino de San Pedro (The Road of the Mountain Summit of San Pedro), a good canyon road, Ojo de La Casa but a mile away and prospectors drifting in now and then to look over the old Montezuma Mine. Then Tejón was about three and a half miles down the Tejón Cañón. A finer location for a trading post could not be found, was the opinion of the business-wise Juan. So the sala grande was extended considerably.

It was at this juncture that a mysterious stranger, a gringo, found his way into the placeta of Juan Armijo. He was Wes Courteny and that was all he ever said of himself. He was a large, fine-looking young man of German descent, well educated and an interesting storyteller. He spoke Spanish fluently. In the evenings when the clan beneath the roof of Juan gathered in the placeta, Wes regaled them with delightful tales of the outside world, for the hospitable roof was also offered as shelter to the stranger and a place at the table was made for him. An idea was again simmering in Juan's head. Placitas had teachers, good ones who had taught the children to read and write in Spanish. Here was a man who could add a little English learning to the Spanish as he went along. And so it was that Wes Courteny became a teacher. One of the first things he did was to marry one of his pupils, the pretty Pablita, daughter of Juan Armijo. Pablita was devoutly Catholic; she must be married by the priest at Bernalillo. Wes was agreeable and accepted her faith as his own. For a while the school teacher and his bride lived in the house that Juan built. Then in due time they moved to a small house built in the mode of the day. Meantime, Juan's plans for a trading post went forward. The sala grande was no more, it was ready for the reception of its store of merchandise when it should arrive.

And then the Grim Reaper suddenly closed the earthly account of Juan. He was buried in Bernalillo.

Lupe gallantly rose to the occasion and tried to be a competent head of the family. Those of her children who had not died were married. Pablita with her two tiny girls, Beatriz and Adelaida, was home with Lupe, her dream of happiness dispelled with the sudden and unaccountable disappearance of the mysterious gringo Wes Courteny. To this day the people in Placitas, the older ones living who knew him, believe he was murdered in some strange place and their respect for him still holds.

The fortune of Lupe was fast dissipated by her sons who undertook to carry on the various activities their father had left. Not one of them inherited his ability in any line. In 1888 Lupe was buried in Bernalillo with Juan. Her two remaining sons, Andrés and Augustino, took possession of the house that Juan built. They partitioned the sala grande into rooms and each took one half of the big house. Thus, Andrés established himself in the south and east rooms and Augustino occupied the north and west rooms. The placeta went to Andrés. The place where the corral was built became the property of Augustino, who further added to his number of rooms on the west by enclosing the zaguán. The daughters, Miquela, María, and Pablita, so they say, received nothing of the estate of Juan and Lupe.

Many years have passed since the burial of Juan, which exact date is uncertain, though it is thought to be about the year 1879. The house he built has passed from the hands of his descendants. The childless widow of Augustino still dwells in his portion of the old dwelling. The other part of the house is owned by Frank Pearce, an old-time Albuquerque businessman. And strange are the ways of fate. His part of the old sala grande is now occupied by The Placitas Trading Post.

SUBJECT: Life in the Old House, Part III
WPA: 5-5-49 #15
April 7, 1939
Words 2432
Sources of information: José Librado A. Gurulé, Patricio Gallegos, Magdalena
Gallegos, Catalina Gurulé.

LIFE IN THE OLD HOUSES: PART III
The Story of Néstor and Maruja Pais

In the intimate history of villages there usually appear the tales of their lazy
men who hate to get up in the morning and who loaf in front of fire or out in
the sun during the winters and in cooling shadows in the summers, and whose
families are the objects of village sympathy and charity. And so in Old Placitas there was Néstor who would not exert himself if he could possibly avoid
it and whose abiding alibi for side-stepping his family responsibilities was an
ailing back. He was a large man with plenty of reserve strength, which
cropped out only in cases of self-preservation. Maruja, his wife, was a small,
thin woman who was ever alert for opportunities to earn a measure of corn or
wheat here, a sheep there, a goat elsewhere, and material for clothing anywhere. She must support her children, and there were three of them: Juan,
Rita, and Tony.

Néstor and Maruja lived in a small house built by the side of the winding
road at the edge of the village, where it turned off to meander to the mountain
foothills—the place men and boys went for wood. Their field lay behind the
house. Each spring Maruja's old uncle José prepared the field for her to plant
her onions, peas, corn, chili, and melons, as Néstor had neither plow nor an
animal to pull it. José would bring his oxen and arado, a plow made from a
heavy, stout forked branch of an oak tree, the forks forming the handles of the
plow and the place from which they sprang being sharpened to a point to dig
the furrows in the soil. The point was often protected by a flat piece of iron,

which also increased the facility for digging. (In those days men searched for scraps of iron with hope and diligence, just as they searched for gold a decade later, and pieces of iron were about as scarce and as difficult to find).

Alone Maruja cared for her garden, that is, until her children were able to help. Besides this Maruja did extra work at the big house of Juan Armijo. For pay she took goats. In this way she accumulated a small herd for her son Juan to tend. In seasons after that when Maruja had the milk of her goats, she made cheese and carried it in a tinaja on her head to San Felipe Pueblo and exchanged it for blue cornmeal. Her small patch of corn in her garden fell far short of her family's needs. Then in the harvest seasons Maruja, with a few other women who needed to supplement the family supplies of necessities, went to the plano (the wide, smooth stretch of land beyond the deep arroyo on the south side of Placitas) and there cut the tall, brown, tender grass and tied it into neat bundles and exchanged it for whatever they could get in Bernalillo. They say Maruja was a fine laundress. For this work she received various things in exchange, which aided her in caring for her family. Little money was paid for labor in those long ago days prior to the big mining excitement in the middle seventies.

Maruja's life was not all drab. There was the help-yourself laundry in the big arroyo where the women met and gossiped as they beat their clothes with sticks on the smooth rocks when the water came down and covered them. For soap they used the roots of the amole plant, which grew so abundantly in the vicinity. Nor were the long leaves of the plant wasted. They were torn into long, slender shreds, laid out to dry, and when they were thoroughly toughened by the sun, they were greased and straightened out and lo, there was thread with which to sew the coarse cloth. Thread with which to tie the red chili pods together when making them into ristras (strings, or files) to hang them up to dry. Every family needed this thread made from the leaves of the amole, for poor beyond poor were the ones who did not have ristras of red chili to hang against their adobe walls to dry in the warm autumn sun. Manta, the coarse creamy cloth from Mexico that was made into suits for the men, was often sewed with this thread. Manta was also made into suits for the boys and was sewed with this homemade thread. Every mother and daughter knew how to make this thread and use it, for every garment that the women and children wore at that time was made by hand, and most of the garments of the men. This coarse cotton cloth called manta was used so extensively for men's and boys' wear that the suits made from them were called mantas. They consisted of two pieces, calzoncillos and camisa (drawers and shirt). The drawers were so called because they were fastened about the waist by a drawstring, which was made of the manta also. The shirt of these suits pulled down over the tops of the drawers. These garments were so universally worn after the breeches of animal skins were abandoned that they were recognized as a native costume. As well, the wide gathered skirt worn with a shirt made in the same manner as the camisa of the men, except the ruffle or pleats sewed to the bottom of it for trimming, which was so generally worn by the women, was recognized as a native dress. This feminine dress was mostly made of merino, woven in the old houses from the wool of the goats until cotton cloth brought up from Mexico became attainable in the middle seventies, and then it was only those who could afford to pay the price of the imported material who made the change. The finer cloth that was brought over the Santa Fe Trail from Los Estados was possessed only by those who were of the more fortunate class. Of these there were some in every village, but Maruja and her family were of the poor that villages have with them always. Her dress was made of merino or the coarse manta. Her grandmother who lived in Algodones helped her with her clothes problem. This old lady, name long ago forgotten except Delorica, was an expert weaver. She gathered up all the old rags she could find, unraveled them, rolled the threads so carefully knotted together into balls, and then rewove them into cloth. This reconstructed material was by no means as durable as the original, but it had wearing qualities that warranted the work it cost. Her delight was to reweave the bright red ravelings obtained from worn-out petticoats of the bayeta (red flannel), which was brought from Mexico. Usually she put this thread into blankets.

It was old Delorica who practically raised Maruja's son Juan from the dead when he was fifteen. He lay delirious, his body burning with fever and none of them knew more to do than had already been done. Doctors had no part in the life of the people at that time. Then someone thought of Delorica and went to Algodones to bring her. When she arrived she found the boy's condition alarming. The family and friends gathered around his pallet believed he was dying. At once Delorica set to work. There were certain things she must have, things she must do with them after they were assembled. She needed poleo (dried pennyroyal) but that was a simple matter, for every household had some. She required an egg. One was brought from a neighbor. (José Librado Arón Gurulé said that chickens had been in Placitas about as long as the people). Then Delorica must have some paper. That was not so easy; paper was rare and the little there was in the village was held a treasured possession. Nevertheless, someone produced what was needed. Maruja had salt in her house.

Delorica took three small pieces of paper and pricked holes in them with a cactus thorn. She whipped the white of the egg, mixed it with the poleo and spread it on the papers and sprinkled salt over it, then she laid a piece of cloth over each of the three poultices she had made. She placed one on the sole of each of the boy's feet, the paper side to the flesh and bound them there as a bandage. Then she waited for the fever to start downward. In due time she applied the third poultice to his head and bandaged it there. These poleo applications would break the fever, she said, and cure Juan.

Meanwhile, Maruja devoutly offered supplications to San Antonio, the patron saint of the village. She made a vow that if the good saint would hear her prayers and heal her son, she would bring him into her house and never while she lived would she allow him to be taken from it.

Juan lived, and both saint and poleo poultice were accorded the credit and to this day are considered powerful healers in cases of fever. Maruja kept her vow, and a little hand-carved image of San Antonio had a prominent place in her house. It was not known who carved the image nor what became of it when Maruja passed away, which time was thought to be about 1880.

But this healing of Juan was not the only miracle that befell the house of Néstor and Maruja. While Juan lay ill of the fever, Néstor found himself forced to tend the flock of goats. At that time, around 1875, the Sandía mountains were well populated with bears. They were a menace to the herds of sheep and goats and a terror to the herders. Always they must be on the alert for the animals, and though they carried bows and arrows and Virola Amarias, the name given the few guns in the community at that time, the herders seldom ever waged war upon these ugly bears. The arrows were too ineffectual, and the guns that fired but one slug or ball at a time consumed too much time in reloading. An angry bear which had been injured only by a shot could destroy the assailant before he could reload his gun. So the bears were allowed to take toll—a sheep or a goat—and go away while the herders sought safety for themselves. On one particular day Néstor left his herd to pursue a deer. He was greedy for deer meat. He never bothered himself with the hunts and accepted readily of the meat friends offered him. But now was his chance to kill a deer for himself. In his plunge through the tall pines he came face to face with a big bear. In his fright he acted upon his first impulse. He fired at it but succeeded only in frightening it. On it came. They grappled, so said Néstor, and the bear got Néstor's head in his great mouth. Néstor prayed as he never had prayed in all his life, prayed to God and to San Antonio to deliver him. He vowed that he would no longer neglect his family if he was saved from the bear. While he prayed he thought of the hunting knife in his belt. He seized it and ripped the stomach of the bear open. The animal fell to the ground writhing in agony. Néstor's throat and head were torn and bleeding. He wandered about, not knowing which way to go, so far up the mountain he had pursued the deer. Then he stumbled upon a trail. It led to La Madera. There friends washed and dressed his wounds and went with him to find his herd and then brought him home, where he told the exciting tale of his adventure and of his vow which is told to this day.

It was shortly before Maruja's death that Rita gave her father his chance to prove the sincerity of that vow. The son of a worthy family in Algodones had seen Rita while she was visiting her grandmother Delorica there, and he had fallen in love with her. He wrote a letter to Néstor telling him of the state of his heart toward his daughter and asked for her. Néstor could not read the message so he carried it to José Librado Arón Gurulé, the young school master in Placitas, who read it to Néstor and then wrote the reply he dictated. Soon came the young man to make arrangements for the big baile (dance), and he wanted it to be a grand affair. Néstor's house was too small for the affair, but there was the sala grande (large room) in the house of Juan Armijo where many guests could be entertained. In those days the refreshments for all festivities, except weddings, were wholly liquid—wine and plenty of it. And so the important event took place. Two fiddlers furnished the music. It was during the cuadrillo (the quadrille) that the prendario (betrothal ceremony) was performed. As they danced, Rita and her lover exchanged rings and placed them on each other's fingers, thus signifying that the two would very soon be married. In a few days they were wedded by the priest in San Felipe. It was Néstor who provided Rita with the ring she must give her groom-to-be. It was Néstor who provided the means wherewith to dress his family for the wedding. It was evident that he had kept his vow.

The prendario of Maruja and Néstor's time is gone with other pretty, quaint customs attending marriages those and earlier days.

Rita went to live in Algodones. After Maruja's death her remaining family went away, just where no one seemed to know. Years have passed since that day but the story of Néstor and Maruja still lives. Perhaps it was the miracles which happened to them that keeps their story alive.

SUBJECT: Life in the Old House: Part IV
WPA: 5-5-49 #16
May 5, 1939
Words 2769
Sources of information: Conception Archibeque, José L.A. Gurulé, Nicolás Gurulé, Avelina Gurulé, Fermenia Durán, Patricio Gallegos. Conception Archibeque was the daughter of Francisco Gonzales and Conception (Chonita) Tafoya de Gonzales of this story. José L.A. Gurulé was the son-in-law of Francisco and Conception. Nicolás Gurulé is the grandson of Francisco and Conception. Avelina Gurulé was the niece of the Francisco Trujillo. Fermenia Durán married Salomé Gonzales, son of Francisco and Conception. The grandfather of Patricio Gallegos, Cassimero Gallegos, was a friend of Francisco.

LIFE IN THE OLD HOUSES: PART IV
(Interwoven with the story of Francisco Gonzales)

As nearly as can be estimated, Francisco Gonzales was born in the year 1818, for they say he was just past one hundred when he died. He was buried in the little cemetery at Placitas in 1919. The place of his birth was also an uncertainty, but it was either in Algodones or the vicinity of Alameda. He married Conception Tafoya (she was always called Chonita) in Alameda and there three first children were born. They probably moved to Placitas about 1861. The house they built was a small one on the winding lane right in the heart of the village.

He was no sooner settled in this house than he answered Governor Connelly's call for volunteers to "resist an armed force from the state of Texas." His oldest child, Margarita María, was eight years old and there were other children. They said Francisco left his family with plenty to carry them through

177

his absence. Also they say it was his intense patriotism that prompted him to go to war. It must have been that, for he was a man of deep religious sentiment, a kind and charitable neighbor and a friend in need, always of cheerful disposition and ever ready to enter the spirit of the simple pleasures of the village. He was the one and only médico (doctor) that Placitas ever had. He could successfully set any broken bone no matter how bad the break. God blessed him with this gift, his neighbors believed, and in those old days of hard work and wild animals and hunts there was much need of his expert services. But he could never be induced to administer remedies. According to his belief, nothing was more potent than the power of the saints, the poleo (pennyroyal) poultice, the tea of an herb, called cota, the bandage for the head, dripping wet with salty vinegar. These, in his opinion, were ultras in the cure of human ailments.

But Francisco will be remembered for other things than his patriotism and his God-given gift of bone-setting. He had a full, rich voice, a wonder voice, and he loved to sing. His favorite song was "Indita El Tecolote" (Indita The Owl), which was an Indian song. When he sang, the whole village gathered about his house to hear him. And often in the evening he sat outside his house and sang. In fact, he led the voices that filled the evening air with music. In those days community singing was much more popular than it is today. There were not so many worried in those days, they said, for the people did not want so much and they were more eager to sing, because they had nothing else to do but sing and dance. And Francisco Gonzales was accounted the best dancer in the village. He was a very tall man with broad shoulders and shapely body, they said, and very good-looking. All the girls and women liked to dance with him. Fermenia Durán hinted that there might have been much family trouble in Placitas in those old days had Señor Gonzales not been such a good man.

The old-time dances are recalled with pleasure by the elder people of the village. In those days dances were frequent and most informal. No one really dressed up for them, unless they were at fiesta or special occasion times. In those days every head of the family considered it his social obligation to open his house for a baile (dance); consequently, these informal festivities were common. As well, those who had musical stringed instruments and could play them held it their social duty to furnish the music gratis. They said Pedro Sarna, the teacher of Ojo de La Casa, possessed a very old and beautiful violin and always he could be counted on to play it at all the dances. Miguel Archibeque was a young man with musical accomplishments. He played the guitar, and there was Eliju Lucero who joined in with his accordion. Very little work was required on the part of the host or hostess to make the house ready for the baile. Seating the guests was no trouble at all. There being no chairs in those days, large logs were laid along the mud floor against the walls for seats. The niches in the adobe walls of the room were filled with candles, a tinaja (pottery vessel) was filled with wine and a gourd dipper was put into it, and all was ready for the guests. In those days the twilight was the time to gather for such pastimes. The very small children who could not be left at home were brought along and laid on pallets on the floor of another room. The women arranged themselves on the huge logs along the walls. All those who wished to dance brought a square of sheepskin with them and sat on it. When a man desired a partner for the dance, he saluted some lady sitting on a piece of sheepskin. Most women who did not wish to dance brought with them their torno de hilar (spinning wheel), a little handmade affair operated by hand power which they used to spin their wool into threads. Throughout the evening these busy spinners chatted to each other, sang with the musicians, and accomplished much-needed work. If the musicians and the wine held out, it was nothing unusual to dance until dawn.

Francisco Gonzales, they said, was very gentle with all children, and he believed that the boys should learn to read and write. He would have sacrificed his last goat or sheep for its hide to be dried and stretched and made into writing material for the boys. It was with dried skins for slates and charcoal for pencils that Pedro Sarna taught his pupils, the little goat and sheep herders, to read and write, as they tended their flocks in the mountains in that long ago day.

Each Sunday brought in a real holiday. Early in the morning everyone attended prayers. Before they had a church they met at the different houses for prayers. In the afternoons Francisco encouraged everybody to sing to the tune of guitars, and always on Sunday there was dancing and some drinking. But there was no feasting on Sunday. Housewives did not spend Saturday over hot fires cooking feasts for Sunday. No one worked on Sunday; therefore, there was no need of gorging. Save the food for days of labor when they needed it, and to this day the people of Placitas observe this economic custom of their fathers.

In 1870 Francisco and Chonita had their last child, Conception, named for the mother. But fate decreed that Conception and her mother should be separated by death before the child was old enough to realize her loss. A motherly neighbor, Gabrielita Gallardo, took the little girl and kept her until she was grown and married to Benino Archibeque. Chonita Gonzales also left a small son and four other children, whom Francisco cared for and provided for the best he could, being both father and mother to them until they were all settled in homes of their own. Chonita Tafoya de Gonzales will live in the memories of the people of Placitas for years to come, for the same reason her memory is so green in the minds of the last few generations. When she died, weather conditions prevented carrying her body to Bernalillo for burial within reasonable time. When it could be taken, tragedy attended the ceremony. The bearers of the ladder holding the body became ill. One was so sick that he stumbled; the body was cut in the fall and the bearers were bloodstained, so they said. Somehow they got their burden to the cemetery, where it was interred.

An indignation meeting was held in Placitas. Every adult person able to be out attended. Too long had they been forced to carry their dead to Bernalillo or San Felipe. They had the right to have a cemetery of their own. They appointed certain men of the community to confer with the priest at Bernalillo and demand that he come at once to Placitas and bless ground for the burial of their dead. And so it was that Chonita Gonzales was the last one to be buried in the cemetery at Bernalillo—unless from choice. The first one to be laid to rest in the new cemetery in Placitas was a little girl, last name Gonzales but first name long ago forgotten. She was of another branch of the Gonzales family.

It was in the early eighties that a schism rendered asunder the social life of the people of Placitas. The enmity that ensued was like a community wound, and lifelong friends and even members of families joined by intermarriages were separated by a chasm of bitterness. Francisco Gonzales stood steadfast in the ancient faith of his fathers, while his two closest friends, Nicolás Gurulé and Francisco Trujillo, and his own son-in-law, José Librado Arón Gurulé (who had married his daughter Rosita), deserters of the faith, followed the inspired proselyte, Ernesto Perea, a zealous young Presbyterian missionary. Ernesto was the son of the wealthy Don Juan Perea of Bernalillo. The youth had been sent east to school. He came home with an assortment of new ideas. One of them was to become a missionary and spread the doctrines of the Presbyterian church. He found an enthusiastic disciple in José Librado Arón Gurulé, whose ideas had long since conflicted with the established church. When he was about fourteen years old, José's aunt, Petra Gurulé, a very pious lady and devoted to her saints, was called from Placitas on an extended stay, which lengthened into years. She possessed a valuable collection of old saints. She could not take them with her so she gave them into the keeping of her sister-in-law, Catalina Gurulé, José Librado Arón's mother. For a time José kept his hands but not his mind off the images. But finally he declared that he could not sleep with them in the house. They were idols and he did not believe in idols. His mother chided him and told him she did not wish to hear any more of the matter. But he insisted that they worried him and that he could not sleep. Time passed in which his complaints did not cease. Then one day his mother was away from home. He gathered up the images and buried them in widely separated places all over the village, buried them deep and tamped the ground that covered them. None at his house missed them nor thought it was strange that at last he had quit his complaints of them. The one day Petra came for her saints alas; they were not to be found. José readily admitted that he had disposed of them and told how. He honestly tried to recollect the various places he had buried them, but his efforts were vain. Only a few of the valuable collection were ever unearthed. The name Librado was added to the name of José in his early youth. His courage, his search for freedom of thinking, brought him the name and it has been used ever since. Librado for delivered. And so it was José Librado Arón Gurulé who became the leader in Placitas of those who joined and helped build the little Presbyterian mission. The first resident missionary of the church in Placitas was Antonio Pérez. It was thought the date of his coming was 1882. Following the opening of the mission came the establishment of a school. The first teacher was Lucette Fenton. The mission school was a success from the start. Today more than half the families in Placitas are members of this church, and though long ago the school was abandoned, most of their children have been sent to Santa Fe to the Presbyterian school.

They say it was years before Francisco Gonzales regained his old familiar cheerfulness and was himself again, ready to sing and dance, eager again to tell jokes on himself. The tales he told of his short stay with the army under General Canby are still remembered. He had never tasted real coffee nor real butter. There seemed plenty of these staples in the commissary. He liked both. It was in the winter of 1862. The butter in the packs was firm and hard. The native New Mexicans liked to have it in slices, and it seemed they were given it thus. They ate thick slices of butter on thin slices of bread. They ate too much of it. Francisco said the butter made him very sick. It made him sick to even think of it. He never tasted butter after that, the thought of it turned his stomach. All of his neighbors in Placitas teased him about it. Whenever he visited at a house, before he left there came the tormenting question, jokingly,

"Señor, will you have some butter?" Always he replied in the spirit of fun, "No, but I'll take coffee, please. I had all the butter I wanted in the army."

Francisco was in the battle of Valverde, where General Canby and men met the forces of General Sibley. Francisco said of the battle, they fought hard all day and everybody tried to kill everybody else. Then all the men with him started to run, all of the men from New Mexico. The other side was running them home, the war was over. Nobody stopped running. He never stopped until, footsore and weary, he arrived at his home, a distance of about one hundred and fifty miles. José Librado Arón still laughs when he tells the story of how Francisco Gonzales thought the war was over and ran all the way home without even stopping to get a bite to eat, and he was carrying his gun with him, one of those old percussion guns with the long, heavy barrel, a load in itself. Never in Placitas had they seen such a firearm. All must see it, touch it. After all curiosity concerning it was satisfied, Francisco hid it away and brought it out only on occasions. He took it with him on hunts when he had the caps for it. The ammunition was another matter; he always had that. The old Montezuma Mine was nearby. There was plenty of lead ore and it was easy to smelt, and after that, the lead could be melted and poured into a mold and formed into balls for the gun. Not always did he bother to mold the balls; often he made the lead into sticks and cut it into the proper-sized pieces. When the little Catholic church was built, not many years later, Francisco kept the gun there. It was thought that he believed its presence there would keep the evil spirits away from the whole vicinity of the holy place. For years the gun remained there. Everyone in the village realized its significance. Then one morning it was gone. A wide and diligent search failed to locate it. Mystery surrounded its disappearance, a mystery never solved.

Of all those who have lived out a long life in Placitas and died there, none have left behind them so many colorful and pleasant memories as has Francisco Gonzales.

SUBJECT: Life in the Old Houses: Part V
May 19, 1939
Words 2022
WPA: 5-5-49 #17
Sources of information: José Librado Arón Gurulé, Patricio Gallegos.

LIFE IN THE OLD HOUSES: PART V
Sports and Pastimes

Life for the lowly native New Mexicans at the time of the American occupation and for long years afterward was barren of things except those which were born of their own ingenuity. Of necessity they were self-reliant and resourceful. From nature's bosom they plucked the raw materials and with nothing but their own bare hands made them into the things which sustained them. They were a light-hearted people and regardless of droughts, Indian raids that often impoverished them, and diseases that laid them low, they sang, danced, and played. They prayed fervently to the saints for life and security but at the same time believed that what was to be would be and that there was nothing they could do about it. In those days their sports and pastimes were joyous and free in the broadest sense of the words. They most thoroughly enjoyed them and they cost nothing. The love of betting, the adventure of staking their all on the outcome of a game, was the high spirit that inspired the play. The greatest of the old games and the one on which high stakes were laid was the game called La Pelota (The Ball).

No football game ever offered more thrills nor received more cheers per viva than this game of La Pelota played between the teams at Placitas and Ojo de La Casa in those long ago days when American influence was still weak in New Mexico. In this game seven players took part on each side. They were the toughest, huskiest, swift runners each village could muster. Frequently the victory went to the team with the best racer. Each player possessed himself of a good stout stick with a crook at one side of it, a decided crook amounting to a right angle. Such sticks were not easy to find; consequently, players were ever on the alert for them. The mountains were searched for just the right sticks for La Pelota. Much depended upon the fitness of the stick and many a game was won because of just the right angle of a certain player's club. It was necessary for each youth to have several sticks. A misdirected blow might shatter the stick into splinters if it struck the hard earth. The ball, too, was important. Its outer cover was usually of buffalo hide. This cover enclosed stuffing of the same material, for the stuffing must be such as to make the ball hard, solid, and well-rounded. The cover was sewed with tough strips of raw hide. It required time to make a perfect ball that was also durable. And for La Pelota, it must be just that to make the game worth playing.

When the sun told them the hour for the game had arrived, the players took their sticks and the villagers followed them to a point midway between Ojo de La Casa and Las Placitas where the game was to begin. The teams lined up, their rooters at a safe distance. Each team faced the home village of its opponent. The referee with the ball stood in the center of a space between the two teams. The captains of the teams took their places on each side of him. He tossed the ball high in the air. As it descended, the captains struggled to strike it with their clubs and send it in the direction of their own teams. The game was on. The goal of each team was its own village. To win the game, they must get the ball there. The ball could be tossed from one player to another, struck with the clubs and sent along, seized and carried by a player, but never kicked. When a player ran with it, the work of his opponents was to catch him, seize the ball, and start for their own goal. Often, when the players were skillful and well matched, neither team succeeded in getting more than a few hundred feet from the starting point. At such times swift runners showed their superiority over others. Once they got the ball, the chances were good for a home run and victory for their side. Then it was that the north end of the Sandías echoed with the shouts and cheers of the spectators. And the betting! Everyone who had anything to stake on the game put it up. Silver coins were scarce, but those who had any gleefully matched them with his neighbor's corn or chili, or with a good goat or lamb. Such was the betting in the sixties and seventies: in the eighties, when the gold fever was at its height and prospectors and mining promoters were hiring men to do the assessment work on claims at the Old Montezuma mine at Ojo de La Casa and at San Pedro, there was money in the villages. Then the betting on the game was exciting, for the stakes ran high. This brought improvement in the skill and technique of the players and gave the bettors a real show for their money. The games drew crowds who shouted and cheered and cried out encouragement to their favorite teams. The way between Las Placitas and Ojo de La Casa would be dotted with people running first in one direction, then in the opposite, keeping up with their teams as they approached their home goal or retreated from it in pursuit of the ball in the hands of their opponents. It was a great sport and throats were sore from yelling.

One Sunday a game was played that still lives in the memory of the older people of both villages. The game was close, the boys played hard, the stakes were large, and those who had gambled on the game were anxious. Neither team seemed able to get the ball within sight of its goal. Then a change of luck, and the Ojo de La Casa boys got possession of the ball and started for home, the Las Placitas team in hot pursuit. Merijildo Martínez of Las Placitas seized the ball as a player struck it with his club. Instantly he was on his way, the ball tucked under his arm, his head thrown back, his rather long black hair streaming out behind as he fairly cut the wind. Never, they said, had any of them seen such running. He went so fast they could not see his feet touch the ground. He made the goal in five minutes. The distance was nearly a mile. Merijildo was the hero of the hour and the dreaded opponent from then on, for Ojo de La Casa had no runner who could match him. He also caused a change in the betting on the game.

Next to La Pelota in popularity was the game called Chueco (head of a bone), a first-rate gambling game requiring only the simplest equipment, a smooth stretch of ground at least twenty feet long, a large bone not less than twelve inches long, perfectly flat at one end and the other to be planted at the end of the ground which would keep the backs of the players to the sun, and the other things required were tejas (roof tile). In this case they were small stones, about the shape and size of a silver dollar. If the bottom of the arroyos did not yield up such stones, they could be made by grinding them with harder stones into the desired size and shape. Each player needed a teja or two.

Now for the game. The players stand on the cleared ground about fifteen feet from the bone, which is firmly placed in the ground and protrudes upward at least eight inches. The spectators gather anywhere on the sidelines. The first move of the game is to determine who shall be first to cast his stone in the play. So each one throws his stone; the one to come nearest to the bone wins the first place, the other players are numbered according to the proximity of their rocks to the bone. Each player's teja or stone has an individual mark upon it. Number one now opens the game by placing any amount of money he chooses on the top of the bone. The others match the sum or withdraw, and when all coins are placed upon the bone head, the excitement begins. Number one tosses his teja at the coins, the others follow in order. All have aimed carefully, almost breathlessly, while on the sidelines bets are made as to who will win this or that or who will hit the bone or who will come the nearest to the scattered coins. When all the players have tossed their tejas, there is a rush to see results. All coins are now on the ground and those nearer the bone than to any teja are again laid atop the bone. The other coins then go to the owner of the teja nearest them. Sometimes only a hair's breadth determines the winner. Then the game is resumed. Number one again places his ante, adding it to what is left on the bone—if any. The other players follow with the same size coin and the play is on again. Coins change hands many times in the course of a game of Chueco. Some carry home a pocket full of coins, others have lost all they had, but what is the difference—there was much fun in the game and many a sunny day was whiled away in throwing tejas at the bone head.

Then there was the annual thrill on San Juan Day when the people of Ojo de La Casa and Placitas gathered together and walked to Tejón where the saint's day was being celebrated. They would start early in the morning to be there for the mass and to join the procession which marched all about the quaint walled town. The distance to Tejón was but three and one half miles, the road was rough, and a part of the journey was through Cañón de Tejón, which was strewn with loose stones and boulders. But who in those old days bothered about such trifles as bad roads? Always at Tejón on their fiesta day there was an abundance of wine and music and dancing. Those were rewards enough to compensate for any hardships in arriving there. The older ones still living who used to go to Tejón on San Juan Day still recall with pleasure the merry times they had there and how they would start home at dawn and sing all the way and then when they reached home how they would say they had too much fiesta and would sleep all day long.

Then the time came when they walked to Tejón no more, for some of them at Ojo de La Casa and Placitas had acquired oxen and carretas and then came burros. And in a yet later day, but still far removed from the present time, there appeared in Placitas and Ojo de La Casa real wagons and horses. Then it was that the people filled the wagons with hay and rode to Tejón. They called them hayrides. It was thus that they attended the last fiesta day held in old Tejón.

In those long ago days the men and boys at Placitas had an educational pastime peculiarly their own. From somewhere, probably old Mexico, someone brought a shaft of iron about thirty inches long and about an inch in diameter. At the time José L.A. Gurulé, now eighty-eight, was a small boy. He said someone in Placitas made it a part of a shooting device, which was in fact from his description a weapon closely resembling an ancient arbalest, a sort of crossbow. He said the men and boys used it until they were all expert with it. The weapon had but one imperfection; it did not send the arrowhead far enough. However, that did not detract from the pleasure they had in it and it belonged to the community. From their land grant, San Antonio de Las Huertas, it was the first and last thing in common they ever held. The old weapon was prized and guarded, and it was never abused nor mislaid in all the years they used it. And the exciting contests they had with it. The gambling there was on the events, and when it was worn out, that old weapon that was so nearly like an arbalest, was missed as if it had been a playfellow.

SUBJECT: Life in the Old Houses: Part VI
WPA: 5-5-49 #18
June 9, 1939
Words 2602
Sources of information: José Librado Arón Gurulé, Rumaldita Gurulé, Predicando Calves, Patricio Gallegos.

LIFE IN THE OLD HOUSES: PART VI
Hunts of the Old Days

From time unknown up to the 1870s, wildlife abounded in the Sandía Mountains. Tracks of deer, antelope, bear, and wild turkey led everywhere. Perdizo Cañón (Grouse Canyon), which was the old Cija del Camino de San Pedro, the main road from Bernalillo and the north end of the Sandías to Tijeras Cañón (Sissors Canyon), in those days was alive with grouse, and in the vicinity of Placitas and Ojo de La Casa they were found in no other place than this Perdizo Cañón. In those old days of plentiful game. Bow and arrow was the only weapon of the people, but because of the large numbers of deer and antelope, they were able to bring them down with it in spite of the short distance they could send their arrows. The Sandía hunters cautiously avoided the bear. If they sighted one they gave him a wide berth. None of the villagers considered him as food in those days.

From the Indians, the men from Ojo de La Casa and Placitas learned to set traps in advantageous points through the mountains for the capture of wild turkey. The traps were boxes made of sticks. They were about two feet square and some twelve or fourteen inches high and were perched upon a tricky tripod of sticks, which collapsed without warning when anything attempted to scratch out the grain scattered in the places where the sticks of the tripod rested on the ground. When the sticks fell, the heavy box came down and entrapped birds feasting upon the inviting grain. Always the owners or watchers of the traps were concealed in blinds nearby, and instantly they removed the trapped fowls and bagged them, then reset the traps and returned to their hidden retreats. In this way a plentiful supply of wild turkey was kept roasting on the home fires in the old houses. The grouse was trapped in the same manner and more often, for Perdizo Cañón emerges from the Sandías on the doorstep of Ojo de La Casa and was therefore a preferred place to trap wild fowl.

In spite of the fact that before the sixties, game abounded in the region of Placitas and Ojo de La Casa, the men from these villages went on distant buffalo hunts. According to José Librado Arón Gurulé, the buffalo disappeared from this section of New Mexico long before 1800. He said the only signs of their existence anywhere near Placitas were the skulls of the animals around a spring near the San Felipe Pueblo. He said there were few buffalo hunts after 1865, but many of them during the fifties. Men from Ojo de La Casa, Placitas, La Madera, Tejón, Algodones, and Bernalillo would make up a hunting party and set out for Llano Estacada (Staked Plains), which extended from east of the Pecos River into Texas somewhere. And it was into Texas that these expeditions went with oxen and carretas and scant provisions of dried peas and beans, onions, raisins (dried grapes from their own vineyards), and ground corn. The trips extended over a period of three months. The buffalo slaughtered were dressed on the spot, the hides prepared and the meat cut into small strips and dried that they might be packed for the journey home. These buffalo hides were important and necessary to the lives of the people in the old houses. From them were made most of the clothing of the men in those faraway days of the past. The tewas (moccasins) for everybody were more lasting when made from buffalo hide. The harness for the oxen teams was made of it and rugs for the floors. The women who had no combs for the combing of their wool had but to turn their buffalo rugs upside down and wipe off the smooth side and lay their wool upon its clean, hard surface for the beating of the wool with sticks, which they gave it instead of the combing. Then there was the festive sport La Pelota (The Ball), which required the durable, tough hide of the buffalo from which to make the ball for the game. So it was that the hides were perhaps more an addition to their lives in the old houses than the dried buffalo meat that was brought home, because of the game to be had in the Sandías. In those early days of the buffalo hunts, few of the men had guns to take with them, but the weapons that were taken along were made to count so that there was always a plentiful supply of dried meat and cured hides to bring back home. But these hunts became fewer and fewer. They learned that anything might happen on the plains to them, or back in the villages to the families in the course of three months. Besides, the families were steadily increasing the size of their own sheep and goat herds, which made the buffalo hunts less necessary. Those who had made the hunts the answer to that call in the blood for adventure now turned to making trips with oxen and carretas or wagons over the Santa Fe Trail to the markets at Los Estados (The States), for themselves or Don José Leander Perea, their wealthy patrón at Bernalillo.

It was after the Civil War that guns made their appearance in Placitas and Ojo de La Casa, except the one brought to Placitas by Francisco Gonzales, the Civil War veteran, in 1862. These guns were muzzle-loading guns, and pellets of lead cut from pieces of the smelted ore was the ammunition they used. These weapons were called Rifle Fulminante which meant guns fired by caps, but for some unknown reason the people called them Virola Amarilla, a name that seems to have no meaning whatever relative to a weapon. But with the introduction of a few of these firearms into the vicinity of the Sandías, the hunt for deer and antelope became more effective; consequently, there was a gradual decline in the size of the herds, then fewer herds were seen roaming the mountains. The virola amarilla was taking toll of the game. Finally Ojo de Osha, the Osha Springs near the top of the West Sandías of today, became the last refuge for the deer on the Placitas side of the Sandías. That was in the seventies sometime. The antelope had quitted the region and herded together around San Pedro Mountain off to the northeast. They virtually disappeared during a terrific blizzard around the San Pedro area, which was thought to have occurred in the winter of 1878. The fierce wind from the east and the blinding snowstorm accompanying it carried the helpless antelopes along right down to San Felipe. There the Indians slaughtered them and feasted upon them for many days. From that time forth, antelope were few and far between in the Placitas region. Deer, too, were by now exceedingly scarce in the Placitas side of the Sandías. In the early eighties, José Martín of Placitas and Bill Bruce, a prospector at Ojo de La Casa, got a doe near what is now known as The Ellis Ranch in the Sandías. They sold it in Madrid for thirteen dollars. As far as any one now living in Placitas or Ojo de La Casa could recall, that was the last deer anybody in either village had captured or killed.

But not all about the Sandías was a hunters' paradise. Bears big and little roamed the mountains and frequented the watering places. The hunters with the Virola Amarillas, and the sheep and goat herders with their sticks, gave them right of way. No man, unless he knew absolutely that he could slay the bear with a single discharge of his muzzle-loading gun, ever took the chance of firing at it unless he was crazy, or so they said. However, there were accidental encounters with the shaggy animals, and Juan María Gallegos met with such a one. It was very early one summer morning, though the year was somewhat uncertain but thought to have been in 1878. In those early days cabins on stilts were built in the mountains for the protection of the men and boys who cared for the sheep and goat herds. Each cabin had a small porch in front of it with the saplings supporting the roof, projecting. These projecting ends afforded hangers for the cheese, which they made from the goats' milk in seasons, and that was a necessary part of the herders' diet. As it was made in huge quantities, most of it was taken at intervals down to the villages. On this occasion a large sack of manta (coarse cotton cloth) full of the cheese was suspended from one of the saplings. A noise startled Juan María from his pallet. He went cautiously to a peephole of a window looking out onto the porch. There he saw a bear mounting the stilts. He was very near the sack of cheese. It would not be long until he had his paw on it. Juan María picked up his loaded gun. He had to take careful aim and did it. A flash and a roaring sound, and the bear fell in a heap at the foot of the stilts he had climbed. Juan María rushed to it. He said of himself when he saw it, that he was disgusted. There lay a small black bear, and when he saw it climbing for the cheese, it looked like a great big bear. But regardless of size, bear hides were prizes.

One man in Placitas, Juan José Archibeque, was the one remembered hunter who deliberately planned to kill a bear. His marksmanship was good, his gun only fair, but he was adventuresome enough to wish to be rated a hunter of bears. One day he went to Cañón de Agua (Canyon of Water), which is in the Sandía Mountains between Sandía Pueblo and Bernalillo. The place was a bear haunt. Without too much walking he was sure to meet his quest. He said he kept his gun in readiness and his eyes wide open. He would not go back to Placitas without his bear and become the butt of their jokes. He later acknowledged that he had not felt so brave there alone in the canyon with so many bears. But he did get his bear. The tales of bear hunts or kills were so few that they stand out in the memories of the older inhabitants and are told with pride, if it happened that it were an ancestor who played an important role in the tale.

A story of a wild turkey rout was recalled. It happened in the early days when Valentine Zamora, one of the founders of Ojo de La Casa, and his youthful son, Juan María, were tending their flocks high up in the Sandías. Juan María was but thirteen years of age. As he was born in 1851, the date of the adventure would be 1864. Evening was upon them and they found themselves in a grassy cañón above La Madera. As they prepared to make their camp their attention was drawn to a fine pine tree. To their surprise the lower boughs looked to be full of wild turkey. Valentino and his son were overjoyed at the sight and they kept very quiet. Juan María, in his youthful enthusiasm, wanted to rush the birds at once and get one of them before they all flew away. Wise Valentino said they must wait quietly until dark, then he would see what could be done.

"But how can you get a turkey after dark?" was what they said the boy demanded. And Valentino said, "Wait and see."

When darkness fell, Valentino moved quietly about making his preparations. He gathered some dry brush and piled it under the tree. He crawled about on his knees digging up the fresh earth, making a ring encircling the pine. In those early days the grasses in the cañóns grew high. It was in the fall and everything was drying and turning brown. The tall grass beneath the pine would aid him in his plan. Now that his fire guard was finished, Valentino produced his ever-ready pieces of flint rock and some quelite. Quelite was an herb that the people in the old houses gathered in abundance in the summer time, soaked in water and dried. When dried it was crisp and easily ignited as paper. It was stored away in large quantities in every household. It was needed in the building of fires. And so Valentino clashed his two pieces of flint together, and the falling sparks set fire to the quelite (which was the way all their fires were lighted in that long-ago day). The burning quelite set fire to the brush and the brush spread flames to the grass. Smoke and tongues of fire rose under the sleepy birds. Some of them, frightened and dizzy; dropped to the ground. Instantly Valentino rushed in and rescued them before any damage to them was done. Other birds flew away. In all, Valentino captured over a dozen turkeys. He kept what he and Juan María could eat and sent the others to the families in Ojo de La Casa by a sheep herder.

Once in the long-ago days of the early eighties they had what they called a big surprise hunt. It was during an icy blizzard in the dead of winter about 1880. Don José Leander Perea of Bernalillo had many flocks of sheep in the Sandía region. One of the larger flocks was in the path of the storm. Nothing could prevent them from drifting with it. The half-frozen herders could not stay with it so they sought shelter in a rocky cave and saved their lives, for they were far from properly clad for such zero weather combined with a blizzard. The next morning found their scattered herd over a wide area of the mesa between Placitas and Bernalillo. Don José was notified. Immediately he sent out runners to notify all those in Ojo de La Casa and Placitas who wished to take away the frozen animals for meat to come at once for them. The animals must be taken at once, and the pay for them was the animal's fleece, which each taker of the sheep must remove and deliver to the man in charge of the frozen flock. Thus, Don José saved only the pelts of his flock and the villagers had all the mutton they could care for and more. Word was sent to other places for help in removing the fleece from the frozen sheep and taking away the meat. The don's loss and their gain is still recalled by the older citizens of Placitas and Ojo de La Casa.

And now no longer is there pasturage in the Placitas area for big herds of sheep or goats. The herds of deer of the old days have vanished. The bears that menaced the region are now reduced to but a few, and those few are seldom encountered. The Placitas side of the Sandías is now a forest reserve and for the last few years deer are again seen at the watering places—not many but a start of a new herd. Turkeys are now being conserved in the mountain reserve. All these things are reminiscent of the days of long ago only—no longer can the villagers go at will to hunt and trap the game. The wildness of the Sandías is gone forever.

SUBJECT: Life in the Old Houses: Part VII
WPA: 5-5-49 #19
July 5, 1939
Words 2940
Sources of information: Rumaldita Gurulé, Barbarita Lucero, Conception
Archibeque, Patricio Gallegos, Magdelena Gallegos, Predicando Chaves,
José Librado A. Gurulé. Rumaldita Gurulé was the daughter-in-law of the
Gabrielita of this story. Barbarita Lucero was the granddaughter of the
Gabrielita of this story. Conception Archibeque was the foster daughter of
the Gabrielita of this story. Patricio Gallegos was the son of Juan María.
Magdalena Gallegos was the daughter-in-law of Juan María of this story.
Predicando Chaves was the head of the house Plácida and Preciliano
(of this story) built by the side of the road.

LIFE IN THE OLD HOUSE: PART VII
Gabrielita and Plácida

The name Gabrielita Gallardo, born about 1826 at the little village of
Nacimiento, which now is the old section of the present Cuba in Sandoval
County, is still glowingly alive in Placitas, and the memory of her good deeds
has lived after her. At what date she came to live in Placitas was not known,
but the name Gallardo was among the names of the settlers residing at Placitas in the year 1843, according to a record inherited by José Librado Arón
Gurulé from his father, Nicolás Gurulé. The first Placitas home of Gabrielita
was the community house where the families of that early date dwelled
together, each family building their own one-roomed apartment. They constructed this community house for the security of their lives and property, for
in those early days the Navajoes raided at will and the mountains were full of
wild animals, including the lion who was in truth lord of all he surveyed, as

194

the only weapon the people of Placitas possessed in those days was the bow and arrow.

In her early teens Gabrielita was married to a man named Felipe, but she was always known as Gabrielita Gallardo. Nothing was known of Felipe, except that it was before 1850 that he and Gabrielita built their own first house in what is now the west side of Placitas, and it was set well off the meandering lane which was the highway through the village. Their daughter Plácida was born there in 1850. Some of the ruins of that house are still standing. A small but hospitable house it was, and within it hung many blankets and animal hides, which were made into pallets at night for the many children who lived there. As the years went by, Gabrielita gave birth to a large family, and she was that sunny type of woman whose home was a gathering place for all the children big and little in the whole community. And it was not only that, but her house more and more became a temporary refuge for children whose mothers were ill or were forced to leave them for a time. It was Gabrielita who took in the tiny daughter of Chonita Gonzales when she died, and kept her until she was grown. This child, who is now Conception Archibeque, cherishes the memory of Gabrielita Gallardo, who was a wonderful mother to her and taught her all she knew. But of Gabrielita's own children there are none left to sing her praises, yet the memory of four of them, still fresh in the minds of the older inhabitants of the village, help keep alive the memory of Gabrielita. Her two sons, Mariano and Eliju, were natural-born musicians, they said. Mariano played the violin while Eliju's soulful manipulation of his accordion charmed the villagers and sent them into dancing ecstasies with his fandangos and tarantelas. Always Mariano and Eliju were willing to play from dusk to dawn at those happy, free dances of the old days. And many a bride of those early days in Placitas danced to their music at her wedding baile (dance). Then there was Gabrielita's daughter, Antonia. She could sing. They said there has never been in Placitas one who had so beautiful a voice. When the Presbyterian mission was built in 1882, it was Antonia who led the singing. It was Antonia's voice that brought many a sinner to repentance. But it was Plácida who was her mother's helper and who carried on her good work as a neighbor and sympathetic friend in Placitas, who was best remembered.

In spite of her many duties in the house of many children, Plácida found time to keep an eye on the tall and handsome Presiliano, who was building a house nearby, a house with a patio facing the winding road. The boughs of a giant cottonwood across that road shaded the patio and kept the sun's glaring light from shining into the house door in the summer time. An impressive small house it was and the builder was happy that Plácida was interested in it, for it was his house of dreams and it was for her; even though he had said nothing to Gabrielita of his desire for her daughter. He would tell her when his house was ready. And so it came about that Gabrielita gave the willing Plácida to him, and the prendorio (an exchange of rings between the lovers) was celebrated at a baile where the music was furnished by Mariano and Eliju, uncles of the bride-to-be, and Pedro Sarna of Ojo de La Casa, who owned a fine violin and knew how to play upon it. Where Gabrielita procured the ring for Plácida is not known, for Gabrielita had no money. In fact, in those days in villages like Placitas, money was all but nil. But money or no money, brides must have wedding clothes, and often it happened that neither parents nor groom-to-be could supply the trousseau, even though it was an ancient custom for the future husband to present his bride with her wedding finery.

In the fifties and sixties only the fortunate could purchase wedding things; yet brides must have bridal clothes. So it was that in Placitas the more privileged daughters had met this difficult situation. Those who possessed wedding gowns and the things to go with them gave of these precious belongings until there was a chest holding a complete wedding outfit. A sort of community chest it was, owned by no one yet to be used by anyone who needed it. The gown was shortened or lengthened, seams taken up or let out, according to the size of the girl who was to wear it. The veil was also made to meet her requirements. The wedding veil of the time was attached to one side of the head and fell over one shoulder to the length of the skirt of the gown. The popular bouquet was made of feathers. Though feathers of beautiful colors could be found, the brides preferred that they be white; so a coat of yeso was applied and the resulting bouquet was snowy white. It was suspended from the waist line at the front. And the shoes in the chest could be endured for the occasion regardless of fit. No one now living in Placitas knew who started the chest nor when it was last used; but they had it from lips long sealed in death, that it brought happiness to many girls in that gone by day, who otherwise would have been wed without a bridal dress. Thus, in this chest Plácida found her wedding dress, and as were all the brides of her day, she was married in the church at San Felipe.

And so it came about that Plácida went to live in the new house by the side of the winding lane. Slowly she accumulated tinajas (pottery vessels) to fill her tapanco (porch built in the kitchen to be used as a cupboard). In time the small adobe bins built parallel to one of the four walls of her kitchen became filled with blue corn, wheat, beans, onions, chili, and other food necessities. She acquired blankets even though she could not weave them. But she could trade the products of her garden and fields to Juan Armijo, the weaver of Placitas, for his work of weaving her wool into blankets for her. However, she could and did weave the cloth that she made into garments for her family in the first years of her marriage. She wove the layettes for her first babies, layettes that consisted of a few squares of cloth, the babies' one garment, called mantilla, and used to wrap them in until they could toddle about.

In the pursuit of these duties Plácida spent the early part of her life while Presciliano labored to accumulate more fields. Then came the middle seventies. Trips of the men of the village to the faraway markets of Kansas City and to Chihuahua, Mexico, aided in bringing about changes in the way of living. Women put aside the spinning and weaving contrivances, all of which were homemade, and bought the coarse cotton and other cloth from which they made the clothing for the family. Before the close of the seventies much of the sewing went out of the house. The coarse cotton cloth suits for men called mantas could be bought. Women chose material other than manta for their dresses whenever possible. Many discarded their tewas (moccasins) and bought zapatos de Castellano (shoes of Spanish style). Curves for the women came in with the early eighties. Plácida now wore a dress of calico that was fashioned with a very full skirt gathered on to a snug fitted bodice and with this new mode she wore many petticoats. But Gabrielita vowed she would not pinch in her body for any new style, and clung to the sack-like skirt and the shirt that pulled down over her skirt at the hips. She never laid aside her moccasins.

Plácida had a table and some benches in her kitchen, homemade ones. They were made of rough boards split from trunks of pine trees, and in her cuarto de dormir (sleeping room) she had a bed of wood made to look like a bench. Now that she could spare cloth for purposes other than clothing, she made a large slip or cover of manta and filled it with wool, which she had carefully washed and beat with sticks until it was light and fluffy. Then she sewed it inside the slip. Thus she made a mattress for her bed and in the same way she made pillows. These modern frills cost Plácida much work, because twice each year the wool must be removed from the slips, washed and again beaten with sticks until it was light and again put into the covers. If this was not done, these pillows and mattresses became hard and lumpy. Plácida had as many copper kettles in her tapanco at this time as she had tinajas in which to cook.

Gabrielita scorned this new fangled bed and stayed with her pallets until death found her on one. She insisted that the mud floors were warmer and more comfortable than the board benches with their wool mattresses, which got all in lumps. She never bothered with tables and benches. Her kitchen floor was kept clean and smooth, a new mud floor was laid frequently; it was comfortable to sit upon and besides, the floor afforded plenty of room for many children and grownups to sit about a great tinaja of meat and chili.

And so it was that the younger women changed their houses; finally tearing out the tapancos and the adobe bins and bringing in wooden cupboards made at home. The older ones held to the old ways and things. But all these changes the younger ones were making were not brought about merely because of long trips the men made to the great markets nor the trading posts that sprang up here and there, but because work. Jobs opened up to men by the influx of gold seekers and the labor required by law, which they must do or have done on their mining claims, and also the opening up of coal mines, for now the railroad had entered New Mexico. Money was no longer an unknown quantity in Placitas. The Golden Age of Placitas was the short but paying era of the gold fever around the old Montezuma Mine at the north end of the Sandía Mountains and around San Pedro northeast of Placitas.

But the seventies witnessed changes other than those which changed the old houses into dwellings where makeshifts resembling furniture were introduced, and those which gave the younger women a different silhouette. The toilers in the fields of Placitas were growing weary of the dull, slow, heavy oxen. These beasts took too much time to plow a field, too long a time to take a carreta places. They wanted burros. Burros were by nature adapted to the trails and arroyos all about Placitas. Burros were costly; a span would come close to fifty dollars, and they would have to be guarded. Burro meat was much more preferred by the roving Navajoes than the tough meat of the oxen: so the initial outlay would not be all the price which must be paid for the burros. The men who finally decided to make the change from oxen to burros got together and talked the matter over. They decided to purchase the animals and hire a burroteer to herd the beasts in green pastures and by good waters when they were not being used. Each owner of the burros would pay the herder a certain amount per head. And so an energetic son of Plácida became the first burroteer and his mother profited more than he, for often half his pay was corn or wheat.

Thus, the burro reduced the need of the ox. Yet a few continued to plow with the clumsy creature. Juan María Gallegos was one of these and he profitted by it. His was about the last remaining ox in the vicinity. One day while he patiently followed his ox and plow, a gringo rushed up the road on a horse. He saw Juan María in his field, he climbed from his mount and joined him. His survey of the ox was critical. Finally he offered Juan María forty dollars for it. Juan appeared to consider but found the offer unsatisfactory. Why should he sell his big, fat ox unless he could make enough to buy a team of burros? He told the gringo he did not wish to sell. The gringo was the owner of the butcher shop at San Pedro. He needed beef. His town was full of prospectors and sightseers who must be fed, and meat was the dish. He had no time to stand in the field and parley with Juan María. "What do you think that beast is worth?" was what Juan María was asked, and courteously the owner of the ox replied, "The señor can have it for whatever he wishes to give. But the price is sixty dollars." The gringo, they said, wished to give the sixty dollars and did. Juan María pocketed the money, unhitched the ox from the plow, and the gringo drove him to San Pedro. Thus went the last ox from Placitas.

Before the close of the eighties a few horses were pulling the plows which cultivated the fields of Placitas, but they were very few.

At the close of the eighties, a few pieces of real furniture appeared in Placitas, though it was believed that years before that, Juan Armijo, Francisco Trujillo, and Presciliano Baros, and Casimiro Gallegos of Ojo de La Casa had brought back various pieces from Kansas City when they made trips there in the early seventies. It was said that about 1920 a man came to Placitas seeking old furniture, and the members of these families, with the exception of Francisco Trujillo, sold pieces to him and received what seemed high prices to them, but which they have since realized was nothing compared to their real value.

Gabrielita, who lived a happy and useful life, died in the late eighties. Whether she lived to help wage that futile war upon the scourge that struck down so many of the children in the late eighties is not known. It came swiftly and terribly. It defied the power of the time-honored herbs and teas; it defied the magic remedies of the witch doctors. The throats of the children swelled and burned, they said. The children in a frenzy would rush from their beds and pallets into the open and run screaming and pulling at their throats until they fell dead. When it had run its course, there was a dearth of early teenage children in the villages, and many, many new graves in the little cemeteries in both Placitas and Ojo de La Casa bore evidence of the tragedy. Many years have passed since that day but they still talk of it and none seem to know even yet what manner of disease it was.

Plácida was one of the mothers whose family was reduced in numbers by the dread malady. Plácida herself died in 1911 in the month of August. And strange it was that her husband Presciliano should go, too, in the same month of the same year. Their house by the side of the road was left to their son Juan and his wife, Rumaldita.

SUBJECT: Life in the Old Houses: Part VIII
WPA: 5-5-49 #20
July 21, 1939
Sources of information: Predicando Chaves, Fermenia Durán, Conception
Archibeque. Predicando Chaves was a son of the Juan P. of this story.
Conception Archibeque was a daughter of Francisco Gonzales of this story.

LIFE IN THE OLD HOUSES: PART VIII
Fiesta Days

The Celebration of San Antonio Day at Placitas in the year 1872 might have passed uneventfully, and now be wholly forgotten by those yet living who participated in the festivity, had it not been for the drunken merriment of José Chaves, who carried his idea of fun too far and almost precipitated a tragedy.

For this long-remembered San Antonio Day there were the usual preparations. Women spent weeks in sewing, cleaning, and washing. But for months they had saved and gathered together food and things with which to make the celebration a success. Such necessities were few and time was required to accumulate them, or a sufficient amount of them to honor fittingly their patron saint San Antonio. So whatever of sacrifices they made in celebration of the event were but works of love.

For months the small quantities of sugar, syrup, and raisins (their own homemade products) possessed in the average household were hoarded, for such luxuries were needed for sweetness in the making of sopia (bread pudding with piñón nuts and cheese of goat milk) and bizcochos (cookies made with lard and little sweetening and cut into fancy shapes). These dainties were considered fiesta complements and no housewife would think of not providing them, especially on San Antonio Day.

While food and drink (wine) were the fiesta indispensables, there was yet another thing which custom had made mandatory. The visible or outer garments worn at their Saint's Day celebration must be new. In those old days, they said, no one showed his face on fiesta day unless he wore new things. At this date the accepted suit for the men and boys was the manta. Most all of them were made by the women at home. So this meant workday, in their preparations for the fiesta. New tewas, and zapatos de Castellano (their name for shoes bought at the store) were worn on every foot that marched in the solemn procession on fiesta day. In those days most of the dresses and suits were of the manta, which was white, but there were some of the women who were lucky enough to have a bright-colored calico dress. These colors besides, being the envy of all the women and girls, were the highlights of the festive day.

The day before the fiesta was an extraordinary workday. Fires blazed in the outdoor ovens at dawn. The bread must be baked, quantities of it. Wheat had been hoarded for this fiesta bread. There was meat to cook. The men had tramped over the mountains in search of wild game to make savory dishes for their hospitable table, or floor, whichever the case might be. But at this date the floor was the popular serving board. There were tortillas to make of the blue meal. As there was little or no coffee in the village, much of the meal of the dried pea was made ready to brew into a substitute. Chili was made in abundance, hot and tempting to the palates of those long accustomed to its high flavor and taste. Feverish work it all was to achieve the real fiesta atmosphere.

Then there were the final touches to add to the little church, which was so very small as to hold only a small percent of the worshippers at one time. Already the walls had been washed with yeso and were gleaming white. The ceiling had been scrubbed as well as the little wooden altar. There were no pews, but a fresh mud floor had been laid. A snow white cloth covered the altar, and there was the wooden image of San Antonio in his capilla (tiny chapel) and he had on a new robe of blue. No one knew of what manner of material it was, they only remembered that it was blue. Now on the altar they arranged all colors of wild flowers in pottery jars of water. Early fiesta morning they would gather fresh ones and suspend them from the low ceiling and make wreaths for the walls. This little church, the first built in Placitas, is now a part of the house of Gregorio Gutiérrez, which is on the winding road through the village at the place where it makes a right angle bend. He bought it when the people built their present church.

While the women were thus engaged, the children went to places where grasses grew rank and sweet and brought great bundles of it to make a carpet from the church door to the road, for the priest to walk upon when he should come to hold the mass, the prelude to the day's festivities. That evening when vespers were said, everyone was most careful not to trample the carpet, for that would take all the freshness out of it. In those old days there was deep respect and high honor paid to the person of the priest, and they took much pains to imitate the pomp they believed should be a part of the reception for him. Therefore, his feet must walk upon a ground covered with fresh and fragrant grasses. Inside the church there were many long, slender sticks carefully wrapped in strips of white cloth. Bound to them were posies the women and girls had made of every scrap of bright-colored cloth and bits of paper that fell into their hands. Now they needed only an abundance of fresh flowers to complete them for their use in the ceremony; and these would be added early on the morrow.

After vespers, bonfires were lighted all along the winding ways and there were fireworks, an inexhaustible supply of them. From every quarter of the village came the clink of rock striking rock, flint rocks they were and myriads of sparks fell everywhere. They illuminated dark places and looked like fiery eyes. Thus, the night before the fiesta day ended in showers of sparks and songs and the twanging of guitars as bands of players and singers wended their way from one bonfire to another.

The village was up with the dawn. Children hastened to the foothills of the mountains and to the shadowy cañoncitos (small canyons) to fetch wildflowers for the church and the white-covered sticks, which were to be decked with them. The early morning hours sped. Then came the deep booming of drums. Up and down the lanes went the drummers, calling the people to the mass. The church had no bell, so they must be warned of the arrival of the important hour. The priest was coming! Every soul in the village, unless he be upon a bed of sickness, flocked to the church in all the new fiesta things and stood outside to see the priest step from the carreta in his resplendent priestly robes. An even number of girls, clothed in white of course, lined up on both sides of the long carpet, each girl carrying one of the flower-spangled sticks. They faced each other across the grassy way and held their sticks aloft, the points of directly opposite sticks touching, forming an arch of flowers under which the reverend father passed with benign dignity to the church door, then on into it to his place near the altar. Those close to the door now hastened inside and filled up the standing room. The remaining ones outside stood near the door, quietly and solemnly, straining their ears to catch the words of the mass and the good father's harangue which followed. When he had finished, Francisco Gonzales took up his muzzle-loading gun from its place of security within the church and walked to just outside the door with it. The people outdoors moved back. Francisco lifted his weapon and fired. There was a loud explosion and a volley of lead pellets sent the evil spirits that were hovering about the place back to the dark regions from which they came. Now was the way clear for San Antonio. Out of the little church came the procession. First, four men bearing a white canopy beneath which walked another man carrying the capilla in which stood San Antonio in his blue robe. Next came the priest leading the chant, which was taken up by the altar boys in his wake. Queer little vestments they wore resembling shirts, and then came the girls lifting their voices in the chant as they marched two by two. Now the worshippers dropped in behind, following in twos as the procession marched solemnly to the little piñón bower to the south part of the village. There the saint was set on a tiny rude table covered with flowers and candles, which was the altar. The priest entered, then retired. The next hour was spent in paying homage to San Antonio, the patron saint and deliverer and protector of the San Antonio de Las Huertas Grant and the people living upon it. Did they not beseech him to deliver their grant from the hands of the raiding Indians and from drough just as they beseeched him to deliver themselves?

Now that the religious ceremonies were over, the day's feasting and drinking began. In groups they made the rounds of the hospitable boards. Wine flowed in abundance. They called such lavish serving of wine, Spanish style. The day waned and dusk came. The fiesta dance was in the sala grande in the house of Juan Armijo. The gaiety was at its height when José Chaves tumbled into the room. They said he sat there for a moment as if thinking, then he went outside. None of the dancers saw him return but when he came in again he had a large tinaja (pottery bowl) of wine. They said that by that time few if any of the merry dancers would have noticed him anyhow. He moved about among them sprinkling the mud floor with wine, giving it a drink. It was fiesta day, why not give everything a drink of wine? How many tinajas of wine he emptied upon the floor no one knew. But by the time he had finished his hospitable task the feet of the dancers began to grow weary in the steps. They found themselves sliding, slipping, landing in each other's embraces, each of them trying to steady himself and his partner. Finally they discovered that the new tewas and the new shoes they wore were heavy with mud. Now some of them sprawled on the slick adobe floor, others fell in trying to aid the fallen ones to their feet. A general brawl ensued. A few were covered by blows and came to a sudden realization of what had happened. There was a general move toward the door. Suits and dresses were bedraggled with mud. The gay new fiesta clothes were a sight to behold. Anger stirred their muddled brains.

Someone remembered, vaguely perhaps, that he saw José with the tinaja of wine. He cried out, "Go get José, go get José Chaves!" The angry crowd took up the cry, as they started the hunt. "Kill him," came from all of them, it was said. José's brother, Juan P., heard the shouts. They had a sobering effect on him. He left the maddened crowd and started on a quiet hunt. He must not call, he must just look until he found his brother before the people discovered him. From all parts of the village now went the cry, "Find José Chaves! Kill him."

They said Juan P. stooped down so none of them could see him and ran as fast as he could go. José might go to his house but Juan P. could not risk going into any houses. Should the crowd see him, they were certain to make him go along with them to hunt José. So he searched all the out places where he thought there was a chance of finding José. While he was at the search, all he could hear was, "Get José! Kill him!" It suddenly came to Juan P. that before this they had found José asleep under the big cottonwood tree across the road from the house of Plácida, when he had imbibed too much wine. Plácida's house was at the other end of the village. At once Juan P. was on his way there. He almost stumbled over the inert body of José in the road. Juan P. tried to wake him but he was too drunk at the moment. The cries of the mob sounded nearer. He must get José to the arroyo, but there was no time to go around the path which led down into the deep arroyo. He must make a straight line for it. So he started dragging José behind him. The rough treatment proved good for José; it sobered him considerably. He became himself sufficiently to demand what it was all about. Juan P. explained his plight. José was scared stiff, and tried his best to run to safety. At the arroyo Juan P. made him sit on the bank with his legs hanging over, then he sat down beside him. There was but one thing to do—slide down that bank, for the shouts of the maddened crowd came closer and closer. "Get José!" Together they went down the steep side of the arroyo and landed on a heap of stones. But they could not remain there; the angered villagers were coming. It was a popular hiding place for those who got themselves into trouble. It would be searched. So they limped on fast as they could go, the cry, "Get José! Kill him!" growing fainter behind them. North to Las Huertas Cañón they went. The going was easier. On they hurried down the cañón until they came out on Camino Real (Royal Road), which was the main highway along the Rio Grande. There the brothers separated. José went hobbling along to Algodones, where he was to hide in the house of a friend until Juan P. should send him word that it was safe for him to return to his home. Juan P. walked back to Placitas. Though the sun was long up, he saw no signs of life in the village. He knew he was safe for they were all sleeping off the effects of their fiesta indulgences. But they did not sleep off their rage against José, whose prank had spoiled their fiesta raiment, brought their revelries to an untimely end, upset things generally. Neither could they forgive him for his wanton waste of the good wine. The more they talked together of the mischief he created, the more determined they were to make him pay. And so it was that José received a warning from Juan P. to flee Algodones and find refuge with relatives in the vicinity of Santa Fe. It was months later before Juan P. sent a message to his brother that he would now be safe in returning to his house in Placitas.

SUBJECT: Life In The Old Houses: Part IX
WPA: 5-5-49 #21
August 11, 1939
Words 2368
Sources of information: Patricio Gallegos, José L.A. Gurulé. Patricio Gallegos
was the son of the Juan María Gallegos of this story.

LIFE IN THE OLD HOUSES: PART IX
Fiesta Days

In past years, the fiesta day of San Juan was really the play day of each of
them, and that was especially true after the middle eighties following the passing of the plodding ox and the introduction of the horse for general use in the
villagers' economic scheme of things. With the coming of the horse, San Juan
Day took on new meaning. It became a day of dangerous sport, a day when
injuries of varying kinds and degrees to the participators in the festivities were
inevitable, and violent deaths were not unusual toll. It was during the final
years of the eighties and the very early nineties that the San Juan Day celebrations were at their roughest and most hazardous.

One of the most eventful and most daring, and likewise one of their last
death-courting celebrations in Ojo de La Casa and Placitas was in the year
1888. A memorable and regrettable day it was for many in those two villages
and they wore the scars of the day's frays, for such the celebrations really
were, until their dying days. In those days the gallo (rooster) was the thing,
and the horse racing was the main event. Each Juan in the village who had
attained the dignity of head of a household must have a chicken to offer the
first one or group to call at his house on San Juan morning or pay a forfeit of
silver. The manner of passing out the fowls was left entirely to the fancy of
the Juans, and more glory to those who conceived the ways most likely to
endanger neck or limbs of the ones who tried to capture them. Men rode hard
and fast in those days. The gallo race was the place to show off their horse-

manship. The more daredevil the riding, the more hero the man. The idea was to stick on their mounts bareback or in the saddle, regardless of the capers of the animals. Bets ran high on San Juan Day races for they became an exciting gambling game.

Weeks and sometimes months before San Juan Day, the men and youths in Ojo de La Casa and Placitas who possessed horses with any show of speed put their animals through severe paces. All the narrow roads, trails, and crooked byways in and around the two villages became temporary race tracks. To condition the beasts, to harden them into endurance, was their aim. The horse that could hold out against time had almost an equal chance with the speedy ones; besides, to be able to emerge triumphant at the finish of the race, and fight, which was always a part of the game, with the rooster or with whatever part was left of it, certainly did require endurance in an animal as well as in the rider. Then, too, the horses must be made beautiful to look at as well as trained into physical fitness and paces. Their coats were washed and brushed until they glistened and their manes and tails were made to look soft and flowing. Pride accompanied the riding of a well-kept, good-looking horse, and often advantageous cash offers for certain such animals followed a San Juan Day race. Then there was the feeding of the horses during the training. They must have plenty of corn and oats even if peculiar and extraordinary means had to be employed to procure it. Usually the peculiar and extraordinary means in those cases was the deliberate transgression of the Sixth Commandment.

On this particular San Juan Day, the elder Juans of Ojo de La Casa and Placitas were up with the dawn and ready with their sacrificial offerings, their sturdiest roosters, to offer the first contingent of riders who came with the day's greetings. Some of the Juans held their fowls aloft and threw them into the midst of their mounted guests, eager for the race and victory. Others buried their chickens in shallow holes by the edge of the roads and covered them with small stones and sticks leaving their heads and necks sticking up, that the riders might try their luck in jerking them from their holes as they swept by. Dangerous sport, that. The riders were lucky indeed if they did not fall from their horses and incur serious injury to their own necks, or cause some of the pursuing horses to pile upon them if their own mounts should chance to break pace. These two methods of putting the roosters into circulation were the most popular.

On this San Juan Day the sun had not yet peeped over the Sandías into the little window of the house of Juan María Gallegos at Ojo de La Casa, when twenty horsemen came tearing down the narrow rocky road leading to

the village. Juan María was ready to receive them. He climbed the ladder leaning against his house to give him a height from which to launch his rooster.
As the squawking fowl fluttered downward, Marijildo Chaves rose in his stirrups and snatched the rooster from the air and away he dashed. In the twinkling of an eye the other horses were in pursuit. Marijildo's mount was one of
the swiftest in the village. He kept well abreast of his pursuers going up the
hill. He came out on the road that is now a part of the famous Loop Drive and
headed toward Placitas. Now the lead horse of his nineteen companions was
gaining on him. Gently he spurred his mount. It leaped forward. In those days
there were many sharp turns and deep ruts and fixed and rolling stones in that
road, and moreover it was precariously narrow. Marijildo knew he must put
more distance between himself and the other racers. Again his horse felt the
dig of the spurs. Now it bounded sidewise. Its foot struck a sharp rock. It
stumbled. The next thing its rider knew, a hand shot out in passing by on a racing horse and seized the rooster. But that was not all Marijildo knew. He was
falling from his horse. He managed somehow to free himself of his stirrups as
the other riders rode past him, but he could not save himself from the sudden
dash to the ground he received as his horse gave an unexpected lurch to gain
its feet, then sent them pawing the air. Marijildo was carried on a ladder to his
house where he lay on his bed for many months. They said he had a broken
head, a leg, and arm, which Francisco Gonzales, the bone setter of Placitas,
fixed and bandaged. He was cut and bruised and broken until it seemed that
he would never be himself again. In that same race two other riders were seriously injured. But for all that, none of the other seventeen still a-horse lost
their ardor for the sport. On they raced over road and trail with first one and
then another seizing the prize, the rooster, from an erstwhile victor whose
horse outstripped his own. And so it went through San Juan Day until the
dusk. Racers struggling for the possession of el gallo, and in the doing, fairly
shedding one another's blood for it. Fist fights were common as they raced
along; a bash over the head from an eager contestant for the fowl was a common injury to those who refused to release the rooster without resistance.

Meanwhile, another race was in bloody progress. Juan Archibeque of
Placitas had planted a rooster with neck and head protruding, for the passing
riders to snatch—if they could. Over a dozen riders went for it, with hardy,
fairly sure-footed mounts. Each rider well knew the danger to life and limb of
such a race. El gallo was planted about one mile from the village on the road
to Bernalillo. Between Placitas and that point there were three deep arroyos
and any number of sharp angles, endangering the safety of racers. But what

mattered? It was all a part of the San Juan Day sports. Come one, come all, and take the risk!

And so they did, more than a dozen racers on that narrow way, striving for the lead to outdistance the others in order to have a chance at el gallo. It was after several had failed when a determined rider came upon the squawking fowl, its neck already clean of feathers jerked out by preceding riders who had tried to drag it from its grave in passing. None now in Placitas remembered his name. He was a visitor who took part in the day's sports. As this unknown rider came upon the spot where el gallo stretched up his long-necked neck, the rider bent low, seized the rooster's head, jerked him free. Somehow the man lost his balance. His horse reared. The oncoming rider piled upon them; he had no time to avert the tragedy, nor was it possible to clear the spot at that point. The unknown rider was crushed fatally. The next man coming at full speed reined in his mount, the sudden stop sent the rider into the air. He came down head-first and suffered an injured back. As for el gallo, his life was stamped out by the foot of one of the horses.

At the very moment of these happenings, another such race was on in another direction from Placitas—the old road between there and Algodones, which was by the way of the ruins of Las Huertas and down the Las Huertas Cañón. In this race the rooster had been pulled from the hole by the very first rider, they said, but he lost it to the next man before he had fairly got it tucked under his arm. For hours the riders in this race for el gallo tore it from each other's hands until the rooster had been dismembered, his feathers scattered to the four winds. The winner came in with naught but the fowl's bloody head, but a hero—the winner of a gallo race of endurance. He had proven that he was a daring rider as well as a most excellent one. But this race which started at sunup and ceased at dusk was not without its share of mishaps. Dislocated wrists, shoulders, and fingers. Cuts and bruises and swollen heads. All were results of first combats during the struggle for possession of el gallo. They had crippled horses to get back into working condition. And one animal sustained a broken leg as he lost his footing on his way down an arroyo. His rider was severely hurt. A great day it had been, barring the accidents, which were the usual things on San Juan Day and to be expected in the course of the day's events.

To add to the general daredevilishness of the festivities of that long-ago San Juan Day, some enterprising saloon-keeper at Bernalillo caused a demi-john of very desirable whiskey to be buried, neck protruding, in a spot on the old road midway between Placitas and Bernalillo, in the same manner as el gallo was buried and for the same purpose. It was for the racer who could grab it from the shallow hole and hold it against all comers until the day was done. The size and rare contents of the jug made its well worth the while and struggles of the many horsemen who contended for it. It was not so easy to manage on a fast galloping horse, the possessors of it soon learned: they also learned that the fights between riders for its possession had a spirit of treachery in them. It seemed to be, get the demijohn by fair means or foul. After eight hours of hard racing and bitter fights, one man from Bernalillo was thrown from his horse and died of a broken neck.

The race for the demijohn of good whiskey may have had much to do with keeping the memory of that certain Juan Day of the past alive in the minds of the older people of Placitas and Ojo de La Casa, who participated in it or heard the tales of it firsthand from their fathers. But the deaths and the number of serious accidents that befell the racers in that day's sports will be remembered and recounted as long as any of those who lived through that long ago fiesta day have a mind to retain them and a tongue to repeat them. A memorable day it was indeed. They recall the weeks and even months those unfortunates injured in the races were in the mending, and they still shake their heads and sign over them as if they were living again those old days. But they enjoy the retelling of the fate of the roosters, how they would be brought in at the close of the day's festivities by the winners, who had nothing of them left in their hands but a wing, a leg, a head, a foot, or a bunch of feathers, to prove their victory.

But true it was that this eventful day of the long ago was one of the last of its barbarous kind. And probably it was not altogether because the law of the state took a hand. The aftermath of the day of daring sport awoke the people themselves to the awfulness of the human sacrifices exacted each San Juan Day in the cause of exciting sport and gambling.

In the old days there were two other saints' days which were observed in the villages of Ojo de La Casa and Placitas. San Lorenzo Day, the fiesta day of Bernalillo, was always kept in a quiet way at home, but all who could attend the festivities at Bernalillo did so. The fiesta day of San Isidoro, the patron saint of the farmer, was always observed by resting from all manual labor.

SUBJECT: Life in the Old Houses: Part X
WPA: 5-5-49 #22
September 1, 1939
Words 1989
Sources of information: José Librado Arón Gurulé, Patricio Gallegos, Fermenia Durán, Predicando Chaves. Patricio Gallegos was the nephew of Juan Chaves and Calletano Chaves of this story. Predicando Chaves was the son of Juan Chaves in this story.

LIFE IN THE OLD HOUSES: PART X

The Christmas festivity was a happy, carefree occasion in the old houses and especially so until the middle eighties. There was no revelry in gift-giving: no rivalry in the kinds of food served upon the Christmas tables. It was the arts and talents of the cooks alone, which made the feasts differ. During the Christmas season there was a spirit of peace on earth good will toward man; there was a religious fervor and a sincere expression of charity.

The important event of the Christmas of the old days was the Velarium (Belarim they call it). A community affair it was, made possible by good-will and free-will offerings. Someone must offer his house for the celebration of the Velarium, which was held on Christmas Eve from 9 o'clock until midnight. Some must give the wood for the luminaries (huge bonfires), which must be lighted about the house to illuminate it so all might see it and come to it, for there they would find the Christ Child in the manger. Some must give food to be taken there to be distributed among the aged poor. Thus, the Christmas was celebrated in Ojo de La Casa.

The last remembered Velarium celebrated in Ojo de La Casa was in 1885, and it was typical of all the Velariums before it in that village. Juan Chaves gave his house for the occasion. It was a large adobe dwelling on the brow of the hill, overlooking Ojo de La Casa from the south. High above the other houses it was, and with the luminaries (made by laying two-foot lengths of wood in corn crib fashion to the height of several feet) sending their fire upward into the night, lighting up the house and the bills about it, it was a grand sight.

The day before Christmas, Juan's large room at the front of the house was made ready for the service. A small wooden altar was set up and the Holy Family, the Infant Jesus in his crib, and the donkey, all in image, were placed up on it. On this occasion the images were brought from the church at Placitas, it was said. Also other preparations to receive the guests who would come to the house of Juan that night were made. Meanwhile, housewives all over the village were cleaning their houses and cooking their Christmas feasts. Plenty of meat they had to prepare: deer and wild fowl. Frijoles (pinto beans) and chili was an important dish and corn in various forms, the fiesta bread pudding, and cakes for the wine which would be served everywhere. This feast was more elaborate and plentiful in sweets than those were at Christmas in the earlier days in the village, because sugar had become a necessity, whereas in the early days it had been a luxury almost beyond the average household.

During that day of preparations, the resador (the one chosen to lead the Velarium and prompt the songs and prayers of those who came to celebrate the birthday of the Christ Child) was busy with his own preparations, and the arrolladoros (the two boys appointed to assist in the work) devoted the day to their own particular purpose. Carrying the Infant in his crib along with them, they made a house-to-house call through the village, repeating set prayers and singing set songs and issuing invitations to each family to attend the Velarium that night at the house of Señor Juan Chaves. Also they asked for and received whatever each family chose to offer. Other boys, sort of sub-arrolladoros with burros, accompanied them on their visits and gathered up these free-will offerings of food, and gifts for the aged poor, and candles and firewood to be used at the Velarium and delivered them to the house of Juan. Nearly always among these free-will offerings were gifts to the Christ Child, which were given to the support of the church.

About nine o'clock in the evening the luminaries were set afire. The house where the Infant Jesus lay was seen clearly from all parts of the village. Every villager who could walk and some who could not, but must be carried thither somehow, hastened to the illuminated house of Juan where the infant

Jesus lay, to adore him. The resador took charge and the ceremony began. He led the singing, he prompted the worshipers in their parts of the prayers, and thus the adoration continued until the booming of a gun outside the house announced the midnight. Then there were hurrying feet going forth in every direction, homeward bound. Another Velarium was over, and as it happened, the last one in Ojo de La Casa. The two boys who last served as arrolladoros were Cándido Chaves and José Peis.

Early on Christmas morning, long before the sun peeped over the Sandías into the hidden village of Ojo de La Casa, the villagers were on foot again, rushing to this house and that, leaving Christmas greetings and taking away in turn gifts of food, prepared the day before by the women of the households, and apples and dried fruit which had been put away against the coming of the Christmas. Wine flowed freely throughout the day as they visited each other in the old houses. The Christmas baile (dance) was an institution, and as the shades of evening crept down the mountainside, another house, the house of Calletano Chaves, was opened for the merry event.

Across the Sandías on the old Cija de la Camino de San Pedro (the high-way between Bernalillo and Tijeras Cañón, Scissors Canyon) was La Madera, the village settled by the cousins of the founders of Ojo de La Casa. There they had their own interpretation of the celebration of the Velarium. They made a game of it. After the passing of the ceremony from Ojo de La Casa, it was a simple matter for them to make the little journey of four miles to La Madera and join in the play with their cousins.

In La Madera the house was offered for the celebration of the Velarium. The altar was erected and set with images, enough of them to tell the whole Christmas story, and these images were all molded of clay by some artistical-ly minded and fingered man or woman of the village. The last one to make these clay images at Christmas time was a woman whose first name was Cesaria. Her last name and the date of her death were not remembered. While this little stage was being set, the resador and the arrollodoros were busy with their parts of the preparations. The arrolladoros called at each house in the vil-lage giving the invitation to attend the Velarium and naming the place where it would be held. They also collected the free-will offerings which were gifts to the Christ Child and were to be used for the church. Silver was the usual gift. Very few, they said, ever failed to offer a gift of silver to the Infant. After them came other boys who collected firewood and candles to be used in the service of the Infant and so the room was lighted and the luminaries were built.

When the luminaries were fired and the house illuminated where the Infant Jesus lay, it was time to seek him out. So forth to the place they went. The resador prompted them in their parts as the service progressed. On each side of the altar stood an ever watchful guard, a man and a woman. They were the padrinos and they must watch the Infant. Those who went to the altar to adore must go in twos, husbands and wives together. The young unmarried men chose maidens to walk to the altar with them. In this way unsuspected budding love affairs came to light, they said, and caused much amusement as well as speculation. After the young people had prayed in twos at the altar, the children followed, likewise in pairs. Thus the remainder of the night wore on. At about the hour of midnight the padrinos feigned drowsiness. The worshippers appeared to nod their heads in sleep. The padrinos made efforts to keep awake and guard the Infant. But at last sleep overpowered them, and the Child was left unprotected. It was then that one secretly chosen by the Padrinos stole furtively into the room and tiptoed noiselessly to the altar and snatched the padrinos' charge and as quietly crept from the room with it. The seconds passed and within the room all was as silent as death. Then in due time a noisy roar from a gun aroused the slumbering ones. They looked at the altar to behold the vacant spot here the crib had been. With the padrinos in the lead they dashed from the room to find the house from which the gun had been fired. There they would find the Infant. The padrinos made a good pretense at aiding in the frantic search but to no avail. But at length the Infant was found in the house of the one who carried him away. Shouts of gladness rang out on the night air. Now the padrinos must redeem the Child. The unlawful possessor must name the price. No set ransom was insisted upon in this game, though usually the one who stole the Infant asked for a dollar, a baile to be given for him at the date he named, or for a rosario to be said on a certain date for a departed relative. When the ransom had been promised by the padrinos, the Infant was given into their hands, and they led the procession back to the house from which it was stolen and restored it to the altar. Thus the Christmas Celebration was concluded, or rather, that part of it which was made into a Christmas game. This Christmas game is a part of the Christmas celebration in the village of La Madera to this day.

In the old days there was little celebration of the New Year. They said that usually there was wine enough left over from Christmas to keep those merry who wished to stay awake to participate in the killing of the Old Year. At the moment before midnight there was a roaring of guns—the Old Year was shot. In the very early days when guns were very few, only one shot was required.

Later in the eighties when guns were common, there was much merrymaking they said, at the expense of those who fired their guns an instant too late. They were accused of killing the New Year. All day they were the butt of the joke and were asked what would they all do, now that they had killed the New Year.

WPA: 5-5-49 #42
January 5, 1940
Words 2262
Sources of information: Ferminia Durán, Magdalena Gallegos, Conception
Archibeque.

LIFE AND PLAY OF THE CHILDREN
(In the Old Houses)

In the early days in the first houses built in Las Placitas, the life of the little children was a "natural course of events" affair. There was nothing special for either diet or play. When the child left the mother's breast, the food for him was atole (milk and meal of ground roasted blue, or pueblo corn). If there was no milk, then a gruel of the meal was made. This cornmeal provided pabulum for them from the beginning when the mothers failed to have the natural milk. As the child advanced in months, soup from frijoles (beans) was added to his diet, and broth from meat and bits of tortillas. There was a gruel made from wheat but it was not in favor as was the atole. Chili was a staple food for the children before they reached the age of three. Wine was given freely to the little children and whatever kind of "coffee" was served to the elders, the little children drank also. In other words, what made a good food for the man made good food for the baby.

The clothing for the babies was a very simply fashioned one-piece affair. A square of cloth called a mantilla it was, and it served to dress the little ones until after they learned to walk abroad. After that the dress was a replica of that worn by the older people.

Then as not, there were so many children to a family that labor was simplified rather than complicated. The more children they had, the more food they were able to hunt and grow. Farming was toil of the severest kind in the old days because the plows, which were only forked sticks, made but scratches in the irrigated soil and labor must be spent to make the land productive.

217

Then wheat and corn must be ground by hand. In fact, it took many hands to make a living in the old days. Nine year-old children made just that many workers. The smaller children played games, though often the older ones, when off duty, joined them in their fun.

In those long ago days the little children spent much of their play time about the small house of the motherly Gabrielita Gallardo. She taught them to play and often led their games. She set them to playing one particular favorite: ¿Qué es chícharo? (What is peas?). Because they need not leave the spot where she started the game, that made it simple for her or the older girls helping about the house to keep an eye upon the little ones as they worked. And too, it was a lively game and afforded an outlet for the little players' energies.

❧ ❧ ❧

¿QUÉ ES CHÍCHARO?
(What is peas?)

One child who started the game was chosen by popular acclaim. At once that child became the starting point of a circle of children. Scuffles ensued as all wanted to be near the leader. When the circle was completed, the leader thrust the thumb of her right hand into her right cheek and waved it back and forth in fan motion while exclaiming in all her power of voice "¿Qué es chícharo?" The child to her right followed the leader's motion and joined her voice in unison, calling out lustily "¿Qué es chícharo?" Then the second on the leader's right dented her right cheek with the thumb of her right hand and fanned her hand vigorously crying out with the other two, "Qué es chícharo?" Number four joined in and the one next in the circle was waving his hand form a thumb and crying out "¿Qué es chícharo?" The circle became a jumping, hopping, dancing circle going round and round with voices in all ranges singing out "¿Qué es chícharo?" And thus the children, hand in hand, went round until their throats "croaked" and their heads were dizzy. Then it was that the circle came to a stand. The leader at once stopped her cry and the circle stood silent. Suddenly the leader squatted down; again her right thumb was thrust into her right cheek and as she fanned her hand she cried "¡Este es chícharo!" (This is peas). In order as before, each child in the circle followed her motion and took up the new refrain "¡Este es chícharo!" When all were squatted in the circle, it once more became a lively circle and a noisy one. Around and round went the children in a duck walk, waving their hands from their right cheeks, calling at the tops of their voices, "¡Este es chícharo!" The circle was naturally waddling and some fell outside and some inside of the circle and of course they were all convulsed with laughter. But round and round they waddled until they could go no more. Then again the leader stilled her voice and brought silence to the circle. Then again the leader came to her feet, again thrust her thumb in her cheek and fanned her hand while crying "¿Qué es chícharo?" One by one in order the children came to their feet and again the circle was a jumping, hopping, dancing one, going round and round until it was brought to a stop, to again be made into a circle of children squatting on the ground doing the duck walk. And thus it went until the little children were too tired to play longer.

🐝 🐝 🐝

COYOTITO
(Name given the boy who played coyote)

A rough and popular game was Coyotito. Somewhere not too far away there must be a cave, the home of Coyotito. The side of an adobe house or a corral served as the home of the mother and her children who were the victims of Coyotito in the game. The mother was always the oldest girl in the game. She must take her children for a walk and, knowing of the terrible Coyotito, she had her children walk along one after another with their arms clasped firmly about the waist of the child in front. At the terrifying approach of Coyotito, the head and tail of the line joined and a circle was formed, the mother in the center from where she tried to defend her children when Coyotito came and tried to find a weakness in the circle and drag out a child. He would pull and push and try to wrench a child free of the hands that grasped it about the waist, and at the same time fend off the blows directed at him by the mother within the circle. But the game was to take one of the children from the circle so Coyotito bent his energies to the task while the mother sought to chase him away. He yipped in all coyote ferocity and, using his fingers as claws, sought to keep the mother off while he tore at the hands that bound the children together. The battle went on until he had broken the bonds and seized a child. He took it up in his arms and went leaping and jumping and racing toward his cave, yelping in a coyote manner. The children broke their circle, the mother went flying after Coyotito. Only she could catch him. No child could touch Coyotito, so went the game. Now the race was on. To save her child the mother must intercept the kidnapper before he reached the safety of his cave. If she did not, then she must pay Coyotito's price for the return of her child. Coyotito might ask her most prized possession. That must not happen. So the mother spurred on to the chase, her other children racing with her, but avoiding a direct contact with the evil Coyotito. How the game ended depended upon the superiority of swiftness of foot of the mother or coyotito. Should the mother catch him and retrieve her child, Coyotito was in for a beating, thus it was up to Coyotito to reach his cave. In either case the loser paid. After the debt was paid the game was repeated. Coyotito was a great and exciting game and in high favor among not only the smaller children but the older ones. "Pára, suelta la niña" (stop, turn the child loose) was the cry of the mother and the children as they pursued Coyotito and the child.

🦋 🦋 🦋

TAN TAN
(Knock Knock)

This game was played by children who are now the grandfathers and grandmothers of the younger fathers and mothers now in Placitas. There are few of this older generation left, and none of the present generation ever heard of the game.

In Tan Tan the boys and girls stood in a circle and the oldest girl playing the game was the mother. She was called Madre de Los Colores (Mother of the Colors) and the children were called Los Colores (the Colors). The oldest boy in the game was Comprador de Colores (Buyer of Colors). He approached the circle singing out "Tan Tan." From the mother of the colors came "¿Quién es?" (Who is it?). His reply was "La vieja Inéz." (The Old Woman). The mother then demanded, "¿Qué queres?" (What do you want?) The buyer of colors answered, "Yo quiero un listón" (I want a ribbon). Then he added the name of the color he desired. Each child in the circle had been given the name of a color by the mother, at the outset of the game. If there was a child named the color the ribbon buyer named, then that child ran from the circle pursued by the ribbon buyer. They ran anywhere and as long as they pleased and finally finished with either the child uncaught back in the circle, or the buyer catching the child and taking him off to his prison, where he was kept until the game was started anew.

If the color named was not in the circle, the buyer must return, or else he returned for a new color. On his second return the calls differed in places. So approaching for the second time he called "Tan, tan" (Knock, knock). When the mother asked, who is it, he now replied, "La vieja loca" (An Old Crazy). On his third return after calling "Tan tan," the mother answered, "¿Quién toca?" (Who knocks?). The return from the buyer was "Un preso" (A Prisoner). From the mother came, "¿Qué crimen comitó éste?" (What crime did you commit, prisoner?). The buyer returned, "Masqué el hueso pero no tengo pruebas del hueso" (Chewing a bone but I have no proof of the bone). Then followed the "¿Qué queres?" with the buyer asking for a ribbon and naming the color.

There were at least ten different phrases used by the buyer of ribbons in introducing himself to the mother of the colors, but the three related above were the only ones which could be remembered. There were also various ways in which the mother inquired of the identity of the buyer of ribbons, but no one seemed to recall but the two given above.

❧ ❧ ❧

ASOTE
(Whip)

Asote was a sort of hide and seek game. It was played with a large piece of cloth that was to be hidden in a "good place" that was difficult to find. The ones to hide it were chosen by the players. The child about to hide the cloth commanded the players to shut their eyes tight and cover them with their hands. That done, he ran away and hid the cloth. No one could look until he returned and gave the command. Sometimes the "good place" took hours to find when the older children played the game. The reward to the finder of the cloth was the privilege of whipping the other players with it, if he could catch up with them. There was where the fun came in, and many a scrap also, if the one lashed with the cloth truly believed the whipper was spitefully using the cloth. This game gave the childish feet plenty of exercise and taught somewhat of good sportsmanship.

❧ ❧ ❧

MUÑECAS
(Dolls)

To play muñecas, and the children played this game often, only a big pile of adobe mud was required, but mixed just right. When the mud was ready, the children gathered about the pile and took what they needed for the dolls they were to make. There was more to this game than just molding pieces of mud in shapes to fit together to look like dolls, then laying them in the sun to bake. There was a spirit of rivalry among the little players to make not only good dolls, but each desired to have his doll the best made during the day's play. Ferminia Durán said that she could remember how many of the little children worked to have their dolls attract the attention of the older people, and to hear words of praise of the dolls they made was the reward of the game. She made many dolls herself when she was a little girl.

SUBJECT: Folktales
WPA: 5-5-49 #'s 34 to 37
January 26, 1940
Source of information: Magdalena Gallegos.

THE WISE DONKEY

Long, long ago two wise men learned in the science of the sun, moon, stars, and the weather, climbed to the highest point of the Sandía Mountains to study the stars and solve some of their astrological problems. With them they carried their instruments for their studies, and their blankets and food.

Evening was coming on. A fair evening their instruments promised, just as the day had been fair. A wonderful night it would be to study the stars. As they came close to the top of the mountain they saw a neat little ranch. A donkey was grazing nearby and an old woman stood in the doorway of the small house. When she saw the two wise men, she greeted them and inquired their mission.

"We are here to study the stars tonight," said one.

"You would be much safer to bring yourselves and your belongings in under my roof. It might rain tonight," said the old woman.

"Huh, there is no sign of rain tonight," scoffed both the wise men.

At that the old woman appeared amused. "But to be safe," she insisted, "I think you would be safer to bring yourselves and your belongings in under my roof. It will rain tonight."

"She is a crazy old woman," whispered one wise man to the other. "Our instruments show no indication of a change in weather, and we see nothing ourselves to warn us of rain. Let's thank the old woman for her advice and be on our way."

They set up their instruments ready for their observations and unpacked their blankets. Then all of a sudden a harsh wind rushed through the pine trees. The next thing they knew dark clouds were spreading over the sky. Then came the rain. It beat down harder every second. The wise men gathered up their belongings, for there was no time to lose. Back they ran to the shelter of the old woman's house.

"Tell us," demanded one of the wise men. "How did you know it would rain tonight? We are wise men and read all signs. We saw no sign of rain."

"Because this afternoon my donkey told me," she said simply. "He went running and jumping all around the place. That always foretells rain very soon."

Early the next morning the two wise men left the house, and the old woman went outside to see them off. To her surprise they turned to go back down the mountain.

"You are not going to stay to study the stars?" she asked.

"We are going back where we came from," answered one. "What's the use of all our scientific studies and our instruments to guide us, when a burro knows more about the weather than science?"

"Who knows what God tells the animals?" the old woman inquired.

❦ ❦ ❦

Words 2723
Sources of information: Patricio Gallegos, Magdalena Gallegos, Ramón Nieto,
José García.

CAPITÁN GRANDE, AGUA
(Great Captain, Water)

It was many years over a century ago when Pedro Viejo (Old Pedro) and his
wife Elena lived in Las Huertas Cañón (The Gardens Canyon). They were a
very devout old couple who never neglected their prayers or the saints. In fact,
Elena repeated her prayers even as she swept and cleaned her house every
morning.

It happened that one winter day Pedro Viejo went to the mountains for
wood. As he hunted around in the snow for his wood, he came upon a small
spot where there was not one flake of snow. The strange thing caused him to
stop and wonder what it meant. Then right in the center of the small dry area
he spied a peach seed. He picked it up. It was the biggest and prettiest peach
seed he had ever seen. He put it in his pocket and carried it to his house to
show Elena. When he showed it to her, she vowed it was different than any
peach seed she had ever seen and they laid it on the table, for they both decided to keep it.

The next morning Pedro Viejo went out with his sheep, and Elena went
about her housework. As she swept her floor she repeated her prayers aloud
as she always did. At the sound of her voice the peach seed jumped about on
the table, and there was a knocking at the little window and the door—a loud
and furious knocking. Elena dropped her broom in terror as she hushed her
prayers. Then when her voice was still the peach seed lay suddenly quiet on
the table just where she had put it and the knocking stopped. Now all was

silence in the room. Elena was so frightened she ran outside but the cold soon drove her into the house again.

When Pedro Viejo returned, she told him all about it. To her dismay, he laughed at her and told her she had been dreaming. But she insisted that the story she had told him was true. Then Pedro Viejo had a bright thought. He commanded his wife to do just what she had been doing when the strange thing of which she told him had happened.

So Elena took up her broom and started to sweep the floor, and as she swept she said her prayers. Then Pedro Viejo was as frightened as much as his wife had been, for the peach seed jumped about on the table and there was the loud knocking at the little window and the door. And as before, all was quiet again when Elena stopped her prayers. Pedro Viejo shook his head and said that they must arise early in the morning and carry the peach seed to the good priest at the Pueblo of San Felipe and tell him everything they had seen and heard.

When the priest heard their story and carefully examined the peach seed, he told them that it was a very strange story they told and that he could tell them nothing until he had seen the thing for himself, that he would go back with them and they must show just how it all happened.

When the three of them came to the house of Pedro Viejo, Elena took up her broom as Pedro Viejo placed the seed upon the table as before. Then Elena swept her floor and repeated her prayers. As before, the peach seed jumped about on the table and there came the knocking at the window and the door. The good priest was much disturbed.

"In God's name I must ask for the story of this peach seed," he said. Then he prayed for enlightenment. Very soon the devout old couple were astonished to hear a strange new voice in the room. It was like low, sweet music and the soft whispering of the wind in the trees. When it ceased the priest said, "God has listened to my prayer. Now I shall tell you the story of the peach seed, which God has caused you to find.

"Once a poor ignorant Navajo heard of God and baptism. Every day his mind dwelled upon his misery, for he had not been baptised. Each day as he rode his horse over desert and mountain he cried out, "Capitán Grande, agua," and he patted his head as he looked upward for God to send the waters of baptism upon him. The years went by and still each day he cried out, "Capitán Grande, agua." At last the Navajo died and his doomed soul passed into the peach seed and the little devils entered it to torture the soul. It was the prayers of Elena that caused the peach seed to dance about on the table as the devils rushed out of it to get out of the presence of prayers to God. They knocked their heads against the window and the door in their frenzy to run out of sound of her voice. Now it is God's will that you take this peach seed and come with me to the church that I may receive it from you, the padrinos (godparents), for baptism."

And so Pedro Viejo and his wife Elena took the seed and went back to the Pueblo of San Felipe, where the priest gave the soul of the Navajo the name the padrinos chose for him (and which has long since been forgotten) and sprinkled holy water upon the seed in baptism. And as the water touched the seed, it opened and a tiny snow white dove sprang from it and raised its wings and flew up and up into the heavens.

🐾 🐾 🐾

THE PHANTOM RAIDERS

A strange thing happened at Tejón in the days when the Navajos roamed and raided at will and even killed. The citizens of Tejón felt safe enough from the raiders when they were within their walls, for Tejón was a walled town. But most of their lives were spent outside those walls. Water and wood must be carried in, livestock must be herded in the mountains for grazing, the fertile land around the vicinity of the walls must be cultivated. To help safeguard life and property outside the walls, two of the citizens at the same time served as guards for a given term and without salary. They were chosen by the vote of the citizens as the majordomos in the native villages are chosen today. These guards were ever on the alert for signs of the enemy and to warn the town. Their duty was to give alarm if they even sensed danger. But in spite of this precaution they were not always able to save their harvests and flocks of sheep and goats from the invaders.

It came about early one morning that Juan Nieto rode into the town on a magnificent black mare. Both rider and mount looked much worse for wear. Juan was an adventuresome youth of questionable exploits; the possession of the fine horse was one of them, but no one in the village dared inquire of Juan how he came by such a fine mare. They all gathered about him and admired the animal and congratulated him upon his safe return to the village; he had been gone about a month, none of them knew where.

For a few days all went well. Juan kept constant vigil over his prized possession in the daytime and at night secured it in the corral adjoining his house. But feed was very scarce and even pasturage was scant, so Juan found that his horse must be tethered out at night where the short grass grew. Then it was that one of the guards saw a lone Navajo clothed in a robe of animal skins standing on the brow of the hill where Tejón Cañón emerged from the mountains just outside the plana (plain) where Tejón was built. The Navajo was signalling someone far behind him. The guard ran to the town to give the alarm, for what could the Navajo be doing but sending signals to a band of Indians planning a raid upon them?

In no time at all the men and boys, armed with whatever manner of weapons they had (and mostly those were bows and arrows), ran to the spot where the guard had seen the lone Navajo. But there was nothing to be seen, not even the lone Navajo, so they went home, the mystery unsolved.

The next day about the same time, which was mid-afternoon, the lone Navajo was again sighted upon the brow of the hill signalling to something to the right and to the left of him and to the rear of him. Again the alarm was spread in the town, and again the men and boys fared forth, but this time determined to hunt down the Navajo and his band of raiders.

Again they saw nothing of the Navajo nor any band waiting to invade their fields and drive off their flocks, but they found tracks of Indians everywhere over the hillside, down the mountain slope, and in the cañón. A mystifying confusion of tracks leading everywhere but nowhere. They returned home weary and baffled.

Juan ran at once to his horse, or to where his horse had been. He sent up a cry that brought the citizens of Tejón from their houses. The animal had been stolen while they scoured the hills for the Navajo.

Old Juan Antonio Chaves, grandfather of Juan, spoke up: "We have been fools. One Navajo has tricked us from our homes. One Navajo made all the tracks to deceive us. One Navajo took Juan's horse." He laughed at the joke that had been played upon them. His neighbors joined in. "That one Navajo wanted the horse just for himself." He addressed Juan in these words:

"Que es bueno para uno es bueno para otro." (What is good for one is good for another).

☙ ☙ ☙

RICARDO'S DEER

San Juan Day was drawing near. Ricardo must make a trip to the mountains to kill a deer for the feast. Deer meat was the most fitting dish to serve upon San Juan Day.

So he arose long before sun rise and set out. He walked along without making a noise, lest he frighten the deer and cause them to run high up in the mountains. But in spite of his precaution there was not a deer to be seen. He thought it looked as if someone had told them he was coming. So he went climbing higher and higher.

Then came high noon and he was weary with the hunt. As he looked about for a place to sit and eat his lunch, his eyes fell upon a young deer. It was stretched out on the ground, fast asleep. Ricardo raised his gun to shoot it. No, he would take it alive. That would be easy with such a small deer. He laid down his gun and crept along on his knees to seize it by the neck. As he reached out his arm, the deer suddenly grew to huge size. It struck him with a powerful kick of a hind leg, opened his forehead and sent him tumbling down the mountain slope. There he lay for sometime, collecting his senses. Finally his head cleared and he realized what had happened. He moaned aloud: "What a fool am I! What a fool am I to leave my cachana behind. If I now had it in my pocket, this would not have happened to me."

Now his cachana was a small piece of the root of a wild bush the Indians called cachana. It was sewed up in a little bag that it could be fastened to the clothes one wore or carried in a pocket. Cachana was the most potent charm there was against the power of witches. Scarcely anyone in the old days was foolish enough to go without his cachana either day or night.

Bemoaning his fate, Ricardo got up and started back up the slope to get his gun. He had taken only a few steps when he came face to face with Doña Euphemia, who lived in the mountains just above Ojo de La Casa. She carried his gun. But Ricardo did not want any more dealings with Doña Euphemia away up there in the mountains. He turned and fled, leaving his gun behind.

When Ricardo reached his door, there stood his gun, but he did not so much as touch it until he had his cachana in his pocket. Now he was safe from Euphemia and her kind. Never again would he leave his cachana behind.

And it is true that there are people to this day who have a little sack fastened somewhere inside their clothing or in their pocket. They call it cachana and it is to protect them from the power of the witches.

SUBJECT: The Trader of Ojo de La Casa
WPA: 5-5-49 #53
March 1, 1940
Words 1801
Sources of information: Patricio Gallegos, Terecita Baca. Patricio Gallegos is the son of Juan María. Terecita Baca is the granddaughter of Juan María.

THE TRADER OF OJO DE LA CASA

Juan María Gallegos, like his father, Cassimiro, was a born trader. Before he was fifteen, he aided his father in handling his flocks and in bartering and in making successful cash sales, wherever there was money to be had. Never was one of his race more successful in wheedling, extolling unfair gains from the Americano, in the old days with his ingratiating, "Whatever the señor wish to give," when asked the price of his sales. This gainful practice he continued until his death in his eightieth year, which was 1930.

It was in the summer of 1865 that Juan María and his father drove their sheep and goats to Santa Fe for the last time. That summer they had more than a thousand sheep and around four hundred goats. Santa Fe offered a profitable market for lambs and kids and goat milk and cheese during the summer months. In the old days there was always money in Santa Fe. There the trades were more advantageous than anywhere else, where there was no cash. All around Santa Fe, pasturage was most excellent, and nearly always there were the summer rains to keep the plentiful grass green.

But this traders' paradise was not without its serpent for Juan María and his father. They were from the País Bajo (Low Country), which in the old days the native New Mexicans called the Middle Rio Grande Valley and vicinity. Santa Fe and vicinity was called the País Alto (High Country). There was a spirit of rivalry in trade and games among these two peoples and a contention as to whose social and economic ways were the wisest and best. Many a fistic combat was averted by some timely native diplomacy, or a barrel of wine.

But Juan María and his father were just the types to stand the jibes and even insults and pass on some of their own. One day as Juan María peddled his goat-milk cheese from a large tinaja (pottery vessel) he encountered a group of men from Santa Fe. They were engaged in their favorite pastime—rolling and smoking punche wrapped in corn husks. These cigarettes were no fewer than six inches in length. Skill was required to make them hold together. One of the group said to Juan María, "My son, how many times do you people of the low country lick your cigarette with your tongue to make it hold together?" Juan María replied, "Señor, we people of the low country lick our cigarettes three times with our tongues to make them stick together. But we have heard that you people of the high country run off at the mouth so much that you never have to lick your cigarettes with your tongue." Then he smiled and passed on quickly, not waiting for the reaction of his thrust.

At the close of that summer of 1865, Juan María came back from Santa Fe with money enough to pay for his wedding to María de Los Ángeles Zamora of Ojo de La Casa. After the wedding they built their house and Juan María settled down to make a living at home and roam no more with his father's flocks. His father presented him with a small herd each of goats and sheep, and after that he turned his attention to converting animal skins into things to use and to wear. Mostly his workshop was his front yard, where he had plenty of room and sunlight. But the room at the southwest corner of his house where there was a fireplace was his cold weather shop. This house built by María de Los Ángeles and Juan María stands today just as it was built in 1866, and the room where he displayed his art remains in every detail as it was then.

He used great care in preparing his skins and cured them with a weed that the Indians used successfully. In his shop he had tewas of all sizes: soles of oxhide, uppers of goat or deer hides. He used correa, or thread, made of deer skin for the sewing. This correa was not easy to prepare. It required time and patience to roll the slender strips of deer hide into pliable, round thread after it was properly soaked. After it was finished and ready for use he threaded it into an iron needle he himself had made. (His grandfather used a needle made of deer horn but he worked the correa in the same manner). Now he sewed the uppers to the oxhide soles with cross-stitch, which was both ornate and durable. The tewas were made while the hides were wet, and when they were finished they were placed into a water hole to remain until the ones who had them made called for them. The time for the call was set by the maker of them. When they came for the tewas, they put them on their feet direct from the water hole and wore them away. Thus, as the tewas dried, they were shaped to the feet.

He anticipated one of the mothers' aids of modern times. He made a soft, pliable, waterproof skin to be used on the bed for mothers and, when cut into small pieces, was used as protectors for babies. They called it gamuza (antelope) and it accomplished all the purposes of the rubber sheeting of today. After the disappearance of the antelope he made goat hides do the same duty.

After he had thoroughly cleaned and scraped the animal hide, he worked salt and rabbit brains into it. This was done thoroughly also. Then he stretched it out to dry. When the drying was complete, he soaked the skin and spread it out on the back of a clean buffalo hide. With a heavy wooden hammer or mallet he beat it until he could crush it in his hands, then he worked it with his fingers until it was as soft as a piece of their home-woven merino.

He made large and small talegones (pouches for tobacco, or punche). They were works of art. When finished, the pouch was shaped like a bottle and a wooden cork was attached to the neck of it with a little strap of the same skin. The talegón was cut in two sections and sewed up the sides with correa with neat coarse stitches. In the same manner, he sewed the fine leather he had tanned into cubiertas para cuchillos (covers for hunting knives) after he had cut the skin in the shape of the knife. In later days he made holsters for revolvers. And to go with these he made belts. In the early days they were fastened by threading the correa through the holes made in the belts and tying it.

He made leather ropes that "wore like iron." When his oxhide was ready for cutting, he laid it flat and started his work. He cut round and round the hide going from the outside to the middle and making the cuts some two inches wide. When he reached the end, or the center, he put the hide in water and soaked it. In time he took it from the water and stretched it out into one long strip and this he cut into two equal pieces. He fastened them together at one end and tied that end to a pole where it would be held firmly. Then he started to intertwine the two pieces, pulling them as tightly together as his strength would permit. Thus, the two strips were put together and then pulled out as far as they would go and the other ends fastened together. Again it was put into water, then stretched out and dried. By splicing the strips or cutting them, ropes could be made any desirable length. When they shrunk or showed signs of weakness, they were soaked and dried again and looked like new. Thus were made the ropes used in those days of long ago in Ojo de La Casa and Las Placitas.

And then came the burro. As long as he cost from thirty to fifty dollars, he was few in number in the villages. But when his price fell to twenty he mounted in number. He had no competitor when it came to bringing wood down from the mountainside. But he must have a pack saddle. Juan María made them. Like cradles they were made of small, round pieces of wood, matched pieces cut from the pine trees and put together with ox or goat hide straps and the bands that held this saddle in place on the burro's back were made of the hides he had prepared for use.

Then he made the hides of sheep and goats into rugs for the mud floors. But these he could not trade. Every householder of those old days had his flocks; consequently, every housewife had her rugs made at home, for this was not a difficult task and anyone could clean and dry a hide with the hair on it.

In his young days he wore clothing made of deerskin. He made them for himself. But as far as can be learned he never made them for barter.

But he gave the community yet another service, and for that one he will be remembered as long as any of those he served are among the living. After they no longer wore the tewas, he gave at least two extra lives to the shoes they bought from the store. He would carefully trim the uppers from the worn-out shoes, using the soles for patterns for new ones to be cut from tough oxhide. Then he soaked the new soles and the old uppers and sewed them together with correa just as he sewed the tewas. He earned many a measure of blue cornmeal, and frijoles and many a ristra of chili, making over store shoes, and of course always with these he sold enough correa for laces, or rather traded them, for Juan María was a born trader.

Thus, it was because of his barter in things made of hides that he possessed oxen long after his neighbors were without them. He long boasted of his one big cash deal in a hide. It was his last ox. He sold it to a butcher in San Pedro for sixty dollars.

SUBJECT: The Terror of Ojo de La Casa
WPA: 5-5-49 #52
March 15, 1940
Words 2412
Sources of information: Patricio Gallegos, Magdalena Gallegos, Terecita Baca, Antonio de Lara.

THE TERROR OF OJO DE LA CASA

The days of the early eighties brought good money and bad men to Las Placitas and Ojo de La Casa. The stirring mining activities in that vicinity and the thrilling tales of gold hidden in the mountains there turned the thoughts of the village men from sheep and goats to mines. At Ojo de La Casa and Las Placitas, at Tejón and San Pedro, strangers with and without money staked mineral claims and hired native labor to tunnel the mountainsides in search of the yellow metal. At Ojo de La Casa, the old Montezuma Mine was reopened and new workings were made all along the north end of the Sandías.

On the tide of this excitement came men seeking easy money, men who would kill to get it. There were other men who wanted good horses and cattle as well as gold, and were ready to shoot for them. In those old dangerous days many a good man died defending his wallet or his horse. And many a bad man dangled from the end of a rope in some village plaza for his crimes.

On this tide of excitement came Merino Leyba to Ojo de La Casa from Puerto de Luna. He brought his wife and little boy with him. Ostensibly he came to visit his wife's father, Florentino Chaves, brother of Juan P. and Calletano Chaves, early settlers of Ojo de La Casa. But his real motive was to find a new hunting ground in which to pursue his dark and sinister ways of filling his pockets with money without working for it. Leyba was a man of powerful build, towering height, but carried no excess weight. He had large, hard black eyes and a heavy, upward-curling moustache, as was the mode of that day. He was an expert shot and horseman.

From the start he made a point of putting the fear of his gun in the heart of every family in Ojo de La Casa, Las Placitas, and San Pedro. He was not the bullying type, but one that made it clear what he would do in certain cases, and if necessary carried out his threat without ceremony.

It was during those days of the early eighties that an eastern company with valuable mining property in San Pedro came to New Mexico with plans for developing their interests. They were handicapped in the placer mining region (a region which seemed to promise golden wealth) by a dearth of water with which to carry on operations. The company hit upon a scheme to bring an abundance of water from the Sandía Mountains to San Pedro.

And so it was that one morning the people of Las Placitas and Ojo de La Casa awoke to find great, heavy wagons drawn by spans of big mules and loaded with sections of twelve-inch iron pipe moving slowly along through the villages, mountain bound. At that time the main road to the higher Sandías went through Ojo de La Casa as well as Las Placitas. Men and boys from both villages trailed the wagons to learn what it was all about. And they did; and some of them remained to help do it at a goodly daily wage. A construction camp was being built of logs just five miles up the road in the mountains where abundant springs provided a huge water supply. A line was being surveyed from the spot to San Pedro via La Madera and San Pedro Viejo, a probable distance of fifteen miles. A trench for the twelve-inch pipe was to be dug along this line.

Then word came to Juan María Gallegos that the superintendent at the camp wanted a man to carry the company mail from Bernalillo to San Pedro and back. After duly considering Merino Leyba and his ways, Juan María decided to go up to the camp and ask for the job. He believed he could handle Leyba diplomatically and with a friendly loan of a little cash now and then, which of course would be accepted as a gift. Juan María's keen, quick eye and his way with a gun and a horse won him the contract to carry the company mail during the time of construction of the pipe line. When he signed the contract, he was told to shoot to kill if any one tried to molest the mail, and the company would take all the responsibility. The company furnished him with a good gun and a good horse, and he must provide himself with another gun and a good saddle horse. The distance from Bernalillo to San Pedro by La Madera was about thirty miles. He was to start from Bernalillo each alternate morning for the camp where he delivered the pouch. When it was ready he carried it on to San Pedro where he remained all night. Next morning he was given the pouch to return it to the camp. When it was made ready he carried it back to Bernalillo. Thus, he passed through Ojo de La Casa each day, where he made a brief stop. There are none now living who remember, if they ever knew, how much money was paid for this carrying of the company mail.

Until the construction was well under way, this trail between the terminals was a long and lonely one. Especially did the lone native horseman, or traveler on foot, have a distaste for the eerie vicinity of San Pedro Viejo, the place of the ruins of an ancient pueblo. That ghosts and witches held revels there, was the belief of the native Mexicans in all the mountain villages round about. They said even horses pricked up their ears when they passed that way.

One day as Juan María watched the busy blacksmiths at their work while his mail was being made up, a well-dressed American man rode up to where the men were working. All the mechanics on the construction work were Americans brought from Colorado by the company. The superintendent came out to greet the stranger, and all about Juan María there was talk that he could not understand, for he spoke not one word of English. But he learned later that the man was a government inspector from Washington, and that a few hours after Juan María was gone, he rode on toward San Pedro where he had business.

As usual, as Juan María went through Ojo de La Casa, he halted. He saw no one in particular and soon rode on for Bernalillo. The next day on his trip when he approached San Pedro Viejo, Juan María was disturbed by the sudden, unexpected movements of his horse. The animal shied, pricked up his ears, and his rider was forced to use his whip to make the animal go forward. Juan María could see nothing unusual about the place, though the actions of his horse made it evident that there was something whether he could see it or not. The next morning as he came from San Pedro, his horse stopped short, pricked up his ears, and snorted and had to be forced forward when they reached the place near San Pedro Viejo, just as he had done the day before. Juan María did not stop to investigate. He got out of there. On the next trip to San Pedro it was the same.

But that day at San Pedro it was not the same. There was excitement in the air. The government inspector had never reached the place. Searching parties were out. The next morning on his return trip to the camp, Juan María passed a party of men just where his horse had tried to tell him in horse-language that something was wrong. But the mail had to go through, in spite of the mail carrier's desire to stay and see.

It was at San Pedro the next night that Juan María heard the story in his own tongue. The party he saw at San PedroViejo discovered evidence of a fire not far from the trail in a sort of hidden spot. They combed the place with sticks and they found a gold ring and it showed that it had been in a fire. That was all anybody knew. But later at San Pedro, Juan María was told that the ring had been identified as the ring worn by the government inspector at the time of his disappearance.

At Ojo de La Casa, Leyba was gone from Florentino's house on the top of the hill overlooking Ojo de La Casa. He was away on a visit, the family said. The visit lasted a month. Leyba came back in good new clothes. But that was not all; he had a new horse and saddle.

At San Pedro the next night a masked man held up a saloon. None of them needed to be told that it was Leyba at his old tricks. But no one dare mention the fact that he knew it was Leyba. The thriving saloons at San Pedro paid regular tribute to Leyba in this manner and, strange to say, no one did anything about it. The fear of Leyba's gun was as a pall over San Pedro.

At Ojo de La Casa, Leyba went his usual ways as the months slipped by and no one heard more of the fate of the government inspector. They all thought, as did Leyba, that this case was like the other cases of mysterious disappearances and murders that had happened around the country. A few weeks of excitement and some talk, and after that the whole affair died down, and was brought to life no more.

Then one night in the dark Leyba talked. Whether he talked because he must or because he could not resist boasting is not known. But peace was no more in Ojo de La Casa when his story was told. If the truth got out, which ones of them would Leyba make pay? Besides, the tale he told gave them all a greater fear of him than they had known before.

In detail he told of the gun battle he had with the government man. How he first saw him when he stepped from the train at Bernalillo. How he shadowed him about the town, saw him take his wallet from his pocket, learned at a livery stable that the man would leave on horse the next morning for the camp in the Sandías and go on to San Pedro. He told how he followed the man as far as Las Placitas and then cut off the road and went by Tejón Cañón to the San Pedro Trail. He came upon him near San Pedro Viejo. He found that the man could shoot as good as he could. In the exchange of shots Leyba's horse was killed. As he went down, he fired at the government inspector but missed. He got behind his horse to protect himself from the inspector's next bullet. Leyba's next shot felled the inspector's horse; then from the ground behind the bodies of their dead mounts, they waged a gun battle until the inspector was shot through the head. Leyba said he searched his body, took his wallet, which contained over three hundred dollars. Then he built a fire encircling the man and his horse and another to burn his own horse. All night he kept the fires going low and hot and by morning he had nothing left but ashes. He covered them and hid out until night, when he came to Ojo de La Casa. He hid in the house of Florentino, just waiting to see what happened. As he heard of nothing, he went away for a time. When he came back he heard rumors here and there to the effect that the government at Washington had taken a hand in the affair of the missing inspector. Leyba became suspicious of his neighbors. From his doorway high above the village, from where he commanded a view of every house in Ojo de La Casa, he watched them. The villagers knew they were watched and took care that they never spoke his name. Often when two or three of them were talking together, they would suddenly become aware of the big man's presence. He said nothing but they had no trouble reading meaning into his actions.

The rumors were persistent. Leyba took a trip to the little village of Manzana in the Manzana Mountains. He remained there for months, or long enough, as he thought, for the matter to be dropped again. And, strange to say, no one in Ojo de La Casa heard further rumors. Miteria, Leyba's wife, had a way to warn Leyba should she hear anything, so as the murderer heard nothing from her, he decided to return home.

But things happened in Santa Fe while Leyba tarried in the remote little mountain village of Manzana, none of which Miteria ever heard. It was known in Ojo de La Casa by one man. And that one man, Juan María, never let word of it escape his lips. The government of the United States had offered a reward for Leyba dead or alive.

Leyba returned to San PedroViejo. At least he reached that place on his journey home. There he was met by two horsemen. One he knew well. As the two rode close to Leyba the friend dismounted and stood close to Leyba to shake hands. As he grasped Leyba's hand, the other rider shot Leyba dead. The reward was theirs. Joaquín Montoya did the shooting.

These two men it was said were not known in Ojo de La Casa. They told how they had planned to take the murderer of not one man but several. They said they knew no one could ever take him alive. This much Juan María heard in San Pedro and that the two men were from Santa Fe.

SUBJECT: El Bandolero de Las Placitas
WPA: 5-5-49 #24
April 5, 1940
Words 1681
Sources of information: José L.A. Gurulé, Rumaldita Gurulé, Venturo
Escarcida. José Gurulé was the brother-in-law of the Rosalía of this story.

EL BANDOLERO DE LAS PLACITAS
(The Bandit of Las Placitas)

It was in the year of 1872 that the crimes of Fernando Sarna brought him to the close of a short and colorful career. During his course, brief as it was, he kept courageous United States marshals and their doughty deputies in a state of wary, watchful waiting.

While Sarna flourished, there was no barn, no corral, no lock strong enough to protect good horses, cattle, or sturdy burros from him if he desired them. His business it was. It enabled him to live like a caballero, to maintain a little fortress of his own high up in the Sandía Mountains, just to the south of Las Placitas at a place locally known as Ojito Blanco (Little White Springs). It enabled him to jingle gold and silver in his pockets, to buy feminine finery to win favors from the many señoritas he knew. But above all, to lavish gifts upon the one girl he wanted to marry but could not. She was Rosalía Gonzales, daughter of the Civil War veteran of Las Placitas, Francisco Gonzales. He would have none of Fernando Sarna.

Fernando Sarna was but twenty-two in that year of 1872. He was gay and handsome, hot-tempered and daring. He feared neither God nor man. He was cautious and elusive. Had he possessed a magic carpet he could have done no "smoother acts" of sudden appearances and disappearances.

Sarna the Infernal, he became known among the peace officers, who were never eager to risk their lives in any of the death traps Sarna contrived in the vicinity of his fortress especially for them. Moreover, his eye nor his nerve never failed him, and his gun never missed its mark.

Sarna's downfall came about through a herd of good burros that he rounded up under cover of dark nights and finally sold to a man who was under contract to carry supplies to a mining camp high in a mountain region near Santa Fe. In the early seventies good, strong burros brought any where from thirty to fifty dollars a head. To steal them was considered grand larceny. For a time after the sale of the beasts Sarna lay low, but not long enough. His longing to see Rosalía led him to Las Placitas. He was with friends when the place was suddenly raided by a marshal and his deputies. When those inside the house realized that it was not friends in the doorway, it was too late for the young bandit to draw his gun. He was captured and taken to the jail at Santa Fe.

In that jail of the days of 1872, Sarna made friends of three bad characters awaiting trial for their crimes. One night they lured the jailor into a gambling game. The five players appeared absorbed in the game, when suddenly the four prisoners seized, disarmed, and gagged the jailor and bound him up. They found a file and away they went. They hid only long enough to file apart the chains that bound their shackles together. There was no time to free their ankles of the bands, but with the chains cut, they had free use of their legs. Sarna fled in search of a horse. He found one, and clinging to its bare back, he sent it galloping for his fortress in the Sandías. He arrived there early in the morning. He gave a bird call, and José Mora, the one-man garrison of the miniature fortress, crept out to investigate.

Now in his stronghold the youthful bandit had too much time on his hands. He sent José Mora to Las Placitas to tell Rosalía, and her alone, that he had escaped the jail and was in his place in the mountains.

Rosalía did just what Fernando Sarna knew that she would do. She sent word that she would come to him. That night José Mora went for her. Then the three of them took up the watch.

Week followed week with no sign of an enemy attack. But Sarna was taking no chances this time. He would allow plenty of time to pass before he ventured abroad again, and never again would he be surprised napping. He boasted now to Rosalía and Mora that he would get the man who tried to take him. If he failed in that, he vowed that he would never be taken alive. And thus they waited while the months went by.

Meanwhile, the officers of the law were biding their time. There was not a peace officer in the district who was not wary of Sarna, who feared neither God nor man and who was never known to miss his mark. Only a suicide squad would chance a raid on that mountain hideout. This was one of those cases where discretion was the better part of valor. So they watched, listened, and waited.

Then one day Sarna and Mora slaughtered a steer. Sarna held a keen hunting knife in his hand. The assaulted animal gave a vicious kick, which struck the knife and drove it into Sarna's leg. An unfortunate accident it was, which disabled Sarna for some days. Rosalía was the nurse who cared for his wound and redoubled her watch. Sarna kept his gun at his finger tips day and night. Close friends of the trio in the hideout learned of the accident. News of it finally leaked out. The waiting peace officers heard of it. They decided it was time to strike.

One night three of them climbed the trail on the backs of burros. They decided not to walk into the trap until early morning. They knew the occupants of the place would be on guard at night. But a daylight attack might surprise them.

But in that they were mistaken. Sarna's "super-powered" ears caught the noises in the night and he was prepared. His alert eyes sighted them as they crept toward the house. He was ready to fire.

Rosalía dashed from the place and stood between the approaching officers and Fernando Sarna. She pleaded with him not to add murder to his crimes, pleaded with the men not to fire at Sarna, that she might persuade him not to shoot. There stood the pretty, slender girl, herself a target no matter from which side a shot might come. Shots were deferred, a parley ensued, while the girl stood her ground.

The marshal commanded Sarna to surrender his weapon. The bandit refused but he promised that he would not use his gun unless he saw them start to draw a gun on him. That brought the parley to a standstill. The situation looked most unhealthy for the arms of the law should they attempt to take the youth. The one of them who tried to take him by force was as good as dead before he started. Should the three of them rush him, one of them at least was certain to be sacrificed. It was out of the question to retreat. That would leave the law in contempt. It was clear that Sarna was in a position to dictate terms of his surrender, if he could be forced that far.

As Sarna and the officers faced each other with less than a hundred feet of distance between them, and with tenseness and uncertainty in the air, Rosalía, who knew that Sarna would shoot to kill if one of the men so much as moved his gun, remained in the space between them and pleaded with Sarna not to add murder to his crimes. She told him if he gave himself up the judge was sure to give him a shorter sentence. She would go with him to Santa Fe. She would wait for him there.

Sarna pondered the matter. Why he ever considered it while he had all the advantages of the situation in his favor, was a mystery to all his friends. However, he offered to give himself on his own terms.

He refused to surrender his gun. He ordered the officers to ride on ahead and to take Rosalía with them for their protection. He would follow with his friend, José Mora, and he would say how far behind he was to ride. The officers could take his terms or leave them, just as they pleased.

There being little else the marshal could do, he accepted the terms. Burros were brought by Mora for Rosalía, Sarna, and himself. Sarna kept guard and mounted last. The cavalcade moved down the steep trail in the manner ordered by the bandit.

In the rear Sarna was talking in low tones to José Mora. "I always said nobody could take me alive." Then he told José that he was not going to Santa Fe. That if he did he would kill Judge Jesús María Salas, the judge at Santa Fe who would try his case. "He would have no mercy on me," Sarna said. "If I kill him then I would be a murderer. Quick, José, give me my mother's blessing. I will kill myself instead. Quick, José, give me my mother's blessing."

José did as his friend bade him. No sooner were the words spoken than Fernando Sarna raised his gun and fired a shot into his own heart.

SUBJECT: Felicia the Bruja
WPA: 5-5-31 #2
April 19, 1940
Words 2144
Sources of information: Magdalena Gallegos, Terecita Baca, María Chaves.
Chaves married into the family of Felicia The Bruja. The husband of Julianita
is her distant cousin.

FELICIA THE BRUJA

It was sometime in the late seventies that Felicia and Roque with their family came from Taos to Ojo de La Casa. They had bought the tiny house nestling at the foot of the mountain on the east side of Cañón de Las Huertas. A pair of burros would not have been overly comfortable in the small one-room adobe, but neither Felicia nor Roque minded the inconveniences of their cramped quarters; they both had outside interests. Besides, in time they would build a better house.

From the beginning of their residence in Ojo de La Casa, Roque made himself unpopular by his frequent, mysterious, nocturnal forays, and Felicia forgot to hide her witch doll when her first caller entered her house.

It so happened that the caller was María de Los Angeles Gallegos, a devout Christian and a kind and truthful woman. But she feared the brujas (witches) as she feared the devil. In all haste she left the house of Felicia when she caught sight of the witch doll hanging behind the door. She never entered it again, though Felicia did not die until 1925, and lived in Ojo de La Casa through all her days.

When word was whispered about that Felicia was a witch, her neighbors were filled with fear of her, though they well knew that they must meet her with friendliness and they must allow their children to play with her children. If they offended her, what might she not do to them? Brujas had power—evil power; they could even make one die.

And so the people tried to be neighborly, but they were always on their guard and suspicious of every act of both Felicia and Roque. Felicia sent gifts of food to her neighbors as they exchanged gifts of food among each other. But the food from the house of Felicia was feared and those who received it threw it away. Brujas mixed food with strange and dangerous herbs. Who could foretell the evil effects of such food?

One day Felicia called the small boy of a neighbor to carry a pint tinaja of warm goat milk to Ignacita, who lived in a house just above the spring in Ojo de La Casa and was ill. Felicia warned the boy not to tell where he got the milk, but to let Ignacita think his mother had sent it. Felicia had learned that her offerings to her neighbors had been thrown out; she had revenge in her heart. Obediently the frightened child delivered the milk to Ignacita with Felicia's message that she was to drink it at once while it was warm, that it would cure her.

But fortunately for Ignacita the child was seen by María de Los Ángeles. With all speed María ran to the house of her friend Ignacita. She seized the tinaja from Ignacita's lips just as she started to drink, and dashed the contents into the brisk fire in the little corner fireplace. There came a hissing, moaning sound, and a white foam rose from the fire. It lifted the pot suspended from a hook over the fire, then set it back, lifted it again and again, each time returning it to its place. In a panic the women fled from the house, dragging Ignacita with them.

Some time after that, on a cold, snowy January day, a little girl appeared at the door of old Sarita. Sarita had said she was hungry for a piece of nice, tender meat. And what did she behold on the dish the child offered her but a piece of tender meat, a slice of young goat. So amazed was Sarita at having a slice of kid at that season of the year that she did not see the child disappear. She wondered who had brought it. Who in her vicinity would have a kid to kill at this season of the year? Mystified, she set the dish upon the table and left it. She felt uneasy about it. As usual, her little dog, her only companion, slept near her on the floor that night. When Sarita arose from her pallet the next morning, she uttered a loud scream. There near her was her little dog. He was not only dead but in a fearful state of decay. The meat was gone from the dish.

It was all too evident to all of them what had happened. Felicia had sent the meat. It was bewitched. Sarita had escaped Felicia's curse.

Now more than ever the people of Ojo de La Casa distrusted Felicia. They said Felicia grew uglier with each passing year and bolder in her evil practices. Always there was a cactus thorn thrust somewhere in the body of her witch doll, which always brought pain to someone. All she must do to give suffering to the one she disliked or wished to punish was to stick the thorn in the part of the doll's body where she wished the pain to come to the person she thought about. In no time at all, that person was ill or in pain.

Julianita in Las Placitas was a frequent visitor at the house of Felicia. Because of her temper and selfishness, Julianita turned many of her neighbors and even members of her family against her. She wanted to learn the ways of the witches. In that way she could bewitch those who turned against her. She begged Felicia to teach her all she knew. Felicia consented. She showed Julianita what herbs to prepare and how to make them bring desired results. She helped her make the many little bags and stuff them with the hair of every different animal and of people, which she must fasten inside her petticoat and wear at all times, to save her from the power of other witches. She taught Julianita how to make and use a witch doll. It, too, was filled with hair from every living thing they could find.

Then one day Felicia told Julianita she must come to her that night in the darkness and she would give her the last lesson. She would teach her how to go forth in the night like the wind. Julianita came and the two women stood at the door of Felicia's house.

Felicia said, "Now raise your arms up as I do and rush out calling, 'I go without God and without the Holy Virgin'."

With the words Felicia went from the door, Julianita after her. But Julianita could not say "without," she was very much afraid. So she said, "I go with God and with the Holy Virgin." She realized that Felicia was gone and that she herself was flat on the ground just as if someone had thrown her there. She saw many lights which looked like cat's eyes in the darkness, and heard a strange wailing of the wind. Frightened almost out of her wits, Julianita raised herself to her feet and ran the mile to her house in Las Placitas.

She avoided the house of Felicia for a time, then her curiosity as to how her witch-friend would receive her brought her back again.

She found that Felicia had troubles of her own. That fall there had been an abundant crop of chili. As it required time and labor to pick her chili, and more of each to tie it in bunches and string it on the strong strips of the leaf of the amole prepared especially to make into ristras of chili, Felicia found that she must have help. All of her neighbors said they had their hands full with their own chili and could not help her at any price. So Felicia went to the Pueblo of San Felipe and bargained for labor. She promised to pay in chili.

For that wage she had no trouble obtaining help. Three Indians returned to Ojo de La Casa with her.

When her ristras (strings) of chili were all made and hung upon the outside walls of her house to dry, she became greedy and broke faith with the Indians. She refused to pay them in chili, but insisted on giving them peas for their labor. The Indians, furious at her deception, acted rather than quarreled with her. They put a curse upon her. For the rest of her days she would suffer. And she did. Soon after the departure of the Indians, Felicia felt peas being poured into her stomach. Always there was that sensation of peas, being emptied from a tinaja into her insides. Time passed but the peas continued to be emptied into her stomach. Then one day she felt a sudden heavy weight inside herself. Instantly she knew it was a metate (flat stone for the grinding of peas or chili peppers into powder). She knew the Indians had caused this unbearable misery. She did not long survive the horror of that heavy stone in her stomach.

The sad fate of Felicia was soon forgotten by Julianita, who thirsted for revenge, upon those she called her enemies. Her gifts of food were politely accepted, then buried. None wished even to risk their dogs' lives, for who knew what Julianita had done to the food she carried to them. Then Julianita changed her tactics. She made good wine in her house; everyone knew of her wine. She sent gifts of bewitched wine. Many who drank of it fell ill; for they had not the power of mind to refuse the clear, purple liquid she sent them.

Then Julianita's daughter fell in love with Miguel's nephew. Miguel had land and houses at Tecolote, and old settlement about a mile from Las Placitas, on the road to Tejón. Miguel had no children; his nephew was his heir. All this would be good fortune for Petra, the daughter of Julianita. But Miguel feared such an alliance and sent his nephew away for a prolonged stay. The dismayed Julianita decided to take a hand in the affair.

One day Julianita cooked some pozole (thoroughly cooked large, white grains of corn). What she mixed into it will never be known. That it was bewitched was all that was evident. She called in one of the few friends she had in Las Placitas, when she had the pozole arranged on a dish. She asked the friend to carry it to Miguel. The friend thought it wise to agree to comply with Julianita's wishes. The friend was Teresa.

On her way to Miguel's house, Teresa thought the matter over. She decided that if the pozole was good for Miguel, it would be good for Julianita. Somehow she had an uneasy feeling about the gift. She returned to her own house. There she prepared some pozole of her own. She mixed some of it with that intended for Miguel, and placed it on the dish. In due time she carried it to the house of Julianita. "It is a gift from Miguel to you," Teresa explained. "He had some for his dinner. He said he would exchange the gift of pozole."

Julianita's joy at having evened scores with Miguel was short lived. In bitterness and suffering she was to learn that her supposed moment of triumph was also her moment of doom. She ate the pozole Teresa returned to her, the pozole intended for Miguel. Nothing could save her. She died by inches for over three years, the final inch succumbing on San Antonio Day, 1939. Her death put a blight on that day's festivities. It was the fiesta day of Las Placitas.

Julianita was buried in the little cemetery at Las Placitas. In her coffin with her was every rosary, crucifix, image of Santo Niño, and piece of cachana that could be obtained by her family and few friends. These would protect her from the witches who would otherwise enter her casket and eat her away bit by bit.

And thus the halfway witch of Las Placitas passed away.

Strange as these tales may sound, stranger still is the fact that those who related them said: "Of course we do not believe these things, but they really happened just as we have told them."

SUBJECT: An Old Native Custom: Guadaloupe's Transgression
WPA: 5-5-49 #38
Sources of information: Rumaldita Gurulé, José L.A. Gurulé, Cristiana Baros,
Jose García, Antonio García y Sánchez. García y Sánchez had this story of
"An Old Native Custom" from his father.

GUADALOUPE'S TRANSGRESSION
(of an Old Custom)

When the Stars and Stripes was planted upon New Mexico soil, the old men at Tejón and Las Placitas talked together of the change in a casual way. "Now that we belong to the rich country maybe we shall see some money, who knows." That was about all it meant to them, according to José Gurulé. Life in the villages went on as before and old customs remained unchanged.

In that year of 1846, Guadaloupe García was four years old; Tejón, her home, was but six years old.

Like all other children of her day, Guadaloupe left off being an idle child at the age of six and became her mother's helper. She looked after the younger children and learned to cook and clean the house and to wash the family clothes and help in the garden. By the time she reached her twelfth year she could manage babies and a house. Then it was that her skirts, made exactly as the skirts of her mother were made, were put down to her ankles and her hair arranged in a single braid down her back, the mode of hair dress that was the symbol of maidenhood.

Now she could no longer appear in the plaza, nor outside the walls of the town, nor in chapel, nor anywhere abroad without a chaparone. At all times in public she must walk demurely by the side of her chaparone, her eyes downcast, her body erect and dignified, and often she clasped her hands in front of her as she minced along. Under no circumstances must she meet masculine glances, nor even speak to one of the opposite sex, unless they be members of

248

her intimate family. Conversation with any man outside her family was absolutely forbidden. More than that, she must take no part in the conversation of visiting elders, though she could sit quietly by and listen. Never must she gossip with her elders in any public place. Never must she thwart the wishes of her father—not even in the question of her marriage. Yes, life for the maidens of those long-ago days was a straight-laced affair from which there happened sad deflections.

But be it said that the maidens of that long-ago day publicly toed the mark set for them by custom. When they walked abroad they looked like angels with their shy, downcast eyes and smiles and silent tongues. But the more angelic they could manage to appear, the more they were praised for their maidenly conduct, and the more the chaparones delighted in them. "The little hypocrites," their great-great-granddaughters of this day call them.

When Guadaloupe was fourteen she gave her heart to a youth in Tejón. So sly about her heart affairs was the maiden that no one even suspected her of a secret romance. Then one day her father told her of his plans for her future.

It was the custom of that day for the parents to arrange the marriages of their children. If the fathers agreed upon an alliance, the young man was sent to ask the maiden's father for her hand. If the father consented, plans went forward for the marriage. The girl was never consulted about it. Many times the maiden never saw her husband-to-be until the day of the prendería (dance where the betrothed pair exchanged rings), which was the night preceeding the wedding day.

The padrinas (godmothers) were given one month plus a certain number of days to produce the evidence of the bride-to-be's virginity. Meanwhile certain preparations went on. But the maiden's wedding outfit could not be completed until the padrinas gave proof of her maidenhood. That was the custom.

Time passed, the days of waiting were fulfilled. Guadaloupe was found to no longer be a virgin. Because human nature dwelled within the walls of Tejón there were "Ahs" and "Ohs" whispered everywhere and shocked madres and padres on every side of the plaza.

But the wedding plans went on just the same. The morning of the eventful day dawned. The wedding party climbed into a carreta, and the oxen plodded down the Arroyo de Tonque which brought the party to San Felipe.

Yet there was something amiss with the wedding party. The little bride-to-be was without veil and flowers. Such a shorn little bride she would be. But it was the custom. Should a maid be found without her virginity, straightway she forfeited the right to veil and flowers or bouquet of any sort at the altar when her marriage service was said.

After the ceremony the party returned to Tejón and to the usual wedding festivities. Wine, wine, and more wine, and cakes and then a feast. After that the padrinas took the bride away. They removed her wedding dress, replaced it with another. They arranged her hair in a knot on top of her head. They returned her to her husband, a matron in good repute. Such was the custom of that day, nearly a hundred years ago, a custom that did not survive the Civil War period.

Subject: An Old Native Custom: El Indio Viejo
WPA: #52
May 19, 1940
Words 1797
Sources of information: José L.A. Gurulé, Cristiana Baros, Benino Archibeque,
Ferminia Durán. José Gurulé was one of the pupils of El Indio Viejo.

EL INDIO VIEJO

In the long-ago days of the middle sixties there came to Las Placitas one Señor Martínez, El Indio Viejo (The Old Indian), as he became known in the village. He hailed from Galisteo, an ancient village on the old wagon trail leading from Las Placitas to Las Vegas. He was a resador or prayer man.

In those old days priests were scarce and their parishes large. The few who were able to receive the services of those good padres in their last hour of life were blessed indeed. But in nearly every village there were men eloquent in prayer who could ably attend to the spiritual needs of the dying, and who were worthy to deliver the souls of the departing to God, as was the custom.

Señor Martínez was such a one. He was so good at his chosen callings that he came to Las Placitas as a teacher, not of the three Rs but of his three arts: praying, singing, dancing. For a time Señor Martínez was called to the spiritual aid of the dying in preference to the old resador, one of the builders of Las Placitas, old Andrés de Aragón.

One morning old Andrés did not arise from his pallet. He refused his breakfast—atole (a drink made from the meal of blue or pueblo corn and goat milk). He lay restless and muttering throughout the morning and steadily grew worse. Old Andrés was dying. El Indio Viejo was summoned.

At once he started his prayers. As was the custom, he stood at the open door and shouted his prayers, his lungs giving of their power as if his words must reach the ears of God in the high heavens. Again and again he shouted; "Jesús, favoresca! Jesús lo ampure!" (God's favor. God help him!).

251

His voice penetrated to every corner of the village. It was like a call to prayers. Mourners came from every direction to intermingle their weird dirge with the shouted prayers of the resador. It was the custom.

Just before his last breath, old Andrés gasped out that he wished to make a sacrifice. He wished to be buried only in a blanket or else wrapped in a cloth. That branded him as a member of the order of Los Hermanos Penitentes, an order which flourished in the Sandías in the old days. In those early days of the life of Las Placitas a morada, a huge wooden cross leaning against it stood on the very spot where now lives Ferminia Durán. In fact, the old morada is incorporated within the walls of her house. The crucifixion cross was planted on a hill in the mountains just south of the village.

(In those early days one man's fanaticism inspired him to offer himself to be sacrificed upon that cross one Easter. He hung there too long and died as the result of it. All Las Placitas mourned the tragedy. This story was told to Ferminia Durán by her mother, Julia Pacheco, who came to Las Placitas with the retinue of Juan Armijo in late 1859).

Now back to old Andrés. When he breathed his last and lay back on his pallet, the wailing of his family could be heard far beyond the place of Ojo del Oso. It was the custom to lament over the bodies of the dead. The louder the lamentations, the deeper the grief was supposed to be.

At the cessation of the bewailing, preparations for the wake began. In those days a death in the village was more or less of a community affair. A wake resembled a social gathering at which the deceased was guest. In cases where they had requested a sacrificial burial, as had old Andrés de Aragón, it was the custom to lay the corpse upon the floor in the room where the feasting was held. The wake broke up at daybreak.

As the body must be carried to Bernalillo, the funeral procession left Las Placitas as early as could be arranged. Wrapped only in a serape the body was laid on a ladder. Four men lifted it up and the march to the cemetery at Bernalillo was on, the mourners filing behind the litter. El Indio Viejo helped bear the dead. At each stop for rest he led the mourners in prayer and song. A rude wooden cross or a mound of stones was left to mark the place where they stopped to rest and prayed and sang. It was the custom.

(It was said that at Bernalillo a charge of four dollars, in grain, or other desirable commodities, or money, must be paid to the priest before the body of the dead could be laid in the grave. In those old days of scarcity and hardships almost all of the villagers went to the church at San Felipe Pueblo, where the services of the priest were given them free of charge, whenever they were needed).

Now that resador Andrés de Aragón was no more, El Indio Viejo, with no rival prayer man to hold him to the conventional custom, struck out on an uncharted course, as far as the villagers were concerned. Being in favor he found it easy to pursue his chosen way. So the artful teacher announced that he was ready to teach the children to pray, to sing, and to dance. As all three arts were a vital part of their daily life, the children were sent to him willingly.

He divided the children into two bands: one of boys, the other of girls. Each band had a leader, El Capitán. El Indio Viejo gave each child two ears of corn, a blue one and a white one. These ears of corn became their music instruments. In unison they learned to click, strike, and rasp them together as they held them above their heads and in front of them, while the steps and movements of their bodies timed with the rhythm of the corn. Strange, fascinating dancing it was, but with no hint of the steps of the familiar cuadrilla, valce, polca, or redondo. The elders shook their heads as they watched the dance of their children and listened to their songs and prayers. Something in the dance appealed to them. They allowed the teacher to go on.

At last El Indio Viejo considered that his pupils were ready for the first public appearance. It was on a Saturday. They looked like a small army descending upon the village but coming with flags of truce, for the captains carried little white flags El Indio Viejo made for them. Then came the surprise. They approached a house and with no ado whatever raised their ears of corn, above their heads and clicking and rasping them together made a sort of music for their dance. Forward and backward and around they moved in the dance Señor Martínez had taught them. The people came to their doors and looked on in amazement. The paganish dance caught their fancy, they cheered. In the excitement of the moment, El Indio Viejo passed the word to the captains and at once they followed him to collect alms from the houses nearby.

The response of the people was generous. All manner of food went into the coarse cloth sack of the teacher, as well as gifts of goat hides.

Soon the children were repeating their performance in other parts of the village. When El Indio Viejo considered he had collected a sufficiency for one Saturday, he led the children to the little chapel where the offerings were spread out upon the floor before the altar, whereon stood the wooden image of San Antonio in his capilla, the one carved from the big root of a cottonwood long years before in old Las Huertas.

That night a dim light was seen in the little chapel. The curious villagers in their tewas swarmed noiselessly into the chapel, or as many as could crowd into the small space. Those who could not get a footing inside stood outside, craned their necks and strained their ears to learn what was going on.

There before the altar where the offerings were spread, was El Indio Viejo. His low voice could be heard in a chant and in the dim candlelight they saw him moving about in a dance—the dance he had taught the children. He was so absorbed in his devotions that he paid no attention to his uninvited guests.

"María lucente star	Mary bright star
Patrona de este lugar	Patron of this place
Nosotras para contento	We to be content
Ahora queremos bailar."	Now we want to dance
Señor Martínez también	God cares for Señor Martínez
A Su Merced	Naragne and also for you
Tue yo soy un pobre Indio	I'm only a poor old Indian
Y vengo a bailarle a usted."	Come to dance to you.

It seems strange that the words of the old Indian's chant should be remembered in the village where he danced to it some seventy-five years ago. (The word Naragne could not be explained nor why it was in the translation).

On that night of long ago, when the old Indian finished his chant, the villagers slipped from the chapel as quietly as they had come and vanished into the night.

In time the Saturday dance and alms-gathering became a fixed weekend feature. But as the Saturdays rolled around in seeming endless alms-gathering, the people of Las Placitas grew weary of the dance and poorer from the drain on their simple resources. One by one the old Indian found his pupils missing from the rank until there were none.

Then it was that Señor Martínez, whom God cared for, took his coarse cloth sack and what of his spoils he had left and disappeared. Then it also was when the people of Las Placitas searched within the village for another prayer man. A resador they must have. It was the custom.

SUBJECT: An Old Native Custom: Madrecita Piedad

WPA: 5-5-2 #40

June 3, 1940

Words 1580

Sources of information: José L.A. Gurulé, Rumaldita Gurulé, Magdalena Gallegos, Cristiana Baros, Terecita Baca. José Gurulé was a nephew of the Juanita Gurulé de Zamora of this story. Rumaldita Gurulé knew the younger children of Piedad and Feliciano of this story. Magdalena Gallegos was the wife of Patricio Gallegos, who was a nephew of Piedad, of this story. Terecita Baca's great-grandmother was Juanita Gurulé of this story.

MADRECITA PIEDAD

It was in the early sixties in Ojo de La Casa that fourteen-year-old Piedad made ready for the coming of her child. The sacred stone, "sarydacia," which is so called to this day, was sewed into a little cloth sack and tied securely about her neck. Her young husband, Feliciano, had just brought it to her from the church at San Felipe. It was a chip from the blessed stone which lay upon the altar (a large and beautiful piece of sardonyx), or so thought Piedad and Feliciano.

The sardonyx was a coveted stone in days of old. In Bible times it was one of the precious stones in the breast plate of the high priest. It kept its wearer from woe and sorrow and brought him good fortune. No evil could touch him when the sardonyx was worn upon his person.

Piedad, as all mothers of her time, reposed implicit faith in the blessed stone. Nothing could possibly go wrong with her or the baby to come as long as the precious "sarydacia" was worn about her neck.

But what Piedad did not know about her blessed piece of sardonyx was that it did not come from the large piece upon the altar. That sacred stone upon the altar was kept covered and none knew that the small stones they received

255

were not pieces of it, but substitute stones blessed and given them. In later days it became burdensome for the priest to furnish these stones. He then told the people that in the mountains around Ojo de La Casa they could find pieces of it, should they search for it. They did search and they found beautiful pieces of agate, resembling the stones brought from the church at San Felipe, which they carried to the priest at San Felipe to have them blessed. Thus, they saved the price of the stone and paid only for the blessing.

Now as Piedad's hour approached, the women of the village gathered outside her house and as many as could find a place, stood at the tiny windows, looked in and sang to her. Simple little songs, which were prayers for the deliverance of her child, were sung over and over to her, even though directed to San Ramón Nonato no Nacido. It was the custom.

As they sang outside the house, old Eufemia, the midwife, sat on the floor near Piedad's pallet and pulled ravelings from a snow-white cloth, which she twisted tightly together by rolling them between her fingers until they formed a cord, the cord that would be needed later on. In the kitchen Señora Juanita Gurulé was busy making atole, the drink of goat milk and blue cornmeal that custom decreed should be given every woman immediately after the birth of her child. In the room with Señora Gurulé sat Feliciano, waiting for Eufemia to tell him when to fire the salute that would announce the birth of his child.

(Before the advent of the gun, runners were sent to every house to announce the births, and the custom has never entirely died out).

When the infant was three days old, it was taken to San Felipe for baptism. That was the custom of the day. Piedad and Feliciano chose Señora Gurulé de Zamora and her husband Valentino to be the infant's padrinos (godparents). It was their problem to get the three-day-old child to the priest and back again. The round trip from Ojo de La Casa to the Pueblo of San Felipe by way of Las Huertas Cañón was about fourteen miles. Señor Valentino had oxen and a carreta; but that was far too rough and joggling a vehicle for baby. So they walked to San Felipe. Señor Valentino wrapped himself in a serape, tied it about the waist, and made a pocket for baby upon his breast and folded the serape in such a manner as to hold the infant firmly in place. Thus they made the trip.

When they reached the Pueblo of San Felipe, they went directly to the church and in due time the good padre came to them. The padrinos delivered the infant into his hands for baptism and gave him the name of Juan.

Soon after this ceremony little Juan raised his voice and announced his hunger. His padrinos made a tour of the pueblo with him in search of an Indian mother with a child but a few days old. When she was found, Juan received his dinner from her breast. At her invitation the padrinos joined her family circle at the big tinaja for their own repast. While the sun was still high, Señora y Señor Zamora departed for home, that they might reach there well before dark.

At Ojo de La Casa they found Feliciano with a gun ready to clear their path to his door of evil spirits. One shot was sufficient. Inside the house old Eufemia was ready to serve wine and bizcochos (small, slightly sweetened biscuits) to all who might call.

Upon entering the house, the padrinos went to the pallet, and Señora Zamora repeated this verse as she returned the infant to the arms of his madrecita (little mother).

Aguá está, esta flor	Here is this flower
Que de la inglesia salió	That came out of church
Con los santos sacramento	With the holy sacrament
Y la agua que resivió	And the water received
Comadre, resiva al niño	Comadre, accept your baby
Se llama- (here name is given)	Whose name is Juan
"Juan."	

The godmother, or madrina, calls the mother of her godchild (ahijado or ahijada comadre).

After this verse was said, Feliciano sent another gun salute into the air. The significance of this salute was not remembered. To this day, some variation of the above verse (which came from no one knows where) is repeated by the madrina when she returns the child to her comadre.

When little Juan was thirteen months old, his madrecita prepared for the coming of another baby. It was Eufemia who came again to care for her, to roll the ravelings into a cord, and to prepare and serve bizcochos and pour the wine. But all did not go well with Piedad. Day after day passed and the women of the village were not called to sing at the tiny windows. Day after day Piedad moaned in almost unbearable pain.

In those old days it was the custom to consider the new life that was yet unborn before attention was centered upon the suffering mother. Though eight days had passed since Eufemia said the child would be born, Piedad had not lost faith in her prayers and the "sarydacia." But her husband deemed it time to run to the Pueblo of San Felipe and consult the good padre; for in those days the padre advised in all matters, and he rated baptism above all earthly affairs.

When Feliciano recited his story to the priest, he was commanded, not advised, to race back to Ojo de La Casa and to sever whatever part of the infant was thrust from the mother into this world, and straightway take the holy water and baptise it. That would assure the salvation of the baby.

Feliciano sped home to execute the bidding of the priest. When a tiny arm came into the world, he severed it with his hunting knife and baptised it.

Now old Eufemia, who was born about 1790, and who bothered less with Christian doctrines, and more with pagan practices, flew into action. She knew exactly what to do. At once she dispatched Feliciano to the field to dig up some caballas (in this case, wild onions). She called upon the sister of Piedad, who was a virgin, to sacrifice some of her hair. When the roots of the onions and the hair of the virgin were placed into a tinaja and lighted, the smoldering pot was placed under the blanket near Piedad. In due time her life-less baby was born, just as old Eufemia knew it would be. Then, as was the custom to bring the afterbirth, old Eufemia gave Piedad a drink made of water and piedra pomez (pumice-stone).

Piedad and Feliciano lived many years in Ojo de La Casa and reared a large family. In the late nineties they went to Albuquerque to live the remainder of their days with a daughter. But there is still left in Ojo de La Casa a pile of tumbled rock and adobes that mark the outlines of the little house that Piedad and Feliciano built, the house wherein old Eufemia saved the life of La Madrecita.

☙ ☙ ☙

SUBJECT: An Old Native Custom
WPA: 5-5-2 #39
July 20, 1940
Words 3397
Sources of information: José García y Trujillo, María García, Antonio García y Sánchez, Lola García de Salazar, José Librado Arón Gurulé, Rumaldita Gurulé.

EL PELÓN Y LA PELONA

In 1740, a band of men with their families settled in the place called Las Huertas and founded a town. They named it San José. Years later, these families were joined by others, and together in 1765 they petitioned the King of Spain for a grant of land, which they designated at the San Antonio de Las Huertas Grant, and whereon San José was located. In 1767 these families were given the grant, and at once they started the construction of the walled town of Las Huertas. Every man in that band wore his hair long and arranged it in two braids. That was the custom of the day.

Those braids proclaimed him a good and honorable citizen. He was proud of them. He would fight to preserve them. He would rather die than part with his braids. Without them he would be called "El Pelón" (the hairless one), and that name applied only to the criminals, for in those days only the criminals who came from the prisons had shorn locks. Their short hair was a brand, a silent declaration of their dishonor. Short hair identified a man as an outcast. A man's long hair or braids set him apart in the social and moral scale, and he did not fraternize with los pelones, or the criminals. Such was the custom in those hard, inflexible times.

All women of that day wore their hair long and knotted it upon their heads. The maidens wore one long braid. In those days should a maiden or a matron fall from virtue, her hair was cut and she was called la pelona. She was not only ostracized but persecuted as well. Consequently, no good woman or

259

maiden ever parted with her long hair. Death would be better for her than the loss of that symbol of honor.

Those men and women of Las Huertas, and all other native New Mexicans of that day, held to this custom, kept their hair long, and in righteous indignation mercilessly punished those who fell from grace and lost their long locks through that decree of custom.

Then a new man appeared on the New Mexican scene. Lo, he did not wear his hair long, nor was he a criminal. He was what was called los exploradores y los negociantes (explorers and traders). He hailed from Los Estados (The States).

It requires time for a new idea to percolate through the human brain. Moreover, custom is custom—something handed down for generations. After the advent of the new man with the simpler hair dress, it was but rarely copied until that grand entrance into Santa Fe of the short-haired ones in 1846, who raised the Stars and Stripes over the old Palace of Governors. Even then the change from the two long braids to hair bobbed just below the ears was gradual. However, the association of short hair and criminals as one and the same was being questioned by many of the natives who favored the views of the newcomers from the east.

In Las Placitas, Nicolás Gurulé, father of José Librando Arón Gurulé, wore his hair bobbed, while his close friend, Francisco Gonzales, clung to his two braids and his belief that the braids did make a difference in men. Men with braids were less liable to become criminals, according to José L.A. Gurulé. José also said that there were several men in the village who had bobbed their hair.

Then came the Civil War and its spread into New Mexico. The ill feeling the New Mexicans nursed against the Texans was turned to the advantage of the Union when Governor Connolly called for men to help resist an invasion from the state of Texas. Eager to right the wrongs suffered by the New Mexicans at the hands of the Texans, men enlisted for the combat from nearly all the villages along and adjacent to the Rio Grande, men who wore their hair in two braids. According to all those who contributed information to this story, many who departed with their braids, returned without them. But in 1863 braids outnumbered the bobs.

At the close of the Civil War in New Mexico, the problem of settling the Navajo question was taken up and prosecuted with unabated vigor until Washington (D.C.) and some Navajo chiefs smoked the pipe of everlasting peace. That was in the year of 1868.

The number of men who came from the native villages to fight the Texans was trivial compared to the number eager to help put an end to the Navajo. In Las Placitas and Ojo de La Casa they had grievances against the raiding Navajoes, and memories of the outrages they visited upon their forefathers at Old Las Huertas. Every man who could leave his family went to fight. The heavy fighting was in 1864. Kit Carson was in command. Under him was one El Capitán Lizarra commanding a company of natives.

Benino Zamora was in this company. He, as most members of the company, wore two long braids. In this war upon the Navajos, there was no time for personal "clean-ups." They all became infested with parasites. The men could not sleep for the suffering inflicted upon them by the pests. They scratched their heads until they broke out in sores. The efficiency of the company was at low ebb. As a last resort, El Capitán ordered the men to cut their hair.

Benino Zamora said the men wept and begged to be allowed to keep their long hair. The belief among the natives at that time was that short hair and criminals were closely related, even if all los pelones were not from the prisons. The old custom was dying hard. But El Capitán was unrelenting. The braids were cut. Undoubtedly this order to cut off the braids was also carried out in the whole enlistment; for that date, according to José Garciá y Trujillo, marked the disappearance of the braids from the heads of the men, except for the old men. They refused to part with their braids.

As for Las Pelonas, they too, found the old custom relaxing for them from that date, seventy-five years ago.

ಜಿ ಜಿ ಜಿ

THE FALL OF PAQUITA

In those old days of harsh customs, Paquita Gurulé and Juan de Aragón lived in Las Huertas. Remnants of their tragic story still live in the memories of some of the very old people whose forefathers received the San Antonio de Las Huertas Grant and who helped to build the walls which enclosed the village. It was in the days of Spanish rule, about the year 1800, that the story of Paquita and Juan began. Because Paquita defied her father, a thing that simply was not done in those days, and Juan defied custom, a ruinous, if not dangerous act in any day, their story has endured.

Social life within the walls of Las Huertas was anything but tranquil in those days. Every able-bodied man in the village was a "minute man" so to speak. He must hold himself in readiness to respond to the governor's calls to help repel the all-too-frequent raids of the Navajos upon the settlements along the Río del Norte and the adjacent mountain villages. He must be available at any time to give the work of his hands or his oxen, if any, in the construction of public roads and bridges. At home he must be on guard constantly in order to save his flocks of goats and sheep, and the harvest of his fields from the ravaging Navajos.

These unalterable conditions brought hardships upon the women, after they were left to carry on within the walls as well as outside of them, with only the aid of the small boys and the old men.

Then there was the tax levy, which took heavy toll of their varas of wheat. (Varas, not acres, was the land unit in those days. A vara is 2.78 feet). Many times this tax payment of wheat resulted in privation for the people in lean years.

But all these things, severe as they were, became trivial matters compared to the social upheaval within those walls, which resulted from the "Fall of Paquita." Paquita was beautiful like the French women, or so she was held in memory by her far-removed descendants. Her grandfather was a Frenchman. He came to the Spanish territory of Santa Fe, or into that vicinity about 1720, José Gurulé said. Paquita's glossy, black hair was worn in one, long braid down her back. That was the mode of the day and a symbol of her purity as well. It was according to the custom of the time.

Her mother wore her hair tied in a knot on top of her head, just as all of the virtuous, respectable matrons of the day wore their hair, and in which fashion all pure maidens hoped someday to dress their locks. Paquita's father arranged his hair in two braids, which fell over his shoulders—likewise did Juan de Aragón and his father, Antonio. That identified them as honorable men. That was the custom.

Paquita and all other maidens of her time were called "Flowers." They were deemed pure as the lily—until proven otherwise. Paquita was reared strictly according to the custom of her time. She never appeared in public places unchaperoned. In the plaza, outside the village walls, at the fiesta, at the baile, to the church at San Felipe, whether she walked or jogged along in an oxen-drawn carreta, a watchful chaperone was at her elbow. Never must she raise her eyes to return male glances. The custom forbid! Never must she converse with any male, except those in her family circle, not even in the dance. Wherever a maiden lived, no man outside the immediate family, though he be the most intimate friend of the father or guardian, could enter the house in the absence of the father or guardian. In short, the maidens were guarded against close contacts with the entire male population, aside from the members of their immediate families. In those days, virtue was the price of social security: the cost of violation of virtue was obscurity and misery. Such was the custom of that long-ago day.

Paquita was restrained by another custom of her day, and was reconciled to it. She knew her father would please himself in the matter of her marriage.

When Paquita was fifteen, her father said it was time she thought of her future. And while he looked about to find a suitable husband for her, one entirely to his own notion, Paquita's heart was set aflame by a dashing trifler who played the violin. His music raised the temp of the maidens' pulses and even caused matronly hearts to skip a beat. His home was wherever dancing feet gathered at fiesta and baile. He first saw Paquita at Angostura (a village settled in 1745 near the junction of Cañón de las Huertas y El Camino Real, which is still inhabited).

Little did Paquita's chaperone dream that the maiden had a lover, lingering in Angostura, and that every time they passed through the place on their way to mass at San Felipe, the enamored youth contrived to talk to Paquita with his eyes, and that she shifted an eyelid just enough to receive the message and return one. Neither did stern padre Gurulé have an inkling of the nocturnal trysts outside the walls of his own village. Parents and chaperones in those days gave little thought to such highly improbable state of affairs, that is, if they had done their duty by their children, taught them the social catechism, properly painted the verbal pictures of damnation of those who fell short of it.

At length padre Gurulé announced that Paquita's husband-to-be was Juan de Aragón, son of his compadre and godfather (padrino) of Paquita.

It must have been at that moment that Paquita's head cleared and chill almost stopped her heart, as in terror she thought of her future. She also thought of Juan and how, since she was thirteen, she had hoped that her father might choose him for her husband. He was industrious and had flocks of his own. She realized, now that it was too late, that the light-hearted violinist in, his passion, had swept her from the fear of all her parents had taught her. Poor Paquita! He had even caused her to forget Juan.

While Juan's family planned for the wedding, which was the custom of that day, Paquita remained in seclusion in her father's house to live the last days of honorable womanhood she would ever know, the days which must pass before the padrinas (godmothers) chosen for her could offer the proof of her maidenhood; and no one in that village entertained a thought in the matter other than that Paquita was as pure as the lily. But dark days those were for Paquita, who must live through them without comfort or hope. She was terror-stricken at what she knew must come, yet there was nothing she could do about it but face it, and alone. Should she try to escape, she would be hunted down.

Then came the dawn of Paquita's judgment day. She had been found to be without virtue. A social storm broke about the head of the unhappy girl. She had dragged the good and honorable name of her father into sin, and her family were equally guilty with her and would become despised and looked upon as social outcasts unless they publicly confessed their daughter's guilt and publicly denounced and punished her. Through this confession and punishment, the sin of the family would be absolved from the guilt by God and they would be restored to their honorable estate in the community; but the sinful Paquita must suffer for her crime, and her sin would be visited upon her children for generations.

The people of the village gathered about the house of padre Gurulé, demanded that he do his duty as the custom of the day decreed. Their harsh voices cried out, not for the blood of Paquita, but for her long black hair.

In fancy can be pictured the scene of that long-ago day: the walled town, the righteous, indignant citizens milling about the plaza, their hands and voices both raised to high heaven as their cry, "Cut her hair! Brand her La Pelona! Ostracize her! Cast her out!" echoed through the hills and down the Cañón de Las Huertas. Padre Gurulé at his door, with hands outstretched as if to silence the accusers. Paquita, pale and shrinking, within his house awaiting her doom, the horror of it already breaking her spirit. Her mother, sisters, and brothers stand removed from her, condemning and scorning her for bringing this disgrace upon them, and hardening their hearts against her, that they might properly mete out the punishment public sentiment demanded of them—public sentiment founded upon the unreasonable zeal of the intolerant religion of that day.

And where would we picture Juan? They said he loved Paquita. Then he would not be among those frenzied ones in the plaza. It is possible that he fled the village that he might not witness his loved one's disgrace. And away from it all, where he could reason with himself, Juan made a momentous decision. He would marry Paquita and suffer with her. Such a resolve was practically unheard of. So it was this decision of the loyal Juan that put a soul in the story of Paquita and Juan and caused it to live.

But Juan's family was among the leaders of those bent on destroying the helpless girl. Padre Gurulé yielded to the clamor of his neighbors. Paquita lost her long, glossy locks. She was branded La Pelona, a criminal. She became a slave in her father's house, to be scorned and punished by every member of her family. Only in this manner could they appease God and society for the sin of their child. Such was the custom of that day.

When Paquita stood before her judges and accusers, condemned, degraded, ostracized by both the church and honorable citizens, society was not yet done with her. She was commanded to speak the name of her seducer. Those who related her story, as it had come down to them, said that the soiled and broken "Flower" stood silent and defiant before them. Overwhelmed at the thought of the shame and misery that had befallen her, she was of no mind to bring the wrath and judgement of her people upon another, so it was out of pity for her betrayer and not sentiment that she withheld his name.

But in those old days there was a remedy for such stubborn resistance; a third degree. She was forced into a small space, presumably one of the lesser adobe bins ranged along the kitchen wall to hold supplies. Wherever security of covering was required, a space was over-laid with heavy timbers. As Paquita was kept within her father's house, it was more than likely that a bin so roofed became the maiden's torture cell. (In the walled town each family had a house, and a corral adjoined it and extended to the wall of the house of the next family. There were no lofts, nor attics in those dwellings, nor spare room for building cells; so the adobe bin must have been the place).

Once folded up in that small space, her limbs and back and neck unnaturally cramped, it would no longer be a question of whether she would yield up her secret, but when she would. Poor, wretched Paquita, beautiful and spirited still, but doomed.

In time the agony she suffered from her cramped body drove her betrayer's name from her lips. No sooner had the enraged manhood of the village learned the identity of the one than the hunt was on, Paquita's brothers and their male relatives, and Juan's brothers in the lead. Juan remained at home to plead with his father for permission to save Paquita from the life of a slave, which custom decreed should be her lot in the house of her father. Juan loved Paquita and that love would not die.

The gay trifler had not lingered in Angostura after he learned the fate of the maiden. Crazed with fear he fled into the mountains. There the frenzied citizens sought him, undismayed by the miles of arroyos and cañoncitos and the all but inaccessible caves high up in the rocky ledges. Men from Angostura and Algodones joined them in the hunt, for they were one in a common cause; the law was with them—the unwritten law. Neither government or church interfered.

The search for the fickle lover did not relent. The wise old men reasoned that such a one as the gay violinist would not long be able to resist the pleasure places where dancing feet gathered at baile and fiesta. They spread the hunt and one day they trapped the despoiler of virtuous maidens. They cut off his hair and branded him "El Pelón," and where they took him and what they did to him became but another mystery of the ages. But never more was the gay youth seen nor heard where dancing feet gathered at fiesta and baile, nor at any other place where mortals came together.

But before the hunt for Paquita's betrayer had ended, Juan had taken his own affairs in his own hands. His father's firm "no" to his request to take the girl he loved as his wife forced Juan to break with his family. That brought the righteous wrath of the community down upon his head. Even Paquita's family ridiculed him as a fool for taking on her crime. But Juan believed that in spite of her sin, Paquita loved him and that he would be happier in sharing her shame and misery than he would be in standing by and watching her endure such a life alone.

And so the day Juan took Paquita to the little house he had prepared for her within the walls of Las Huertas, that day his father publicly denounced him as a criminal, branded him one by cutting off his braids, and cast him out. Likewise, society turned its back upon him. They said, in effect, that birds of a feather flock together, and that both were criminals indeed. The church would have none of them; they must dwell together in adultery and their children would be born in sin with no hope of baptism. Within the walls of the village every soul would be against them. With ceremonial regularity their hair would be cut as a constant reminder to society that they were transgressors of the law of God and man. They would be shunned by all throughout their days, and their sin would be visited upon the heads of the children of their unholy union.

There was nothing that Paquita and Juan could do but bow to the judgment put upon them, and accept their lot. The old Spanish law forbade settling outside the walls of a village; those walls were built for their protection, they must live within them. Juan had no reason to petition the king for a grant of land; he had land whereon to live and make his living. If he had not, others would not join him in asking for a grant of land. Should they leave their native village for another, their short hair would at once brand them as outcasts and they would find no welcome, even if permitted to take up residence there. There seemed no hope for them.

So Paquita and Juan dwelled in Juan's little house. He tilled his fields and tended his flocks. Paquita, as all maidens of her day, had been taught to keep a house and meet its rigorous demands. She could even rebuild her home should a storm tear it down. She could clean the wool from Juan's flocks, card and spin and weave. She could make her own dress after weaving the cloth and help Juan dry the skins for his clothing. She could make coverings for their pallets, cook the meats Juan brought from his hunts, grow, roast, and grind the blue corn into fine meal. But they always worked alone, even at harvest times. There were not community gatherings at their house for jollifications and community work. Alone Juan and Paquita must work out their own salvation.

Children did come to Paquita and Juan, the first one unduly. Paquita grieved that there was no baptism for them, that no child within the walls would ever play with them, that there was but scorn and ostracism for them so long as they lived. But the real horror of their degradation came to Paquita and Juan when their children became of marriageable ages and the urge to mate was upon them. Within the walls of Las Huertas there were no fathers who would seek wives for their sons and husbands for their daughters among the children of Paquita and Juan, nor could such fathers of sons and daughters be found for them at Angostura, Algodones, or Bernalillo; for in all these places the children of Juan were deemed evil.

To save his children from each other, Juan searched and found mates for them: undesirables they were, who like Juan's own family were outcasts, cut off from church and society. And what of their children? A like fate awaited them. They too, must pay for the sin of Paquita and Juan.

Time passed, Paquita and Juan went stolidly on, for life must be lived. Paquita old and broken at thirty-eight, wearing her strength away in labor and in aiding her children to rear their children; no others would aid them.

Then came the fateful order of 1823, issued from the Palace of Governors at Santa Fe by the Mexican Governor José Antonio Vicarrea. (Spanish rule was overthrown in 1821). All citizens of the mountain settlements were ordered to abandon their towns and settle in villages along El Rio del Norte, where they would receive land for their sustenance, the order to become effective at once. Their safety demanded it. Hostilities of the savage Indians were increasing, there was no time to be lost. The alcalde at Alameda sent officers to deliver the command.

It was then that Paquita and Juan awoke to their opportunity. With the other families of Las Huertas they made preparations to abandon their home. When their flocks and movable household goods were ready, they and their children escaped into the Sandías. Now, with all the settlers of the mountain districts commanded to leave and take up abode in the communities along El Rio del Norte, there would be nothing of importance to attract the red-skin marauders to the mountainous regions and even less to cause officials of the government to penetrate the wilds. Thus, Juan and his family had but one enemy—the savage beasts that infested the sierras. But Juan and his sons and his sons-in-law were well armed with stout bows and plentifully supplied with arrows of obsidian. Where this weapon could not be used effectively, their native sagacity must be relied upon to save them.

The wanderers found abundant pasturage for their flocks; thus, they ate well of meat, cheese, and fat, besides they had plenty of goat milk. The mountains provided them with leaves and roots for teas and greens for food.

So eluding dangers, and with God preserving them from sickness (Juan and Paquita carried some santos with them; neither the church nor society could prevent that), they traversed the length of the Sandías and entered the Manzano Mountains. They were in no hurry; for they must allow time to grow their hair long enough to be proclaimed honorable citizens. Juan had chosen a new home for them, where they could live honorable lives and where his grandchildren would find their chance. That place was Socorro (Help). There they would find aid to rise again. And Juan's dream and Paquita's prayers came true. That was well over a hundred years ago.

And in that village where no one knew them, nor ever heard of their story, the descendants of Paquita and Juan lived and prospered. In later times some of them moved to Old Albuquerque, but even that happened in the old days. These descendants of Paquita and Juan came to know descendants of their brothers and sisters, and thus has the story of Paquita and Juan been kept alive.

SUBJECT: An Old Native Custom: La Curandera

WPA: 5-5-49 #45

August 5, 1940

Words 1764

Sources of information: Aurelia Gurulé, Gracia Gurulé de Trujillo, Catalina Gurulé, Rumaldita Gurulé, Natividad Gurulé, José García y Trujillo, Lola García de Salazar, Cristiana Baros, Magdalena Gallegos, Terecita Gallegos de Baca. Aurelia Gurulé was the niece of Jesusita, Gracia Gurulé de Trujillo was the grandniece, Catalina, Rumaldita and Natividad were all friends of Jesusita.

LA CURANDERA

In the days of long ago when there were no médicos in the now land of New Mexico, nor none trained scientifically to care for the sick and the suffering, self-appointed healers called curanderos played important parts in the life of the native communities. Their cure-alls were of the lavish gifts of nature and free to all who collected them. From the traditions of their people, those who collected them knew of their curative powers and how to administer them.

In the earliest days of Las Placitas a little house nestled close to Cerro Negro, the hill of black rock carved with Indian symbols, just to the north of the village, a house that became a kind of sanctuary for weary souls and a little temple of health for the sick. It was La Casa de La Curandera, Jesusita.

The name Jesusita, and all of its forms, have since been banned by the church. This Jesusita was a pious, honorable curandera devoted to the saints and her remedios. She had high faith in each of them.

She kept her house fresh and clean from the vigas, which supported the ceiling of latas and the adobe mud roof, down to the hard earthen floor. Her walls were snow-white with yeso and the hand-hewn timbers of her wee windows and dwarf door were scrubbed to a saffron tint. Those who still have memories of La Curandera also tell of her house. Just inside her door stood a smooth, stout stick with grama grass bound tightly to one end of it by a piece of correa (leather string). That was her broom and first aid to household cleanliness in those old days.

La Curandera was a very small person, with slender, graceful hands with which she did half of her talking and much of her healing. She wore many petticoats, made of cloth she wove herself, and always she kept them fresh and clean. To one of them she fastened a little sack filled with the hair of every different form of life she could find. This would save her from the power of the witches as would the piece of cachana she wore about her person. A small piece it was with a hole pierced in it through which to run a string. This charm against witches was worn for many years upon the person of La Curandera and finally given to a grandchild to preserve her from the power of the witches. Jesusita feared the witches even more than she feared the devil; but then she was born in 1830.

Always there was a pleasant suggestion of a flower garden in the air in La Curandera's house. But, "entren todos y mirren alrededor ustedes" (enter all and have a look around).

Those vigas that supported the roof were festooned with drying herbs which restored health, eased pain, and saved life. When they were dried, they would be taken down and carefully put away for use. There was yerbabuena (mint), guaco (birthwort), berraza (water-parsnip)—all superior remedies for dolor de stomago (hurt of stomach) as all stomach ailments were called in those days. But not all the yerbas good for this ailment were dried. There was chan (an Indian word), which was eaten when green, a pinch of salt added. There was ramo de sabine (twig of savin). Boil the leaves and make strong tea. Both these remedies were sure cures for cramps of the stomach. Yerba de zorra (fox-weed) also made a desirable tea for stomach disturbances.

From the vigas hung much poleo (pennyroyal). It was the magic fever reducer. But an egg white, well beaten, added to the dry poleo and well mixed, a little salt sprinkled over it, was what really made the poleo effective. And it was effective, when spread as a poultice on a piece of cloth and covered with an equal-sized-piece of pin-pricked paper. This poultice was bound to the forehead and soles of feet—paper side down—and it brought quick relief to victims of high fevers. So good a remedy was it that it is used to this day. A strong tea made from the reddish flower of the dried saffron (yerba de azefrán) was also an aid in reducing fever. It required some sort of sweetening for best results. Raisins made from the grape at home were used before the advent of "yellow sugar." Azefrán relieved colic.

La Curandera's house was sweetly scented by the drying cilantro (coriander). She would receive extra special gifts, perhaps a lamb or a kid for those precious aromatic seeds so coveted for flavoring soups, puddings, and bizcochitos (small biscuits).

La Curandera dried mansanilla in abundance (good old camomile in English). That yerba was the baby medicine. It made excellent tea for the cure of colic, and it was considered a food substitute.

When dried, cota (proper name should be macha and it is lamb's lettuce) made a very popular drink, good for almost any disposition toward general debility. It is popular to this day. Also it was cota that was dried in abundance in the old days and stored for using to light a fire when flint rocks furnished the sparks. Suspended from Jesusita's vigas was a plentiful supply of that yerba.

But not all of La Curandera's cure-alls were hung from the vigas to dry. Packed away in all those tinajas inside and upon the tapanco (the cupboard of the old days) were quantities of all the important roots and wonder-cures of her time. Prominent among the roots was yerba del manza, which was indeed a lifesaver, a killer of infections. The root was thoroughly boiled and bath water was made strong with it. The infected parts of the body were soaked in this water, not once, but many times. No infection survived those repeated, sustained baths. To this day it is declared that the doctors of medicine who came to the territory of New Mexico in the early days had no germ destroyer to compare with yerba del manza. Much of yerba del lobo (herb of the wolf) was stored in the tinajas This root made a tea that was given to ease the first pains of childbirth

Another tinaja contained tronkos del calabazas (stems of the pumpkins). When La Curandera was summoned to relieve dolor del garganta (hurt of the throat), regardless of the specific hurt, the sufferer's throat, both inside and out, was plastered with a paste made by mixing toasted and powdered tronko del calabaza with fat and sal de Zuni. This salt did not come from the region of the present Estancia. This sal de Zuni was the outstanding eye wash of La Curandera's early days, when dissolved in water.

In those old days rheuma was a common complaint. The local remedio was Alonzo García (a short, sturdy plant with purple blossoms). It was well boiled and the water from it used as a bath. But there was another remedy for rheuma (rheumatism), and a most effective one it was. It cost more chili, frijoles, wheat, or more of whatever was given to pay for it. But the compensation for the service or remedios of la curandera or el curandero was called gifts, because these were free-will offerings; but there was a definite under-standing among the people concerning the rarer cures. Hedionda (fetid) was the favored cure for rheuma. La Curandera traveled far to gather it. It was a vile-smelling herb but a sure remedy. It was boiled and boiled and the strong water was used as a bath.

Also La Curandera traveled mile upon mile to fetch the one true remedio for dolor del corazón (hurt of the heart). It was almagra (Indian red) from near a place they called Azabache (jet) on Mesa de Chaco, which was near to two hundred miles from the house of La Curandera at the foot of Cerro Negro. In those old days los curanderos y las curanderas made pilgrimages in the direction of the setting sun into the land that is now the state of Arizona. There they found hedionda, almagra, sal de Zuni, and azabache from which charms were cut. These black charms protected their wearers from witches. It was the custom for curanderos and curanderas to keep a supply of charms on hand for their customers.

Those must have been merry pilgrimages, for many of them went together with oxen and carreta to bring back the precious yerbas and metals they found, and the prized almagra (Indian red), which was neither yerba nor metal but a substance akin to pumice that looked very much like the real almagra (red ocher), which came from Spain.

La Curandera powdered the almagra and wet it with sufficient water to knead it, then she worked it into small loaves and put them away for use. When it was required for her patients, she broke a small piece from a loaf and mixed it with water until it was the color of the heart, then it was taken for dolor del Corazón. Needless to say, it was an effective cure, for La Curandera used her mind and her hands as well as her remedios. Her words, "No tener miedo" (Have no fear), were powerfully reassuring and cures in themselves: a philosophy the old Southwest borrowed from the old East—or was it the other way?

Always when los curanderos y las curanderas returned to their villages with their wonder-cures and charms and their tales from the outside world, they received as royal a welcome as the villages could afford, for what would they do without these men and women who "dispensed" health and assistance in time of need?

La Curandera had another supply of roots in her tinajas, a goodly quantity. It was called inmortal (endless) for the commonest of all the ailments she was called upon to heal, colds. This root induced sneezing, an almost endless number of sneezes. But that was the cure. The more the patient sneezed, the sooner would he be cured of the cold.

If the cold got beyond bounds and ended in dolor de pecho (hurt of chest), a more severe treatment was given. A poultice of cebollas y sebo de oso. (Grease of the bear thoroughly mixed with shredded onions was how the poultice was prepared, and then it was put into a small cloth sack and laid on the chest). This was the treatment for pneumonia, as they came to call the most acute pain of the chest in later days.

🐝 🐝 🐝

SUBJECT: La Curandera
WPA 5-5-2 #47
August 19, 1940
Words 3345

Friegue (rub) was the name La Curandera called her treatment for colds she gave the small children who rebelled against her yerbas. The patient was told to stand rigid and cross his arms upon his breast. Then he was thoroughly rubbed on his arms, shoulders, and neck. That completed, La Curandera placed her cupped hands under his elbows and raised him from the floor and shook him vigorously. This was repeated twice; then followed a short rest, and the treatment resumed until she considered her small patient had enough of it.

For the older ones who preferred to have their colds cured by means other than taking yerbas, there was "remojos de pies" (steeping the feet). Into a bath of steaming hot water La Curandera forced the cold-victim's nether limbs. She squatted down beside the tinaja or copper kettle, whichever was used, and cascaded hand fulls of the water down her patients legs. When he was well heated from the rising steam, she wrapped him in a hot blanket and had him lie on a pallet. Soon he was in a sweat. If he obeyed La Curandera and remained in the blanket until she released him, his cold left him. If he obeyed his own impulse and kicked off the heavy home-woven cover, he was worse off than he was when La Curandera started the treatment.

In the old days the prime remedy for building blood was sangre del berendo (blood of the deer). When a deer was slaughtered, the blood was caught in tinajas and set aside to dry. When it was hard, it was sealed into the tinaja with jara y peño de teá (willow and pitch from the pine), and buried to keep it fresh for use. When needed, a tinaja was removed from its grave, opened and the needed piece broken off. This piece was dissolved in water and then water added until the fluid was the color and consistency of human blood. The patient drank it. Both the taste and odor of this cure was almost beyond the patient's ability to endure, but he downed it for his blood's sake.

The pine tree offered aid in the cure of infections from bad burns, a remedy that never failed. So it happened that La Curandera was not baffled by a serious infection resulting from a burn. She merely walked to a pine tree where she was certain to find gusano excremento (excretion of worms that delved into the pine) and scraped out what she desired. This was mixed with candle tallow and sprinkled lightly with salt, spread on a cloth and bound to the infections. To prevent infections in deep cuts and hasten the healing, gusano excremento was mixed with bear grease instead of the tallow.

La Curandera knew exactly what to do for asthma. Select a tender branch from el álamo (the cottonwood), peel off the bark and boil it in water until but one quarter of the water remained. This made an excellent tonic which was administered regularly.

For the cure of hemorrhoids (La Curandera had no name for that affliction, except to describe it), there was a yerba which gave relief to those hardened enough to take the treatment. The dried añil del muerto (yerba of death), a poisonous herb that was a source of indigo, and was obtained in Mexico, was reduced to a powder, and for use it was mixed with hot grease and applied hot to the afflictions by rubbing, then covered with a hot cloth so hot it was just short of smoldering.

All around La Cerro Negro, La Curandera found la calavacia (the evil-smelling wild gourd) which she boiled and boiled into a mash and bound by strips of cloth to swollen joints to reduce them. Such an effective cure it was that many use it to this day.

La Curandera was never selfish in the matter of her time when laboring over a victim of viruelas (smallpox), the scourge that wrought such havoc among the Indians. It was a dreaded disease but its marks were feared more than the plague itself. There was no one in those old days who worked harder to prevent her smallpox patients from carrying the scars of the disease all their days. She made a small mop of a rag well covered with the carbon from the fireplace and soaked in bear grease. This rag was folded into a cloth on which she had rolled tortillas many times and which was saturated with grease and sprinkled with sal de Zuni. She placed a heated stone on the floor near her patient's bed and knelt by it. Then she started a treatment that was to continue without ceasing until its purpose was accomplished; and that was the total absorption of all pus so that no pockmark be left in the wake of the disease. Hour after hour through day and night she heated her hand mop on the stone and pressed the pustules on her patient's body until they were clean and dry. When she fell exhausted upon the floor, some member of the patient's family or some friend carried on. Thus went the treatment until all danger of permanent markings upon the sick one was past. Wood ashes were the final touches to the treatment. The one yerba given in cases of smallpox was verranza, a cure for constipation. Where the patient could not swallow, the dried herb was rolled into pellets and with the aid of grease and fingers, was injected into the intestinal terminal.

La Curandera had her treatment for tired, weary "bones" and aching muscles. Machucones, she called it, literally interpreted into "making old men into young men."

The candidate for youth (and strange to say it was always an old man) bared his body and lay prone upon the floor. La Curandera knelt beside him and with her clenched fist, her thumb projected upward, pounded the muscles up and down his body until all the soreness, stiffness, and aches were banished, and the body lay relaxed. And in rhythm to her padded beat upon the body, she mumbled or chanted, "En el nombre de Dios te voy a curar" (In the name of God I cure you). After hours of this dual treatment, the old man who painfully stretched himself upon her floor fairly sprang up from it. In this manner La Curandera kept her own husband young in body. The women in those long ago days had no time for keeping youthful.

In her flourishing days, La Curandera healed paralytics. From anís Mexicano (anise seed grown in Mexico and different from the American garden variety) she made a powder that she used as if it were soap. She moistened it and massaged the lather into the pores of the body of the patient, not once but many times. Tea made from the water in which the anís seed was boiled was given the victim of paralysis to drink. This cure required both time and patience but it did restore the helpless to active life. This and her low-voiced chant, "En el nombre de Dios te voy a curar."

Dolor del espaldo (hurt of the back) came in for its share of attention in the old days. For all of them, lime water was the cure. Always there has been a kiln where local limestone was burned into lime. There was great need of it, not only for el remedio but for putting into the water in which the white corn was soaked to remove the cáscara (the viscid covering of the grains). The pozole made from this corn was one of the health foods of the long-ago days, and still is.

Cara de vinagre (vinegar compact) was an item of importance on La Curandera's list of cures, and it is a leading household remedy to this day. No headache went without a vinegar compact. No bruise or minor cut could possibly heal without one. Stiff necks, sore hands, sore feet, toothache, and nausea came in for their share of vinegar cures. Sprains were bathed in vinegar and bandaged. In later times when whiskey was available, it supplanted vinegar in the treatment of cuts, sprains, and nausea. It was used also to kill infections.

SUBJECT: A Tale Of Witchcraft
September 12, 1940
Words 1751
Sources of information: Auralia Gurulé, Gracia Trujillo, Catalina Gurulé.
Auralia Gurulé is the grand-niece of La Curandera of this story. Catalina
Gurulé is a friend of La Curandera.

THE STORY OF LA CURANDERA
(A Tale of Witchcraft)

It was shortly before the year 1830, and during the days of hostilities between
the Spanish and French in New Mexico, that the family of Alary, including a
daughter, Victoria, and three or four other French families came from France
and settled on a grant known as El Rancho de Montoya, a grant from the king
of Spain to Capitan Gonzales for service rendered the crown. The French families settled in that part of the grant called Corrales (little corrals), the place
where Capitan Gonzales had once rounded up his livestock. Corrales is across
the Rio Grande from Bernalillo and about ten miles from Las Placitas.

From the Alary family came Jesusita, daughter of Victoria, and heir to her
mother's beauty and red hair. Jesusita was educated by her scholarly grandfather, and she created in Las Placitas a taste for good manners and for their
entertainment she told them the glamorous Arabian Knights, which are told to
the children of the village to this day, along with their own folklore, until Ali
Baba and the Forty Thieves, Sinbad the Sailor, Aladdin, and the rest of them
are one with the heroes of Mexican tales.

But Jesusita never told a more fascinating tale than the story of her own
life and adventures, which is now told by her direct descendants.

In her early teens she married a native youth, Junario, who settled her in
a humble little adobe dwelling and gave her nothing but hard work and privations. The spirited girl found such an existence intolerable and without cere-

mony gave him an Indian divorce (ordered him from the house and threw his belongings out after him). Not long after that a wealthy stockman and merchant discovered her, rid himself of his own wife, and married the red-headed girl and forthwith became her slave. From Corrales he took her to Azabache, where he had a store and thousands of sheep and was neighbor to the Navajos and lived in peace with them.

There Jesusita acquainted herself with the ways of the Indians and endeavored to learn of their cures. But the Indian, then as now, did not talk of himself and his affairs; so the French lady learned only what they chose that she should know. However, Jesusita was not confined to the semi-desert country around Azabache during the years of her sojourn there. Her husband, Eugenio, took her on many of his trips to Santa Fe and Mexico.

In her twenty-fifth year, fate abruptly changed the pattern of her life. Eugenio decided to spend that year on his rancho in Corrales near his wife's people. Victorio was hale and hearty at the time. One afternoon soon after their arrival, Jesusita felt weary after a day of house cleaning and went into the patio to rest.

As she sat there, a stranger came in and made herself very agreeable. She remarked that Jesusita looked very tired and offered to make her a cup of coffee, which would revive her instantly. Jesusita agreed and together they went into the kitchen. When the coffee was ready, the stranger carried it into the patio to serve it. Instead of drinking with her hostess, the stranger begged to be excused and hastened away.

No sooner had Jesusita drained her cup of delicious coffee than she was bereft of her senses. She ran screaming from the patio, tearing her clothing from her body and trying to hide from those who came to quiet her and learn of what had happened.

In the days that followed her family discovered the cause of her madness. She was bewitched. Her guest had evil intentions toward her. The coffee was mixed with a potent drug. Eugenio's scorned and deserted wife hated the beautiful Jesusita. This was her revenge. On this the whole family agreed. Poor Jesusita!

Eugenio thought the familiar things at Azabache might restore his wife's mind, so back they went to that place among the Indians. But in that he was mistaken. Her mental condition remained unchanged. She raved and tried to run away and tore up all the beautiful clothes he had the serving maids put upon her.

Eugenio took her to Mexico City. There he squandered half of his fortune upon the vain quest of a cure for his wife, while his men left in charge of his interests betrayed and cheated him out of a goodly portion of the other half.

On his return to Corrales, Jesusita's own father and sisters took her case in hand. Against her will she was taken to El Arbolario (meaning the madcap, but applied to Indian witch doctors) who lived on his rancho in Cañón del Oso (Bear Cañon on the maps of today, in the Sandías about midway between Albuquerque and Alameda). The name of the Arbolario was Juan and his wife was Josefeta. Bear Cañon was an eerie and lonely place where brujas (witches) in the form of owls made the night ghostly. Bears, lions, and wildcats added to the terror of the place. But Juan and his wife lived there unmolested and received and healed victims of witchcraft.

Here Jesusita lived for two months alone with Juan and Josefeta, except for her young niece, whom the Indians permitted to remain with her. Many pieces of gold Eugenio paid for this privilege, and many more for the services to his wife. From this niece, as well as from the bewitched woman herself, has come this story of the restoration of the mind of Jesusita.

The cure progressed for sixty days. The mad woman was forbidden to speak of her illness, and compelled each day to say that she was better. A charm of cachana was made for her and hung about her neck. That would ward off all witches. About her person pieces of osha roots were fastened; they protected her from the power of Indian witches. Each day Juan mixed the heart of a chili pod with sal de Zuni and burned it and then dissolved the ashes there in water and gave it to her to drink. This was a purifying drink and a recovery aid; this was impressed upon her mind. Juan and Josefeta held a velorio (wake) over Jesusita two days of each week during her cure, on Thursdays and Fridays. All day they watched over the patient to ward off the brujas. Her recovery would be accomplished one of those two days. They must be on their guard lest a witch try to interfere. One those days of el velorio, Jesusita lay on a pallet, relaxed and listening to the droning voice of Juan, though she had no idea of what he said. Added to all this, Juan repeated daily that she was getting well. In time, Jesusita spoke the same words with conviction.

So passed the days with the unceasing impressions left upon the consciousness of the patient that she would find herself entirely cured on an approaching Thursday or Friday.

Then one Friday Juan conducted her to a secret place encircled by concealing ledges of rock. In the center of the small place was a limpid lagunajo (pool). Juan made her sit down and look into the pool until a face appeared.

She would recognize the face and at that instant her mind would be wholly restored. Then Juan dropped his cuchillo (knife) into the water and sat down beside her. In time the troubled water calmed, and together they gazed steadfastly into its clear depth. Again he told her she must be able to see a face and it would be the face of the one who had bewitched her—but to know that the moment she saw the face that she would be cured.

Hours passed. Then Jesusita did see a face. It was the face of Eugenio's cast-off wife and she was in the act of passing a cup of coffee. Jesusita felt calm. The sixty days with Juan and Josefeta had brought her that. She knew that she that was healed. All through the days of treatment that fact had been kept alive in her mind. And now she was herself. She had no desire for revenge against the woman who had sought to destroy her.

Eugenio now no longer was a merchant and sheepman. But he salvaged enough from the sale of his rancho in Corrales to buy land at El Cerro Negro just across an arroyo from Las Placitas. There he built a home and there he and Jesusita lived out their days. They pursued the lowly ways of their neighbors, and she spent her days doing good. From Juan and Josefeta she learned much of cure-alls, where to obtain them and how to use them. But her yerbas and other cures were second to her faith in God and in her own mind. Many were the healings she made with a cup of cold, clear water, which she gave them to drink with the words "en el nombre de Dios te voy a curar" (in the name of God I shall cure you). But never did a patient know that the cup contained no yerba.

But throughout her life La Curandera never overcame her fear of the brujas and she wore all manners of charms to preserve her from their power until her death.

To this day in Las Placitas and round about, people fear the brujas, and to this day many go to the arbolarios at the Sandía Pueblo for their cures, regardless of the nature of their ills. Yet in spite of this fact, there is a prevailing fear in the heart and mind of most of the people, even those who go to the pueblos for cures, that they are in danger of being bewitched whenever they are in a pueblo. They fear the Indians, even if they claim them as amigas who cured them, for they believe that none are safe from the power of the witches. And they believe that the Indian witches have more and mightier power over their victims than any other witches.

SUBJECT: An Old Native Custom: Camila
WPA: 5-5-49 #55
February 12, 1941
Words 2309
Sources of information: Rumaldita Gurulé, Benino Archibeque, Conception
Archibeque, Fermenia Durán. All the above were born in or near Las Placitas.
They told the story of the old native custom and Camila as it had been related
to them.

CAMILA

Camila was born at Las Placitas in the community house more than one hundred years ago. She was just one of the many children born to Felipe and María Montana, or so they thought until she started to grow up. Then they discovered that she was different, and what was accepted by their other children was usually questioned or rejected by Camila. But after all she was their child and must be brought up according to the customs of the day, whether she would or no.

To Felipe and María, the customs of their time constituted the pattern of life by which a child's life should be molded. There were no exceptions, from their point of view. They had been brought up according to the ways of the day. They would bring up their children according to those same customs. It was the way of life in those times.

In those days the parents held authority over their children until death, regardless of the ages of those offspring. Always the parents dictated, the children obeyed. Even if those children had children of their own, they harkened to the voice of their parents. It was the custom of the time. Should they consider it necessary to inflict physical punishment upon their adult children, there was nothing for those men and women to do but submit, and without question. Belief in the infallibility of their elders was a part of their religion; if they did not believe it they lacked the courage to declare themselves. This dumb submission was termed "respect for their elders." But in any case, the elders had their way. Even where there were children who rebelled against the beliefs and customs—and they were few—their elders still managed to hamper them until their lives were reformed, outwardly at least, or wrecked.

Camila's madrina (godmother) was Felipe's widowed sister. As such she was obligated to promote the welfare of the child. The madrina was a servant in the great house of Don José Gonzales at Bernalillo. So it came about that Camila spent much of her childhood there, especially after she was of an age where she could be of service—and that service to be rendered without pay.

But Camila was alert and ambitious, and her natural beauty had given her ideas of her own that were not in accord with those of her family. So in the great house she learned much besides kitchen drudgery. She learned to sew and to weave. But more than that she learned to put color into the natural-colored cloth woven by her people and the manta (unbleached, coarse cotton cloth) that came from Mexico. These two materials made all the garments worn by both men and women, as well as the children, at Las Placitas. Everyone looked more or less alike. There was no romance in that drab dress. Camila hated it, yet she must wear it.

Nevertheless, she learned to use the two dyes possessed locally. With piedra lipis (rock with much copper in it) a green dye could be made. If piedra lumbre (which was spar) was boiled with the piedra lipis, the dye was made fast. Then to get a gay orange color, azafrán (saffron) blossoms were boiled with piedra lumbre and there was a fast orange color.

Camila also learned how to sew her dress that she might have a slim waistline and wear a sash. She hated the loose sack-like garments worn by all the women and girls in the village. They pulled down over the hips and fitted just like the shirts of the men. She also learned how to dress her hair as the ladies did at the house of Don José. She could not wear her hair dressed so until she was married. Custom dictated that maidens among her people wear their hair in braids until they became matrons. But when she was married she would brush her hair and pile it up with a large comb. Yes, she dreamed of marriage, and with Andrés, the son of a trusted servant of Don José. They were in love with each other. Though she had never spoken to him—custom and her aunt would not permit that—they had talked much together with their eyes.

But Felipe had other plans for his daughter, though he knew nothing of Camila's dreams. However, it would not have altered padre Felipe's plans had he known. His heart was set on marrying her to Ramón, the son of his old friend. And that old friend was as eager to have Camila for a daughter-in-law as Felipe was eager to have Ramón for a son-in-law. On that they were agreed. Accordingly, the betrothal was arranged.

So her padre went to Bernalillo and fetched his daughter home. There he told her of her future wedding and of her husband-to-be. Camila's heart sank but there was nothing she could do about it. She did not know that Ramón was no more willing to have her as a wife than she was to have him as her husband. The custom of the day had prevented any speech between them. Poor Camila. Sad Ramón, for he, too, had dreams of his own.

And so, they were wedded at the chapel in San Felipe by the good priest who gave them his blessing. They returned to Las Placitas to set up housekeeping in the apartment added by the community to the community house for them.

But from the beginning nothing went right. Camila grieved in secret for her lover in Bernalillo, and Ramón went indifferently about his share of the community work. Madre María thought her daughter ill, and as the months passed by and Camila's spirits did not revive, she called in La Curandera. Then the daughter showed some spirit. She refused to have La Curandera's yerbas, but prescribed for herself. She would work for herself, work to make herself beautiful. She would return to clothes—an age-old remedy for women grieving over lost dreams—though, of course, Camila did not realize that.

By hook and by crook she accumulated all the wool that she could. She cleaned, washed, carded, spun, and wove it into cloth—cloth to be dyed green and gay orange for dresses that would have snug waist-lines.

She piled up wood for her fire, she searched the arroyos and mountain foothills for just the right piedras de lipis y lumbre. She knew just the quality and quantity of these rocks needed to make the dye. She procured a sufficiency of azafrán blossoms, and a huge tinaja. In this vessel she would make the dyes and dye the cloth she had woven on her own loom. She was happy in this work and the old sparkle returned to her eyes. As she boiled the rock of copper and the rock of spar together and kept up her fire, she had many visitors to see what she was about. Madre María did not think she should waste so much time on cloth that was serviceable and could be kept clean, if the housewife was industrious. But there was no unwritten law against dying cloth, so the best she could do was to discourage the wasting of time, which was no argument at all. Didn't they all spend happy, peaceful hours just leaning against the sunny sides of the adobe houses in the winter, and in the shade of them in the summers?

At least Camila had a pretty green dress and a joy of a dress of gay orange color. They were not made in the mode of the day, as worn in the village. But they were slim and trim at the waistline. They did in truth make Camila different. She also put work on her face. She ground terra firma (yeso) with the metate until it was a very fine powder for her face, and she made a dark rose-tinted paste from the seeds of a plant, which they called sesame. With this she painted her cheeks. This paste was called alegría (a paste of sesamum and honey). And her hair came in for its share of beauty treatment. With her brushes (made by firmly attaching small pieces of buffalo hide to pieces of wood) she brushed brilliance into her hair, then dressed it in the manner of the ladies at the house of Don José.

Now the troubles of Camila really did start. There was not one other married woman in the village who would have gone to all the work and painstaking care to do for herself what Camila had accomplished. At once they condemned her vanities and declared that it would lead to no good. Padre Felipe berated her for her vanity. She listened to him, but did nothing about her offending manners. At that failure of Felipe to make Camila cease her frivolities, a whispering campaign ensued to which Ramón gave ear. Not that he believed his wife meant any harm. He did think that she should be like the other women of the community—be content to give her time to her house and her husband, and to her share of the community work. He did not seem to realize that Camila had done all these things and gave time to herself as well. He thought she should not be doing the things that made her the talk of the village—whether it was warranted or not. He tried to reason with her as her father had tried to do and then commanded her to end her vain pursuits. Camila refused to listen to him.

Then they quarreled. Their bitter denunciations of each other grew more bitter as the months went by, but Camila did not change her ways. Her first baby arrived. That event made no difference either in Camila nor the stormy family life. Now everybody condemned Camila and openly pitied Ramón.

El abuelo, or coco, took a hand in their affairs. It was his self-imposed duty to promote public and private welfare. He made sudden visits to their home, knocked their heads together with intent to hurt, but with no results.

Then Camila and Ramón decided that they did not want each other. Yet what could they do about it? There was the priest. Camila's parents must be reckoned with, as well as the parents of Ramón. There was the custom of their time; when once you married, you stayed married till death did you part. There was no such thing as divorce; custom forbade that.

But in spite of all these obstacles, Camila and Ramón went to the house of her parents and begged that they be allowed to separate. The indignant

Felipe berated them for their disgraceful conduct and for their unnatural desire to live apart. He commanded them to return to their home and live together in peace. In vain they tried to obey the command given them.

Desperate, they sought permission from Ramón's parents to separate. All they had from them was a scolding and another command to return to their home and dwell together in harmony.

They did return to their home; they did try to follow the advice of their elders. But very soon they found that it was easier for them to fight and quarrel than it was for them to try to dwell in harmony. So padre Felipe took them to the priest at San Felipe. But they found no relief there. The good padre reminded them of their holy vows, which united them in wedlock until death. He lectured them roundly and bade them go home and live together somehow. It was their duty.

Without hope Camila and Ramón returned to their home. They could not live together peaceably. They wished to be free of each other. Their quarrels became more violent. Ramón listened to the gossiping tongues. Camila wept throughout the days and neglected her household duties.

Then it was that padre Felipe made the ultimate in decisions. He publicly flogged his daughter, just as the father of his son-in-law flogged Ramón. That was the custom. Then the couple was taken home and commanded to abide there in harmony.

That was the last straw for the broken Camila. She vowed to herself that she would no longer endure life with Ramón, who accused her of all the things her jealous neighbors said of her. One day she took her two babies to the house of her mother and left them. With her clothes tied into a bundle, she stole from the village and walked to Bernalillo. She told her aunt of her miseries and her sufferings. But all that aunt could do was to advise her to return to her husband. Camila went her way.

That way was not back to Las Placitas. Camila evidently preferred any fate to that. She went to her lover and together they fled from Bernalillo. The enraged and outraged Ramón hunted them down. There was no compassion in his heart for the beautiful Camila. He laid her lovely head open with a stone machete, without weighing the justification. The custom of the day allowed one to kill an unfaithful mate. Church and society condoned it. The church buried the slain, the law did not touch the slayer. Such was the custom of Camila's day.

SUBJECT: An Old Native Custom: Señor Flores comes to Las Placitas
WPA #85
March 12, 1941
Words 1745
Sources of information: José L.A. Gurulé, Patricio Gallegos. José Gurulé is
the son of Nicolás Gurulé and nephew of Lucas Gurulé.

SEÑOR FLORES COMES TO LAS PLACITAS

It was in the spring of 1860 that Señor Flores brought his family to Las Placitas to live. One morning the village woke up to find them just standing in
their midst, waiting to hear a cheery good morning and "welcome to our village."

And the greeting and welcome did come. The Flores family wore better
clothing than was possessed by the average family in the village, and they had
a wealth of possessions with them. One especially gave them a financial rat-
ing—a burro. A good animal it was, well worth fifty dollars. They had a goodly supply of provisions and plenty of seed to plant. All Señor Flores desired
was land to plant, a place to build a house, and pasture for his flocks. Yes, he
had sheep and goats. As soon as his family were housed and his seeds in the
ground, he would go to fetch his flocks.

The villagers talked together, decided that the Flores family would be
quite an addition to their community, invited them to settle down, and forgot
to ask for references.

According to the custom of the day, the community turned out to help
build the new house, which they made of rock, and a stout corral adjoining it,
which would secure the flocks Señor Flores was to bring.

Soon the spring work was on; plowing and planting the fields. The new
neighbor worked along with the men and his wife, Clarita, worked side by
side with the women of the community. Their fourteen-year-old son and their
two daughters helped with the work, as did the other children of their ages.

When the planting was finished, Señor Flores went for his flocks. He told them he would be gone for several days, or more. His flock was away off in the mountains. No one asked him where.

Señor Flores was gone several weeks, not days. But when he came he brought a flock of good sheep, all marked and ready to add to the community herd. And very soon he went for more of his sheep. It would take some time for him to move the whole flock.

The days were growing hot and the weeds vied with corn, beans, peas, and chili for supremacy in the fields. Clarita now took her husband's place in the fields; he was either gone from home or very ill. The villagers saw little of him. They were really becoming accustomed to missing him.

Then something strange and unprecedented started happening about the village. Nothing left outside the houses at night was ever found in the mornings. Sharp stone axes, tinajas, boards which someone had labored over to smooth and make usable. Even the washings left out to dry disappeared. Spy as they might, no thief could they catch. It was all perplexing. Then the peaceful villagers grew wary and suspicious of each other. Their bailes and games lost the spirit of gaiety, community work dragged. In short, community life was ill. Lucas Gurulé, who was ever a courageous soul, advised them all to protect their possessions and watch. And above all, not to quarrel with their neighbors until they had something to quarrel about.

The green corn clung temptingly to the stalks, but the families ate sparingly of it. Corn was needed to carry them through the winter and the next spring. They must let most of it dry that it might be stored away.

Then it was that they heard it in the night—the visitation. The still night air was vibrant with the sound of it. That blood-freezing, unearthly too-tootle-teetoo, the whistle of the penitentes. That weird refrain over and over, which raised the hair straight up on their heads. How they feared it! It was a warning that the penitentes marched, let none behold them. And none of them did. Every villager kept within his house and dared not even look out in the dark when he heard that whistle. Las Placitas had no penitentes at that time, but the region of La Madera across the mountains was a hot bed of them. Whether the people of Las Placitas heard that whistle by day or by night they fled to the security of their houses or caves, or in fact, anywhere out of sight of the fanatics.

The whole village, excepting Señor Flores, who had gone to Sandía Pueblo to consult El Albolario (the Indian witch doctor), was up and about very early the next morning, talking together of the eerie night sounds that sent them to cover. It was not until later in the day that they discovered that their corn fields had been raided. The green corn they had denied themselves had been stolen. Some thief had taken advantage of the march of the penitentes to rob them of much of their green corn. Angry citizens searched everywhere for traces of the thief but there was simply no clue. The corn had been whisked away as if by magic.

Different men watched the fields at night. Weeks past without alarms and in time the watch was discontinued. The harvest time was coming on. The usual fears of Indian raiders kept the villagers alert, and with the work and problems of the succeeding days, the hectic night of the march of the penitentes was forgotten.

And then one dark night it came again. That too-tootle-tee-too, shrill, startling, paralyzing it came, warning them to clear the path and to spy not upon los hermanos de luz. Danger, or perhaps death, lurked for those who defied that weird warning. In those old days the penitentes had ways of their own to enforce their whistled commands. Few risked the consequences of being caught spying upon the brotherhood. So to the security of their houses went the villagers, with no thought but to save themselves. Yet, one villager did fling a challenge at that frightening refrain. It was the ever-courageous Lucas Gurulé. He had a mind to see for himself about the sudden repetition of the too-tootle-tee-too whistle of the penitentes.

Armed with a stout oak club he stole noiselessly along the byways. He paused briefly at the house of Señor Flores. Even the burro was gone. Now and then he crouched low. He had no desire to be seen. Swiftly he moved along until he came to the edge of the community fields. There he strained his ears in an effort to hear the footsteps of the "penitentes."

Presently he heard something in the distance. Now and then came the shrill refrain from the whistle. Lucas crept low among the corn stalks in the direction of the sounds. Soon he was near enough to make out a faint silhouette. It was a shrouded man and burro with a large crib on its back. Almost without sound corn was being broken from the stalks and deposited in the crib. Lucas moved cautiously. It was most difficult to remain unheard among the drying leaves of the corn. But he did accomplish it. Then without warning he sprang up, bringing his poised club down upon the bent figure before him. Another blow he delivered before the sheeted figure fled through the rustling corn stalks. The burro sped from the place like a wild thing. Lucas found he could not keep up with the fleeing figure, but he was satisfied with his night's work and ready to go to his house and get in a few hours' sleep.

He was the first man to be astir when the day broke. He roused Nicolás Gurulé and José Mora and together the three went to call upon Señor Flores. They found the weeping Clarita preparing breakfast. Her husband was very ill, she told them. They asked to see him. La Señora said he was much too ill to be seen. She stood at the door of the sleeping room, as if to bar their passage. Almost rudely they put her aside and entered.

The three men stood looking down at the form of their neighbor well covered with a blanket. Lucas snatched the cover from the sick man and the callers gazed upon his swollen head, his bruised back, showing a ridge-like mark across it—the mark of the club wielded by the hand of Lucas.

Unceremoniously they jerked the man to his feet and forced him from the house.

As they moved along with their unwilling companion, a crowd of men and boys joined them. On they went down the winding trail to Arroyo Colorado, crossed over and came to halt at the spot where an old carreta wheel lay. Lucas produced pieces of strong leather lashes and a cuarta (short whip).

The men bound the struggling Flores to the heavy wheel, while he protested loudly against such unfriendly treatment and demanded explanations. But there came no explanations, only accusations that painted him as the thief who attempted to rob them of their corn the previous night and who did raid their corn fields in mid-summer and who stole all the things missed about the village since his arrival in it.

After the accusations Lucas administered a thorough flogging. That was the custom of the time, and the only punishment for petty theft. Now and then Lucas gave him a particularly stinging blow, settlement in part for frightening the villagers out of their wits at dead of night by using the pentitente whistle while he robbed them of their corn.

Soon after the flogging, the Flores family disappeared from Las Placitas. The villagers never heard of them again. From whence they came and where they went none of them ever knew. Señor Flores and his family still live in the memories of a few of the older ones of Las Placitas, because he was the first and only one ever to be flogged for petty theft in the village—with or without benefit of the too-tootle-tee-too of the penitente whistle.

SUBJECT: An Old Native Custom: The Cruel Moon
WPA: #40
April 9, 1941
Words 1633
Sources of information: Rumaldita Gurulé, Magdalena Gallegos, Catalina
Gurulé, Florinda De Lara, Ferminia Durán. Catalina Gurulé had the story
from her mother, as did Florinda de Lara. Ferminia Durán grew up with the
children of Paula.

THE CRUEL MOON

It was early springtime in the year 1864. The rush of spring work was on. There was as much work to be done by the women as there was for the men to do. It was during the rush of this spring work that Paula prepared for the coming of her child, along with the other things that she considered her share of the work that she must do.

So while Andrés, her husband, helped do the community ditch work, and helped clean out the tanque (tank) that held the irrigation water, Paula cleaned her house, laid new adobe mud floors, put on new walls of yeso, and scrubbed the rough woodwork of her house. While the men plowed the fields and planted corn and beans, the women dug their gardens up with stout sharp sticks, planted their chili and peas. So while Andrés worked with the men, Paula planted her garden.

Plowing and planting went on, but many of the men must go with the sheep and goats; the kids and lambs were being born. Andrés was one of the men to go with the herd. That left Paula to shoulder a little more than her share of the work. Often she was tired and weary. Without thinking she had gone outside to rest in the softness of the warm spring night and the moon light had shone upon her.

Alas for poor Paula! But then, any woman in her right mind would never have gone out in the moonlight when she was carrying her child. As surely as she did, the cruel moon would nibble at her child and it would be born with some part of it missing, the part nibbled off by the moon.

Poor Paula, her utter helplessness to change the sad fate to befall her unborn child, the foolishness of her in allowing such a thing to happen to her, and the probable defects of the baby-to-come, became the gossip of the day. Paula's mind dwelled upon the tragedy, and its certainty was so real in her mind that all her prayers to the saints went amiss.

La Curandera used the heavy work of the spring rush as an excuse for not promising Andrés and Paula that she would attend the expectant mother during her ordeal. La Curandera had never before resorted to excuses at such a time, but she was vexed at Paula for her carelessness, which would probably bring sorrow to them all, and especially make the delivery most unpleasant. Paula could not expect to have a perfect child. Giving the moon such a chance at her, La Curandera turned from her in her need, Who would help her? Paula went about her work, growing weaker and looking more pale each day.

In the villages in those long ago days, births were a community affair. There was something that each willing worker could do. And so it was that La Curandera was the first to rush to Paula when the call came. Women were needed to watch and pray at the window outside the house. La Curandera could well use the help of several women in the house. So it was that a few willing ones accompanied her to the house of Paula.

At the house were some of the elderly women. One acted in the capacity of hostess, in a way. Later she would prepare a meal for those in the house. La Curandera lost no time in getting things in readiness. Paula had the things for the baby in readiness. The layette of the day consisted of squares of manta (coarse, unbleached cotton cloth). They were pinned about the infant in the manner of a pañolón (shawl) and was the only garment worn by the infant. A small tinaja of grease, or oil, was ready also. It was not definitely known what oil or grease was used in those days, aside from sebo de oso (bear grease). As well, a small vessel of eye wash was ready for use. It was sal de Zuni in a weak solution (salt brought from somewhere in Arizona). Another vessel contained an indispensable remedy that saved many a mother in those old days from blood poisoning. It was called Piedra de pómez (rock of pumice in water). It was given to remove the afterbirth and was highly effective.

La Curandera found Paula in great distress. Hastily she brewed some well-washed roots of yerba de lobo (herb of the wolf) and gave the tea to Paula to drink. That was the remedy for childbirth pains. The tea was given at intervals as the expectant mother endured her pains stoically.

La Curandera then took the long, tough rope of rawhide and threaded it between the latas and a viga at a place near the center of the ceiling. She pulled the end down, then she properly adjusted both ends, one end coming much shorter than the other and at a distance from the floor to be best suited to the needs of Paula. Under the rope, La Curandera laid Paula's pallet. Then she helped the expectant mother to her place on it, to kneel in a position directly behind the ends of the leather rope. Then Paula grasped the ends of the leather in her hands, one coming just where she could press her head against it, the other end reaching to her waist or a little beyond. In the agony of her pains, Paula strained against that rope which she clutched in her hands.

Hour after hour passed while Paula moaned and strained at the rope, while the women outside the window sang prayers to God and the Holy Mother, and those on the inside of the house waited and watched. And through it all, each woman wondering in her own mind just what Paula's baby would be. None of them expected it to be all there; some part would be missing because Paula had carelessly let the moon shine upon her. Had she only worn a string of keys around her waist, that would have protected her child from the moon. But alas, Paula had not even remembered to do that. Of course a string of keys was not owned by many in the village, but there was one or two, and those who owned them gave them to any expectant mother to use, in case she must go out into the moonlight.

But at last the child of Paula was born. It fulfilled the expectations of them all. It came without most of its legs, but also it came dead.

La Curandera immediately gave the infant to one of the women, then she placed Paula gently in a position where she could drink the piedra de pomez. In a short time La Curandera administered the all-important cota (a tea made from the plant called cota, a tall slender-stemmed plant, with narrow, dull green leaves growing thickly along the stem, and a small yellow flower at the tip). The tea is made from the whole plant. No one would think of omitting the cota at the time of childbirth. It was absolutely essential to the well-being of the mother.

After the cota, the mother must have a dish of atole. That was another item of diet that no curandera neglected to give her patient. Upon that dish of atole (a drink made of milk and roasted ground blue corn) depended the mother's future health.

Now Paula was relaxed and lay upon her pallet asleep. La Curandera had done all that any conscientious curandera could do. She was free to help the woman with the stillborn baby. They had a duty to do by that infant. It had not been baptized. Wherever there was a birth there must be a baptism. In the cases of stillbirth, the infants must be buried where baptism would come to them. That place was where the adobe roof of the house drained. So at the back of the house of Paula and Andrés, the women dug a grave and buried the infant. That was the custom and still is the custom.

And there was another custom of that day that still exists in a more limited degree. Paula must not be bathed with water until the sixtieth day after the coming of her child. Under no circumstances must she allow water to touch her body until the proper number of days had passed. No woman in the native village of those long-ago days was daring enough to disregard that custom.

The coming of the railroad brought spikes into the villages. These were driven into the vigas and the leather ropes were fastened to them instead of being threaded between the latas and the vigas of the ceilings. To this day, these spikes are to be seen in many of the old houses.

SUBJECT: Community Work
WPA: 5-5-49 #26
November 20, 1940
Words 1533

COMMUNITY WORK

The Indian raiders, who left devastation and even death in their wake in the old days before the close of the Civil War, practically constituted the yardstick by which the standard of life was measured in the old communities where livestock, corn, and wheat were raised. Every such village of those old days had its Indian raid, its tragic one that it could not forget. But few are the men and women yet among the living who went through them and can tell the story.

The first work done by the settlers of Las Placitas was community work and it was the building of a community house, where they could all dwell within common walls and thus better defend themselves in case of Indian raids. Each family had a small apartment in this big house, which was built of rock and mud, mostly mud. Each family had a tiny window set well up in the wall and a small door, both designed as protection against Indian invaders.

The exact date of the construction of this community house and the names and number of the families who built it are not known. Antonio Gurulé, who died in 1858, left a list of the families living in Las Placitas in the year 1843. This was a list of the families using the community irrigation system at that time. What it was originally written on is not certain, but in all probability it was inscribed on goat skin. Who transferred it to paper was none other than a priest at San Felipe. The list finally came into possession of José Librado Arón Gurulé, grandson of Antonio Gurulé. If history is carried on in no other way, it will be handed down from generation to generation in these lists of owners of water rights in the community irrigation systems, for such lists are kept by the mayordomos.

Whether this old list was the first ever made in Las Placitas is not known. The roll contained the name of the heads of sixteen families.

As the settlement must be self-protecting, the community must organize its defense. Their lives and property depended upon their ability to outwit or defeat the savage Indian raiders whenever they chose to descend upon them. So the men of the settlement elected an alcalde, or justice of the peace. He in turn selected certain men as sentinels, or at least to act as such—one man at a time, for stated periods. These men must be ever on the lookout for warnings of Indian raiders or signs of the presence of Navajos in the region. Then certain other men were selected to be prepared to rush to the defense of the settlement at a moment's notice. A sort of home guard squad. These, with the sentinel on duty who warned them of probable danger, constituted the first line of defense. Always they were ready with stout bows and sharp arrows, slings, and clubs. In that first line, too, were the big savage dogs, which always dashed into the fray.

Then there was the community tanque y acequia madre (tank and main trench), which must be kept in usable condition by community work under the supervision of an elected mayordomo. This official was paid in produce or hides of goats by those he served for his services. It was his duty to make and preserve a list of all users of the water, to notify each one when it was his turn to have the water. He must see that the whole irrigation system was in good condition, and to call out all the users of water to work when storms or other causes damaged the tank or ditches. He was elected in the spring, in the old days, and his first duty was to notify all men of the community work of cleaning the reservoir, and repairing it if necessary—with adobe mud and logs—and clearing debris from the main ditch.

The spring plowing, rolling the soil, and planting was community work in those long-ago days, even though each man possessed fields of his own. While there were many stout, forked parts of oak trees that would make good plows, there were only two or three oxen to break up the ground with them; consequently, the men worked together, plowing up the fields as the owners were ready to have the work done. After the plowing, a heavy log was drawn across the fields to smooth them over for the planting. When the ground was ready to receive the seeds, the men worked together in sowing the seeds, all of them going to the designated fields together. This community work not only lightened the burdens of each family, but made time for fetching wood for the fogón compaña (family fireside) or the corner fireplace inside the house, and the horno (oven) outside, where bread was baked, corn roasted.

This outdoor oven required huge quantities of wood to heat it to the right degree. Also more time was found for hunting wild game, which abounded in the Sandías.

Community work was at its height at harvest time. Families worked together to gather in and preserve what they had brought to maturity. That was the time of year when the sentinels were most active. Every day those people felt their insecurity more keenly as they piled up the fruits of their labors. What a tempting bait for the Navajos, who stole their corn and wheat instead of raising it for themselves.

But this harvest was not the only lure to the raiders at this season. There were the herds of sheep and goats with their young now strong enough to be driven off. These flocks had been combined and put under the protection of several herders and a man in charge, enough to make an effective guard in case of attack. The youth in the community took their turns tending the combined flocks and herding them to pasture. Theirs was a responsibility; they reckoned with it and as far as possible, stood ready to defend their charges. However, they were not to risk their lives on the spot. Better to let the Navajos drive off the herd, then join the men from the village in a pursuit. If they were hard pressed, they were to flee, and hide in the secret caves prepared for them in the herding areas.

The date of the building of the first individual family dwelling is not known, though it was known to be long enough before the year 1854 for houses to be considered old. In that year Francisco Trujillo of Las Huertas bought a house in Las Placitas he called old, and a part of which house is still occupied by his descendants.

In the building of those first houses, the community took part. When a family wished to leave the community dwelling, the head presented his desire to the others, and together they labored to construct it. What oxen the community possessed were taken to the mountains to fetch the vigas, the trunks of large pines, which would span the walls of the house and support the ceiling and roof. The ceilings were slender aspens. The roof was adobe. The walls were of rock and mud—many small rocks and quantities of adobe mud, though many large stones were used here and there in the construction. When the men had finished this work, the women, working together, plastered the house, inside and out, with adobe mud and straw, or a certain tough grass found around Las Placitas. The floors were of adobe, smoothed and allowed to dry until they were as hard as rock itself. These floors served nobly as long as only tewas were worn on the feet. The inside walls of the house were made snow white with yeso. This yeso helped light the dark interior of those old houses, which had but one peephole of a window to a room. The women built the fireplaces and outdoor ovens and whatever inside features were needed in the keeping of the house. However, it was not uncommon in those old days for the women to build the houses.

In that long-ago day the fiesta of San Antonio was kept. There was an altar placed in the homes of the various families to receive the saint when it came their time to have him. Also, wherever the saint and altar were, there the people went to pray.

The dead as well as the living came in for their share of attention in those old days. It may have been because they were few in number in the mountain villages in the turbulent days of Indian invasions a hundred years ago, or it may have been because birth and death were the all-absorbing events of community life in those long-gone days. Together the women brought their children into the world. Together the men prepared the dead for burial. Together they implored their patron saint to protect and prosper them. In years of abundance they shared together their plenty; in lean years they struggled together, sharing their little to live until spring again.

SUBJECT: Clotilde And Francisca

WPA: 5-5-71 #25

January 29, 1941

Words 5111

Sources of information: Benino Archibeque, Conception Archibeque, José
L. A. Gurulé, Pedro Gurulé, Magdalena Gallegos, Patricio Gallegos. Benenino
Archibeque, 75, was the son of the Francisca and Salvadoro of this story.
He was born after the death or Marcelino. José L.A. Gurulé and Pedro Gurulé
were sons of the Nicolás Gurulé of this story.

CLOTILDE AND FRANCISCA
(The Story of an Indian Raid)

The year 1863 was one of the most tragic in the annals of Las Placitas. That was
the year of the Indian outrage in the vicinity of Algodones and Las Placitas,
which is even now recalled with sorrow by the descendants of those who lived
through it. The villagers put up a valiant fight, for they were not caught off their
guard, but there was little they could do to protect themselves against the ruthless raiders when government authority over the Indians was so weakened.

At no time since the American occupation had the towns and villages
been more vulnerable to attack by the Navajoes. During the Civil War in New
Mexico, most of the military posts scattered over the territory were abandoned
that the forces might be concentrated at Fort Craig, Santa Fe, and Fort Union.
Thus, wide areas of the territory were left defenseless, a condition that offered
unlimited opportunities to the Navajoes to wage their own devastating and
cruel warfare whenever they desired, or wherever they found what they
desired. They wanted food, they coveted horses, they thirsted for revenge.

In 1863, Juan of Tecolote was alcalde of Las Placitas and Lucas Gurulé,
uncle of José L.A. Gurulé, was what might be called captain of home guards.
Both men wore heavy mustaches. That hirsute adornment was of paramount

lost them and were not able to again pick up the trail. S
their starting point and took up the trail of the sheep. They h
hen they discovered one of the animals nibbling at the short
it along with them. Now and then they picked up others tha
m the flock or had fallen out from sheer weariness. Soon the
ck with them.

hours had passed since the men left Las Placitas. They were
y. They could push on no further without rest and food. So
eltered place, built a fire (they always carried flint rocks in t
slaughtered a sheep, cooked and ate of it. After a brief rest
e trail again—the trail that crossed the mountains to Ojito Bla
Nicolás and his man arrived at Las Placitas, they found the vil
he old men who were left there, the women and many of the c
e to sleep, moved about in the darkness like shadows. Even J
Salvador were among them awaiting the dawn, when they co
d search for the lost shepherds, the search they were forced to ab
se of the darkness.

e moment the gray dawn streaked across the sky, the men were
, where they would pick up the trail. They discovered several trai
nade in the earth by dragging some object over it. They follow
t its end lay the body of the brave little Marcelino. His arrows we
and nearby was his bow. His small body had been whipped in
th the keen las jaras (the willows). The bloody switches we
about the spot. Salvadoro uttered a terrible cry and fell down besid
f his son.

men carried the body back to the village. The people saw them an
ing to meet them, Francisca and Clotilde among them, lifting thei
eaven in grief, for they could see that they boy being returned was
and that he was dead. As they moved toward the house of the heart-
ther, the whole village joined in the dirge that echoed and echoed
e cañons and up and down the mountainsides. The wailing and
ns rose higher and higher as the body was borne into the house.
refused to be comforted. She had wept throughout the night, pray-
lling for her son. Now she seemed crazed with grief.

Nicolás and his men, thirsty for revenge, were on the trail again,
picked up at La Jara. Tracks led in many directions, and every-
found slaughtered goats and sheep; animals wantonly killed just
shepherd had been. But no trace of Jacobe could they find.

importance in selection of leaders of the people in those old days. It denoted judgement and wisdom, and it seemed that these virtues increased as the mustaches grew. A heavy mustache with long ends curled up to meet the ears was facial decoration both cultivated and coveted. Smooth-faced men were never accorded a hearing in the public meetings; they had neither wisdom nor judgment, according to the ideas of their time.

Lucas Gurulé was ever aware of the dangers of a sudden descent of the Navajoes upon them. He knew they were ever on the hunt for horses. In Las Placitas there were five good animals. Where they came from no one now could tell. Nicolás Gurulé possessed two of them. Another was owned by José Mora, the ownership of the remaining two was not known. Then there were the flocks of sheep and goats, always a magnet to attract the raiders.

All the flocks owned in the community were divided into two herds. One was a small herd, consisting of the lambs, kids, and weaker sheep and goats. Small boys cared for this herd, pastured in the green and brown grassy plots near the village. The large herd was taken to the pasturing grounds around Cerro Pelón, in upper Cañón de Las Huertas. Men and some boys watched this herd, which was kept in the mountains where water and forage were plentiful.

Then upon this scene dawned a day the fates had marked for tragedy. As on all other mornings, Francisca gave her twelve-year-old son, Marcelino, her benediction, handed him his ear of roasted corn, his noon-time lunch, and sent him forth with the three other boys with the smaller herd. From another home on that morning went Jacobe, the son of Clotilde. She gave him her benediction and an ear of roasted corn and sent him to Algodones to carry a message to her brother. In the mountains the men and the two boys with them tended their flocks as before. On that morning, Nicolás Gurulé drove his two horses to Cerro Pelón, where he was to remain with the herd of sheep and goats for a few days. And so the day passed with no hint of the evil brooding over them.

At dusk the young herders had not returned, and neither had Jacobe. There was uneasiness in the village. Lucas Gurulé called the men. They must go at once to learn what had befallen the shepherds and their flock. They had gone but a short distance when they saw two of the boys creeping along from tree to tree as if trying to escape from an enemy. Salvadoro Archibeque was with the men. He did not see his son.

"Where is Marcelino?" he asked the frightened shepherds.

They sobbed out a story of some Navajoes who came suddenly and without warning upon them and started to drive off their sheep. The boys said that they were so frightened that they ran away as fast as they could go and hid behind some rocks. Marcelino would not leave the herd. He stood his ground and shot arrows at the Navajoes. They did not know what happened to him, and they were afraid to stir from their hiding place before dark for fear the Indians would steal them.

The frantic Salvadoro and Juan Tomás, father of Jacobe, went on while Lucas and the few men with him returned with the little shepherds to the village. There Lucas would rally all the men, and they would hunt the raiders down and restore the two boys to their mothers; for it was clear they had been captured by the Navajoes.

But when they reached the village they found it in a state of confusion. The Navajoes had swooped down upon them, rained arrows at their houses, and forced every one of them to run for their lives. No one dared stick his head out his door for fear of being made a target. The siege just lasted long enough for the raiders to round up the three horses corralled in the village. They made off with them toward the mountains, and they shot arrows back at any fool who dared show himself, until they were out of sight.

"Arm and race for Cerro Pelón!" Lucas shouted. "They are after our herds. Nicolás and his men will be killed." In no time the able-bodied men, armed with stout bows and plenty of arrows, were ready. There were two or three muzzle-loading guns in the community but they would never risk those weapons in an emergency. Now they were off, taking shortcuts and steep trails in hopes of beating the raiders to Cerro Pelón. But swiftly as they moved, they heard the barking of the savage sheep dogs while they were yet far away, warning them that the Navajoes were already upon the sheep camp.

Nicolás and his son José, and the others of the small party at their supper heard it. Instantly they were armed and hunting hollow places where they could hide, and made ready to shoot. The huge dog belonging to Nicolás Gurulé uttered a low growl and dashed out into the dark. At once came the sound of his savage snarls and the yells of the redskins, which told of the battle he waged out there in the night. It was only by force that the men with Nicolás restrained him from rushing to his dog's defense. A much loved-dog he was and a great fighter. The greatest and bravest dog that ever was owned in Las Placitas. A protector of their sheep and goats and a friend of every child in the village. All at once came a yell of pain from an Indian, followed by a bark and then a pitiful whine from the dog. Then into the hollow crawled the dog and lay quivering at his masters's feet. Nicolás ran his exploring fingers over the animal's body until he found what he sought, and that was an arrow. He removed it as gently as he could. No sooner was the dog rid of the thing

hat hurt him than he was off again to the defe Nothing could stay him.

Then from the dog's throat came sharp, gl and his men crept forward; they knew that m had arrived and the dog knew them. Now the

Lucas and his men showered arrows at th in the dark. The dog snarled and leaped at th went down; an arrow in his heart silenced h short, all the men knew it and revenge burnt an and his men crept out and joined their comra they routed the Navajoes, but they could not nor the sheep the Indians had cut out of the he of hearing. The Indians that fled had remaine of sheep, but they went without them. The m too soon. These Navajoes were only a part of itas and drove off the horses. The two bands v place south of Las Placitas called Ojito Blanc

There was no time to lose. Lucas picked with the herd. He sent Nicolás and his son wi to Las Placitas to track down the raiders if pos the missing flock and the little shepherds, all Jara where they had gone for pasture. With th started off in pursuit of the Indians they had ju mountains.

They well knew there was little they could move along cautiously and listen for suspic enough to pick up a trail. But as they went alor ing their weapons ready, they heard nothing th hint of the whereabouts of their enemies. Not did they discover tracks. They followed them. where the earth had been much trampled upon the rocks nearby and upon the ground. That arrows showered at the Indians had found its m of bringing the enemy upon them they would umphant yells.

They saw the hoofprints of the stolen hors sheep, but all seemed to go around the place where the prints of the hoofs led off over the r

There the
returned t
gone far w
They drov
strayed fr
a small fl

Many
and hungr
sought a s
old days),
were on th

When
yet astir. T
dren unab
Tomás an
go forth ar
don becau

But th
for La Jara
One was
that one. A
beside hin
ribbons w
strewn all
the body o

Some
came runn
voices to h
Marcelino
broken m
through th
lamentatio
Francisca
ing and ca

Soon
which they
where they
as the littl

With some tewa tracks leading off toward Las Huertas, they discovered a track of a tewa much smaller than the others. They followed it to the vicinity of Algodones. There they lost it. Juan Tomás identified the tewa print as that of his son. It was clear that the Indians had taken the boy captive. After they lost the trail, they returned to Las Placitas and picked up more tracks. This time the hoof marks of the three horses stolen from Las Placitas were discovered. They could be seen here, then there. For a time they would lose them, then suddenly come upon them again. Up and down the foothills of the mountains south of Las Placitas, then higher up, they went until they suddenly spied something far below them, that caused them to drop down on their knees and crawl to a vantage point. The Indians!

They were atop a sheer cliff of some fifty feet. Below them grew tall pines; a protection for them once they climbed down the face of the cliff, which was not to be seen from that particular spot they discovered in the protected hollow of Ojito Blanco.

Nicolás followed his son José, who never found any cliff too steep to climb or descend. The men followed. Not a sound did they make. They crept to a position where they could easily conceal themselves, yet have a straight and effective path for their arrows. When they were well in place, they studied the scene yet below them.

The Navajoes were settled comfortably in a circle around a tinaja from which they helped themselves with their fingers. They were eating greedily as if half starved and spoke only a word or two as they stuffed their mouths. Bows and quivers of arrows were lying about on the ground and there also lay a serape.

Without warning came a shower of arrows into their midst. With a wild and startled yell, the Indians leaped to the ground and took to their heels. It was then that Nicolás and his men saw two of the horses, their riders speeding away on them.

Nicolás and his men came cautiously from their hiding place. But there was no need for caution; to a man the raiders had fled leaving their dinner and their belongings behind them. Nicolás and his men came upon the carcass of José Mora's horse. The Indians had slaughtered it for meat. Values meant nothing to them. They were encamped at Ojito Blanco to await the coming of the other band with the sheep; but they had no taste for the wait and they did have a taste for horseflesh. They were hungry so the fine horse was sacrificed.

The men knew they were beaten, they could never catch up with the thieves. They knew the other two horses were gone forever. They were also satisfied that Jacobe was not with the raiders. So they gathered up the things the Indians left behind and made their way back to Las Placitas.

Meanwhile, Lucas and his men pushed on, now and then adding a stray sheep to the flock they were accumulating along the trail. But this flock was proving to be troublesome. Lucas selected a man to drive it back to Cerro Pelón, and after that he and his men made better time.

But Lucas, too, was doomed to failure. They came upon a place where horses' hoof prints marked the ground. Strewn about were many dead sheep. The course of the Indians' trail veered, then doubled backed on the path they had come. They tried to track the horses and lost the trail in an arroyo. They finally gave up, not knowing that the Indians they were pursuing had been warned by the Indians routed from Ojito Blanco by Nicolás and his men. They returned to Las Placitas by way of Cerro Pelón.

Nicolás and his men arrived at the village several hours ahead of Lucas and his companions. From the wailing of the women heard from afar, Lucas and the men knew some sad fate had befallen the shepherds. But they were not prepared for the tragedy they found. So with the coming of the new mourners the whole village broke afresh into loud lamentations and weird wailings. The rise and fall of the voices in the sad dirge continued throughout the day and night. Never before nor since had anything like it been heard in Las Placitas.

At dusk the neighbors gathered at the house of Salvadoro for the velorio. They lighted candles about the board on which the body lay and old Andrés de Aragón led the prayers and the singing. Long since his voice had lost much of its power and sounded rather quavery at times, but he knew the prayers and could instruct the rest of them in the responses and he could still inject a certain eloquence in his voice. For many years Andrés had been the resador at Las Placitas and had served his neighbors faithfully and freely. No one had been able to supplant him.

Now he lifted up his voice in the prayers. As the sound drifted out on the evening air, wailing voices were raised in every quarter of the village. Hour after hour the praying and the singing continued. No brujas would dare enter the place with prayers in progress.

Midnight approached, the hour when the brujas were at their wickedest. A fire at midnight served to keep the evil ones away; so a fire was kindled on the ground very near the house. Midnight was also the time for the watchers to retire from the room and partake of the refreshments provided by the family, or relatives. But not all of them could leave together. The brujas might enter during their absence and work some evil upon the body, or even spirit it away. So, some of them went, while the others remained to pray and sing.

Those who went out for refreshments found everything ready outside by the fire. Atole was brewing and cornbread was baked. They ate and drank (the atole was a drink), rested for a time and then returned to the room of the dead to watch, pray, and sing while the others came out to the fire for rest and refreshments. And thus passed the darkest and most fearsome hour of the watch. At dawn the velorio was over. The watchers departed to get a few hours of sleep before the march with the dead to the Pueblo of San Felipe.

In those old days the women had no part in preparing the bodies for burial nor in burying them. They did not even attend the funerals. San Felipe was between eight and nine miles away and the going was rough. Through the cold and the snows of winter; through the rain, the slush, and the mud of spring; through the heat and the dry winds of summer; through the cold, sharp winds and the cold, chilling rains of autumn, their dead must be carried to the sacred burial ground at San Felipe. The women and the children could not keep pace with the men on that sixteen-mile trip.

So the men wrapped the little shepherd's body in a blanket and secured it with leather strings that it might not be loosened on the journey. One man went to fetch the escalera (the ladder) from the house of the last user of it. Always the one who used it kept it safely until the next to need it came for it. This ladder was made by the men of the community. It was constructed of light, tough timber that it might be strong, yet not too heavy to bear with its burden. The poles were about eight feet or a little longer than that, with notches but close together and in the same places in each pole. From logs, flat boards some six inches wide and about two feet long were hewn with sharp stone axes. These boards were fitted into the notches along the poles and fastened securely with leather string. Thus the ladder was made. The ends of the poles made to rest upon the shoulders of four carriers were sometimes padded with pieces of goatskin to render the carrying easier. The body of the boy was laid upon this bier and all was ready.

Old Andrés was also ready to take his place behind the escalera and lead the prayers and the songs. Nicolás Gurulé and three other men lifted the ladder to their shoulders and the funeral procession started off, with all the men who could be spared marching in twos behind, and joining their voices in the prayers and songs. Lucas and the other men remained behind to guard the lives of those in the village, for who could tell whether the Navajoes still lingered about, to make another raid on them.

The sad little funeral train turned west from the door of Salvadoro and followed the winding trail to Arroyo del Horno. There they turned to the north, past Cerro Colorado and Cerro Negro and on to Cañón de Las Huertas. There they faced the Río del Norte and moved on. Now and then they halted just long enough to shift the burden to a rested shoulder, and the man thus relieved dropped back in the procession. And all the while as they went along, they prayed and sang. Then came the time to make a complete rest. The ladder was placed upon the ground. The resador said a prayer, and when they were ready to go, they brought stones and piled them up into a moument that would mark the spot where the body had rested on its way to the grave. Now they were again on their way, singing and praying as they went. In time, when the shoulders of the men ached from the strain put upon them, they rested the body upon the ground and relaxed themselves. A monument of stones was erected there to mark the spot. And thus moved the funeral train until it came through the gates of San Felipe.

The body was placed in the chapel, and the men went to the cemetery to dig the grave. It was made according to specifications given by the priest. In time they reached the required depth. At the head of the vault and on a level with the floor a niche was dug and made smooth, after every particle of loose earth had been removed. Into this niche would be placed the head of the body, when it was laid into the vault.

Now that everything was ready, the blanketed body was brought forth and properly placed in its last resting place, covered with earth, and a little mound raised above it. Only a wooden cross was set up to identify the spot, a cross with not a name upon it.

The sad rites over, the men took the escalera and returned to their homes. At the sight of them, the sad dirge again rose and fell as the people came from their houses to meet the men who had done all there was to do for the little shepherd.

Now it was for Clotilde to hold the only ceremony possible for her lost son. As friends and family gathered about her in her house, she took up her Santo Niño and addressed him. She prayed him to return her son to her, and made a vow that she would imprison him in the darkness of her chest and keep him there until he did return her boy. After she made her vow, she lifted the heavy lid of the chest, removed the contents therein, placed the little Santo at the bottom, and replaced the things she had removed, leaving El Santo Niño well hidden from the light. Then she closed the lid of the chest and fastened it. There he must remain until he brought Jacobe back to her. The ceremony over, the witnesses went home.

Each day after that Clotilde prayed and reminded Santo Niño of her vow, while Francisca went about the village looking more like a ghost than a live woman, grieving her heart away, and crying for revenge upon the Indians who killed her boy.

And while the mothers prayed and wept, other small boys tended what remained of the small herd. But no longer did they go alone. Marcelino had not been sacrificed in vain; a man now went with them. And the men and the two boys continued to keep the large herd at Cerro Pelón, where they missed the brave dog of Nicolás, and tried to train another dog to take his place. And Lucas and the home guards continued to be on the alert for signs of the murderous raiders. And while life thus moved on in the village, a change that would vitally affect them was going forward in the territory.

When the Confederate soldiers withdrew from the territory of New Mexico, General Carlton found himself in command of several thousand troops, itching to spend their energies and ammunition on the Indians. The General knew that something must be done. He decided upon a policy of concentration for the Indians, with the idea of teaching them to farm. He chose a place called Bosque Rodondo, or the roundup. It was located on the Pecos River near Fort Sumner. The noted scout and pathfinder Kit Carson was to command the fighters.

Kit Carson marched straight into the Navajo stronghold at Chelly Cañon, waged battle with them, disarmed them, and started to drive them to the Bosque Rodondo. In the general exodus an enslaved boy saw his chance to make a break for liberty and took it. He was only half clad, and there were scars upon his body. A triangular piece was cut from one of his ears—an identification mark. But he still had spirit enough left to want to be free, and he could still run like a deer.

Some of the Navajoes saw him go. Two of them eluded guard and pursued him. If they had to work at Bosque Rodondo, more than ever they would need slaves. But the boy had the advantage of a good start, and keeping himself hidden as well as he could, he struck out in the general direction of his home. The two Navajoes knew the country. They took a short cut for Algodones, from which vicinity the boy was taken. Late one afternoon they were seen on the outskirts of the village. Immediately the people were on the defensive and stood ready to defend themselves.

Into this scene, the boy crept silently, under cover of darkness, into the house of his uncle. When he learned that the village was surrounded by Navajoes; for such the people thought they were, the boy knew the Indians were there to get him. At once he decided to get away while it was yet dark. He had seen no Indians on his way to his uncle's house. He chose that same path out. Silently he moved along very close to the ground until the village was behind him, then he found a place of safety where he could hide until the morning. That place was in the hills north of old Las Huertas. At dawn he surveyed the land, saw no signs of Indians, and with all the strength he had left he went for home.

That morning at dawn a strange sweet sound awoke Clotilde. It was the ringing of little bells. She listened. The sound came from the chest in her house. She arose from her pallet and peeped inside the box. But the sound had died out and she saw nothing strange inside the chest; so she closed and fastened it again. But no sooner had she left the room than she heard the ringing of the bells again. Clotilde was frightened. What did it mean? The sound of ringing bells, where there were no bells? The sweet tones of the bells filled the air. Again she went to the chest to look inside. But there was still nothing there that she could see.

Then came to Clotilde a vision. It was of Jacobe. Clotilde lifted up her voice. "He is coming. I know my boy is coming. It is for that Santo Niño rings the bells!" So great was her faith that she released the Santo from his dark prison. Then she ran outside her house and strained her eyes in every direction to catch sight of her boy. He was yet some distance away when she saw him. "There he is! There comes my boy! God be praised!" And she ran to meet him. Her voice had carried to the far parts of the village, and there was a grand welcome for Jacobe, who would forever bear the marks of his enslavement to the Navajoes.

SUBJECT: Los Pedlers
WPA: 5-5-49 #50
April 23, 1941
Words 1744
Sources of information: José Gurulé, Rumaldita Gurulé, Benino Archibeque,
Conception Archibeque. José Gurulé saw the early Arabes in the house of
his father, where they kneeled down to pray. He is the only one now left in
Las Placitas who saw those earliest peddlers. Rumaldita Gurulé remembered
the peddlers and the wonderful things they brought to see. Benino
Archibeque remembered the peddlers as did Conception Archibeque.

LOS PEDLERS

In the early days, especially before any of the men of the villages made trips to Los Estados with the wagon trains of their patrons, the villagers knew little, if anything, about the outside world. So whatever came to them from the great unknown would was a source of wonderment, curiosity, and brought to them new ideas of what made up the world, particularly God's world.

In fact, the first peddlers, whom the natives called "Arabes," brought God to them in a new way. In those days village life revolved around religious teachings and symbols of spiritual things. Songs and prayers to the saints occupied much of their time. Their annual fiesta day was a saint's day. Their patron saint was the paramount factor in their social existence.

So because symbolic religion inspired most of the villagers' thoughts and actions, the "Árabes" appealed to that easily aroused emotion in them.

Those olive-skinned peddlers came to the village in twos or threes. They wore long, flowing robes. Turbans covered their heads, and often they entered the village barefooted. They looked very much like the pictures of priests in the region of the Holy Land of many centuries ago.

Upon entering a house, and they were admitted to most of the homes in the village, they kneeled upon the floor, made the sign of the cross and offered a prayer for the welfare of the household. After that ceremony, they squatted upon the bare adobe floor with the family and showed them their wares, speaking the while, for all los Árabes spoke Spanish fluently.

The small pack was spread out. The light from the small window and from the open door fell across the display, bringing out the beauty of the rosary beads, the gold-colored medals and chains and the crosses and crucifixes. Those were the things for which the villagers would part with their last tortilla and the peddlers knew it. The most popular seller was the rosary made of seeds or berries, which closely resembled cherry seeds. They were brought from afar and of course had certain curative qualities. That made them doubly valuable. They were costly, considering the time and the estate of the lowly native villager, the price being fifty cents each. But so prized were those rosaries that nearly every family managed to purchase one of them.

The medals (medallas) were silver or copperish color with chains attached to them. They were decorated with the images of santos y santas. It was a valued possession when it bore a favorite saint, and was worn about the neck with pride. The vari-colored rosaries made of glass beads were also highly prized. Then there was a wide assortment of them in order to tempt the buyer. Almost any color could be had.

Should the household appear to lose interest in his wares before he considered he had profited enough at one household, the Arab knew just how to revive interest in himself and his wares. At such times, he arose to his feet, raised up his flowing sleeves one at a time, and displayed the wonderful tattooing that covered them. Pictures of saints in beautifully colored robes. The very saints whose images he had on the medals. On his chest there were tattooed pictures. There was one of the Holy City of Jerusalem. What a wonderful scene it was. It never failed to arouse the deeper emotions of those whose love of art was always stirred by pictures of the Holy Jerusalem.

The peddler now had created an appeal for his holy sand, brought from the Holy Land of Jerusalem. The sand was in little bags, and naturally the sand possessed healing qualities. Think of it, sand from the Holy Land! The peddlers always left a goodly supply of those little bags in the villages where they stopped. How they pointed out the various holy places in the pictures of the Holy Land tattooed on their chests was enough to make a reality of the Holy Land in the imaginations of their audiences, and make every one long for a small bag of sand dug up from the holy place.

Then there was another and holier phase of their good work. Now and then one of the Árabes carried a most beautiful image of the Christ Child. It was small and so perfect and lovely as to inspire worship. It imparted a blessing or granted a prayer of all who touched it. But to even touch that precious Christ Child one must wash his hands seven times. The image was carefully wrapped in cotton to keep it perfect and clean. So while the wrappings were being removed, the first to be allowed the privilege of reverently touching it was busy washing his hands seven times. This washing the hands seven times was a ceremony and took time. While the families were large, much time was consumed. What was given the Árabes for this great favor was not remembered.

Los Arabes accepted almost any barter as exchange for their wares. In not demanding money, they profited much more. These priestly robed men, after a house-to-house visit at Las Placitas, left the village looking like walking bazaars, and taking with them the goodwill of the people who watched them depart. The people were uplifted spiritually, and made happy by the symbols of their spirituality they had been able to purchase from these strange men, because they would take anything they raised in payment for the "beautiful" rosarios, crucifijos, medallas, and arenilla bendita (blessed sand). And more than that, los Árabes left with the people something to talk about and to remember of the Holy Land, which was the Mecca of all Christians who found the highest degree of help and comfort in a graphic religion. So long as those people lived, they would never forget the wonderful pictures of the Holy Land los Árabes had tattooed on their breasts. These strange men seemed to belong to that land.

Those colorful peddlers passed with the advent of the Civil War period. They were missed by the villagers, and are remembered to this day by those who have well over four score years.

In the seventies came another type of peddler. He was of olive skin and the people called him Árabe. From his head to his feet, he was clothed in the fashion of the day. He appeared smart and businesslike. He demanded money for his wares, but he was very friendly and won the confidence of the villagers. He, too, carried trinkets that appealed to the religious sentiments of the people of Las Placitas.

Besides the small pack of such wares, he carried two large and heavy packs on his back. They were filled with alluring feminine wear, men's wear, and colorful decorations for the home. The contents of those two bags were never displayed at Las Placitas. They cost much money. El Árabe was on his way to San Pedro with them. San Pedro was then a bustling, thriving town;

the gold rush was on. There the peddler would find men with money, men seeking gold, women, saloons, and dance halls. There he would dispose of the treasures in his two large packs. Las Placitas was but a stop on the way to San Pedro. El Árabe made it a paying stop. He brought to Las Placitas the things he knew they could not resist, and yet have a few coins with which to pay for them.

And so it was that when el Árabe arrived in the village, the people gathered about him suggesting a placita here or a zaguán there as a fitting place to display his goods. The peddler had not the time to make a house-to-house canvass. He must take the people in groups, for he must be in San Pedro before dark, and there was Tejón, another paying stop on his way.

When he had his wares spread out to advantage, the people gathered round. He had many saints and santas of plaster, beautiful figures they were. He had medals and rosaries, crucifixes and crosses. His rosaries were of more brilliantly colored beads than the early peddlers carried. He also had pictures of the saints and santas, which the buyers found most attractive.

But his best seller was a cross suspended from a metal chain. It was made of wood, a dark-colored wood, and at the intersection of the two pieces that formed the cross, there was a small square of glass. It was a magic glass. When they looked into it, lo and behold, they saw wonderful things. One was the inside of a grand cathedral. It was a magnificent place and they seemed to be looking right inside of it. The beauty of it was breathtaking, and the picture so real. That is why older ones can tell of it to this day.

Most all of the families managed somehow to buy one of those magic crosses. However, no one seems to remember just how much they cost. But then, that happened a long time ago, when el Árabe made his first stop on his way from Bernalillo to the booming town of San Pedro in the first glorious days of the gold rush.

that hurt him than he was off again to the defense of his master and the flocks. Nothing could stay him.

Then from the dog's throat came sharp, glad barks of recognition. Nicolás and his men crept forward; they knew that meant that men from Las Placitas had arrived and the dog knew them. Now they could save their herd.

Lucas and his men showered arrows at the forms of the Indians they saw in the dark. The dog snarled and leaped at the throats of the raiders. But he went down; an arrow in his heart silenced him forever. Nicolás knew it. In short, all the men knew it and revenge burnt anew in their hearts. Now Nicolás and his men crept out and joined their comrades from Las Placitas. Together they routed the Navajoes, but they could not save the two horses of Nicolás nor the sheep the Indians had cut out of the herd. They were already well out of hearing. The Indians that fled had remained to cut out another small flock of sheep, but they went without them. The men from Las Placitas had come too soon. These Navajoes were only a part of the band that raided Las Placitas and drove off the horses. The two bands were to meet in a well-protected place south of Las Placitas called Ojito Blanco.

There was no time to lose. Lucas picked out two men and a boy to stay with the herd. He sent Nicolás and his son with a few of the other men back to Las Placitas to track down the raiders if possible and to aid in the search for the missing flock and the little shepherds, all of which disappeared from La Jara where they had gone for pasture. With the remainder of the men, Lucas started off in pursuit of the Indians they had just routed, who had fled into the mountains.

They well knew there was little they could do in the pitch-darkness but to move along cautiously and listen for suspicious sounds until it was light enough to pick up a trail. But as they went along straining their ears and keeping their weapons ready, they heard nothing that gave them even the slightest hint of the whereabouts of their enemies. Not until it was light enough to see, did they discover tracks. They followed them. Soon they came upon a place where the earth had been much trampled upon. There were blood stains upon the rocks nearby and upon the ground. That meant that at least one of the arrows showered at the Indians had found its mark. Had it not been for the fear of bringing the enemy upon them they would have lifted their voices in triumphant yells.

They saw the hoofprints of the stolen horses, tracks of Indians and of the sheep, but all seemed to go around the place in circles. Finally they found where the prints of the hoofs led off over the rocks toward a mountain spring.

There they lost them and were not able to again pick up the trail. So they returned to their starting point and took up the trail of the sheep. They had not gone far when they discovered one of the animals nibbling at the short grass. They drove it along with them. Now and then they picked up others that had strayed from the flock or had fallen out from sheer weariness. Soon they had a small flock with them.

Many hours had passed since the men left Las Placitas. They were tired and hungry. They could push on no further without rest and food. So they sought a sheltered place, built a fire (they always carried flint rocks in those old days), slaughtered a sheep, cooked and ate of it. After a brief rest they were on the trail again—the trail that crossed the mountains to Ojito Blanco.

When Nicolás and his man arrived at Las Placitas, they found the village yet astir. The old men who were left there, the women and many of the children unable to sleep, moved about in the darkness like shadows. Even Juan Tomás and Salvador were among them awaiting the dawn, when they could go forth and search for the lost shepherds, the search they were forced to abandon because of the darkness.

But the moment the gray dawn streaked across the sky, the men were off for La Jara, where they would pick up the trail. They discovered several trails. One was made in the earth by dragging some object over it. They followed that one. At its end lay the body of the brave little Marcelino. His arrows were beside him and nearby was his bow. His small body had been whipped into ribbons with the keen las jaras (the willows). The bloody switches were strewn all about the spot. Salvadoro uttered a terrible cry and fell down beside the body of his son.

Some men carried the body back to the village. The people saw them and came running to meet them, Francisca and Clotilde among them, lifting their voices to heaven in grief, for they could see that they boy being returned was Marcelino and that he was dead. As they moved toward the house of the heartbroken mother, the whole village joined in the dirge that echoed and echoed through the cañons and up and down the mountainsides. The wailing and lamentations rose higher and higher as the body was borne into the house. Francisca refused to be comforted. She had wept throughout the night, praying and calling for her son. Now she seemed crazed with grief.

Soon Nicolás and his men, thirsty for revenge, were on the trail again, which they picked up at La Jara. Tracks led in many directions, and everywhere they found slaughtered goats and sheep; animals wantonly killed just as the little shepherd had been. But no trace of Jacobe could they find.

behind some rocks. Marcelino would not leave the herd. He stood his ground and shot arrows at the Navajoes. They did not know what happened to him, and they were afraid to stir from their hiding place before dark for fear the Indians would steal them.

The frantic Salvadoro and Juan Tomás, father of Jacobe, went on while Lucas and the few men with him returned with the little shepherds to the village. There Lucas would rally all the men, and they would hunt the raiders down and restore the two boys to their mothers; for it was clear they had been captured by the Navajoes.

But when they reached the village they found it in a state of confusion. The Navajoes had swooped down upon them, rained arrows at their houses, and forced every one of them to run for their lives. No one dared stick his head out his door for fear of being made a target. The siege just lasted long enough for the raiders to round up the three horses corralled in the village. They made off with them toward the mountains, and they shot arrows back at any fool who dared show himself, until they were out of sight.

"Arm and race for Cerro Pelón!" Lucas shouted. "They are after our herds. Nicolás and his men will be killed." In no time the able-bodied men, armed with stout bows and plenty of arrows, were ready. There were two or three muzzle-loading guns in the community but they would never risk those weapons in an emergency. Now they were off, taking shortcuts and steep trails in hopes of beating the raiders to Cerro Pelón. But swiftly as they moved, they heard the barking of the savage sheep dogs while they were yet far away, warning them that the Navajoes were already upon the sheep camp.

Nicolás and his son José, and the others of the small party at their supper heard it. Instantly they were armed and hunting hollow places where they could hide, and made ready to shoot. The huge dog belonging to Nicolás Gurulé uttered a low growl and dashed out into the dark. At once came the sound of his savage snarls and the yells of the redskins, which told of the battle he waged out there in the night. It was only by force that the men with Nicolás restrained him from rushing to his dog's defense. A much loved-dog he was and a great fighter. The greatest and bravest dog that ever was owned in Las Placitas. A protector of their sheep and goats and a friend of every child in the village. All at once came a yell of pain from an Indian, followed by a bark and then a pitiful whine from the dog. Then into the hollow crawled the dog and lay quivering at his masters's feet. Nicolás ran his exploring fingers over the animal's body until he found what he sought, and that was an arrow. He removed it as gently as he could. No sooner was the dog rid of the thing importance in selection of leaders of the people in those old days. It denoted judgement and wisdom, and it seemed that these virtues increased as the mustaches grew. A heavy mustache with long ends curled up to meet the ears was facial decoration both cultivated and coveted. Smooth-faced men were never accorded a hearing in the public meetings; they had neither wisdom nor judgment, according to the ideas of their time.

Lucas Gurulé was ever aware of the dangers of a sudden descent of the Navajoes upon them. He knew they were ever on the hunt for horses. In Las Placitas there were five good animals. Where they came from no one now could tell. Nicolás Gurulé possessed two of them. Another was owned by José Mora, the ownership of the remaining two was not known. Then there were the flocks of sheep and goats, always a magnet to attract the raiders.

All the flocks owned in the community were divided into two herds. One was a small herd, consisting of the lambs, kids, and weaker sheep and goats. Small boys cared for this herd, pastured in the green and brown grassy plots near the village. The large herd was taken to the pasturing grounds around Cerro Pelón, in upper Cañón de Las Huertas. Men and some boys watched this herd, which was kept in the mountains where water and forage were plentiful.

Then upon this scene dawned a day the fates had marked for tragedy. As on all other mornings, Francisca gave her twelve-year-old son, Marcelino, her benediction, handed him his ear of roasted corn, his noon-time lunch, and sent him forth with the three other boys with the smaller herd. From another home on that morning went Jacobe, the son of Clotilde. She gave him her benediction and an ear of roasted corn and sent him to Algodones to carry a message to her brother. In the mountains the men and the two boys with them tended their flocks as before. On that morning, Nicolás Gurulé drove his two horses to Cerro Pelón, where he was to remain with the herd of sheep and goats for a few days. And so the day passed with no hint of the evil brooding over them.

At dusk the young herders had not returned, and neither had Jacobe. There was uneasiness in the village. Lucas Gurulé called the men. They must go at once to learn what had befallen the shepherds and their flock. They had gone but a short distance when they saw two of the boys creeping along from tree to tree as if trying to escape from an enemy. Salvadoro Archibeque was with the men. He did not see his son.

"Where is Marcelino?" he asked the frightened shepherds.

They sobbed out a story of some Navajoes who came suddenly and without warning upon them and started to drive off their sheep. The boys said that they were so frightened that they ran away as fast as they could go and hid

SUBJECT: Easter Tide
WPA: 6-19-41
June 18, 1941
Words 1707
Sources of information: José Gurulé, Rumaldita Gurulé, Benino Archibeque,
Conception Archibeque, Patricio Gallegos, Terecita Gallegos de Baca.

TIEMPO DE PASCUA
Easter Tide 1863

It was late February in the year of 1863. The Lenten season had begun. Likewise had the sacrifices of the zealous penitents, who garbed themselves in
flowing robes, called themselves Sirvientes de Dios (Servants of God), and
sought to make their flesh pay for the sins on their souls—and while they were
about it, to make such sacrifices as would bring purification to their families
and friends, and to the whole world, just as the Master had done when he
prayed and fasted in the wilderness.

They were not members of Los Hermanos de Luz (Penitente Brothers)
who were outlawed by the Catholic Church. They were a small group of religious fanatics who desired fervently to do penance the hard way—and did.
Only by the grace of God did they survive. But only at Easter Tide did this
religious zeal possess them, a zeal that found release only in a sojourn in the
mountains, where they fasted and prayed.

They carried nothing whatever with them. God would protect them from
the wild beasts. God would direct them to caves where they would be safe and
warm. God would lead them to places where they would find nuts and edible
roots. They had nothing to fear, for as Servants of God, he would care for them.

Thus, it came about in that long-ago Easter Tide that two of the religious
fanatics paused at Las Placitas on their way to the mountains. There was none
in the village who sympathized with their cause, or thought it anything other
than pure insanity. No one in the village sought to stay them from their mis-

sion, for they knew such efforts would be futile. So they watched the two men continue their way.

Soon the wayfarers came to Ojo de La Casa. There they rested at the friendly house of Valentino Zamora. As they spoke of their assumed duties of sacrificing themselves for others, their zeal-inspired courage proved to be infectious. It was Señora Juanita Zamora who felt the moving power of it. The idea grew within her mind and would not let her rest. She had many children, and many times that number of grandchildren. She grieved over their sins, as well as her own. As the days passed she felt the courage rising within her to go into the mountains to fast and pray, and through bodily suffering, redeem herself and loved ones from their sins.

Holy Week was approaching. Father Gaspari came to Las Placitas from Bernalillo. He wished to select several boys to play the part of angels in an Easter pageant at Bernalillo. Everyone in the village was brim-full of excitement. Never before had boys from their own families been chosen to take part in the pageants at Bernalillo. Mothers anxiously awaited the good padre's decisions. Thirteen-year-old José Gurulé was one of the fortunate ones. When they were ready they walked to Bernalillo with Father Gaspari. There they would remain the eight days until Easter Sunday, and prepare for their parts, and have their robes made for them—very fancy clothes they were to wear in the role of angels.

All this happening served to fan the flame of fanaticism in the mind and heart of Señora Zamora. She felt that she must escape her family and go to the mountains to fast and pray. And she did. She went empty-handed, with only the clothes upon her back for warmth. She fairly ran to put as much distance between her house and her destination as she possibly could, before her family should discover her disappearance.

Her family, thinking she was visiting at some neighbors, did not become alarmed until the darkness fell. When calls about the village failed to reveal her whereabouts, the family were alarmed. But Señor Zamora realized then where they must search for her. She had confided in him her earnest desire to do penance in the mountains. He had rebuked her and forbidden her to do such a rash thing. But now she was gone, without food nor proper bodily clothing to protect her from the cold and freezing weather of the mountains, for it was yet the month of March.

So into the mountains went Valentino and his sons. They searched all through the night and came home exhausted. Señora Zamora had not been found. After refreshing themselves, they set out again. But the day's search was as futile as had been that of the night. The next day the search was resumed, and other men joined the party. Still no sign of the missing Juanita Zamora did they find. Holy Week was at hand. On the first days much cooking must be done. Food must be prepared for the week, for after Wednesday there would be no time to cook. Festive food they must prepare with eggs. All the good housewives had saved as many eggs as possible for the Easter celebration, eggs and quelites (a tender-leafed plant of early spring—quelite is probably an Indian word). This green was boiled and served in the manner of spinach. It was served with chili when desired. The favorite egg dish for the Easter celebration was forejas. This required bread. The bread was slicked and cut into small squares and dipped into egg batter. The squares were then fried in fat on both sides, then boiled in a syrup. As sugar, which they made from cane, was very scarce, the syrup was made largely from raisins, which they made from their grapes. For flavoring they used anís and cilantro (coriander) seeds, which they raised. This was a very festive dish and caused a few eggs to go a long way. Eggs symbolized the resurrection; therefore, eggs formed a very important part of the feast. Sopa (pudding with bread as the foundation), a fiesta-day favorite, was also made and served at the Easter feast. In those old days, the bread was unleavened. In every household could be heard the sound of the mano on the metate. There was need for much ground dried peas. From it was made the "coffee" of which everyone partook in abundance. This drink was second to vino, the homemade wine of the grape. Also, the women spent time and work in the making of many candles to be used in the little chapel. And all through the labor preparation, men and women thought with gladness of the boys in Bernalillo, and with sadness of the tragedy of Juanita.

But at last the cooking and baking was over. The food was ready to be served. Early Thursday morning entire families, except the smaller children, arose early and went to fast and pray at the little chapel. All morning they prayed. The chapel, so tiny it was, that only a few could enter at a time. So there was one continual procession in and out of the door.

Then came noon. Every woman hastened to her house. Throughout the hour, or perhaps more, people were hurrying about the village bearing gifts of food and drink to bestow upon one another. Food was exchanged; food was sent to those who were old and not able to attend the services. There was a general feasting until the time came to return to the little chapel to pray.

Then dawned Good Friday. Early and without food the people went again to the chapel to pray. Now they prayed at the stations. In bright-colored pictures was told the story of the betrayal, arrest, trial, crucifixion, and burial of

Jesus. Each picture was a station. These pictures became real to those who agonized before them. They became so real that the emotional almost broke under the strain of their own agony. And thus they went through the morning. Then again the people retired to their homes, and again they gave gifts of food or exchanged food with one another and feasted until the hour to return to the chapel, where the procession to the stations continued.

At length it was finished and they were all gathered together for the velorio. They would watch until the dawn. At just about dawn it was when the weary and almost broken Valentino with a few faithful searchers came upon the exhausted body of Señora Zamora. She was famished and nearly frozen. She could not speak and was only half conscious. She had found a secluded cave much off the beaten trails. But hunger and cold had driven her out. She had lost her way. She prayed as she had never prayed before for her sins and the sins of her family to be forgiven, but mostly she had prayed to be led safely to that family for whom she so eagerly sought to sacrifice herself.

And on that long ago Easter morning there was a loud rejoicing over a risen Savior. But there was also a rejoicing over the living Juanita, the good mother, wife, and friend, whom they had mourned as dead and who seemed resurrected on that Easter morning.

No longer do the people of Las Placitas keep the Easter Tide in the old and gracious way. No longer do they sacrifice to bestow upon one another gifts of any kind. In those old days, food was all they had to give, and they sacrificed and gave liberally of what they had at Easter. There are only a precious few yet alive who remember those old days of Easter Tide agonizing, feasting, and fanatical sacrificing of the body to win forgiveness of sins.

SUBJECT: The Year It Rained Tortillas
WPA: 5-5-49 #54
February 13, 1942
Words 1357
Sources of information: Pedro Gurulé, Grace Trujillo, Dave Trujillo.

THE YEAR IT RAINED TORTILLAS

It was many years ago that old Diego and his wife, Sareta, lived near old Las Huertas. Diego the Dull, Sareta the Bright, they were called.

Old Diego listened much to the tales of buried treasure told by the Indians. Long before the coming of the cruel Spaniards, the Indians worked in mines dug into the Sandia Mountains, which threw long shadows not far from Diego's door. When the Spaniards came, they enslaved the Indians and forced them to work in the mines. Then came a day when the Indians rebelled against their Spanish masters and drove them back to Mexico from whence they came. Then, too, it was that the gods told the Indians to fill up the mines and hide their treasure and never to open them again lest other cruel masters come and again enslave them and force them to again work in the mines and take out the gold for the masters.

The thought that buried treasure lay somewhere in the mountains nearby intrigued Diego and gave him something to dream about. Many times he loitered in the warm sunshine dreaming when he should have been watching his sheep or his goats.

Perhaps it was while he was dreaming that his very finest goat wandered away. When Diego brought in his flock that evening, he discovered his loss. He resolved that he would search until he found the animal and told Sareta to call him very early the next morning that he might be on his way. He said that while he was about it he would gather wood to bring home.

And so it was that old Diego set out the next morning, a pair of nicely roasted ears of corn tucked in his serape to satisfy his hunger when the sun should look straight down upon him.

Also it was that old Diego set out on the great adventure of his life. In his search for his goat he tramped over hill and arroyo, investigated every cañoncito and viacito as he climbed farther and farther and higher into the mountains. But no sign of his goat could he find. He squinted straight up at the sun, then dropped to the ground to eat his lunch. As he dug his teeth into the parched corn, his eyes roved about the place. Suddenly they stared at a strange sight in a bosque of oak on the side of a steep slope opposite him. For an instant old Diego thought only of running from the place. Then his curiosity overcame his fear, and he climbed up the slope and stood there looking at the skeletons of two mules all tangled up in decayed harness holding them fast to a wrecked carreta.

Old Diego sank weakly upon the ground. He was thinking, recalling the story of the lost carreta carrying some gold to Mexico. It was about ten years ago. At the news of it everybody went searching for it. Two men had come asking the people if they had seen the carreta. Then came the whole exciting story. Someone had uncovered some of the golden treasure of the Indians. Three carretas drawn by mules had come up from Mexico to get it and take it to Mexico. One carreta dropped behind, the muleteer lost his way and was never heard of again. Each of the carretas held some of the treasure. Diego was up instantly with a stick digging about under the upturned wreck. He drew back as he unearthed the skeleton of a man. Now it was clear to old Diego what had happened. The mules had become frightened, had run away, got tangled up in their harness and had been dragged down the slope where the carreta overturned and killed the muleteer. Furiously, old Diego returned to his digging. And he found it! The gold!

He would not bother with wood, it would be all he could do to drag the treasure home. Oh, what would he not buy! What would his friends say of all his good fortune? And Sareta, what would she say?

When Diego reached his house it was very late and he found Sareta weeping for him. She feared he had been hurt, or perhaps killed by some wild animal. When Diego told her his story and dazzled her eyes with the treasure, she was overcome with joy.

"See how rich we are!" exclaimed old Diego. "What will our friends say? We shall go to Santa Fe and buy many fine things like the rich people do."

"No, no, Diego. Let us bury it in a corner of the kitchen, first. Then you drink this warm atole and go to bed. Tomorrow we shall see."

With Diego soundly asleep, Sareta set to work. All night she kept up her fire and made tortillas. She hid them as she made them lest Diego awaken and find them. At daybreak she carried them outside and scattered them everywhere. Then she called to Diego.

"Wake up, wake up! Come and see what has happened. Quick, quick, Diego!"

Old Diego got stiffly from his pallet and hastened outside. He stood staring at the tortillas all over the ground.

"See, Diego, this is the year it rained tortillas. You will never forget it. The year it rained tortillas was the year you found the treasure. Come, let us hurry. This is the year you must go to school. Today you must go to the priest at San Felipe and ask him to teach you to write your name. All rich men must know how to write their names. The year you found the treasure was the year you went to school."

So in no time Diego was speeding down Cañón de Las Huertas toward the Pueblo of San Felipe to beg the good padre to teach him to write his name. When he returned he was so full of joy at being able to put his name on a smooth piece of goatskin that he almost forgot his golden treasure.

Soon the news of Diego's good fortune traveled like wildfire. His friends and neighbors flocked to his house to hear all about it. Diego and Sareta made feasts for them and when they were filled with wine and food, Diego said, "Remember the year it rained tortillas? The year I went to school and learned to write? That was when I found my treasure and we buried it. Only now I choose to spend it." His friends and neighbors shook their heads. None could remember the year it rained tortillas. Oh, that must have been many, many years ago, for Diego was now an old man. And they saw him write his name. Surely it was long, long ago since he went to school.

And then the news of Diego's find reached the ears of those searching for the lost carreta. They came to the house of Diego.

"And when did you find this treasure?" they demanded.

"Do you remember the year it rained tortillas? It was the year I went to school." spoke old Diego.

The strangers spoke together. They could not remember the year it rained tortillas. It must have been many years ago if Diego went to school that year, many years before they were born. The carreta was lost but ten years ago. This treasure of Diego could not be the treasure lost in the carreta. In all the ten years it had been lost it had not rained tortillas.

And so they went away, leaving Diego the Dull and Sareta the Bright to enjoy the golden treasure. The treasure that had been buried by the Indians centuries ago and that someone found, and lost, and Diego found again.

SUBJECT: How Juan Brought Art to Las Placitas
WPA: 5-5-49 #11
February 27, 1942
Words 1171
Sources of information: Adelaida Chaves, Merlinda Chaves, Benino
Archibeque, Conception Archibeque. Tomás Lucero was Adelaida Chaves'
uncle by marriage. Benino and Conception Archibeque were friends of
Juan Armijo and of Tomás Lucero.

HOW JUAN BROUGHT ART
TO LAS PLACITAS

It is well over eighty years ago since Juan Armijo came to Las Placitas with
his household gods, his livestock, and his peons and built the most artistic
house that has ever been built in the village. He brought his loom with him,
for Juan and his loom were seldom separated. A weaver was Juan, a true artist
and he may well be called the father of art in Las Placitas. He put something
besides mere living and bare necessities into the houses of his neighbors at a
price within the reach of all.

None of his work can now be found in Las Placitas, but there are many
who remember various pieces of it owned by long departed members of their
families. And there are many descendants of Juan who remember his weaving.

Juan made his serapes to order. His customers had but to bring their wool
and their ideas; Juan did the rest. He had no dyes, but the wool from the goats
furnished contrasts just in its natural state. Some was snowy white, some a
grayish white, some a light brown, and there were two tones of black. With
these contrasts, Juan wove background and any figures of animals or birds his
customers might choose. He wove the figures into any portion of the serape
or in any position desired by them. The serape with a dog or horse woven into
it was always a favorite. Juan's woven creatures might lack balance; legs

might be four lengths instead of one, heads might be too long or too bulky, bodies might be too short or too thick, tails might grow unnaturally but however it was, the likeness to the original was unmistakable, and always they would be expertly shaded. Juan wrought wonders in natural wools. There was a brown horse on snowy background, a snowy white goat on a coal black ground. Some serapes had a border of animals, or ones in a panel. Some had only stripes—bars of white beside bars of black, or bars of brown, drab white and black in groups. No two of Juan's serapes were ever alike. He preferred to weave animals into them. He studied animals and strove to weave them in action. However he did it, his clients were satisfied and gladly parted with the wool, the goats, the beans, the wheat, the blue corn, the cane or whatever of their commodities he accepted in return for the serapes.

Juan's serapes were never laid upon the adobe floors of the old houses. They were used as bedding or were worn as coats in the colder weather. In the old days, serapes were handled with care. When not in use they were hung over long poles built into the rooms for that purpose. They were frequently washed in plenty of water with amole (a plant) for soap.

Juan wove many tilmas. Tilma is a Mexican word that means a cloak fastened by a knot. To Juan and his people, tilma was a woven piece much smaller than the serape and much thicker. Its purpose was wholly decorative. A tilma or two put life in a room. A rude table made of pine boards roughly hewn from a pine tree with an axe—mostly in those old days the axe was of stone—took on a festive air when a tilma was laid on its top. More than that, it became a thing of beauty in the old house, which had so little in it that was not purely essential. Scarcely a house but possessed some of those precious tilmas, scarcely a house but possessed a chest hewn from pine and put together with wooden pegs. These rude chest and the tilmas were beautiful together. They brought art right into the houses. Those tilmas were the first real luxuries in the old houses. It was almost impossible for the overworked housewives to spare wool for the making of anything that was not to be put to real use. Clothing, bedding, threads for sewing, a few sacks absolutely needed—those things required more wool than the housewives could supply, as the wool must be washed, dried, combed, carded, spun, and otherwise prepared for actual use by their hands, in addition to all the other labors made necessary in the care of a house and rearing and feeding their families. Tilmas were fairly loved by the women of old Las Placitas, and are to this day, especially the older ones, who tell of the way tilmas added beauty to the old houses.

But those tilmas were more familiar to later generations because they were woven long after Juan had departed this world to join his fathers.

Juan's daughter was given in marriage to a youth named Tomás Lucero, who came to Las Placitas with Juan. Juan's daughter, María, and Tomás lived very near the big house of Juan. To Tomás, Juan taught his art. Tomás did not weave very many serapes, especially the large ones, but he did weave many tilmas. So it is the art of Tomás Lucero and not the actual work of the master weaver Juan, which is best remembered in Las Placitas by even the older people.

In his day Juan Armijo kept his loom busy. Even though he was a man of business interests, he kept at his loom. When he died he left that loom to María and his son-in-law and friend, Tomás Lucero. Tomás kept the old loom busy for many years, or until changing times made his serapes and tilmas out of date, as values were estimated when new things came in. Cotton cloth could be bought. The old worn-out garments need no longer be pulled into threads to be rewoven into cloth. This the women tore into strings and wove them into colonial, or rag rugs. Later they had large wooden needles and with them, they were able to crochet the spare and worn-out cloth into rugs, and later they could buy thread and then they made lace. Lace window panels, lace covers for chests and table tops, lace edges for garments. This handwork was utility and beauty to put into the houses. And so the new things—new to them—replaced the serapes and the tilmas of Juan and Tomás. But always there must have been something of beauty or art in the houses. Art was to brighten and gladden life and save it from being stolid and dead to beauty.

SUBJECT: Antonia and Her Saints

WPA: 5-5-49 #9

March 13, 1942

Words 1779

Sources of information: José Gurulé, Benino Archibeque, Conception
Archibeque, Patricio Gallegos. José Gurulé is a grandson of the Antonia
of this story and a nephew of Juana, whose old saints he buried. Benino
Archibeque helped take care of the old saints for so many years. He bitterly
opposed exchanging the old saints of this story for new saints. Conception
Archibeque, a member of the church, who well remembers the capilla of long
ago. She opposed giving up the old saints for new ones. Patricio Gallegos
helped build the new church in Las Placitas and who opposed exchanging
the old saints of Antonia for new saints.

ANTONIA AND HER SAINTS

Many, many years ago within the walled town of Las Huertas there lived a
pious and saint-adoring maiden whose first name was Antonia. Her maiden
name is long since forgotten. But she is remembered as Antonia Gurulé as she
became the wife of Antonio José Gurulé around the year 1815. With her family Antonia moved to Algodones in 1823, when the Mexican government
ordered all mountain villages evacuated to save the citizens from the ravages
of the Indians. When Antonia left Las Huertas, she took her saints with her.

These santas and santos were carved of wood and of yeso. Among them
was the patron saint of San Antonio de Las Huertas Grant, San Antonio. He
was carved from a root of a cottonwood tree, as well as was his capilla (little
chapel) by some unknown artist of old Las Huertas. In all probability some of
the other saints of wood and of yeso were made in Las Huertas but this is not
definitely known. Antonia had many saints, all very old. But there are none

living today of her descendants or friends who know where Antonio got her collection of old saints, except her wooden San Antonio.

None now living know the exact date of the coming of Antonia and her family to Las Placitas. The name of Antonio José Gurulé appears on a preserved list of heads of families living in Las Placitas in 1843. But the community house was built in Las Placitas several years before that date, and Antonia lived in the community house and Antonio José helped build it, according to his older living descendants.

But the important thing is that Antonia brought her saints to Las Placitas. She stowed them away the best she could in her crowded apartment and kept some on her family altar. To this family altar came her neighbors to pray and to seek blessings.

Whether it was due to the uncomfortable crowding of her neighbors at her altar or because the pious and saint-loving Antonia believed that a people needed a house of worship will never be known now. All that is known by her descendants is the story passed down to them.

One morning the people of the community house awoke to find Antonia busy with a heavy, sharp stick scratching out a trench wherein to lay the foundation of a capilla. Around her were stones of every size and shape. A little ditch brought water to the spot for the mixing of adobe mud. All day Antonia labored with her mud and rocks. Early the next morning they found her at work, and the next and the next. When the people saw that Antonia was determined to build a capilla wherein to put some of her saints, the women, then the men joined in the labor in a spirit of true dedication of work to the saints, and soon a neat little church stood on Las Placitas ground. The inside was plastered a snowy white with yeso and all around the walls were niches wherein Antonia would rest her old saints, and wherein also there would be candles in snowy white holders made of yeso. And thus the capilla was built, and thus many of the saints of Antonia became the property of the church.

The years passed and with them passed Antonia and Antonio José. Their children prayed and sought solace in their sorrows in the little chapel, where there was just standing room for the people when they held their festive services there. These children passed away, and their children came to worship in the house that Antonia started to build. The old and loved images of the saints still stood in their niches and San Antonio in his capilla stood on the altar.

Then came the world war, which brought new ideas even to the little mountain village of Las Placitas, for at least six of her sons had gone out to train or to fight for their country.

Not long after that first armistice day there was a fiesta day in the village. A small fire was started in the capilla from the flame of a candle and some damage was done to the church, and the little chapel of cottonwood holding San Antonio was scorched. Though the damage was trifling, the people talked together and decided to build a new church, on new ground.

And so it came about that the present church was built in Las Placitas. Before the present pews were built and the other furnishings were placed, a visitor came to the village. He knew art when he saw it. He knew also antiques and their value when he saw them. He was the good father from Bernalillo. He carefully inspected Antonia's saints. No one need tell him that San Antonio and his capilla were long over a hundred years old. The old yeso saints in the little old chapel were aged and looked it. The hair and the features on them were stains of the long-ago, brown stain made by boiling the bark of paloduro (a very hard wood that grew in the Sandías) until it was an ink. It was then eternally indelible when applied to wood or yeso. The faded red stain was made from almagre, Indian red, made from a red pumice-like substance found in what is now called the Navajo country. The secret of how a permanent dye was made from almagre is lost, as far as the descendants of Antonia are concerned. But the saints of Antonia were decorated with both that brown and red ink as her descendants describe the stains.

The good father from Bernalillo praised the new church the people had built. He assured them that such a fine new church should have new saints in it. The old ones, he assured them, would be good for one purpose: to turn into ashes to be used in making the sign of the cross on the foreheads of these devoted ones on Ash Wednesdays.

The younger ones, devoted ones, were for filling the new church with new saints. The older ones, devoted to the old and faded saints Antonia had placed in the chapel so many years ago, stood firm against turning those precious old saints into ashes. Conferences, arguments, and even quarrels disrupted the people of the church. But finally the moderns won out, and the good father from Bernalillo took all the old saints, including San Antonio in his capilla, to Bernalillo.

The present church at Las Placitas has not one of its old saints left. The very old people still remember the feud and are still resentful that their old and revered images were taken from them and in their places there were but factory-made ones. A few of the older people of the church in Las Placitas believe that their old saints were not turned into ashes but that they are now in collections at Santa Fe.

But all of Antonia's saints were not in the little chapel in the village. She kept as many as she gave to the church. The others remained her sacred treasures until she died. She left her beloved images to one of her daughters, Juana. Juana was as devoted to her saints as her mother had been before her. But Juana was a mystery señora if ever Las Placitas had one, at least she was the first mystery lady in the annals of Las Placitas, just as her mother was the first collector of antiques in the village. Juana made frequent trips from her home; none ever knew where she went nor why. Sometimes she made brief stays. At other times she was away from her home for years.

Just before one sudden departure she gave her saints into the keeping of her brother Nicolás and his wife, Catalina. They, too, revered the old saints and put them carefully away. Feeling that they were safe, they gave them no more attention.

Strange it was that in a family of saint-loving people there should be one member who abhorred them, and that member a mere child. His name was José, after his grandfather. José took advantage of every opportunity to get at the hidden saints. One by one he stole them out of the house and buried them in various places about the village. He left not one in the hiding place.

In due course of time Juana returned and asked for her saints. Lo, there were none. Her grief was so sincere that the boy repented, confessed his sin, and did all he could to try and locate the graves and dig them open. But in the years that passed while Juana was away and the saints, forgotten, lay in their graves, even the places he had put them were hazy in the boy's memory. So, few of them were ever found and even those were devoid of the beauty they had possessed. In the ground they had deteriorated and were of little or no value. Juana took what was left of them and sorrowfully left the village, never to return.

The name Antonia and her story keep green in the memory of the people of Las Placitas, except in the minds of the younger generation. As time goes on, those who willingly sacrificed Antonia's saints realize the more the value of the things they caused to be lost to Las Placitas forever. All those images were made by human hands, of long ago. True artists they were, who created those saints. They have been forgotten long generations ago. They lived no one knows where, they created Antonia's saints no one knows when. Thus speak those of the church at Las Placitas who realize now what fame Antonia's collection of ancient saints would have brought to their church.

SUBJECT: El Cajón Bonito
WPA: 5-5-55 #3
April 10, 1942
Words 1509
Sources of information: Adelaida Chaves, Ferminia Durán. Adelaida Chaves
was a niece of the María of this story. Ferminia Durán was an intimate friend
of María.

EL CAJÓN BONITO
(The Beautiful Box)

It was well over a hundred years ago when a young man named Juan Lucero
set to work to materialize in wood a vision he had. He was not only an ambitious youth but he had skill in his fingers and art in his soul. He also possessed
a love, and for that love he determined to make his dream of a box come true.

In every age there are luxuries and necessities in all households. In Juan's
day and for many years after Juan was gone and forgotten, except for the box
he made for his love, boxes were a household necessity in the homes of Juan's
people. And so it was that Juan made a box, not an ordinary box but a box that
was called el cajón bonito for many many years by those who saw it, and to
this day is so called by the few old people yet living who remember it.

Juan selected the finest pine he could find in the mountains from which
to make boards to put into his box. He made it about twenty-six inches long,
about twenty-two inches wide and around eighteen inches deep. The boards
were fitted smoothly and perfectly together and fastened with stout wooden
pegs. No one knows how long Juan spent in sanding the surfaces of those
boards. But they were sanded until they looked as smooth and glossy as satin.
Juan decided upon a change from the flat tops or the curved in tops of the
boxes he had seen. He measured a piece of wood about six inches thick, and
with the width and length of his box and from that he literally sanded into

being a dome-like top for his precious box. Juan had no tools with which to work but those he made himself of flint rock and pieces of iron picked up by Juan on El Camino Real on his frequent visits to Alameda, where Juan's ancestors were born.

This top seemed to roll upward from the four sides of the box, and its surface was highly polished until the sunlight upon it made it look somewhat like a reflector. The front of the box was decorated with hand carving and was then stained. The effect was beautiful, for the roses on the box were Spanish roses, which all the women loved and which grew in many places where they could enjoy them. The stains were faded red and a soft brown, the only stains Juan knew in those old days.

Juan made wooden pins with heads to hold the dome-like top on the box. The long, stout pins were inserted through holes drilled into the lid along the edge and down into the corresponding holes made in the edge of the box at the back, formed hinges as they spoke of them—wooden hinges. The heads of the pins were just large enough for the thumb and forefinger of a hand to grasp and pull from their places in the holes. The heads of the pins in Juan's box were worn and misshapen from the generations of fingers that pulled them out and replaced them in their holes.

These wooden pegs were the only hinges known to the people of Juan's day and for years afterward. How many times a day patient fingers pulled out the pins and replaced them is unknowable, but they did that task with the same patience as the modern woman lifts the lid of her cedar chest.

And so to Juan's love went this beautiful box. It was the envy of every woman who saw it. Proudly she displayed it and lovingly she tucked her treasures away in it. Then came a day when she would open it no more. And strange to say, of all her children she chose her youngest son, Tomás, to inherit it.

Both Juan and his love died in Alameda. Tomás brought the box with him when he returned to Las Placitas. It seemed that the women welcomed it back as they would have received a treasure of their own. Feminine hearts yearned for that beautiful box and again caressing hands smoothed its glossy surface. As time passed, its surface took on a saffron hue and the stained roses and scrolls on the front mellowed. There was not a maiden in Las Placitas who did not pray that some day that box might be her own.

Time passed. Tomás became a youth. He wished to marry María, the daughter of Don Juan Armijo. But he had no one to carry on his affair, so he boldly presented his own suit to María's father, nor had he any fear for the outcome. Juan Armijo had been one of his father's closest friends. Juan readily agreed to give María, lazy María, in marriage to the youth. María was "lazy María" only to her family in those days. Little did the youthful Tomás or her family dream that before she departed from this world forever, she would be lazy María to the whole village.

So it came about that el cajón bonito came into the possession of María. Tomás built a little house across the winding lane from the great house of her father, and in her best room rested the box where all could see and admire it. It held her wedding finery and other treasured possessions, and in time it also held the fiesta clothes of her children.

In old Las Placitas many a wife and daughter sought vainly to inspire a husband or a father to make for them a box to match María's beautiful box. Many boxes were made and made well. Choice pine was used in the making; they were well put together with strong wooden pegs, they were well rubbed with sand, and their lids were securely fastened to them, but somehow they all fell far short of the beauty and the workmanship of María's box. None possessed the flowing lines in the lid and none had that satiny finish. Truly, they said, old Juan, whom many of them remembered, must have had some great gift that none of them possessed. So the matrons and the maidens went on envying María her beautiful box. And their hands continued to caress its satiny surface, which as the years went by made that lovely surface even more satiny.

Time went by. Changes in household necessities and luxuries crept into the village, as the gold rush and its flow of money was felt by many of the families of Las Placitas, especially in those where the men were energetic or ambitious. With money women could buy material to make things for their houses. A craze seized them to possess homemade lace pieces: panels for the windows, homemade lace edges to sew on various things, such as snowy white sheets used as bedspreads. In short, handmade lace became the rage as well as patchwork quilts. A home without a handmade patchwork quilt was a poor home indeed. These precious fads cost both work and money. They cost less money if they were made by the hands that were to possess them, or if they came as gifts, which was rare. The cost of making these handmade things was greater than the cost of the material used in them, so it behooved all the matrons and maids to learn to make them.

But not so with María. Fine handwork was hard to do. María was too lazy to undertake such tasks. María coveted patchwork quilts and those beautiful fine lace panels with flowers, angels, or saints worked into their lacy designs, as much as the feminine population of the village had coveted her beautiful box. Somehow she would find a way to buy them, or have someone make them for her.

And the way did come. One morning a collector of antiques came to the village. He was from Santa Fe. Whether he just chanced to come to María's door or was directed there no one knows. But when he came from her house, he was helping carry the beautiful box to his buggy. María was not guilty of selling the beautiful box for a song, but no price that she might have realized from the sale of it would have even quieted one of the many sad thoughts and even more regrets that Tomás suffered at the loss of the beautiful box his father made for his mother years before he came into the world. Perhaps there was some compensation in the knowing that his mother's treasure was added to a worthy collection of old things made in New Mexico and kept on display in Santa Fe.

SUBJECT: How Señora Petra Clothed Her Family

WPA: 5-5-49 #8

April 24, 1942

Words 1570

Sources of information: José Gurulé, Ferminia Durán, Benino Archibeque, Conception Archibeque. José Gurulé was a nephew of Petra. Ferminia Durán's grandmother was a friend of Petra. Benino Archibeque remembers how the telar and malacate belonging to his mother were made. Conception Archibeque remembers the telar and the malacate. She has a malacate that was made by her husband.

HOW SEÑORA PETRA CLOTHED HER FAMILY

The people who built Las Placitas made their village of the material they found on the ground and they put the material together with their own hands. Likewise all the food they ate and the clothing they wore were the results of their own efforts, and they possessed nothing aside from the fruits of their own labors. The women contributed much of this labor. In the matter of clothing they produced every step in the process, but one. The men sheared the wool from the backs of their sheep and goats and handed it over to the women who prepared it for the backs of their families.

Señora Petra was a model housewife and an expert weaver of wool. More than that she always had the wool her husband gave her ready for the loom days before the other housewives in the community house. Besides doing all that work, Petra had a large family that required much of her time.

The women of the village went in groups to the arroya to wash the wool. They used large stones as washboards were later used. As the wool was very dirty, the work of cleansing it was not easy. So many days were spent in the washing. Not from sunup to sundown, because of the other work to be done, but many hours each day were spent at the arroya until the wool was clean and all the dirty water pressed from it.

Señora Petra had a large buffalo hide. Some of the women possessed only goat hides; but to dry the wool, animals skins were a necessity. Señora Petra laid the skin, hairy side down, in the best corner her largest room afforded. She scattered the wool on the skin and left it there to dry. Each day she turned it over and rescattered it until it was dry.

When it was dry, the real work started, combing it. The herders tended their flocks, but they could not keep them out of briars, burs, and other prickly seed cases that so tangled up the animals' hairs as to be almost impossible to remove. These labor-hardened fingers of Petra did much of the task but there yet remained work for the carda (comb), which Petra made for herself. It was a rough piece of wood about one and a half inches thick, which enabled her to get a good grasp upon it. The piece of wood was about eight inches square. The rougher the wood, the better it was for the combing.

With the combing finished and the wool left clean and fluffy, the next step toward a garment for one of Petra's family was the spinning. The malacate (hoisting machine) and Petra's expert hands accomplished that tedious task in time. The malacate was a very simple contraption, but whether Petra or her husband made it will never be known, as Petra lived more than a hundred years ago; but until recent years, some of her descendants could have told of Petra's malacate, from firsthand knowledge of it. There yet may be some of these malacates in Las Placitas, for there were one or more of them in every family as recent as seventy-five years ago, or even later.

The material needed for the making of the malacate was a stick about an inch in diameter, or a trifle less, and about twenty-four inches long, and a piece of wood, about three-quarters of an inch thick, made round and measuring close to five inches (more or less). This rodundo, as it was called, had a hole in the exact center, just large enough to slip down the stick and a wooden pin held it in place about four inches below the center of the stick. The stick and the rodundo were sanded until they were as smooth as polished stone. Then a tinaja (pottery bowl) was used to stand the malacate in, for the malacate must have a smooth, confined surface in which to be whirled round and round. And thus was made the thing on which the spinning of the wool was done. In those days when so much cloth was needed for the clothing of the family, and the process of securing it was so slow and hard, the malacate was almost a constant companion of the women. At the bailes in those old days, the señoras took their malacates with them, and as they sat on the thick vigas

ranged on the floors against the walls to serve as seats, they set up their malacates in front of them and started them to working. In case a señora wished a
partner in a dance, all she had to do was to place the small piece of animal
skin she brought along to sit upon, out in front of her alongside her malacate
and soon she was asked to dance.

How well a malacate turned out the work depended upon the degree of
skill and nimbleness of the fingers on the hands which operated it. One hand
held a fluff of wool at the top of the palo, or stick, and sorted it in single, double, treble, or more threads, or hairs, according to the heaviness of the thread
desired, rolled them together and started them downward on the palo in such
a manner as to twist them together round the stick, as the other hand twirled
the stick round and round. The fingers at the top of the malacate must always
be ready to join more threads to the long one being twisted on the palo that
was coiling up on the rodundo.

At intervals, depending on the speed of the worker, the thread was taken
from the rodundo, else it tumbled off, and the long, continuous thread was made
into a modeja (skein) of woolen thread and put away. When there were enough
of these modejas to make the garment most needed or desired by the family, it
was time for the telar (loom). It was a happy day in those households of the old
days when enough wool came from the malacate to make a new garment.

There was a telar in most homes of Old Las Placitas. Some women could
not or would not weave. Those women paid in commodities to have others
weave for them. Señora Petra excelled as a weaver of cloth and as such was
able to add to the family supplies of wheat, corn, peas, and probably cane for
sugar, as that was a prize commodity. Petra made her own loom and it was
well made. It served her and some of her children, for she left it to one of her
daughters. It required but four pieces of timber and many ganches (hooks)
made of wood. The uprights of the telar were called vigetas and were thick
enough to stand up without supports, about six inches in diameter. They were
about thirty inches high. At the top and bottom of each one, corresponding
holes were made to hold the palos or sticks, which would hold them together
and give width to the loom. These sticks were about the size of our present
broomsticks and they were about thirty-eight inches long. Petra's loom was of
encino (oak), though most looms were made of pine. Those cross sticks were
called vara alto and vara bajo (high stick and low stick). Down the length of
the vigetas, and at the exact point on each one and very close together, were
the hooks that held the warp of the cloth to be wove, or the thread that would
run crosswise. Then came the arranging of the threads to run lengthwise. Each

thread to be used—and that depended upon the width of the cloth to be woven—was rolled on a round wooden pin, which they called rodillo (roller). Now the preparations were complete. The weaving of materials enough for Señora's naguas (petticoats) took many months, for the petticoats were very wide and numerous. For Señora's calzones y camisa (trousers and shirt) less time was required, and as both Señora Petra and Señor Gurulé, her husband, wore camisas made exactly alike and worn over the tops of their lower garments, the same amount of time was required in the weaving of cloth for them. Less time was required for the weaving of cloth for the garments of the children, which were but smaller patterns of the garments worn by their elders. Señora Petra's loom was never put away, nor was her malacate; they were always handy as the work of making clothes for her family was an eternal one.

What has become of all the old looms that were once used in Las Placitas is a question answered by one word, the word explains why there are no antique chests, nor boxes, nor blankets, nor old saints left in the village. That word is—collectors—of antiques.

SUBJECT: La Cuna y La Muñeca

WPA: 5-5-49 #28

June 5, 1942

Words 2332

Sources of information: Conception Archibeque, Benino Archibeque, Feminia Durán, Nina Montoya de Pearce. Conception Archibeque was the daughter of Chona of this story. Ferminia Durán was the descendant of the Pancho Pacheco of this story. She saw some of the dolls he made. Nina Montoya de Pearce's mother had one of the dolls.

LA CUNA Y LA MUÑECA
(The Cradle and The Doll)

Even in the long-ago days of privations and extreme hardships when the first houses in Las Placitas held little aside from the bare requirement of existence, there were women who found the time and the medium through which to express their innate love of something above drab necessities, something that cheered them and gave them a sort of vision of what they might accomplish with their own hands.

The two most important of these few "somethings" were the cradles and the dolls they created for their children. Upon these two things could be lavished their greatest efforts and enthusiasm. And among those women of long ago who made cradles and dolls that inspired other mothers to imitate them was María de La Conception, whom they called Chona. When she came to Las Placitas is not known, but it was many years before the Civil War, as her husband, Francisco Gonzales, went to fight at the battle of Valverde, leaving behind his children old enough to carry on his work in the fields at home. The memories of her cradles and her dolls lived long after her.

There was but one way to make la cuna (the cradle). But it was the care and selection with which the materials were assembled and the way in which

336

they were put together that made the difference between just a place to put the baby and a delightful and pretty nest wherein to keep and cuddle it. The cradle Chona made was a pretty thing to see and a comfortable bed and play-place for her child.

Chona spent many hours preparing the animal skin that formed the most important part of la cuna. She chose the hide of a white goat for it made the prettiest cradle. Long she worked with it to remove the burs, briars, twigs, and mud that matted the hair. When that was done she washed it and rewashed it until it was thoroughly cleansed. Then came the drying, the stretching, the kneading, which was a softening, toughening process. This required time and patience, but at length it was finished. Then Chona turned her attention to the hair of the now cured skin. She combed it with a rough piece of board until it was out at full length. Then she put the finishing touch to it with a warm water and amole (soap made from the amole plant) wash. Over and over again she washed it until it was snowy white and soft as the finest wool and was as satin to the touch. The skin was ready.

Four slender, but stout poles were required in the making of la cuna, and many, many strips of goat hide made into straps of semi-pliable leather called correa. Many times ox hide was used to make those straps but Chona preferred straps or correa of goat skin. The two longer poles for the cradle were about four feet long, the shorter ones were about two feet in length. They were smoothed and polished by rubbing them with sand, another tedious task. When they were ready for use, they were securely tied together with correa, about two or three inches of each pole extended beyond the point where they crossed and were tied. When the prepared skin was carefully and expertly laced to the poles in such a manner as to allow a depth in the skin sufficient for the baby's safety and comfort, more correa was attached to the places where the poles crossed for the purpose of hanging la cuna from the vigas that supported the roof of the room, where baby would spend his cradle days.

Not just any place in the room would do. There was a special spot in those old houses where la cuna hung. It was a spot about four feet and just to the right of where some member of the family knelt throughout the daylight hours, and many candle-lit hours, with the metate and the mano (a stone for the grinding of corn and wheat and dried peas). There it was a simple matter for the mother or any other member of the family to lift a hand and set la cuna swinging whenever baby became fretful. In those old days there was little time to cuddle a baby in the arms of anyone. The baby actually lived and had its being in la cuna. It was taken from the place only when necessary. It slept there, unless it was ill, then it was taken to rest in the arms of the mother or grandmother, or some other adult member of the family.

Chona prepared truly beautiful wrappings for her baby. A serape of the softest white goat hair. Not all the serapes woven for the cradle were snowy white. The grayish white ones and the brown ones (all were woven from the natural-colored wool) were easier to keep clean and all housewives did not have the time or the desire to keep la cuna snowy white.

Chona had some truly beautiful skins on the baby's cradle. That was the day of the deer and the antelope. An antelope skin, with proper curing, could be made as soft and fluffy as a soft kid glove. Those skins could be put next to a baby's skin, so very soft they were, and warm, too. The baby of Chona's day wore but one garment, a square of cloth folded diagonally and fastened about it in the manner of a mantilla (shawl); in fact, that was what an infant's dress was called. Those squares of cloth were made from the finest of goat hair. Such fine, soft wool was called sayalete (thin flannel). When the antelope's skin was made into a wrap for baby, it was called gamuza because it was as soft as chamois. Those chamois-like robes on baby's cradle gave then an air of luxury.

Chona and those ambitious, industrious, beauty-loving women of that long-ago day had it within their possibilities to create a thing of real beauty when they made a cradle for their infants.

Señora Chona could make muñecas as well as cunas. She made them with the same painstaking labor and with the same careful selection of materials as she did the cradles. She spent the same time and effort in putting the doll together, and the results were dolls that are still remembered by the surviving few who saw them.

There were two classes of dolls in Chona's day: the female dolls and the male dolls. Women like Chona made the female dolls for their children; the male dolls were made by someone who could carve wood. A woodcarver who was really gifted could make male dolls that were works of art. Such a one earned many a measure of wheat and corn and chili and added many a goat or lamb to his flocks in return for a muñeco (doll-male).

So it was that Chona left behind her only female dolls, or rag dolls. But they, too, were works of art. And to make even one doll required hours of extra labor as cloth represented hours of work whether it was new or old. In Chona's day the old garments of the family were unraveled, the threads twisted together into long ones for weaving, and were wound on the rolling pins ready for the loom just as was the new thread. The cloth thus woven was very much less durable than new cloth but the process saved the housewife the labor or preparing the raw material for the loom, which was a long and back-breaking process. So cloth taken for the making of a doll meant a sacrifice. Chona stuffed her doll with cloth because the cloth made a prettier doll. Many mothers stuffed the dolls they made with cáscara o perfilla del maís (corn husk). Always there was a quantity of this cáscara on hand. When it was soaked in water and properly dried, not in the sun, it became pliable, and while in this condition made a fairly good stuffing for the dolls, and it saved many hours of preparing the cloth required for the padding.

Chona never made large dolls, nor did the other mothers. The doll about ten inches in height with width in proportion was the most popular size. The cloth was cut out and sewed, or merely sewed into shape and then stuffed. The more care used in the stuffing of a doll, the more perfect the doll. Chona made dolls that pleased the eyes of her children as well as gladdened their hearts. The making of the features of the doll and the hair was important. Thread was used in the natural state, white, grayish white, black, and brown. Stains were used; the brownish stain made from the bark of the palo duro and the red stain made from the pumice-like stone almagre. The eyebrows were made and shaped as nearly lifelike as Chona could make them. Perhaps she tried to copy the features of her own child, for her dolls had pretty faces. The eyebrows, eyelashes and the eye itself were neatly outlined with thread the desired colors, then threads put in to make the hair, and so arranged as to make long bangs and a chongo (braid) at the back. Chona used an abundance of thread for the hair and thus gave the doll the appearance of having thick hair. Straggling threads ruined the appearance of the doll and made it ugly. Chona seemed not to mind the quantities of threads she put on the heads of the dolls she made. When the doll was finished, arms and legs well padded as well as the head, it was ready to be dressed. That meant more cloth, sometimes new, sometimes old. The doll was an exact copy of its little owner when it was dressed: many petticoats, a full gathered skirt, all long, and a camisa with rounded neckline and ruffled bottom and drawn over the doll's head and down over its skirt top, just as was the little girl's and the little girl's mother's, too, for there was but one pattern for feminine dress. This completed doll was a work of art and to this day the older women, the great-grandmothers now living in Las Placitas, recall them with fondness and pleasure.

There were rag dolls in almost every home, but the wooden doll was found only when parents or members of the household were able to give some commodity in exchange for them, or when they were received as gifts, unless a member of the household was a wood carver himself. This case was rare. In those old days when Chona made her pretty rag dolls, old Pablo Pancho Pacheco carved selected pieces of wood into dolls for those who could afford to part with food, or with material for clothing, or with some other commodity necessary to their existence in return for them. Because of the price old Pablo set on his art, which was not exorbitant for such fine hand carving and other expert workmanship that he lavished upon his dolls, he was not called upon to make a great number of them, and in consequence there were but a comparative few of his dolls as compared to the number of rag dolls they had.

Old Pablo made his doll of pine. Unlike the Indian doll it was not made in one piece. The arms and legs were made separately and holes were drilled in the places that were to be attached to the body, as well as in the corresponding places in the body of the doll. Then they were put together with correa (strings of tough, pliable cured animal skin). Thus the wooden doll had movable arms and legs. The beauty and value of Pablo's doll were in the perfection of its form and features. It was a perfect replica of the human male anatomy with dominantly featured male characteristics. Hair on the body of the doll was realistically accomplished by the use of ink (brown fluid made from the bark of the palo duro). This stain was permanent and so closely resembled the human hair when Pablo's expert hand applied it that it gave the male doll a great advantage over the female rag doll. Those wooden dolls of Pablo tempted his neighbors into the sacrifices some of them made to obtain one.

There are very few left in Las Placitas who remember Pablo's dolls, for he carved his last ones a generation before the present oldest generation were born. The last of his dolls disappeared from the village nearly seven years ago—whether to collectors, no one knows.

Old Pablo was a real artist and a rival of Chona and a few other mothers who loved beauty and possessed the ambition and talent to create something that added a touch of loveliness and pleasure to the drab life of their day, something that brought genuine happiness to the children of their day and is remembered to this day, the rag dolls with their many petticoats, the wooden dolls that were never dressed.

SUBJECT: El Horno
WPA: 5-5-41 #39
July 3, 1942
Words 1341
Sources of information: Conception Archibeque, Benino Archibeque,
Fermina Durán, José Gurulé. Conception Archibeque was the youngest
child of Francisco. Benino was his son-in-law as was José Gurulé.
Ferminia Durán's first husband was also Francisco's son.

EL HORNO
(The Oven)

In those first days of Las Placitas, and for many generations thereafter, the family dwelling consisted of three inseparable and indispensable units . The family dwelling was not complete until all three were finished. La casa, la fogón compaña, y el horno (the house, the family hearth, and the oven) were the parts that constituted the whole. The fireplace, or family hearth, was always built in a corner of the living room; the oven was always built outside the house at a place deemed most convenient for the housewife.

El horno was of utmost importance. It baked the bread that substantially sustained the life of the family and, in a manner, it was related to the generosity and hospitality of the family, particularly at fiesta times, unless such acts of God as droughs, floods, and Navajo raids intervened.

The life of the outdoor oven, its efficiency and convenience, depended mostly upon the skill and excellence of the plasterer. It was Francisco Gonzales in those long-ago days of Las Placitas whose plastering gave years of service to the mud outdoor ovens of his family and to others who sought the help of that much envied artist who so expertly mixed and applied both adobe and sand plaster. His ovens stood intact through wind and weather; they gave efficient heating; they baked the bread with no extra bother and worry to the housewives throughout the long years of his life and for many years after him. In those long-ago days, to be a fine plasterer was to be rated an artist and a real benefactor, for in the all-important building of el horno, the plastering was the thing.

The family of Francisco was large and hospitable; therefore, his oven must be large. He laid out a foundation for his oven that would give it an outside circumference of approximately twenty feet. He marked off that area and set to work. A good foundation must be laid. It must be thoroughly dried, for the foundation was a most important feature of the oven. It was made of a layer of rock, then a layer of mud, another of rock, another of mud and so on until a height of eighteen inches was accomplished. Then it was left to dry. That drying process required a week or ten days, or even more, all depending on the weather. The top of this foundation became the floor of the oven and on it all the bread to be baked must be laid.

When the foundation was ready, the adobes, thoroughly dried and smoothed off, were laid around the foundation handy for the laying in place. Those adobes were eight inches long. At one end they measured six inches and at the other end they were four inches. The adobe was four inches thick. This wedge-shaped adobe gave the oven, when finished, a beehive appearance. The first twelve inches of adobe was laid with straight up and down side and allowed to dry out thoroughly before another layer was added. After that, Francisco started on the real work of the oven. Each successive course of adobe, set in plenty of mud of just the right consistency, was set inward about an inch, and each course was allowed to dry before another was added. A properly constructed oven was not built in haste. The building of it required time. In the construction two openings were made; one was the door that measured about eighteen inches high and the same number of inches in width, the other was a humero (flue) built about halfway up the side and at a point about midway between what would be the front and the back of the oven, using the door as a measuring point. El humero was about eight inches in diameter, and when the heat was being retained in the oven, it was plastered over with mud. After the adobes were all set, another drying period was allowed before the application of plaster, the master-work in the building of el horno.

In those long-ago days, there was more than one reason for the growing of wheat. Bread was paramount, but straw for the making of adobes, for plastering inside and outside walls of houses, and for the essential work of plastering the ovens, was almost as important. Without straw or a good substitute, the plaster of adobe dried out and in short time crumbled and fell from the surfaces it covered. But with straw mixed with the adobe mud, plenty of it, too, the plaster held firm and did not crack. An oven covered with poorly made plaster was a poor oven indeed.

So in the manner of an expert plasterer, Francisco mixed mud and straw and put on the first coat. It was a good thick coat of adobe mud, and required from a week to ten days for perfect drying. The oven was then ready for the second coat of adobe and straw, but that coat of plaster was not so heavy as the first. When it was thoroughly dry, the last coat was applied. That last coat was made of adobe and sand. It was well mixed and applied thinly and even-ly with the hands, and not with llano (trowel) as were the first two coats. When dry, that finishing coat looked and felt like hard clay. There were no cracks in it and nowhere was there a place for the heat to escape from the inside.

Satisfied with his outside plastering, Francisco set to work to plaster the inside of the oven, and that was a difficult job as he must work on the inside. Being a large man, he was not able to force his body into the oven, so he directed the work of his wife, who had no trouble in creeping through the door admitting to the inside of the oven. A first coat of adobe mud was applied. There was some straw used in it. After it was sufficiently dried, another coat of adobe mud was put on, with only straw enough to make it adhere to the first coat. That meant using as little straw as was possible. The floor of the oven was then finished.

Francisco hewed down a sizable chunk from a pine tree into a door to cover the outside of the opening through which the oven was entered. It was very thick, probably around four inches and made sufficiently larger than the open-ing in the oven to allow it to be fitted against the doorway outside. This wood-en door was held firmly in place by a large stone. With that, the oven was done.

But the work of Francisco was not done. If the oven were to be used, he must make una pala (a shovel) which was a necessity for the placing of the loaves of bread into the oven and the removing of them from it. La pala (the shovel) was made of one piece of timber. Francisco hewed it out with his hacheta (little stone axe). The piece of wood overall was about six feet long and wide enough to leave the scoop of the shovel at least a foot wide. He hewed into shape a scoop twelve inches wide and eighteen inches long. He hewed the remaining length into a long handle and rounded it that it would be easy to handle. He put a very sharp edge on the scoop of the shovel by grind-ing off the wood with sand, and he sanded and smoothed the whole shovel. And then his usable oven was completed.

SUBJECT: La Era (The Threshing Floor)
WPA: 5-5-49 #10
July 17, 1942
Words 2083
Sources of information: Benino Archibeque, Conception Archibeque, Patricio Gallegos, José Gurulé. Benino Archibeque's father, Salvadoro, helped with the community era. José Gurulé's grandfather, José Antonio Gurulé, helped make the first community threshing floor in Las Placitas.

LA ERA
(The Threshing Floor)

In the early days of Las Placitas, la era (the threshing floor) was of the utmost importance. It was made by the men of the community to be used by the community, for grain must either be raised by every family in the community or else procured by barter from the Pueblo Indians. The people held la era as a common possession because the making of one as well as the threshing of the wheat on it was a many-men job and not a one family. So it was that in Las Placitas long over one hundred years ago, they made a threshing floor that served them well; also many generations of their descendants used it. The making of it required about twenty-five poles of approximately eight feet in length and four inches in diameter, at least three-hundred-eighty feet of rope, which was both reata de correa y reata de crin (rope of animal hides and rope of horsehair). Rope of horsehair was borrowed from el patrón (the man who held most of the Las Placitas men in peonage) as only the rich possessed horses at that time. The rope of animal hides was the pooled correa of the community. Then they needed azadones (digging tools as wooden hoes) and stone axes and a flock of goats, plenty of water, adobe, and fair weather, and a plot of ground at least thirty feet square.

The ground was cleared and leveled off and filled upward from edge to center until it was a mound, then it was measured off and a pole set in the center. A measuring rope of fifteen feet was attached to it, and with that rope pulled out at full length, the circumference of a circular floor was marked, which had a diameter of thirty feet. The canto (rim) was then slightly curved inward and the first pole was planted at its outer edge. Four feet from that point on the canto another pole was set; another approximate four feet was marked off on the rim and another pole planted—poles standing some six feet above the ground and in firmly enough to withstand the contacts of any animals and not yield an inch. About four feet farther on another pole was set, another four feet, another pole. That process was repeated until the area was encircled by poles. Then the rope was placed around the poles; four lengths of it, the first length around the poles very near the ground, the other lengths around were put about sixteen inches apart. The rope was bound to the poles with scraps of correa and thus a secure fence was made around the threshing floor.

When that fence was done, a place was left between two poles to form a gate. The flock of goats as driven into the area through that gate, which was replaced by again fastening the rope to the poles.

With the fence finished, water was poured all over the surface of the mound-shaped floor and dug up as it was mixed with the adobe, and then the goats were driven in to tramp it down. With sticks and long lashes of leather the goats were kept on the run, round and round the circular floor. They were driven in at dawn, they were kept racing round and round until the sun announced high noon. Then they were driven out to be watered and allowed to graze while the men ate their lunches. There was only a short rest period for the men after the refreshments. Again the goats were sent into the arena, again the men forced them to a trot and a run around the floor. That work was kept up until twilight when both animals and men were almost exhausted, but the floor was firm and hard.

The next day water was again poured all over the area; again the goats were driven in on it. Another day of racing round and round, of pounding hooves on the wet, then damp, then dry adobe, and the threshing floor was as hard as cement, a lasting, efficient floor for the work of threshing out the grain, which furnished the daily bread for that community of long ago. The rain would slide from it, the sun would dry it harder and harder and with annual upkeep, which was labor of men, and the era was always ready for the hard usage to which it was put.

Every autumn when their grain was ready, and after all the grain of el patrón was threshed on his own floor and the cleaned grain was sacked in bags of buffalo hides and stored, all the men, except the few out with el patrón's sheep, set to work to thresh out their own grain. And for this work they needed horses; mares were used in those old days for the threshing. But there were no horses in Las Placitas, so the patrón's horses were used whenever he saw fit to loan them, and the price for this service was not remembered by any of the descendants of those people of long ago who borrowed el patrón's mares to thresh out their wheat.

The dried gavillas de trigo (sheaves of wheat) were brought and piled atop the mound. The mares were driven inside the arena and the tramping out the golden grain was begun. Wise men choose moonlight nights for this labor, as it was easier on the mares, and the men, too. The men must stand at the canto (rim) of the floor, ready with the wooden shovels or their bare hands, to throw back la barcia (the chaff) or las gavillas (the sheaves), which were thrown out to the rim or beyond by the flying hoofs of the horses. That was backbreaking work for it was unending so long as the horses were kept racing around the floor trampling out the grain. At short intervals the gate was opened and the horses driven out for a period of rest. At the same time, wine (made from the grape) and bizcochos (small biscuits) were served to the men and boys. Those old threshing parties often became real revels along about daylight.

When the horses were through their labors, the tramped-out mass on the floor was gathered up and stored away either in adobe bins in the house or in tinaja, according to the wishes of the family to whom it was allotted. There it was kept until a favorable wind, a brisk wind that would separate the grain from the chaff when it was dropped, by handsful, from a certain height to a cloth or an inverted animal hide spread upon the ground. That was another wearisome task, for days were spent at the work—days when the wind was favorable. As the grain was cleaned it was stored in tinajas, or pottery bowls of jars. It was then ready for the hands of the girls and women.

The grinding of this wheat into flour was one of the torturing labors forced by necessity upon the women of that long-ago day. Down on their knees they were at work with their grinding stones, the metate and the mano, at all hours and for long hours at a time, that their families might have their daily bread. There was constant need of flour and there was no other way than grinding it, to meet the demand. As the families were large, with very few exceptions, the need of flour kept some woman of every household busy with the grinding stones. At fiesta times the demand for flour was even greater.

The day preceding a fiesta day in those long-ago days was truly a busy one. Much bread must be baked and many bizcochos. The baking of bread required time even when la levadura (the leaven) was already prepared. It was made by mixing flour, salt, and water together, making the mixture into small cakes and drying it in the sun, and afterwards storing it in some cool place until it was needed. Utmost care was taken in the use of the levadura as it was exceedingly potent and therefore liable to cause the bread to be sour. Sour bread was most unpleasant food, but few families could afford to throw away a baking because it was too sour. So housewives made certain that they used just the right number of the cakes to raise their bread. The cakes were mixed with the warm water before it was poured into the flour, salt, and water, which was to be kneaded into dough. The more kneading the dough was given, the lighter would be the bread. When it was sufficiently kneaded, it was greased all over the surface, covered with a cloth, and set in a warm place to rise. That was a process that required from five to six hours, all depending upon the temperature of the room, or the place it was put.

And while the bread rose, the fire was laid in the oven outside. El horno (the oven) was not easy to heat. First, a thick layer of dry pine needles was spread evenly over the floor of the oven. Next, a thick layer of dry twigs and brush was added. On top of that and well distributed, was a layer of small sticks, and that in turn was topped by a layer of larger sticks, then small pieces of wood were laid on and covered with larger pieces. As the layers increased, the wood used was correspondingly larger. When just the right height was reached, the pine needles at the bottom were ignited by sparks from two pieces of flint rock. The flame spread and rose. An opening was made in the flue at the side of the oven and the heating of the large oven was well under way. Outside the oven was a great pile of wood to be added to the flames as the heating would require around two and a half or three hours, with an ever-increasing fire. The amount of wood needed to heat el horno was the equivalent of an entire day of wood gathering, for the plaster of the inside of the oven must glow red before it was properly heated.

And at a certain point in the heating the raised dough was made into loaves and placed on a board for an hour more of raising. There were twenty loaves, the capacity of the oven, allowing space for the placing and removal of the bread with the wooden shovel, that was, the larger ovens.

At length it was time to test the oven. The flue was again covered with adobe mud. A wet cloth bound to a stick was used to remove all the ashes and clean the floor for the bread. When that was finished, a handful of goat wool was wrapped about a stick and thrust into the oven. Should it be too brown when withdrawn, the oven must stand until another wool test was made, and another, if necessary, for the oven must be just right or the bread would be burned. When all was considered right, the shovel was produced and one at a time the loaves were placed inside the oven with it. When all were in position, the heavy wooden door of the oven was well wrapped in wet rags and stood in place and made firm by placing a heavy stone against it. Then the baker must be on the watch. The sun was her clock. She knew to the inch how far the shadows must travel before her bread would be done. When that time arrived, the door of the oven was removed and, one by one, the wooden shovel brought out the perfectly browned loaves of bread. They were again laid on the board, but to cool.

Then the oven was again heated for another oven full of bread; much bread and bizcochos were needed for the fiesta. Bizcochos baked quickly.

SUBJECT: El Platero (The Silversmith)

August 14, 1942

Words 1236

Sources of information: José Gurulé, Patricio Gallegos, Dave Trujillo. José Gurulé was a small child when old Narvez made jewelry for the people of Las Placitas. He knew how the old man made it and what it looked like. Patricio Gallegos recalled seeing the ruins of the little smelter near the old Montezuma Mine and remembers how it was built. Dave Trujillo knew from his parents that silver and other ores taken from the old Montezuma Mine were smelted nearby and made into jewelry, though he could not remember the name of the silversmith.

EL PLATERO
(The Silversmith)

In the long-ago days of Las Placitas when the barest necessities were obtained only through hard work, many long hours of it, the women somehow managed to work a little harder to raise surplus commodities in order to barter for prenderia. Those precious treasures of personal adornment, which were made of silver, of copper, of iron, were all hand-wrought.

In those days old Narvez (none living today remember his family name) gladdened the hearts of the feminine members of the village with his handiwork. Whether his rings and bracelets were of silver (few could afford the silver), or copper or iron, they were all works of art, crude though they were, and they all bore designs, and never were two ornaments carved alike. To keep a piece of stolen jewelry made by old Narvez was almost impossible. By the design on it, the owner was certain to know it.

Old Narvez lived at Algodones, but much of his time was spent at or near Las Placitas, for there he found his materials: metals, a whole mine of them at the fabled old Montezuma Mine, and there he found coal which he could reduce to coque (coke), and there he found barro (clay) of just the right kind, and there he found plenty of piñón wood abounding in resina (pitch) needed to raise the heat units of his fire, which he must have in his fundidor (smelter).

In making his fundidor, Narvez dug a very shallow place in the ground as large as he wished the base to be. He lined it with rock and clay, then built it up to the desired height, making it with thick walls and using plenty of adobe mud to hold the rocks together. He molded a bowl-shaped crisol (crucible) of the clay, and when it was finished, it was as hard as rock and no degree of heat could damage it, that is, the highest degree of heat he needed for his smelting. The crisol became the top of the fundidor. Two small holes were made at the base of the fundidor. They were directly opposite each other and permitted a free circulation of air, which fanned the fire to greater heat.

When his fundidor was ready and his ore piled near it for fusion or smelting, Narvez piled up his fuel. He had cut down an abundance of piñón wood and cut it into proper lengths with his hacheta (small stone axe). That wood was full of resina (pitch), which would raise the heat units of his fire. A mound of coque (coke), which he had made by burning the coal until combustion was greatly reduced, was ready and some dirt and clay. Narvez laid brush and dry leaves in the bottom of his smelter; on that he piled the pieces of piñón and covered them with coke. He knew how to sprinkle adobe dirt over the top to compact the fuel space, and how to set the crisol and pack the clay about it to hold it firm. He struck his flints together, ignited the dry brush at the bottom of the smelter, and his fire was built. Into the crisol went the intended ore and the melting process was on.

Old Narvez made most of the jewelry of iron because there was much the greater demand for it, even for rings. But into that iron went pyrites, both of iron and copper. Those pyrites glitter like gold; in fact, they are known as fool's gold. When they were smelted into the iron, rings and bracelets made of it dazzled in the sunlight and the candlelight. Then Narvez dropped pieces of copper ore and a little chunks of silver ore into crisol with the iron and got gaily flecked molted stuff from which to hammer and cut out rings and bracelets.

As different metals required different heats to melt them, they were in different states of molten mass. But when in an adorning piece of jewelry, that roughness, knobby appearance, and general mixed-upness added to its worth and beauty.

When his molten mass was ready, Narvez poured it out on a flat smooth stone as he kneaded it and tooled it and cut it with stone tools. Upon the rings and bracelets he carved figures of animals, birds, reptiles, flowers, and geo-metric symbols. The plain pieces made from iron alone were carved with the same skill and artistic touch as those rings and bracelets which would bring him more beans, chili, peas (both black-eyed and Spanish), and wheat or blue corn. The silver rings were beyond all but a few, unless they were to be bought at great sacrifice. But there were those who made the sacrifices and adorned themselves with silver rings, silver bracelets, and even silver earrings which, were all highly polished and carved.

Narvez used pumice for polishing as well as smoothing down his melted metals. After he had labored with sand or pumice, even the roughest rings and bracelets took on a finished appearance.

In those old days there was a demand for rings of iron and the iron made to glitter by the addition of pyrites, for it was the custom of the day for engaged couples to exchange rings in a dance called la prenderia given at the home of the bride, or some place chosen by her family, on the night preced-ing the wedding. A tragedy it was for a girl's family not to provide her with a ring to give her husband-to-be on that great night amid festivities and the eyes of friends. Then the young man would be a poor lover if he did not bring a ring to slip on the finger of his wife-to-be as they both moved to the center of the floor in the dance and came very close together to exchange rings. That ceremony meant much to all concerned and rings must be had for it. That old custom brought happiness to brides and developed the art of making jewelry in the village of long ago.

Narvez has long since passed away but his memory still lives among those who are left who wore his precious jewelry, or those who saw some of it bought by barter by their ancestors. Sad it is that the artistic work of el platero viejo (the old silversmith) can no longer be found in Las Placitas. Like other things from the hands of the artists and craftsmen of old Las Placitas, his creations, crude but beautiful, have disappeared and newer, modern machine-made ornaments of personal adornment have taken their place.

SUBJECT: El vestido de Venado Cuero de Juan
WPA: 5-5-49 #76
August 28, 1942
Words 1128
Sources of information: José Gurulé, Ferminia Durán, Patricio Gallegos.
José Gurulé's father, Nicolás, wore a suit of deerskin. Also he could
remember the fine clothes of deerskin worn by Juan of Tecolote on an official
trip to Santa Fe. That suit was made by Juan's wife. Ferminia Durán knew
from her mother how suits of deerskin were made, and how the deerskins
were prepared. Patricio Gallegos's grandfathers Valentino Zamora and
Casimiro Gallegos wore deerskin suits made by the women of their families.

EL VESTIDO DE VENADO CUERO DE JUAN
(The Deerskin Clothes of Juan)

In the Las Placitas of a hundred years and more ago all the women made vestidos de venado cuero (clothes of deerskin) for their men. It was a hard task for those busy women whose work was rearing children. And helping their men provide for them kept them toiling early and late. And though the men prepared the animal skins for their clothes, there was yet much work for the women to do before garments could be called ready to wear.

In those long-ago days the winters were much colder and the snows very much deeper than they are today, say all the old people now left in Las Placitas, so it was necessary that the men who were out with herds of sheep and goats wear the suits of deerskin to keep them from freezing. So the women made those suits, made them by hand. A few of those women, in spite of all the other things they had to do, made such beautiful garments as to keep the whole art of making them fresh in the memories of their descendants.

One of those few who excelled in the making of vestidos de venado cuero was la esposa (the wife) of Juan of Tecolote, who was one of the leaders of the people in that long-ago day. An outstanding alcalde, farmer, and business-man of Las Placitas when times were difficult and Navajo raids frequent. He was large in stature and was very imposing-looking. He made much of those gifts, according to those who knew him and handed down stories of him. So, it was not strange that he wore the finest deerskin suit ever made in Las Plac-itas, and it was made by his wife, María.

Juan killed the deers and prepared the skins. He scraped the hair from them with a very sharp stone and a rough board, which he held easily in his hand. He washed the skins thoroughly, then started the real work of preparing them for the garments. He made a thick solution of amole (soap root) and seso de el venado (brain of the deer) and spread it on the skins and worked it in with his hands until the skins were soft and pliable. It was a tedious job, for every inch of the skin must be well kneaded and smoothed until it had the feel of chamois skin. When that work was accomplished, the skins were hung up in the proper place to dry—a place where they would dry slowly. Then Juan took all the nervios (sinews) and cleaned and shredded them to the proper thickness for sewing. He used only those tendons taken from the backbones of the animals.

With her materials ready, Señora María set to work. She had no scissors, but there were a precious few cuchillos (and those were hunting knives) in the village and there were stones with edges sharp enough to cut the skin, but which Señora María used in cutting out her Juan's deerskin suit was not remembered. The skins were laid out and smoothed, then placed on a reversed buffalo hide where María could best cut them out. Her pattern, which was in her mind, contained seven pieces. Her measurements for the cutting of the skins were Juan's waist measure, the length of his body from ankle to waist-line, the length from his shoulder to his hip, the length around his torso, and length for sleeves and for a collar. Each leg of los calzones (trousers) was cut from a folded skin, the fold for the outside of the leg. María cut each leg on the inside by curving upward from the bottom and downward from the top until they met, which points were joined in the making of the calzones. The back and the front of la camisa (shirt) were cut very much alike excepting around the neck. The back was round neckline, while the front was a V-shape. The skin was cut deep on the shoulders and she cut two pieces for sleeves to attach to those shoulder pieces. The collar was a straight piece cut just as long and wide as she desired it.

María had no needle, but she did have a lesna de hueso (a punch of bone). With that well-pointed and polished bone, she pushed the nervio through the doubled skins where she formed the seams. The seams were made from one and a quarter to one and half inches inside the edges of the skin. With the lesna she punched the nervio through the skins at evenly spaced sections, and always she doubled back to the center of the space she had finished to begin the new length of the space she was to cover with the nervio. Thus reinforced with the nervio or thread, the garments were made almost rip-proof. When el calzones and la camisa were sewed, María cut that inch or so from the seams to the edge of the skin into slits, thus forming a real finish that looked like fringe. The edges of the collar and sleeves and the tail of the shirt and the bottoms of the calzones were all likewise slit up the same distance, which made a fringed edge on them. The camisa was pulled down over the hips. The straight and evenly spaced stitches, the perfectly and uniformly cut fringe on the edges, the softness, the smoothness, the pliability of the perfectly cured skins—all combined made a very handsome suit for Juan.

The rain and the snow made sorry spectacles of those deerskin suits of long ago. The calzones drew up to the knees, the camisa crawled up to the armpits, and the sleeves crawled up somewhere near the elbows, and both garments were shrunken to skin tightness. But with patience the women stretched, kneaded, smoothed, and otherwise worked those shrunken garments back to their original size and beauty.

Thus were made and kept in good condition, the dress-up suits of the men of the Las Placitas of over a hundred years ago.

SUBJECT: La Tinaja de Lemita
September 11, 1942
Words 1074
Sources of information: José Gurulé, Benino Archibeque. Benino Archibeque
knew from his grandfather how the tinaja de lemita was made.

LA TINAJA DE LEMITA

When the forefathers of the builders of Las Placitas built the walled town of
Las Huertas, they found several springs nearby but none with a volume flow
that would bring water close enough to them to supply their needs when the
need was immediate. That condition worked a hardship upon the busy housewives in the bad seasons. To remedy that lack of water for household purposes, to be able to have it without delay, they made jarrones (large jugs) in which
to store their water. With storage, they could carry water from the springs
when they had the time. That water was carried in tinajas (earthern or clay
jugs) balanced on their heads. That water was, like everything else they possessed, hard to get. The storage jar was hard to make.

The people of that long-ago day called the huge jar a tinaja, which means
a clay or pottery jar. But that large tinaja was not made of clay, but of the twigs
or switches of a shrub they called lemita, which grew in the vicinity of old Las
Huertas. The switches of la lemita are long, slender, and pliable as are las jaras
(the willows). But unlike the willow, the twig of lemita is barbed, and bears a
fruit, which is called lemita. The fruit is about the size of a large pea. When it
is ripe, it is deep red and has a refreshing taste of a lime, plus a suggestion of
salt. The people of Las Huertas relished this fruit, just as their descendants in
Las Placitas do today. But to those people back in the old town of Las Huertas, the lemita meant utility as well as enjoyment. It helped to give them their
tinaja for water storage.

The word tinaja is of Philippine origin. It means pottery or earthen jar but
it also means a liquid weight of about twelve and two-thirds gallons. The tina-

ja de lemita made in Las Huertas over one hundred and eighty years ago held close to twelve gallons of water.

In making that tinaja, lemita was used rather than the willow of which they made many things: baskets, carriers for the backs of oxen, and bows were some of them. They used lemita because it was barbed and the barbed switches could be made to stick together much more securely than the willow. Many of those switches were required in the making of one of the large jars, and much trementina or resina (resin) from the pine tree for it was that substance which made the tinaja of lemita possible. The tinaja was about thirty-four inches high. It measured around thirty inches in diameter at the bottom, about twenty-four inches in diameter midway of the height, and about eighteen inches in diameter at the point which would mark the water's height, or the capacity of the jar. As the tinaja slanted in toward the top, fewer switches were required. Long ones were used at the base and turned upward at the place that would form the circumference of the bottom. Lemita was tough, strong, and pliable and bent easily, just as did the jara. When the switches had been placed side by side and pressed firmly together into the form of the tinaja, the switches at the top were bent inward about an inch and a half, then upward a little. That formed a bottle neck that would hold a wooden plug. When the tinaja was all formed, the resina was heated until it was in a flowing state, not too hot to work with the hands. Then it was pressed into every joining place of the switches. It adhered firmly to the barbs. It glued every part of the lemita together, then it was pressed and smoothed over the entire inner surface of the tinaja. Not one spot escaped a thorough coating. When that was done, the tinaja was placed in the coolest corner of the house and left there until the resina was dry and shiny. And there it was, the finished tinaja de lemita, strong, durable, waterproof. It would remain that way so long as it was kept in a cool place. And the house was that place—the house of rock and mud walls two feet and more thick, with thick adobe mud roofs and with very small windows, never more than one wee one to a room, and small doors never high enough to admit any one over sixty inches tall unless he stooped. Such a house was certain to be cool in the summer and cool in the winters, too, in the corners fartherest from the inadequate little corner fireplaces.

And so it was that those tinajas de lemita lasted throughout the years, for any leak could be stopped instantly, should one happen, by an application of warm resina and given sufficient time in which to harden.

When the people of Las Huertas were ordered to abandon their town in 1823, by order of the governor at Santa Fe (to save them from Navajo raids), those large jugs were left behind, or at least some of them were found therein by the children of the first settlers of Las Placitas, a dozen years later. The best of them were carried to Las Placitas and used for a time. But they were not needed there as they had been needed in Las Huertas. In the mountains just back of Las Placitas was the wonderful Ojo del Oso (Bear Spring), with such a force of water that it swept down the mountainside and rushed through the many ditches that supplied the houses first built at Las Placitas.

And so the art of making the tinaja of lemita was lost among the descendants of those sturdy founders of Las Huertas, and the last of those they left behind in their deserted town soon fell to pieces where they stood out in sun and rain. That such a tinaja was ever used as well as made by their people is known only to the very old ones yet living in Las Placitas.

SUBJECT: Mateo y Raquel

WPA: 5-5-49 #12

October 9, 1942

Words 2016

Sources of information: José Gurulé, Benino Archibeque, Conception Archibeque, Nina Montoya de Pearce. José Gurulé's father was a contemporary of Mateo, as were Benino Archibeque's maternal grandparents.

MATEO Y RAQUEL

Had it not been for the tragic fate of José María, the story of Mateo y Raquel would not have been remembered, nor would the story of his sufferings, nor of others of his class (los peones) who suffered wrongs and injustices as did José María, be remembered to this day by their descendants.

José María was held in bondage by Don José Leander Perea. A debt left by his father put him in bondage and kept him there, a debt José María's son would inherit because José María would never during his lifetime be able to pay that debt to his patrón. It was the privilege and the custom of the rich dons to see to it that such obligations grew rather than diminished. The law was on the side of the rich dons; in fact, they were a law unto themselves. They must have the labor of the poorer class (los peones) and they laid down all the rules of the game. The peón received five dollars a month—an average of about sixteen and two-thirds cents a day. His hours of labor were from sunup to dark, regardless of seasons. The sheepherders had no days off. The laborers on the rancho or at other jobs had Sundays off, providing there was no urgent work to be done. Food, of a kind, was furnished to the sheepherders wherever their flocks happened to be. The day laborers were given their midday meal. Many attached to the rancho was fed other meals as their presence was required there at all hours. The food given to the peones was inferior and in amounts just to keep them going. When the peón was ill or old, he was kicked out and forgotten.

But the thing that kept los peones in bondage for debt was the patrón's store. It was the law that the peones must buy what they needed from the patrón's store. It was the patrón's system to charge plenty for everything bought and to see that things were bought. It was the accounts at his store, just debts, that bound the poor to his sheep, his goats, and his fields, as well as to his wagon trains, which made their annual trip to Los Estados (the states).

José María knew well of the patrón's law regarding delinquent peones. He had often been an eyewitness to the lashings, beatings, and kickings dealt out not only to delinquents but to any others of the peons who had incurred the enmity of el mayoral (the foreman) or had failed to show the proper respect for him. Any peón who failed to report for duty promptly when called by el mayoral received a lashing; any peon who committed the offense twice was lashed without mercy. No reason was sufficient to cause a peón not to appear when called for duty. A peón dare not lag behind because he was tired. No peón dared to forget that el patrón had a store with things in it for him to buy and have added to his account.

Yet knowing all that, José María failed to report one morning when summoned. José María was not lazy; he merely remained at his house to do some work on his own plot of ground. He could not make a living for his family without his small crops. The sixteen and two-thirds cents a day, with payments on his debts subtracted, left his family with only about two dollars a month. They all must work if they were to live.

But no sooner had José María got into his work than his patrón's man was there to take him into the presence of el mayoral. The distance from Bernalillo to Las Placitas was but ten miles by the crooked old road. On the rancho grande of his patrón he faced el mayoral, and then came the lashing that José María knew he would receive—a lashing with the long, stinging whip across his back. Then José María was asked to declare aloud that he would not remain away again when called to work. For some reason José María refused to make that declaration. The lash was again applied with two-fold fury and in the presence of many of the peons who trembled and muttered "Diós mío!" El mayoral was making an example of poor old José María. After that, he was taken up in the Jemez Mountains to el patrón's big sheep camp. Morning found José María a deserter from his patrón's sheep camp.

José María knew the patrón's law concerning deserters. He knew all about his debt to his patrón and how his patrón held money far above the life of any peón. But he hated his patrón. All the peones hated and feared him. Perhaps in his hatred, rebellion, and longing to get even with his patrón, he did not stop to reason but just got up and ran, or so those who still remember his story say.

Secretly the word of his flight was taken to his wife and his son. They ran all the way to Bernalillo, for they well knew that José María could not escape. They knew el patrón would not permit him to escape.

Concerning those who fled to escape payment of their just debts, the law, the law of the rich dons, held that a warrant could be issued for the deserter and he could be arrested wherever found within the confines of the territory, or the land known as the department of New Mexico under Mexican rule, and could be brought back to his patrón to stand trial. As every peón was in dept to his patrón, that warrant covered any and all cases of desertion. Debts must be paid. It was considered a crime to try to beat a debt.

And so it was that José María was hunted down and dragged back to face trial. No self-respecting don would consider such a crime lightly. The whole system of making and keeping peones and preserving the rights of rich dons to become richer at the expense of the peones' bondage to them was at stake. The right of don to mete out justice as it would best serve himself and interest would never be questioned. There was the alcalde, one of the don's own handpicked men, to see that justice was done. José María was condemned to be hanged.

His wailing wife threw herself upon her knees, begged and pleaded for mercy, for her husband's life for the sake of his many children. She was answered not in words, but by rough treatment by men ordered to remove her bodily from the place. Her wailings were heard far and near but to no avail. The law of the dons was the law of the land. And so the body of José María was hanged upon a great cottonwood tree for all to see and take heed.

No sooner was José María dead than his young son, Mateo, aged about seventeen years, was ordered to take his father's place in bondage to el patrón and work out the debts of his father—and likewise buy from el patrón's store. And so started the tale of Mateo, in bondage for life to work out a debt he did not contract and to contract a debt that would enslave his own son, should he have one, and of course he would, for all self-respecting peones married and raised families. That was about the year 1836, ten years before the American occupation, which in no way affected the status of the peón until twenty-one years later.

When Mateo was about eighteen years of age, he was married to Raquel, whose family lived in Algodones. As was the custom of the day, Raquel was chosen for Mateo, and neither of them had a voice in the matter. Raquel was about fourteen years old and she was very industrious.

In time, Raquel had a small adobe house of her own built near the adobe house of Mateo's mother, and Raquel shared the land José María had chosen for his family when Las Placitas was being settled.

In time, babies came to Mateo and Raquel. As was the custom, Raquel's mother helped out by taking one of the older, if not the oldest one, for her own. (This custom may have come from the Indians.) This custom prevails in Las Placitas to this day.

When his family was young, Mateo became one of the hundreds of sheepherders for el patrón, who had countless thousands of sheep and goats. He had no time to help his wife plant or harvest and his sixteen and two-thirds cents a day, or approximately that, was of no help to her, for it was always applied to Mateo's debt or the debt of his father. During his life, Mateo never had even one cent in his hand that he earned from his patrón; and that was contrary to the words of the contract that bound him to the patrón's service. By the terms of that contract, he was to receive a percent of his earnings in money, each month.

Mateo wished to buy a lamb from his patrón. The privilege was denied because he had not enough money to pay for it. There were weak lambs in the herd that dropped behind. Mateo could not care for one and keep it as his own. Many lambs were left without mothers. No peón might rescue and care for them. They must be left to die. El patrón could not allow (if he could prevent it) any peón to accumulate a herd of his own. That herd might in time free the peón from debt. That would menace the institution of peonage.

But Raquel knew her needs and if Mateo could not meet them, she would meet them herself. Her children needed milk, they needed more clothing, they needed more tewas (moccasins), they needed more fat, they needed more bedding, which the skins of the goats supplied. So Raquel set to work to acquire goats, for above everything else, her children needed goat milk and the cheese made from it. Early and late she knelt on her smooth mud floor, grinding her blue corn into flour. Blue corn and goat milk made atole. Atole was good for young and old alike. At San Felipe she could exchange the blue flour and some wheat for goats. So her grinding stones ground on and on until her tinajas were filled. One at a time she carried them on her head to San Felipe and soon she had a few goats of her own. In another year, those few would become multiplied. In another year she would grind more blue corn and raise more wheat to trade to the San Felipe Indians for goats or kids. And year after year,

Raquel slaved to add to her small herd of goats. And each year the increase of kids brought numbers to her flock. Two of her small boys tended them where other small boys cared for their small flocks. In spite of patrónes, the mothers were slowly building up small flocks of goats and sheep.

With the help of the women, the men, by means of their wits, added to the community herd, where each owner of the herds that made up the community herd took turns at tending it. Of course there were men, and more than a few, in those old days in Las Placitas, who were able to buy a few goats and sheep each year, and their increase eventually gave them a good herd. But most of the herds were started by the women.

And while Raquel reared and provided for her large family, and built up a small flock of goats that would supply her family needs, Mateo was bound to his patrón's herds. Instead of his debt to his patrón diminishing as time went by and his five dollars a months applied in whole on it, the debt had increased so amazingly that the sum bewildered poor Mateo, and he well knew that never in his lifetime nor the lifetime of his oldest son, would the debt be paid.

And while Mateo struggled on, hopelessly bound to a debt and his patrón's sheep, Raquel carried on at home, struggling to feed, clothe, and teach her children. She taught them how to turn raw materials into necessary things, which made their existence possible.

In the summers, late spring, and early autumn, the sheep were herded throughout the bear-infested Jemez Mountains. Always Mateo and the other herders were on the lookout for the dangerous animals. There was little they could do except move the herd from place to place in an effort to elude the bear.

The winters were spent on the range in the vicinity of El Río Puerco, near the Navajo country. There the snows were heavy and the blizzards fierce, but soon the snows melted away and the blizzards died down and the sheep could feed until the snow again fell and another cold wind raged. And while the snow lay deep on the range the herd went hungry. And while the deep, cold snows lay over the range, sheep and sometimes herders froze to death. Herders were often forced to get down with the sheep and keep close to them to keep themselves alive during a fierce snowstorm, when neither man nor beast could move. And whenever the snow was gone, there were the menacing Navajoes, who never hesitated to shoot an arrows into the hearts of herders who ventured to interfere with their thievery. Often on the cold winter nights, the herders were forced to forego the warming pleasure of a campfire for fear of betraying their whereabouts to the Navajoes. All winter long Mateo and his companions had nothing to eat but meat and corn. There was never a cheering, hot drink for them, on that great sweep of cold land. But there were many days when the warm sunshine cheered them and the clear air gave them long-range vision to see the Navajo should he approach, and gave them time to hide themselves in arroyos or among the flock, well towards the center, for the Navajo took his prizes from the outer herd.

Then one summer Mateo became very ill. He could not work. His pay was cut off and he was told to get out. And as all the curandera's yerbas failed to cure him, he was ordered to send his son Juan to take his place and assume the just debt to the patrón, and likewise add to the account at the store.

And so it was poor Mateo, broken in health stayed at home and helped with the planting and harvesting, and helped tend the flock of sheep and goats that Raquel and her children had accumulated, while his son Juan went away to spend his youth and the best part of his manhood in the service of the patrón, or so they thought. But fate had it otherwise mapped out for Juan.

Late in the fall, before going with the herd to the range bordering the Navajo country, Juan came home to get fixed up for the winter. His mother helped him with his clothes just as she had helped his father.

She made his calzones of deerskin, well cured. But they were in no way made like the dressup ones worn by men in Las Placitas. Raquel cut them in one piece and just large enough around the waist for Juan to get into. The legs were made by slitting the skin upward in the middle at the bottom, and then sewing the slit edges together to form legs. She sewed them with correa and used a punch with which to do it. The legs were made skintight and came to just under the knee. A broad sash was made of the skin and attached to the waist line and then tied tightly around the waist. Juan's camisa (shirt) was pulled down over it. There was no opening whatever in the calzones. Juan wore tewas (moccasins) made of deerskin and with tough buffalo hide soles sewed on with stout correa (leather string). Over his tewas he wore what he called snowshoes. They were made of sheepskin, woolly side in. They were shaped just like a sack and cut high to reach his knees. They were folded well about his legs then wrapped about from knee to ankle with a binding made of the amole leaves, which they called palmito. The leaves were tied end to end to secure the length. A wrapping of them kept the water from soaking into the snowshoe top. Then a seam was taken in the middle of the part that covered the tewa. It ran from the toe to the ankle and made the shoe fit. It held the shoe firmly in place and close to the tewa and thus kept the herder's feet warm. Around his shoulders Juan wore a serape woven from the wool of a goat and woven long and wide enough to serve him in the coldest of weather. It was bound to his body at the waistline with a heavy piece of correa. Then it was lifted up and pulled around his shoulders, folded crosswise across the front and the ends tucked securely under the serape where it covered the tops of his arms and his shoulders. There it stayed and kept him warm. When he needed to use his hands, he unfolded the serape, let it fall about his hips like a skirt, for it could not come loose from his waist. Then Juan wore a gorra (cap). It was made of sheepskin, woolly side out. It was cut in three pieces. The front piece, which covered the front part of the head from temple to temple, was cut deep enough to fold in front and give two thicknesses, to be pulled down in the severest of weather. The other two pieces, which would be sewed together in the back, were cut with a full sweeping skirt that would fall around the shoulders and thus prevent snow, rain, or cold from chilling the neck or shoulders. In shape it resembled the hood worn in the long ago days of the men in armor. And thus arrayed, Juan went forth to tend his patrón's sheep on the cold plains of the Río Puerco.

It was a cold and hard winter. Icy winds froze the snow. Sheep froze in the tracks, and the herders struggled to keep moving. Some sheep strayed; herders tried vainly to drive them back to the herd. Juan was one of those. When the storm had passed, Juan was found frozen to death. Word of his death was carried to Mateo and Raquel many weeks afterwards.

And then in 1867 came the abolition of the crime of peonage. But even so the patrón forced labor from those who were in his honest debt. But things grew better for the once-bonded servants. Money could be paid on debts, as much or as little as they could manage. And enforced buying at the store of the patrón ceased until finally the peón was no more.

SUBJECT: La Orquesta Antigua
WPA: 5-5-49 #47
October 23, 1942
Words 1604
Sources of information: José Gurulé, Benino Archibeque, Conception
Archibeque, Ferminia Durán. José Gurulé was a descendant of the harp;
maker, Benino Archibeque was a descendant of the guitar maker. Conception
Archibeque was a descendant of Francisco Gonzales one of the early
musicians, and Ferminia Durán was a descendant of the flute maker.

LA ORQUESTA ANTIGUA
(The Old Orchestra)

There was never a time in the days of long ago when the people of old Las
Huertas and Las Placitas did not have their music. Without music a fiesta would
have been but an occasion to feast and drink all the wine they could contain and
perhaps more. But music they had aplenty. La orquesta made music for los
bailes (the dances). Without dances life would have been a drab and monoto-
nous affair, for bailes were their only happy recreation in those old days.

In those olden times, the men who furnished the music for the merry-
making were considered men of importance. Talented artists they were and
skilled, for they must make the instruments upon which they played. And
merry men they had to be, with wit and voices for song, and tireless players
and singers they had to be to carry on till the break of day or high noon,
depending upon the whims of the dancers. And all that was without pay,
unless plenty of wine could be considered compensation.

It was well over one hundred years ago that Casimiro and his brother
Felipe, skilled makers and players of stringed instruments, delighted the villagers with their music. Valentino played with them upon the flute he made
himself, and Andrés accompanied them upon his big drum, and thus com-

pleted that orquesta of long ago that made many, many happy hours for the great-grandfathers of those who are now grandparents in Las Placitas.

Casimiro made his guitarra (guitar) upon which he played. Of all the instruments they made in those days, the guitar was the most difficult to make. It was a matter of expertly cutting and fitting together thirteen pieces of select- ed encino (oak), and of making good strings, and strong keys upon which to wind them.

So it was that Casimiro went to the mountains to fetch the oak that would be suitable for the making of his precious guitarra. Besides the encino he needed nervio (tendons) from the backbone of an animal, properly treated, to make his strings and he needed gluten (glue) with which to glue the parts of the guitarra together. No wooden pegs were used to put that guitar of long ago together. That gluten was made by boiling a certain quantity of cured oxhide down until it was dissolved into a substance that looked very much like jelly, though it was a milky color. It made a long-lasting glue.

With his sharp hacheta (little stone axe) Casimiro split and shaped his oak. The top and the bottom of the guitarra were cut exactly the same and in very much the same shape as is the modern guitar. From end to end it meas- ured eighteen inches. At the widest point, it was about nine inches. A hole about an inch and a quarter in diameter was made in the top of the guitarra a little below the center of the top and directly in the middle. Spaced directly between that hole and the end of the upper part of the instrument was affixed the wooden piece that would anchor the strings. That piece was just the length as the narrowest width of the top. It was glued in its place. The neck of the guitarra was about two-thirds of an inch thick and as wide as the hole made in the top of the guitarra. It was around fourteen inches long and extended beyond the body of the instrument about half its length. At the end was fas- tened the small V-shaped piece of oak, into which holes had been drilled to hold the keys that would hold and adjust the free ends of the strings. It was put onto the neck at an angle, pointing downward.

The most difficult of all the work was to fit the top and the bottom into shape. For that, a width and length of oak was cut very thin, around three and half inches wide. The length was cut into eight pieces and placed in water to soak. There it remained until the oak was so pliable that it could be put into any shape. With those wet pieces Casimiro made that part of the instrument that formed the hollow inside of it and joined the top and the bottom of the guitarra. The wet pieces were shaped to conform to the outline of the top and bottom and end; each piece was pressed tightly together, and all were tied into shape and left to dry. Then they were glued together, the top and bottom were glued firmly to the dry perfected pieces thus joined and there was the body of the guitarra. The neck was glued in place on the top part of the instrument. The keys were cut from oak, the strings were made fast to the board made for them, and the keys fixed them in place and held them firmly. And then Casimiro had his guitarra ready for the baile.

His brother Felipe made a good arpa. The frame he made of oak—an open frame it was, and put together with wooden pegs. It was cut in the shape of a triangle. The base, or stand, was about eighteen inches long, around eight inches wide, and about an inch thick. The upright was about thirty inches high, about four inches wide, and around an inch in thickness. Another piece of oak about half that width and about an inch thick fastened the top of the upright and the base, slanting diagonally. Thus the triangle was formed. The holes for the strings of the arpa (harp) were made in the center along the length of the base and at equal distances apart. There were usually twelve strings on the arpa. Along the center, lengthwise, of the hypotenuse, holes were made to correspond with the ones along the base. Keys were made for the upper holes. The strings were made of nervio, and each string was of different length, growing shorter and shorter as they approached the base. Very sweet music came from la arpa when Felipe played upon it as he squatted upon the old adobe floors, or outside the house where the ground was clean swept. The arpa was an indispensable piece in the orguesta antiguo and one of the oldest. Nimble fingers upon an arpa cheered many a heavy heart in the days of long ago.

The memory of a certain Valentino lives because of his flute. He made it of a piece of cane. In those old days every household had its little patch of cane. He called the piece of which he made his flute a caña. La flauta (the flute) was about ten inches long and had holes cut at intervals down the surface along the length at the top, and it contained a mouthpiece cut to suit the player's own notion. Valentino knew how to make sweet music on his flute. The flute was the easiest of all the old instruments to make, providing the maker knew how and where to place the holes. It blended in with the music of the guitarra and the arpa in the music for los bailes.

And there was Andrés, who knew better than all the others in those old days how to make music with his drum. He made a big drum. It measured about two feet in diameter and was about twenty inches high. It was made of a section of a pine tree log. The log was hollowed out until there remained a wall of not more than an inch thick. Before the hollowing out process was finished, the log was sanded and smoothed down until it was made with a uniform circumference from top to bottom. Andrés cured the deerskins that he used to cover the open ends of his drum. They must be made tough and durable to stand the stretching and the poundings they would get. When he cut out the skin to cover the ends of the drum, he cut them long enough to reach down each side to one third of the distance, which left a third of the drum's side uncovered—that is around the middle. About halfway between the drum head and the edge of the skin, he made holes all around the skin about three inches apart. When the skins were put in their permanent position on the heads, the holes were so arranged that the correa (leather lacing) would run slantwise, always assuming V shapes whether running up or down. Andrés played upon his drum with his hands. His muffled beats made an alluring accompaniment to the music of the guitar, the harp, and the flute, and added that barbaric touch, which the people of those old days loved, just as their descendants love it today. And to this day, the drum is a part of the home orchestras that play for los bailes in Las Placitas.

SUBJECT: La Cosecha de Maíz (The Harvest of Corn)
WPA: 5-5-49 #27
November 6, 1942
Words 1560
Sources of information: José Gurulé, Benino Archibeque, Patricio Gallegos.

LA COSECHA DE MAÍZ
(The Harvest of Corn)

In Las Placitas in the days of long ago, the sight of fields of waving caña de maíz (corn stalks) cheered the hearts of the people, young and old, and gave cause for much prayers and thanksgiving. Especially were there prayers and rejoicing when the waving corn had turned dry and brown and was heaped high in safe places after the harvest. San Antonio, guardian of El San Antonio de Las Huertas Grant—their own land grant—had been good to them and saved their corn from the drough and from the thieving Navajo.

Truly it was a time of rejoicing, for the maíz, the blue Indian corn, was the life-sustaining food of those old days. Without it they would have perished. It was good for infants, for the growing children, and for the men and the women who labored throughout the year to keep nourishing food in their houses. They must so process that corn that it might sustain them from harvest to harvest. That meant much work for everyone, but it was a festive time also, the time of wine making. The new wine, the newly roasted maiz meant feasting and bailes. The relaxation and merrymaking after the strenuous plowing, planting, irrigation, hoeing, harvesting.

For the drying of the corn, much wood must be gathered. It required many days to pile up enough to heat el horno (the outdoor oven) and to prepare properly el tajo (the trench). As for the corn, it needed only to be heaped up in handy places for those who were to roast the corn, which must be done with great haste lest the effectiveness of horno y tajo be lost.

So the outdoor oven was cleaned and the little hole that was the chimney was put in place. Small sticks and dry brush was placed on the oven floor. When the fire blazed, more and more wood was piled on, and yet more and more, with larger sticks being used as the pile grew. At length when the oven was filled with wood and the flames rising upward, it was left to heat to the proper temperature, which would be indicated by the flame-red color of the plastered wall inside the oven.

In the roasting of the corn, the trench was as important as the oven. More corn could be roasted with one good fire, though the corn thus roasted was not so good as that put into the oven. Where outdoor ovens were small, el tajo was necessary. The length, width, and depth of the trench depended upon the amount of corn to be put into it. The earth removed from it was piled up along the tajo as it was being dug, and care was taken that it remained there. When el tajo was considered of the proper size for the heap of corn that would be roasted in it, the length of the trench was covered with dry brush, with leaves and small sticks at the bottom. Then a layer of larger sticks and more brush was laid upon that, another layer and another, the wood used being heavier and thicker and longer as the pile mounted up. When there was heavy wood to some height—that determined by the size of the trench—the fire was left to burn, with watchers to see that the embers gathered and sank to the bottom of the tajo. The corn to be roasted in the trench was piled along the length of the trench that it might be placed with no loss of time. Also large tinajas of water were placed alongside the corn. At each end of the trench, the place was left clear at a midway point or so. Those clear places were where the surplus embers and smoldering wood and excess ashes would be removed from the trench when the time was ready.

If there were not enough members of a family to attend to the work of roasting the corn, families combined and helped each other, for it took a small force of helpers when corn was placed in the trench and the greatest factor in the success of this method of roasting corn was haste.

While the fire in the trench was being guarded, the changing color of the inside plaster of the oven was watched. When it glowed red, the shovel made of oak or pine was brought out and hastily the oven was scraped clean of ashes. The oven was made ready to receive las espigas (ears of corn). Las hogas (the shucks) of the corn and el cabello (the corn silk) were left just as they were when the corn was gathered. Las espigas were laid as thickly as was practical for roasting, all over the oven floor, leaving only enough space for a huge tinaja of water, or plenty to supply the needed moisture for the perfect roasting of the corn inside the shuck. When the oven had enough ears in it, the wooden door to the oven was wrapped in a thickness of wet cloth, fitted tightly against the outside of the opening in the oven, and fixed there firmly with a large stone. There it was to remain for the full period of twenty-four hours.

The oven process of roasting corn was all a very simple procedure compared to work involved in making and roasting it in a trench. With the trench all must be ready to do their part with absolutely no waste of time. The trench was cleared of all except the red embers considered sufficient to do the roasting. Then it was, "Ready, go!" Las espigas were laid in the hot trench by some, others dashed water over the corn the instant it was in place from the handy tinajas, while yet others pushed the earth back into the space over the corn and tamped it smoothly, leaving no places open. Thus, at almost the same instant without any loss of heat, the trench was filled and covered, to remain untouched for twenty-four hours.

And while the corn roasted in the oven and in the trench, long slender poles were set up, lengthwise, and high enough from the ground to keep the menacing ratones (rats) and puerco espins (porcupines) from doing too much damage to the corn, which would be dried there. Plenty of correa (strings of the leaves of the leather) and palma (strings made by shredding the amole plant) were needed to tie the corn to the wooden line.

The sun told the time when the oven and the trench should be opened. The roasted corn was taken out and the work of preparing it for the drying was on. The husks were peeled back and suspended from the poles by pieces of correa or palma. Pole after pole was loaded with the corn where it would remain until it was thoroughly dried. Neither rain nor snow could damage it after it had been roasted. And when the corn was dry, it was taken from the poles and stored. Some had the husks removed, and some was left with the husks by which it would be tied to vigas (beams supporting the roofs) to keep it ready for use throughout the long winters. Much corn was stored in the adobe bins built along the inner walls of the kitchen. There it was safe, as well as handy for the use of the family, for it was eaten in large quantities without further preparation. An ear or two was the only food taken by the shepherds, or the wood hauler, or hunters, to refresh them at midday. Mostly it was the lunch of all the children.

One of the most popular dishes of that long-ago day was chicos (little or small). Chicos was the name for the kernels of corn after they were removed from las tusas (the cobs). They were cooked with meat and were one of the sustaining foods of the day. To this day in Las Placitas, the descendants of those early people make chicos and enjoy them as did their ancestors. Also the ears of roasted corn are enjoyed and considered a light refreshment at any hour. The most nourishing and life-giving food for the children was made of this roasted corn (which is the blue or pueblo corn). Ground into a meal, cooked well, and served with goat milk, it was called atole, a highly nutritious food for young and old alike that is relished to this day in Las Placitas.

And so it was that corn made a sturdy race in those long-ago days, and the men and the women survived to great ages in spite of the privations, the hardships, and the unceasing labor, their heritage, from which there was no escape a century and more ago.

APPENDIX

(BATCHEN)

SUBJECT: Juan of Tecolote
WPA: 5-5-49 #55
September 25, 1940
Words 8005
Sources of information: José L.A. Gurulé, Rumaldita Gurulé, Pedro Gurulé, Catalina Gurulé, Benino Archibeque, Conception Gurulé, Patricio Gallegos, Lucas Salazar.

JUAN OF TECOLOTE

A mile north of Ojo de la Casa in Cañón de Las Huertas are still to be seen the ruins of the Tecolote (Indian name for owl) of long ago. Tecolote is still inhabited and on the maps, but the old Tecolote is gone along with old Las Huertas, and nothing but ruins remain to tell the tale of the long-ago town except the stories of their people, which live only in the memories of the older living generation who had forefathers there. It is their belief that the two towns were settled about the same time. That date is about 1740. Old records give the names of those who settled Las Huertas, and the town before Las Huertas, which was San José; but only tradition tells of the probable settlers of Tecolote, and it might be that Tecolote anti-dated the settlement of San José.

Tradition says there was no Sandía Pueblo when San José was settled in 1740. The historian Coan says that Sandía Pueblo was abandoned in 1680 and that some of the people went to settle in the Moqui Country. He also says that they returned and rebuilt the pueblo in 1748. But there is nothing said of what became of the Sandía Indians who did not go to the Moqui Country. So the tradition of this region is that the people who settled Tecolote may have been Sandía Indians. At least, Juan, who did not know exactly from where his people came, said they might have been Sandías. Long before Las Placitas was settled by the present inhabitants, the whole place showed unmistakable signs of having been occupied by Indians, and those signs and symbols are still there. Moreover, the legends of the buried treasure at Las Placitas and at Sandía are similar.

Juan of Tecolote, whose last name was Salazar, married Petra Gurulé, a maiden born in Algodones not long after Las Huertas was abandoned in 1823. She was an aunt of José Librado Arón Gurulé. She married Juan of Tecolote when she was yet a child and they dwelled alone in the Cañón de Las Huertas, for those were the days before Ojo de la Casa was settled.

In those days there were good springs at Tecolote and Juan was an industrious farmer. He also had herds of sheep and goats. But then pasturage was abundant in the cañón and he need not take his flocks so far from his house except in dry years.

In time Las Placitas became a sizable village and some families returned to rebuild their homes at Las Huertas. All of them raised wheat. Wheat must be ground into flour; that required a molino (mill). Juan knew how to build one, he had oxen with which to drive it. Besides, all the people, even as far as Tejón, could bring their wheat to him to grind for them instead of carrying it to San Felipe and trading it for meal or flour, or for whatever else they might offer.

And so it was that Juan built a mill. Who helped to construct that primitive molino is not known but it served the people for many years. The huge grinding stones used in it have been seen by many of the people now living in Ojo de la Casa and Las Placitas.

The materials for the project were assembled. From the higher mountains the necessary pine timbers were dragged by oxen. After they were on the ground, they were dried, then the bark taken from them and most hewn into planks. Even at that day, the sharp stone axe was used to advantage when hewing the large timbers into boards. A log about ten feet in length was left intact.

Two wooden wheels were needed. They were fashioned of tough oak. A long oak pole some five or six inches in diameter was used. One wheel was three feet in diameter, about six inches thick, and the plies of oak were put together with wooden pins. A hole five or six inches in diameter, or rather a hole through which the oak pole could be run, was made in the very center of the wheel. Around the circumference a groove was cut, wide enough to hold a thick, four-inch belt made of buffalo hide. The second wheel was greater in circumference by at least one foot. It was made up of a heavy hub joined to a rim, proportionately heavy, by thick, wide treadles. One end of the hub was constructed to operate the four-inch belt placed in a groove. The hole through the hub was drilled in such a manner as to allow the axle to stand perpendicular, yet to have the wheel at an angle of about forty-five degrees. This axle was of tough oak, one end of it dressed to a sharp point that it could be driven far enough into the ground to remain firm while the wheel was in motion. Wooden pins held the hub in place on this axle.

Skill was required to shape and dress the stones needed for grinders. They must be large, hard stones, which approximated eight feet in circumference when perfectly rounded. There were two of them; the bottom one must be at least six inches thick, the top one was made cone-shape, graduated from two inches at the outer edge to six, where a hole was drilled in the exact center of the stone. This hole was made to encircle the oak pole, which was to turn it round and round. The underneath stone had a somewhat larger hole in the center, that the pole would be cleared, as it was a stationary stone. These stones were rubbed and polished with harder stones until they were smooth and even, for they must fit very closely together, face to face.

This process of grinding wheat into flour required a funnel, through which the wheat must drop through the outer edge of the hole drilled into the top stone and which found its way in between the stones as the top one was moved irregularly about in a circular motion. This top stone was secured to the pole by means of wooden pins. Then sieves were required to give certain refining to the ground mixture, as well as to separate the grains from the hulls. This funnel and the sieves were made of toughened hides. The sieves, after they were perforated with the required holes, were sewed to wooden frames with correa (flexible leather string).

The housing was made of pine logs, boards, and adobe mud plaster. Four huge logs were deeply planted in the ground. They projected upward about eleven feet. This constituted the foundation and skeleton of the house, which was some ten feet square. Then logs were notched and carefully fitted together and strengthened by wooden pins at a point five feet above the ground level. These held the four corners firmly together and provided a base for a wooden floor upon which the stones were to rest. The tops of the poles were treated to the same method of joining together, then a roof was added. All sides were boarded up with the boards hewn from the logs; but one side contained a door. The door had no hinges but was held in place by wooden pins, removable from the outside. A hole was made in the very center of the floor and in direct line with the holes of the stones, now set one upon the other in the center of the floor. The tough oak pole was now pulled through an unfinished place in the center of the roof and guided through holes made for it.

Underneath the housing a thick log had been laid prone and half buried. A hole was dug into it large enough to make a snug and sufficiently deep fitting for the oak pole, but where it could run, or turn easily. Over this hole the large wooden wheel made with the hole in the center was placed, so that the two holes came together. The oak pole was put through these and grounded in the log. Wooden pins held it firmly to the wooden wheel so that it might revolve with the wheel. The upper stone was likewise clamped to the pole, and the rotation of the wheel below also set the top stone in motion. Just clearing the housing at one side, the larger wooden wheel was set. A thick, sturdy oak supported it in its slantwise position. In that position it must support the weight of an ox borne by its front feet.

Now another pole was planted in a place near the wheel that would be fairly in line with the hub of the wheel and back of it. To this pole was hung an open sack of grain and also the ox was tied to the pole with a leather strap so short that the animal's front feet were kept on the treadles.

The walls and floor were plastered with a thin coat of adobe mud, put on thinly that it would stick to the boards. Over this, when it had completely dried, was spread a coat of yeso (gypsum), of which there was an abundance one mile east of Tecolote in Tejón Canyon. This made the housing clean for the reception of the ground wheat.

When the molino was completed, Juan invited the men round about him to bring their wheat to him. He would take a percent of it in pay for the flour, which he would deliver to them. The amount of this toll was not known, but the prevailing toll in the Las Placitas region now is, and has been since the oldest can remember, one part out of every five. It was probable, they said, that this twenty percent, or one part out of every five, was established in that long-ago day by Juan de Tecolote.

Now to run the molino. A sack made of hide, and therefore easily adjusted to any position, was filled and the bottom of it attached to the ceiling at a certain distance from the center. The bag was much smaller at one end than at the other. The small end was drawn over until it fitted into the rigid funnel. They came together at such an angle that there was not a free dropping of the grain. Then a pin projecting from the center pole at just one side struck the bag just above the funnel as it turned round and round. Thus, the grain was kept pouring into the funnel and on down through the hole and into the stones.

The tough belt was now put into the grooves of the two wheels that were made to receive it. The feed bag was ready, the ox was drawn up until its front feet rested on the treadle nearest the ground, and hastily the animal was tied in that position, for no sooner had his feet touched that special treadle until it moved down and the animal was forced to fumble for a footing on the one brought in front of him. As his feet came down on that one, it moved on and he tried for the next. Hitting that one, it swung off and he floundered for the next one—and so on. Thus the wheel was turned, and as it turned, it set the belt moving, which turned the other wooden wheel and the pole and in like manner the top stone was set in motion; the grain spilled through the funnel, and the stones crushed the hulls from it, and in time it was pushed from between the stones to the floor. When there was a sufficiency of it on the floor, the door was taken out and the crushed wheat removed and placed in large tinajas. Now it was ready for the coarser of the sieves. This separated the wheat from the chaff. The wheat was put through other sieves until it was considered a finished flour. Naturally it was necessarily coarse. It was carried from the molino in tinajas.

This mill powered by oxen took heavy toll on the animals. Confined in one position, with front feet above the ground and continuously striking for a hold upon the moving treadles, soon wore them out and they were of a consequence, short lived. Many of them died before they could be dragged from the treadles.

In later days when burros were cheaper, they were used to power the molino. For some reason, they did not wear out so readily. But even so, burros were valuable and indispensable property in those days. And Juan decided to make over his molino to run it by water power. Somewhere in the Jemez Mountains he saw one powered by water.

It was in the year 1868 that Juan removed the two wooden wheels and everything connected with them from his molino, and then set about the task of modernizing it. In those old days water flowed throughout the seasons in Arroyo de Las Huertas Cañón. At a place along the arroyo above his mill, Juan engineered a ditch in which he would bring water to run his molino. The ditch ended in a narrow outlet about eight feet from it.

He then excavated a much deeper and wider ditch underneath the housing and extended it far beyond to a lower place where the water coming through it might return to the arroyo. This was some distance below the point where he dug the ditch to carry the water to the mill.

A wheel with wide paddles was required now. Juan made it about nine feet in circumference. The paddles were set into the hub slantwise so that the full force of the water might turn them freely. As in the old mill, a thick log was laid prone under the housing, but now it was half buried in the ditch. There was also a hole in it in line with the one in the floor of the mill. The new wheel was laid flat on top of this log; the hole in the log matched with the hole through the hub. Now a new and much longer oak pole was started downward from the roof, threaded through the holes in the stone grinders, the hole in the floor of the molino, through the hub of the new wheel, and grounded in the hole in the log underneath. Then the proper connections were made by plac-ing wooden pins through the pole and into the parts to be moved by it.

Juan hollowed out a log just wide enough to connect with the narrow mouth of the first part of the ditch. It was secured in its place by heavy stones. It was made to slant downward at a sharp angle where it ended just short of the slanting paddle, which was in position to receive the force of water from the log that was to set the wheel in motion. As the paddle moved, the next one came under the water's driving force and so on, moving the hub and the oak pole, which set the grinder to work. Juan's new molino with its smoother motion and quicker action was a success. He was able to handle more wheat in a given time. His molino became a popular meeting place for more than small local wheat growers. Juan's just toll filled his own adobe wheat bins to overflowing. He was rated a successful businessman.

But this molino was not the only public service offered by Juan of Tecolote. He also built and operated la machucadora, which was a press for the extraction of syrup from cane.

In those long-ago days, what sweetening the household possessed, they must grow themselves. So there was a patch of sugar cane somewhere on each family's land. Securing the syrup from the cane pulp was more than a one-man job; therefore, there was a demand for the machucadora of Juan, for he and his son were always on hand should more help be needed.

This machucadora was constructed of one long log of immense girth and three stout poles not less than twenty feet long and eight inches in diameter and one tough, forked pole at least fourteen inches in diameter. The length of this pole depended upon the height of the press, or machucadora. The huge log was cut into two pieces. The shorter one, about eight feet, was hollowed out to within some eight inches of one of the ends. This end now became the bottom off a barrel. Certain-sized holes, about four in number, were drilled at the bot-tom of this barrel to allow the syrup to ooze out as the cane pulp was pressed down. Another section of the log was hewn off and made perfectly flat at both ends. It measured about four feet and was shaped to fit into the barrel as a cork, but from a point about halfway up the cork, it was tapered toward the top. The barrel was set in place. The two long poles were firmly planted at one side of it at about ten inches apart. These poles were set so deeply into the ground as to defy ordinary force to shake them. On the opposite side of the barrel the forked pole was planted at just the point where a lever laid in the angle of the fork would extend across the top of the barrel and on between the two upright poles, which would hold it in line as it was moved upward and down. One of the long poles became the lever. It was held loosely in the forked pole by strips of leather, but in a manner that gave the lever plenty of play.

The remainder of the huge log was split in two, lengthwise. Each section was hollowed out and these became troughs in which the cane was placed after it had been broken up into small pieces. Then it was pounded into pulp with wooden hammers.

When the pulp was ready it was removed from the troughs in large tinajas (in later years, copper kettles) and dumped into the barrel. When the barrel was piled high with the massed pulp, the top of the barrel was set in place: the lever was set angling from the crotch of the pole upward across the cork and into the grove between the two poles.

Two men climbed upon the barrel and set their feet on the lever, bracing themselves by holding to the upright poles. As they bore their weight down upon the lever, the cork beneath it began to lower. The men stamped down with all their force, they tramped up and down, they jumped up and down on the lever, forcing the cork downward into the barrel. The syrup trickled from the holes at the bottom of the barrel into the tinajas, and when these vessels were filled they were removed and others set in their places. This process went on until the cork was well into the barrel and the syrup no longer dripped from the holes. Then the men descended from the barrel, removed the lever, took out the cork, cleaned out the debris, and otherwise prepared to repeat the syrup-making process from the beginning.

And so it was that Juan earned many a pint of syrup, for which there was always a good price as barter. Juan's utility business prospered until about 1876, when drought forced a shutdown for his molino and a vacation for his machucadora. He never again set the wheels of his mill in motion. The cane press was operated for only a few seasons after that, when abundant rains once more caused crops to flourish in Cañón de Las Huertas, for by that time commercial "yellow" sugar was within the reach of all.

But Juan of Tecolote continued to be a good farmer and a successful sheep man. He was known throughout his region for the good condition of his herds and the fine quality of his melons. He always planted and cultivated his sandías (watermelons) himself, even after he was a very old man. He personally supervised his flocks until he was no longer able to totter up the mountain trails with his staff.

In the high tide of his youth, Juan constructed a crib far up in the Sandía, where the grass grew rank and wild animals were fierce. It was a fortress for himself and his young herders during the seasons when lack of water and pasturage in the lower areas forced them to the higher mountains with their flocks.

Alone Juan built that place of refuge. He cut down the huge timbers with his stone axes. He hewed them into even lengths of some ten feet, properly notched each one at the ends that the corners of the structure might be rendered unmovable. The fortress was built corn-crib fashion to a height of between four and five feet. The lower it was built, the more resistance it offered to furious attacks of disgruntled bears, for within the security of the crib, it did not become a matter of life or death to take a shot at one of the animals with the old muzzle-loading gun they called "virola amarilla." Should the bear be wounded, he could wreak his vengeance upon the unresponsive logs and not upon the poor marksman.

In his later years Juan of Tecolote spent many days and some nights with the young herders in his old refuge. Often he was in a reflective mood. Then it was that he told bits of wisdom to the young herders. Juan told the boys that every good herder studied the clouds, the birds, and the animals, for all of them were true friends of the herders and warned them of the coming of foul weather, that they might prevent suffering among their flocks, and even loss. That was, they could save their sheep and goats if they were wise enough to heed the warnings.

One warm spring afternoon Diego and Pedro were tending their patrón's sheep on a flat, grassy area several miles from the timber back of which rose the Sandía. Diego had cared for his patrón's sheep for many years. Pedro was a young and inexperienced tender of flocks. He contented himself in the warm sunshine just watching the sheep and chasing the wandering ones back to the herd by frightening them with his rattle (made by filling a calabaza vinatera with small stones, then closing the opening of it with a stick). A calabaza vinatera is a bottle-shaped gourd.

All the while clouds were gathering over the mountains. Diego eyed them anxiously. He was not to be deceived because the sun was shining. Then suddenly he cried out, "Hurry, hurry, get the sheep to the timber! It's the only thing. Quick! La vaca morena! (The black cow). We have no time to lose! The storm will catch us. Hurry, hurry!"

Pedro gazed at the bright sun. "Diego is loco. But I must do as he says. He is the boss!"

And so they started their sheep on the way to the timber as fast as they could go. But the snow caught them on the way and the sheep tried to turn back and scatter, for it was a fierce storm. Four inches of snow lay upon the ground before they reached the shelter of the timber.

"How did you know the storm was coming when the sun was shining?" Pedro demanded of Diego.

"Watch the clouds. Even when the sun shines, watch the sky. When you see the dark clouds getting together, see what form they take. If they run together in the form of a cow, that is the sign of a heavy storm. La vaca morena! Every sheepherder knows that sign."

Ojo de buey al pomiente	Bull's eye by the setting sun
Suelta tus yuntas y xente.	Leave your yoke and come on.

At the time of sunset when clouds were gathered around the sun, should a spot of color appear in any of the clouds it was called a bull's eye and for certain foretold rain within a short time.

Cuando cabra viejo rotosa lluvia copiosa (When the old goat begins to play, plenty of rain.) This was an old Indian prophesy. It is repeated in Las Placitas to this day.

No matter how warm the day nor how clear the sky, wise herders watched their flocks for warning of coming storms. If the sheep should suddenly break into a panic and set to crying out on the sunniest day, when there was not a cloud in the sky, beware, and start at once for a place of safety. A storm was on its way.

In Juan's day it was the belief that only the north wind brought death to the flock and the fruits in the spring. Should there be wind from any other direction at bedtime, there was no concern. Should the fruit be frozen in the morning, or any other damage done from freezing, then of a certain they knew that the wind had changed to the north and that it was the north wind that had brought the destruction.

To safeguard the ripening crops in the autumn and save them from undue exposure, watch the corn. If the husks showed brown markings on the inside, look out for early frosts.

If los gallos (the cocks) crow at off hours during the day or night, take heed, for certain there will be a change in weather.

When the coyotes send their bloodcurdling yip-yips into the night, it is not always an alarm that they are in pursuit of sheep and goats. Just as often it is their warning that heavy rains are due.

Not often does the águila (eagle) descend from his high places. But when he does swoop over lower areas and above mountain villages, it is to cry out a warning of storm. Rain always follows such visits.

The grullas (cranes) prove their worth to the farmer by warning him of coming frost. When they fly in great flocks on their journey to the south lands, they keep up such a clatter that everybody knows they are on their way and that they are warning farmers to look after and protect their ripening crops yet in the fields, lest the frost take them.

In the late winter those who wish to sow and reap during the coming year keep a sharp look out for the arrival of the golondrina (swallow). If swallows come at that time, it is to tell them that there will be an early spring.

Always watch the sunset for a forecast of the morrow. No matter how dreary nor cloudy nor rainy the day, if the sky suddenly clears in the west and the sets clear, the morrow will be a fair day.

Burros are dependable weather prophets. Whenever you see a burro kick up its heels and frolic about like a lamb, get ready for a rain. It never, never fails.

The tórtola (the turtle dove) was one bird that did not help the farmer nor the herder. It was too busy with its own affairs. But they all loved the tórtola and said, "pobre tórtola." Ages and ages ago when God talked to men and birds, he commanded that the tórtola rise very early each morning to receive God's blessing before the sun got up. On each and every morning, therefore, all the tórtolas were up in the cool hush of the shadowy mornings. But things do not all go right all the time. Tórtolas overslept and missed God's blessing. God had to punish them. When they slept until after sunrise, they forfeited God's blessing and could have not one drop of water until before sunrise the next morning. So without God's blessing and thirsty throughout the day, the tórtolas cooed sadly. A melancholy, dismal call it was, so full of sadness as from a breaking heart. Some also said their sad call was a mourning over the sins of mankind. All around Las Placitas and Ojo de la Casa and Tecolote the tórtolas send their plaintive calls out on the air to this day. A sad and mournful coo and the people pause and listen and say, "pobre tórtola" (poor tortola).

Then there was another bird, a dreaded and feared one. La lechuza, the bruja (witch), defied death and could not be killed. Just to listen to them as they moved sent shivers over these who heard them. They moved along together, hop, hop, hop, stop. Hop, hop, hop, stop. On and on with never a break in the sounds, and the pauses of their hop, hop, hop, stop.

They brought bad news, bad luck, and even death to those whose doorsteps they visited at dusk. Often when no one was about, they would rap on the door, and when someone came to answer the summons, they would utter a harsh, mocking laugh and go hopping away, all together in perfect time. Often they would gather about a house and all together laugh mockingly at those on the inside. In the long-ago days no one ever came outside to chase them away. No one dared. Inside each of those feathered creatures was a bruja come to do them harm. So the lechuzas (barn owls) were left to deride and taunt all they pleased, undisturbed, for those inside the houses were afraid. They never knew what curse a lechuza might lay upon them, and they never knew what terrible thing might happen to them after a visit of these lecuzas.

But there are always a few courageous ones. Probably only a few would dare challenge the lechuza. But there were a few who went out in those nights of long ago and sent arrows into their midst. They could hear that hop, hop, hop, stop, over and over until the noise vanished into the night. But never a dead lechuza did any of them ever find.

In later days, and even to this day, men have shot into their midst with guns. All they heard was that hop, hop, hop, stop, and so on until they were gone. But a search where they were revealed not one dead lechuza left behind. Either the lechuzas cannot be killed or they take their dead away with them, for no one has ever seen a dead lechuza.

An interesting story Juan of Tecolote left his people was a queer version of the Sodom and Gomorrah episode of the Bible.

Many, many years ago when the world was new there was a very wicked city. The people called it Gomorrah. At first the people were good and followed the laws of God. But they forgot God and did nothing but look for pleasure. They neglected their duties. The men paid no attention to their families and the women neglected their houses and children. Everybody just went looking for a good time. The men made so much wine that everybody had more than they could drink. But everybody did not want to drink wine and get drunk. Half of them wanted to dance. So all they did was dance while the others drank and drank. The town grew very sinful, as the people spent their days and nights in drinking and dancing. At last, God became very angry with them. He decided to punish them for their sins. One day he came and turned all those who danced into bears. And all those who did nothing but drink, he turned into hogs. And that is the way bears and hogs came into the world.

In the year 1860, a law was passed in the territory of New Mexico establishing a public or free compulsory school system. A tax was to be levied to pay the teachers a compensation amounting to the sum of fifty cents for each pupil taught. These schools were to be managed by the alcaldes of the local districts. They selected the teachers and removed them for causes they deemed sufficient. They inspected the school, saw to it that attendance of the pupils was enforced for the prescribed term of five months, which started on November first and ended April first. The schools were under the general supervision of the probate judges of the various counties.

The qualifications of the teachers were practically nil; many of the first ones could neither read nor write, not even could they sign their own names. Then the wealthy strenuously objected to paying for the education of the poor, and that matter was settled by making it obligatory upon the part of each family to pay the fifty cents for each pupil they sent to school. This worked out to the disadvantage of the teacher in many cases, as it became a matter of the parents who paid, to decide how much in quantity of the various commodities they used for pay to the teachers, constituted the equivalent of fifty cents. But in some instances the teachers were able to turn this method to their own account and often profited thereby.

Sometime after this compulsory school law passed, the alcaldes of the precincts of districts were somehow notified to appear in Santa Fe for special communications. It so happened that at the time that Juan of Tecolote was the alcalde of the Las Placitas district. Juan was greatly mystified by the summons and consequently suspicious of it. He decided to be prepared for any emergency. And while he was about such preparations he evidently decided to make them impressive. So it was that Juan of Tecolote made ready a fine suit of deerskins and an extra well-made pair of tewas. A war bonnet of eagle feathers finished his costume. He made the headdress himself. Juan was a very large man, and with his especially designed costume, and armed with his strong bow, he presented a somewhat menacing figure. However, he felt himself to be ready for any emergency. He had no faith in the gringos and Santa Fe was full of them. He took the precaution to see that his quiver was well filled with sharp, shining obsiniana (obsidian) arrows. But at the last moment he discovered that he yet lacked the courage to face the gringos in Santa Fe. So he persuaded his compadre Nicolás Gurulé to climb into his carreta and go along.

And thus Juan of Tecolote arrived in the City of the Holy Faith. They left their carreta in a safe place and walked about seeking the meeting place where Juan of Tecolote was told to present himself. In the quest, some gringos with pistols at their belts approached Juan and his companion. One look at their weapons and Juan of Tecolote prepared to send an arrow at the one who took a step nearer him. One of the gringos shook hands with him and Juan of Tecolote and invited them to eat and drink with them. So without further ado and without yet inquiring the object of Juan's summons to Santa Fe, they went with the gringos. After Juan had partaken of a drink, the like of which he had never tasted before, he boldly asked for more. He became merry; then as he imbibed more of it, he grew sullen, then lapsed into a dangerous mood. He threatened the gringos. Trouble seemed inevitable. Nicolás advised against plying Juan with more whiskey, for such was the drink that had conquered Juan of Tecolote. After that, the inert Juan, war bonnet and all, was loaded into the cart, and Nicolás started with him on the well-over two days' journey to Las Placitas, with Juan knowing nothing whatever of the business that summoned him to Santa Fe.

This tale of Juan of Tecolote has lived because Nicolás Gurulé could not keep it to himself. Juan was an unusually temperate man for his day. That fact added zest to the story, and in time, even Juan enjoyed the recounting of it.

It was not known just how or when Juan received notification of his new responsibilities relative to the school to be established under the compulsory public school law in his district. Though Juan was ranked as a smart man, he was illiterate. But he did have one outstanding qualification for his new job. He adhered religiously to the maxim "This is the IDEA: make the family mind," a much-repeated phrase by men of Juan's kind in that long-ago day. It applied to wives as well as the children. It used to be that obedience was counted a major virtue, and too, reverence for the old people was not only taught but insisted upon. This also was a main point with Juan of Tecolote. He believed in work. So all considered, Juan was not a bad choice for the duties of district school supervisor.

It was November 1864, when Juan finally got around to the hiring of a teacher. Being an Indian himself it is not strange that the honor of being the first teacher under the new law in Las Placitas should be El Indio Viejo, Señor Martínez of Galisteo. Galisteo was not so many miles from Las Placitas. It was an ancient pueblo visited by Oñate in 1598, and was on the old route to Las Vegas in the days of trade over the Santa Fe Trail.

It is more than likely that the old Indian never saw the inside of a book. He could not even write his own name. But he could and did teach his pupils to obey, honor their elders, to dance, sing, and pray, and he did know how to gather in his own pay. This he did with ceremony on each Saturday.

Part of his pay (and for those following him) was a room in which to live and to conduct his school. This caused him to make frequent moves as the families took their turns in "lending" him a room for the use of which he credited certain amounts as tuition paid.

Bare but clean were the rooms to accommodate teacher and pupils. Each child brought his own seat with him: a square of goat hide. If a pupil insisted upon a better seat, he brought a section of log. There were no books, slates, paper, nor pencils in those first schools. The first writing materials were smooth goat skins and charcoal; but those were not introduced until later when teachers could read and write.

The medium of teaching in the first schools was verse, taught by rote. Those verses possessed certain values to be impressed upon the growing minds. Juan Gutiérrez of Bernalillo, teacher number two hired by Juan of Tecolote, so impressed the verses he taught upon the minds of his pupils that some of them are remembered to this day.

This one taught the lesson of grim fortitude:

Todo fiel Christiano	Every faithful Christian
Está muy obligado	Is very much obliged
A comer asemita y	To eat bran bread
Aguantar callado	And suffer hunger in silence.

This one stimulated the imagination and taught love of beauty:

En una redoma de oro	In a flask of gold
Traigo almendras de cristal	I bring nuts of crystal
Para darle cuando llore	To give when it cries
Al pájero cardinal.	To the cardinal bird.

This verse was to teach love for family and home:

Cuando salí de mi Tierra	When I left my country
Voltié la cara llorando	I turned back my face crying
Y le dije a mi mamá	And I told my mother
Que lejos te voy dijando	How far behind I am leaving you
Le dije que volvería	I told her I would return
Pero no le dije cuando.	But I did not tell her when.

A spirit of reverence was taught by this verse:

Que lúcido resplendor	What a beautiful reflection
El de La Virgen María	Was on the Virgin's face
En aquel dichoso día	In that happy day
Quando nació el Redentor	When the Redeemer was born.

En el nombre del padre, del Hijo, del Espíritu Santo, Dios bendiga.

It was quoted by the elders and not by the children. It was the benediction "In the name of the Father, of the Son, of the Holy Ghost, God bless you." This benediction was repeated in every house in the morning, before the family scattered for the day's activities. The children knelt down before the mother; she made the sign of the cross and repeated the words. When the children entered the house at noon and in the evening, they came together, knelt before the mother, and she repeated the benediction. At any time a child met an elderly person in the road, the child knelt down before him and asked a benediction. This was one of the ways in which respect and reverence was taught to children for their aged ones.

In the first schools a household art was taught; and it was done as an aid to the busy and overburdened mothers. The children brought roasted blue corn and metates and manos to school, and the teacher gave them practical lessons in grinding their corn into meal. Each child also had his tinaja in which to carry his meal back home.

There seemed to be a sort of regulation dress for school children. (In those days the smaller children were considered the school class.) The uniform was a one-piece affair made to pull down over the head, and the bottom of it came midway between ankles and knees. It was made of the heavy unbleached cotton called manta, which was brought from Mexico or woven on the home looms. This single garment was all that was worn, except in the winter, then a serape was wrapped about the child.

Cleanliness was enforced to a degree. Children's hands must be clean and their fingernails must be short; long nails were not tolerated in those days. The first child to arrive at the school room in the morning was delegated the honor or duty of examining the hands and nails of each child as soon as school was called. The symbol of authority was the palmeta. It was a paddle, made round and with a handle, all carved from one piece of wood. It was used to hit the ends of all the dirty fingers and the too-long nails. This punishment was not trifling matter, nor was it meant to be. The other parts of the body might be as dirty as individual tastes dictated, but the hands must be scrupulously clean and the nails must be trimmed close.

In fact, punishments were never mild in those old days. The lash was applied to the backs of all children who failed in asking a benediction of the old people they met in the highways and byways. However, punishable offenses were few in that long-ago day.

So it was that Juan of Tecolote saw and directed the first steps of the public school system in Las Placitas. Juan lived to a ripe old age, about ninety-eight years. Until the last he personally cultivated his melons, until the last he feared the power of the witches and decorated himself with charms to save him from the evil ones.

In those last day Juan had an exceptionally fine crop of melons. One night he and the inmates of his house were awakened by the sounds of arguing voices outside the house. At once they were all alert. Juan's sight and hearing were keen to the last, they said, and it was no effort for him to catch the words from outside.

"I'll take the big ones, you take the little ones," came the high-pitched voice. "No, I'll take the big ones, you take the little ones," came the reply in a gruff voice. Over and over came that argument to the ears of those inside the house.

Juan said, "It's the witches. They are after us!"

By us he meant himself, his old wife, and a room full of great-grandchildren.

"The big ones mean me and you," he said to his wife, "the little ones mean our grandchildren. We must run and hide. Run for our lives and hide from the witches. But we're too old to run," he addressed his wife.

"We'll hide here, and the children can run."

So with caution, old Juan opened a little window and helped the children to escape, and they ran and ran until they came to some big rocks near to the foothills of the Sandías back of Juan's house. There they hid until dawn. Juan and his wife hid in the tapanco (a sort of built-in cupboard) and kept still as images until the darkness disappeared.

And what did Juan find when he crept forth and went outside his house? All of his melons, both big ones and little ones, were gone. Poor Juan.

Juan of Tecolote is buried in the little cemetery at Las Placitas.

OVER THE SANTA FE TRAIL IN 1868
A Trip from Las Placitas to Kansas City

It was in February 1868, that José Gurulé, then a lad of seventeen, went adventuring to Los Estados, which was the common name for Kansas City.

Esquípulo Romero, El Capitán of José Leander Perea's freighting outfit, came to Las Placitas to look over Perea's men for the purpose of selecting the most able-bodied to make the annual trek over the Santa Fe Trail to Kansas City with the many thousands of pounds of wool, and then to bring back the golden returns to Perea, who was at that time one of New Mexico's wealthy and powerful men and an outstanding political boss of Bernalillo County. In those days most of the men in the village were Perea's men, and his ledger showed most, if not all of them, to be in his debt, and therefore at his command.

Esquípulo could tell at a glance a trail-worthy man, a man who could keep going. Youth offered possibilities for these endurance trips, for that was exactly what they meant. There was husky Joaquín Trujillo, a strong and well-developed man, though he was but nineteen. He was told to get ready for duty. Juan Bautiste had proven his mettle on a previous trip, as had Nicolás Gurulé. Both were chosen. José Gurulé, son of Nicolás, had grit and was as tough as a pine knot. He wanted to go, and was taken. There were others picked from the men of Las Placitas, but who they were and why they were chosen has long been forgotten.

For the journey they needed clothing to stay on their backs for at least three months and shoes or tewas, whichever they could afford. And each man must take his own bed roll. These were usually serapes woven on the village loom, or home-woven Mexican blankets. The men's suits were mantas (drawers and shirt of coarse white cotton cloth) and underwear made of goat hair woven into cloth on the household looms. The serapes (men's shawls) served as coats. But the greatest preparations for the trip were in the cook-house of the José Leander Perea place in Bernalillo. There, tortillas were made by the hundreds and packed away. Bushels of dried peas were finely ground between stones to make "coffee!" Huge quantities of mutton and goat meat, onions, frijoles, black-eyed peas, and chili were amassed. All these supplies were put away in the rolling commissary from which Esquípulo would dispense certain amounts. Besides, each man was allotted a limited quantity of cube sugar and tobacco, which he carried with him.

At the appointed time some ten wagons from the Perea train rumbled through the village. Heavy wagons were loaded with wool, each of them drawn by five spans of oxen, for the roads were heavy with mud, especially on the plana (level ground). In February or early spring, when the wagons left for Los Estados, the road through the village and on toward Tejón was a popular route. The men from Las Placitas joined the procession as it passed through. The route was through Tejón Cañón, in all probability one of the ancient trails in New Mexico. In the region of San Pedro Mountains, which is a relatively short distance from Tejón Cañón, is the ruin of San Pedro Viejo, an early pueblo. Across the Rio Grande at Bernalillo is an old pueblo now being restored. Tejón Cañón is part of a natural road between these places.

But to get back on the trail. When the wagons rattled through the gate of the town of Tejón, the villagers swarmed about them, saying farewells and wishing their friends a safe journey. Some accompanied the expedition as far as Golden, the next village. The men trudged along, skillfully using their long sticks to keep the plodding oxen going and in order. From Golden the train swung to a northerly direction, but that was after a night spent somewhere near that place. The next village on the route was Galisteo, then Cerrillos. They continued toward Glorieta until night, when they camped. The route through the mountains was slow and difficult for the snow was deep, but at length they passed through Glorieta and headed for Las Vegas.

Las Vegas was the starting point of the big adventure as well as the meeting place for those who wished to add their wagons and carretas to the train. By the time all were assembled, there were about four hundred carriers. Each outfit held its own place in the caravan. The Perea layout were well in the lead with more than fifty wagons of various sizes, beside those loaded with feed for the mules and oxen. Several wagons were required for the commissary and many more to carry the firewood when there was none along the route. This saved time. On these trips to the wool market, time was important.

About the middle of February the caravan started. José Librado Arón Gurulé said the trail taken was a shortcut made by Obrey, and that at the beginning it was like a great ranch. In those days the poorer native New Mexicans knew no English, and they had their own way of interpreting English names they heard. From his description of the route followed, it was doubtless the one followed by Josiah Gregg.

From the beginning of the march, both men and animals were pushed to the limit. A schedule was set and every effort was made to maintain it. The drive was kept as near a continuous eighteen hours as was possible. The halt came at ten in the morning, or as close to that time as could be arranged. There was a rush and a bustle to feed man and animals and get in some sleep. The animals were unhooked from the wagons and often almost fell to the ground from exhaustion near the latter part of the last lap to the Cimarrón. Within six hours from the halting moment the train was again in motion. This order was not relaxed until after the Cimarrón was reached and crossed. Until that time the trip was filled with unjustifiable hardships. Maintaining the schedule was mostly to blame for the condition of both men and beasts. The scouts looked for camping grounds where there were no signs of prairie dogs. That meant that the area would be absolutely barren of vegetation and no fires could menace them. Often the train was raced to reach such a place. The men who guided the oxen with their long goads must run to keep the pace. During each twenty-four hours, there was but one full meal, supplemented by two light snacks, the first consisting of a tortilla and an onion in the hand to be taken on the run—the second, an onion and a tortilla eaten likewise. The men were drawing heavily upon previously stored up energy. This army of hirelings was traveling on their feet with very little assistance from their stomachs, according to the picture painted of it by the one who endured the experience and related it. The stops made for feeding the mules and oxen were brief, and all hands were busy hurrying through the labor.

One afternoon a near panic was caused in the Perea section of the caravan. Frightened oxen brought a heavily loaded wagon to a tipsy angle. The animals and wagons following were brought to an abrupt halt. An exhausted man who had stretched himself upon the tongue of the wagon preceding the one tip-tilted by the frightened oxen, had fallen into a dead sleep and rolled off to the ground. He was trampled to death before he could be rescued. A solemn pause was made while the victim was buried. This tragedy happened in other outfits on that journey. Under the strain of eighteen-hour marches the men were giving way. "Too much awake, too little water to drink, too little frijoles, men go to sleep anywhere," was the comment of the narrator.

One morning just after the halt of the caravan, Indians were sighted across the plains of Kansas. They were on the march. There was a hasty conference among the captains and excited talk and anxiety among all the others in the train. On came the Indian band, looming large and ominous in the distance. Nearer they came. The order went out from the captains not to fire or make a move until the word came from the proper authority. But as the band bore down upon them, the ordeal of waiting proved too much for a few near the point of approach. They fired. At once, the fire was returned and one man near the Perea outfit went down. For a moment it looked as if the situation were out of hand. But Esquípulo and a few other courageous ones stepped forward and made signs of friendship to the Indians. At once, all appearances of hostility vanished and the band advanced. Some were on foot. Some drove mules hitched to queer-looking conveyances built exactly like ladders: two stout poles with strong cross pieces. One end of the ladder was harnessed to the mule, the other dragged the ground. Bundles, pots, and small articles of wearing apparel were tied to the poles and dangled down. Children and women sat on the cross pieces of the ladders as if they were seats in a wagon. Many of the Indians rode horses, the prizes for which they would murder and plunder. Luckily the caravan boasted no horses, and there was a reason. It made the trips less hazardous in cases like the one they were experiencing. The train contained little to tempt the Indians. One old woman drove her mule and ladder close to the spot where José Gurulé was standing. She dismounted and approached him, her eyes upon the cube of sugar he held untasted in his hand. He sensed her desire and at once took another of his scanty hoard from his pocket and gave the two cubes to her. She thanked him, or he supposed that was what she said, for he had no understanding of her language. Then she went to her ladder and untied a bundle. From it she took a pat of ground meat and came back and gave it to him. He thanked her in his own tongue. She smiled, and returning to her seat on the first cross of the ladder, took up her lines. In time the band passed peacefully on its way, bound for Dodge City (Huertas Douche), another of the New Mexicans' interpretations of an English name. They were going to get "gifts" (rations) from the United States government. On the remainder of the caravan's journey to Kansas City, José Gurulé was the butt of many jokes. The old Indian woman was referred to as his sweetheart, who had come so far to bring him some choice meat, and as his grandmother, who had come to see him, and seeing how hungry he looked, gave him her meat. At last the caravan, on time, rolled into the appointed grounds in Kansas City. Then there was more work for the men: unloading and carting the wool to storage and conditioning the mules, oxen, and wagons for the homeward trip. On the first day of their arrival some of the men wandered idly from the camping grounds. They walked along hoping to see wonderful sights. The very first thing they saw was a huge, bright-colored picture of an Indian on the front of a wooden building. He was wearing a war bonnet. The words under the Indian: TOMASITO, THE FAMOUS WARRIOR OF THE FAMED VILLAGE OF TAOS. "We all laughed," José said, "to find Tomasito in Los Estados."

After enjoying the colorful likeness of the Taos warrior, they wandered on. They heard a welcome sound. It was music, and they hurried on to find it. What music! It was a Negro band. The Negroes wore white pants and tall hats. They played outside a place where there was a minstrel show. The men had no money with which to buy tickets to go in, so they just stood around and listened. José carried money enough to pay for a worsted suit out of a store and nothing could tempt him to part with one penny of it. He had boasted around Las Placitas that he would bring back a suit of clothes from Kansas City, and he had sold some of his goats to get the money.

The stay in Kansas City was short. Too soon Esquípulo checked them over to find who needed clothes and shoes to wear back. He found most of the men in tatters and outfitted them with new mantas made after the same pattern as those they had worn on the long trip. "Linens," they were called in Los Estados and listed as such in the Perea books, where they were charged for "linens," not mantas. Everyone in the outfit needed shoes, another item to enter in the Perea accounts to be paid for in due course in labor imposed by Esquípulo or others in charge of the Perea interests.

Once again the train was on the march, but westward now. Wagons were loaded with merchandise of every description. The men who goaded the oxen, drove the mules, and otherwise met the grueling demands of the trip knew little of what awaited them.

The time was late June, the days were moist, windy, and blazing hot. Somewhere on the Kansas prairie the Perea band dropped out of the caravan. José Leander had taken a contract to furnish wagons, teams, and men to work on the railroad that was built across the state. A rough camp was set up and everything put in readiness for the cook. This was important; what he dished out to the men was to be the tie that bound them to the job. The commissary was well stocked with real coffee, enough sugar cubes for all, white flour for bread once a day, and butter to spread on it. There was ham and bacon and there would be fresh meat. It was to be a delectable handout three times a day.

Men and animals went to work. For a time the new and hitherto unsampled food and the shifting scenes about them kept the native New Mexicans going their placid ways. But soon there was distress in camp. The hard manual labor was taking its toll of strength. No one living all his days in the mountains of New Mexico could sleep during the hot, blistering July nights in Kansas. The water was disagreeable; the food remained good in quality but dwindled in quantity. Men were worn thin, but kept on their feet. Men and animals were driven to the point of exhaustion, but the contract must be fulfilled.

At last it was over, and again the Perea band turned westward. The trip home was a nightmare. The men were weak and ill, the animals drooping. And then what José Gurulé called a "plague" broke out among them. Those who went down were laid in the wagons; those who stayed on foot kept the caravan moving. But soon there were not so many wagons, for a large number of the animals had fallen by the way. They just crept along, making frequent stops to rest. There were other stops to make, and always after these they left one of their number behind under a mound of earth. Many died of the plague, José said.

It was December before what was left of the Perea outfit dragged into Las Vegas. "A dejected-looking outfit," said the storyteller, "with maybe a third of it left somewhere on the way." In another week they were back in Bernalillo.

The entire trip had consumed almost eleven months. Each man who survived it was paid eight dollars in cash. The food they had eaten in the railroad camp was pay for their labor. It is not known whether the families of the men who died on the way received any part of the eight dollars that would have been paid to them had they returned with the caravan.

José Gurulé was a man of eighteen when he reached home. And he made good his boast. He brought home a suit of worsted from Kansas City and donned it for the admiration of the whole village. It was the first real suit of clothes ever worn in Las Placitas.

SUBJECT: The Panic of 1862
WPA: 5-5-49 #49
March 16, 1941
Words 2544
Sources of information: José Gurulé, Twitchell Vol. 2 , John Vaughan,
History of New Mexico.

THE PANIC OF 1862

The aged ones in Las Placitas still recall their own particular panic that befell them in the spring of 1862. It was a hectic week that followed the return of the Perea family from Colorado, where they had fled before the advance of the victorious Texans up the Rio Grande Valley.

The Perea family were rich and influential. Their power extended throughout the length and breadth of the extensive region then known as Bernalillo County. A small army of natives at and around the town of Bernalillo were practically in bondage to Don José Leander Perea, head of the family. To them his word was the equivalent of the law of the land.

La Hacienda de Perea (the landed property of Perea) was just north of the small village of Bernalillo, and lay between El Camino Real and El Río Grande. The house was a large adobe building containing huge living rooms, sleeping rooms for the family and Navajo slaves, and a large storeroom. In fact, the room was a store, which supplied the needs of the Perea household, and at which every peon round about had a charge account.

The peons lived in little adobe houses of their own, on land outside the Perea estates or in the native villages in the vicinity. Those who labored on the Perea estate walked to and from their long days' work and what they earned was applied on their accounts at the Perea store. Eight dollars a month was standard wage for the men.

Yet in spite of the ease and grandeur (for that time) in which the family lived, they had their fears and worries—fears for their lives and worries over their property, personal and real, just as the poor natives feared for their lives and their possessions. Only there was a difference. The poor natives feared the cruel Navajoes who preyed upon them, and never had the courage to steal from the rich and powerful, nor attack them. The rich and powerful feared the raids of Los Tejanos (the Texans), who were just as ruthless as the Navajoes, but far more ambitious; they were out for big stakes. But then the Texans were hated and feared by all New Mexican natives—the rich for what they had suffered at the hands of the Texans, the poor for what they had heard of the Texans. Texas raiders had taken heavy toll of the rich.

In the very early days the Tejanos built up a reputation for lawlessness, all up and down the Río Grande Valley and on the Santa Fe Trail. The upper class New Mexicans called them meddling foreigners who had taken Texas from the republic of Mexico and who wished to join the department of New Mexico to Texas. The New Mexicans blamed the Texans for their internal troubles of 1837, when the government at Mexico supplanted a native of New Mexico department governor, by a governor from Mexico, who tried to install a system of taxation. They did not like the idea of the taxes, nor the interfering Pérez, who was the new governor. Under the leadership of General Armijo, Pérez was routed and beheaded. Then followed a catastrophe. General Armijo did not have the courage to seize the government himself, and the victorious mob, made up of the followers he could recruit from anywhere, elected José Gonzales, a Taos buffalo hunter, as governor. Armijo quickly reorganized his forces and overthrew Gonzales and executed him because he had threatened to call the Texans to his aid, or so it was charged. Anyhow, the desired result was obtained, and hatred of the interfering Texans flamed anew.

In 1841, an armed band from Texas raided the village of Mora and killed five citizens of New Mexico. In the spring of 1843, Colonel Jacob Snively with a band of one hundred-eighty Texans attacked the spring caravan on the Santa Fe Trail.

Even after the conquest of New Mexico by the government of the United States, the native New Mexicans continued to hate and distrust the Texans. The rich feared them, the poor took up their quarrel, and to this day the natives in the villages refer to the Civil War in New Mexico as the war with the Texans.

In 1861, Captain Baylor with his Texas army invaded the southern part of New Mexico and occupied Mesilla and other villages. In 1862, they won a glorious victory at Valverde and completely routed the Union forces of New Mexico. Then they started their march north.

News of their victory and march spread like wildfire up the Río Grande Valley. The whole territory was thrown into confusion. It was February; the great spring caravan of wool was on its way to Los Estados (the states) and it was time to start the spring work.

At Bernalillo, Don José Leander Perea viewed the coming of the Texans with alarm. The victorious Texans would rob them of all they had and take the men as prisoners of war. He knew other heads of noted families would be forced to protect themselves just as he must do. They must flee the territory. They must go to safety in Colorado. There was no time to lose. He told his family to prepare themselves for the journey.

The peons were rounded up and set to work to expedite the preparations. Carretas were packed with clothing and valuables and supplies. The fine horses and carriages were made ready for the flight of the family with their Navajo slaves. The great house was barricaded and orders issued right and left by the patrón, Don José.

Two youths were left to guard the house and adjoining property. They were to stick to their duties, no matter what. The boss of the peons was to start the spring work and see that the peons "kept their places." And with that, the Perea family, slaves, bag, and baggage, were off with a flourish and a dash, bound for Colorado, where they would remain until they had the word that all was quiet along the Río Grande.

At the very time that the Don's carriages were traveling the route of the caravan into Kansas, in order to avoid the heavy snows and almost impassible mountain passes, on the shorter route to Colorado, the Colorado army, Pike's Peakers, were braving their way over those deep-snow covered mountains to aid the New Mexico army men, Indian fighters, and volunteers to repel Baylor and his Texas army.

By the last of April all danger of further invasion by the dreaded Texans was past. They had been driven steadily down the Río Grande finally too make their escape.

It was really springtime in the Río Grande Valley when the Perea Family returned to their house at Bernalillo. The house was reopened and the work of cleaning inside and out was started. But a few days had passed when "the devil broke out" in Bernalillo.

Without warning, the youths left to guard the house were dragged into the fearsome presence of the Dons, José and his son Pedro. They were scared half to death, and in their minds connected whatever was happening to them with the dreaded Texans, for at once both the men accused the boys of theft, of digging up the earth in the old chicken-house yard.

The boys declared their innocence, begged for mercy, and vowed that no Tejanos had been around the place, and that the army had just marched up El Camino Real. But that was not the answer the Dons wanted. They threatened the youths with floggings if they did not confess—and it would have been floggings if they did. The men demanded of the fear-crazed boys, who had dug up the chicken yard, if they had not done it.

The boys saw their way out. So, it was not Los Tejanos, it was somebody else.

They had not done it themselves, but someone who knew the place had done it. To save themselves, they named some peons who worked around the place. After that, they were told to go.

With little loss of time, the men they named were summoned, accused, and in spite of their protests of innocence, were flogged. The flogging brought no confessions. The men evidently had nothing to confess.

This happening threw the vicinity into a panic. Word of it was carried to Las Placitas, where the panic spread. Nearly all the men there were Perea men. What would happen to them? Lucas Gurulé pointed out that most of the men of Las Placitas took care of the Don's sheep, and all during the time of his absence were away up in the Jemez Mountains. The others in Perea's service who lived at Las Placitas had been busy at Cerro Pelón with their own herds and had not gone to Bernalillo or were gone with the caravan to Los Estados.

But the flogging of the men did not end the affair, but rather was but the beginning of it. The boys were again called before Don José and Don Pedro. Again they were accused of the crime of digging in the chicken yard. Then they were asked what they did with the treasure they dug up. Again the boys cried out their innocence. Trembling with fear anew, they begged not to be flogged. Once more they were commanded to name the guilty ones. Again to save themselves they gave the names of three men, ones they knew to be none too honest.

Forthwith the men were ordered to appear before the Dons, and Perea aides went to hasten them on their way. But the three men protested their innocence and no amount of accusations by the Dons could force them to change their minds.

Don Pedro was fast losing patience. The treasure had been dug up from the chicken yard. He would find out who did it. He had a pillory built. When it was completed, the people round about eyed it with fear in their hearts. It meant that the Dons were not through with them yet. Again they blamed Los

Tejanos. They were the ones who had stolen the treasure. Los Tejanos were always robbing the great dons.

The boys were forced to give more names when they were again dragged into the presence of the Dons. By now they had learned that the one sure way to keep the wrath of the Dons from their own heads was to name probable guilty ones. They grew generous in the manner of giving lists of suspected ones; they even named a few against whom they had a grudge.

All those named were rounded up and brought before the patrón and his son. All were punished; some were flogged, others put in the pillory where they remained at least two days, when they denied the accusations of having taken part in the theft of the treasure from the yard of the old chicken house. The panic-stricken people knew not what to do. They could not flee; it would only be the worse for them. So they grimly waited their turns, praying the saints to save them from the dire punishments for things they did not do, or for crimes they did not commit, and all the time living in terror of being called next into the presence of the Dons. The orgies endured through the week at Bernalillo. Then one morning the worst spread to Las Placitas. Into the village walked seven of the Perea aides demanding that Manuel and José Chávez accompany them back to Bernalillo. Don José Perea commanded it.

There was a loud protest from the villagers. There were no more honorable men among them than Manuel and José. The Chávez family was one of the families who built old Las Huertas and received the San Antonio de Las Huertas Grant. A loud wailing went up from the lips of the Chávez women, who knew that their men had not been near Bernalillo during the absence of Don José from Bernalillo.

Lucas Gurulé knew that, too. He decided that it was about time that someone besides the Pereas took a hand in their inquisition; and that somebody might as well be himself. He sent for the Chávez men; he called Nicolás Gurulé, and then announced to the Bernalillo delegation that the four of them would accompany Don José's men back to Bernalillo and to the presence of the Don. And so it was.

When they were all conducted into the place where the Dons held their secret sessions, the Dons scowled upon the intruders and made it plain to Lucas and Nicolás that they were not wanted. The two men stood their ground and remained with their friends, the Chávez brothers. Lucas could have it so. He had never had his name on the Perea account book. But Don Pedro did not allow the presence of Lucas and Nicolás to delay the matters at hand. At once he turned his attention to José and Manuel and accused them of the crime of digging up a treasure from the chicken yard. He informed them that they had been named as the guilty ones and now demanded their confession.

Before they could make reply, Lucas demanded of the Dons that they send for the alcalde at Bernalillo and give the men a lawful hearing. He told his two friends to save their statements until the arrival of the alcalde.

The Dons were speechless for the moment. Perhaps they had never before been defied by the lowly, and had no special and immediate remedy in mind for the unprecedented act. Without apology or explanation the four were dismissed. Lucas' inspiration had saved the day for his friends. As well, his courage and his subtle threat to invoke the law brought an end to the panic of 1962 in Bernalillo and Las Placitas.

It was some time before the Perea secret leaked out, and the cause of the panic of 1862 was really known.

When the Perea family fled before the advance of the Texas army, they did not desire to carry all their gold with them. Perhaps they thought it would be safer at home. So choosing a time when they believed they were absolutely unobserved, Don José and Don Pedro buried two leather bags, each one containing three thousand dollars in gold. They were buried in widely separated spots. After their return from Colorado they had gone out secretly to dig up the gold. They discovered that there had been much digging about the yard. To their sorrow they were able to find only one of the bags.

Then it was that they started in to find the thieves in any way they could. Strange to say, and in spite of the lash and pillory, they were never able to wring a confession from any of the accused. And never were they able to find a clue outside their own domain. They never found the gold.

SUBJECT: Out of Bondage
May 7, 1941
Words 2153
Sources of information: José L.A.Gurulé, Benino Archibeque, María Chávez, Catalina Gurulé, José Trujillo. José Gurulé knew the José de Luz of this story, as well as the conditions that existed after the abolition of peonage. Benino Archibeque knew of the condition of the people after the abolition of peonage in 1877, through his father, and also of the story of the adventure in this story. María Chávez was a descendant of the José de Luz of this story. José Trujillo is well acquainted with the legend and facts concerning the hidden treasure at Sandía Pueblo.

OUT OF BONDAGE
(José de Luz Seeks His Fortune)

Peonage was a recognized institution in the Spanish colonies of the Southwest. There were laws giving recognition to both patrón and peón. Though it never got further than the books in which such rights privileges and obligations were written, there was a definite obligation on the part of the patrón to the peón. Whatever the peón bought at the store of the patrón, he was to pay the market price for it. Then there was another: only two thirds of the peón's wage per month could be credited to his accounts. The other one third, or $2.66, (if the peón received $8 per month) or $1.66, (should his monthly wage be $5), was to be paid each month to the peón. Neither of these particular provisions was observed. The prices charged at the patrón's store for every item bought at the store were enormous. This kept the poor peón in debt. There were no way he could ever pay out and still live. There was no set amounts if any paid the peón in cash, as part of his monthly wage. But there was one provision of the law that applied to the peón which was kept to the letter. The

402

patrón saw to it. The peón could bind his children to his patrón to work out his debts to the patrón. This, the peón was forced to do.

This custom prevailed so long in the Southwest that the peons had few if any dreams of life beyond that of being bound to some great family who would keep them from actually starving to death. However, the patróns were in no way obligated to see that their peons did not starve. It was to their advantage to see that they did not. This tiny hold on social security kept the peón laboring on, binding his sons to the same sort of life he led himself, with no time of their own, or means with which to do anything for themselves. Such was the status of the lowly peón when he found himself suddenly cut adrift from his patrón in 1867 when the system of peonage was abolished. Or that was, the peón would be released as soon as his indebtedness was canceled. That brought about an immediate change: less credit, that debts could the sooner be wiped out.

All peons were not affected equally. As men are different, so are they differently moved by the same circumstances. When some of the peons realized that what little security they had was taken from them by a law they had not sought, they were paralyzed with fear for the future. They stood humbly before their patrón and cried to be "occupied" again. Others, fearful of being upon their own, took refuge with their families in the pueblos with the Indians where they had blood ties. Yet others calmly accepted their fate, turned their faces steadily in a new direction of living for themselves, sought to clear and cultivate new land and acquire flocks of their own. There were yet others who, while in the occasional service and debt of the patrón, were still free enough to make most of their living for themselves independent of him.

Most of those in Las Placitas belonged to these last two groups. They could yet find occupation with Don José Leander Perea, receive credit, and take off time to follow their personal pursuits. These were the sort of men who did find employment with the patrón after the abolition of peonage and credit.

But while the former peons were struggling for readjustment, there came a great new adventure in the way of labor. The railroad was coming! Some of the huskier, more ambitious ones found work, work that paid cash for labor done. It was hard labor but wonderful wages to the peón who had given all he had in the way of strength and loyalty for $5 and $8 a month.

But there was another and greater adventure, from the new freedman's point of view, which brought work and money right into his midst. It was the rush and the excitement of the mining boom, the hunt for gold. He could help the gringos hunt rocks and dig holes into the sides of the mountains and get paid for it. The gringos knew where there was gold to be found in the mountains, but they must find the right spots and dig deep enough and in the right direction. There was lots of digging to do.

Some of the men worked for the gringos at Las Placitas, where much assessment work was done. One of those men was José de Luz Montoya, once peón in the service of Don José Leander Perea, who reached his year of freedom about three years after the law of 1867, as it took him that time to work out his obligation and keep body and soul of his family together. José de Luz was one of those, too, who, when separated from the little security he had, was full of fear for the future. He knew not which way to turn. With but a house and a small plot of ground of his own, and with no blood ties in any of the pueblos, his outlook was bleak indeed. When he found that his once patrón would not employ him further, he went to work as many others did, cleared and planted a few fields and hunted wild game. Somehow his family carried on, even though José de Luz lost rather than accumulated ambition as he went along.

Then came a gringo to Ojo de la Casa. He knew he would find gold in the vicinity of the old Montezuma Mine. Old legends told of gold being found there. He hired José de Luz to help him find it. José de Luz delved into the mountainside, and received one silver dollar for each day he delved. His wife fixed up their old adobe house, and he spent silver dollars to buy desirable things with which to fill up their stomachs to capacity—a luxury hitherto denied them.

But this new and costly standard of living could be maintained only by some daily ten hours of delving by José de Luz. He was wholly unaccustomed to such strenuous labor. In service to his patrón he herded sheep. It was a leisurely existence compared with handling heavy pick and shovel all day long. He cast about for a change of employment. By this time he felt that the prospector, the gringo who knew that he would find gold in the region of the Montezuma, had told or taught him all there was to know about the business of finding gold.

So it was that José de Luz decided to find gold for himself. And as a sideline, he accumulated a small herd of goats, which he would herd about as he scoured the arroyos for the right kind of rocks and thoroughly investigated every hole or cave he came upon. There would be excellent pasturage for the goats: they would grow fat and make fine eating, or fetch a good price if he chose to sell them. The only real trouble he would have, would be keeping clear of bears. While herding his patrón's sheep he had learned much about bears, mainly to keep clear of them.

Fate seemed to favor José de Luz in the matter of bears and mountain lions. He did keep out of their way. Farther and farther he wandered from the old herding ground at Cerro Pelón. He explored each cave or mine working he passed; he gathered samples of rock with a gleaming yellow streak in them. His dreams of finding gold would surely come true.

One day José de Luz lost some of his goats. He started to track them down. He entered strange territory as he climbed the higher mountains and descended slopes he had never known existed. Grass grew rank there and he saw goats feeding in the distance, his lost goats of course. He set out to herd them back.

On his way he spied a cave. He approached it. It went far down into the earth and there was a ladder leading down in to it. Without debating the matter in his mind, José de Luz set his feet on the top crosspiece and hastily descended into the cave.

But he was to be frightened half out of his wits before he had been there long enough to make it all out. Swiftly, silently, something surrounded him, covered his head with a blanket, seized him, and dragged him back up the ladder. But that was not all. He was rushed so fast over the ground that he could scarcely keep his feet.

He did not know into whose hands he had fallen. He fearfully, suddenly knew the reason. At once he knew he had little chance of his life. He was in the clutches of the Sandía Indians. Unwittingly he had invaded their private domain.

"What did you see down in that cave?" demanded an angry voice right in his ear.

"Nothing, nothing," protested José de Luz. "I did not have the time. It was so dark my eyes could not see."

The Indians demanded over and over what he had seen while in the cave. Over and over their prisoner declared that he had seen nothing. Handling him as roughly as they pleased, they could not shake his statement from the original words he spoke to them.

Then things came to a halt. Angry voices sounded all about them. The cover was jerked from his head as suddenly as it had been flung over him. He was completely surrounded by angry, menacing Indians, some shouting, "Kill him! Kill him!"

What chance had he? Trembling violently he protested loudly, "I saw nothing. I could not. It was dark. I was there too short a time. My eyes could not see!" But the angry voices about him continued to say, "Kill him!"

Then José de Luz saw one friendly face. It was his compadre. This Indian was the padrino (godfather) of the first son of José de Luz. He looked at José de Luz sympathetically, and the poor, frightened man saw a ray of hope. When the Indian asked him whether he had seen anything in the cave, he stuck to the story he had told the other Indians. At that, the friendly Indian merely said to his companions, "I say, let him go."

Reluctantly they released José de Luz. But he was not permitted to go for his goats. The grateful man was not much troubled by the refusal. He was happy to make a hasty departure from his would-be killers, and he lost not one moment in covering the ground between the pueblo of Sandía and his home at Las Placitas.

José de Luz forthwith lost his taste for investigating caves, or even hunting rocks streaked with shining yellow. He accumulated more goats and more fields to clear and till. He became a quiet, stay-at-home man.

Not until after the death of José de Luz was the story of the adventure repeated outside his immediate family. Fear of the consequences sealed their lips, for he did see something of what was in the cave. There was an altar adorned with beautiful images, small ones they were. And other bright-colored things he had not the time to make out.

To this day, if the story is repeated, it is spoken cautiously. And the reason? It is believed that it is the cave that holds the treasures hidden there by the Indians, when the Spaniards were driven out. It is guarded to this day. Anyone entering that vicinity is watched by the Indians with hostile eyes. None from Las Placitas would go there.

There is scarcely a native in Las Placitas but believes that the tragedy that happened to the two American boys in that vicinity a very few years ago, was not an accident. They were too near the treasure. The treasure is always guarded by zealous and hostile Indians. Both boys were found dead in that vicinity.

SUBJECT: Juan y el Oso Ladrón

May 21, 1941

Words 2142

Sources of information: José Gurulé, Benino Archibeque, Patricio Gallegos, Venturo Escarcido. Benino Archibeque is the youngest brother of the hero, Juan Archibeque, of this story. Benino was born after Juan was grown up. Venturo Escarcido knew Juan Archibeque and grew up with his younger brothers.

JUAN Y EL OSO LADRÓN
(Juan and the Robber Bear)

The beauty, the grandeur, the strength of the eternal hills (the Sandía Mountains) around Las Placitas afforded very little if any pleasure but created many problems for the villagers in the old days.

Wild turkey and deer were plentiful throughout the region and that was especially true around the watering places. But also in those same mountain retreats lurked the bear. A four-hundred-pound bear was not a rare inhabitant of the Sandías. The bear was an enemy of the hunter and the herder. They could not cope with the bear; they could merely keep out of the bear's way, or outwit him in any manner they could devise. When the bear came upon their flocks of sheep or goats, there was nothing they could safely do, but to allow him to depart with a loudly protesting member of the flock. The bear was out to get himself a dinner. If he were allowed to take it peacefully, he carried it off and there was an end to his thieving, at least for the time being. Meanwhile, the herders removed their flocks to another region and protected them the best they could.

Always the shepherds carried bows and arrows, and a gun if they had it—and plenty of lead slugs. But the muzzle-loading gun was no weapon to turn upon the bears. But then, few indeed were foolhardy enough to tempt providence or the saints by such an act. When herders were compelled to remain in the mountains with their flocks, they constructed strong refuges with heavy logs, laid upon the ground and built up in the manner of a corn crib. These places were made so low (for the purpose of strength) that they were comfortable only when the occupant was lying down. But there were other places to give safety and built for more comfort—cabins atop tall, heavy stilts. The occupants of those cabins perched so high from the ground always had a gun. But then there was a chance to take careful aim at any bear found climbing one of the poles and also there was time to reload the old gun, should the first shot (slug) miscarry. The bears that attempted to climb those poles leading to cabins must have been few, as but one instance can be recalled. Juan María Gallegos of Ojo de la Casa killed a small bear, about a two-hundred-pounder, when it attempted to climb the pole that led to a point of the cabin where a sack of cheese of goat's milk was suspended.

However, these cabins did not become refuges from bears until after there were several guns in the community. It does seem strange that in Las Placitas and immediate vicinity, located at the very foothills of the Sandía Mountains where bear abounded, that there should have been but one famed bear hunter. To this day, the older citizens like to tell of his exploits. His name was Juan Archibeque. He did not seek to avoid the bears: he openly hunted them. His only weapon was one of the old muzzle-loading guns. He was a good marksman and quick as a flash at reloading his gun. But even at that, hunting bears with such a weapon was dangerous business. Who could tell when something would go wrong, right in the face of a bear that had been injured by the shot and not killed? So his family and friends worried about him whenever he picked up the old weapon and announced that he was going bear hunting.

In the Sandía Mountains in the region of Alameda was a cañón infested with bear: Cañón del Oso (Bear Canyon). Juan was determined to go there. He told the women of Las Placitas that he would bring them some bear grease from Cañón del Oso, and he did not mean it as an idle boast.

Nicolás Gurulé and José Mora, his two close friends, tried to dissuade him from making the dangerous attempt. He laughed at their fears, so they decided to go along with him. When they reached the bear-infested cañón, Juan had little difficulty in dissuading them from entering the cañón with him. They knew only too well that few hunters even with good guns risked their lives in hunting bear in Cañón del Oso.

So it was that they watched their friend enter the place as he called back to tell them not to worry about him, that he would get his bear and so make good his word to the women of Las Placitas.

Nicolás and Juan passed the first few hours of the wait very pleasantly. But as time passed and the afternoon shadows grew long, they became anxious. Could it be that Juan had met his last bear? But they stayed outside the cañón because there was nothing else for them to do.

Then suddenly he appeared. What did he bring? Something heavy all wrapped up in a beautiful bear hide. They hastened to meet him. What a bear hide it was! Juan was as good as his word. He had killed a bear. It was a huge animal. He had taken off its beautiful coat, carved many choice cuts and plenty of fat from the carcass, and there it all was. He would show the women of Las Placitas that he meant what he said. The three men divided the burden among themselves. Each portion proved to be as much as any man could carry the long way back to Las Placitas.

Now Juan was a hero for true. He had got his bear in Cañón del Oso. What more than that could any hunter do to prove his prowess?

After that, Juan went away to hunt, to hunt bigger and meaner bear, and herd sheep in the interim. He was gone several years—years that wrought a change in the life of the people of Las Placitas, abolition of peonage and the centralization of the Navajoes on a reservation, brought about by new laws. With the menacing Indian raiders safe in the hands of the government, the villagers need fear them no more.

And now that the people no longer could turn to the patrón's store and receive credit unless they were employed by the patrón, the very fact that they were well rid of the thieving Navajoes gave them heart to clear and cultivate land wherever they could find it—that was within reasonable distance of the village.

Just to the south and to the west of Las Placitas lay a flat area abundantly watered by the stream from Ojito Blanco (White Springs). The land was studded with oaks and brush and stones. They called the place Los Montes (The Wilds). A low range of hills concealed it from most of Las Placitas. But that mattered little under the new conditions. So the men set to work to clear the land, and to divide it into fields. It was rich soil for corn, and with water to spare, the place was a real Promised Land. In the very early seventies it became a land of waving green corn, a welcome sight to the corn-hungry people of Las Placitas.

But it happened, as it usually does, that the serpent came to this Eden. Men irrigating the fields found precious ears of corn broken from the stock. Many ears yet green were lying about the fields. Woe to them, a thief was invading their fields—a thief in many ways more difficult to deal with, from their point of view, than the treacherous Navajo. They must now fight and kill a bear—a big bear, if the tracks about the fields told the truth.

They improvised a trap. The bear cunningly sidestepped it. They ingeniously prepared falls, but never a bear track did they find in those vicinities. Yet the corn was stolen or wasted. The situation grew desperate. Not one of them would risk his life in attempting to kill the animal with a gun. Something must be done.

Then they decided to send a runner into the Jemez country to find and fetch Juan, their own great bear killer. Who but Juan could help them in this kind of trouble?

It is not remembered how many days passed before Juan came in haste to Las Placitas in answer to the summons. It was recalled that he lost no time in surveying the lay of the land and in making his plans to kill the raider. So before dawn of the morning that followed his return to the village, he went to Los Montes and hid himself on top of a low hill, at the lower southwest part of the land. From that vantage point, he had an unobstructed view of the fields as well as the trail from the mountains. In that cool of the very early morning he weighed the bear's approach. He was indeed a huge bear, and he seemed hungry for his breakfast, as he was coming at a lively pace.

Juan waited motionless, measuring distances with his eye and waiting for the bear to attain a good position from the hunter's viewpoint. But the bear had scarcely penetrated the outlying cornfield when he paused to take observations. Juan felt that the moment was right for him to take aim. He moved. Before he had time to fire, the bear was headed full speed up the trail to the mountain.

With but one thought in his mind, Juan leaped down the hill and went in full pursuit. He would not be outwitted by that bear. Up the mountain trail he dashed, the bear ahead of him, bent on keeping his distance. The trail grew steeper, more narrow; but on went the bear, trailed by his pursuer, the hunter who had no notion of giving up the chase. He had killed bears before, and he would kill this one. He kept his weapon ready in case the animal should turn on him.

Now they had reached the giant pines. It became harder to keep track of the bear, as the great trunks of the trees became hiding places. Between trees,

Juan thought he had found his chance. He took aim and fired. The slug missed its mark. For the first time in his hunting career, Juan missed his bear. For a second he was stunned. But he had no time to think of his bad aim; he must give all his attention and energy to the matter of saving his life. The injured bear was at him. Juan dodged behind the trunk of a tree. The bear was the pursuer now. Juan stepped lively, then fairly leaped around the tree, that race track of some twelve and a half feet. The bear made fearful sounds and Juan could almost feel his breath as he came on, round and round the track, as determined to get Juan as Juan was to get him.

As Juan ran around the tree he refilled his gun. He gave a bound, put a wee more distance between himself and his enemy. He whirled about and fired. There was a flash. That was all. In a twinkle of an eye, Juan had jerked himself about and was on his way again. What had he done? Nothing. That was the trouble. In his excitement and worry (he was worried now) he had forgotten the slug—the powder was all he had put into his gun.

Juan felt like a condemned man for just an instant. Then he reloaded his gun again. Keeping his mind upon what he was doing, he skipped around the track, a jump ahead of the suffering bear, a bear infuriated and eager to kill him.

As the bear kept his pace, there was nothing for Juan to do but speed up, put enough distance between him and his enemy to take another shot at him. He had to get the bear this time. He had to do it, and he did.

But with that victory came a general slump in Juan's overtaxed mind and body. And it was thus that his friends Nicolás and José, who had tracked him to the spot, found their more famous than ever Nimrod, his faithful weapon, and the big brown bear, the thief of Los Montes cornfields.

SUBJECT: The Fury of 1869

June 4, 1941

Words 2316

Source of information: José Gurulé. José Gurulé's family never left the grant. He is the Arón of this story.

THE FURY OF 1869

It was in the year 1869 that the young scholar Arón made his last stay in the pueblo of San Felipe. He lived in the house of Juan Bustos, where he earned his board and keep, but he pursued his rudimentary education under the tutelage of the good priest Father Baron. So it was that he had access to whatever books were to be found in the church or the house of the priest. That was the one great privilege the youth craved.

Arón was ambitious. He craved to be able to write letters and to read books. But he was not selfish in his ambition. He earnestly desired to teach others to read and write—in Spanish of course. That was the only language he knew. It was the language of the world, as far as he was concerned.

Arón did teach the small children at the pueblo. The chili, the corn, the beans that he was paid for his services, he gave Juan Bustos for his board and keep. But no reading and writing were required in the daily schedule. Rather, his energies were spent in the teaching of religious songs and verses, in prayers, in adoration of the saints, in reverence for the church, and respect for their elders. If there was a stress laid on any particular thing taught, it was the respect, which included implicit obedience, the children must pay their elders.

In his pursuit of learning, young Arón often entered the church. There were some books there, mostly records. Those books intrigued him. He had a longing to find the entry of his own baptism. He wanted to be certain that his parents had remembered the exact date of his birth. He knew many parents who never knew the dates of their own birth, and in as many instances they

412

were not certain of the dates of the births of their children. Dates made little difference in those long-ago days of pre-1860. Events were what counted.

But Arón found it most difficult to do the desired research in the record books in the church. Whenever he went there, he either found a few Indians, who watched his every move as if they were guards; or he was followed there and his every move noted. It was as if they divined his intention and were there to prevent it.

After a lengthy period of watchful waiting, he found the opportunity for which he had actually prayed. An Indian event from which he was excluded left him to his own devices. He stole to the church, got the book upon which he had cast his longing eyes so many times, hid himself, and started the search for the entry of his baptism. He found it. But he also found something else: a lengthy entry that was not easy to read. He must have time to make it all out.

What he planned to do was not exactly honest, yet his intentions were good. He wished to learn what was in the book. It was clear that he could not do it in the pueblo. There would be neither time nor privacy. He must take the book and go to his home in Las Placitas. He would guard the book, see that no harm came to it, and he would work out the meaning of all the words in that long record. He would waste no time and would be back with the book before anyone had a chance to miss it.

So it came about that he reached the house of Juan Bustos with the record book and hid it. That night he would go to visit his mother at Las Placitas. He would make it known that he was to go home for a short time; no one would give the matter a thought. That portion of his plan he carried out with precision. He arrived at the house of his father, Nicolás Gurulé, and his mother saw to it that he was not disturbed in his studies, for such she thought his request meant to be left strictly alone.

Thus, without hindrance, Arón set about reading and copying the stirring entry. He found no date that he could decipher. But he found later in his life, things that led him to believe that the recorded event took place many, many years before the American occupation, perhaps as many as fifty.

The recorded event as Arón copied it was in his possession for many years, and then one day he went to his desk and found that his papers had been disturbed. He knew someone was trying to get the story he would never tell. He had expected that very thing to happen, and had hidden the copied record. The secret was guarded through the years.

Here's how the record read: "The old priest at San Felipe Pueblo fell ill. He raved day and night with a tormenting pain in his head, and his body was covered with sores. The Indians said he was stricken with leprosy. At times a paroxysm of pain shot through the body of the poor old priest, and seemed to come from every sore on his body and settled at the very top of his head. There was nothing he could do to bring relief from his suffering.

Another priest came to care for him and look after the mission. He knew the malady was not leprosy, and was much puzzled by the nature of it, but did what he could for the old priest and said nothing of what he thought.

All the servants about the house of the priest were Indians. One youth lived in the house. His duty was to run errands and be on hand at all times, and particularly at night. It so happened that the new priest had need of him one night and called him. There came no answer. The priest went to the Indian's sleeping place. There was no sign of the youth. The priest made sure that the Indian was nowhere in the house before he gave up the search.

The next morning the priest found the young Indian in his bed and aroused him. He demanded of the youth where he had spent the night. The boy did not hesitate to speak. He spoke truthfully, too. The old priest had taught him that it paid to tell the truth. He told the padre that he had sat up watching two Indians burying something just outside the cemetery. He also told the good padre that the Indians were saying that the old priest would die before night.

Leaving the young Indian to his chores, the padre took two Indians and started the work of finding the place the boy had told him about, a place where he saw two Indians burying something. It took only a short time to locate the spot. The padre gave orders to dig and see what they could find in the hole. Without hesitation the Indians set to work. It was clear to the padre that they were not in on the secret of the burial place. As the Indians dug into the loose earth, the padre kept his eyes upon the spot, fearing to lose any clue of what deviltry the Indians were up to, for he felt that such was the case.

He heard a stick strike a something. He bent down low and watched the Indians drag out a soil-covered object. The priest stared at it. It was a perfect image of the sick priest. The robe was a copy of the one the good old father wore. But there was a perfect network of strings coming out the top of the head of the image. The visiting priest closely examined the strings. He found that each string was threaded through the eye made in each of the cactus thorns driven into the body of the image. The thorns thus were controlled by the strings coming out the head of the image. When the mass of strings projecting out the top of the head of the image were jerked about, the thorns scraped the body of the image. The new padre gasped.

He was not slow in realizing the awful truth. The old priest was bewitched. Everywhere one of the horrible thorns was thrust into the body of the image, the priest had one of those terrible sores. Whenever the strings on the head of the image were pulled, the good padre suffered death with the sores as well as the head, where all the pain concentrated. They had buried the image and willed that the sick priest die.

Without loss of time the priest hastened to the bedside of the dying priest. He washed each sore upon his body with ashes. Immediately the old priest was healed.

And then came the retribution. The pueblo was combed to find the evil witches. Punishments were meted out until the two witches were identified. Then a great heap of dry grass and sticks was piled up and the image placed on top of it. The whole was crowned with the two Indian witches, bound head and foot. The dry grass at the bottom was set ablaze. The fire ate its way rapidly upward, as it became the funeral pyre of the two Indian witches."

Arón had no sooner finished the copy than he hid it away and prepared to carry the book back to the church at San Felipe. It was at that very moment that an ear-splitting, bloodcurdling yell from Indian throats fell upon the ears of the citizens of Las Placitas. The next thing they all knew, an invading mob of angry Indians came marching into the village. They carried clubs and shook them violently. No sound could be heard above their angry shouting. They demanded to see Arón. They marched on to the house of Nicolás and his wife, Catalina. Fearful that the Indians meant harm to Arón, some of the men of the village sought to break through the ranks of the mob to reach the house of Nicolás and warn him. But these men were roughly held back. Some of the Las Placitas men sought to reason with the mob, only to be brusquely pushed aside.

What was it all about? None in the village knew. Why should those friendly Indians from San Felipe turn against them in this way? It all seemed very mystifying and very serious.

It was most serious to the angry Indians. Their sacred place had been robbed. They were the zealous guardians of their church and all the holy things in it, whether it meant anything to them or not. The church and everything belonging to it was their own. No one should molest it. The leader among them had worked them into a fury over the desecration of their holy place, the place the priest called holy. The missing book to them was a place where the padre wrote down the facts of their births and baptisms and deaths. Outside the padre, no one had a right to touch it, let alone steal it. Religiously awakened zeal recognized no limits. It is often cruel. This Indian mob at the height of an awakened religious emotion was ready to kill—if need be—for their righteous cause.

Lucas Gurulé could not stand idly by. He fought his way to his brother's house. He was determined that whatever Arón had done, he would save the youth from the fury of those Indians.

The Indians, shouting and shaking their fists and their clubs, were coming on. Lucas stood at the closed door of his brother's house and faced the mob defiantly, courageously.

Behind him he felt the door being removed. From the opening came Catalina. In her hands she carried a book. With upraised head and with a firm and determined step, she advanced to meet the oncoming mob.

There was but little distance between her and infuriated Indians. But she showed no fear of them. Why should she? Her son had committed no crime. He was a good and smart and obedient son. They dare not touch him.

Perhaps the keen eyes of the leader read the face of Catalina Bustos de Gurulé. And whatever it was he saw there caused him to halt the mob. She approached him, addressed her greeting to them all as she laid the book into the hands of the now much becalmed leader.

With the precious book in their possession, the leader had little difficulty in swaying the mob to the cause of peace. They had won! Back to San Felipe they went, to restore the book to its honored place.

But not for long did it rest there, that is, not for many years. One eventful Sunday as the good padres of San Felipe took their usual Sabbath recreation, a walk into the nearby mountains, a sudden rainstorm came up. It was one of those furious, beating, sheet-like rains that seems bent on destruction. When the padres reached the pueblo, they found the walls of the church badly washed out. One place where the adobe wall connected with the roof washed out was directly above the niche which held The Book. It was smeared with adobe mud and was water-soaked, as were other books kept there. The books were sent to the pueblo of Sandía for safety. No one in Las Placitas now knows the whereabouts of that book which holds so many entries of the baptisms of the long ago babies of old Las Placitas.

SUBJECT: Dos Hombres Sabios de Las Placitas
WPA: 5-5-49 #56
June 30, 1941
Words 1964
Sources of information: José Gurulé, Rumaldita Gurulé, Fermina Durán, Onofre Gonzales, José Trujillo.

DOS HOMBRES SABIOS DE LAS PLACITAS
(Two Wise Men of Las Placitas)

In the days of long ago, every well-regulated village had its wise man who spoke knowingly of sun, moon, and stars and advised the people upon the most vital of all their problems—the sowing and reaping of the sustaining substance called crops. Each spring he called the farmers together and told them when, what, and where to plant. He was indeed the dictator in this all-important matter, and none there were who lifted a voice against his decisions. He knew about such matters. He was the wise man. The responsibility of feeding the people became his. And where did he acquire all this wisdom? No one knew then. In those old days wisdom indeed was power, and no one possessing it disseminated it until the proper time, and then it was given to but one he deemed the proper person, or such was the belief of the people.

It was only fitting that the wise man of the community should be chosen alcalde. As the alcalde, he kept such records as were accumulated in the village. He kept the calendar and proclaimed the feast days. The wise man of the village was in truth a busy man. And above all, the wise man must be a good weather forecaster. Therein was his wisdom, and therein lay his success or failure in the pursuit of his high calling.

Within the memory of the oldest now living in Las Placitas, one of the wisest of the long-ago alcaldes, if not really the wisest, was Francisco Trujillo. He was born in Old Las Huertas. He fought the Texans in the Battle of

Valverde, and before that and afterward made trips over the Santa Fe Trail to Los Estados.

In those old days all the houses faced the east. That was the custom. The sun shone in at the open door, and throughout the morning hours the time could be told by the position of the sunlight upon the adobe floor. That is one of the reasons why it is still recalled that all the houses faced the east. Another reason for remembering the fact was that regardless of weather, the wise man mounted his roof each morning and faced the east at the moment of sunrise. He stood there like a statue observing the heavens, making deductions, adding them to the results of his observations of the sky, the wind, the moon on the night before. Soon he would descend from his high place, summon the men, and in the manner of an oracle, utter the weather forecast. Thereafter the plans of the day's activities could be made.

The wise man was especially busy in the pre-planting weeks. Much depended upon his reckoning. The moon, the rain-band, the scurrying clouds— all had their part in causing a wet or dry season. When all the signs were favorable to a more than ordinary degree, then the wise man bade the farmers to plant fields plentifully with seeds, whether such fields were under irrigation ditches or not. There would be a copious rainfall throughout the season and the harvests would be abundant. Should all signs point to dry weather, he told them to plant seeds only on land under ditches. Thus forearmed, the people made few mistakes in their sowing. Anxiously Francisco awaited each "new moon" to see whether it foretold rain or drough. Should the crescent ride flat in the sky, that clearly indicated dry weather, as no water could spill from it. Should the crescent dip, clearly there would be rain, for water could easily spill from the crescent. Early and late, the wise man studied the heavens and the heavenly bodies so that his weather forecasts might be accurate, or wise ones.

Francisco kept a day-by-day calendar. He never proclaimed the fiesta days publicly, but he told this one and that one of the coming event and asked that the word be noised among the people. Had he not kept a day-by-day calendar, he still could have called the fiesta days. He knew how the wise men of long ago reckoned them. Those men were students of the heavenly bodies. They foretold the days by the position of the sun, moon, and stars. Once, generations ago, the people lost track of the days. There were no priests nor wise men near their remote village who kept a calendar. But one old man remembered a date from which they could reckon. They must wait for the harvest (October), watch for the new moon, then count fifteen days forward. That day would be the feast of Las Cabañas (Cabins), or the Jewish feast of The Tabernacle, when they spent seven days in the cabins. That feast day would be the fifteenth day of October, and thus they could find their calendar again.

In the old days they made weather forecasts in August for the following year. They spoke of Las Cabañuelas pointing the right or the wrong way, but no one in Las Placitas now, can explain what was meant. Nor do they know how their people of so very long ago knew of the feast of Las Cabañas or how to reckon it, and thus set their calendars aright.

In the long-ago days their calendars were inscribed on properly prepared animal hides. Down through the years those calendars were preserved. It would be strange should none be among the old records at Las Placitas, yet no one speaks of the existence of such relics. Alcalde Francisco did leave some records. If his descendants yet have them, they are hidden away and not brought forth for exhibition.

There was one fiesta day Francisco favored, and himself saw to it that the whole village was up early to usher the day in with the proper ceremony. That was June 24, the feast of San Juan Day, the jolliest, most carefree day of the year for the villagers of long ago.

In the dewy freshness of the morning of San Juan Day, every man, woman, and child of permissible age was astir, making ready for the event that would properly launch the festivities of the day. When all was ready they went forth from the village in a body, following the trail that led to the nearest arroyo of deep, running water. Now with one accord they walked into the water and went down on their knees and completely immersed themselves in the water. This was to commemorate the baptism of Jesus by John the Baptist. When all had been immersed, they made their way back to the village, and the day's merry-making was on. This old custom of repeating the baptism of San Juan morning has long since been abandoned. Likewise has the old custom of choosing the wise men to direct and advise them. The advent of politics and the influence of money have set a new standard.

While Francisco was yet in his prime and a wise and honored alcalde of Las Placitas, there was another wise man in their midst. He was old Rafael, a dreamer of dreams and a seer of visions. El adivino (the prophet) he was called. In those days of long ago el adivino was born, not made. He announced his divine calling even before he was born. Only those destined to become prophets or soothsayers sent out a cry while yet they were in the mother's womb. So it was that the parents of the unborn baby who was to be baptized Rafael, knew that their child was to be a prophet. He cried while in his mother's womb.

From infancy Rafael heard sounds and saw things that the other children neither heard nor saw. He grew up not wise in practical affairs, nor caring for them. He wanted only to be left alone and to be permitted to go his solitary way in peace that he might see visions of the things to be. Talk of things to be some day was of vital importance to him. So fanciful were the word pictures he painted of the visions that came to him, that the villagers gathered about him to hear him tell of them.

None of the very old people who yet recall anything of what he foretold, doubt the sincerity of his stories. He did see visions. Of that they feel certain.

The old man spent much of his time in meditation. He withdrew from his friends and family and would sit for hours on the brow of a lonely hill, just gazing into the heavens. Or he would sit by an arroyo and watch the tumbling waters and not move even a finger for hours at a time. He would take his staff and climb the mountain trails to sit beneath some lofty pine, there to see and think.

Always after such sessions he was ready to tell them of some vision he had revealed to him. He made two predictions that have caused the descendants of the people of his day to believe that he was in truth a prophet and that he foretold his coming by crying in his mother's womb, after the manner of all true prophets.

Once after a period of meditation in the mountains, he told the people that some day those who were living would see strange things come to pass in Bernalillo. He said the babies of his day might witness them. Then he painted for them in word pictures the vision he had beheld. In Bernalillo many men were tearing down the houses and corrals that stood in the middle of the town from north to south. They cleaned all the rock, adobes, dirt and poles from the place and made it clean. The people who had lived in the houses had to go to other parts of the village to build new homes. Then strange men came and they brought strange looking things to work with and they built a great highway. The highway was not like any road he had ever seen. It looked bright in the sun and the rain could not wash it to pieces.

In those old days El Camino Real was the main highway through Bernalillo and the only main road connecting it with the outer world. It was an ancient highway that was narrow, rough, and winding. It lay to the east of Bernalillo. Such were the roads Rafael knew.

A few of those who were infants at the time old Rafael told of his vision of things to come to Bernalillo did live to see the modern highway put through the town. Houses and corrals were torn down to make way for it, and all happened just as the wise man foretold, so many, many years ago.

Once he told the people that the time would come when great birds would carry passengers through the sky.

There may have been other adivinos in Old Las Placitas, but only Rafael is yet remembered. And all because nearly eighty years ago he foretold the present great highway through the village of Bernalillo, and the aeroplane.

SUBJECT: Salvadoro, El Constructor de Arado
WPA: 5-5-55 #2
March 27, 1942
Words 1087
Sources of information: José Gurulé, Benino Archibeque, Conception
Archibeque. Benino Archibeque is the son of the Salvadoro of this story.

SALVADORO, EL CONSTRUCTOR DE ARADO
(Salvadoro, the Plow Maker)

In the early days of old Las Placitas the men and the women were forced through necessity to make every tool and implement with which they worked. Consequently, those who possessed vision as well as skillful hands became of importance in the village. What they created that brought better living to the people was long remembered by the descendants of those who used the creations. So it was that Salvadoro has long been remembered for the plows he made.

Salvador came to rebuild a long deserted village, with others whose forefathers received the San Antonio de Las Huertas Grant. They named the place Las Placitas. Salvador possessed a keen sense of land values. He chose the most desirable spot in the new village whereon to build his house. It still remains a most desirable spot. He picked out good fields, and he made himself a good plow, which would cause his land to yield abundantly, if weather conditions were favorable, that is, abundantly for his time.

Salvador's plows were his pride. He made them with utmost care and skill and they performed the work he built them to do. Much depended upon the pine tree he selected from which to make his plow. He spent many days tramping through the hills and cañoncitos in search of just the right trees. After he found them, there was the work of chopping them from the limbs he selected, and the dragging of the limbs to his workshop behind his house, a somewhat protected place in the great outdoors. When the limb for a plow was trimmed and smoothed, it must measure about six inches in diameter. One of the forks must be about thirty inches long, the other about thirty-six inches long, and the angle of the fork of the limb must be around seventy degrees. The longer portion of the forked limb was called el cabezo, the head. That part of the fork became the part of the plow that was pulled over the ground. The shorter length of the forked limb became the mano and stood up; it became the handle of the plow. One of the most important features of the plow was the point (la punta). It was made of piñón wood. It corresponded in size of diameter to the cabezo, and was cut to a good, strong point and attached to the cabezo at an angle, downward, with pins four inches long made of encina (oak). These pins were stout and thick. Whenever a point needed to be removed from the cabezo, for replacement with a new point, usually new pins were used.

The next feature to be added to the plow was the frame (la telar). It also was of piñón, and was placed upright and attached to the middle of the head with strong oak pins. Its function was to support the timón (beam which was attached with huge oak pins to the angle of the fork). This timón was of piñón, at least ten feet long and of a thickness to stand the pull or strain that must be put upon it, as this timón was the equivalent to a wagon tongue, by which oxen would draw the plow. Then there was the yugo (yoke), or llugo, as Salvadoro himself spelled it. He made them also. A plow was useless without a llugo, which was a smooth, straight pole about seven feet long or more if needed and of a thickness needed, which depended mostly upon the size of the oxen. This llugo was tied to the horns of the oxen and the center of the pole was tied to the hip to the timón with a rope made of leather, which the aged son of Salvadoro spelled "collundo" and pronounced it so. It evidently comes from the word collerón (harness collar), for the leather rope was the harness which fastened the plow to the oxen.

The only other farm implement used was el cavador (the digger). It was made simply by sharpening to a point, a stout stick. Not a very good substitute for a hoe; but it was all they possessed and its efficiency depended altogether on the strength and energy of the man who wielded it.

Salvadoro used as much care in selecting a cavador as he used in his choice of limbs of his arados. But Salvadoro loved his fields. He tried to out do his neighbors' yield of precious grain and corn, and did it. But Salvadoro did more than make better plows. He was also a maker of arcos (bows). He made most excellent bows from the materials right at hand.

Regrettable it is that not one of his bows is to be found in Las Placitas. More than that, there are but two living in Las Placitas who seem to know just how he made them. The making of this arco, which at one time was the sole weapon of defense in the village, is a lost art.

Salvadoro needed but two things from which to make an arco: palo de poñel and a cord. Poñel, like jara, are species of the willow which grow in the vicinity of Las Placitas. Unlike jara, poñel does not grow on every ditch and watering place in the area. It is found at Las Huertas and in an isolated spot not far from the spring from which the people of Las Placitas have always received their water. Poñel has thicker growth of wood than the jara. It was just the proper thickness for a good bow. The cord for the bow was made of a fibrous substance found under the backbone of the animals they killed. This nervio, or llerbo, as it is spelled and pronounced by the lone direct descendant of old Salvadoro, was kneaded and dried until it was tough and pliable and highly durable. With such a cord the ends of the poñel were held in position to form the arco. The arcos were made in various useful sizes.

In a few more years all memories of the old arco will be vanished from Las Placitas. But in their day los arcos were works of the hands of the men they were made to protect, and also los arcos brought down the meat for their families.

SUBJECT: Miguel y Su Carreta
WPA: 5-5-49 #43
May 8, 1942
Words 1112
Sources of information: Benino Archibeque, Conception Archibeque.

MIGUEL Y SU CARRETA
(Miguel and His Cart)

Miguel Archibeque was born about 1815 somewhere in the Valle del Río del Norte (Valley of the River of the North). In his youth he settled at Algodones, married, and reared his children there. Miguel was of Indian descent, the son of a prisoner of war.

He was energetic and ambitious. Among his possessions was one thing that marked him so. That thing was the carriage of the day, a carreta. Only the ambitious and energetic owned a carreta unless they had the money with which to purchase one or hire one made for them.

The making of a carreta required both labor and time. Those who must make their own carretas, if they had any, were compelled to build them in the winter months when there was less work of other, more necessary kind. Just how long Miguel's carreta was in the making is not known. It is only known that he built one and that it served his family and their families for many years.

Miguel had but one tool with which to build his carreta and that one he made himself. It was la hachuela (a little axe) made of stone and fastened to an oak handle with a tough, stout string of cured animal skin. The stone was about seven inches long, and some three inches wide, and where the handle was tied on, it measured between two and three inches in thickness and diminished in thickness from that point to the end where it was ground to a sharp edge with sand. This little axe was an efficient tool in the hands of Miguel and his people in that long-ago day. Many a giant pine was brought to the ground with it.

To make his carreta, Miguel cut down a pine tree about three feet in diameter, for la rueda (the wheel) must be at least three feet in diameter. From the trunk of this tree he cut two wheels about twelve inches thick. Next he made a hole in the exact center of each one large enough to hold the pole that would form the axle tree.

Aside from the wheels Miguel made his carreta of encina (oak). He hewed down the best and largest oak trees he could find. He needed one pole about seven feet long to form the axle tree. Its diameter was around six inches. Another pole was required for the lanza (pole for wagon). The length of this timber was gauged by the length of the carreta box plus the length required to harness it to the oxen. From the oaks he hewed out the equivalent of one hundred eighteen board feet from which the box was made. The box measured eight feet long, five feet wide, and three feet deep. The boards were mainly dressed through the expert use of the hachuela, and after that they were sanded into shape and smoothness. The finished boards were put together with pegs made of encina. During those winter days Miguel cut out many, many pins of varying sizes for use in the making of his precious carreta.

When the box was finished, Miguel was ready to assemble his cart. The axle lanza was laid in place, the length of the middle on the bottom and securely fixed with stout oak pins. Across the middle of the width of the box and fitted over the lanza, the axle tree was fastened, and then the wheels were put on and firmly secured by means of crosspieces affixed to the wheel at the places where they would best hold the axle tree where it protruded through the holes in the ruedas (wheels) cut for them. Stout oak pins were used everywhere to assure long and hard wear to the carreta.

In those long-ago days a carreta was treated with respect, and on the occasions of starting on journeys in one, there was real ceremony. Carretas used by the native people were never called just carreta, but carreta Católico. Always the Indians called them carreta Católico, and the native people learned to make them from the Indians, so they, too, called them by the name the Indians gave them, carreta Católico. Any carreta owned by others than Indians or natives of the land of New Mexico were referred to by them as carreta Mexicano.

Under no circumstance might anyone, even an infant, ride in a carreta Católico unless he had been baptized. Whenever an unbaptized one climbed into a carreta Católico, he was immediately thrown out. Consequently, carretas Católicos were held in a sort of spiritual esteem.

A carreta Católico carried six people very comfortably when they were seated upon the floor. Animal skins and serapes covered the floor and thus the women were the better protected. But at best the riding was rough and very bumpy, and the creaking and rumbling of the cart was so great that the passengers could scarcely hear the sound of their own voices. After a long journey—twenty or thirty miles—they were sore and stiff.

It was an important occasion when the carreta Católico was made ready for a journey. The men approached it with bowed and uncovered heads. The master of the carreta saw to it that none entered the carreta who had not been baptized. He did it as conscientiously as if the fate of the journey depended upon him in this matter. When the passengers were all seated on the floor, the driver stood up in his place among them and started the oxen and the journey was begun.

It was with such ceremony that the carreta Católico of Miguel was set on its way from Algodones to Las Placitas, the village that one of Miguel's sons helped to build. That journey was made over one hundred years ago. At that time there was no other carreta in the newly resettled village. There were never but a few carretas in the village, and now among those older folk yet surviving there are but a precious three or four who have any memories of the carreta Católico or the carreta Mexicano of the days of their grandparents.

In those old days the carreta Católico was used as a carrier of harvests from the fields to the house and the starting off was without ceremony, but none without baptism could ride in it. The carreta Mexicano had no baptism qualifications nor were they started on their journeys with ceremony.

SUBJECT: Nicolás Goes to Market
WPA: 5-5-49 #4
June 19, 1942
Words 1160
Sources of information: Benino Archibeque, Conception Archibeque, Patricio Gallegos. Benino Archibeque remembers how the packsaddle was made and fastened to the back of an ox. He played with the younger children of the Nicolás of this story. Conception Archibeque remembers seeing the old packsaddle. Her father was a friend of the Nicolás of this story.

NICOLÁS GOES TO MARKET

It was in the early years of the American occupation that Nicolás set to work to make una albarda (a packsaddle) for his buey (ox). With such a saddle he would be able to take his one surplus commodity, uvas (grapes), to market and get them there in good condition.

To make the packsaddle, he required a certain-shaped limb from a pine tree, enough jara (shrub of tough, pliable willow-like switches), and plenty of correa (straps of buffalo and goat hides). In those long-ago days a good pack-saddle was more the result of expert hunting than of the skillful handling of timber and hacheta (small stone axe). And so it was that Nicolás started the work on his packsaddle by taking his lunch of two ears of dried blue corn and going up into the mountains to arch out a properly shaped limb of a pine tree, which would form the foundation of the saddle. That was not an easy task. The limb must be about thirty-four inches from tip to tip. That thirty-four inches must be at least one foot in diameter, it must contain a middle section of about eighteen inches that was straight, and the portions of limb at each end of it must curve upward at an angle of around forty-three degrees. Difficult as it was to find such a timber, it was a much simpler matter than it would have been had Nicolás attempted the making of such a foundation for his saddle with his own hands. Nicolás knew he would find what he needed, so he searched until he found it. When he discovered it, he hewed it from the tree and took it to his house. With his hacheta he cut off the curved ends to the desired length of some eight inches; he hewed the three naturally formed sections of the timber down to a thickness of around one-and-a-half inches and there was his form measuring around twelve inches in width. He carefully cut off the ends, shaped them as he cut until they were perfectly rounded. This process took very little from the length. At the base of each curve and on the outer side of the curves or angles, Nicolás hewed out a little shelf wide enough to support the leather straps that would help to hold the saddle in place on the back of the ox. On the inside of each angle and at a point in the center of the width, a hold was drilled large enough to carry a three-inch correa (leather strap). That done, Nicolás took sand, rubbed the surfaces of the saddle with it until all was even and smooth. With sand he shaped the bottom of the saddle to fit the contour of the animal's back. The foundation of una albarda was finished. Nicolás next piled up his small branches of jara and set to work. There must be a safe carrier for his grapes. He called it la guatol. (The word is not Spanish but it was used instead of the Spanish word jaula, which means cage. Where this guatol originated was not known but it is still recognized as a word meaning cage.) Nicolás took care in the weaving of the cage, made it both durable and strong. It was about the length of the seat of the saddle and about the same width. The height was a matter of preference. The bottom of it was tightly woven, the sides closely woven, for the grapes must be protected. The weaving was firm and strong to stand wear and strain. It was a perfectly balanced carrier and fitted firmly on the seat of the saddle between the ends at the bottom. In fact, it fitted so snugly that it needed no further securing when the saddle was girded firmly and immovable on the back of the ox.

The correa used in fastening the saddle was three inches wide. It was tough and sufficiently pliable to make knots secure. One piece was drawn lengthwise along the seat of the saddle and was threaded through the holes drilled for it. The ends of that piece were attached to the three-inch-wide pieces held in place by the little shelves. Those pieces of correa were long enough to reach half the distance around the bottom of the saddle and allow for knots. The two lengths came together at a point that marked the middle of the sides. At that point on each side of the saddle, more three-inch correa was added. Those two hanging straps were tightly cinched under the animal's body and made secure. Thus was the packsaddle laced to the body of the ox and la guatol held firm.

The grapes were gathered while just sufficiently ripened to allow for the time to be consumed in the journey. The guatol was packed with skill and the grapes were found in good condition at the time of sale; and in those long-ago days there was a market for grapes. In the autumn many an ox carried grapes to Santa Fe, where there was a ready market. The time required to make the journey was fully a week. In those old days that was a profitable venture, for the expense of the trip was nil.

Once when Nicolás drove his ox to market he was fortunate enough to make some extra money. His son, a youth in his early teens, was tending the animal. Two men from the east came along and were puzzled as to just how the saddle was fastened to the animal. The correa was so skillfully adjusted that it defied the average understanding of such matters; to those who knew nothing of how it was done, the fact that the saddle remained in place was baffling. The two men offered to pay liberally, according to the boy's notion of finances, to see just how the thing was done. So for fifty cents the youth removed the outfit from the back of the ox and replaced it. That incident still lingers in the memories of the few remaining old people in Las Placitas, and probably because of that memory, the memory of the old albarda and guatol and of Nicolás himself, and his trips to market are still remembered with pleasure by those precious few.

SUBJECT: The Rope Maker
WPA: #38
July 30, 1942
Words 1627
Sources of information: Benino Archibeque, Conception Archibeque, Patricio Gallegos. Benino Archibeque was a descendant of the family of Mariano and Juan, who were among the early settlers of the village of Algodones. Conception Archibeque well remembers the rope makers of her childhood days. Patricio Gallegos is a descendant of the old Valentino of this story.

CONSTRUCTOR DE REATA
(The Rope Maker)

In the Las Placitas of long ago, reata (rope) was as essential to the people in carrying on their simple mode of living as were their serapes (blankets). So the art of rope making was just as necessary as was the art of weaving; an expert rope maker was as important in the community as an expert weaver and both were looked upon as craftsmen.

Horsehair and the hides of animals were the materials from which rope was made. But there was no reata de crin (horsehair rope) made in the Las Placitas community for the community. That kind of rope was made only for the rich, for they possessed horses.

The making of the coveted horsehair rope, reata preciosa (precious rope) they called it, was made by the skillful hands of youth whose fingers had not been hardened and stiffened by toil. Hands that made rope must be quick and skillful in the handling of even a single hair from the tail or the mane of a horse. The homemade spinning apparatus for the making of horsehair rope was constructed on the same principle as the malacate, which was made for the use of the women in spinning their wool into thread.

The spinning implement for the hair was called una tarabilla (a holder). It was made of two sticks: one about seventeen inches long and around an inch in diameter, the other about a foot in length and around a quarter of an inch in diameter. That stick was called the mango (handle). Both sticks were sanded down until they were perfectly smooth. An eye was drilled through la tarabilla (the holder) large enough to push the mango through it and have sufficient room left to turn it. The eye was placed about three inches from the top of the holder. A knob was cut at the end of the holder to prevent it from going clear through the eye. And thus was made the implement on which the hairs were spun into rope. Rope of varying sizes were made on those tarabillas aided by two pairs of skillful masculine hands.

Once each year the horses on the ranch of el patrón were brought from the stables to a cleanly swept spot to be properly cropped. Certain men in the employ of el patrón were skilled in that work, for el patrón wished his horses to look elegante (stylish). Their manes and tails were cropped short. There was the hair for the rope all over the clean area. Then was the time when the rope makers set to work. Young Mariano and his much older brother, Juan, were el patrón's most skilled rope makers. They gathered up the hair, carried it to the outdoor work place under the shade of a spreading cottonwood tree, and washed the hair until it was clean. When it was sufficiently dry, they piled it up on an inverted animal skin, where it would be handy for them, as there must be ever-ready strands for the tarabilla. Each strand was composed of either three single hairs, or strands made of various sizes of other strands put together in triples, all according to the thickness of the rope desired.

Mariano held the tarabilla by the handle, took the three hairs that Juan had fastened together at the top, and placed the knot directly under the point where the handle was joined to the tarabilla. With his right hand he revolved the handle. That set the other stick, the holder, in a rotary motion. Mariano kept his left hand busy holding the three hairs together and making them go tightly together around the holder in a way that twisted them together as they moved down the polished surface of the holder. As the hair was wet, the twisting process was easily accomplished. As the hair was taken up by the tarabilla, or holder, Juan stood ready with another triplet of hairs for Mariano to get attached to the end of the first three as they coiled about the holder. When the second three were nearing the end, Juan handed a new three to Mariano to fasten on to the descending end of the strand of three single hairs. That process was repeated until a length of ten feet was acquired. Thus was completed the first single strand of three, which would require two more such strands before it could become a part of a rope. A very slender rope it would be but a very strong one.

When those three strands were done, they were fastened together at one end placed in position on the holder. Mariano twirled the handle again and the holder went round and round, twisting the wet strands about it until the end of the strands were off the holder. The rope was less than ten feet, for the last spinning had taken it up. The strand, or rope, if that size was desired, was then dipped in water and the ends fastened to sticks or poles that would hold it firmly into the twists the tarabilla had made in it until it was perfectly dried, when the twist would be permanent.

To make a thicker rope, Mariano and Juan set to work to make many more single strands of triple hairs and then combine them into thicker strands and unite them until they attained the desired thickness. The repeated process of making the first strands of three hairs each, in any thickness of the strands, resulted in various thicknesses of rope. These ropes were enduring.

El patrón needed this stout rope for the animals in his wagon trains on their annual trips to Los Estados over the Santa Fe Trail. He needed them for his great wagons of wool, he needed such rope to fence in his threshing floor, to suspend great leather bags of wheat from beams in his storehouses. He needed enough to loan to those who labored for him to fence in their own community threshing floors. The need of reata de crin was great, and while his fingers were nimble, young Mariano was kept busy making it. Day after day, year after year in fair weather, cold or hot, Mariano stood up or squatted on the ground, putting aches in his back and cramps in his arms at the unending labor of spinning hairs into ropes.

Making rope of animal hides was a much simpler matter. In Las Placitas rope of leather (correa) was needed in every household. Such rope was just as good, or bad, as the hands of the rope maker made it. Rope of leather was stout and durable if made so. It was used for harness to hitch the oxen to the plows; much of it was used along with the borrowed horsehair rope to complete the fence around their threshing floor. They needed much correa to tether their animals. They required quantities of it, made into slender rope, for fastening parts of their harness together, for tying stone implements to their handles, for binding various things together, and for fastening saddles to animals, the wooden saddles served as carriers . Slender rope in those old days took the place of nails in that they were used to join things of wood together, where wooden pegs were impracticable.

Rope of correa was durable and stout only when the hides used to make it were properly cured. Old Valentino of the long-ago Las Placitas earned many a goat to add to his herd because he took great care in the curing of his hides. Ropes made from the hides he cured were desirable ropes, and his care in making the ropes made him an outstanding craftsman.

When the hide was ready, Valentino spread it out and knelt down beside it. With a sharp stone, he made a mark in from the outer edge of the hide, the distance he wished for the width of the leather strap he was to cut. Then he cut the hide to that point. That was the starting place, and using that short distance for the width of the strap, he started cutting that distance all around the hide in an unending circular movement. He cut round and round, keeping the certain width until he reached the center of the hide. Then he stood up, straightened out the strip he had cut into one long length. He required three of such lengths. When he had them, he fastened them together firmly at one end and put them in water to soak for many hours, which meant that he knew just when they would be ready for the rope. When that time arrived, Valentino took them from the water, fastened the joined ends to a tree trunk, then twisted the three straps into one stout rope, just as the tarabilla twisted the strands of horsehair into one rope. All the time he used all his strength to keep the leather rope pulled taut. When the straps were together firmly in the rope, Valentino needed help for one man could not do a perfect job of fastening the free end of that wet, taut rope to another anchor, where it would dry into a perfect rope, strong, durable and a credit to its maker's skill.

A SELECTED BIBLIOGRAPHY

Books:

Archives of the Federal Writers' Project. Series One: Printed and Mimeograph Publications in the Surviving FWP Files, 1933-1943, excluding State Guides. A Listing and Guide to Parts One, Two and Three of the Harvester Microfilm Collection. Sussex, England: Harvester Press Microform Publications, 1987.

This is a guide to the records of the Federal Writers' Project in the Library of Congress. Part One, "Contents of Reels," lists the publications by state, titles, authors, date of publication, and notes on the series. Part Two is a list of the publications from the East, the Midwest, and New Mexico. Part Three concludes the list from the rest of the states not in Parts One and Two. Also includes the administrative files, 1936-1944, and the Records of the Folklore Project, 1936-1939. Title and author indexes complete the guide.

Archives of the Work Projects Administration and Predecessors, 1933-1943. Series One: The Final State Reports 1943. A Listing and Guide to Part One of the Harvester Microfilm Collection. Sussex, England: Harvester Press Microform Publications, 1987.

A guide to the surviving files in the Archives of the Federal Writers' Project, Record Group number 69. The Final State Reports include, among others, reports for the Federal Music, Arts, Crafts, Theater, and Federal Writers' Programs. Excluded are the State Guides and the manuscript/typescript Surveys of American Life and Culture, which is unpublished material and is in the FWP Archives in the Library of Congress.

Batchen, Lou Sage. *Las Placitas: Historical Facts and Legends.* Placitas, N.M.: Tumbleweed Press, 1972.

This book consists of eleven of the stories and legends Lou Batchen collected as a field worker for the New Mexico Federal Writers' Project. Most of the stories are descriptions of life and culture in the villages of Las Placitas and Tejón.

Brewer, Jeutonne P. *The Federal Writers' Project: A Bibliography.* Metuchen, N.J.: Scarecrow Press, 1994.

This "working bibliography" gives major sources of information about the Federal Writers' Project. Includes items about the Writers' Project found in records about the Historical Records Survey and the Federal Theater Project .

Brown, Lorin W., Charles L. Briggs and Marta Weigle. *Hispano Folklife of New Mexico: The Lorin W. Brown Federal Writers' Project Manuscripts.* Albuquerque: University of New Mexico Press, 1978.

This book presents the material Lorin Brown collected as a field worker for the New Mexico Federal Writers' Project. Part I is a biography of Lorin Brown and an ethnohistory on Córdova, New Mexico, where he concentrated his activities. Part II is a chronicle of village life and lore in Córdova that includes a brief story of Tía Lupe, the village church keeper.

Cabeza de Baca, Fabiola. *We Fed Them Cactus.* Albuquerque, NM: University of New Mexico Press, 1954.

A story of the life and culture of Hispanos in early New Mexico, written as an endeavor to preserve a history of daily life in the Llano country. Similar stories appear in the New Mexico Federal Writers' Project.

Córdova, Gilberto Benito. *Bibliography of Unpublished Materials Pertaining to Hispanic Culture in the New Mexico WPA Culture in the New Mexico WPA Writers' Files.* Santa Fe: New Mexico State Department of Education, 1972.

The first part of this bibliography consists of names of the authors, transcribers, and contributors associated with the WPA files. The second part is the bibliography itself while the last part is the subject index. The bibliography lists nearly 600 unpublished manuscripts, briefly annotated.

Córdova, Lorenzo de. *Echoes of the Flute.* Santa Fe: Ancient City Press, 1972.

Lorenzo de Córdova narrates three personal stories that describe the life and culture of Córdova, a northern New Mexico Hispano community. He briefly mentions Tía Lupe, the village church caretaker and source of the many stories and legends collected by the author. Marta Weigle contributes a place names list and glossary.

Delgado, Edmundo R. *Witch Stories of New Mexico: Folklore of New Spain—Cuentos de Brujas de Nuevo Mexico: Folklore de la Nueva España.* Santa Fe: E. R. Delgado, 1994.

This collection of witch stories is based on the folktales collected by Lou Sage Batchen, Lynn Bright, and Annette Thorp for the New Mexico Federal Writers' Project.

Deutsch, Sarah. *No Separate Refuge: Culture, Class, and Gender on an Anglo-Hispanic Frontier in the American Southwest, 1880-1940.* New York: Oxford University Press, 1987.

This is a study of the dynamics between Hispanics and Anglos at the time when Anglos were moving into traditionally Hispanic lands. Deutsch includes a chapter, "At the Center: Hispanic Village Women, 1900-1914," to illustrate, using some of the stories about women in the New Mexico Federal Writers' Project, the roles Hispanic women played in village life and culture.

Dickey, Roland F. *New Mexico Village Arts.* Albuquerque, NM: University of New Mexico Press, 1949, 1990.

Chapter Three, "Parlor Pieces," of this portrait of New Mexico life as seen in 1949, includes descriptions of the New Mexican adobe home and the work life of the Hispanic woman performing such activities as plastering and whitewashing her home. The stories are similar to the "cuentos" collected for the New Mexico Federal Writers' Project.

The Federal Writers' Project. Following Marta Weigle's "Reader's Guide with Maps" in *New Mexicans in Cameo and Camera.* Albuquerque: University of New Mexico, 1985.

A guide to the materials, including photographs, in New Mexicans in Cameo. Items are identified by "title, collector, informant, word and page count, date of writing, date of receipt in Santa Fe and the location(s) of the documents."

Federal Writers' Project. New Mexico. *Calendar of Events, Compiled and Written by Federal Writers' Project.* Santa Fe: Works Progress Administration, 1937

This calendar of events includes Indian dance rituals, Spanish fiestas and religious ceremonies, and Anglo-American celebrations. Some of the annual events held are told as stories collected for the New Mexico Federal Writers' Project—for instance, "Los Pastores" and the Feast Day of Nuestra Señora de Guadalupe.

Forrest, Suzanne Sims. *Century of Faith. One Hundred Years in the Life of the Las Placitas Presbyterian Church.* Albuquerque: Desert Dreams Publishers, 1995.

A history of the Presbyterian Church in Las Placitas and the families who founded it. In the first chapter, "San Antonio de las Huertas," Forrest draws upon some of the WPA histories for her background. In the second chapter, "The Seeds of Presbyterianism," she comments on the inter-relationship of Lou Sage Batchen with the community and on some of Batchen's interview methods. In Chapter Five, Other Founding Families, she also makes use of the Batchen Las Placitas materials.

Forrest, Suzanne. *The Preservation of the Village: New Mexico's Hispanics and the New Deal.* Albuquerque, NM: University of New Mexico Press, 1986.

This book places New Mexico and its Mexican-American population within the context of Anglo-American-ethnic-history. The study characterizes the New Mexico Federal Writers' Project as an effort to record, preserve, and revive interest in the oral and written heritage of Hispanics.

Griego, Alfonso. *Good-bye My Land of Enchantment: A True Story of Some of the First Spanish-speaking Natives and Early Settlers of San Miguel County, Territory of New Mexico.* n.p. 1981.

This story is about the author's ancestors and his life in Las Vegas, when New Mexico was still a territory. His narrative includes stories about preserving and preparing food, and health practices of the people of the time. For example, he tells how the community depended on the curanderas and parteras and their herbs. His stories resemble those collected for the New Mexico Federal Writers' Project.

Gurulé, Bill F. *Fleeting Shadows and Faint Echoes of Las Huertas.* New York: Carlton Press, 1987.

Gurulé's ninety-five page book is a personal narrative about his family life and the History of the San Antonio de Las Huertas Land Grant and the village, Las Huertas, where his ancestors lived during the early days in New Mexico. He includes his experiences as a soldier and a prisoner of war in World War II.

Jaramillo, Cleofas M. *Shadows of the Past/Sombras del Pasado.* 1941; reprint, Santa Fe: Ancient City Press, 1980.

This is a collection of vignettes, written by the author to preserve some of the Hispano folklore of New Mexico. The chapter "A Bit of New Mexico Folklore" mainly consists of witches tales similar to those that appear in the New Mexico Federal Writers' Project.

Kutsche, Paul. *Survival of Spanish-American Villages.* Colorado Springs: Research Committee, Colorado College, 1979.

A collection of essays presented at a symposium on Mexican-American affairs. One of the essays briefly mentions Lorin Brown's work on the village of Córdova in New Mexico, the Hispano community he portrays in his book *Hispano Folklife of New Mexico.*

Lea, Aurora Lucero-White. *Literary Folklore of the Hispanic Southwest.* San Antonio, TX: Naylor, 1953.

This compilation of New Mexico folklore consists of folk songs, songs, prayers, and folk stories. Aurora Lea was associated with the New Mexico Federal Writers' Project for some time and was responsible for collecting some of the materials for the Project.

Mangione, Jerre Gerlando. *The Dream and the Deal: The Federal Writers' Project, 1935-1943.* Boston: Little, Brown, 1972.

Inez Cassidy, director of the New Mexico Federal Writers' Project, is briefly mentioned in this comprehensive history of the Federal Writers' Project.

McDonald, William F. *Federal Relief Administration and the Arts: The Origins and Administrative History of the Arts Projects of the Works Progress Administration.* Columbus: Ohio State University Press, 1961.

Chapters 26 to 28 of this volume are a history of the Federal Writers' Project, its origins, philosophy, purpose, and the people involved with its creation and direction. At the core of the Project was the production of the American Guides for all the states. Other projects included Folklore Studies, Slave Narratives, Social-ethnic Studies and Negro Studies, for example.

Minton, Charles Ethridge. *Juan of Santo Niño: An Authentic Account of Pioneer Life in New Mexico, 1863-1864.* Santa Fe: Sunstone Press, 1973.

In the preface Charles Minton gives a brief history of the early settlement of New Mexico and the communities established. Vaguely ficitionalized, the book is the story of Juan, one of the early settlers, his family, relatives, friends, and neighbors and their daily lives in the village of Santo Niño. Minton bases Juan of Santo Niño on the stories collected by Lou Sage Batchen, a field worker for the New Mexico Writers' Project, but never mentions her or the informants by name.

Otero, Nina. *Old Spain in Our Southwest.* New York: Harcourt, Brace, 1936. Rept., Rio Grande Press, Chicago, 1962.

This book is an attempt to preserve a record of life and culture in early New Mexico as remembered by the author. Some of the stories in one of the chapters, "Songs and Stories," are like the ones recorded for the New Mexico Federal Writers' Project.

Penkower, Monty Noam. *The Federal Writers' Project: A Study in Government Patronage of the Arts.* Urbana: University of Illinois Press, 1977.

This is a social history of the WPA's Federal Writers' Project and its ties to the cultural mood and environment of the Depression era. The book's intent is to establish the FWP's concern with the trends of the period, such as regionalism and an expanding interest in minority groups and socioethnic studies.

Pláticas del Pasado/Conversations of the Past. Placitas, NM: Tumbleweed Press, 1976. Sponsored by the Public Library of Placitas.

A series of conversations with Barbarita Baros Lucero, Aurelia Gurulé, and Antonio DeLara with Christina Gonzales and Vivian DeLara, about life in Placitas and food customs. It also contains recipes.

Rebolledo, Tey Diana and Eliana S. Rivero. *Infinite Divisions: An Anthology of Chicana Literature.* Tucson: University of Arizona Press, 1993.

The authors use a historical framework to introduce "a heritage of oral and written traditions" to feature women's writings before the Chicano Renaissance. Chapter 1, "Foremothers," consists of some of the narratives collected for the New Mexico Federal Writers' Project, among other early works.

Rebolledo, Tey Diana. *Women Singing in the Snow.* Tucson: University of Arizona Press, 1995.

Tey Diana Rebolledo discusses the history of Chicana literature and criticism, the different standpoints from which the critics engage their subject, and the characteristics that influence contemporary Chicana literature: oral traditions and folklore, for example. In the chapter "Early Hispana/Mexicana Writers: The Chicana Literary Tradition," Rebolledo includes a section on the oral histories related to the New Mexico Federal Writers' Project.

Robe, Stanley L., ed. *Hispanic Folktales From New Mexico: Narratives From the R.D. Jameson Collection.* Berkeley: University of California Press, 1977.

R.D. Jameson's collection of folktales and other narratives were gathered over twelve years and organized into the New Mexico Folklore Archive. The tales consist of animal stories, ordinary folktales, jokes and anecdotes, and formula tales. The introduction gives a brief history of the State's early settlement and the Hispanics' efforts to maintain their attitudes, way of life, and their oral traditions.

Smith, Andrew T. "The People of the San Antonio de Las Huertas Grant, New Mexico, 1767-1900." Unpublished M.A. Thesis, Colorado College, 1973.

An ethno-history of the Las Placitas area that draws largely on the Lou Sage Batchen Las Placitas materials, locating them within a larger historical frame. He comments on Lou Sage Batchen's recording and interview technique.

Weigle, Marta, ed. *Hispanic Villages of Northern New Mexico: A Reprint of Volume II of the 1935 Tewa Basin Study with Supplementary Materials.* Santa Fe: Lightning Tree, 1975.

The United States government conducted a sociological study of the Tewa Basin area of the Indian pueblos and the Spanish-American villages. Weigle compiled an eight-part bibliography of materials related to the anthropological and sociological aspects of New Mexico. Part II is a selected list of materials on Hispano folklore.

Weigle, Marta, ed. *New Mexicans in Cameo and Camera: New Deal Documentation of Twentieth-Century Lives.* Albuquerque: University of New Mexico Press, 1985.

This is a compilation of portraits gathered from throughout New Mexico by artists, writers, and photographers involved in WPA projects. The book consists of selected photographs, life and oral histories, and narratives from various New Deal agencies, including the New Mexico Federal Writers' Project. "Rebozo and Resolano: Old Historic Lifeways" is a descriptive account of the Hispano communities and their "vanishing way of life."

Weigle, Marta. *New Mexico Artists and Writers: A Celebration, 1940.*

This newspaper-type publication honors the artists and writers who made Santa Fe and Taos their artists' colonies. Among the writers noted are Ina Sizer Cassiday, writer, poet, author of *Art and Arts of New Mexico,* and known as director of the New Mexico Federal Writers' Project, and N. Howard Thorp, writer and author of *Cowboy Songs* and *Tales of the Chuck Wagon.*

Thorp was also known as the husband of Annette Hesch Thorp, field worker for the Writers' Project.

Weigle, Marta, ed. *Two Guadalupes: Hispanic Legends and Magic Tales From Northern New Mexico.* Santa Fe: Ancient City Press, 1987.

Guadalupe Gallegos and Guadalupe "Tía Lupe" Martínez are the sources for the many stories and legends collected by Lorin Brown and Bright Lynn as part of the New Mexico Federal Writers' Project. Brief biographies of the two Guadalupes are included along with photographs of family members, Lorin Brown, Bright Lynn, community churches, and church members. An appendix describes the New Deal projects and project workers. A list of sources and notes supplements the texts.

Weigle, Marta, ed. *Women of New Mexico: Depression Era Images.* Santa Fe: Ancient City Press, 1993.

This volume compiles a collection of eighty-six photographs taken for the Farm Security Administration (FSA). Twenty-five excerpts from the New Mexico Federal Writers' Project accompany the photographs. The photographs and excerpts are organized in categories that depict life and cultural activities: weaving and sewing, food and cooking, and public events. The introduction includes sketches of Reyes N. Martínez and Annette Hesch Thorp, both field workers for the New Mexico Federal Writers' Project.

Weigle, Marta and Kyle Fiore. *Santa Fe and Taos: The Writer's Era, 1916-1941.* Santa Fe: Ancient City Press, 1982, 1992.

This volume chronicles the history and ambiance of the art colonies in New Mexico and includes the period when the New Mexico Federal Writers' Project was active. The book also includes some information on Reyes N. Martínez, Lorin Brown, Bright Lynn, Lou Sage Batchen, and Annette Hesch Thorpe, who were field workers in the Writers' Project.

Weigle, Marta and Peter White. *The Lore of New Mexico.* Albuquerque: University of New Mexico Press, 1988.

This is a compendium of the Native American, Hispano, and Anglo folklore, songs, rituals, and artifacts in New Mexico. This 523-page volume explores the major symbols and themes in the State's travel, tourism, and spectacle, and visual, verbal, and musical folk arts. The last part is a study of the folklife representative of the three major cultures.

Wood, Nancy. *Heartland New Mexico: Photographs from the Farm Security Administration, 1935-1943.* Albuquerque: University of New Mexico, 1989.

Using photographs taken by FSA photographers, the author documents life in New Mexico during the New Deal years. In the chapter "Three Hispanic Villages," Wood shows how the Hispanic people struggled to preserve their way of life and culture.

Wroth, William, ed. *Russell Lee's FSA Photographs of Chamisal and Peñasco.* Santa Fe: Ancient City Press, 1985.

This collection of photographs records life around a "Spanish-American home," with the women performing their household duties, many of which are mentioned in the stories collected for the New Mexico Federal Writers' Project.

Articles:

Batchen, Lou Sage. "La Curandera." *El Palacio* 81.1 (1975): 20-25.

This is the story about Jesusita, la curandera. Batchen describes Jesusita, her house, and the remedios she used from the herbs collected in the area.

Bryan, Howard. "Off the Beaten Path." *The Albuquerque Journal* 28 (1973): E-12.

Howard Bryan interviewed Mrs. Lou Sage Batchen about her work on the history of Las Placitas. Mrs. Batchen collected the stories and legends of the old village of Las Huertas, a community near Las Placitas, but her manuscript was never published. Eventually her work was produced as *Las Placitas: Historical Facts and Legends.* Bryan retells the story of Eufemia and how she saved her community from an Indian raid with her sopapillas.

Dumont, Andre. "Ina Sizer Cassidy and the Writers' Project." *Impact: Albuquerque Journal Magazine* 19 (1982): 12-14.

The author presents a brief biography of Ina Sizer Cassidy, who was the director of the New Mexico Federal Writers' Project. He claims that Cassidy's work for the Project has been overlooked, and with this article he strives to bring some recognition to her leadership.

Dwyer-Shick, Susan. "Review Essay: Folklore and Government Support." *Journal of American Folklore* 89 (1976): 476-86.

The author reviews *The Dream and the Deal* by Jerre Gerlando Mangione, who chronicles the history of the Federal Writers' Project. Dwyer-Shick describes the books as useful for telling the comprehensive story of this government effort. She suggests that Chapter Seven, "Varieties of American Stuff," might be the most useful for those interested in folklore.

Gonzales, Barbara. "Women's Stories of the WPA." Paper presented at the National Association of Chicana/Chicano Conference, Mexico City, June 1998.

Márquez, María Teresa. "El Diablo a Pie: Historias de las Mujeres Hispanas de NuevoMexico." Paper presented at the ALDEEU Conference, Leon, Spain, 1996.

This is a sketch of the stories about and by Hispanic women collected for the New Mexico Federal Writers' Project. The study focuses on stories that illustrate women's lives and their social and cultural activities.

Rapport, Leonard. "How Valid Are the Federal Writers' Project Life Stories: An Iconoclast Among the True Believers." *Oral History Review* (1979): 6-17.

This narrative is about the author's experience with the Southern Regional Writers' Project as a writer. He collected and wrote a few life stories for the Project, but his main task was to write a book on tobacco and the tobacco people in the south. He recalls that he did not view the Writers' Project with the same degree of seriousness as others did.

Weigle, Marta. "Guadalupe Baca de Gallegos' 'Las tres preciosidas' (The Three Treasures): Notes on the Tale, Its Narrator and Collector." *New Mexico Folklore* Record 15 1980-81, 31-35.

This article includes one of the tales told to Lynn Bright by Mrs. Guadalupe Gallegos of West Las Vegas, New Mexico, who was one of the informants for the New Mexico Federal Writers' Project. Lynn Bright was a field worker for the Writers' Project. An extensive biography of Mrs. Gallegos and an autobiographical sketch of Lynn Bright are part of the tale "Las tres preciosidas."

Weigle, Marta. "Some New Mexico Grandmothers: A Note on the WPA Writers' Program in New Mexico." *In Hispanic Arts & Ethnohistory in the Southwest: New Papers Inspired by the Work of E. Boyd.* Edited by Marta Weigle, Claudia Larcombe and Samuel Larcombe, Santa Fe: Ancient City Press, 1985; Albuquerque: University of New Mexico Press, 93-102.

Marta Weigle relates what happened to the stories and life histories collected by Lou Sage Batchen and Annette Hesch Thorp, field workers for the New Mexico Federal Writers' Project. Batchen collected her material, folklore, and ethnohistory, in Las Placitas and the other small communities nestled at the foothills of the Sandia Mountains. *Before Your Time,* a children's book, and a three-hundred page illustrated manuscript, based on Batchen's material, were not published. Annette Thorp's manuscript of the life stories of the old women still alive in the villages was not published either. Thorp's work was not ready for publication by the time funding for the Writers' Project was cut.

Weigle, Marta with Mary Powell. "From Alice Corbin's 'Lines Mumbled in Sleep' to 'Eufemia's Sopapillas': Women and the Federal Writers' Project in New Mexico." *New America* 4.3 (1981): 54-76.

This article chronicles the history of the New Mexico Writers' Project and its female staff, headed by Ina Sizer Cassidy, who was assisted by Alice Corbin Henderson. The article also focuses on the work done for the Writers' Project by Aurora Lucero White.

GLOSSARY

Acequias-	canal, trench or drain
Ahijado/a-	godson or goddaughter
Ahora-	now
Alabados-	hymns
Alado-	to the side of, on the side of (correctly as al lado)
Alao-	(see alado)
Albarda-	pack saddle
Alcalde-	mayor
Almendras-	nuts
Alva (Alba)	dawn, daybreak. Son of praise to the dawn
Americanos-	applied to any non-Spanish-speaking whites
Ansina-	(see así)
Arado-	primitive plow
Arpa-	harp
Asemita-	bran bread
Así-	like this, this way, thus
Atole-	ground blue cornmeal
Azadons-	digging tools (like a hoe)
Bailes-	dances
Bancos-	form or bench without a back
Barcia-	chaff
Bastimiento-	food to take on hunting trips
Bautismos-	baptisms
Bendija-	bless
Berraza-	water parsnip
Bizcochos-	small biscuits
Bosques-	forests
Buñuelos emmielados-	a kind of fritter with honey
Cabello-	corn silk
Cachana-	charm made of a small root

449

Calabasas (also (spelled calavasas)-	squash or pumpkin. Dar calabazas-to reject or turn down a man's proposal of marriage
Calavacia-	evil-smelling herbs
Calabaza vinatera-	bottle-shaped gourd
Canto-	rim of something
Cañón-	canyon
Capilla-	chapel
Carda-	comb
Carne seca-	dried meat or jerky
Carreta-	cart
Casorios-	weddings
Católico-	adjective for Catholic
Chicos-	kernels of corn removed from the cob
Chongo-	long braid
Cibolero-	buffalo hunter
Comadres-	the mother of a godchild and the godmother
Correa-	animal hide
Correa-	straps made of buffalo or goat hide
Corrida del gallo-	the running of the rooster, or rooster pull
Creo que-	I believe that . . .
Crianza-	child rearing, bringing up
Crin-	horsehair
Crisol-	crucible
Croque-	(see creo que)
Cuajo-	water made by steeping the stomach of a young animal (goat or calf) used for making cheese, rennet
Curandera-	healer, also witch (varies)
Davidosa-	the unselfish one
De pidimiento letter-	letter asking for a woman's hand in marriage, usually delivered by the man's male relatives to the father of the woman.
Despencias-	storage room or pantry
Día de Santiago-	St. James's Feast Day
Día de fiestas-	feast days
Duende-	dwarf
Era-	threshing floor
Escrivano-	person who wrote and read letters for those who did not know how to read or write
Esquite-	toasted corn

Espigas-	ears of corn
Espins-	porcupine
Los Estados-	the United States
Fanega-	a measure of grain and seed of about a hundred weight
Flauta-	flute
Fogón Campaña-	wood burning stove or fireplace
Fundidor-	smelter
Gavilla-	sheave
Gente (sometimes spelled jente)-	people
Gringoes-	Anglo people
Hacheta-	small stone axe
Hachuela-	little axe
Hogas-	shucks of the corn
Huertas-	gardens
Humero-	flue
Inocente-	innocent
Jara-	willow
Jara-	tough but pliable wood
Jarrones-	jars
Jefe-	boss, employer
Lagunajo-	pool
Lanza-	pole
Lemita-	shrub whose branches are tough and pliable
Levadura-	leavening
Llano-	trowel
Lumbago-	lumbular rheumatism
Luminaries-	bonfires
Machucador-	machine used for extracting syrup
Madrina-	godmother
Malacate-	hoisting apparatus
Maleficiada-	bewitched or made ill through witchcraft
Maleficio-	spell
Mango-	handle
Mansanilla-	chamomile
Mayoral-	foreman

Merienda-	light afternoon meal
Mesa-	table; the flat top of hills or mountains
Metate-	grinding stone
Miel-	honey or molasses
Mieleros-	molasses maker or place where the honey is made
Muchachos-	youngsters
Munchos-	(correct spelling is muchos) many
Músicos-	musicians
Muy grande-	very big
Naguas-	petticoat
Nicho-	niche; a recess in a wall to place a statue in
Niño-	a child
Obligado-	obligated
Ojas-	leaves
Ojito-	spring of water
Ollas-	clay jars; pots
Orno-	outdoor oven
Padre-	father; priest
P'alla-	(see para allá)
Padrino/a-	godfather, godmother
Pajero (pájaro)-	bird
Panocha-	a pudding made from ground wheat grain that has been sprouted
Para allá-	Over there
Parado-	either standing or stopped (varies)
Parao-	(see parado)
Partera-	midwife
Pero-	but
Pezole, posole-	posole
Piñón-	nut pine, the pine nut
Plana-	level ground
Platero-	jewelry maker, silversmith
Prendario-	betrothal ceremony
Prendería-	jewelry, also a dance between two engaged persons when they exchange rings
Preso-	prisoner
Puellas-	iron skillet

Quelites-	tender-leafed plant similar to spinach
Ranchito-	little ranch
Ratones-	rats
Razo-	even, or level
Reata-	rope
Redoma-	flask
Remedios-	herbs
Resador-	person in charge of the prayers
Resplendor-	reflection
Ricos-	rich people
Rifle Fulminante-	gun fired by caps
Ropón-	christening robe
Rueda-	wheel
Sabine-	savin
Santero-	carver of saints
Santos-	saints
Sarape-	shawl
Sarydacia-	sacred stone
Sayalete-	thin flannel
Serape-	rug or throw rug
Sopa-	bread pudding
Talegon-	pouch for carrying tobacco
Tapanco-	porch
Tarabilla-	a holder
Tecolote-	owl
Tejas-	roof tile
Tewas-	moccasins
Tilma-	cloak fastened by a knot
Tinaja-	large earthenware jar
Tinaja-	large jars
Torno de hilar-	spinning wheel
Tortillas de maiz-	corn tortillas
Trementina-	resin, sap
Trijo-	wheat
Tusa-	cob
Vara-	unit of measurement used for land

Velorio-	bonfire meetings among men in which conversations concerning horse trading, planting of crops, and hunting took place. Also wake.
Vigas-	wooden roof supporting beams
Vinatera-	gourd
Vino-	wine
Virola Amarilla-	muzzle-loading gun
Xente-	vente (come here)
Yerbabuena-	mint
Yeso-	gypsum, used to whitewash the inner walls of an adobe house
Yunta-	yoke
Zorra-	foxweed